Theodore B. Gates

The ``ULSTER GUARD``

Theodore B. Gates

The ``ULSTER GUARD``

ISBN/EAN: 9783741114885

Manufactured in Europe, USA, Canada, Australia, Japa

Cover: Foto ©Andreas Hilbeck / pixelio.de

Manufactured and distributed by brebook publishing software
(www.brebook.com)

Theodore B. Gates

The ``ULSTER GUARD``

THE

"ULSTER GUARD"

[20th N. Y. State Militia]

AND THE

WAR OF THE REBELLION.

EMBRACING

A HISTORY

OF THE

EARLY ORGANIZATION OF THE REGIMENT; ITS THREE MONTHS' SERVICE;
ITS REORGANIZATION AND SUBSEQUENT SERVICE; A CHRONOLOGI-
CAL RECORD OF EVERY MARCH, PLACE OF ENCAMPMENT OR
BIVOUAC, WITH DISTANCES MARCHED; ACCOUNT OF PRO-
CEEDINGS OF DETACHMENT ON VETERAN FURLOUGH;
FLAG PRESENTATIONS, &c.; COMPLETE ROSTER
DURING ENTIRE SERVICE; OFFICERS AND
COMPANIES ON SPECIAL DUTY; LISTS
OF KILLED AND WOUNDED; &c.; &c.

TOGETHER

WITH A BRIEF TREATISE UPON THE ORIGIN AND GROWTH OF SECESSION;
THE MILITIA SYSTEM, AND THE DEPENDENCE OF THE FEDERAL
GOVERNMENT UPON IT IN THE BEGINNING OF THE WAR;

WITH A

CRITICAL HISTORY

OF THE

FIRST BATTLE OF BULL RUN; CAMPAIGN OF GEN. POPE; McCLELLAN'S
MARYLAND CAMPAIGN; BATTLE OF FREDERICKSBURG; HOOKER'S
CHANCELLORSVILLE CAMPAIGN; GETTYSBURG CAMPAIGN;
AND A GLANCE AT THE CAMPAIGN FROM THE RAP-
IDAN TO APPOMATTOX COURT HOUSE.

BY

THEODORE B. GATES,

COL. AND BVT. BRIG. GEN. U. S. V.

New-York:
BENJ. H. TYRREL, PRINTER, 74 MAIDEN LANE.
1879.

the Memory

OF THE GALLANT OFFICERS AND MEN WHO SEALED THEIR DEVOTION

TO THEIR COUNTRY WITH THEIR LIFE'S BLOOD WHILE

FIGHTING UNDER THE COLORS OF THE

"ULSTER GUARD,"

AND TO THE

SURVIVORS OF THOSE DEAD HEROES WHOSE COURAGE ON MANY

BATTLE-FIELDS TESTIFIED THEIR READINESS TO MAKE THE

SAME GREAT SACRIFICE IN THE SAME GREAT CAUSE;

THIS WORK IS

REVERENTLY AND GRATEFULLY INSCRIBED

BY THE AUTHOR.

ERRATA

1. For "Appendix A," at bottom of second paragraph on page 69, read "Note II."

2. For "Maulius," on page 193 and 196, read "Manlius."

3. In connection with the account of the operations of the Fourteenth Brooklyn, Ninety-fifth N. Y. and Sixth Wisconsin, on pages 430 and 431, read extracts from official reports of Generals Fowler and Wordsworth, Appendix H.

PREFACE.

———•———

I PRESENT this work to my old comrades in arms with a confident reliance upon their indulgent judgment. I submit it to the public at large with great diffidence. I was not ambitious to undertake the labor of writing the history of the "Ulster Guard," and, as most of its old members know, another pen was expected to perform that service. But I confess to having had a love for the task, which has grown in strength as the work has progressed, until, I fear, the volume has reached unpardonable dimensions: and there still remains so much unsaid that the book seems to the author very incomplete. There are a thousand incidents of the march, the camp, the bivouac, and the battle-field, which I have been forced to exclude, upon being informed by my publisher that the volume already overran 600 pages —100 more than I deisgned the book should contain. It had been my intention to illustrate the work with likenesses of the officers of the regiment; but it was found to be impossible to do this except to a limited extent, and that would have subjected the author to the charge of having made invidious distinctions between different officers.

The members of the "Old Twentieth," and the thousands of its civilian friends, have felt that its services entitled it to a historical record ; and, so long ago as 1862, Mr. Archibald Russell proposed that the Ulster County Historical Society should undertake such a work, and his proposition was adopted [see page 57], but never carried into effect.

I am fully conscious of the many imperfections of this work. As the advance sheets come from the press, I see much that I would be glad if I could have spent more time and care upon. Frequent and often protracted interruptions have not only delayed the publication, but have forced me to devote the heat of summer to labor which I hoped to have completed during the preceding winter ; and latterly the cry for "copy" from my publisher, and my desire to have this book issued before I meet my old comrades face to face again, at our annual Re union on the 17th of this month, and again have to apologize for its non-appearance, have prevented that degree of care which such a work should command at the hands of its author. But,

> " What is writ, is writ,—
> Would it were worthier ! "

The high regard in which the regiment has always been held by the people of Ulster County, has led them to manifest much interest in the promised history of its origin and service in the field. Their hearty, practical and untiring interest in its welfare and reputation, has been one of the pleasant memories connected with its five years of service, under the Federal Government. They so identified themselves with the organization that any truthful history of it must necessarily identify them with its career.

Some readers may object that my subject did not require me to discuss, as I have, many of the operations of the armies of the Potomac and of Virginia, and several of the battles fought by those armies. But it must be remembered that the regiment is the lowest unit in the army organization, and it acts in conjunction with its brigade, division and corps, and, finally, with the army of which it is a component part. To attempt to describe the individual operations of a regiment in such battles as those participated in by the "Ulster Guard," would be like asking you to judge of the merits of a great painting from a fragment of the canvas. A history of any given regiment must be at least a miniature history of the war. It is but one of the united implements in the hands of the Commanding General, and its acts are always influenced by its fellows. But beyond all this, I designed to give the work something more than a mere local interest, and to make it, so far as I was able, an accurate history of the great events with which the regiment was connected.

I have claimed no merit for the "Ulster Guard," that was not freely ascribed to it in the army in which it served—I have sought to do it only simple, naked justice. I am persuaded its deserts were greater than I make them appear, but my relation to the regiment as its commander during a considerable part of its service, seemed to me a reason why I should not be its eulogist. I have not, however, felt that delicacy required me to exclude from these pages the cordial commendations of others.

In the discussion of battles and the general operations of the armies, I have endeavored to be accurate, fair and impartial. I have consulted the best authorities, both Union and Confederate, and have striven to arrive at just conclusions. While the criticisms I have felt constrained to pass upon some of the leaders of the Union Army may be distasteful to many of my readers, yet they will find it difficult to deny their justice, in view of the facts upon which they are founded.

T. B. G.

42 FIRST PLACE, BROOKLYN,
    September, 1879.

CONTENTS.

CHAPTER I.

CHAPTER II.

CHAPTER III.

CHAPTER IV.

CHAPTER V.

CHAPTER VI.

CHAPTER VII.

CHAPTER VIII.

CHAPTER IX.

CHAPTER X.

CHAPTER XVII.

CHAPTER XVIII.

CHAPTER XXII.

CHAPTER XXIII.

CHAPTER XXIV.

CHAPTER XXV.

CHAPTER XXVI.

CHAPTER XXVII.

CHAPTER XXVIII.

CHAPTER XXIX.

CHAPTER XXX.

CHAPTER XXXI.

CHAPTER XXXII.

CHAPTER XXXIII.

CHAPTER XXXIV.

CHAPTER XXXV.

CHAPTER XXXVI.

CHAPTER XXXVII.

NOTES.

NOTE I.

NOTE II.

APPENDICES.

APPENDIX A.

APPENDIX B.

APPENDIX C.

APPENDIX D.

APPENDIX E.

APPENDIX F.

APPENDIX G.

APPENDIX H.

CHAPTER I

THE FEDERAL CONSTITUTION—ITS INCONGRUOUS ELEMENTS—POLITICAL
PARTIES—GROWTH OF ANTI-SLAVERY SENTIMENT—THE CASE STATED
BY MR. LINCOLN—BY ALEXANDER H. STEPHENS—THE SOUTH WEDDED
TO ITS IDOL—STATUS OF THE SLAVE—THE SOUTH CONTEMPLATE SEP-
ARATION—STATE'S-RIGHT DOCTRINE—ITS APPLICATION ALWAYS ONLY
A QUESTION OF TIME—ELECTION OF LINCOLN—SECESSION ENSUES—
ORGANIZATION OF CONFEDERATE GOVERNMENT—SEIZURE OF FEDERAL
PROPERTY—INAUGURATION OF LINCOLN—ATTACK ON FORT SUMTER—
DESTRUCTION OF PROPERTY AT NORFOLK—MERRIMAC AND MONITOR
—THE NORTH AROUSED—SOUTHERN LEADERS SURPRISED BY UNANIM-
ITY OF LOYAL SENTIMENT AT NORTH—THEY CANNOT RECEDE IF THEY
WOULD—WOMEN STRONGEST SECESSIONISTS—THE SWORD THE ONLY
ARBITER.

IT WAS impossible for the Government to go on har-
moniously for all time in the exact form in which our
fathers had constructed it. The Federal Constitution
was adopted by the several States hesitatingly, and, in
some instances, by barely the requisite vote ; not more
than two of the original thirteen States cordially accepted it as the fundamental law of the new nation.
Experience had taught them to be jealous of extraneous
authority, and they were averse to stripping their several States of any one of the functions of independent
government, which they had become accustomed to,
and conferring them upon a federal legislature and federal officers. The Northern States were quite as inimi-
cal to the Constitution in the beginning, as the Southern States were ; but they gradually became reconciled
to it, and cheerfully acquiesced in the later interpretations of the instrument, which tended to confer upon
the General Government even greater powers than were

at first supposed to be lodged in the Congress and Executive Department of the nation.

The incongruity of a system of involuntary servitude, with a form of government professedly founded upon the principles of civil and political freedom and equality, was too patent to be overlooked by the merest tyro in political economy, and the utmost the framers of the Federal Constitution would accord to it was a recognition of its existence, under the obscure phrase of "persons held to service." As time went on slavery languished, and finally utterly died out at the North, rather because it could not compete with the growing volume of free labor, and hence became unprofitable, than because of any sentiment that it was morally and politically wrong, in the mild form in which it existed, and which amounted to little more than a condition of involuntary apprenticeship. Abolition at the North had little moral or political significance, because the motive lying at the bottom of it was only mercenary; but there soon began to grow up new views as to the moral aspect of slavery, and public sentiment throughout the civilized world gradually arrayed itself on the side of human freedom, the slave-holding States of this Government constituting almost the solitary exception.

In this country, the Whig party—in its latter days, and after its dissolution, the Republican party—were the political exponents of this humanizing idea; but neither organization, as a party, claimed that the General Government had authority to abolish, or in any wise interfere with the institution of slavery in the States, but only that it had the power, and that it was its duty, to exclude it from the national domain, because it was an abnormal condition of society, inconsistent with our theory of government; and that while it was protected under the Constitution wherever it already existed, it could not be established in the territories without express enactment therefor by Congress, and that such authority ought to be forever withheld.

As time went on, this anti-slavery sentiment broadened and strengthened, and surged up against the American Slave-holding States, with no other effect upon them than to excite the apprehensions of the slaveholders, as to the perpetuity of their cherished institution, and to stimulate them to devise and carry into execution, so far as they could, by friendly legislation, protective measures.

The position of the Republican party on the question of slavery was stated with great force and perspicuity by Mr. Lincoln, in the course of his great debate with Judge Douglas, in these words :

"We have in this nation this element of domestic slavery ; it is a matter of absolute certainty that it is a disturbing element ; it is the opinion of all the great men who have expressed an opinion upon it, that it is a dangerous element. We keep up a controversy in regard to it ; that controversy necessarily springs from difference of opinion, and if we can learn exactly, can reduce to the lowest elements, what that difference of opinion is, we perhaps shall be better prepared for discussing the different systems of that policy that we would propose in regard to that disturbing element. I suggest that the difference of opinion, reduced to its lowest terms, is no other than the difference between the men who think slavery a wrong and those who do not think it wrong. The Republican party think it a wrong—we think it is a moral, a social and a political wrong. We think it is a wrong not confining itself merely to the persons or the States where it exists, but that it is a wrong in its tendency, to say the least, that extends to the existence of the whole·nation. Because we think it wrong, we propose a course of policy that shall deal with it as a wrong. We deal with it as with any other wrong, in so far as we can prevent its grow-

ing any larger, and so deal with it, that in the run of
time there may be some promise of an end to it. We
have a due regard to the actual presence of it amongst
us, and the difficulty of getting rid of it in any satisfactory way, and all the constitutional obligations
thrown about it. I suppose that in reference both to
its actual existence in the nation, and to our constitutional obligations, we have no right at all to disturb it
in the States where it exists, and we profess that we
have no more inclination to disturb it than we have the
right to do it. We go further than that ; we don't
propose to disturb it where, in one instance, we think
the Constitution would permit us ; we think the Constitution would permit us to disturb it in the District
of Columbia ; still we do not propose to do that, unless
it should be in terms which I don't suppose the nation
is very likely soon to agree to—the terms of making
the emancipation gradual, and compensating the unwilling owners. Where we suppose we have the constitutional right, we restrain ourselves in reference to the
actual existence of the institution and the difficulties
thrown about it. We also oppose it as an evil, so far as
it seeks to spread itself. We insist on the policy that
shall restrict it to its present limits. We don't suppose
that in doing this we violate anything due to the actual
presence of the institution, or anything due to the constitutional guarantees thrown around it."

The views of so conspicuous a leader as Alexander
H. Stephens, the Vice-President of the Southern Confederacy, and now a member of Congress from Georgia,
are in singular contrast with those of Mr. Lincoln, and
seem at this day almost like irony   Mr. Stephens was
by no means a "fire-eater," but belonged to the more
moderate class of Southerners, as will appear from a
brief quotation from an address he delivered before the
Legislature of Georgia, November 14, 1860, wherein he
deprecated secession. He said: "The first question

which presents itself is, shall the people of the South secede from the Union in consequence of the election of Mr. Lincoln to the Presidency of the United States? My countrymen, I tell you candidly, frankly and earnestly, that I do not think that they ought. In my judgment, the election of no man constitutionally chosen to that high office, is sufficient cause for any State to separate from the Union. It ought to stand by and aid still in maintaining the Constitution of the country To make a point of resistance to the Government, to withdraw from it because a man has been constitutionally elected, puts us in the wrong. We went into the election with this people, the result was different from what we wished, but the election has been constitutionally held. Were we to make a point of resistance to the Government, and go out of the Union on this account, the record would be made up hereafter against us."

After the Confederacy was established, he made a speech to the citizens of Savannah, in which he gave an exposition of the principles on which the new government was founded. He said : "The new Constitution had put at rest forever all agitating questions relating to our peculiar institutions—African slavery, as it exists among us—the proper status of the negro in our form of civilization. Jefferson in his forecast, had anticipated this, as the 'rock upon which the old Union would split.' He was right. What was conjecture with him, is now a realized fact. But whether he fully comprehended the great truth upon which that rock stood and stands, may be doubted. The prevailing ideas entertained by him, and most of the leading statesmen at the time of the formation of the old Constitution, were, that the enslavement of the African was in violation of the laws of nature ; that it was wrong in principle, socially, morally and politically It was an evil they knew not well how to deal with ; but the

general opinion of the men of that day was, that somehow
or other, in the order of Providence, the institution
would become evanescent and pass away. This idea,
though not incorporated in the Constitution, was the prevailing idea at the time. The Constitution, it is true,
secured every essential guarantee to the institution while
it should last, and hence no argument can be justly used
against the Constitutional guarantees thus secured, because of the common sentiment of the day Those
ideas, however, were fundamentally wrong. They rested
upon the assumption of the equality of races ; this was
an error. It was a sandy foundation, and the idea of a
Government built upon it was a wrong. When the
' storm came and the wind blew, it fell.' "

" Our new Government is founded upon exactly the
opposite ideas ; its foundations are laid ; its corner-stone
rests upon the great truth that the negro is not equal to
the white man ; that slavery, subordination to the superior race, is his natural and normal condition. This,
our new Government, is the first in the history of the
world based upon this great physical, philosophical
and moral truth. This truth has been slow in the process of its development, like all other truths in the
various departments of science."

*   *   *   *   *   *   *

"In the conflict thus far, success has been on our
side, complete through the length and breadth of the
Confederate States. It is upon this, as I have stated,
our social fabric is firmly planted, and I cannot permit
myself to doubt the ultimate success of a full recognition of this principle throughout the civilized and enlightened world."

The South readily accepted such doctrines, and was
practically a unit on the question at issue between itself
and the advocates of non-extension of slavery. The
liberal and modern view of the natural rights of man,
negroes included, obtained no foot-hold among the plan-

ters, and found very little favor among the non-slave-holding whites of the South. All classes of whites were wedded to the system, and could see only good in it. This was but the natural result of the Southerner's education and associations. His fortune, often, and he believed his happiness and prosperity, were largely dependent upon the perpetuity of the institution, as it existed in the Southern States. Upon it was founded the industrial interests of his section, and even his domestic establishment seemed impracticable without the glamour conferred by slavery

This unanimity of sentiment was an element of strength in politics, and it proved itself capable of dictating party platforms and achieving some notable triumphs in Congressional Legislation, and was not without great influence in the highest judicial body in the nation, as witness the national platforms of the party with which the pro-slavery masses of the South acted in 1852, 1856 and 1860 ; the repeal of the Missouri compromise measures ; the Kansas-Nebraska Legislation, the fugitive slave law and the Dred Scott decision.

The institution was a powerful element in our political fabric, and was the foundation for a large Southern representation in the House of Representatives, while, at the same time, our highest Court had declared that a slave or the descendant of an African slave could not be a citizen in the sense of the term as used in the Constitution of the United States, nor could he have any political rights ; from which it followed that the three-fifth slave representation was a *property* representation. And the Southerner insisted that his slave *was* a mere chattel, and that his title to him rested upon the same broad principle of right, and was governed by the same laws that applied to any other kind of personal property, and that therefore he had the absolute right to take and hold this property But all attempts to de-localize the institution, finally failed, and it became

evident that the sentiment of the country was irrevoca-
bly fixed against the expansion of slavery

The South now began to look forward to a possible
separation of the slave from the free States, as the only
certain means of securing the perpetuity of their cherished institution. With this eventuality in view, the old
question of the powers vested in the Federal Government and the reserved rights of the several States, were
diligently discussed and industriously propagated by
Southern leaders in politics, business and society.
Their theory practically denationalized the Government,
and left it the mere representative of the co-partnership
of sovereign States, any one or more of which could
withdraw at pleasure. Stability could scarcely be hoped
for, if the organic law were really of this character.
And if it were clearly otherwise, so long as a large and
influential section of the country believed its inter-
pretation to be the true one, the practical application of
that theory was only a question of time and circumstances, depending on some real or assumed provoca-
tion.

The election of Mr. Lincoln in 1860 was made the
pretext for the inauguration of the fore-ordained experiment of secession of the Slave States; it was the practical application of the doctrine of State's Rights. President Buchanan doubted the power of the General
Government to obstruct this process of disintegration,
or to "coerce a Sovereign State." The Cabinet, Congress, and the officers of the Army and Navy, were
largely in sympathy with these views, while many of
them actively espoused the Southern cause.

Thus it came to pass, that between the date of Mr.
Lincoln's election, in November, 1860, and his inauguration on the fourth of March, 1861, secession had made
formidable progress, and a so-called Southern Confederacy had been actually established, with Jefferson Davis
at the head of it, without hindrance or obstruction

from the General Government. The seceding States had taken possession, without opposition, of the U. S. Forts at Beaufort and Wilmington; Forts Caswell and Johnson; the Arsenal at Fayetteville; Fort Barrancas, and the Navy Yard at Pensacola; the Arsenal at Little Rock; the U. S. Mint at New Orleans, and had practically dispossessed the parent government of its property and symbols of authority in a half-dozen Southern States, while the Administration of Mr. Buchanan looked on in a dazed and resistless condition.

In the meantime the South had organized an army and prepared for war; Sullivan's Island, in Charleston Harbor, had been fortified, with works bristling with hostile cannon pointing toward Fort Sumter, over which still floated the Stars and Stripes, and which was garrisoned by a small body of United States troops, under command of Major Anderson, a loyal Southerner. Every other Fort, south of Virginia, had already fallen into Confederate hands, without the firing of a gun, excepting only Fort Pickens.

On the fourth of March, 1861, Mr. Lincoln succeeded Mr. Buchanan, and even he entertained hopes of some adjustment that should preserve the integrity of the country, and save it from the horrors of civil war; but it was not to be. In the Providence of God the time had come to recast and mould anew this Nation, and as the first gleam of light, on the morning of the 12th of April, revealed the grim walls of Sumter to the anxious watchers on Sullivan's Island, the boom of cannon rolled out from the brazen throat of a Confederate gun, and the last hope of a peaceful solution was crushed by the iron hand of fratricidal war. Battery after battery followed this signal gun, until Sumter was enveloped in fire, and stone and mortar trembled with the roar of artillery, and crumbled under the iron deluge that poured upon them.

Quickly following this disaster came a self-inflicted blow upon our Navy At Norfolk, were the powerful forty-gun steam frigate Merrimac, the Cumberland, the Germantown, the Plymouth, the Raritan, the Columbia, the Dolphin, the huge three-decker Pennsylvania, the Delaware and Columbus, with over two thousand cannon ; quantities of small arms, and immense supplies of war material and naval stores, valued at $10,000,000. These vessels, with one exception, were scuttled and fired, and the property abandoned by Captains McCauley and Paulding, of our Navy, who then, at four o'clock on the morning of the 21st of April, fled from the scene of their suicidal exploit, on board the Cumberland, lighted on their way by the nation's burning Navy

As a thrilling epilogue to this disgraceful abandonment of the most valuable war material of the Government, it will be remembered that the rebels raised the Merrimac, and converted her into a powerful iron-clad ram, and that on the 8th of March, 1862, the monster came out from Norfolk Harbor on her mission of destruction.   The escaped Cumberland and the Congress fell a prey to the fury of this novel and uncouth leviathan, whose mailed surface beat back the shot and shell which our devoted vessels poured upon it, as though they were rubber pellets.   Indeed, but for the opportune arrival in the waters of Hampton Roads of the little Monitor and the gallant Worden, it is doubtful whether we could have held Fortress Monroe against the assaults of this almost impervious engine of destruction.

These untoward events alarmed and aroused the people in the non-slave-holding States, and led them, at last, to believe in the possibility of an internecine war between the Government and the revolted States. The effect was electrical.   Party lines disappeared before the higher duty of patriotism.   The uprising of the masses in favor of sustaining the just prerogatives of the

Federal Government, and maintaining the inviolability of the Union, was a grand spectacle. The universality of this sentiment of loyalty surprised and disappointed the Southern leaders. They were bold and able men, and most of them were sincere in their belief in the abstract question of the right of a State to secede. Behind them stood a constituency who had inculcated this dangerous doctrine from their youth, and who would tolerate no suggestion of its fallacy The women of the South were even more tenacious of the rights of slavery, and the ultimate right of a State to withdraw from the Union, than the men were, and the moral influence they imparted to the cause was tremendous. To recede would have been political and social ruin to the leaders, and it remained only to settle the great issue they had thrust upon the country by the terrible arbitrament of the sword.

CHAPTER II.

THE Federal Government could scarcely have been
less prepared for war than it was on the day the
Confederate batteries opened their fire on Fort Sumter.
The army contained but ten thousand seven hundred
and fifty-five officers and men ; many of the former disloyal. This little force was chiefly distributed in Southern States and the Indian Country General David E.
Twiggs, who commanded that portion of the army
stationed in Texas, surrendered his force to that State,
together with $12,000,500 worth of public property, and
was very indignant because President Buchanan dismissed him from the army, "for treachery to the
flag of his country " He addressed a letter to Mr.
Buchanan, which reveals a singular state of mind on the
part of the writer, as to his duty towards the Govern-

12

ment which had educated and supported him, and to which he had taken an oath of fidelity. He says: "Your usurped right to dismiss me from the army might be acquiesced in, but you had no right to brand me as a traitor. This was personal, and *I shall treat it as such*—not through the papers, but *in person*. I shall, most assuredly, pay a visit to Lancaster, for the sole purpose of *a personal interview* with you. So, sir, prepare yourself. I am well assured public opinion will sanction *any course* I may take with you." Could insolence further go?

The navy was as weak and unavailable as the army. The report of the Secretary of the Navy, July, 1861, showed that of the 90 vessels belonging to the navy, but two of them, carrying 27 guns and 280 men, were within reach, and likely to obey the orders of the department. Mr. Toucy, Mr. Buchanan's Secretary of the Navy, had sent 5 of our ships to the East Indies, 3 to Brazil, 7 to the Pacific Ocean, 3 to the Mediterranean, 7 to the Coast of Africa, and others to other remote stations, where they were of no use in our great emergency. As early as February, 1861, a Congressional Committee had been directed to investigate the conduct of the Secretary, and this committee reported that the Brooklyn, 25 guns, and the store-ship Relief, 2 guns, were the only vessels available for the defense of the Atlantic Coast; the latter vessel, even then, under orders for Africa. The committee say nothing like it ever occurred before. Such disposition of the navy, at so critical a period, was pronounced extraordinary The committee also arraign the Secretary for neglecting to put in repair and commission a single one of the 28 ships dismantled in port, although he had $646,639.79 of the appropriation for repairs, unexpended.

Mr. Cameron, Secretary of War under Mr. Lincoln at the outset of his administration, thus speaks of the condition of the War Department, when it was turned

over to him at the end of Buchanan's administration:
"I found the department destitute of all means of defence; without guns, and with little prospect of purchasing the *material* of war. I found the nation without an army, and I found scarcely a man throughout the whole War Department in whom I could put my trust. The adjutant-general deserted, the quarter-master-general ran off, the commissary-general was on his death bed; more than half the clerks were disloyal."

The Richmond *Enquirer* stated, that under a single order Secretary Floyd sent, during the preceding year, 114,868 improved muskets and rifles from Northern to Southern Arsenals. The Memphis *Appeal* boasted that by the transfers made by Floyd, and by the seizure of forts and arsenals, and some purchases abroad, the Confederate States had, in the spring of 1861, 707,000 stand of arms, and 200,000 revolvers; a pretty good out-fit.

The seceded States appropriated, without scruple, the government's war *material*, and there was no arm of the service in which they were not thus very well equipped. The abandonment by the federal forces of the Norfolk Navy Yard, one of the most extensive naval depots in the country, threw into the hands of the rebels nearly 3,000 cannon of the most formidable and efficient kinds — many of them Columbiads and Dahlgrens. They were spiked, of course, by our people, but that is an idle ceremony, except to avoid *immediate* use of the guns. Shot, shell, revolvers, carbines, and small arms, in vast quantities, were cast into the harbor, to be fished out again, with almost as much ease and certainty as they were thrown in. From these combined sources the Confederates were enabled to confront the Unionists, at the beginning of the war, with a decided superiority, both in quantity and quality of arms.

On the other hand, the South boasted of its readiness for war. On the 18th of February, 1861, a member of the Military Committee of the Confederate Congress, said : "My colleague, however, greatly errs, when he states we are unprepared for war, and have no arms, and I am unwilling to let the assertion go undenied. Sir, we have arms in abundance, though no armories. Every State has amply provided itself to meet any emergency that may arise, and is daily purchasing and receiving cannon, mortars, shell, and other engines of destruction, with which to overwhelm the dastard adversary. Organized armies now exist in all the States, commanded by officers brave, accomplished and experienced ; and even should war occur in twenty days, I feel confident that they have both the valor and the arms, successfully to resist any force whatever." But in addition to all this, the South was educated up to the undisturbed contemplation of a state of war between itself and the Federal Government ; and victory, to the Southern arms was the unquestioned and undoubted result. The Charleston *Courier* was disposed to have the Confederacy treat the *Northern* States as insurgents, and deny them recognition. Still, if the North quietly acquiesced in secession, the South, after transferring its seat of Government to Washington, might possibly condescend to recognize what might be left of the old Confederacy, in order to enable it to maintain a feeble national existence.

The South Carolina leaders but expressed the truth as to the state of the Southern mind on the question of a separation, when Mr. Inglis said to his colleagues in the convention : "Most of us have had this subject under consideration for the last twenty years." Mr. Keitt said : "I have been engaged in this movement ever since I entered political life." Mr. Rhett said : "It (secession) is not produced by Mr. Lincoln's election, or the non-execution of the fugitive slave law. It is a matter which has been gathering head for thirty years."

Senator Douglas, in his great speech before ten thousand people at Chicago, on the first day of May, 1861, said: "There has never been a time from the day that Washington was inaugurated first President of the United States, when the rights of the Southern States stood firmer under the laws of the land than they do now ; there never was a time when they had not as good cause for disunion as they have to-day What good cause have they now that has not existed under every administration ?

"The slavery question is a mere excuse. The election of Lincoln is a mere pretext. The present secession movement is the result of an enormous conspiracy, formed more than a year since. Formed by leaders in the Southern Confederacy more than twelve months ago.

"But this is no time for the detail of causes. The conspiracy is now known. Armies have been raised, war is levied to accomplish it. There are only two sides of the question. Every man must be for the United States or against it. There can be no neutrals in this war ; *only patriots or traitors.* I know they expect to present a united South against a divided North. They hoped, in the Northern States, party questions would bring civil war between Democrats and Republicans, when the South would step in with her cohorts, aid one party to conquer the other, and then make easy prey of the victors. Their scheme was carnage and civil war in the North."

The Richmond *Enquirer* of April 23, 1861, urged an attempt to capture Washington, and declared it entirely feasible ; why such an attempt was not made in the spring of 1861 is one of the unsolved riddles of Confederate policy That such an enterprise would have had many chances in favor of its success, cannot be doubted. While it is possible that such a movement would have inflamed the North, and extinguished the last spark of sympathy with the rebel cause in the loyal states ; on the other hand, it would have been likely to carry the border states over to the Confederates and secure to the Confederacy the recognition of foreign governments.

Well authenticated facts show that a secret organization existed, from which the Capital was in danger of capture, for a month after Mr. Lincoln's inauguration. The plan involved a march upon the city by 3,000 Virginians, an uprising by the Washington Secessionists ; while the Baltimore Rebels were to cut off the communication by telegraph and rail with the North, and march upon the beleagured city in such force as they could command. If this movement proved successful, the Confederate government was to advance its troops and occupy the captured town; but if the Federals developed unlooked-for strength and the assailants were repulsed, the Confederate government would stand in a position to shirk all responsibility, and treat the affair as the exploit of unauthorized partisans.

The Federal government knew enough of this scheme to appreciate the danger to which it subjected the Capital, and to be induced to make such provisions against its success as were possible, with the limited means at hand. The situation of the President, his Cabinet, and the various officers, archives and property of the several departments of the government, were anomalous. The population of the city was largely and bitterly opposed to the administration, while of the clerks in the departments, about eighty per cent. were from the South, and nearly every one of them was disloyal. The city of Richmond, itself, could hardly have been more hostile to the administration, and Mr. Lincoln and his Cabinet, in so far as sympathy was concerned, might as well have been set down in the latter city. But there were a great many transient inhabitants in Washington at this time—men who were loyal and

2

friendly to the administration. These men met, by notice quietly communicated, in the old church in rear of Willard's Hotel, on the evening of April 18th ; the oath of fidelity was administered, and the celebrated "Cassius M. Clay Battalion" was formed. This organization consisted of about 200 men; they were from the best ranks of society and represented the culture and wealth of the land. This battalion was divided into squads, and each under an efficient commander, patrolled the streets of the Capital. Another party of three hundred men was quietly gathered in the east room at the White House, under command of Gen. Lane, of Kansas; and for three weeks this improvised garrison occupied these quarters. The veteran General Scott took possession of the capitol building with a few hundred men, and converted the structure into a citadel, which he supplied with provisions and military stores, adapted to a siege. The long bridge across the Potomac was under charge of a body of dragoons, and a detachment of artillery had its guns planted on the Washington side to sweep the structure.

All these preparations were very inadequate to defend the city against so formidable an attack as was believed to, and probably did menace it. Why the meditated blow was not struck is now only a matter of conjecture.

These circumstances revealed a state of affairs humiliating to a just national pride, and endangered for a time the very life of the Republic. To see a government of 38,000,000 of people, rich in all the resources that tend to make them great and powerful, ranking second to no nation of the earth, so denuded of its proper martial puissance that it could not set a squadron in the field, even to save its capital from capture, was unspeakably humbling.

The lesson of 1861 ought to have taught our national Legislators that we are not so isolated from the rest of the world, nor so safe from internal violence that we can dispense with an army and conduct this government on *high moral principles alone.* But we are advancing now toward the same condition of impotence that covered us with mortification and imperiled our existence eighteen years ago. And still our "reformers" demand a further reduction of the army, and would take from the Federal Government the authority to control what little there is left of it.

With new-born zeal for economy, they tell us the army costs much money. True, it does; but how many tens of thousands of human lives, and how many millions of dollars has the non-existence of an army cost us? Does any man believe that the war of the rebellion would ever have been inaugurated if the disloyal element had not known that the Government was practically powerless? Does any one believe that the war of the rebellion would have been fought if this Government had had an adequate, a loyal and an efficient army in 1861? NEVER''

It is an unwise policy, if it is not a false and dishonest pretence, which, in the name of economy, allows our ships of war to rot in their ports and our army to be reduced to a single corps. Such policy invites insult and invasion from without, disorder and insurrection within.

Not till those halcyon days shall come, "when nations shall learn war no more," can a great Government afford thus to disarm itself before the world. We believe in all just measures of economy, and in that reform which looks to the elevation and prosperity of the whole country; but we do not believe in depriving the Government of the power to enforce, at home and abroad, on sea and land, on the plains among the Indians, or among the strikers and rioters in Harrisburg and Baltimore, respect for its authority

The thunder of preparation for war had rolled up from the South for months. Her States had seceded and formed a new Government. They had possessed themselves of the forts and war material of the nation. They had organized armies for the avowed purpose of resisting the authority of the Federal Government. They had erected batteries and mounted heavy cannon to re- duce a Federal fort in Charleston Harbor. Their pur- pose had been openly declared on the floor of Congress ; in the Cabinet of Mr. Buchanan ; by words and deeds, all over the country   There had been no concealment of the rebel purpose since November, 1860. It was a dissolution of the Union and the erection of a separate and independent Government, composed of some or all the slave-holding States. This and nothing less, was the programme defiantly and insolently flaunted in the nation's face, through all the winter of 1860-1 ; and no one called it treason. Indeed, our form of Govern- ment seemed to be either not a subject of treason, or without power to punish it.

Mr. Buchanan could find no authority in the Consti- tution to justify an attempt to arrest the disintegra- tion. His Attorney-general concurred in this view of the question. His Secretary of the Interior boasted of the fact that he had telegraphed the rebels at Charleston, that the Star of the West was on her way to re-enforce Major Anderson, and that "the (rebel) troops were then put on their guard, and when the ship arrived in Charleston Harbor she received a warm welcome from booming cannon, and soon beat a hasty retreat." His Secretary of the Navy had paralyzed that arm of Gov- ernment power, as already shown. His Secretary of War had been equally successful in neutralizing that department, and he even had the effrontery to protest to President Buchanan against the transfer of Major Anderson and his men from Fort Moultrie to Sumter, and to demand that the President should allow him to issue an order for the withdrawal of Major Anderson from Charleston Harbor, thereby surrendering it to the rebels. And because Mr. Buchanan refused to permit such an order to be issued, Floyd resigned his portfolio, and betook himself South.

On the sixth of January, 1861, the Senators from Florida, Georgia, Alabama, Louisiana, Arkansas, Texas and Mississippi, then, and for weeks afterwards, holding their seats as United States Senators under their oath of fidelity to the Government, met together and adopted resolutions advising such of their several States as had not already done so, to secede and form a Confederate Government, not later than the fifteenth of February, then next ; the time being so fixed "to enable Louisiana and Texas to participate." Senator Yulee, of Florida, who communicated this resolve to his constituents, said in his letter accompanying it : "It seemed to be the opinion, if we left here, (Washington) force, loan and volunteer bills might be passed, which would put Mr. Lincoln in immediate condition for hostilities. Whereas, by remaining in our places until the fourth of March, it is thought we can keep Mr. Buchanan's hands tied, and disable the Republicans from effecting any legislation which will strengthen the hands of the incoming Administration." Senator Iverson, of Georgia, in withdrawing from the United States Senate, said : "Georgia is one of six States, which, in less than sixty days, have dissolved their connection with the Federal Union. Steps are now in progress to form a Confederacy of their own. If you (the United States) acknowledge our independence, and treat us as one of the nations of the earth, you can have friendly relations and intercourse with us ; you can have an equitable division of the public property and of the existing public debt of the United States. But if you make war upon us, we will seize and hold all the public property in our borders, and in our reach ; we care not in what shape or form, or under what pretext you undertake *coercion ;* in whatever shape you make war, we will fight you." Still, nobody ventured to utter the word "treason." With the conclusion of the trial of Aaron Burr, treason seems to have been practically blotted out of the statutes of the United States.

The inauguration of Mr. Lincoln produced no immediately apparent change in the bearing of the Administration towards the South, but the views of the new President were very carefully expressed on the great questions towards which all thoughts were directed. He said : "To the extent of my ability I shall take care, as the Constitution itself expressly enjoins upon me, that the laws of the United States be faithfully executed in all the States. The power confided to me will be used to hold, occupy and possess the property and places belonging to the Government, and collect the duties and imposts ; but beyond what may be necessary for these objects, there will be no invasion, no using of force against or among the people anywhere."

This was the modest programme of the new President, and it did not look very belligerent. To the Secessionists he said : "In your hands, my dissatisfied countrymen, and not in mine, is the momentous issue of civil war. The Government will not assail you. You can have no conflict without being yourselves the aggressors. You have no oath registered in Heaven to destroy the Government, while I shall have the most solemn one 'to preserve, protect and defend it.' I am loath to close. We are not enemies, but friends ; we must not be enemies. Though passion may have strained, it must not break our bonds of affection. The mystic chords of memory, stretching from every battlefield and patriot grave to every living heart and hearthstone all over this broad land, will yet swell the chorus of the Union when again touched, as surely they will be, by the better angels of our nature."

Though these words were pacific, and held out the olive branch to the South, yet they fully covered the situation, and the conviction was general that Mr. Lincoln would live up to his solemn pledge, and at the proper time would act with decision and boldness. Although it might have been said that the South had already committed numerous acts of war against the Federal Government, yet each side wished to leave to the other the fearful responsibility of firing the first gun, if war must come.

As time went on, and the Federal Government adhered to its inoffensive policy, the leaders of Secession became apprehensive that the way to reconciliation might be opened or that the Secession ardor might abate, and they, therefore, resolved to put an impassable barrier between North and South. To this end, on the morning of the twelfth of April, they opened fire on Fort Sumter, and the gauge of battle could no longer be disregarded by Mr. Lincoln. The last hope of a peaceful solution expired with the reverberations of the first cannon that sent its shot against the walls of Sumter, and aroused the nation at last to a partial consciousness of the imminence of the danger which threatened it.

Our fathers regarded the militia of the several States as the true source of military strength in such a Government as ours, and the Constitution makes provision for calling out these citizen soldiers for service under the Federal authority It was feared, however, that the "cankers of a calm world and long peace" had left our militia organizations in anything but an efficient condition. Nevertheless, they had to be depended upon in this great emergency, and, perhaps, the result afforded the highest evidence of the wisdom and foresight of the fathers of the Constitution, in thus placing in the hands of these patriotic and voluntary organizations the ark of the Federal Constitution. At all events, they did not disappoint any reasonable hopes reposed in them, from the opening♦to the end of the rebellion.

[Some reader who thinks it witty or popular to laugh at the militia, (always excepting the New York Seventh and a half-dozen other crack regiments, here and there) is expected to turn up his nose at this general commendation, and ask : "How about the first Bull Run ?" We answer unhesitatingly, that veterans have seldom fought better under like conditions than our militia did on the 21st day of July, 1861, at Bull Run. In proof of this, we propose to present, by and by, some facts for the consideration of the reader.]

Under the authority thus conferred, Mr. Lincoln, on the fifteenth day of April, issued his proclamation, setting forth that certain States were engaged in obstructing the laws of the United States, by combinations too powerful to be suppressed by the ordinary course of judicial proceedings, and that he therefore called for the militia of the several States, to the aggregate number of seventy-five thousand men.

The Bay State displayed most alacrity in responding to this call, and on the day following the promulgation of the proclamation, the 6th Massachusetts regiment, completely equipped, left Boston for the National Capital. Baltimore lay like a dragon across their line of march, and while passing through that city, the regiment was attacked by a furious mob of rebel sympathizers, and several of its men were killed or severely wounded.

Following this event, the railroad bridges over Gunpowder, Bush and Canton Rivers, between Baltimore and Havre de Grace, were burned, and the Government was obliged to find other routes for transporting troops and war material, from the east and north to the Capital.

Now, however, inflamed nearly as much by the brutal and unprovoked assault on the 6th Massachusetts, as by the attack on Fort Sumter, prodigious energy was displayed in the forwarding of troops, and in a few days the Administration felt that all danger of its expulsion from the Capital was over, and that the nucleus of an army was encamped around the city.

Considering the fact that the Rebellion was quasi-political, the uprising of the masses of the people of the loyal States, irrespective of party, was something wonderful in the history of revolutionary movements. The southern leaders supposed that the ties of party would bind to their cause a considerable body of men in every State, and that if they did not act with them, they would at least openly sympathize with them. And they believed that this course would seriously hamper and embarrass the administration : but instead of this, political ties with the rebel South were snapped asunder without a moment's hesitation, and Democrat and Republican stood shoulder to shoulder in support of the Government.

The country had just passed through an unusually heated and exciting political canvass, and it was the purpose of the secessionists to strike the blow for dissolution before the blood, warmed up in the political contest, had resumed its cool and wonted flow. But its effect upon their political allies was the reverse of what they looked for, and really, of what they had reason to expect. No other age or country has ever presented the exact parallel of such an inflexible line of demarkation as between the rebel and loyal States. True, the people of the so-called border States were divided on the question ; but passing these, either way, there were no contending factions ; practically, on the southerly side all the whites were rebels, and on the northerly side *all* were loyal.

The impression that prevailed so generally at the North, in the early days of the war, that a large proportion of the whites in the Southern States were opposed to secession and wanted to see the Union preserved, was a baseless delusion. There may have been many, who like A. H. Stephens, were averse to a separation, but when the deed was done, they, like him, gave their whole souls to the cause. Exceptions here and there, like the case of John Minor Botts on the rebel side, and Vallandingham on the Union side, were striking chiefly because of the rarity of such instances.

It required a few months to effectually dispel another Northern delusion, in which the "hope was father to the thought." We could reason upon the fall of Sumter without necessarily plunging the country into war, and we tried hard to believe that when the South saw the government arm for the strife, it would find some way by which diplomacy might avert the impending conflict, and restore the revolted States to their allegiance to the Government. But Bull-Run extinguished this fond hope, and as the news of that untoward battle sped over the country, the Administration and the people saw the struggle was inevitable and that it would assume herculean proportions, and it and they prepared to meet it.

The revolted States embraced an area of 783,144 square miles, with a white population of 5,672,272 and 3,279,320 slaves. The slaves, who were counted upon in the beginning, by our Northern people, as an element of weakness to the South, really constituted one of the rebels' most useful factors in carrying on the war. Their fidelity to their masters, under all the circumstances, was most extraordinary, and enabled the white population to send all its able-bodied men into the field, while the industry of the negroes provided for the wants of the non-combatants, and very largely also for the Confederate armies. Moreover, the negroes were employed by the Confederates in various quasi-military occupations in the commissary, quartermaster's and ordnance departments, whereby an equal number of whites were relegated to the ranks.

This condition of things enabled the Confederates, with a white population greatly inferior to that of the loyal States, to rally around their standards during the first two years of the war, armies quite as large, and sometimes larger than our own.

The magnitude of the attempt to coerce these people, and constrain them to acknowledge and respect the federal authority, can only be measured by the vast area of their territory, the number and the circumstances of the population, and the severity and duration of the contest.

CHAPTER III.

THE Constitution of the United States declares that a well-regulated militia is necessary to the security of a free State. The Constitution and Laws of the State of New York provide for the creation and maintenance of a militia organization. But there had been nothing to arouse the military ardor of our people for more than a quarter of a century after the close of the last war with Great Britain, and our militia organizations drooped and degenerated until they became mere burlesques. Long years of peace and habits of thrift and industry had practically extinguished the martial spirit, except in our cities, where favorable conditions enabled the organizations to flourish.

The war with Mexico stimulated the military sentiment in a gentle way, but produced no permanent results. Again, a long period of peace ensued, and it seemed as improbable that war should visit our peaceful land as that the sun should cease to shine upon it, or that its rich soil should refuse to return to the husbandman the rewards of his industry We were at comity with all the world, and never dreamed of treason. Why then, should our artizans and farmers, our merchants and lawyers, play their brief hour at soldiering once or twice a year? Why should our intensely practical people mimic the "pride, pomp and circumstance of glorious war," who never more should see "battle's magnificently stern array?"

The militia organization of which the "Twentieth" was the successor, was known in its day as the 245th Regiment, and it did nothing to impress itself upon the annals of its time. The very number it bore proves its absurdity. Like its fellows, it had neither cohesion or discipline, uniforms or equipments. It occasionally helped to amuse the people at "general trainings," which events usually resulted in a general train.

This was not the fault of its commanding officer, but of the system upon which these regiments were organized and maintained, and the inevitable demoralization resulting therefrom. The 245th was the peer of any of its fellow country organizations, and probably superior to many.

Colonel Christopher Fiero, then and now a resident of Saugerties, Ulster County, was commissioned by Governor Silas Wright, colonel of the 245th, January 13th, 1845, and continued to command it until a re-organization took place, under an act of the Legislature, passed in 1847, whereby the counties of Ulster and Sullivan were constituted a new regimental district, to be known as the "Twentieth Regimental District," and Colonel Fiero, as the senior commandant, was commissioned colonel of the new organization, April 28th, 1848.

The two counties were sub-divided into eight company districts, according to population, and with the following result : First Company—Saugerties and Woodstock. Second—Kingston and Shandaken. Third—Hurley, Olive and Marbletown. Fourth—Rosendale, Esopus and New-Paltz. Fifth—Rochester and Warwarsing. Sixth—Lloyd, Plattekill and Marlborough, for Ulster County ; and Sullivan as follows : Seventh—Rockland, Neversink, Callicoon, Liberty and Fallsburgh. Eighth—Cochecton, Bethel, Thompson and Lumberland. There were to be two flank companies raised in the district at large, one of artillery and one of rifles.

The first regimental roster was as follows: Christopher Fiero, Colonel; Henry A. Samson, of Samsonville, Lieutenant-Colonel; John D. O'Neil, of Fallsburgh, Major; John L. Butzel, of Saugerties, Adjutant; Jason Gillespy, of Saugerties, Quartermaster; William Hornbeck, of Ellenville, Paymaster; Abram Crispell, of Rondout, Surgeon; Rev. Silas Fitch, Rondout, Chaplain.

The line officers were: First Company--Francis Haber, succeeded by Abram H. Martin, Captain; Seaman G. Searing, First Lieutenant; William B. Dubois, Second Lieutenant. Second Company—George F Von Beck, Captain; soon after promoted to Brigade inspector, and succeeded by Adam Metzger. Nicholas Kreitel, First Lieutenant. Third Company—James A. Gillespy, Captain, Stone Ridge. Fourth Company—John Van Ostrand, Rosendale, Captain. Fifth Company—M. D. Freer, Ellenville, Captain. Sixth Company--John Bodine, Modena, Captain.

An additional company was organized at Kingston, with Teunis H. Haulenbeck as Captain, T. V G. Folant as First Lieutenant, and George Van Keuren as Second Lieutenant. A company was organized at Samsonville, of which James E. Gay was Captain, J. P Schoonmaker, First Lieutenant, and Samuel Penneman, Second Lieutenant. Of the artillery company, Dennis Carroll was Captain, Michael Maher, First, and James Diamond and Patrick Kinney, Second and Third Lieutenants. John Derrenbacher was Captain of the rifle company, and Jacob Hersch was First, and F. G. Horst was Second Lieutenant.

On the nineteenth of May, 1855, Gideon E. Bushnell, of Clarryville, Sullivan County, was commissioned colonel, in place of Fiero, resigned. Colonel Bushnell had some time previously been appointed lieutenant-colonel in place of Samson, who had been promoted to the command of the eighth brigade.

To show the interest still felt in the organization by its first regimental commander, I take the liberty to copy the concluding paragraphs of a letter recently received from Colonel Fiero :

"My active connection with the regiment ceased on my resignation in 1855, when I was succeeded by Lieutenant-Colonel Bushnell. Your intimate acquaintance with the period immediately succeeding, will no doubt furnish you abundant materials for further details after that date.

"I must, however, be allowed to express the great degree of satisfaction afforded me in learning of the probable speedy completion of the story of the old 20th, in whose early history I indulge a pardonable pride, which is intensified by the fact, that in its subsequent career, it more than fulfilled the hopes of its friends and outdid the expectations of its founders.

"It is a source of hearty congratulation to those interested in the organization, that it is to find a historian, not only from among those who are familiar with its career during 'the piping times of peace,' but in one who was actively connected with it 'in the days that tried men's souls,' and who was in a position to learn the facts which will now enable him to do full justice to its merits. Wishing you abundant success in your undertaking,

I remain yours very truly,
CHRISTOPHER FIERO,
Late Col. 20th Reg't, N Y S. M."

On the eighteenth of October, 1878, an anonymous writer published in the *Kingston Journal* an article on the early history of the Twentieth, which contains so many interesting historical and biographical facts, that I insert it. It is as follows :

"The brief history of the Twentieth Regiment given

in a recent article in the *Journal*, in connection with an
account of the reunion of the veterans, has not only received warm commendation as a faithful and correct
sketch of its record during the rebellion, but has called
out reminiscences of the days before the war, and awakened interest in the story of the organization of the
' Ulster Guard.'

"We therefore recall some of the facts connected with
the formation of the regiment, which to many will re-
vive associations and call up recollections of scenes and
faces once as familiar as "household words;" premising
that the intimation contained in the previous article,
that the regiment was formed in 1857, related to its consolidation with the Twenty-eighth Regiment, which up
to that time had existed as a separate organization, into
a single command, under Colonel Pratt, rather than to
the date when it assumed the form and took the name
under which it has been a source of honor and just pride
to the citizens of Ulster.

" The Twentieth Regiment was organized and established in 1851, under the direction of the State military
authorities, by Colonel Christopher Fiero, then and still
a resident of Saugerties, under the militia law of 1847,
and succeeded a military organization which had been
known as the Two Hundred and Forty-fifth Regiment,
of which Colonel Fiero was the commandant at the time
it was disbanded, and by virtue of his rank became
Colonel of the new regiment, and, as such, supervised
the enlistment of the men and recommended the appointment of the officers ; and in 1852 many of the men
who were for a long time prominent in social, business
and military circles, and some of whom afterward distinguished themselves at the front among the bravest of
the brave, began their military career.

"Prominent among the first officers was General Henry
A. Samson, who was appointed to the Lieutenant-Colonelcy, in which position he always took a most intense

interest in military affairs, and which position he filled
until, at a later date, he was promoted to the rank of
Brigadier-General, commanding the Eighth Brigade,
which included the old regiment.

"Major George F Von Beck received his first commission as Captain of an infantry company of the Twentieth, which he was active in recruiting at Rondout, and
which he commanded until appointed Brigade-Inspector
upon the staff of General Samson, with rank of Major,
thus obtaining the military title by which he was best
known—a position which he filled for a considerable
period.

"Dr. Abram Crispell was the first regimental Surgeon,
and how long and how creditably he filled that office is
a matter the recollection of which is not confined to
those alone who recall the days before the war, and his
connection with the command dates from its infancy to
the days when it made history.

"Captain John Derrenbacher was closely identified
with the enlistment of one of the companies, of which
he was the principal promoter and earliest commandant,
while other companies were organized at different points
throughout the county, including Saugerties, Rosendale,
Stone Ridge and Ellenville.

"Among the company commanders commissioned at
this time is Captain John Bodine, who has since achieved
so enviable a notoriety as a representative American
rifleman, and whose wonderful nerve at Dollymount won
the admiration of Europe and America. Captain Bodine commanded the company recruited at Modena, and
in his present position as Division-Inspector of Rifle
Practice, doubtless contemplates with no little pleasure
the proficiency in marksmanship of the members of the
Twentieth Battalion, when he recalls the fact that they
are the successors of the organization of which he was
once a conspicuous member.

"Shortly after the completion of the regimental organ-

3

ization. Colonel Fiero, having arrived at the age when
military service was no longer obligatory, resigned his
commission, and was succeeded by G. E. Bushnell, who
had succeeded to the Lieutenant-Colonelcy on the promotion of General Samson.　By this vacancy General T.
B. Gates, who had been connected with the regiment as
a member of the staff, was promoted to the rank of Major ; and that the General was one of those to whom
the Twentieth owes much of its early progress is almost
forgotten in view of the later events in its history, in
which he figured so prominently and acquitted himself
so creditably　In this connection it may be appropriate
matter for congratulation that in him the regiment is to
find a historian who has personal knowledge of all the
facts and circumstances of its early history, as well as
personal experience of the perils of the bivouac and the
field, and who can mingle with the calmness of the critic
the enthusiasm of the soldier, and add to the dignity of
history the vivid impressions of a spectator, and the
correct recollections of an observer.

" At a later date Colonel George W Pratt, having removed from the territory in which the Twenty-eighth
Regiment had been recruited, took command of the consolidated regiments under the designation of the Twentieth, and devoted himself to the drill and discipline of
the command, so that as he rode down Broadway at
their head on the march to the front, he might well feel
that he was leading one of the crack regiments of the
Empire State.　Yet he perfected what another had
planned and organized, and under Colonel Fiero was
formed the nucleus of that splendid corps whose battle-
stained banners tell so impressive a tale of the dangers
and the triumphs of so many hard-fought fields.　And
it is enough of honor to the memory of Colonel Pratt,
that with one of the finest military organizations of the
State, brought to a high state of efficiency by his untiring labors, he led the way to the front while thousands

hesitated, and enough of glory that those who followed
—dying—were worthy of the baptism of fire to which
he led them, and—living—ever cherish the memory of
the hero of Bull Run.

"To the successors of the Ulster Guard is transmitted
all the responsibility as well as the glory of their brilliant record, and it is safe to say that the present organization can be fairly expected to keep up the reputation
of the 'Twentieth.'"

Gen. Henry A. Samson, who was promoted from the
Lieutenant-Colonelcy of the regiment to the command
of the Eighth Brigade, was a very enthusiastic militiaman
and a most energetic officer. It was through his influence, chiefly, that the great encampment was held near
Kingston, in August, 1855. He always attended the
parades and encampments of any troops of his brigade,
and exerted himself to the utmost to increase the numbers and improve the condition of the force under his
command. He was a plain, uncultured man, and
really knew very little of military tactics or science, and
did not pretend to. But he was a true, earnest man,
faithful to every enterprise in which he embarked, and
loyal to his friends. His energy was tireless, and his
disposition was of that unusual quality of consistency
that his attachments for persons or occupations never
waned. He had a great fondness for the pomp and pag-
eantry of military life, and the infrequent occasions
when he could review his troops or go into camp with
them, were epochs of genuine pleasure. Nor was this
a childish pleasure—a mere love of spectacle; but it
was a pleasure derived from a consciousness of power—
of the command of men. While he would assume great
austerity towards officers who were remiss in the
discharge of their military duty, he had not the heart
to inflict punishment. He would terrify a delinquent
by the severity of his manner, and at the very climax of
the scene would relent and condone the offense. On

the occasion of a parade of the "Twentieth," at Kingston, in 1855, B Company tarried in the village, instead of reporting at the parade ground, as was its duty, and Gen. Samson was exceedingly indignant. Captain Teunis Haulenbeck, who commanded the company, was ordered to report, forthwith, to General Samson at the Kingston hotel. In the parlor of that old and popular hostelry was seated the General, belted and spurred, and surrounded by his gorgeously uniformed staff. To these enter Captain Haulenbeck, six feet three inches tall, and looking every inch a soldier, but as solemn of visage as a Crusader; he walks to the center of the room, halts, and gives the General a military salute. For a minute or two no one speaks or moves, but the General is looking at the towering culprit as though he was deliberating upon the various modes of execution, with a view to select the one capable of inflicting the most suffering upon the victim. At length, in tones hard as iron, he demanded of the Captain the reason of his failure to appear on the ground at the proper time. The Captain set up as his excuse for his breach of discipline some trivial matter of military etiquette, which, in his judgment, justified a disobedience of orders on his part, but which really was of no force as a justification. The General then began what was intended to be a severe reprimand, but his heart softened before he had gone far enough to hurt the Captain's feelings, and he concluded with inviting the Captain to take a glass of wine, and then directing him to march his company to the field.

On another occasion, and while the Eighth Brigade was encamped at Poughkeepsie, in 1857, the General ordered the field officer of the day to be arrested upon the ground that he had gone outside the line of sentinels during the night. The incident occurred at midnight, and the General and his staff had congregated at the guard tent to see the order executed. The officer of the day denied the justice and legality of the order, and insisted that, as officer of the day, it was his right, and might often be his duty, to pass the line of sentinels, and that they had no right to stop him, knowing him to be the officer of the day. The General finally became convinced that he was wrong, and apologized to the officer for the threatened indignity, and there the matter dropped. The officer shortly afterwards found a basket of champagne deposited at his house, without ever knowing from whence it came, but he always suspected General Samson. It was a libation in atonement for an unintentional offense against the rules of the service, and was delicately made.

The General would have gone into the field at the breaking out of the Rebellion, if physical infirmities had not disqualified him. In his death Ulster County lost a worthy and valuable citizen, and the National Guard one of its most liberal and earnest friends.

CHAPTER IV

GEORGE W PRATT was born on the eighteenth day of
April, 1830, at Prattsville, Green County, New York.
His father, Colonel Zadock Pratt, had acquired a fortune
in the business of tanning leather, and had achieved
considerable reputation as an energetic and sagacious
business man. He had represented his district in Congress, and had filled various minor positions of honor
and trust. Illiterate himself, he, nevertheless, appreciated the advantages of education, and gave his son the
best facilities for acquiring a thorough knowledge of

books and men. His education, begun here, was completed in Europe. When but seventeen years of age he traveled over the larger portion of his own country, and a year later crossed the ocean and made the tour of the Continent. He ascended the Nile, and spent much time on its historic banks—not in idleness, but devoting his opportunities to the acquisition of knowledge, and especially in studying the Arabic language, in which he became proficient. Returning home in 1850, he was made a captain in his father's regiment of militia, and assumed the duties of cashier of his father's bank at Prattsville. A few months later he again went to Europe with his sister. In 1850, when he was but twenty years old, the First University of Mecklinburgh conferred on him the degree of Doctor of Philosophy.

Young Pratt returned from his second European tour in 1851. His father observed, on the occasion, that he came back "in good health and much improved. This trip and that previously made by Captain Pratt cost about sixteen thousand dollars, but it was money well spent."

On attaining his majority in 1853, his father gave him fifty thousand dollars, and one-half of the Samsonville Tannery, the other half of which was owned by General Samson, and from that time until Pratt's death they continued co-partners.

Pratt had not been spoiled, as so many other young men have been, and will continue to be, by the affluence which surrounded him, and the indulgence with which he was treated. His habits were industrious, and his tastes studious, with a fondness for literary pursuits. He was an earnest, tireless worker at whatever he set himself about, and possessed an ability for the comprehension and arrangement of the details of business that was as valuable as it was unusual.

On the thirty-first of May, 1855, young Pratt was married to Miss Anna Tibbits, daughter of Benjamin

Tibbits, Esquire, of Albany, by the Right Rev. Bishop Potter, of Pennsylvania. Soon thereafter he removed to Kingston, where he resided a few years, and then settled upon a farm which he purchased, on the banks of the Hudson, in the town of Esopus, in Ulster County.

From the moment Pratt took up his residence in Kingston, he identified himself with the affairs of the county, and was foremost in all works of a public character, and especially in those voluntary movements designed to promote the development of the historical riches of the county—a kind of study of which he was very fond, and in which he would delve with tireless zeal. He was a member of the "Ulster Historical Society," and I cannot better show the character of the man, and the estimation in which he was held by some of the best known and most distinguished men of the county, than by incorporating into this work the proceedings of the society, at its meeting held on the sixteenth of October, 1862—a month after Colonel Pratt's death ; moreover, these proceedings show in what estimation these gentlemen held the regiment which Pratt had commanded, and what they proposed to do to perpetuate the memory of its heroic services. May their design be carried out ere "the opium of time deals with the memories of men."

Hon. A. Bruyn Hasbrouck, LL.D., President, in the chair ; Reuben Bernard, Esq., Treasurer and acting Secretary. After the transaction of necessary preliminary business, Henry H. Reynolds arose and said :

" MR. PRESIDENT : Limited as may seem to some to-day our historic field of labor and the interest taken by others in our efforts, none here are unconscious of the events passing about us, making up a momentous history, in many respects, of sad and solemn importance. One of these is upon all our hearts to-day, as we contemplate a vacant place, never so before, but at the call of patriotism or duty. Of him who filled it, the

lips of the strongest among you were too tremulous
first to speak, for such knew him best and longest, and,
therefore, loved him most. So it has not seemed presumptuous in me to accept the charge in offering the
resolutions I am about to present. No one who has
known our history or him for whom we mourn this
day will deem these resolves a mere formality, or
doubt the deep emotion with which we seek to add one
more wreath to his grave, one more tribute to his
memory. We could have said far more in like sincerity, nor blush in after years to speak of it to each
other, for to no other man has this Society owed so
much. The efforts of others have been earnest and
effective ; the desire to do honor to your noble ancestry
has prompted to honorable labors and sacrifices, and
yet amidst them all, again and again, as you have
marked the unwearied and unselfish perseverance of
our noble comrade, and responded to his earnest and
courteous appeals, you have freely passed to him the
tribute of commendation offered to all, and claimed
only for yourselves, that

" ' The trophies of Miltiades will not let me rest.'

"It is too early yet for us to speak to each other of
the nature and extent of our loss ; and besides there is
too much that is sorrowful and sad in this and other
events about us to permit us to do more than cheer
and encourage one another. And so we need, in some
degree, to antedate our consolation as we strive for submission to the Divine allotment. As the captive tribes
of Israel, amid all the depression or the prosperity of
their Babylonish condition, ever left some part of their
dwellings—palace or hovel—unfinished or broken, to
remind of the desolation of Jerusalem, we shall not be
without mementos of our loss, and do best for the
past, the present and the future, by recognizing in them
the hand that writes all history

"Eight hundred years ago, in a cause then deemed more sacred than the love of country, a mixed multitude went forth from Southern Europe to rescue the Temple and the Sepulchre. In the market-place of Clermont the eloquence of Urban awoke from an hundred thousand lips the shout, almost of triumph, 'God wills it! God wills it!' and so that host went forth to the field of conflict and of death. That unearthly battle-cry is the utterance, though far more sad and low, that with muffled voice and sobbing, here and elsewhere, speaks of our wise counselor and faithful fellow-laborer. It is the assurance of our consolation in the day when we may dare to speak of the great inheritance of which we are co-heirs—the memory of such a life, the witness of such a death. Nor even now may we forget, that as on the forms of ancient Christian martyrs—Andronicus and his fellow-sufferers—a fond tradition said the stars came down to rest; so were such a witness given to our honored dead—not those alone that on his country's banner told its past history and advancing glory would be there, but those, to our tearful vision, the brighter for its darkness—that gem, a crown more unfading and enduring than the laurel.

"To our own section of land he loved so well he gave no small portion of the earnest sympathies and labor of his most active life; to the whole of that land he gave the sacrifice of that life; and thus to both a memory more enduring than either, and beyond which neither shall have a trophy of history more priceless.

> " 'They never fail who die
> In a great cause—though years elapse,
> And others share as dark a doom;
> They but augment the deep and sweeping thoughts
> Which overspread all others, and conduct
> The world at last to freedom.' "

"Mr. Reynolds then submitted the following resolutions:

" *Resolved*, That the Historical Society may well claim a place among the multitude of mourners over the honored grave of Colonel George W Pratt, its late Secretary, and record its sense of the great loss sustained in that of one to whose ardent and unwearied labors in its behalf, it owes much of its prosperity, if not its very existence.

" *Resolved*, That while we bow in sorrowing submission to the Divine dispensation which has removed from the midst of us a scholar and patriot, we would recognize, with devout gratitude, his unsullied example, as an incentive to earnest effort, as well in our especial field as in every other of usefulness and philanthropy

" *Resolved*, That such efforts in behalf of institutions so dear to him, will be among the best tributes we can render to his commanding excellencies, and best witnesses of the respect and affection with which he was regarded by all who knew him.

" *Resolved*, That the Executive Committee be requested to obtain a portrait of Colonel Pratt, suitable for preservation among our archives."

The President, A. BRUYN HASBROUCK, said :

" GENTLEMEN : It is known to the members of the Society, that a memoir of the life and character of Colonel Pratt was in preparation to be read to us at this meeting. Our associate, the Rev Mr. Temple, who had kindly undertaken the task, was obliged to decline, from not being able in due time before this meeting to procure such particulars of the earlier life of Colonel Pratt as he deemed necessary for the completion of his work. I cannot but hope, however, that the reverend gentleman will, at an early day, favor the Society and the friends of Colonel Pratt with the result of his inquiries, which cannot fail to be both interesting and instructive. As it is, we are left to review the character of Colonel Pratt only in its more general aspect, as it was exhibited in his brief intercourse with the world

and in his connection with this Society Enough, however, remains to confirm the opinion of his friends and
of those who intimately knew him, that he was no ordinary man ; to justify the warm eulogium expressed
in the resolutions now offered for adoption, and the
many public demonstrations of regard which have been
made since his death. I might, perhaps, after what
has already been said by Mr. Reynolds, have contented
myself with a mere cordial assent to the passage of
these resolutions. But it seems to me that the pro-
prieties of the office I have the honor to hold among
you require something more than a silent vote ; that
my official and personal relations with Colonel Pratt
demand some open demonstration of my regard, some
outspoken expression of sympathy with the Society in
the loss it has sustained. I have often been struck at
Masonic funerals with the simple ceremony I observed
there, where each member of the Order throws a sprig
of evergreen into the grave of a departed brother.
Without understanding the meaning of this act, I can,
at least, catch its spirit ; and I would now, with all of
the recollections of the past, with all of the regard and
of the hope which it seems to imply, venture to offer
to the memory of our departed associate the poor
tribute of my reverence.

"It was my melancholy gratification, with some of
the members of this Society, as its representatives, and
with many citizens of Ulster, to be an attendant at the
funeral of Colonel Pratt. And as the procession moved
from the church to the distant cemetery, with muffled
drum and solemn dirge, through the crowded streets of
the Capital, amid ranks of soldiers, at mournful, military rest upon their arms, past long lines of sympathizing members of the Masonic brotherhood, I could not
but recall the familiar line, which, though poetry, I then
felt to be no fiction—

" ' The paths of glory lead but to the tomb.'

But after the last sad rites had been performed, and as
the mourners went about the streets, each carrying to
his home the lesson of mortality taught by the occasion, when the sun, on the very verge of the horizon,
suddenly shone through the clouds and illumined the
whole western sky with the rich tints of an autumnal
evening, I forgot the despondent sentiment of the elegist
in remembering the equally familiar but exultant strains
of the Christian poet :

> " ' See truth, love and mercy, in triumph ascending,
> And Nature all glowing in Eden's first bloom ;
> On the cold cheek of Death smiles and roses are blending,
> And beauty immortal awakes from the tomb.'

" Yes, it is indeed consoling to know, that here is
not the end of our being—that the grave is but the portal
to another world.   For we have an assurance, which has
sustained many a stricken mourner and been a balm for
many a wounded heart—which will exert its influence,
too, till the battle of the warrior is no more heard, and
garments are no longer seen rolled in blood ; an assurance higher than the inspiration of mere human
poetry—a *Divine* assurance, that this corruption must
put on incorruption, and this mortal must put on immortality   In the providence of God, the Angel of
Mercy is thus made to move swiftly on the footsteps of
the Destroyer, and survivors are consoled and cheered
in knowing and believing, that all our friend's graces
of character which so attracted our admiration ; that all
his amiable qualities, which so won and fixed our regard ; that all his talents and acquirements, which
blossomed so thickly ' in the dew of his youth,' and
gave such ' hopes of unaccomplished years ;' that all
his ardor of patriotism, which shrunk from no sacrifice,
even of life itself, have not been consigned to lie in
the cold obstruction of the grave ; but that they will
awake from the tomb, to be clothed upon with immortality.

"Among the personages of a former period, whom history has delighted to honor, and around whose memory are clustered the choicest tributes of eloquence, of poetry and romance, stands conspicuous the name of Sir Philip Sidney I trust I shall not be suspected of an undue or exaggerated estimate of our friend's merits, when I say, that I find much in his life and character to remind me of that distinguished man. Both possessed of the advantages of wealth and high social position ; both passing through early life, amid the dangers and temptations incident to such a condition (so often, alas ! fatal to young men), with untainted morality and habitual virtue ; both dying at an age when most men have but just put on harness and are yet hesitatingly treading the arena of action ; honored in their day and generation, and mourned at their death, beyond the measure accorded to few of their years ; with habits and pursuits nearly identical, and talents and acquirements different only in degree ; both, amid the love of books and the calmer pursuits of polite literature, still intent upon the knowledge of tactics and the study of all the arts of war ; both tearing themselves away from troops of friends, the caresses of society, and the endearments of home to endure the privations of the camp, and to meet the stern realities of war on the perilous edges of battle—falling, wounded on the battle-field, at precisely the same age, and alike carried away by sympathizing soldiers to die of their wounds at no distant day, among kindred and friends ; it needs but the touching incident of the cup of cold water declined by Sir Philip in the extremity of his distress, and proffered to a dying soldier at his side, to complete the parallel. From what we know of Colonel Pratt's character and the impulses of his nature, we may be sure, had the occasion presented itself, that the cup of cold water and the generous offer would not have been wanting still more to strengthen the resemblance.

"I need not, surely, remind the members of this Society, how, with his whole heart, Colonel Pratt devoted himself to its interests. One of its founders, its first and hitherto its only Secretary, he labored to give it character at home and a name abroad, with a degree of success that outstripped the exertions of the best of us. Coming to reside among us, almost an entire stranger; descended from a family that had never struck root or fibre in the soil of our county since its earliest settlement, he yet labored with the zeal of a native to explore its early history, and to exalt its character. He came to seat himself, at once, with the familiarity of kindred and descent, at what the poet has called 'the fireside of our hearts;' and listening there, with filial interest, to the tales and misty traditions of former times, he garnered up his materials, not to gratify an idle curiosity, or to enrich the pages of some future romance, but for profit and instruction ; to present them to us in the nakedness of truth—to fix them in the dignity of history. His paper, published in our collections, on the expeditions of General Vaughan up the Hudson, and the consequent destruction of Kingston by the troops under his command, has been pronounced by those best qualified to judge, a highly valuable contribution to the History of the Revolutionary War. I can myself bear witness to the patience he exhibited, amidst much doubt and perplexity, in the preparation of that work ; to his liberal expenditure of time and money, and to the earnestness with which he sought to verify every statement he made—extending his inquiries even to the *paper offices* in London—all, at last, to result in a narrative of charming detail, and undoubted authenticity—honorable to himself and to this Society In my sober judgment, if Colonel Pratt had no other claim ; if there were no faithful discharge of duty, no generous public spirit, no patriotism, no loss of life in his country's service to speak of, his interest

in this Society and his contributions to it would alone
entitle him to the lasting gratitude of the people of
Ulster.

" Gentlemen : It is no light thing to tell of a man
after he has gone ; it is something that will ' blossom in
his grave and smell sweet ' in after days that, amid the
occupations of a busy life and in a period of great political anxiety, he could turn aside to devote his time
and talents to rescue from neglect the piety, the sufferings, the bravery and the patriotism of an humble and
almost forgotten generation ; that he illustrated in his
own conduct, even to the bitter end, the love of liberty
and the devotedness to his country, which he found
exhibited there.   That he taught us by his example, in
the words of his own chosen motto of our Society—
*Gedenkt aen-de-dagen-van-ouds—to remember the days
of old ;* that we, too, might learn there, lessons of conduct, and gather courage and hope in the troubles that
so thickly beset us now.

" Gentlemen : Colonel Pratt's course is finished ;
' his warfare is accomplished.' Having himself passed
into history, let us do for him what he has done for
others ; let us enroll his name among the worthies of
the country Let the resolutions be entered on our
minutes, that those that are to follow us, in these our
labors of love, may know how highly we esteemed our
associate—how truly we revered his memory, as a man,
a citizen and patriot soldier. For he was, indeed, an
embodiment of Shakspeare's conception of a finished
man :

> " ' His years but young, but his experience old ;
> His head unmellowed, but his judgment ripe,
> And in a word,
> Complete in feature and in mind,
> With all good grace to grace a gentleman.'

" Mr. William Lounsbery, having been requested,
from his acquaintance with Colonel Pratt's public life,

seconded the Resolutions. He advocated their adoption as follows :

WILLIAM LOUNSBERY'S REMARKS.

"MR. PRESIDENT : The Ulster Historical Society, at this day of its assembling, commemorates the burning of Kingston, and the sufferings of our early settlers in their first struggle for independence. The resolutions which have been proposed are equally suggestive of patriotic sacrifice, and strike us with a closer sympathy. They commemorate the loss of one of our founders, who has lately fallen in another contest to preserve the liberties and Government handed down to us by the heroism of our ancestors. This Society would be unequal to its trust, if it passed by in silence a loss so vital to the country and itself.

"It is with no ordinary feelings that I have undertaken to respond to the resolutions just offered, and to utter an appropriate tribute to the worth, enterprise and heroism of our late secretary, Colonel George W Pratt.

" Government is the work of mortal man. The social fabric is sustained and held together by the enterprise of individuals. And when a man of intelligence and active virtues falls, either by the ordinary decay of age, or, more suddenly, by violence and war, we feel the structure crumbling, and see the beauties of the edifice defaced. In the death of Colonel Pratt a column has fallen in the temple of liberty The decorations which art and learning and civilization have added to it, have been marred and mutilated, and are not to be quickly repaired.

"Some lives do not perform very vital functions in the community A retiring or selfish nature works in quiet—out of sight of associates, and does not mingle in such efforts as society puts forth for its advancement

4

by the combination of multitudes. I do not say that
such are useless, but their death is not so much felt.
Their little circle of action revolves upon itself, and its
destruction does not jostle and unhinge the public aspirations, or break up the social progress. They are
not missed from the world—their death is not counted
by so large a value. So many of such do not seem to
die. The poet utters this conviction when he says:

> " 'The good die first, and those
> Whose hearts are dry as summer dust,
> Burn to the socket.' "

"Colonel Pratt was a man of active and busy enterprise. He had the inspiration of a genius that works
and accomplishes. He set to work and did not look
back. He had the elements of a great man, which only
failed to ripen into eminence by the accident of his
early death.

" I recollect when the plan to form this Society was
first revolved in his mind. I think it originated with
him, though the materials for the work were not lack-
ing either as to the field of operations or the workers
that were called out. He saw that Ulster County was a
rich field for historical research, and he undertook to
lead and stimulate the action of the people in that direction.

" I was one who distrusted the project and express
ed the fear that a society, organized simply for plodding among dusty records, or turning up memorials of
the past, could not be sustained by a practical and
working people, however intelligent. This was suggested to him when we were going in company to attend
the meeting to organize this Society. He thought dif-
ferently, and it is proved that he was right. The half-
dozen that assembled in the Dutch Church, at New
Paltz, have grown into an organization that has made
its mark upon the literary character of the age. How

much of this is due to the personal efforts of Colonel Pratt, the members of the Society, here assembled, are the witnesses. He was ably seconded by men of a high order of intelligence and spirit, but the organization and direction of the enterprise were his, and its present prosperity is a part of the glory that clusters about his memory

"The spirit in which this enterprise was accomplished was only a type of his other efforts. The Ulster County Regiment was organized and equipped into a military corps, and when the war broke out he marched at the head of his men by the side of the regiments of New York City. It was his glory and the glory of his country, that he took to the field the only regiment of the State Militia, outside of New York and Brooklyn, and the one equipped under the eye of the State authorities, at Albany

"In the years 1858-9, Colonel Pratt represented Ulster County in the State Senate. At that time the Senate Library was being removed from its old room in the Capitol, to the new building erected in the rear for the purpose. The work of arranging the State collections was entrusted to a committee of the Senate, of which Colonel Pratt was the working head.

" I have lately had occasion to admire his work in the arrangement of the invaluable archives there collected by our great State. It shows the master hand of a faithful and intelligent worker, and will furnish for ages a curious testimonial of his genius.

" After the return of the Ulster County Regiment from its three months campaign, I visited Colonel Pratt at his new residence in Esopus. He pointed out to me his future plans in reference to beautifying the grounds of his new home. I took in the picture which his own fancy was painting for coming years. The happy family circle of his wife and children—the surroundings of fields and shaded walks—the landscape, with the

beautiful river in front—his library, so full of the learning of which already he had imbibed so much—and
wealth to furnish every rational comfort—were all his.

" In view of this picture, I asked if it was his intention to take command of his regiment for the remainder of the war. I felt then impressed with the
extent of the calamity, if his life were sacrificed by such
a resolution. I knew, too, that *he* was impressed with
the fearful nature of the hazard. His wife had plead,
with tears of regret, all she dared urge against her
country His children and his plans of home and
home comforts had been busy in dissuading him. And
his reply was impressive for its earnest sadness. 'I
shall go again,' he said. He made the sacrifice—and
oh, how great !

" Who can replace the fallen column ? Who can
repair the mutilated ornament, or restore to beauty this
shattered ruin ? Who can again fill the place in that
widow's blighted heart ? Who can heal an aged father's
sorrow ? Who can take up the noble aspirations that
were blossoming into bright fruition ?

" Death hath stricken us all. Country, society and
friends have suffered a common calamity, and have a
common sorrow. The grave, so arbitrary in its deal-
ings, hath taken him in the beginning of usefulness.
His youth and virtue—too glorious for a common
death, have given him a sacrifice to our Constitution
and liberties, and insured for his name an illustrious
immortality "

After the passage of the resolutions, Archibald
Russell, of Esopus, submitted a resolution proposing
the erection of monuments commemorative of the services of the gallant soldiers of Ulster.

MR. RUSSELL'S REMARKS.

" MR. PRESIDENT : During the crisis of our country's
history, it is proper that the Ulster Historical Society

should consider whether any duties devolve peculiarly
upon it, and take efficient measures to discharge them.
Our attention is so apt to be diverted from the occur-
rences around us to the war-stirring news from other sections of the country, that we allow the materials of history to be lost, and forget to take proper measures to
ensure their preservation. Already this county has sent,
in connection with Greene, three regiments into the field;
and I question if we have in our archives the roster-roll
of any of them. It is evident, however, that it is the
duty of this Society to pay diligent attention to the part
which our neighbors are taking in the great drama en-
acting around us. Our sons—our young men—are leaving us amid the sound of martial music, and with confident step marching to defend the liberties of their country; but how many of them shall return to recount
their deeds and tell of their toils and sufferings, and to
be cheered by the Christian amenities of the domestic
hearth, after the rough experience of the battle-field ?
The blood of Ulster tinges the sod along the Annapolis
Railroad; it can be traced upon the bank of the Potomac, and on Upton's Hill; it crimsons the field of Manassas, and mingles in the bloody stream which swelled
the waters of Antietam ! And shall the Historical Society sit silent and make no fitting record of the victims
who may have fallen, or of the gallant survivors who
may return ? It is fortunately not too late for us to obtain most of the information which it is important
should be preserved; and I most respectfully urge upon
the officers of this Society, not to lose the opportunity
of doing so. It is proper that the names and positions
of all who enlist should be recorded with, as far as possible, some brief biographical sketch. I would suggest
that suitable books, strong and durable, should be provided; that a page should be appropriated to each individual, and a small fee paid to a neat penman for
entering such particulars as might be furnished con-

cerning each. Few are so friendless as not to have some
one who would be interested in having recorded some
traits of their character and some events of their history ; and their surviving comrades would furnish the
particulars of their death. In after ages, when blessed
with the peace for which we waged this war, how grateful will it be to all connected with its martyrs, to be
able to turn to our archives and trace the part the forefathers took in the National struggle for the preservation of the Union.

" But while we thus make a record of the services
of the sons of Ulster, the manner in which I propose
having it done is necessarily private and devoid of publicity. We should not be satisfied with this—we should
at the same time attempt to raise some public and enduring tribute, which in all future time will perpetuate
the self-denying efforts which our friends have made.
Each regiment should have a commemorative pillar
erected on some conspicuous place, to give prominence
to its services, and recall, as time rolls on, the memories of the past. I am sorry to see so many bodies,
marred and maimed amid the carnage of the battle-
field, returned to their homes, to be buried in the private
grounds and cemeteries of the land. It is a practice
injurious alike, I think, to the living and the dead—to
the living, as exposing to contagion those brought in
contact with remains which have lain exposed and become corrupt ; to the dead, the most appropriate resting place of the soldier being the battle-field.

> " Tranquil amidst alarms,
> It finds them on the field :
> The veterans sleeping on their arms,
> Beneath a blood-stained field."

" But though many are brought back to be buried
among their relatives, more sleep beneath the sod of the
battle-field, or lie in the hastily dug trench, to wait with
their comrades in arms, the dawn of the Christian's hope.

" It is not only to those who fall that I would suggest a commemorative pillar, but to those who have breasted successfully the tide of battle, and return to tell how fields were won. To the Regiment as such, to all who went out to crush the rebellion, this tribute is due, and I hope will be gratefully paid by their friends and countrymen.

" Of the regiments that have been raised among us, one only has as yet been actively engaged in service. Under the leading of as true, modest and conscientious a colonel as ever marshalled his men and led them into battle, it went out one thousand strong. It stood the rude shock of war, and still maintains, with one-fourth of its number, its proud pre-eminence. But the survivors mourn the loss of their gallant colonel ; the staff and commissioned officers miss many of their number ; and the men cluster around their war-worn standards a mere handful. Shall we, who cheered them on their departure and reap the benefits of their sufferings, coldly and calmly hear of their loss, and not raise a tribute of respect ere ' the opium of time (as Sir Thomas Browne terms it) deals with the memories of men ? '

" The most appropriate method of perpetuating the remembrance of the heroic services of the Twentieth Regiment would be to erect, on some of the prominent mountain tops which abound in this picturesque county, a simple stone column, massive, substantial and plain, dedicated to the Regiment. As the county is so large and is intersected by several mountain chains, it would be impossible to select one spot that could be seen from all its towns ; but if a similar monument were raised to each regiment, and judiciously placed, there would be few districts which would not be within sight of one of them. Such a silent monitor, erected on the top of a commanding height, with its outline sharply cut against the sky, braving the storms of winter and heedless of the alternations of our climate, would tell to all time

the grateful estimate which we, the loyal people of
Ulster, placed upon the devoted services of the War of
the Rebellion.

"Should this proposal be deemed worthy of adoption, I would suggest that the monument of the Twentieth Regiment should be erected on the top of Shappawnic, as it overlooks the home of the gallant Colonel
who has sealed with his blood his devotion to his
country's cause. There are few points of land in the
country that are more generally seen. Situated about
ten miles south of Kingston, and about one mile from
the Hudson, it commands a view in almost every direction. To the east, the valley of the Hudson stretches
far into the distance, and any monument erected on
Shappawnic would attract the notice of the tens of
thousands who daily throng this great national highway. To the north, the view is unbroken till the eye
rests upon the Catskills, and easily discerns Rondout,
Kingston, and innumerable smaller towns and villages.
To the west, it overlooks the valley of the Esopus, and
Shandaken and Olive seem to be at its feet. To the
south, it looks upon New Paltz and the other settle-
ments of the earlier Huguenots. It is also of easy
access by a good mountain road, which would greatly
facilitate the transportation of all the material required
in its construction.

"When we consider the number of small but expen-
sive monuments that will be erected over the remains of
those connected with this Regiment, and the very ephe-
meral character of all these structures, the severity of
the climate soon damaging the most elaborate carvings
and effacing in a few years all the inscriptions, it would
seem that a simple, unadorned and effective column,
built of rough mountain stone, and made enduring for
all ages, would, in connection with the records of the
Regiment already suggested, be the most appropriate
method of perpetuating the memory of our national defenders.

" I would after this statement respectfully move :

" 1. That a committee be appointed, with power to raise funds and carry the following resolutions into effect :

" 2. To procure suitable books, in which to record the names and a brief biographical sketch of all the members of the Twentieth Regiment who went to the war ; to make arrangements for the engrossing of the sketches and the preservation of the records.

" 3. To obtain a suitable site on which to place a monument to the Twentieth Regiment, and to erect the same in an enduring and permanent manner."

These resolutions were unanimously passed, and the following committee appointed :

ARCHIBALD RUSSELL,	A. BRUYN HASBROUCK,
JOSHUA FIERO, Jr.,	RUFUS H. KING,
JAMES FITCH,	HENRY H. REYNOLDS,
REUBEN BERNARD,	THOMAS CORNELL,
HENRY A. SAMSON,	JAMES L. HASBROUCK.

EDMUND ELTINGE.

In November, 1857, Pratt was elected State Senator from the counties of Ulster and Greene, which composed the Tenth Senatorial District. He was a Democrat in politics, but of liberal views, and his personal popularity secured him a large Republican vote. His majority in the district was 1,493.

While in the Senate he did much to promote the interest of the State militia, and he was recognized as one of the most earnest, judicious and influential friends of the organization. The State Military Association elected him its President, and he held that office at the time of his death. At the meeting of the Association, in January, 1864, the following proceedings were had in reference to the deceased President :

Upon taking the chair, General Elias A. Brown addressed the Association as follows :

" GENTLEMEN :

" In the orderings of Providence I am called upon for a second time to preside over this Association at its annual meeting. At the last annual meeting, you will recollect that we could scarcely count a quorum, owing to the absence of our members filling their positions in our armies in the field, including our president. It is with diffidence that I assume this official station, conscious as I am of the high qualities of the man whose position I occupy, though I cannot supply his place. Indeed, there are few who can command the respect and lay fast hold on the esteem of this Association, in the de gree and measure of our late chief. He will ever hold a chosen place in the memory of all who knew his worth His deeds have built him a monument for all time ; and the simple inscription which says : ' Here lies GEORGE W PRATT,' will be legend enough for posterity. His name stands resplendent in the galaxy of those heroes given by his native State to their country's cause, and who have gone to a rest only to be broken by the reveille of the last day "

Capt. Roosa moved the appointment of a committee to draft resolutions expressive of the feelings of this Association toward their late president, prefacing his motion with the following remarks :

" In proposing a befitting expression by this Association of their regard for their late president, I trust I may be indulged in a few remarks. There are very many here, doubtless, who knew and valued Col. Pratt aright—comrades in arms and intimate friends, who would pay a fitting tribute to his memory in more eloquent terms than I, who am no public speaker. But I was honored with his warm personal friendship for years ; he was our county commandant, at the head of the Twentieth Regiment, N Y S. M., which, long before it had won the proud name it now has achieved in the history of this war and the Army of the Potomac, was one of the few militia regiments of the whole North, disciplined and ready, with full ranks, animated with the right spirit, to march at the first call to the defence of our threatened National Capital. And that regiment, ‘Ulster Guard,’ was a part, and the best part, of the Brigade upon whose staff it has been my pride and pleasure to serve for many years. You will therefore, I am sure, gentlemen of the Association, pardon me if there is any undue assumption on my part in moving this tribute of respect to the memory of Col. Pratt.

“ It may be said that I speak here for the Twentieth Regiment and for the Eighth Brigade, and for the county of Ulster as well, which has a just pride in the unspotted name and unsullied fame of the leader of its veteran regiment, who fell at its head in the very fore-front of the battle. We, who have more intimately known all his worth, are better able to feel to the full what we have lost in his fall ; and we can say, in the fulness of our hearts, and without fear of challenge, that in the proud roll of the heroic who have given their lives for the salvation of their country, there is not a name which more vividly recalls and illustrates all the high quali- ties which are demanded to make the true hero and patriot, than that of George W Pratt.

“ It is certainly not claiming too much for Col. Pratt to say, that he was among the first to feel, to the full, the responsibilities and duties of the commandant of a regiment in the military force of this his native State. Most of us can remember how the ‘cankers of a calm world and long peace’ had eaten into and sapped the very vitality of the military system and array of the most powerful State of the Union. Here and there were company and even regimental organizations, which showed a discipline and spirit only rendering the general indifference and apathy more striking. From the close of the war of 1812, the nation seemed to have subsided into the pleasurable delusion that we, of all the polities of the civilized world alone, had 'fought our last fight and won our last battle,' and that 'no sound would awake us to glory again.' We never realized accurately, till within three years, the tenure upon which we held our very existence as a nation. The Mexican war, so brief, brilliant, and remote, was hardly felt by the nation at large, and certainly failed, and haply did not need, to call out the resources and strength of the country. Our boundary difficulties now and then darkening our national horizon with the ominous 'cloud, no bigger than a man's hand,' but which might, perhaps, bear in its bosom the tempest of war with our ancient foe and the most powerful nation of Europe, gave us a passing warning, now and then, of our duties and needs. But one by one our impending storms passed away, and serene skies lulled us into fancied security and indifference. Our regular army dwindled to a mere skeleton, barely supplying meagre garrisons for the outposts of our extensive frontiers; and our militia, as a whole, half enrolled and miserably equipped, had barely discipline and numbers sufficient to maintain a nominal existence, and to get up a few parades and nominal inspections. There is no wrong in speaking the plain truth of our wretched and inadequate military system, or lack of system, when its solemn weight has been impressed so deeply by the severe lesson following the startling outbreak of the rebellion of 1861, at once dispelling our dreams and arousing us from our slumbers. We, in the dark and drear days of that sad year, realized in bitter severity which we can now lay to heart, that we, as a people, had failed in our duty to our country in one of the most important responsibilities. We had not prepared in peace for the contingency of war, always regarded as among the imminent probabilities of a nation's life by the sagacious.

" Among those who, years before we had so startling an arousal to our duty, took a comprehensive and clear view of our full duties to ourselves and posterity, was Col. Pratt. And his foresight was not shown by idle words. He was ever eminently practical, and this was more especially shown in his whole military career. He never regarded the State force as a mere machine for idle show and recurrent displays. He replied, when a friend complimented him on the appearance and skillful evolutions of his regiment, many years before it was called into service, that he 'wished that every nominal regiment in the State were at least as well disciplined and organized ; but, superior as it was to most of the New York Militia on that score, the 20th Regiment, as well as every other in the State force, was far below the true standard of thorough efficiency. The nation,' he added, prophetically, 'would pay dearly, and that at no distant day, for permitting its sole reliance for defence to fall so far in arrear of the times.' And he remarked to the same point, one day, that 'one thing, at least, he had learned in his travels in the Old World, and that was, how far we were behind the foremost European nations in military science. We have men and material enough,' he remarked, 'but where is the military pride and spirit, and the discipline and organization which they generate ? '

" Col. Pratt's first exertions to do his share toward arousing his countrymen to a due sense of duty on this score were made in his native county, Greene. We all know that he succeeded there, as he subsequently did in Ulster, in arousing in the people something of the required military spirit, and had not the accidents of party prevented his continuance in the position of Adjutant-General, to which he was called for a brief term, there is every reason to believe that he would have given a new and needed turn to the military system and array of the whole State, and imbued it with something of his own spirit and energy.

" When Col. Pratt took the command of the 20th Regiment, it had little more than a nominal existence. But, entering at once upon a vigorous discharge of his trust, he brought it up to the full measure of efficiency, according to the standard before the war. That regiment was ready at the first word ; and was the foremost regiment north of, or outside of, the city of New York, to march to the Potomac. At the close of its first three-months term, the 20th re-enlisted for three years. Its share in the conflicts which have made Virginia historic ground, you well know ; and the price paid for its name, in the life-blood of so many under its colors, is written in the history of the nation. At the head of the regiment which he had in a great measure created, Colonel Pratt received his death-shot ; and its colors, rent and torn in the storm of battle, are now among the trophies of the State, and will ever recall the remembrance of the gallant leader who fell in their defence.

" In this brief history of the 20th Regiment, N Y S. M., you have almost the entire record of Col. Pratt's military life, which was bound up and identified with that corps. Had he survived, there was doubtless before him a higher position and more conspicuous career. But he could not have achieved a higher place in the regard of all who knew his sterling qualities, or have closed an honorable life by a more heroic death, than that which met him in the very flush and vigor of manhood.

" The older members of this Association will unite with me in a due estimate of the talent and patriotism of Col. Pratt. He ever regarded this body as one of the most promising and efficient agencies toward rendering our State force what it should be, and was most earnest in every word and work to promote its interests. We hoped much from his executive ability when called upon to preside over this Association. But it was decreed otherwise, and we can only record upon his tomb the comprehensive lines graven over one of the best and bravest of another clime and age :

" ' Here lies one without fear and without reproach ! '

"Mr. President, I move the appointment of a committee of three to report resolutions expressive of the regard of this Association to their late president, Col. George W Pratt, and their respect to his memory "

The motion was carried, and Capt. Roosa, Gen. Burnside and Col. Forbes were appointed such committee, who reported the following resolutions, which were unanimously adopted :

"WHEREAS, This Association have been called upon since our last annual meeting to mourn the loss of our fellow-member and president, Col. George W Pratt ; it is

"*Resolved*, That we, individually, record our sorrow at the loss of a friend distinguished for his intellectual endowments and scholarly attainments ; for his high moral qualities, his rectitude of purpose and purity of life ; for his lofty, self-sacrificing patriotism and chivalric courage ; for his courtesy, generosity, and magnanimity, and for all the gifts and graces combining to make up the true soldier and man.

"*Resolved*, That as comrades in the State service and companions in this body, we especially feel the loss of one whose energy, zeal, military spirit, and talent were devoted many years to the advancement of the efficiency of our State militia ; one of the founders of this Association ; the first colonel in this State, outside of the city of New York, leading his regiment at the first call to defend the capital and country against armed rebellion ; and who consummated his labors and sacrifices by laying down his life in defence of the Union on the field illustrated by his heroism.

"*Resolved*, That these resolutions be entered on the minutes of this Association, published in its proceedings, and that the Corresponding Secretary be instructed to transmit copies of the same to the widow and father of our late friend and comrade."

The following proceedings were had in Ulster County in honor of the memory of Colonel Pratt.

At a special communication of Kingston Lodge No. 10, of Free and Accepted Masons, held at the Lodge

Room, in Kingston, on Saturday evening, September 13th, 1862, the death of Brother George W Pratt was announced by Worshipful Brother Warren Chipp. On motion, it was resolved that a committee of five be appointed to prepare and present resolutions expressive of the sense of this Lodge upon the death of Brother George W Pratt. Whereupon the Worshipful Master appointed Brothers John B. Steele, Henry Van Hoevenburgh, William S. Kenyon, Henry B. Luther, and Abraham A. Deyo, Jr., such committee.

On motion, it was resolved that this Lodge attend the funeral of Brother George W Pratt, in a body, and that the Lodge be draped in mourning for the space of sixty days.

The committee reported as follows: which, on motion, was accepted, and the preamble and resolutions were unanimously adopted.

                WARREN CHIPP, W M.,

[L. S.]   ISAAC VAN BUREN, *Sec. pro tem.*

To the Worshipful Master, Wardens and Brethren of Kingston Lodge No. 10, of Free and Accepted Masons.

The undersigned, a committee appointed to prepare and present resolutions expressive of the sense of this Lodge upon the death of our lamented Brother, George W Pratt, respectfully report for consideration the following preamble and resolutions :

PREAMBLE.

Upon the fall of Sumter, as the report "borne upon the lightning's wing," flashed over the land, such an effect upon loyal citizens was experienced as might have been expected had the tocsin of war sounded in their ears or the roar of hostile cannon thundered at their gates. Here, as if the subtile fluid which transmitted the intelligence, had electrified our people, they spontaneously gathered together for counsel and for war. As all such grand impulses need a definite object and aim to become useful, so this noble outburst of patriotism required a practical direction.

A young gentleman of modest pretensions, with stern and high resolve, moved quietly and calmly among the people. He was well known, and it seemed that his appearance had given direction to all thoughts, upon the instant ; the pent-up feelings found expression in prolonged cheers for Colonel George W Pratt. From that moment our course was taken, and in an incredibly short space of time our noble and patriotic 20th, with their gallant young commander, went forth to battle. Their blood has moistened many a hard-fought field, and many a stout heart, which then beat high, is now cold in death. The horse that bore the leader of that gallant band has returned without his rider, and we must now mourn the death of our well-beloved brother, George W Pratt, and mingle our tears and sympathies with those who weep for him.

RESOLUTIONS.

1st. *Resolved*, That in the death of Colonel George W Pratt, caused by fatal wounds received while manfully contending for the honor of our flag and the preservation of our glorious Union, upon the recent battlefields of Virginia, this Lodge has lost a much-loved and worthy brother ; the community a most useful and important citizen ; his family, a dutiful and affectionate son, husband, and father, in whom was justly centered much of hope and pride ; the armies of our country, a brave, intelligent and enterprising officer ; and the Church of God, a highly useful and consistent member.

2d. *Resolved*, That while the virtues, talents, and acquirements of our deceased brother were of that high order as naturally and properly to inspire him with confidence and self-possession, and his ample fortune and social position such as to draw around him many to court and flatter, yet his ability was not more conspicuous than his modesty, and his natural simplicity of habits and manner, genuine goodness of heart, and firm integrity of purpose were proof against all the allurements of wealth and blandishments of society. In his legislative career, while occupying the position of State Senator from this district, he was, as in private life, eminently practical and useful; and when we see one thus gifted stricken down in the first vigor of youthful manhood, we are constrained to say, " Thy ways, O God, are mysterious and past finding out."

3d. *Resolved*, That although we would not detract from the just meed of praise due to any who, struggling against poverty and adversity, have perseveringly encountered and overcome obstacles to success, neither would we be unmindful of the trials and temptations which beset the pathway of such as would devote themselves to a life of usefulness and toil, when possessed of that wealth and position which, so fatally to many, invite to a life of inglorious indolence or more fatal indulgence ; and we

5

feel a natural and just pride in the example of our deceased brother, who, with every inducement and facility to seek his own enjoyment and ease, could, in time of peace, subject himself to the severe discipline of regular business habits, and when his country called to arms, unhesitatingly surrender all the enjoyments of a luxurious home for the privations and hardships of the camp, and, resisting the entreaties of a loving and beloved family, offer himself a willing sacrifice upon the altar of his country.

4th. *Resolved*, That in addition to the usual formalities, this Preamble and Resolutions be entered in full upon the minutes of the Lodge, and properly engrossed copies be furnished to the father and widow of the deceased.

5th. *Resolved*. That such portion of the proceedings of this Lodge, in reference to the death and burial of our deceased brother, George W Pratt, as may properly be printed, according to the usages and customs of the Order, be furnished to the newspapers of Albany, Greene and Ulster Counties, for publication.

All which is respectfully submitted.

KINGSTON, Sept. 13th, 1862.

> JOHN B. STEELE,
> HENRY VAN HOEVENBURGH,
> ABM. A. DEYO, JR.,
> W S. KENYON,
> H. B. LUTHER,
> > *Committee.*

At a meeting of the citizens of Kingston, held at the Court House, Friday evening, September 12th, 1862, for the purpose of paying a tribute of respect to the memory of Colonel George W Pratt, Hon. Wm. B. Wright was chosen Chairman, Dr. H. Van Hoevenburgh and A. B. Preston, Vice-Presidents, and H. D. H. Snyder and H. H. Reynolds, Secretaries.

After an address by the Chairman and Hon. T. R. Westbrook, on motion of the latter, a committee of five was appointed to prepare resolutions expressive of the sense of the meeting.

Messrs. T. R. Westbrook, Rev Dr. Hoes, Rev Mr. Waters, Wm. Lounsbery and H. H. Reynolds, Esqrs., were appointed as such committee.

The Committee reported the following resolutions, which, after addresses by Wm. Lounsbery and Henry H. Reynolds, Esqrs., were unanimously adopted.

WHEREAS, It has pleased an All-Wise Providence, by a vicissitude of war, to remove from our midst Colonel George W. Pratt, of the 20th Regiment, N. Y. State Militia, and

WHEREAS, The deceased was greatly endeared to and beloved by us all for his high social qualities and manly virtues—therefore, in order to testify our respect and love for the departed, be it

Resolved, That in the death of our late fellow citizen and friend, the community in which he lived has lost an esteemed and valued member, the country a wise statesman and gallant soldier, the Church an earnest and faithful member, and his family an affectionate son, husband and fond parent.

Resolved, That we tender to the father, widow and relatives of the deceased our warm and tender sympathy, in this the sad hour of their bereavement, and humbly pray that He who governs and does all things well will administer to them of His own rich consolation.

Resolved, That we cannot and will not forget that the deceased laid down his life for the sake of country and government, and though sorrowful, we point with joy and pride to his great sacrifice, as worthy of emulation and imitation.

Resolved, That upon the roll of our country's defenders, the name of George W Pratt occupies a conspicuous position ; that dying, as a soldier loves to die—defending his country and flag, we are proud to know that that country shall cherish his name and memory forever.

Resolved, That it be requested that the bells of the village of Kingston and of this Senatorial district be tolled during the hour of the funeral of the deceased, or from 2 o'clock P.M. to 3 o'clock P.M. on Sunday next.

Resolved, That a copy of the proceedings of this meeting be sent to the father and family of the deceased, and that the same be published in the papers of the district

In connection with the above, Hon. T. R. Westbrook offered the following resolution, which was unanimously adopted :

Resolved, That while we deplore the death of George W. Pratt, the gallant Colonel of the 20th Regiment, N. Y. S. M., we can not and do not forget the bravery and virtues of every officer and private of that organization, which so recently went from our midst to defend our country and its institutions, but who now sleep with their commander that sleep which knows no waking ; that to us their memories are dear and precious, and their departure is mourned by this Senatorial District with sorrow, deep, sincere and abiding.

On motion, it was resolved that the officers of the meeting, and as many of our citizens as can conveniently do so, be appointed to attend the funeral of Col. Pratt.

The citizens residing at and about Elmore's Corners, in the town of Esopus, convened at the house of William Atchison, on Saturday evening, September 12th, for the purpose of passing resolutions expressive of their feelings at the sad intelligence of the death of Col. George W Pratt, their late neighbor and fellow-townsman. Cheney Ames was called to the Chair, and John W Wheeler and William Atchison appointed Secretaries. A committee was appointed to draft resolutions, consisting of Daniel Freer, William Atchison, John Griffiths and Cheney Ames. The committee then retired, and soon after reported the following, which were unanimously adopted :

WHEREAS, Colonel George W Pratt, a beloved and prominent member of this community, was mortally wounded while commanding his regiment in one of the late battles of Virginia, and has since died in consequence of his wounds,

Resolved, That as members of the community from which he has thus been taken, we regard the event of his death with feelings of deep and heartfelt sorrow

Resolved, That in his death we, as individuals, have lost a good neighbor ; society, a shining ornament ; the Christian Church, a faithful member, and our country, a valiant defender.

Resolved, That earnestly desiring the speedy suppression of this monstrous rebellion against the best government man ever devised, our mourning for the loss of our honored neighbor, is tempered with the consolation that he did not give his life in vain ; that he died in a cause which warmly commends itself to our deepest sympathies ; and that in his self-sacrificing devotion to his country he has left an example which cannot be too generally imitated.

Resolved, That the sympathies of this community are hereby tendered to the family of the deceased, in this their severe and irreparable affliction.

Resolved, That a report of these proceedings and a copy of these resolutions be presented to the family of the deceased, and to the publisher of the Kingston *Argus* for publication.

On the face of the rocky ledge that overlooks the turnpike road, a half mile south of the village of Pratts-

ville, Colonel Zadock Pratt caused to be cut into the
rock a colossal bust of his son, whose right hand is uplifted, and above it the motto, " This hand for my country," being the coat of arms and legend adopted by the
Colonel for the "Ulster Guard." Below the bust are
inscribed the words : "Hon. G. W Pratt, Ph.D.,
Colonel XX. Regiment, N Y S. M., Ulster County
Born April 18th, 1830 ; wounded August 30th, in the
second battle of Manassas, Virginia ; died at Albany,
(N Y.), September 11th, 1862. Good—brave—honorable !" A fond father's commendation of the virtues of
his lost son—and every word is true. Knowing him as
few others did, we can most sincerely repeat his
father's words : " Good—brave—honorable !"

Pratt had succeeded his father as Colonel of the 28th
Regiment of Militia, located in Greene County, and after
his removal to Kingston, the counties of Ulster and
Greene were united in one regimental district, while
Sullivan was detached. The result was that Colonel
Bushnell, who resided in Sullivan, was disqualified to
command the "Twentieth," and on the 12th of September, 1857, Colonel Pratt was appointed Colonel of
the consolidated regiment, with rank from the 1st of
February, 1852. Hiram Schoonmaker, who had held
the position of Lieutenant-Colonel since May 19th, 1855,
and Theodore B. Gates, who had been Major from same
date, retained their commissions. Henry W Smuller
was appointed Chaplain. The other members of the
staff were the same as shown in Appendix A.

The new Colonel of the "Twentieth" gave a fresh
and wholesome impetus to the organization, and it grew
rapidly in his hands. He was a good disciplinarian and
an indefatigable worker. He had the regiment in camp
for about a week every autumn, and improved such occasions by enforcing order and devoting the time to
company and battalion drills. The result was that the

regiment became one of the best in the State, and acquired a reputation of which it had a right to be proud.

Pratt gave the corps the name of " Ulster Guard ;"
a name it always afterwards bore. The citizens of Ulster
County, but more especially the people of Kingston and
Rondout, took a lively interest in the organization, and
to testify, in a manner, their regard for the regiment,
they united in presenting it a stand of colors, on the
thirty-first of August, 1858. The presentation took
place on the green between the two villages, afterwards
known as " The Camp Ground," and Hon. William S.
Kenyon, President of the Board of Directors of the village of Kingston, made the presentation address, and it
was the most perfect thing of its kind ever spoken. In
thought, in imagery, in a forecast of the future, in
beauty of language, it has no peer. It should be preserved among the most durable archives of the "Ulster
Guard." I am glad to be able to give it a place in these
pages. Mr. Kenyon said :

" *Colonel and Officers and Soldiers of the Ulster
Guard :* The vast importance to a free and independent people of a duly organized and efficient citizen soldiery, both in a civil and political aspect, requires at our
hands no proclamation. The Constitution of this great
State, the text-book of our chartered civil and political
rights, proclaims it by a recognized equality between
the civil and military branches of the Government. So
close a relationship is established by constitutional par-
entage between those branches, that the Governor, the
great civil head, is declared to be the commander-in-
chief of the military and naval forces of the State. A
union so complete, an intimacy so vital to each must of
necessity prompt a sense of mutual dependency, and
incite to an open expression of regard. Eminently meet
and natural is it that the civil and municipal authorities everywhere should proffer the right hand of fellow-
ship to the military, and testify before the world to a

recognition of a common origin and one and the same destiny. The corporations of Kingston and Rondout here convened by their representatives, recognizing you as an honorable and distinguished member of that noble body of organized citizens of which the Empire State has reason ever to be proud, seize this opportunity to tender you a testimonial of their high appreciation of your merits as soldiers, and through me to express an abiding sense of your worth as citizens and as men. The flag of his country, emblazoned all over with an ever-increasing galaxy of stars, symbolical of a prosperous union of free and independent States, which God grant may never be dissolved, must to the heart of every American soldier prove a cherished *souvenir*

"Receive these colors at our hands; preserve them in remembrance of an occasion so pregnant with interest, and of a scene in which you act so conspicuous a part. A thousand holy recollections will forever cluster around them. The very heavens that are now smiling down upon you; these old hills that lie crouching all about you with expansive ear, listening to catch the every accent of this scene; the very ground on which you stand, enriched by patriotic blood and teeming with savory memories of revolutionary times, will at sight of them again and again start out before your mind's eye with all the vividness of the present.

"Accept them as they are. *Would that it were possible with a graphic touch to represent upon them your future glories.* When Aeneas received from his goddess mother the shield which Vulcan had wrought out, he beheld with loving eyes all over it a prophetic history of the future achievements and glory of his race. A wise Providence has denied to us the power of tearing aside the veil which hangs between you and the fulfilment of your hopes. You will read upon this simple gift no prophetic revelation, but you will not fail to discover on every fold some divine memento, traced there by the hand of memory.

" Accept them and guard them with a valiant heart, and may they, like that stand of heavenly colors flung out by Israel's God—a pillar of cloud by day and a pillar of fire by night—introduce you to a full and free fruition of your dearest hopes."

In accepting the colors, Colonel Pratt spoke as follows :

" *Mr President and Gentlemen :* In behalf of the Ulster Guard, I thank you for this beautiful gift, and the kind expressions of appreciation with which it is accompanied. The soldiers constituting my command cherish the homes and firesides of their country, and it needs no incentive to earn a pledge of their protection ; but it is a proud pleasure to them, that the municipal authorities of the two largest villages of Ulster have taken this occasion to express their regard. We appreciate the honor you have thus done us, *and we promise that, if this land is ever involved in war, these colors shall wave with credit and glory wherever danger is thickest and the fight is warmest.* Gentlemen, we thank you, and as you have alluded to our revolutionary sires, we trust the Ulster Guard will never be found unworthy of the noble inheritance of honor and virtue they have left us."

Subsequent to this event, and shortly before the regiment left for the war, the City of Poughkeepsie presented a beautiful national flag to it—the regiment going to Poughkeepsie to receive it.

On the evening of the seventh of January, 1861, Brigadier-General H. A. Samson, Commandant of the Eighth Brigade, N Y S. M.; Major Von Beck and Captains Rossa and Davis, of his staff; Colonel Pratt, Lieutenant-Colonel Schoonmaker, Major Gates and six or eight other officers of the " Twentieth," whose names I cannot now recall, met in one of the parlors of the

Mansion House, at Rondout, to confer together as to the course the regiment ought to adopt, in case of an actual outbreak of the then threatened hostilities.

Colonel Pratt addressed the meeting, and stated that he believed war was inevitable, and if it came, he intended to take part in it in some capacity, but that he would very much prefer to serve with his regiment. He foresaw that the Government would be obliged to have recourse to the Militia of the Loyal States in the first instance, and that the "Twentieth" could be soon put in a condition to take the field. He was in favor of tendering the service of the command to the Government, and he believed the officers and men would approve of the act.

After a discussion that lasted until four o'clock in the morning, Colonel Pratt was authorized to tender the services of the regiment to the Federal Government, through the Hon. E. D. Morgan, then Governor of the State of New York.

From this time the work of preparation went quietly forward, and by judicious recruiting the companies had been considerably strengthened by the beginning of April. Company drills were frequent, and the regiment had perceptibly improved in numbers and efficiency

On the twelfth of April, Beauregard's cannon put an end to the forbearance of the Federal authorities, and Colonel Pratt's prediction was verified. The Secessionists had assumed the terrible responsibility of inaugurating a fratricidal war, with a wantonness that has no parallel in the history of nations.

As the reverberations of their guns swept over the country, loyalty shook off its lethargy, and made prodigious strides in preparing to defend the Government. Ignoring party distinctions, Democrats and Republicans united in cordial declarations and acts in support of the administration and in denunciation of secession.

Immediately on hearing of the attack on Fort Sumter, a mass meeting was held in the Court House, at Kingston, whereat Hon. John B. Steele, then a member of Congress from that district, and a Democrat, presided. On taking the chair, he said: "It must never be supposed that the flag could be desecrated without touching the soul of every genuine American; no matter what it must cost, the Stars and Stripes must wave. But one heart beats here, and that is the true loyal American heart." Throughout the war he was faithful to these sentiments. Hon. William S. Kenyon, an ex-member of Congress and a Republican, delivered an eloquent and impassioned speech in denunciation of treason, and in favor of the most energetic measures for its punishment. Hon. Theodoric R. Westbrook, a Democrat and an ex-member of Congress, and now one of the Judges of the N Y Supreme Court, and who probably did more work and made more speeches in behalf of the Government and its soldiers than any other private citizen in the State of New York, spoke at the Kingston meeting, and among other things said: "I lay aside all party lines, all party prejudices, all political bias, and stand for my country alone. I love my party, but, thank God, I love my country better. I am not going to stop to consider who is right or who is wrong; but, right or wrong, my country" Grasping the folds of the Stars and Stripes, he said: "Let it be known that in the nineteenth century, traitor hands and traitor hearts are found among us to disgrace that flag, which had been their shield and protection as well as our own. May God record my vow to stand by, protect, and, if need be, to die for that flag."

Speeches were also made by Messrs. Erastus Cooke, George H. Sharpe, William H. Romeyn and Warren Chipp. Committees were appointed to aid in enlisting soldiers for the "Twentieth," and for supplying the wants of the families of those who needed help during the absence of husband, father or son.

The regiment was deficient in many things that were required for its complete equipment and efficiency, and the State was not in a condition to supply its immediate wants. An application was therefore made to the banks of Kingston to advance the necessary funds to purchase the needed articles. The following response was almost immediately received:

KINGSTON, N. Y., 20th April, 1861.

Colonel George W. Pratt:

DEAR SIR—At a meeting of the officers of the Banks in this town, held this day, on the representation that the sum of $8,000 is needed to prepare your regiment for the field, it was unanimously,

Resolved, That the Banks here represented, viz.: Ulster County Bank, Kingston Bank, Bank of Rondout and State of New York Bank, will each honor the drafts of the Regimental Paymaster of the Twentieth Regiment for the sum of $2,000.

Yours, &c.,

A. BRUYN HASBROUCK,
Chairman.

H. H. REYNOLDS,

    Secretary.

A "Ladies' Army Relief Society" was organized about the same time, with Mrs. Dr. Finch as chairman, whose judicious work contributed very greatly to the comfort of the soldiers.

Another of the agencies organized at Kingston to aid the Government and contribute to the comfort of the soldiers, was the "Ulster Military Relief Committee," of which Mr. Henry H. Reynolds was chairman. In his report for the month of May, 1861, he announces the following donations and monthly subscriptions. No doubt later reports would show a very much larger list, but I am unable to obtain, at this time, a subsequent report:

DONATIONS.

J. F Brower, $1 ; Mrs. Samuel Dubois, $1 ; John J. Davis, $1 ; James L. Hasbrouck, $10 ; N A. Houghtaling, $2 ; Joseph Maton, $3 ; Miss E. G. Ostrander, $1 ; William Shaw, $4 ; Cash, per G. Southwick, $25 ; Peter

Van Buren, $3 ; A. C. Willis, $1 ; C. H. Coutant, $1 ;
Mrs. Peter Dubois, 50c. ; Isaac Decker, $5 ; J S. Joy,
$2 ; L. Low, $1 ; P T. Osterhoudt, $1 ; Jacob Sahler,
$10 ; David H. Smith, $1 ; Wessel Ten Broeck, $5 ; H.
Van Steenbergh, $1 ; F L. Westbrook, $5.

MONTHLY SUBSCRIPTIONS.

G. W Pratt (for regimental district), $100 ; Thomas
Beekman, $1 ; Bradley Burhans, 50. ; Reuben Bernard,
$5 ; Corns. Bruyn, $50 ; Thomas C. Broadhead, $2 ; H.
Broadhead, Jr., $25 ; C. & J. Burhans, $5 ; Edn. Crosby,
$5 ; P J Davis, $2 ; P J. Dubois, $20 , G. W Ewen,
$3 ; Mrs. A. E. Post, $1 ; Samuel L. Frame, $5 ; J. C. F
Hoes, $1 ; M. Hauver, $2 ; P Harlow, $1 ; J. F Jen-
nings, $5 ; John O. Legg, $1 ; James O. Merritt, $5 ;
Augustus Newton, $1 ; A. Near, $5 ; Jacob Osterhoudt,
50c. ; C. M. O'Neil, $1 ; H. H. Reynolds, $4 ; Henry
Rosenkrantz, $2 ; Rev. W A. Shaw, $1 ; W P B. Sharp,
$5 ; J. D. Sleight, $1 ; C. B. Safford, $1 ; J. H. Trem-
per, $5 ; W I. Teller, $3 ; A. L. Vankenburgh, $1 ;
Ab'm Van Keuren, $2 ; G. N Van Deusen, $5 ; James
Wells, $4 ; Miss H. Wynkoop, $10 ; Rev W B. Askam,
$1 ; A. H. Bruyn, $30 ; Benj. Burhans, 50c. ; R. N
Baldwin, $25 ; E. W Budington, $2 ; Joshua Bruyn,
$10 ; B. L. Brodhead, $2 ; Jacob Burhans, $15 ; Howard
Chipp, $3 ; C. D. Crispell, $5 ; J H. Dubois, $5 ; C. I.
Deyo, $1 ; Daniel Eckert, $1 ; John P Folant, 50c. ;
William H. Hamlin, $1 ; P S. Haines, $10 ; W M.
Hayes, $3 , James Joy, $3 ; H. Legg, $1 ; Silas Myer,
$1 ; Peter Masten, $8 ; A. G. Nichols, $2 ; J. E. Ostran-
der, $2 ; J. P Osterhoudt, $15 ; A. B. Paynter, $5 ;
Mrs. H. H. Reynolds, $6 ; Augustus W Reynolds, $3 ;
William Reynolds, $10 ; W F Romer, $10 ; George P
Sharp, $15 ; Justis Shaw, $2.50 ; Henry Snyder, $1 ; W
P Swart, $1 ; J. K. Trumpbour, $3 ; C. P Van Deusen,
$8 ; John Vignes, $1 ; P G. Van Steenbergh, $1 ; P V
S. Whitaker, 50c.

On the 23d of April the following order was issued :

GENERAL HEADQUARTERS, ADJUTANT-GENERAL'S OFFICE, }
                                ALBANY, April 23d, 1861.   }

General Orders, No.   —Major-General John Taylor Cooper, 3d
Division New York State Militia, is hereby directed to detail the 20th
Regiment, Colonel George W Pratt, for immediate service, to report forthwith to the President of the United States, at Washington, until relieved
by proper authority.

By order of the Commander-in-Chief,

J. MERIDITH READ, JR.,
Adjutant-General.

On the same day General Cooper issued an order, in
pursuance of the above, to Colonel Pratt. On the 24th,
General Samson, commanding the 8th Brigade, issued
an order detailing Surgeon Abram Crispell of his staff
to report to Colonel Pratt for duty with the 20th.

Regimental orders were at once issued for the command to prepare to march. The money advanced by
the banks was expended in partially uniforming recruits,
and supplying the most pressing wants of the regiment.
The outfit of the regiment was not as good or as complete as the officers thought it ought to be, when going
into the field. The uniforms of a large proportion of
the men were old and worn, and the arms and accoutrements were of ancient pattern. It was believed these
arms and equipments could be exchanged for more
modern styles, and that new uniforms could be furnished at New York, or forwarded to us in the field at an
early day, and requisitions therefor were forwarded to
the Adjutant-General at Albany, just before the regiment
departed from Kingston. These requisitions came very
near bringing the career of the Twentieth to an untimely
end.

CHAPTER V

On Sunday, the 28th day of April, the regiment
paraded in Academy Green, where, surrounded by
thousands of people, religious ceremonies were conducted by the Kingston clergy, and the formal leave
takings were then concluded. When these were over,
the regiment marched to Rondout, and embarked on
board the steamer Manhattan and a barge, which were
to convey the command to New York. The streets
through which the regiment marched to reach the boat
—a distance of two miles—were thronged with people,
whose voices filled the Sabbath air with cheers, while
flags were waving on every hand.

As the boats swung out into the stream, the regiment gave its friends on shore three rousing cheers, and
then sought the repose which the activity and wakeful-
ness of the last three days made most welcome.

The regiment arrived in New York in the evening of
the same day, and marched to Centre Market Armory
It was vociferously cheered as it went through the

streets of the city, and its welcome in the Metropolis seemed as cordial as were the good wishes which followed it from its friends at home.

It was found that no provision had been made for sending the regiment forward from New York, and it soon became apparent at regimental headquarters that trouble was brewing for it at the Adjutant-General's office in Albany

On Tuesday, the 30th of April, and while the regiment was still at Centre Market Armory, the Major was dispatched to Albany to interview Governor Morgan, and dissuade him, if possible, from sending the regiment back to Kingston, which was believed to be his design.

The following entry in my diary, of Wednesday, May 1st, gives Governor Morgan's side of the case, as I understood it at that time. The matter caused a good deal of talk and newspaper comment, and produced some ill feeling :

" I found on reaching Albany that such a contingency (sending the regiment home) had been contemplated, owing to the fact that, when the Governor ordered the regiment to march, he supposed, upon information received from Colonel Pratt, that it was all ready to take the field, and he was not disabused of this idea until after we had left Kingston, when a requisition arrived for nearly everything a regiment could require, to fit it, *ab initio*, for the field. The Governor was astounded. The articles were not to be had at the moment, and the circumstance placed the Governor in a false and embarrassing position, as he understood it. The general view of the matter would be, that he had ordered a regiment to march, and gotten it a hundred miles from home, and in the way of other regiments going to the front, when it was almost totally unprepared to take the field ; and, moreover, that it would cost nearly as much to equip the regiment for three months as it would to equip one of the new two-years regiments ;

that New York's quota of three-months regiments was already quite or nearly full, and that no regiment had made any such demand upon the State for an outfit as that received from the Colonel of the Twentieth. Nevertheless, the Governor directed that the requisitions should be filled, and I returned to New York with orders to that effect in my pocket."

But the Governor reconsidered his resolution, and on the third of May caused an order to be issued, in which it is said: "The prompt obedience of orders by the organized regiments of the State militia, and the alacrity of the volunteers, fully meeting the wants of the National Executive, having superseded the necessity for any additional regiments of the organized militia, no more regiments of such organizations can be received into service at this time. Accordingly, the Twentieth Regiment, commanded by Colonel Pratt, now in New York City *en route* to Washington, is hereby relieved from that duty, and it will be ordered to repair to Kingston, in Ulster County, whence the several companies will return to their respective districts. Special Orders No. 113, directing the Commissary-General to issue certain arms and equipments to that regiment, are also countermanded. Major-General Sandford is charged with the execution of this order."

It will be seen that the Governor delicately evaded the real ground upon which this action was taken, and assigned reasons which were true in themselves, and with the then existing views of the emergency were quite sufficient to justify the order. He, no doubt, felt that a revelation of the "bottom facts" would be unpleasant to the officers of the regiment, and a disagreeable surprise to their friends. He seems to have been willing to bear a good deal of animadversion, on account of this order, rather than to attempt to justify it by giving publicity to the facts. So much is due to Governor Morgan.

Colonel Pratt had forwarded the requisitions, which caused all the trouble, with the very best of motives, and without intending to have it understood that the regiment could not take the field without the things called for ; and this is proved by the fact that the regiment marched without these supplies. But Colonel Pratt and his officers felt that the regiment would be much better prepared for service, if it could be furnished with new uniforms and arms. Those it had were worn and old fashioned, and while they did very well for home duty, were not just the outfit for a regiment to go abroad with. Having sent in the requisitions and feeling that the regiment was entitled to the articles called for, it then became a matter of etiquette to stand by the action already taken. But when the order to proceed came, it was made manifest that the regiment could take the field in the condition in which it marched from Kingston.

Several influential citizens, from different parts of the State, united with the officers of the regiment, in an earnest appeal to Governor Morgan to allow the regiment to proceed. The corps had made many friends during its sojourn in New York, and its drill and discipline induced the belief that it would do good service in the field. It was urged upon the Governor, that to send it home would tend to discourage other organizations preparing for the field, and that the effect would be bad, in every point of view. The result was, that the Governor revoked so much of the above order as directed the regiment to return to Kingston, and instead, ordered it to proceed to Washington. This latter order was telegraphed from Albany, and reached head-quarters about six o'clock on the evening of Monday, May sixth. It was at once promulgated to the regiment, and the scene that ensued is thus described by the New York *Commercial Advertiser :* "When this news was imparted to the troops, a scene of genuine enthusiasm

6

ensued; cheer upon cheer rang upon the air; the President, the Governor, General Scott, Colonel Pratt, and in fact every name the troops could think of, was wildly cheered. Colonel Pratt was deeply affected at the enthusiasm manifested by his men, and took no measures to check their outbursts of joy After order was restored, the commandant made a few pithy remarks, thanking his regiment for the manner in which they had undergone disappointments, and congratulated them on the prospect of having an opportunity of showing of what material the Ulster County boys are composed. He said that his regiment would come back covered with glory He also exonerated the State authorities from all blame in keeping them back, and said that the principal reason for their being ordered home, was the great number of organized regiments of militia offering, by which the Government was forced to decline one-half the tenders. A few encouraging words to the men, and the Colonel concluded by giving orders to be in marching order, as soon as possible.

"The celerity with which the camp was placed in marching order is one of the very best evidences of what might be expected of this regiment in actual service; the train could not leave owing to the storm, and the men again bivouacked. At reveille the men were all ready in trim, ready to take arms and march; a hearty and substantial breakfast was partaken of, and all the arrangements made, necessary for the comfort of the troops; the order to form line was given at eight o'clock. After inspection by the officers and several military celebrities, who had assembled to witness their departure, the line of march was taken up, and the command wheeled out of the west gate of the park, and filed down Broadway to Cortlandt street ferry The officers were mounted on splendid chargers, and the general appearance of the regiment elicited considerable praise from the spectators; at the depot a train was in readiness to take the troops to Philadelphia."

The reporter does not overstate the manifestations of delight with which the order to proceed to Washington, was received. The motives of patriotism and a desire for military distinction, had united in inducing officers and men to set out upon this enterprise. Some of them had made considerable sacrifices, and all had taken leave of family and friends, with a feeling that they might never meet again, that months, at all events, and possibly eternity, lay between them and a re-union. And now, after a journey of a hundred miles, and without having crossed the borders of their peaceful State, and after an absence of a week, to march back to Kingston and disarm, would have been a great humiliation. I think if the regiment had been fairly out of the State when the order to return came, it would have gone on, anyhow, if it had been obliged to march all the way and forage on the country, but in New York, it had to obey the orders of the Governor, who is the Commander-in-Chief. The men were ready to march within two hours after the final order came ; they seemed to be afraid of a counter-mand before they could get off, every possible effort was made by the officers of the regiment to get under way Monday night, but transportation could not be furnished until next morning.

The regiment took cars at Jersey City, and felt, at last, that there could be no recall. A number of Ulster County friends who had come to take a final leave of us, accompanied us to the cars, and some of them went with us as far as Philadelphia, Messrs. Erastus Cooke and Jansen Hasbrouck, I remember as among the number. Through New Jersey, Pennsylvania, and even in little Delaware, we were treated with great courtesy and attention. At many stations the men were furnished with lemonade and sandwiches, and other refreshments, and crowds of people welcomed our arrival with cheers and

sent their blessings after us. Loyalty was burning warm
and bright in the hearts of the people, and manifested
itself in their looks, words, and acts.

Nevertheless, the journey from Jersey City to Perryville, on the east side of the Susquehanna River, was a
very trying one. Our train was an extra, and we had
to keep out of the way of the regular trains. Moreover, the road was encumbered with troops and army
store trains, and our detentions, from time to time, were
terribly tedious. We did not arrive at Perryville until
one o'clock at night ; whereas, the ordinary time for
the journey is not more than six hours. The Baltimore
rebels had some time before destroyed the bridges, which
carried the railroad over the broad and deep streams
crossing its track west of the Susquehanna, and we were
obliged to embark on two steamboats at Perryville, and
proceed by water to Annapolis. But our boats were
not ready until five o'clock in the morning, and I think,
to most of us, it was the worst night we had ever spent.
The novelty of the situation had ceased to divert, and
the wit and humor that had amused and entertained us
for many weary hours, were exhausted. Patience and
quiet submission to fatigue and discomforts, habits
which we by and by acquired, had not yet impressed
themselves upon officers or men sufficiently to smother
all expressions of discontent, and there was a slight imitation of the bad habit of "our army in Flanders."

But as a bright April sun dispersed the gloom and
fogs of night, so also it restored cheerfulness and contentment to our tired and sleepy men. The waters of
the Susquehanna, which has its source in Otsego
County, New York, discharge into Chesapeake Bay
three miles below Perryville. We were soon on the
broad waters of the Chesapeake, and after steaming
about fifty miles, entered the Severn River, and drew
up in front of the grounds of the Naval Academy, at
Annapolis, Maryland.

Disembarking, we were directed to occupy certain of of the Academic buildings, and we were soon in very comfortable quarters. The buildings extend in a long row across the upper part of the grounds, and are furnished with gas, water, bath-rooms, and all the conveniences of a city house. The grounds are extensive, and slope in a beautiful lawn to the Severn, on the east, and the Chesapeake on the south. The grounds are handsomely laid out, and adorned with fine trees. A granite shaft reminds the visitor of the gallant Herndon, while a white marble monument testifies to the merits of various other naval heroes. The view from the Academy grounds was exceedingly pleasant, embracing, as it did, luxuriant fields of grass and grain ; the waters of the Severn and the bay, and the green-robed forests covering the islands and the shores across the Chesapeake. The Academy grounds are separated from Annapolis by a high wall, and no one was allowed egress or ingress, without a pass from the proper authority The post is called "Fort Severn." At the breaking out of the war, the Academy had seven professors and some eighty midshipmen and students.

The city of Annapolis, which lies just outside the Academy walls, contained less than 4,000 inhabitants, a considerable proportion of whom were negroes. The city is the capital of Maryland, and of Ann Arundel County, and is about 38 miles south of Baltimore. The Annapolis and Elkridge Railroad connects the town with the Baltimore and Washington Railroad at Annapolis Junction, fourteen miles to the northwestward. Annapolis is an old-fashioned place, but it has been famous in its day. Its streets radiate from three centres, which are the sites of the three principal buildings in the place—the State House, St. John's College, and St. Ann's Church. These buildings are not remarkable for architectural effects, but they are considered very important edifices by Marylanders. Dur-

ing the Revolutionary War the American Congress held
some of its sessions in the State House, and the closing
scene in that great drama was enacted in the senate-
chamber of that building, and the room and the appearance of many of the actors have been transmitted to us
with reasonable accuracy, in the picture representing
Washington in the act of resigning his commission to
Congress. This room, in honor of that great event, has
been preserved, in just the condition it then was. St.
John's College was founded in 1784, and just before the
war it had a president, five professors, twelve or thirteen hundred alumni, eighty students, and a library of
4,000 volumes.

We found at Annapolis the Thirteenth N Y. S. M.,
(from Brooklyn), Col. A. Smith, who commanded the
post. Across the Severn was the Sixth N Y., Colonel
Pinckney Along the railroad, from Annapolis to the
Junction, with headquarters at the latter place, was
the Fifth N Y. Volunteers, Colonel   General
Benjamin F Butler commanded the Department, with
headquarters at Baltimore.   •

Our stay at Annapolis was brief, yet there were
some incidents connected with it that impressed themselves very strongly upon my mind ; one of these was,
that Colonel Smith imposed all the guard and fatigue
duty upon the Twentieth, and that some of the latter
work was exceedingly onerous, consisting in the removal of some heavy pieces of ordnance. We were
required to furnish a daily detail for guard duty of 250
men, with a field officer of the day The second night
after our arrival one of our men was stabbed while
strolling through the grounds, and the circumstance
caused great excitement and indignation among our
officers and men. Fortunately, the man was not seriously wounded. About midnight—the same night, we
were aroused by the " long roll " at Colonel Pinckney's
post, across the Severn, followed by the discharge of

fire-arms. Our regiment prepared to turn out, but soon the concerted rocket signal of "all right" was given, and the residue of the night passed without further disturbance. These events would have seemed trivial oc-currences to us some months later, but at that time they were exciting. Colonel Pinckney reported next day that a small body of mounted men attacked a picket post, and, exchanging shots, without damage to his men, rode away, themselves apparently uninjured.

On the morning of the eleventh of May we received an order from General Butler, to march from Annapolis at 12 o'clock, and to relieve the Fifth along the line of the railroad, from Annapolis to the Junction, and es-tablish headquarters at the latter place. We were not sorry of the opportunity to get out of Colonel Smith's jurisdiction, and were soon ready to march; but Colonel Smith had a large fatigue party at work, and although advised of the order, and the necessity of re-lieving the men, he omitted to do so until General But-ler, who fortunately arrived, sent him a peremptory order to relieve them.

AT twelve o'clock, on the eleventh of May, we took up
our line of march for Annapolis Junction. The Annapolis and Elkridge Railroad had been disabled by the
local Secessionists, at about the same time the bridges
on the Trunk road were destroyed ; but a regiment
which preceded us had repaired it. We established ten
picket posts along the line of the road, with a signal
system between posts, and arrived at the Junction, with
the main body of the regiment, in the evening. The
Fifth New York Volunteers departed as we arrived,
leaving their tents standing for our occupation. The
regiment, with the line officers, took possession of the
abandoned camp, while the Field and Staff secured
quarters in the " Annapolis Junction Hotel," which,
with the railroads, constituted Annapolis Junction.
Captain D. T. Van Buren, of the Engineers, procured
a straight sapling, 35 feet long, which was erected in the
front centre of the camp. Colonel Pratt issued the following order : " The ' Stars and Stripes ' will be hoisted
on the flagstaff at half-past three o'clock, and the camp
will be known as *Camp Reynolds*, in compliment to the
zealous and active friend of the Ulster Guard, Henry H.
Reynolds, of Kingston, N. Y " The flag was run to the

peak at the appointed time, amid the cheers of the regiment. Camp Reynolds was located in an open field, near to and in full view of the railroad. The men went to work to beautify their quarters, and the front of the tents were soon adorned with evergreens, which afforded a pleasant shade, and added greatly to the comfortable appearance of their quarters. The grounds were kept as clean as a house floor, under strict police regulations, and the camp was a very pretty canvas village. Above it floated an American flag, seventeen feet in length, and around the borders of the camp constantly patrolled a line of sentinels.

Meantime, the railroad communication on the Great Trunk line between New York and Washington had been re-opened, and Annapolis Junction had become a scene of constant animation. It was a watering station, and almost every train stopped there. Trains were following each other in rapid succession, laden with troops, on their way to the National Capital. They invariably cheered Camp Reynolds, and the men within it gave back a hearty response. The officers at headquarters found acquaintances in nearly every New York regiment, going to the front, and pleasant interviews and little acts of hospitality were the agreeable episodes of every day. Numerous civilian friends from the East visited us, and we were always glad to welcome them. Boxes and bundles, for officers and men, were constantly arriving, reminding us of the thoughtfulness and zeal of those who had bidden us "God speed" on our departure from Kingston. It would require pages to enumerate the various articles thus received while we were at this post. At the risk of being deemed invidious, I will mention a few instances of the kind referred to. Colonel Zadoc Pratt, of Prattsville, Green County, and Mr. Henry Dowey, Andes, Delaware County, N Y., sent us a large quantity of excellent butter of their own make. Messrs. Wales, Van Deusen, Knapp and

Deyo, of Rondout, N Y., forwarded a large and well-assorted supply of medical stores. From the Esopus people, a bountiful donation of under-clothing. A like donation from the ladies of Wilbur. Blankets, clothing, and a large dry-goods box of delicacies for the table, from the ladies of Kingston. Some grumbler in the regiment had written home, complaining of the army ration, both as to quantity and quality, and our friends were led to apprehend that we were on starvation allowance. To relieve their minds on this subject, Colonel Pratt caused the adjutant to send to our home papers, the following statement, which is reproduced for the information it affords, as to how our paternal Government feeds its defenders : "Government allowances of rations : ¾ lbs. pork or bacon ; 1¼ lbs. fresh or salt beef; 18 oz. bread or flour, or 12 oz. hard bread, or 1¼ lbs. corn meal. At the rate of 100 rations, 8 qts. beans, or in lieu thereof, 10 lbs. rice, or in lieu thereof, twice per week, 150 oz. of desiccated potatoes and 100 oz. mixed vegetables ; 10 lbs. coffee, or 1½ lbs. tea ; 15 lbs. sugar : 4 qts. vinegar : 1¼ lbs. tallow ; 4 lbs. soap ; 2 qts. salt. This is not exactly the bill of fare that an epicure would gloat over, but soldiers have no business to be epicures.

The regimental headquarters continued at Annapolis Junction until the 29th of June. During this time the duty required of the corps was neither arduous nor dangerous. The picket posts already mentioned were maintained, and others were established, covering several miles of the Baltimore & Washington Railroad, east and west of the junction. Around the camp was nightly posted a strong guard, and every precaution taken against a surprise. Detachments were now and then sent off to intercept parties reported to be on the march to join the rebels, and the houses of several notorious Secessionists were searched for arms. Alarms were sufficiently frequent at the outer picket posts to keep officers and men on the *qui vive*, and Colonel Pratt would often mount his horse at midnight, or later, and accompanied by one or more of his officers, make the "grand rounds" of the outer picket circle, which in-volved a ride of five miles, through fields and woods, and which was a somewhat dangerous pastime. Our pickets were especially cautioned to be on their guard against a sudden dash of cavalry, and on two occasions they mistook the colonel's party for rebel raiders, and were on the point of firing on them.

While the headquarter's family were at breakfast one morning, a considerable body of troops were seen to be approaching the junction from the direction of Savages. The Annapolis Hotel was between the advan-cing soldiers and the regimental camp. Attention was at once called to the column of troops, and an officer designing to play a practical joke on Rev. Mr. D. ——, the regimental chaplain, whose fear of an attack on the post was constant and notorious, sprung from the table and buckled on his sword, the other officers at once taking their cue, followed suit, with all the appearance of haste and terror they could assume. The chaplain gave one glance at the approaching troops, and one at his hurrying comrades, and, springing from the table, he fled from the house, and was not again seen around headquarters until late in the day, when he strolled in, with an expression of countenance which seemed to deprecate any allusion to the little incident of the morn-ing. The chaplain had learned, meantime, that the soldiers were from our own regiment, and were return-ing from a night's scout.

There was genuine excitement in our camp on the 24th of May, the Federal troops had entered Virginia the night before, and Elsworth had been shot in the Jack-son House, at Alexandria. The most extravagant and startling rumors were pouring into our camp from every passing train. On the 25th, we were assured that heavy fighting was going on at Alexandria and Arlington

Heights. Among our informants was Mr. Thurlow Weed, who said he reached Washington the preceding evening, and that he was then hurrying back to New York, at the request of the War Department, to expedite the forwarding of troops. At ten o'clock on the same night Colonel Pratt received a dispatch from General Cadwalader, who was then commanding the department, stating that the rebels were threatening the railroad track, near Laurel, five miles west of our post, and directing him to protect it. Lieutenant Jacob Sharp, B Co., with 40 men, was at once sent to the menaced point; while Colonel Pratt, the major, and several staff officers, made a personal inspection of the locality. On the same evening, our vigilant friend, Mr. Henry H. Reynolds, arrived from Kingston, with parcels and news from home.

Picket duty is very tedious, and green soldiers have hard work to keep awake two or three hours on a quiet post, especially after midnight. One night the colonel, the major, and Captain Webster, officer of the day, were making the rounds about two o'clock, and came upon a post where two men were stationed. We found them both fast asleep on the ground. We quietly took their muskets, which were standing against a tree, near by, and returned to camp. A detachment of the guard was then sent out to arrest the sleepers, whom they found still asleep, and brought them into camp. The men had been guilty of a very grave military offence, and they were tried by a court-martial and sentenced.

On the 28th of May we received a supply of shoes, socks, shirts, &c., from Washington, but the United States uniforms were not issued to us during our three months' term of service. Subsequently, the Twentieth, like other regiments, was uniformed by the Federal Government; and there never was a large army so well fed and clothed as the Federal troops were during the rebellion. Foreign officers were amazed to witness the

abundance of food and clothing that were issued to our
soldiers. I am satified the men could have lived well
on two-thirds of the Government ration, and would have
been comfortable with half the allowance of clothing.
The chief reason why the Confederates often out-march-
ed us was that they were nearly always in "light marching order,"—probably from necessity rather than from
choice. While a Federal column never could move without a cumbersome train of wagons, which the troops
must cover and protect. Such *impedimenta* rendered
celerity of movement simply impossible, and gave the
fleet-footed men of Jackson and other Confederate commanders great advantage. As an example of the enormous encumbrance with which the Federal armies were
accustomed to move, I will take the army of the Potomac, during the campaign of 1864. That army averaged
about 125,000 effective men. Its transportation consisted of about 4,200 wagons, 800 ambulances, 30,000 horses,
including cavalry, artillery, and draft horses ; 4,500 private horses, and 22,000 mules, making a grand aggregate
of 56,000 animals, or nearly $\frac{1}{3}$ animals to men. The ratio
in our Western armies was even higher than this, and
ranged from $\frac{1}{2}$ to $\frac{2}{3}$. A civilian can hardly conceive the
effect of such an immense train of animals and vehicles
upon the movements of accompanying troops. Time
and again the latter are forced to stand for hours and
hours to allow the train to pass, or to await its movement, while it must always have an adequate guard.
When we consider that an army of 125,000 men, marching in column four abreast, with the usual intervals, extends over a distance of 35 miles, and that each six-mule
team occupies about sixty lineal feet, or ninety teams to
the mile, we see how interminable the line seems to be,
and how difficult it must be to cover such a train, and
protect it against an enterprising enemy. But, to pursue the subject a little further, 6,300 mule teams will
extend about seventy miles, assuming the roads are

good and the teams are kept well closed up—otherwise they will stretch out a hundred miles. Nine hundred ambulances will occupy, on the march, seven miles : add to these the space required for the artillery (say 40 batteries of six pieces each, requiring 7 miles), and we have a grand total distance covered by the army of the Potomac, with 125,000 men, marching in one line, of 119 miles. When Lee surrendered at Appomattox Court House, Grant's commissary gave the 20,000 starving Confederates the first "square" meal they had eaten in seven days, and supplied them with rations to last them until they could reach their homes. I have no doubt the liberal supplies made glad the table of many a poor Confederate, *after* he got home. But our quartermasters and commissaries always had enough and to spare. It was this superabundance that often made our armies slow and unwieldy on the march.

Hiram Schoonmaker, of Rondout, who had been lieutenant-colonel of the regiment up to the first of June, resigned on that day in consequence of the pressing demands of a large and important business at home, which had already suffered greatly in consequence of his absence. According to the Militia Law of New York, the field-officers of a regiment were elective by a majority vote of the field, staff and line officers. Colonel Pratt called a meeting of these officers, at headquarters, on the evening of the second of June, and communicated the fact of the resignation of Lieutenant-Colonel Schoonmaker, and asked what action the officers would take in the matter. An officer moved that the meeting proceed to fill the vacancy. This was seconded, and carried, the election resulted in the choice of Major Gates. The promotion of the major having caused a vacancy in the majority, it was resolved to go into an election for that office, and Adjutant Hardenburgh was elected. Maurice McEntee, 1st Sergeant of

H Co., was appointed adjutant, in place of Hardenburgh, promoted.

On the fifteenth of June the first death occurred in
the regiment, and was the result of an accident. The
victim was Dunbar Schoonmaker, son of the late John
M. Schoonmaker, of Kingston. Dunbar was with a detachment of his Co. (B) at Laurel, and while stooping to
grasp his musket his pistol fell from the pocket of his
coat, and striking the musket, was discharged, the ball
passing directly through his heart. He was an active
and intelligent young man, and was much respected for
his many good qualities of head and heart. His remains
were taken home for interment. On the 26th of June,
John Cooper, private of E Co., died of inflammation of
the brain, at Annapolis Junction. He was buried in a
little oak grove, near headquarters, in the midst of a
terrific thunder storm, with religious and military ceremonies. John Converse Elmendorf, son of Peter P
Elmendorf, of Kingston, went home on sick leave and
died at home, June 8th. He was a bright boy of 13
years of age, and a great favorite in the regiment. He
was a drummer, attached to F Co. His father was a
private in the same Co.

On the 24th of June the lieutenant-colonel went to
Washington, to obtain an order, if possible, for the removal of the regiment into Virginia, where events
seemed to be drawing toward a crisis. He had an interview with General Scott, but that chieftain declined to
accede to the request to transfer the regiment to Virginia.
He said the duty we were performing was important,
and we were better qualified to discharge it than another
regiment new to the work would be. Senator Harris
was finally appealed to, and thus re-enforced General
Scott was again urged to let us cross the Potomac ; but
he peremptorily refused.

It was getting to be very dull and monotonous at the
Junction, and we were anxious to leave. We were tired

of seeing trains of troops pass, and the eternal rumble of cars and screaming of locomotives had become a burden and a nuisance. A bit of unlooked for good fortune befell us at this stage of *ennui*, in the form of an order to proceed to Baltimore, which reached us on the morning of the 29th of June, from General Banks, at Fort McHenry, who was then commanding the department. Colonel Pinckney, 6th N. Y S. M., was ordered to relieve us, and as soon as he did so we took train for Baltimore, on the afternoon of the 29th of June, rejoicing in the vicissitude which had delivered us from Annapolis Junction and its hotel.

WE were delayed by various causes on our short journey, and it was after dark when we reached the westerly suburb of Baltimore, and debarked at Mount Clair. Everybody was worried and fagged out by the hurry and bustle of the day, and ill temper was the dominant condition of officers and men. Our bivouac was an open field, south of the railroad track, where the regiment was formed, stacked arms, and prepared to spend the residue of the night. We did not know our future destination. As it was expected we would reach Baltimore early in the afternoon, no rations were issued for the journey, but they were put into a freight car attached to our train. On reaching our bivouac, Commissary Lounsbery proceeded to perform the difficult duty of getting his rations out of the car, in the darkness, and issuing them to the several companies, in the established order.

The field officers were lying upon the ground, near the right of the regiment, waiting for their own supper, when their attention was drawn to a tumult, near the commissary car. Colonel Pratt sent a staff officer to learn the cause of the disturbance, who soon returned and reported that the officers of a certain company were

insisting that their men should be served out of their
order, and threatened to have their men take possession
of the car and help themselves, unless the Commissary
at once gave them their rations.

Pratt was not a stickler for matters of form, and was
ready at any time to deviate from any established rou-
tine for the comfort or convenience of his command.
But he was a resolute enforcer of discipline, and the
last man in the world to allow one of his officers to be
overrun when in the proper discharge of his duty
He at once went to the scene of controversy, and found
things rather worse than they were reported to be. The
Co. in question had fallen in, without arms, and were
quietly awaiting the course of events; their Captain
was greatly excited, and was applying very strong and
uncomplimentary language to the Commissary, who received it with his habitual imperturbability

Colonel Pratt ordered the captain to march his company back to its quarters, and await his turn for rations. This he refused to do, and the situation, thereupon, became delicate and important, in so far as the
discipline of the regiment was concerned. The issue
was squarely presented between the authority of the
colonel and that of a captain. But Pratt did not hesitate ; he ordered Captain Flynn to put F Company
under arms and march to the scene of trouble. When
they arrived Colonel Pratt told the captain of the Company in question, that if he did not return with his company to his quarters at once, he would order them to
fire upon him. After a moment's hesitation, the officers
returned with their men to their position in the line of
bivouac, while F Company, relieved from a disagreeable duty, returned to its place and stacked arms. The
commissary then proceeded with his work, and all were
finally supplied with their rations in proper order, and
our first night in Baltimore passed without further incident worthy of notice.

The following morning the lieutenant-colonel, accompanied by the adjutant, rode through the city, and thence to Fort McHenry, and reported the arrival and position of the regiment to General Banks. He inquired what route we had taken to reach the fort, and when informed, he said we had had a dangerous ride, and directed we should return by a route that would avoid the city He said that he had arrested certain prominent Baltimoreans the night before, and that the feeling among the rebels in the city toward Union soldiers was very bitter, and that we were liable to be shot while riding through the streets. He directed that the regiment should march through the city, to Patterson's Park, on the east side, and encamp; the two officers, in returning to the regiment, took General Banks' advice, and gave the city a wide berth.

Fort McHenry is situated on the point of a peninsula, at the mouth of the harbor, and is famous for having sustained a 24 hours' bombardment by 16 British ships-of-war on the 13th of September, 1814. While this bombardment was going on, Francis Scott Key, then a prisoner on the British ship Minden, lying near Soller's Flatts, eight miles below, and where the white walls of the unfinished Fort Carroll now rise above the water, composed the national song known as the "Star Spangled Banner." Baltimore was justly proud of the defense of the fort and the city, and well it might be, in view of some contemporaneous events. Superadded to the attack by the fleet, 9,000 troops landed and advanced against the city General Stryker, with the Baltimore brigade of 3,200 men, met the invaders, and opposed them so stoutly, killing a large number, including General Ross, their commander, that they were glad to get aboard their ships again and sail away Battle Monument, in the city, commemorates these events.

We marched through the city with drums beating,

and colors flying, greatly to the disgust of the secession
element.   As we advanced through the streets, we
could see heads thrust out of windows, in front, and
after a hurried look at the approaching troops, the
head would disappear, and the window blinds would be
closed. Men and women retired to their houses, and
the streets and buildings looked deserted. Many of
the people secluded themselves because they were
afraid of another street fight, but more of them did so
because they did not want to see Union soldiers, or appear to take any interest in them. Reaching Patterson
Park, on the east side of the city, we went into camp.

This park contains 56 acres, some portions of which
are covered with trees of large growth, the shade of
which, on a July day, we found very acceptable. The
park is on high ground, which overlooks much of the
harbor, canton, and the surrounding country The
City of Baltimore is built up to the westerly and northerly limits of the park, and ten minutes' walk takes
one into Broadway, one of the fashionable streets of
the city Until eclipsed by the superior attractions of
Druid Hill Park, Patterson Park was a favorite resort
for pleasure seekers, and pedestrians yet resort to it in
great numbers, as a convenient and pleasant breathing
place in warm weather. It is so high it catches the
breeze from every direction, while it affords a view of
city, country and harbor that make up a very charming combination of scenery An earthen fort was constructed in the park, as one of the means of defending
the city, in the war of 1812, and the embankment yet
remains, overgrown with sod and grass. The park belonged to, and was called after the Patterson family, of
Baltimore, whose beautiful daughter Elizabeth married
Jerome Bonaparte, on Christmas Eve, 1803, and who
was deserted by her husband, in order to restore himself to favor with his brother, the Emperor, and who,
on the 12th of August, 1807, at the command of his

brother, married Fredrica Catharine, daughter of the
King of Wurtemberg, while his wife was clasping to
her torn heart, his infant son, in her father's house, in
Baltimore. In Loudon Park Cemetery, near Baltimore,
peacefully repose the remains of the child of that
famous but unhappy marriage. On an imposing granite obelisk is this legend : "Sacred to the memory of
Jerome Napoleon Bonaparte, born July 7th, 1805 ; died
June 17th, 1870, aged 65. *Requiescat in pace.*"

We named the post "Camp Banks," in honor of
the commander of the department, Major-General N P
Banks. Soon after settling down we lost one of our
men,   Dubois, of E Company, who died
of brain fever. He was buried by his comrades.

On the evening of Sunday, July   , Colonel Pratt
received an order to report to General Banks, at Fort
McHenry Returning to the camp about midnight, he
ordered the regiment to be ready to march at five
o'clock Monday morning, excepting a detail of 100
men to be left in charge of the camp.

At the designated time on Monday morning the
regiment marched out of camp, and filing into Broadway, moved down that fine street, until the head of
column rested on Bank street, where we were directed to
await orders. The rain came down in a steady drizzle.
We had no idea what was expected of us, but we saw
we were giving the occupants of the locality a genuine
surprise. As they arose and looked from their windows, the first sight that greeted their eye was a half-
dozen mounted officers and a good sized regiment of infantry, occupying their street, and apparently waiting
for some development. The rumor soon spread that
we were going to search the neighborhood, and especially a church near by, for concealed arms, and I think
we rather fell in with the notion ourselves.

By and by an order came for four companies to
march to the Custom House, in Lombard street. Col-

onel Pratt took D, F, H, and R Companies, and proceeded to that destination, leaving the remainder of the
regiment, A, B, C, E, & G Companies, under command
of the Lieutenant-Colonel, in the street. If our appearance surprised the denizens of Broadway, they were
soon quits with us, by administering a counter-surprise,
different in kind, but equal in degree. Invitations
were received by the Lieutenant-Colonel from a number of families, for himself and officers to breakfast,
and they seemed so cordial and sincere that they
were accepted in such order that a certain number of
officers were permitted to leave the regiment and breakfast with our hospitable neighbors, others following in
their turn, until all had a " square meal."

Among our entertainers that rainy morning, and
often afterwards during our sojourn in that city,
were Doctor and Mrs. Inloes (the former of whom is
now deceased), Mr. Randolf, Captain J. W Hugg and
family, Mr. Harry Wilson and family, Hon. Mr. Leary
and family, Captain ———— James, Mr. Wollen, Mr.
Hunt, Rev Mr. Reese, and many others, whose names
I cannot now recall. They made our stay in their city
very pleasant, and deserve to have their names recorded
in any volume that tells the story of the three months'
campaign of the "Twentieth." Nor should the name
of Mr. John Thomas, now collector of customs of the
port of Baltimore, be omitted. A staunch and influential Union man, he was a zealous and valued friend of
the corps. Captain Hugg was one of nature's noble-
men, and his house was a second home to the writer of
this history ; his hospitality was bountiful and princely, and his warmth of heart in keeping with his grand
physique. On the departure of the regiment for home,
he accompanied it to the borders of the State. When a
military hospital was established in Baltimore, his
eldest daughter devoted herself to the care of sick and
wounded soldiers.

I cannot resist the temptation to insert a letter, written to me in behalf of the regiment's little friend, Neal Leary, soon after the regiment left Baltimore. I know it will be a pleasant reminder of the bright lad to a good many of the officers and men of the corps. It is as follows

BALTIMORE, 12 *Aug.*, 1861.

DEAR SIR :—

My little brother Neal has just received, and begs me to answer your pleasant letter of the 9th inst. He tells me to write that the Wisconsin Brigade encamped in the Park, after the departure of the 20th Regiment, and was without doubt a good and patriotic body of men, but he did not become acquainted with a single member of the Brigade, and he is quite sure that no one can be found in it to take the place of Col. Gates in his affection.

He asks me to write too, that he was very happy to learn from the Kingston paper you kindly sent him, that the regiment would re-enlist and that for the war, he will be very much disappointed if you are not again ordered to Baltimore. He begs you to give his love to all the gentlemen of the 20th that he knew and especially to Geddy and Charley McEntee.

My father, mother and sisters send their compliments, and Neal sends his photograph, which he begs you to keep as a reminder of your little friend in Baltimore.

With much respect,
I am yours,
COL. T. B. GATES,   P LEARY, JR.
    Kingston.

But while I have been indulging in these pleasant recollections of Baltimore friends, the battalion has been standing in the street. At nine o'clock Major Belger arrived with instructions to the lieutenant-colonel to take possession of the station-house on Bank street, and of the public school buildings on the corner of Bank and Broadway, as quarters, and they proved to be just adapted to the purpose.

We had daily drills in Broadway, which is a very wide street, and through which the battalion could march in column of companies. By a preconcerted arrangement Col. Pratt marched down from the Custom House, one afternoon, with his battalion and a section

of artillery, and made a feigned attack upon the post in
Broadway The Lieut. Col's command was under arms
and sallied forth to meet the foe, quite a brisk battle
took place in the street and the Col. was eventually
forced to retreat. A few days afterwards the Broadway
army moved down upon the Custom House and a lively
sham fight took place between it and Colonel Pratt's
forces, in presence of thousands of wondering spectators.
The defense was so vigorous and well conducted, we
were unable to "clean out" the establishment, and
were glad to retire without loss of colors, guns or
prisoners.

It seems we were ordered into the city in view of the
impending battle of Bull Run, and a bold aspect of the
secession element. The population of Baltimore at this
time, was about equally divided between Unionists and
Secessionists, but the latter had been so violent and
demonstrative before troops were stationed in the city,
that they seemed to be vastly in the majority The
Unionists had not dared to openly express their sentiments, and the Stars and Stripes were carefully secluded.
But the moment they felt themselves secure from insult
and violence, by reason of the presence of Federal troops,
the loyal sentiment gushed forth in words and acts, and
on the Fourth of July, the national colors were flying
from hundreds of private houses, where one would not
have been seen if the troops were away, or if they had
been displayed, they would have been torn down and
their owners outraged. Families who had lived side by
side for years and been upon terms of the closest intimacy, had become estranged by their differences on the
great question of disunion, so that even the courtesy of
recognition was no longer observed between them, although meeting each other almost on their very door-
steps, day after day It was easier to be a staunch,
out-spoken Union man in Boston than it was in Baltimore.

Frequent detachments were sent out in search of concealed arms designed for improper purposes, and large quantities were from time to time seized. A large quantity of arms and munitions of war, were found concealed in the building occupied by Marshal Kane. Captain Lent's Co. E. went out at midnight, on the 24th of July, a short distance from camp, on the Philadelphia Road, and fished out from under a hay rick a quantity of arms and war munitions. About the same time Lieut. Jervis M'Entee, H. Co., captured two secession flags, which were about being sent South. In one house where a search was made for arms, was found among other things, a drum belonging to the Sixth Massachusetts Regiment, and which had been captured at the time of the brutal attack upon the regiment in the streets of Baltimore. We took possession of the drum not only, but also of its custodian, and turned him over to the Provost-Marshal to explain the circumstances under which the drum came into his possession. It was *prima facie* evidence of his connection with the rioters who had attacked the Sixth Massachusetts.

Among the families with whom pleasant acquaintance was formed in Baltimore, was that of the Rev Mr. Lyon, of Philadelphia, who were guests of Dr. Inloes. A son, Augustus Lyon, had the misfortune to fall under the suspicion of the Federal authorities, and was arrested as a Confederate officer, but upon application of an officer of the "Twentieth," he was released and escaped incarceration for an indefinite period at Fort Lafayette. Baltimore was a bad place for a young man whose convictions as to his duty to his government were not well established. The young bloods of the city were all Secessionists, and they were eloquent and persistent advocates of the cause. The tone of "society" was decidedly disloyal, and Jeff. Davis could hardly have had more enthusiastic and persuasive emissaries than were to be found among the beautiful women of the Monumental City.

In the latter part of July, the regiment returned to its camp in Patterson Park, and soon after was paid off in gold. Officers and men were glad to exchange the burdensome coin for bills. The three months for which the regiment had enlisted had now expired, and many of its members were anxious to go home. But the Federal misfortune at Bull Run had inspired a fear of fresh trouble at Baltimore, and we were required to remain.

The men were not entirely satisfied with this arrangement. Their term of service was up, and many of them had business and domestic duties demanding their attention at home. Colonel Pratt had the regiment paraded, and addressed the men in an earnest and impressive speech, showing the necessity for their remaining, and appealed to them as patriots and soldiers, to remain at their post until the present danger was over. He submitted the determination of the question to the regiment, but it was not prepared to act at once, when Captain Flynn suggested to the colonel that it would be well to let the men go to their company quarters and decide the matter by separate company action. This plan was adopted, and captains were directed to report the result without delay

I followed Company F to its quarters, as Captain Flynn had acted as the spokesman of the line officers, and I had some curiosity to see how he would get along with his men. I knew some of them were very anxious to go home. When Captain Flynn got on his company ground, he opened ranks and made a stirring speech to his company. He told them that the Capital was in danger, and that their services were now needed as much as they were the day they left Kingston, and it would be disgraceful to leave. The captain then added, in nearly these words: "If there are any men here who are in favor of going home before this emergency is over, let them step three paces to the front, and I warn you to be careful in doing so, lest your comrades shoot or bayonet you ; and any man who goes home with a wound in the back, will be justly considered a traitor." It is needless to say that not a man stepped to the front, but on the contrary, by a unanimous and enthusiastic vote they resolved to stay until the crisis had passed. The other companies came to a like conclusion, and the regiment settled down to bide its time.

On the afternoon of the 2d of July, the ladies of East Baltimore presented the regiment with a beautiful silk national flag.   Hon. Mr. Leary, M.C., made the presentation speech, and Colonel Pratt replied in an exceedingly felicitous manner.

The Baltimore *American*, the leading paper of the city, thus spoke : "The Twentieth New York regiment, under command of Colonel G. W Pratt, now encamped at Patterson Park, will, it is expected, shortly leave this city on its return to the homes of those composing it.   While in this city the regiment has, under the strict discipline maintained by the officers, attained an enviable reputation, there being no such cases of interference on their part with citizens or their property as unfortunately has been exhibited by those belonging to other regiments about the city   The officers, during the brief space of time in which they have sojourned in this city, have made a very favorable impression.   Not only on those who are loyal to the Government, but also on those who are more favorable to the Confederate cause, by reason of their scrupulous desire not to interfere with private rights.   Until the day of their departure, the officers will be obliged to devote their time to camp duties, so that all who wish to see them must necessarily visit the camp at Patterson Park."

By orders from department headquarters, the "Twentieth" furnished a guard of three companies, under command of Major Hardenburgh, to convey Marshal Kane, the Baltimore Police Commissioners, and a number of other Baltimore rebels, to Fort Lafayette, in New York Harbor. They made the journey by steamer, and the major delivered his prisoners and rejoined the regiment on its arrival in New York.

A few days before our final departure from Patterson Park, Simon S. Roos, of Company C., was wounded in the leg by a Minie ball whilst he was lying upon a bench, within a hundred yards of regimental headquarters, and far inside the line of sentinels. No report of the gun was heard, and no one could tell from whence the shot came. The direction of the wound indicated that the ball must have been fired from the north side of the camp, and three companies were soon scouring the country, but failed to discover the would-be assassin.

On Tuesday, the 30th of July, the welcome order came to begin the homeward march, and we were soon on board cars and speeding northward. We arrived in New York Wednesday morning, and proceeded to the Park Barracks, where the regiment was mustered out of service. A large delegation of Kingston friends, with the regimental band, met us in New York, and accompanied us home. Thursday the regiment embarked on board the steamer Manhattan, and debarked at Rondout on Friday morning, August 2d.

The soldiers were met at the point of debarkation by wives, children, and other relatives and friends, eagerly welcoming them home. The two villages were all astir from the evening before arrival, hundreds coming in from the country during the night.

In anticipation of our coming, a meeting was held at the Court House, on the evening of the 30th of July, at which Gen. S. S. Hommel presided. with Messrs. Erastus Cooke, as Vice-President, and L. B. Van Waganen, Secretary A Reception Committee was appointed,

consisting of Messrs. T. R. Westbrook, J. S. Lang-
worthy, J. S. Burhans, A. A. Deyo, Jr., Erastus Cooke,
Samuel Frame, S. S. Westbrook, H. H. Reynolds, J. E.
Ostrander, A. M. Low, S. S. Hommel, L. B. Van
Waganen and A. Schoonmaker, Jr. This committee
did their work admirably

The regiment was received by Brigadier-General
Samson and Staff, the Kingston and Rondout Fire Department, the Kingston National Greys, the Dragoon
Company of the 20th, and a corps of Juvenile Zouaves.
The regiment and escort were formed in Abeel street,
Rondout, and forming column, headed by the regimental band, proceeded up Wurts and Holmes streets
to the Plank Road, and thence to Kingston. Arriving
there, the regiment was formed in line of battle in Wall
street, right resting on North Front, and exercised in
the manual, &c., after which they were addressed by
Hon. T. R. Westbrook, who eloquently welcomed them
home, in the name of the citizens of the regimental district. Complimentary orders from the War Department
were then read by the Adjutant, when the regiment was
marched to Academy Green by companies, where a
bountiful breakfast had been spread by the ladies of
Kingston and vicinity, who personally attended the
tables. This over, the companies were dismissed ;
the soldiers from other towns hurried homeward, to
be again welcomed by their families, neighbors and
friends.

Thus terminated the first experience of the "Ulster
Guard," in the service of the United States. It saw no
fighting and performed no extraordinary deeds ; but it
went forth ready and willing to do for its country whatever brave men might do, and it was not its fault that
it was not among the combatants at Bull Run, or on
some other field where martial honors were to be won.
Its officers solicited a more active field of duty, than
that to which the regiment was assigned. They were

overruled by higher authority, and it was only left to them and their men to perform the more humble role which it has been the object of the preceding chapters to narrate. Such duties as were devolved upon the regiment it discharged with alacrity and fidelity, and it was so fortunate as to receive the commendation of its superiors, of the people among whom its duties were performed, and what was more precious than either or both, of its friends at home.

CHAPTER VIII.

THE hue and cry which rang through the country immediately after the first battle of Bull Run, has, to a
great extent, given color to the various histories of the
affair, and every one of them leaves the impression upon
the mind of the reader that the plan of the campaign
was defective and the conduct of the army pusillanimous. A few words in vindication of General

McDowell, under whom the Twentieth regiment served so long, and of the militia regiments which were with him at Bull Run, and in the reputation of which the " Twentieth" naturally feels that interest which is demanded by a just pride in *esprit de corps*, seem not out of place in a work of this character.

When the President yielded to the popular clamor for an advance of the army, General McDowell was called upon to submit a plan of campaign against the rebel cohorts, who were flaunting their colors almost in sight of the Capitol. McDowell prepared and submitted to the President and his Cabinet such plan. Lieutenant General Scott, then General-in-Chief, General Charles W Sanford, then commanding the First Division, N Y S. M., and Generals Tyler, Mansfield and Meigs, U.S.A., were present. The plan was adopted with scarcely a change in any particular, and General McDowell was directed to carry it into execution. Many of the regiments which were to compose the army, were on the east side of the Potomac, and some of them did not join until the day the movement began. As to the novelty of the situation General McDowell said : "I had no opportunity to test my machinery ; to move it around and see whether it would work smoothly or not. There was not a man there who had ever manœuvred troops in large bodies. There was not one in the army ; I did not believe there was one in the whole country ; at least, I knew there was no one who had ever handled 30,000 troops. I wanted very much, a little time : all of us wanted it, we did not have a bit of it." Here, then, was an army of 28,000 men thrown together in a hurry, none of whom had ever been drilled in evolutions of the line, and who were compelled by the exigencies of the occasion, to advance against a force of at least equal numbers, holding a position which they had spent three months in fortifying. Nevertheless, General McDowell expressed his belief in his ability to defeat Beauregard, if he should not be re-enforced by General Johnson. General Scott promised McDowell that if "Johnson joins Beauregard, he shall have Patterson on his heels."

With this understanding, the march began on the 16th of July, and as the Union troops advanced, the rebels fell back until they were under cover of their works on the west side of Bull Run.

On the 18th of July the van of McDowell's army occupied the Heights of Centreville. Before it, and about five miles distant, flowing in a southeasterly direction, was the historic Bull Run. McDowell had organized his army into four divisions, commanded respectively by General Tyler, Colonel Hunter, U. S. A., Colonel Heintzelman, U. S. A., and Colonel Miles, U. S. A. Each division contained from 6,000 to 8,000 men. The bulk of this army was made up of the advance regiments of three years men, and some of these knew scarcely anything of company or battalion drill—officers and men equally ignorant. They had nobly responded to their country's call for volunteers, and, in time became splendid soldiers. But they went into their first battle without knowing much about the "machinery" of a military organization, and that ignorance placed them at great disadvantage when manœuvering in the field, against an army in position. General J. E. Johnson, the Confederate commander, said on this subject: "The Northern army had this disadvantage, a great one to such undisciplined troops as were engaged on both sides, of being the assailants, and advancing under fire to the attack, which can be well done only by trained soldiers. They were much more liable to confusion, therefore, than the generally stationary ranks of the Confederates."

General Scott telegraphed Patterson: "If not strong enough to beat the enemy, make demonstrations so as to detain them in the valley of Winchester." Again:

" Do not let the enemy amuse and delay you with a
small force in front, whilst he re-enforces the Junction
with his main body." Again, on July 18th : " I have
certainly been expecting you to beat the enemy ; if not,
that you had felt him strongly, or at least, had occupied him with threats and demonstrations. Has he not
stolen a march and sent re-enforcements towards Manassas Junction ?" To the latter telegram, Patterson replied : " The enemy has stolen no march upon me. I
have kept him actively employed, and, by threats and
reconnoissances in force, caused him to be re-enforced."
When this dispatch was sent, Patterson had not only
not caused re-enforcements to be sent to Johnson, but
had given him so little concern, that on the 19th he put
his army in march to join Beauregard, and had himself
gone to Manassas. This was the result of Patterson's
stupidity, cowardice or treason, whichever it may have
been, that had induced him on the night of the 16th of
July to withdraw from a position near Bunker Hill,
within about nine miles of Winchester, where Johnson
lay, to Charleston, 22 miles in rear, and where, Patterson himself says, he could offer no obstacle to Johnson joining Beauregard, whenever he chose. General
Charles W Sanford, who was in Patterson's army with
some New York militia regiments, wanted to be allowed
to attack Johnson, with the men under his command,
but Patterson would not consent. The very day Patterson moved to Charleston, Johnson began to send
off troops to Beauregard. Patterson gives two reasons
for falling back on Charleston ; one was, he wanted to
provision his army, and his wagons were at Charleston, and he thought it was easier to march to the
wagons than to have the wagons come to the army. It
is but fair to General Patterson, however, to say, that
this reason was more especially urged by Fitz-John
Porter, who was Patterson's adjutant-general. The
other reason was, that the enemy greatly outnumbered

him, and he was afraid of being attacked. This danger
Fitz-John Porter considered imminent. He and Patterson both belonged to that somewhat distinguished body
of officers who always supposed that the enemy outnumbered them, and whose demands for re-enforcements
were insatiable. Butler was to watch, and if necessary,
engage Magruder, although little danger was apprehended from that quarter. Orders covering these objects were given, before McDowell set his army in
motion.

Radiating, like the spokes of a wheel, with Centreville as the hub, are three roads descending the slope in
a westerly direction, striking Bull Run at points about
four miles apart, and some five miles from the hub.
The most northerly of these roads is the Warren Turnpike, which crosses Bull Run at the stone bridge. The
middle road leads to Blackburn's Ford, and is the direct route to Manassas Junction, ten miles away The
most southerly intersects the run four miles further
down the stream. From Centreville to the line of Bull
Run the descent is gradual, but continuous, and the
bank along the east side of the stream is generally low.
The westerly side presents a more bold and difficult
shore, and the country in rear of it rises in ridges, separated by smooth intervals of ascending ground, until
it spreads out into the plains of Manassas. On that
side of the run, for a distance of eight miles along its
course, the rebels had spent two months in fortifying,
and had covered the approaches at the fords and
bridges by heavy guns, and had obstructed the roads
on the west side of the stream with *abatis*. The crossing of a hostile force, at either of these points, would
have been attended with heavy loss, if indeed, it could
have been accomplished.

McDowell's original design was to pass Bull Run at
some point below Blackburn's Ford, and turning the
enemies' right flank, seize his communications with

Richmond, and attack his line in flank and rear. But reconnoissances from Centreville disclosed the fact that Beauregard's right was more extended and stronger than had been anticipated, and the country west of the stream impracticable for the movement of large bodies of troops, and, moreover, the unauthorized demonstrations of General Tyler, in front of Blackburn's Ford, on the 19th, had lead Beauregard to be especially watchful on his right, and to concentrate a heavy force there, while at the same time he had neglected the ford at Sudley's, two miles above his left. General J. E. Johnson states in his "Narrative of Military Operations," page 40, that Beauregard had received information, through spies, that the Federal army was to advance by roads eastward of that leading directly to Manassas Junction, and had been governed by such information in posting his army   On the morning of the twenty-first of July, Beauregard's right rested at Union Mills, where the Orange and Alexandria Railroad crossed Bull Run, and extended from thence, up the stream, about a mile above Stone Bridge. Ewell's Brigade was on the extreme right, and was supported by Holmes' Brigade lying a short distance in the rear. D. R. Jones' Brigade was on Ewell's left, in front of McLean's Ford, and was supported by Earley's Brigade, posted in a thicket of young pines, a short distance in rear. Longstreet's Brigade was at Blackburn's Ford, supported by Jackson's Brigade, concealed by a skirting of pines; and behind Jackson was Barksdale's Thirteenth Mississippi Regiment. Along the edge of the pines above mentioned, and with a view to support any threatened position, were the brigades of Bee and Bartow. In the front line, and on the left of Longstreet, was the brigade of Bonham, covering Mitchell's Ford. On Bonham's left, and Gurding Island, Ball's and Lewis' Fords, was Cocke's Brigade, and on his left was the brigade of Evans, covering the crossing at Stone

Bridge, and a farm ford a mile above. Stewart's cavalry guarded the level ground extending in the rear. From Bonham's left to Cocke's right, two companies of cavalry were posted in reserve, in the rear of Mitchell's Ford. Wade Hampton's Legion, six hundred strong, was held in reserve near the Lewis House. This force aggregated 27,833 men and forty guns, and included 6,000 men who had arrived the day before from Winchester, a part of the army Patterson was supposed to be watching.

Beauregard resolved to assume the aggressive and attack McDowell's left and rear, on the morning of the 21st, and issued orders for that purpose. Ewell was to begin the movement, and was to be followed by the brigades of Jones, Longstreet and Bonham, with their respective reserves. But the orders were miscarried, and while Beauregard was waiting, momentarily expecting to hear the outburst of battle on his extreme right, the Union guns opened upon his centre and left. He then countermanded the order for attack, although Ewell had finally thrown his brigade across Bull Run at Union Mills, and Jones and Longstreet were in march to support him. In lieu of the proposed attack, and to " retain and engross the enemy's reserves and forces at and about Centreville, Ewell, D. R. Jones, Longstreet and Bonham were ordered to make demonstrations on their several fronts." These demonstrations were continued during the battle, although the forces engaged in them were largely drawn upon to re-enforce the left. Nevertheless, the Confederate troops remaining at the centre and lower fords, were sufficiently numerous to menace McDowell's communications, and to compel him to detain Miles' division and a brigade of Tyler's on the east side of Bull Run. The fact that McDowell did not bring these reserves into action, has been variously commented upon, but the *fact* that he did not, and the reason why he did not, have been approved by the soundest military critics.

From Centreville, therefore, McDowell's operations were directed against the enemy's left flank, instead of his right. And with the hope of detaining Beauregard's forces in their then positions on his right and centre, until the turning column should strike him in reverse, Miles was directed to demonstrate strongly against the lower and centre fords, with a part of his division, while the residue was held in reserve near Centreville. Tyler was, in a like manner to threaten the position at Stone Bridge. Meantime, Hunter and Heintzelman were to march to Sudley's Ford, about three miles above Stone Bridge, in a direct line, but twice that distance over the " tortuous, narrow trace of road, rarely used, through a dense wood the greater part of the way," and which was the only practicable route open to them. Having crossed Bull Run, they were to sweep down on the west side and take the rebel line in flank and rear. As the turning column uncovered the Stone Bridge, by forcing the enemy out of his works, Tyler was to throw his division across, and join the forces of Hunter. If, however, the movement of Hunter and Heintzelman induced the Confederates to fall back from Blackburn's Ford, Miles was to cross with a part of his division and attack. In like contingency, at Stone Bridge, Tyler was to push across and attack the foe in flank and rear.

Tyler's division, which was lying in front of Cub Run, (a stream rising north of Centreville and flowing into Bull Run, midway between Stone Bridge and Blackburn's Ford), was ordered to march at half-past two A.M., July 21st, and to advance to the vicinity of Stone Bridge. Hunter's division was to follow to a road a mile beyond Cub Run, which leads from the Warrenton Turnpike to Sudley's Ford. Thence by this road to Sudley's. The march of Tyler's division was ex-

pected to mark Hunter's column to the point where it
left the Warrenton Turnpike, and from thence, its
movements would be screened by the woods through
which the road ran. Heintzelman was to close in immediately after Hunter. (It should be stated, by way of explanation of the fact that the rear brigades of this
turning column did not arrive on the field until mid-
day, that a column of troops, marching over a single
road, 10,000 strong, requires five hours to pass any given
point.) The head of Hunter's column was expected to
reach the ford at half-past six o'clock, at which moment
Tyler was to open his batteries at Stone Bridge, as
though he designed to force a crossing there. Hearing
Tyler's guns, Miles was to threaten the enemy in front
of Blackburn's. While thus keeping the enemy in
doubt as to the real point of assault, it was hoped that
Hunter could make his flank march, followed by Heintzelman, and reach the vicinity of the rebel left, before
the movement should be discovered—or, at all events,
before Beauregard could re-arrange his line of battle, in
time to meet the attack.

The plan was admirable, and is admitted so to have
been by the best military judges. The faulty execution
was not chargeable to General McDowell. He designed
to begin the movement at dark on Saturday night, and
position his turning column, after an easy march, near
Sudley's, ready to cross at daylight. But his division
commanders preferred to remain in camp, allowing the
men to sleep the fore part of the night, and start at such
time as would bring them to their several positions in
one march, and, in their judgment, a start at half-past
two, Sunday morning, would be quite early enough.
Yielding to this view, General McDowell directed the
march to begin at that hour. Experienced troops would,
doubtless, have met the expectations of their commanders, but this was a green and inexperienced army, and,
however ready it was to obey orders, it could *not* do so

with the facility of veterans. It was, therefore, long
after the time designated when the march of Tyler's
division began, and Hunter, who was obliged to await
Tyler's movement, was so much delayed thereby, that
when the head of his column reached Sudley's it was
half-past nine o'clock—just three precious hours after
the appointed time. Still, the enemy had not discovered the march of the turning column, but was absorbed
by the demonstrations of Miles and Tyler, whose guns
had been thundering for three hours, and whose pickets
had been skirmishing with the rebels all the morning.

It may be said, perhaps, that this turning column
should have been positioned sufficiently early to secure
its crossing at the designated time. But in addition to
the representations of the division commanders, Mc-
Dowell may have been influenced by the consideration
that its chances of success were in the exact ratio to
the secrecy of its movements. That these operations
were conducted in the enemy's country, and that if
Beauregard were to be surprised, it must be by a sudden
operation, which would out-strip the willing feet of
watchful spies.

The road from Sudley's, over which Hunter was to
march after crossing the Run, is bordered by dense
woods for about a mile, and then passes through an
open country, towards Manassas Junction, crossing the
Warrenton Turnpike, a mile in rear of the left of the
Confederate lines.

About ten o'clock, Colonel Evans, who commanded
the Confederate left, became aware of the approach of
Hunter's forces, and at once divined the real purpose of
the Union commander. Dispatching an aid to Beauregard, with notice of the impending attack, and a request for re-enforcements ; he at once took measures to
oppose the best front he could to the flanking column.
He immediately detached a portion of his forces, and
put them in march for his left and rear, and marching

nearly a mile across the fields, selected a position a little in advance of the intersection of the turnpike and
Sudley roads, in a cover of detached woods, commanding the road over which Hunter must debouch from the
woods through which he was approaching. His artillery was so posted, that it could sweep this avenue of
approach, while a portion of his infantry was within
fifteen hundred yards of the point where the head of
Hunter's column was expected to appear.

Burnside's Brigade, composed of the 1st and 2d Rhode
Island Volunteer Regiments, the 2d Rhode Island Battery, the 71st N Y S. M., and the 2d N. H. Volunteers,
was in the advance, and by reason of the density of the
woods, or some other cause, no deployment was attempted until the open ground was reached, and the
men were actually under fire of both infantry and artillery The manœuvre should have executed, if possible,
under cover of the woods, even if the line had been
disarranged in advancing subsequently Any manœuvre
which exposes the sides or backs of troops to the fire
of any enemy is hazardous, and should be avoided.
Veterans become unsteady under such circumstances,
and raw troops must be composed of exceptionally
good material, who can keep their formations and be
successfully handled under such trying conditions.
Marshal Bugeaud says : " I affirm that I have seen
an entire division in column of regiments, which began
its deployment within range of the enemy's guns,
routed before it finished its manœuvre." And he was
speaking of old soldiers. Burnside's men were thrown
into temporary confusion and began delivering an in-
effectual fire. But they soon recovered from their surprise, and, completing their deployment, they advanced
towards the enemy, with a steady and well-directed fire,
which told seriously upon its ranks.

Colonel Andrew Porter's Brigade, in which were the
8th and 14th N Y S. M., now debouched from the

woods, and deploying rapidly, formed on Burnside's right, while Sykes' regulars took position on his left. Evans kept his guns steadily playing while these movements were taking place, but after the first shock, failed to disconcert the Union line, although his fire was rapid and effective. Hunter was cut down almost at the first fire, and Colonel Andrew Porter assumed command of the division. Griffin's Battery now dashed out of the woods, and getting into position, opened such a vigorous and effective fire on the rebel cannoniers, that they were forced to direct their attentions and their guns towards this battery

But while the Federals had been disengaging themselves from the woods and deploying, Evans was reenforced by the brigades of Bee and Bartow, and Imboden's Battery—a portion of the army of the Shenandoah, which had arrived from Winchester the day before. Wade Hampton's Legion, which had come up from Richmond on the 20th, went into action on Bee's left.

The Confederates had the advantage of position and of a defensive battle, but the Federals were the more numerous. Now, however, began to be experienced the disadvantages resulting from ignorance of the evolutions of the line, and the result was that regiments, and in some cases, even companies, manœuvred and fought on their own account. The division, as a unit, had no cohesion when it once got into action. Neither officers or men of the volunteer regiments understood the gradation of authority, and would receive orders only from their immediate superiors. As these circumstances operated to take the troops, to a great extent, out of the hands of the division and brigade commanders, it will be seen at once that its effect was to render it impossible to manœuvre the division, or even a brigade, so as to throw it on any desired point, or to employ one part to support another. Colonel Averell,

Porter's adjutant-general, says: that although McDowell had 18,000 troops across Bull Run, that there were not more than 6,000 or 8,000 actually engaged at any one time. But there was no lack of courage among the men, and they advanced to the attack with undaunted spirit. The rebel line was well posted, and its fire was well delivered. But it could not check the ardor of the assailants, who, although sometimes staggered by a destructive volley, would return the fire and push on for the goal to which the enemy was clinging so desperately. The 14th N Y S. M. advanced against a grove in which Colonel Bee had posted the 7th and 8th Georgia Regiments. The enemy allowed the 14th to reach the edge of the woods before discovering himself to them, and then poured a murderous fire into their very faces. The surprise and the fatal effects of the volley, threw the regiment into temporary disorder, but the discipline of the men and the efficiency of their officers, soon restored the symmetry of their line, and pouring in their fire, they charged into the grove, and put the Georgians to flight.

For more than an hour the fight raged fiercely along this line, but the pressure of Hunter's Division became so heavy that the Confederates were gradually pressed back across the wide open valley and up the slope on the south side of Young's Branch and the Warrenton Turnpike. The stone bridge was now uncovered, and Tyler ordered Colonels Sherman and Keyes to cross Bull Run, and marching in rear of the line of battle, form on Hunter's right. Meantime, a portion of Heintzleman's Division had debouched from the woods, and following the movements of Hunter's line, joined in the attack. Rickett's splendid battery of rifled guns went into position on the right of Sudley road, and did great execution. At noon McDowell was in possession of the ridge south of Young's Branch, and

the Confederates had been driven back, in rear of their
line of works, a mile and a half

Leaving only sufficient troops in front of his fords
on his right to deter Miles from an attempt to cross,
Beauregard hurried six additional brigades to his
menaced left, and formed a new line of battle on the
crest of the plateau, half a mile in rear of Evans'
struggling line, while at the same time Bonham, Longstreet and Jones were ordered to demonstrate strongly
along their front.

The initial point in McDowell's plan of battle had
been handsomely won, notwithstanding the untoward
delay of .the morning. The enemy's left was turned,
and he was forced to form a line perpendicular to his
elaborate works, and meet the onset of battle from an
entirely unlooked-for quarter. McDowell had now
18,000 men across the Run, advancing upon the foe,
whose entire army was in the confusion and uncertainty
resulting from the nature of the Union assault, and the
necessity for a sudden change of front.

Jackson's brigade of five regiments, which had, up
to this time, been held in reserve, was thrown forward to
relieve the pressure on Evans' retiring and disordered
line. Forming in rear of the discomfited troops of Evans,
with his line dressed as though on parade, Jackson
awaited the shock of the on-coming and exultant Federals. Here Colonel Bee endeavored to check the retreat
of his command, and to stimulate a spirit of emulation,
pointed to the brigade drawn up in perfect order, and
exclaimed: "There is Jackson, standing like a *stonewall;*" and in this scene and circumstance was framed
a sobriquet for one of the Confederate's most gallant
leaders, that will be as lasting as the "Iron Duke."
But even "Stonewall's" bold front melted away before
the steady fire and impetuous advance of the Federal
line, whose right swep. up the slope and seized the
plateau on which stood the Robinson and Henry houses,

and whither the batteries of Ricketts and Griffin were at once transferred.

It was now mid-day The Union army had been afoot since two o'clock in the morning, and the divisions of Hunter and Heintzelman had marched fifteen miles ; and for nearly three hours the division of the former had been continuously engaged with the enemy The day was excessively warm, and the battle-field was enveloped in smoke and dust, almost suffocating the combatants. The inexperienced soldiers in McDowell's army, oppressed by the heat and fatigue of the march, had thrown off their canteens and haversacks, and were now suffering from hunger and thirst. Men left the ranks to find water, and for a half an hour there was a partial suspension of the battle. There can scarcely be a doubt but that the Confederates would have been totally routed if the Federals had instantly followed up the victory they had gained at this time, by a general and vigorous advance of the entire force on the west side of Bull Run. But their delay was the result of the lack of cohesion, growing out of causes heretofore mentioned, and it was pregnant with disastrous consequences.

About 11 A.M., Generals Johnson and Beauregard having sent urgent orders to their commanders on the right of their line, and to their reserves, to hurry forward re-enforcements to the imperiled left—themselves set out from their headquarters, four miles away, and spurred to the point where the battle raged. General Johnson says : "We came not a moment too soon, for the long contest had greatly discouraged the troops of Bee and Evans. Bee had sustained heavy losses, especially in field officers, and the troops of Evans were dispersed or destroyed." They at once devoted themselves to a reorganization of their disheartened and fleeing troops, and to the formation of a new line of battle on the crest above mentioned.

This line was formed along the northeasterly crest of

a broad plateau, known as "Bull Run Hill," and which rises to an elevation of one hundred and thirty feet above the level of the stream of that name. The general direction of this crest where the Confederate line was formed, is oblique to the course of Bull Run, and is about two miles west of it. The approaches from the northeast are intersected by several irregular ravines, bordered with straggling young pines and scrub oak. The Warrenton Turnpike passes a mile to the north of this hill, while the road from Sudley's, after crossing the Warrenton Pike, at right angles, continues in a southerly course over the hill, striking the crest at about the centre of Beauregard's new line of battle. The Chinn House was a few hundred yards in the rear of the Confederate left, and near it was posted a battery, while three other batteries were embrasured in their line. The easterly margin of the plateau was overgrown with dwarf pines, affording excellent cover for sharp-shooters, and into which the Confederate right was thrust ; while the ground to the westward was covered with an oak forest, on which Beauregard rested his left flank. The northerly front was open country, excepting the fringe of pines and scrub oaks, along the ravines above mentioned, and the trees immediately surrounding the Henry and Robinson houses, which, however, occupied portions of the northeasterly surface of the plateau itself, and which the Federals now held.

Meantime the Confederates had been pressing forward to this new line of battle, until nearly their whole force was positioned on it or within supporting distance. A golden opportunity had slipped through the hands of the Union commander. An opportunity that he would have successfully employed, if he could have had his army in hand thirty days before the battle.

The Confederates were splendidly officered.

General J. E. Johnson was one of the ablest of the Confederate commanders, and associated with him was

Beauregard, then already famous as the captor of Fort Sumter. These two exercised a joint command over the Confederate army. Among the brigade commanders were several whose names subsequently became familiar to the world, Early, Ewell, Jackson, Hampton, Longstreet.

McDowell's line of battle was at this time well up the slope of "Bull Run Hill," with its centre thrust forward upon the plateau, and was in possession of the Robinson and Henry houses, to hold which the Confederates had fought desperately Wilcox's brigade, of Heintzelman's division, was on the extreme right, and just west of the Sudley road, in which was planted a section of artillery Howard's brigade of the same division came next in order, with its right near the Sudley road. Then the brigades of Franklin (Heintzelman's division) and Sherman and Keyes (Tyler's division) were posted on the left of Howard, in the order named. The right wing was supported by part of Colonel Andrew Porter's brigade, and the cavalry under Palmer covered that flank. Other supports were stationed in rear of the centre and left of the line. As among the Confederate officers on this field, so also among the Union officers, will be recognized several names which became famous before the war closed, and which will live as long as the history of the country endures.

The Federals were now in possession of all the ground over which the conflict, during the forenoon, had surged. The Warrenton Turnpike was several hundred yards in their rear, and their left overlapped the Confederate works at Stone Bridge. They had fought their way a mile and a half beyond where Evans formed his first line of battle. Their further success demanded the possession of the entire crest of the plateau, where the Confederates had re-established their line, and were rapidly augmenting their numbers. With this view McDowell swung his right flank forward, and ordered the batteries

of Griffin and Ricketts to an elevated position, near the
Henry House. The Fire Zouaves—Elsworth's—and a
small body of marines, were posted in support of these
batteries, while the Fourteenth N. Y S. M., which had
behaved splendidly through the day, and won the en-
comiums of General McDowell, and all others under
whose observation it had come (Colonel Wood having
been wounded, the regiment was now commanded by
Lieutenant-Colonel E. B. Fowler, with James Jourdan,
major), was sent into the oak woods, on the extreme
right flank of the army

The battle, which had for some time languished.
now opened with redoubled fury The Confederates
had posted thirteen guns behind a low undulation,
which partially concealed and protected them, some
500 yards northeast of the Henry House, and in easy
range of Ricketts' and Griffin's Batteries, which were
very much exposed. For nearly four hours the struggle was stoutly maintained—the Confederates to hold,
and the Federals to gain possession of the plateau,
with the prospects of success decidedly in favor of the
latter.

A correspondent of the Charleston, S. C., *Mercury.*
writing to his paper, said : "When I entered the field
at 2 o'clock the fortunes of the day were dark, the
remnants of the regiment, so badly injured, or wounded
and worn, as they staggered out, gave gloomy pictures
of the scene ; and as, up to this time, after four hours of
almost unprecedented valor and exertion, no point had
been gained, the event was doubtful—hope seemed
almost gone." A rebel officer, writing to the Richmond
Dispatch, July 29th, said : "There is no earthly doubt
that our army was overcome several times between 12
and 3, and the bulletins sent by the enemy are in the
main correct. But, alas ! 'The best laid schemes of
men and mice aft gang alee ;' and, in this instance,
verily there was a great slip between the cup and

the lip." A Mr. Boddy, who lives near Centreville, told the writer, when he was there with his regiment, in March, 1862, that he was under guard two miles in rear of the rebel army during the battle, and that at about one o'clock companies and regiments were coming to the rear, in great disorder, and reported that the "Yankees" had whipped them. General Jordan, chief of staff to Beauregard, stated, that just a short time before the giving way of the Union lines, "Streams of stragglers and skulkers from the Confederate army were pouring to the rear."

About half-past 1 o'clock, two companies of Stewart's Confederate Cavalry made a bold and determined charge down the Sudley road, and threw the Union line at that point into disorder. Taking advantage of the confusion, the 33rd Virginia Regiment of Jackson's Brigade, sprang forward and seized three guns of a battery posted near the road, but before they could remove them, the Federals rallied, recaptured the guns, and repulsed the 33d, with heavy loss. A little after 2 o'clock the Confederates made a desperate effort to expel the Unionists from the plateau, much of which they then held. The whole Confederate line made a simultaneous and furious onset upon their antagonists, and after a close and deadly struggle, they pressed them over the crest, and two hundred yards down the slope. The batteries of Ricketts and Griffin were among the trophies of this brilliant success. Pausing a moment to recover breath, as it were, the Federals again became the aggressors, and their onset was so vigorous and well-sustained that they recovered their lost ground and their batteries, and forced the Confederates back beyond their former position, with severe punishment.

General Johnson says of this stage of the battle : "The aspect of affairs was not encouraging." Beauregard, speaking of the same crisis, says : "The whole line, including my reserves, which, at this crisis of the

9

battle, I felt called upon to lead in person, were ordered forward. The attack was general, and shared in by every regiment on the field." At this time the Confederate troops engaged, largely outnumbered the Federals, and overlapped their right by several hundred yards, and re-enforcements were constantly arriving

McDowell now determined to execute a *coup de grace* and finish the battle. He, therefore, directed General Tyler to throw Schenck's brigade, (in which was the 2d N Y S. M., and which brigade had not yet been engaged, except in some desultory skirmishing in the ᵓmorning) across Bull Run, at the Stone Bridge, and fall upon the enemy's right flank. The effect of such an assault would, no doubt, have been very influential in deciding the fortunes of the day, at that stage of the battle, and while the Federals were stoutly maintaining the fight along the entire line. The Confederates had now put every man they dared draw from their works on their right and centre into action, and they, although subjected to much less marching than their opponents had been, were battle-worn and discouraged.

A fresh brigade, impinged upon their flank, would have doubtless thrown their right into irretrievable confusion, which would soon have communicated itself to their entire line, and as their reserves had been brought into action, it would have been difficult, if not impossible, for the Confederate commanders to restore the battle.

But events were transpiring on the farther side of the field that overruled the purposes of the Union commander. When the Federals got possession of the plateau, near the Henry and Robinson Houses, the batteries of Griffin and Ricketts were ordered forward, and went into position west of the Henry House, and a few hundred yards east of a strip of oak woods. The batteries were supported by the New York Fire Zouaves—Ellsworth's—and a battalion of marines. The woods were supposed to be occupied by Federal troops. A most unfortunate circumstance for the Federals now occurred, and proved to be the turning point in this stubborn contest.

There was, as yet, no system of uniforming troops, by which the men of one army could be distinguished from those of the other. In fact, regiments, and even different companies of the same regiment, followed their own fancies, in many instances, in the matter of uniforms. This, perhaps, was more especially so among the Confederates. But on the Union side, there were all sorts of costumes, from the plain United States style of the regulars, to the gaudy, but *not* neat, outfit of the zouaves, and the striking and stylish dress of the "Brooklyn Fourteenth." The colors ran through the several shades in red, blue and gray, as to clothes, and for headgear, hats and caps were worn, indifferently, and of every variety of pattern and material. The flags carried by different regiments were as various as their uniforms, and in the smoke and dust of a battlefield, it was difficult to distinguish the Confederate from the flags carried by the Federal regiments. Some months later the Confederates adopted a battle-flag, which was readily distinguished on the field.

So it happened, about half-past two, that a grievous mistake was made by the Federals as to the identity of a regiment of infantry, which just then emerged from the oak woods on the right front of Ricketts' and Griffin's batteries. At this moment, these batteries were playing upon a Confederate battery only some 300 yards off, and near the Sudley road. Griffin had two of his guns on Ricketts' right, and consequently, was nearest to the woods. He saw this infantry regiment come out of the woods, and an officer, whom he took to be its colonel, stepped in front of the line and commenced making a speech to his men. Griffin believed it to be a Confederate regiment, although there was reason to

believe that some Federal troops were in that locality
He ordered one of his lieutenants to open fire on it.
Two pieces were loaded with canister; the guns directed
upon the regiment, and about being fired, when, at
that fateful moment, Major Barry, Chief of Artillery,
rode up and said to Griffin, "Captain, don't fire there;
those are your battery support." Griffin replied:
"They are Confederates; as certain as the world, they
are Confederates." "I know," said Barry, "they are
your battery support." Griffin then revoked the order
to fire on this regiment, and his guns were turned to another part of the field, whither they had been directed
before this incident occurred. In the meantime, the
officer in command of this dubious regiment concluded
his speech. He then faced his regiment by the left
flank, and marched about fifty yards along the edge of
the woods, when, facing to the front, the regiment advanced towards the right of the two batteries, about fifty
yards, and suddenly opened fire on them. The volley was
most destructive to men and horses, and the batteries
were utterly disabled—either for use or removing.
Colonel William W Averell, who was Colonel Porter's
Adjutant-General, and who witnessed this untoward
event, says: "Probably there never was such a destructive fire for a few minutes. It seemed as though
every man and horse of that battery, just laid right
down and died right off. The destruction of the battery
was so complete, that the marines and zouaves—supports—seemed to be struck with such astonishment,
such consternation, that they could not do anything."
But the guns were not surrendered without a further
struggle. The 14th N Y S. M., and the 27th, and 38th
N. Y V., with fragments of other regiments, rushed to
the rescue of the batteries. Meantime, the Confederate
regiment was re-enforced, and the batteries were captured and recaptured three several times. The fiercest
fighting of the day took place around the coveted can-

non. Ricketts, who was lying on the ground wounded, says the struggle went on over his body—the contending forces surging back and forward, and that his battery was three times taken and recaptured.

Appreciating the advantage the possession of these splendid batteries and the position they occupied would give them, the Confederates made a most gallant and skillful effort to hold the prize. Charging furiously along the whole line to engage the Federals at every point, they massed all the troops at hand on their left centre, and again and again swept the Federals back and swarmed around the guns—to be in turn driven off, as the Unionists with ball and bayonet reclaimed the batteries. The horses having been killed, the guns could only be removed by hand, and the fighting was so close and desperate that neither party ventured to disarm the requisite number of men to drag the guns away

At half-past three the Federals were crowded off the plateau and forced to abandon the cannon to the Confederates. The right centre of the Union line fell back to a broad ridge near the intersection of the turnpike and Sudley roads, while the left and the extreme right maintained their positions. This gave the line of battle a crescent shape, and it was still in good form and temper. The guns of Griffin and Ricketts were lost, but the Federals knew their adversaries had paid dearly for them, and had made an exhaustive effort to retain them, and they still believed the victory would finally perch upon the Union banners.

The whole Federal line prepared to advance about four o'clock, and essay once more the capture of the entire plateau, while Schenck made his flank attack. Beauregard says, in his report of the battle, "they (the Federals) threw forward in fine style a cloud of skirmishers, preparatory to another attack." But now, a new and an overwhelming disaster befell the Federal right. The Confederate commanders had long and eagerly looked for the arrival of the residue of Johnson's army from Winchester, and that general had proceeded some miles down the Manassas Gap Railroad to intercept the train on which they were to come, and to have his men debark opposite the battle-field, instead of continuing on to the Junction. These troops, nearly 3000 strong, and lead by General Kirby Smith, arrived at this momentous crisis. Early's brigade was, at the same time, marched through the woods and formed on the Confederate left, near the Chinn House, out-flanking the Federal right.

Up to this time Beauregard had considered his left flank " much endangered. " But now his adversary was out-flanked, and he had nearly 3,000 fresh and well-drilled troops, with which to make his *coup de grace*, by a resistless assault on the right flank of McDowell's worn-out army. Heat and dust, hunger and thirst, twelve hours of marching and five of fighting, had not broken the spirit of the Union army. But the shouts of 3,000 fresh adversaries, sweeping down upon the flank of the Federals, extinguished all hope of victory General Keyes said : "I thought the day was won about two o'clock ; but about half-past three o'clock a sudden change in the firing took place, which to my ear was very ominous. * * * If Johnson had not come, my impression is we should have won the battle. I know that the moment the shout went up from the other side there appeared to be an instantaneous change in the whole sound of the battle; so much so, that I sent my aide, at the top of his speed, to find out what was the matter. It was the shout that went up from the enemy's line, when they found out for certain that it was Johnson and not Patterson who had come. " Yes, it was Blucher, not Grouchy, who had come.

It was now too late for the success of McDowell's

contemplated *coup de main*, and the march of Schenck was suspended and dispositions made to cover the retreat of the army. The right fell back in disorder under the attack in front, flank and rear, towards Sudley's ford, while the centre and left marched off the field over the Warrenton turnpike and the adjacent lots.

General Johnson says, it was four o'clock and forty minutes when the Union line gave way. He states in his official report, that there were three brigades of the army of the Shenandoah engaged in the battle. These gave Beauregard not less than 10,000 more men than McDowell had expected to encounter; and that these men turned the scale of battle in favor of the Confederates, no one, who reads the story of the fight, can doubt. And, even as against this largely increased force, General Johnson says: "if the tactics of the Federals had been equal to their strategy, we should have been beaten."

General Andrew Porter testified before the Committee on the Conduct of the War: "The plan of battle was admirable; it could not have been better; everything was as well looked to and taken care of as could be." General Sherman says, in his "Memoirs," vol. 1, page 181: "It is now generally admitted that it was one of the best-planned battles of the war." * * "It is easy to criticise a battle after it is over; but all now admit that none others, equally raw in war, could have done better than we did at Bull Run; and the lesson of that battle should not be lost on a people like ours."

A portion of the Federal Army left the field in confusion. But there were many causes conspiring to produce this result, not the least among which were want of drill, discipline and experience. But what added immeasurably to the disorder and to the disintegration of commands was the wild flight of horses, guns and

caissons through the masses of retreating troops.
Speaking of certain batteries, Colonel Averell says:
" What there was left of them, a few limbers and caissons that had live horses to drag them, came galloping
down the hill, right through the mass of troops, and
occasionally a horse would fall and the whole thing
would get all tangled up." He says a great many men
were dying of thirst. Lieutenant Hazlitt, of Griffin's
Battery, speaking of another Union battery, said:
" We saw the battery flying all around, and the horses
with the caissons running in every direction." Imagine
these ponderous vehicles thundering over the roads and
fields, breaking the ranks of the retreating troops and
scattering the men in all directions. Officers were separated from their commands, and men from their companies ; and re-formations under the circumstances
were simply impossible where this disruption had occurred. General Keyes says his brigade came off the
field in perfect order, and of the other troops he says:
" As I approached the line of men in retreat, they were
all walking ; I saw nobody run, or trot even, until
coming down to Bull Run.' The crossing of this
stream added to the disorder, and beyond it the confusion was increased by the flight of ambulances, army
wagons, and everything on wheels, which were now
rushing to the rear. Confusion became worse confounded, as an occasional shell from the rebel batteries
exploded among the troops and teamsters. Men who
all day long had braved rebel bullets, and stood steady
under fire, were now seized with a nameless terror, and
all discipline was gone. At Cub Run bridge, caissons,
wagons and ambulances interlocked and were overturned, blocking the way The men crossed the stream
as best they could, and spreading over the road and
fields, pursued their flight.

So far as this portion of the army was concerned, it
was disorganized beyond the hope of immediate resto-

ration. But soldiers know how just such a state of
things could be produced by just such or similar circumstances, without reflecting upon the *courage* of the
men. They know that even veterans are not panic-
proof. The steadiness of *any* troops depends upon
their cohesion. Break their military formation—separate men from their companies, and officers from their
men—and even regulars would do little, if any better,
than these raw soldiers did.

Finding themselves without officers or military organization, hundreds of these men straggled on towards
Washington; their numbers greatly augmented by the
crowds of civilians who had come out to see the battle;
until it looked as though the whole army was in flight.
Newspaper reporters led the van, and in a few days
they made their readers believe that the entire army
was as badly demoralized as they themselves were.
Members of Congress and other civilian spectators of
the stampede, who did not wait to see the end of the
affair, but, shouting " *sauve qui peut*," dashed away,
assumed that the residue of the army was in as bad
condition as that with which they fled, and flooded the
country with most unjust aspersions upon the conduct
of the troops; and the impression is general, even to
this day, that our army showed the white feather at
Bull Run.

Colonel Don Piatt, in a recent letter of war reminiscences in the *Cincinnati Commercial*, says:

" And here I must enter my protest to a world-wide slander heaped
upon us. Men talk of the panic at Bull Run who gather their information from Congressmen and correspondents who did not witness the fight.
When our men fell back before the re-enforcements of the Confederate
Johnson, there was, of course, great confusion, and so long as they were
under fire suffered the usual demoralization. But this lasted only some
ten or fifteen minutes. When the army re-crossed Bull Run it was a mob
something more disorderly than when we went into the fight, but possessed
of no panic whatever. I was sent into the road by Gen. Tyler, with
other officers, ordered to try and re-form the masses, yet armed, but surg-

ing on in disorder. I found them beyond control, but laughing, singing, and talking in a very indifferent way, while hundreds stopped to gather blackberries, then thick and ripe upon the ground.

"The panic referred to, and so implicitly believed in, happened, I am told, in this way. About 2 o'clock, perhaps later, a company of Con-federate cavalry, called mysteriously the Black-Horse, dashed crazily in on the Warrenton pike, far in the rear of the battle-field. This road was crowded with army wagons, hacks containing Congressmen, and buggies and horses of correspondents, Bull Run Russell among the number. When the charge occurred, Capt. Ayres, then on the eminence command-ing the road, wheeled about two pieces of artillery, and fired grape and can-ister into the entire crowd. Wagoners, Congressmen and correspondents, thus brought, unexpectedly, between two hot fires, attempted to turn their vehicles, upsetting many, and fled in a fearful panic and confusion toward Washington. The stampede was ludicrous. To some it continued 24 miles, that being the distance to the capital ; to others 124 miles, for it is said that quite a number kept on to New York.

"At the very moment this panic happened, our army in the field was under the impression that we had won a great victory, and when some hours later I passed along this road, I was amazed at its condition. I found wagons upset and broken, hacks in ruins, buggies smashed, and amid all, the unfinished lunches of patriotic Solons and scattered note-books of frightened journalists."

General Johnson states that Bonham was ordered to march with his and Longstreet's brigades by the short-est route to the turnpike and intercept the retreat, and adds : " When General Bonham saw the Federal column on the turnpike, its appearance presented so little indication of rout, that he thought the execution of the instructions he had received impracticable. He therefore ordered the two brigades to march back to their camps." He admits that the severe handling the Confederates had received had demoralized and disor-ganized them, nearly as much as defeat had their adversaries.

General Andrew Porter makes honorable mention of the behavior of the Eighth N Y S. M.; and of the " Brooklyn Fourteenth," he says, quoting from the report of Lieutenant-Colonel Fowler : " In the last attack Colonel Wood was wounded, together with Cap-tains R. B. Jourdan and C. F Baldwin, and Lieutenants

J. A. Jones, J. R. Salter, R. A. Goodenough, and C. Scholes, and Adjutant Laidlow The officers, and especially Major Jourdan, were distinguished by their display of spirit and efficiency throughout the action." In his examination before the Committee on the Conduct of the War, he said : " The Brooklyn Fourteenth behaved remarkably well." General Sherman speaks highly of the 69th and 79th, which were in his brigade ; and Burnside says of the 71st, which served under him : " I beg to again mention the bravery and steadiness manifested by Colonel Martin and his entire regiment, both in the field and during the retreat."

General McDowell was, of course, the scape-goat, upon whom the chief volume of vituperation was poured. Three-fourths of the people in the loyal States were made to believe that McDowell was drunk on the battle-field, and many yet believe that that had much to do with bringing about the misfortune of that day to the Union arms. Men are too ready to believe evil of their fellow-men. It is a pitiable human infirmity Officers who were unfortunate in the field were too often the subjects of unjust animadversions. General McDowell neither drinks wine, tea, or coffee. The corps of military critics and self-constituted mentors was very large during the war, and they pronounced Sherman crazy, and Grant habitually drunk. One of them complained to the President of Grant's supposed inebriety Mr. Lincoln asked the grumbler if he knew what kind of liquor Grant drank. " No," said he, " why do you ask ?" " Because," said the President, " I would like to send some of the same kind to the other generals."

General McDowell was in the midst of the fight throughout the day, and shared the perils of the field with his men. No one felt more keenly than he the misfortune that befell his army, not in a personal, but in a national sense ; he had no political ends to subserve, and no personal ambition to gratify, save as it

tended to promote the welfare of his country Among
the Union officers, McDowell had no superior in earnest
whole-souled devotion to his country's flag and cause ;
his habits are almost Puritanic in their simplicity An
article in *L'Opinion National*, thus speaks of him :
"His face is remarkably open and sympathetic, through
its air of frankness and kindness ; he is one of the most
honest, truest, simplest men you can meet." As an
illustration of one of these qualities, I quote his opening words in answering a question put to him by the
"Committee on the Conduct of the War," with reference to the organization of the army into corps : "I am
personally interested in this, I will frankly say to you,
because it will affect my position, and I want you to
understand that it will do so, that you may understand
how much of personal bias there may be in my opinion
upon the matter." Again, on the subject of the staff
organization of the army : "The position of aide-de-
camp on my staff is going begging ; I have not the
highest reputation in the world, but I have some character, and I know very well that so far as I am personally
concerned they would not object to going on my staff ;
they say so ; but they say they command batteries, or
are commissaries of subsistence, where they are captains, while I only propose to make them lieutenants."
Quartermaster-General Meiggs, in testifying before the
same committee and in reference to the staff of a general commanding an army, said : "I think General
McDowell and all our officers at that time (battle of
Bull Run) were crippled by want of sufficient personal
officers to assist them. He had not the proper staff ; I
do not believe he had more than two or three men
around him after the battle began." On the subject of
the battle itself General Meiggs says : "The attempt
was made and it was successful—to turn their flank,
and they marched out of their intrenchments and
fought us. * * * McDowell marched his army to

the right, and actually did turn their left flank, and drove them two miles to the south of the field of battle. In his own opinion he had gained the victory ; and if it had not been for the sudden and unexpected re-enforcements of Johnson's army, he would have held it."

The *Chicago Tribune*, speaking nine years after the battle, said :

"We now begin to feel that we walk upon the solid ground in estimating its heroes and its importance.

"In the first place, we have learned to estimate the character of McDowell, who planned this battle with a cool, wise head, and fought it upon this plan according to the best advantage he could make of the material that lay at his command. No other battle during the whole war was better devised, and none in the East, fought upon the offensive, during the next three years, had more nearly been successful. The Federal commander was assailed for the folly of his troops here as few commanders have ever been, and yet he kept up heart, stood patiently by the cause, took a third-rate place under McClellan, with generous resignation, and gave all the successive men placed over him hearty support; and since the death of George H. Thomas, it is safe to say that there is no man in the United States upon whom we rely for judgment, for devotion, for willingness to suffer above the common fate of all who suffered then, more than Irwin McDowell.

"Last winter, when the Army of the Potomac met at Philadelphia, and McDowell sat quietly among them, thinking himself an unsuccessful man and one set down among the failures of the war, a quiet young officer arose with his glass in his hand, and proposed the health of General McDowell. As he did so, he made a stammering effort to say that since the war had passed by, and we had come to know man for man and man to man, we were equal to the appreciation of the commander of the first Army of the Potomac. At once the whole table rattled with bravos and hearty cheers, and amid more applause than had greeted the name of any man that night, McDowell rose, profoundly moved, the most patient and heroic martyr of the war, and he said, as he had always said, that he knew the justice of his countrymen would come at last; that he had expected it long before, but that he had not complained, because he knew that it would come; and then his cold, regular army nature melting down to the occasion, he gave a little burst of egotism, which was truer than tears, because it was both the occasion and himself. There are more men who fought in the Army of the Potomac who would enlist under McDowell to-day than under any general commander which the war in the East turned out. His great element of character was resignation, never mutinying, never abusing any man behind his back, holding to the cause at the expense of frightful calumnies heaped upon himself, and it is probable that his fame will glow henceforward as brightly as, during the war, it was suddenly obscured."

But it should not be supposed that the whole army ran away from Bull Run; excepting the 4,000 or 5,000 men who were disorganized as above described, the army retired in good order and re-formed line of battle on the Heights of Centreville, where Miles' reserves were posted. It will be remembered that there was really no pursuit, notwithstanding the fearful stories of the "black-horse cavalry." General Johnson, who had superseded Beauregard as his superior in rank, explains the fact in his official report, wherein he says: "The apparent firmness of the troops at Centreville checked his pursuit."

I do not wish to be understood, from what I have said about the popular clamor against McDowell and his army, that anybody designed to do it or him injustice; but the North had counted upon a victory, and they had not yet learned how to accept defeat instead of the expected triumph. In the popular judgment, this unlooked for reverse could only be attributable to some blunder on the part of the commander, or cowardice on the part of the troops. The public at large had no knowledge of the circumstances which inevitably tended to render the Federal army inefficient, but seemed to suppose that, to make a soldier, it was only necessary to arm and uniform a man. When General McDowell had a few brigades drawn up for inspection and review, some little time before marching to Bull Run, he was charged with wanting to make a display, and it was pronounced to be an unnecessary tax upon the troops; neither did the public know anything about the assurances which General McDowell had as to Johnson's army, or of the real causes which led to the defeat of the Federals.

Unless a Union victory at Bull Run would have resulted in a termination of the war, which was not at all probable, it was, perhaps, the best thing that could happen for the final success of the Federal cause that the Unionists should have been defeated. The North thereafter had a truer sense of the magnitude of its undertaking, and while it hurled its men into the field, it was content to allow a little time to its officers and men to learn, at least, the rudiments of the art of war.

CHAPTER IX

REORGANIZATION—IMPORTANCE OF RETAINING OLD RANK—CAMP ARTHUR —"CHAPEL OF THE PREPARATION"—FASTING AND PRAYER—B AND E COMPANIES DISBANDED—REVIEW AND FLAG PRESENTATION—EMBARKATION AND ARRIVAL IN NEW YORK—ROSTER—PHILADELPHIA AND ITS "COOPER SHOP"—THE WAY IT STRUCK THE CHAPLAIN—FROM BALTIMORE TO KALORAMA HEIGHTS—DESOLATED KALORAMA—FROM WASHINGTON TO UPTON'S HILL—GENERAL WADSWORTH.

ON the 5th of August the Field Officers advertised for recruits for three years, and began the work of reorganization. Many of the original officers and men of the command could not go out again, and large numbers were discharged.

Lieutenant-Colonel Gates had had an interview with the Secretary of War, before the regiment left Baltimore, wherein the Secretary expressed a wish to have the regiment reorganize for three years or during the war, and agreed that it should be re-mustered as the 20th N. Y S. M., so that the old officers should be able to serve under their then existing commissions. This was a very important matter, as the welfare of the regiment might be seriously affected by the way in which this question should chance to be settled. It has already been shown how Colonel Jesse Smith, who happened to have an older commission than Colonel Pratt, and therefore ranked him, compelled the Twentieth to do guard and fatigue duty at Annapolis. Now there had gone into the field from the State of New York, while the Twentieth was out on its three months' tour of duty, a hundred volunteer regiments, the officers of most of which had had little or no experience, yet to whose orders the officers and men of the Twentieth would be subject, unless the old commissions stood. Such a state of things might become very serious on the battle-field, where, by reason of the death or disability of a brigade-commander, a ranking colonel of the brigade should succeed to a command he was unable to exercise intelligently, and before higher authority could interpose he might have destroyed or disgraced his brigade. Governor Morgan, whose function it was to commission officers of New York troops, acquiesced in the understanding that the Twentieth should go as the 20th N Y S. M., if it would reorganize and return to the field.

A camp was established on the parade ground, west of the Plank Road, between Kingston and Rondout, to which was given the name of "Camp Arthur," in compliment to General C. A. Arthur, late Collector of the Port of New York, and at that time Engineer-in-Chief and Acting-Quartermaster-General of the State of New York. Lieutenant-Colonel Gates was put in command of the camp. Rigid discipline was enforced and drills were going on in squads by company or by battalion hourly.

By the 18th of September there were about 450 men in camp, and 150 more enrolled. The men in camp had received new uniforms, and their appearance accelerated recruiting. Lieutenant John M. Schoonmaker, a capital bureau officer, was Acting-Adjutant; Captain C. D. Westbrook, Engineer, and Dr. Robert Loughran, Surgeon.

The following observations and Order are copied from the Kingston *Argus* of September 25th : " A few citizens, warmly seconded by the officer in command at Camp Arthur, have erected in the camp a commodious place of worship, to bear the name of "Chapel of the Preparation," (Ephesians vi., 15). Services are held on Monday, Wednesday and Friday evenings. The presence of several ladies, and their aid in the singing, add much to the interest of the gathering. We copy the following Order, issued on Monday :

10

HEADQUARTERS 20th REGIMENT, N Y S. M., }
Camp Arthur, Kingston, Sept. 23d, 1861. }

Special Order No. —

The President of the United States, having appoint
ed Thursday next as the day of general fasting and
prayer, there will be religious services in the Chapel,
at these headquarters, at three o'clock and at seven and
one-half o'clock, P. M.

For the purpose of enabling officers 'and soldiers to
attend these services, and to devote a portion of the
day to the purposes contemplated by the President's
proclamation, the afternoon drills will be suspended at
three o'clock.

By order,

THEODORE B. GATES,

Lieut.-Col. Com'ng.

J. M. SCHOONMAKER,
   Post-Adjutant.

On the 31st day of August, B Company, Captain
Sharpe, and E Company, Lent, which companies had
not participated in the reorganization of the regiment,
were disbanded by orders from Brigade Headquarters,
for ''not having the required number of men to be
effective at this critical period of our national history''

On the 18th day of October General Samson reviewed the Twentieth for the last time. The " Ellsworth
Grays," a military company from Poughkeepsie, was
present on the occasion, and the crowd of spectators
was immense. Ten days previous to this event, the
regiment had visited Poughkeepsie by invitation, when
it was presented with a beautiful silk national flag.

On Friday afternoon, October 25th, 1861, the tents
of Camp Arthur were struck, the baggage sent off, and
at three P.M. the regiment was in march for Rondout,
on its way to the seat of war, 987 strong. Embarking

on the Manhattan, the regiment was landed in New York
at sunrise next morning, and proceeded to the State
Arsenal, where the men were supplied with Enfield rifles.
From thence the command marched to the Park Barracks,
where dinner was furnished, after which they proceeded
to Pier 1, embarked on the John Potter and steamed to
Amboy, where they debarked and took cars for Washington, via Camden and Philadelphia.

The regiment at this time was officered as follows:
Colonel, George W Pratt; Lieutenant-Colonel, Theodore
B. Gates; Major, Jacob B. Hardenbergh. The staff offi-
cers were Lieutenant John M. Schoonmaker, Adjutant;
Captain Cornelius D. Westbrook, Engineer; Lieuten-
ant John S. Griffiths, Quartermaster; Selah O. Tuthill,
Paymaster; Major Robert Loughran, Surgeon; Captain
Robert K. Tuthill, Assistant-Surgeon; Rev Cornelius
Van Santvoord, D.D., Chaplain. The line officers were:
A Company, James Smith, Captain; Charles S. Wilkin-
son, 1st Lieutenant; Joseph H. Harrison, 2d Lieuten-
ant. B Company, Walter A. Van Rennselaer, Captain;
Abram S. Smith, 1st Lieutenant; John R. Leslie, 2d
Lieutenant. C Company, John R. Tappen, Captain;
Andrew S. Schutt, 1st Lieutenant; Martin Snyder, 2d
Lieutenant. D Company, Daniel McMahon, Captain;
Henry Mick, 1st Lieutenant; James G. Wilson, 2d
Lieutenant. E Company, Peletial Ward, Captain;
Albert S. Pease, 1st Lieutenant; Edgar T. Dudley, 2d
Lieutenant. F Company, John S. Corbin, Captain;
Nicholas Hoysradt, 1st Lieutenant; George North, Jr.,
2d Lieutenant. G Company, J. Tallmadge Hendricks,
Captain; Wm. H. Cunningham, 1st Lieutenant; James
M. Van Valkenburgh, 2d Lieutenant. H Company,
Abraham S. Smith, Captain; Ely R. Dobbs, 1st Lieu-
tenant; Martin H. Swarthout, 2d Lieutenant. I Com-
pany, James D. Balen, Captain; John D. S. Cook, 1st
Lieutenant; Demetrius J. France, 2d Lieutenant. K
Company, Ambrose N Baldwin, Captain; Alexander

McFarland, 1st Lieutenant ; John R. Horner, 2d Lieutenant.

The regiment reached Philadelphia at half-past one o'clock Sunday morning, and as they left the ferryboat that had carried them over the Delaware River they were marched into an immense hall near the wharf, called the "Cooper Shop," after Mr. Cooper, one of the originators of the plan of operations there carried on. In this building tables were set for the accommodation of several hundred men at a time, and these tables were spread with the best of bread, meat and vegetables in abundance, while tea and coffee were furnished without stint. It was one of the kindest and most considerate conceptions for the health and comfort of the soldiers of any developed by the war. It surprised the soldier on his journey, and while he was still thinking of the home comforts he felt it so hard to dispense with, and before he had learned to be content with army rations— or, again, in coming home (for no matter which way the soldier was journeying, the Cooper Shop was open to him with a cordial welcome), he enjoyed the feast that awaited him here, as a harbinger of what would be found on the family board—it got the taste of army rations out of one's mouth, as it were.

I will quote from a letter written by the Regimental Chaplain to the Kingston *Argus*, under date of October 30th, to show what he thought of the Cooper Shop, and few men are better judges than he on such matters. And I will also let the chaplain tell, from the same letter, the story of our progress from Philadelphia to Washington. He says of the Cooper Shop : "Six tables stretching the whole length of the apartment, and ample enough to enable a whole regiment to stand around them, were loaded with refreshments, furnished by the hospitality of the city of brotherly love, thus proving the name to be fittingly applied. And *such* refreshments—excellent bread and delicious butter, superb cold beef and ham, potatoes, coffee and tea, pickles of various kinds, etc., urged upon all with a persistent hospitality that seemed to receive rather than to confer a favor. The ministry of gentle hands was conspicuous, as it always is in such scenes as this. Your correspondent being conducted toward the head of the bounteous board, one angel took his hat, another disrobed him of his overcoat, a third took charge of a package or two, a fourth led him to a seat at the table, a fifth ministered to his wants while there. And all with a delicacy and warmth of kindness, that brought forcibly to his mind the pilgrim of Bunyan in the Palace Beautiful, with the ministry of the fair sisterhood there, refreshing and strengthening him for the hardships and dangers of the way that lay before him. No wonder that the soldiers, exulting in this goodly fare, broke forth, company after company, into spontaneous cheers for the city of Philadelphia, which made the rafters of the building fairly ring again. Nor was this ample cheer all. Here the sick soldiers are furnished with comfortable quarters, and receive assiduous medical care, until able to rejoin their regiment, or failing this, are sent home, without money and without price. In addition to all, in a room overhead, writing materials are furnished for those who may desire, during the two or three hours stay in the city, to write to their friends. Your correspondent was urged there several times to write home, which, though much fatigued, and the hour being two o'clock in the morning, he finally did, to show at least how much he valued such attention and kindness. When the letter was written and enclosed, they refused even to let him pay for the stamp. All hail to the city of Philadelphia, for such princely generosity, continued so long, and yet rendered not only without grudging or complaint, but rejoicingly! It will prove a noble and lasting monument to her honor.

"Leaving the good city about 4 A.M., the regiment

reached Baltimore at nearly noon of the same day—a
slow passage—but the length of our train and an inferior locomotive made slowness well-nigh a necessity.
I was curious to scan the faces of the populace in a city
kept submissive and peaceful only by the mighty martial arm of the Government. As we entered Baltimore
there was no enthusiasm apparent, no cheers, perhaps
because the people feared to violate the Sabbath by un-
seemly demonstrations—little waving of handkerchiefs,
and not many smiling faces, such as we saw everywhere
farther north. Stern and scowling faces were plenty
enough, seeming to say : "Yes, ye Northern hordes, we
tolerate you because we must, but our day will come to
sweep you from the soil ye profane—beware of that
day !" We will beware of it, but it never will come.
The only hope of Baltimore is adhesion to the Union
and loyalty If she disregard this, and persist in har-
boring treasonable and rebellious designs, ready ever to
break forth into open hostility to the Government ; her
glory is departed and her doom is sealed. No clear-
sighted citizen, not blinded by passion, can fail to see
this. Would that they all saw it, that this fine city might
find its prosperity restored, and become in all future
times one of the bulwarks of the Union, and a terror to
rebels and rebellion-hatchers of every name and degree.

" The regiment marched through the streets some mile
and a half to the depot of the Baltimore & Ohio Railroad, without the smallest molestation or annoyance.
We found little aid or comfort, however, in the way of
refreshment and cheer, and left for Washington between
3 and 4 o'clock P.M.—traveling on the Sabbath, except
when unavoidable, should be sternly frowned upon. I
believe, with Sir Matthew Hale, that prosperity and a
strict observance of the Lord's day, are, as a general
rule, inseparable. In our case, necessity was laid upon
us to proceed at once to our destination. And as be-

tween the evil of remaining over Sunday in one of the
large cities on our route, and that of going right on, the
latter was certainly the lesser. It was such a Sabbath
as I hope not to spend again, with little to remind one
of the sanctity of the day. In the officers' car, however,
some familiar religious songs were sung, and well sung ;
a few remarks made, and a prayer offered ; and this
constituted all our religious service for the day   We
arrived in Washington about 9 P.M. The men were
marched into barracks prepared for their accommodation, while the officers were allowed to choose their own
quarters for the night in the town. The next morning
at 9 o'clock the 20th took up its line of march for our
present quarters, Kalorama Heights, about a mile and a
half from the White House—the same position occupied
by the Ellsworth Regiment, till its removal a few days
ago over the Potomac. Our regiment marched in coming here, up the length of Pennsylvania avenue to 21st
street, in full dress. I scanned them closely on their
march through the city, and must aver that a finer looking body of troops, hardly excepting the Ellsworth
Regiment, has not left New York for the war. Ulster
County had reason to be proud of her " Guard." All
that is needed is a longer and more effective drill to
make the regiment a noble one, fully ready for a vigorous part in suppressing this infamous rebellion. Its
officers, from our honored colonel, indefatigable in attention to his duties, to the various subordinates, are intelligent, gentlemanly, and well instructed, and are at once
worthy men and agreeable associates. But this letter is
already too long, and at this breathing place I bid you,
for the present, adieu."

Soon after the regiment settled down on Kalorama
Heights each officer and man was presented with a copy
of the Testament and Psalms, neatly bound together, a
gift from the Ulster County Bible Society, and very acceptable to most of the recipients.

Kalorama Heights was not long ago the site of a fashionable residence, and the scene of many social gatherings of Washington's *elite*. The family mansion was large and pleasant, and the grounds around it were extensive and well laid out, with a porter's lodge and a circuitous drive among the trees from the gate to the house.

But the tramp of thousands of infantry, the iron hoofs of troops of cavalry, and the crushing wheels of artillery and army wagons have taken all the beauty out of the grounds of desolated Kalorama, while the noble mansion, where wealth and domestic comfort once reigned, now resounded to the jingle of spurs and the clank of sabres.

On the seventh of November orders came for the Twentieth to cross the Potomac, via Chain Bridge, and report to General McDowell, Arlington House, Virginia. By the latter's orders we proceeded to Upton's Hill and reported to General Wadsworth, into whose brigade we were incorporated.

Chain Bridge is about seven miles north of Washington, while Upton's Hill is eight miles west of that city, so that in reaching our destination, via Chain Bridge, we marched along the easterly side of a triangle to the bridge, and thence along the westerly side of Upton's Hill, making a total distance marched of about fifteen miles. Why we were not allowed to cross the long bridge, or Aqueduct bridge, I never knew.

It became dark before reaching our destination, and as we were in the enemy's country, and knew nothing whatever of our surroundings, the men were ordered to load their pieces, and the march, for the last two or three miles, was made with the circumspection necessary when troops are liable to be attacked. But, fortunately, the only armed men we found that night were Union soldiers, and of these there were a great many, encamped along a line running nearly parallel with the Potomac, and embracing the high ridge which includes in its general course Hall's, Upton's, Munson's and Mason's hills, on the second of which hills we found General Wadsworth's brigade, at nine o'clock in the evening.

Officers and men were glad to hear the command "halt!" for the march had been a long and fatiguing one, and they were tired, hungry and thirsty. Not one of us knew anything about the commander into whose hands we had just fallen, and the locality was a perfect *terra incognita* to all of us. We knew we had reached our destination, because we were halted by a guard drawn up across the road in front of us, and an officer directed us to file to the left, into an open field, and bivouac. We marched into the field, and went to work in the darkness, to make ourselves as comfortable as possible, but the command was by no means in an amiable mood. Each officer and man knew we had marched fifteen miles to reach a point less than eight from our starting place, and that there were two routes no more than half as far as the one we had been required to take, and the consequence was we had arrived at our destination too late to cook coffee or make any arrangements for a comfortable night's rest.

But this feeling underwent a very sudden and unexpected change. Lanterns were seen approaching from what appeared to be a house, a few hundred feet west of us, and a kind, cheery voice called out, "Twentieth, where are you?" The interlocutor was Brigadier-General James S. Wadsworth, who captured the affections of the entire command by his evident anxiety for their comfort and by the practical way in which he manifested it. He had the men supplied with fuel, and the whole regiment was furnished with an abundance of splendid hot coffee, which he had had prepared for it as soon as its approach was announced at his headquarters. He did not turn this good work over to some of subordinate officers and get back into his comfortable house,

out of the chill November air, but he personally superintended it, and left only when he was assured the
men were properly provided for ; many a poor fellow
went to sleep that night blessing General Wadsworth,
and congratulating himself that his regiment had been
assigned to his brigade.

This example of consideration for the men over
whom he was placed was by no means exceptional.
He was the commander not only, but he was also the
watchful friend of the officers and men in his brigade.
There was no matter too trivial for his ready personal
attention, if it concerned the health or comfort of his
men.   The guard-house, the kitchens, the sinks, the
stables ; all were frequently subjected to his inspection
and required to be kept in the cleanest and best possible condition.   The writer of this has been aroused by
General Wadsworth at four o'clock of a winter's morning, and requested to accompany him in a tour of the
camp, to see if the men's huts were properly warmed
and ventilated, and many a soldier of the Twentieth was
surprised, on being awakened in the short hours of the
morning, at seeing his gray-headed Brigade-Commander and his Lieutenant-Colonel inspecting his stove and
chimney and sniffing the air of his hut, as though they
suspected he had the choicest stores of the commissary
and quartermaster's departments hidden away in the
capacious recesses of his eight by ten palace.   General
Wadsworth would stand in the snow and mud
for hours at a time, instructing the men how to build
rude fireplaces and chimneys, and he was especially
exacting in regard to the stables.   He was a lover of
good horses, and he believed the brute deserved a good
dwelling-place, and that he should be well fed and
kindly treated.

General Wadsworth was a graduate of Yale College,
and was distinguished for his scholarly attainments. He
entered upon the study of law, and completed his legal

course under the supervision of Daniel Webster, and, in 1833, was admitted to the bar, but he never entered upon the practice of the profession, and probably had never intended to. His vast landed estates in Western New York gave him an occupation more congenial to his tastes. He brought to the pursuit of agriculture a mind stored with all the knowledge that is required for a successful career as a farmer in the highest and best acceptation of the term. Agriculture with him was a science, and conducted as such he found both pleasure and profit in the pursuit. He was distinguished for his liberality, and the tenants on his broad acres found him a most generous and considerate landlord. Whenever great calamities befel people anywhere, James S. Wadsworth was among the earliest and most liberal benefactors. He furnished a ship-load of food at his own expense, and sent it to Ireland in the days of the great famine there.

He was a Republican in politics, and had been twice tendered the nomination for Governor of his State, but declined to be a candidate. When the Rebellion broke out, General Wadsworth, then being in private life, chartered two ships, and freighting them with provisions sailed to Annapolis, Md., to provide for the militia, then hurrying forward to the Capital. He forsaw that the Government was unprepared to meet this want, and his ever-active sympathy for his kind suggested the possibility of suffering among the men who were hurrying to the front, and the next thing for General Wadsworth to do was to provide, at his own expense, against the threatened danger.

When the army advanced, in June, 1861, Wadsworth, then being fifty-four years of age, volunteered upon the staff of General McDowell. His chief says of him : "The latter, who does me the honor to be on my personal staff, had a horse shot from under him, in the thickest of the fight." He had heretofore declined a commission, but he now accepted the appointment of Brigadier-General of volunteers, and was assigned to command of the brigade lying at Upton's Hill. We shall have occasion to speak of him hereafter, as our history progresses.

THERE are two rugged ascents between the Potomac
and the crown of Upton's Hill. The first occurs immediately after crossing the river, and is short but steep ;
then, having ascended it, a broad plain stretches out toward the west, four or five miles, broken here and there
by gentle undulations, until it reaches the range of
hills heretofore spoken of. The general course of this
range is north and south, but Upton's Hill is thrown
considerably to the front of Hall's and is slightly in advance of Munson's ; Hall's is northeast of Upton's, and
Munson's is about south. Between these hills the country falls to nearly the level of the plain above the Potomac, but the intervals are narrow, and a cannon posted
on Upton's could send a shot to the summit of either of
its neighbors. From the top of Munson's Hill the dome
of the Capitol may be seen, and from this "coign of
vantage" the rebels unfurled their flag after the first

Battle of Bull Run, and thousands gazed upon the disloyal emblem from the Capitol dome, and many trembled
lest it should be borne into the very streets of Washington.

Along the westerly rim of Upton's Hill was a fresh-
ly constructed earth-work, called Fort Upton. It was
a substantial cover for men and guns in case of an
attack, and was one of that class of works which the
experience of the war proved to be the best that could
be constructed. The work itself was protected by a
line of well-set abattis, very difficult for an assaulting
party to pass, and between that and the fort was a wide
and deep moat. Within the work a few guns were
mounted, to sweep the approaches from the direction of
Fairfax or Vienna. General Wadsworth's headquarters were in the Upton mansion, just behind the fort,
and the encampment of the Twentieth extended to
within a few feet of the base of the fort and the general's house. Three miles in our rear, toward Washington, was " Ball's X Roads, " and about an equal distance to the south, towards Alexandria, was the more
celebrated " Bailey's X Roads "—Alexandria itself
lying five miles farther to the southward.

The rebels had occupied the entire country above
mentioned soon after the first battle of Bull Run, and
continued to hold it until the latter part of September,
1861. They had had a battery planted on Upton's Hill,
and had undisputed possession of the surrounding country   When the Union troops began to advance, the
rebels gradually fell back, without fighting, but they
burned some of the houses in the neighborhood upon
suspicion that their owners were Union men.

As the rebels retired, they effectually barricaded the
roads leading to Fairfax Court House, which thereafter became their advanced post, with their picket line
along the woods on the westerly side of the ridge heretofore mentioned, some two miles beyond Fall's Church.

Fairfax C. H. was but eight miles from Fall's Church, and Vienna, where the enemy had a strong force posted, was only six miles northwest of Upton's Hill. The reb-el picket line extended from the Potomac river, two miles above the Great Falls, in a due south course, to the Occuquan river, which empties into the Potomac, at High Point, ten miles below Mount Vernon. A refer-ence to the map of Virginia will show that this line in-tersected every road leading from Washington or Alex-andria into Virginia, and that no advance could be made by the Union troops, occupying the *cul de sac*, formed by the bend of the Potomac, without striking this picket line within ten miles of Washington.

Three miles in front of Upton's Hill is a continuous and uniform ridge, of about the height of Upton's Hill, running nearly north and south, wooded on the easterly side, and which constituted, during the fall and winter of 1861–2, the picket ground of the Union army

Nestling among trees and shrubbery, in the plain be-tween Upton's Hill and the ridge beyond, is the little hamlet of Fall's Church, the only thing of interest about which is the Protestant Episcopal Church ; and not simply because it is a church, but because it is evi-dently a very ancient one ; and the sexton told us George Washington used sometimes to worship there, and pointed out the pew which belonged to him.

The village contained one tavern, three churches (Baptist, Presbyterian and Episcopalian), two black-smiths', one carriage and one paint shop, two stores, one grocery, and about twenty dwelling houses. The place derived its name from the Episcopal church, which is built of bricks imported from England, and is said to have been erected in 1760. It is a plain, square building, with two tiers of windows on each side ; the upper ones surmounted by semi-circular fan lights. It had doubtless been designed to construct a gallery, but the wants of the community have never required it,

and the effect of this arrangement of windows is rather
grotesque. The chancel is slightly raised above the
main floor, at the east end of the building, and is surrounded by a modest railing. The rector's desk is a
very plain inclosure, and the entire structure is in
primitive simplicity In one of the walls are three
tablets, one containing the Creed, one the Lord's
Prayer, and the other the Ten Commandments. At the
right of the desk is another tablet, erected to the
memory of one of the patrons of the church, and bearing this inscription :

" HENRY FAIRFAX,

AN ACCOMPLISHED GENTLEMAN—AN UPRIGHT MAGISTRATE—A SINCERE
CHRISTIAN.

DIED IN COMMAND OF THE

FAIRFAX VOLUNTEERS,

AT SALTILLO, MEXICO.

ON THE 14TH DAY OF AUGUST, 1847.

But for his munificence this church might still have been a ruin. "

There is, to the minds of most people, a sanctity about
an ancient church edifice that begets a feeling of veneration and respect, which involuntarily induces them to
tread lightly on its time-worn floor, and treat with reverence its venerable shrine. For a hundred years devout men and women have gathered within its mouldy
walls, as Sunday after Sunday have dawned upon their
quiet hamlet, and offered up to the Christian's God,
the prayers and thanksgiving of a God-fearing people.
Here have the marriages of their children, for generations, been solemnized, by the beautiful form of the
Protestant Episcopal Church ; here have the infants
been baptized ; and here have been pronounced the
solemn services of the Church over the hundreds of
forms now mouldering in the adjacent graveyard. Infancy, youth, maturity, old age—marriage, life, death
—the highest joys and the keenest griefs, have been

experienced within the walls of this old edifice.
It is the treasnry of a thousand precious recollections.
It is the gate-way through which men and women for
ages have first approached the mercy-seat and learned
the way to life everlasting. And when added to these
associations, which are common to every old church,
was the additional circumstance, that "The Father of
his Country" had worshipped here a hundred years
ago, the quaint and moss-grown edifice was very precious in the esteem of most of us. But some of our
men, not having their feelings touched by such considerations, and probably ignorant of the history of the
old building, defaced its walls by writing their names
and company and regiment upon them, while doing
picket duty in the vicinity It was evidently not done
with a bad motive, or a design to commit an act of
desecration, else they would not have furnished evidence to convict themselves, as they did, by writing
their own names. The colonel soon learned what had
been done, and he ordered the guilty parties to provide
themselves with scrubbing brushes, and soap and
water, and to repair to the church and expunge the
evidences of their ability to write. They did it effectually and neatly, and when the Twentieth bade farewell
to Upton's Hill, the old church looked as solemn and
decorous as it had any time during the last hundred
years. May it survive until the trumpet of the arch-
angel shall arouse the sleepers who repose in the ground
around its foundations !

In the adjacent graveyard were the graves of nine-
teen rebel soldiers, killed in sundry skirmishes hereabout. To these were added many graves of Union
soldiers, during the time the army occupied that neighborhood. The Twentieth made its first interment there
on the 9th of December, 1861, the deceased being private William Cator, of G Company He was not more
than 19 years old, and came from Roxbury, Delaware
11

County, N Y., where his father, a man of respectability
and in easy circumstances, resides. Young Cator's disease was rapid consumption, which skill of physician
or nursing of sympathetic friends could not stay He
was buried with military honors, most of the officers
attending the ceremony

From the time of our arrival at Upton's Hill down
to the last day of December, the weather was magnificent ; days of clear, bright sunshine and nights of
star-lit glory ; an atmosphere as soft and balmy as
the month of May, in the latitude of the Hudson, with
just enough of autumn in it to give the blood a gentle
acceleration, and to make brisk exercise a pleasure. At
any.time, down to the end of December, it was a luxury
to mount without overcoat, and canter ten miles over
the dry, hard roads, that seemed to invite a movement
of the army.

Company, battalion and brigade drills were frequent
and thorough, and occupied most of the time of officers
and men, except when on picket duty General Wadsworth was required to picket about three miles of the
line in front of Fall's Church, and this duty was done
alternately by the different regiments of his brigade:
each regiment marching with two days' cooked rations,
and staying out forty-eight hours, or until relieved.
Alarms were frequent on the picket line, and shots
were often exchanged between the Rebel and Union
pickets. The picket line is not intended as a line
of battle, but only as an alarm line in case of an advance of the enemy, and to administer, if necessary,
a temporary check to such advance, but during the
early months of the war hundreds of Union soldiers
were murdered on the picket line. The burden of the
newspaper report, day after day, was, " All quiet along
the Potomac," and this was but too true as to the army,
but it was bitterly false as to the picket line. To how
many sad households and to how many old veterans

will the following poem recall incidents at "the front,"
and blighted domestic joys at the home far away, in the
rear:

THE PICKET GUARD.

"All quiet along the Potomac," they say,
  Except now and then a stray picket
Is shot as he walks on his beat, to and fro,
  By a rifleman hid in the thicket.
'Tis nothing; a private or two now and then
  Will not count in the news of the battle.
Not an officer lost—only one of the *men*
  Moaning out, all alone, the death-rattle.

All quiet along the Potomac to-night
  Where the soldiers lie peacefully dreaming,
Their tents in the rays of the clear autumn moon,
  Or the light of the watch-fires are gleaming.
A tremulous sigh, as the gentle night wind
  Through the forest-leaves softly is creeping,
While stars up above with their glittering eyes
  Keep guard—for the army is sleeping.

There's only the sound of the lone sentry's tread,
  As he tramps from the rock to the fountain,
And thinks of the two in the low trundle-bed
  Far away in the cot on the mountain.
His musket falls slack, his face, dark and grim,
  Grows gentle with memories tender,
As he mutters a prayer for the children asleep—
  For their mother—may Heaven defend her!

The moon seems to shine just as bright as then,
  That night when the love yet unspoken
Leaped up to his lips, when low murmured vows
  Were pledged to be ever unbroken.
Then, drawing his sleeve roughly over his eyes,
  He dashes off tears that are welling,
And gathers his gun closer up to its place,
  As if to keep down the heart swelling.

He passes the fountain, the blasted pine tree,
  His footstep is lagging and weary,
Yet onward he goes through the broad belt of light
  Towards the shades of the forest so dreary.
Hark! was it the night-wind that rustled the leaves?
  Was it moonlight so wondrously flashing?
It looked like a rifle—"Ah! darling, good-bye!"
  And the life-blood is ebbing and plashing.

All quiet along the Potomac to-night.
  No sound save the rush of the river,
While soft falls the dew on the face of the dead—
  The picket 's off duty forever '

General Wadsworth was very restless under the in-action of the army, and occasionally obtained consent from headquarters to send out a foraging party through the enemy's lines. One such party, commanded by the general in person, and embracing the bulk of his brig-ade, with about thirty army wagons, proceeded at day-break to the vicinity of Vienna, and there entering fields where the corn had just been cut, and in full view of the rebel post at Vienna, proceeded to load our wagons and march away with the valuable prize, without moles-tation.

But sometimes the rebels gave us a Roland for our Oliver. In the latter part of November, a detachment of fifty men from the 30th N. Y V., (not in Wadsworth's brigade) lying near us, went out on a foraging expedi-tion, and after loading their wagons, *stacked their arms*, and entered the house of a Mr. Dulin, to enjoy one "square meal." While engaged in this novel and de-lightful occupation, a body of rebel cavalry swept down upon them, and gobbled up twenty-eight of their num-ber, including Captain Lanning, of Troy, and Lieuten-ant Andrews, of Saratoga Springs. These gentlemen had a very practical application of the trite proverb, that "eternal vigilance is the price of liberty," es-pecially while foraging in the enemy's country

Before we had fairly recovered from the exciting effects of this untoward event, another and a still more agitating episode threw the whole division into commo-tion. The division was on drill on the plain, south of Munson's Hill, General McDowell being in command, when a report came to him that the pickets of the Four-teenth Brooklyn had been driven in and many of the regiment killed and wounded—that the enemy was in large force and threatening the Union works. General McDowell at once ordered several regiments, the Twen-tieth among the number, to proceed with all dispatch to the point of attack, which was a short distance west of

Fall's Church. Before the re-enforcements could reach the ground, the danger had passed, by the withdrawal of the enemy, whose forces consisted of cavalry, and the pursuit of which by infantry would have been useless. The casualties to the Fourteenth proved much less serious than they were at first reported to be. Their loss was two men killed and ten taken prisoners.

On the fourteenth of December, General McDowell accompanied by Governor Morgan, of New York, reviewed his division on the plain near Ball's Cross Roads. The troops looked well and the marching was admirable. Both General and Governor complimented them on their appearance and marching.

But the great review of the war, excepting the final march of the armies past the White House, at the end of the rebellion, was that held by General McClellan, on the broad plain in front of Bailey's Cross Roads, on the 20th of November. The General was accompanied by the President and Secretaries Seward and Cameron, and other distinguished civilians, and a staff as numerous as a squadron of cavalry, and glittering in gold. Sixty thousand infantry, eight thousand cavalry, and one hundred and eighty-six pieces of artillery, each piece drawn by six horses, with one hundred and eighty-six caissons similarly furnished, and the artillerists necessary to this number of guns, made a pageant surpassing in grandeur anything ever before seen on this continent.

Now, surely, said the tens of thousands of civilians who witnessed this superb display of the most superb army the age had produced—now, surely, there will be a forward movement and the enemy must fly or be overwhelmed. This is the final gala-day parade, and henceforth the march of the army is toward the enemy His bold troopers shall no longer come with impunity, within an hour's ride of the Capital of the nation ; his batteries shall no longer blockade the great river that leads from the Capital to the sea. The army is ready ; the

weather was made for a campaign and the roads are as
dry and hard as a Roman causeway—*Forward, Grand
Army of the Potomac!*

No events of importance transpired to disturb the
serenity of the Twentieth for the next three months and
a half. Drill and picket duty—picket duty and drill.
It was a very dull and monotonous existence.

Up to the middle of December the Twentieth had
buried three more comrades in Fall's Church graveyard; Jacob H. Fox, who hailed from Philadelphia, and
who had been in three months service with us; he belonged to Company G; Abraham C. Hinckley, of Mar-
garetsville, Delaware County, member of Company I;
Smith McCoun, of Hunter, Greene County All three
were good soldiers, and the two latter left families. The
sick-list became very large throughout the army, and the
probability is that we lost as many men by sickness,
the result of camp life, as we would have lost by the
casualties of a general engagement, with the enemy supposed to be in front of us. Later in the month Ananias
Hyatt, of Olive County, a member of I Company, died
and was laid besides his dead comrades in Fall's Church
graveyard, and on the 24th of December, Cornelius
Hunt, a private of B Company died, and was sent to
his friends at Kingston, N Y

General Wadsworth's brigade consisted of four regiments of infantry, namely: The Twentieth New York
State Militia, Colonel George W Pratt commanding; The Twenty-first New York Volunteers, Colonel
Rogers, of Buffalo (a splendid officer), commanding;
The Twenty-third New York Volunteers, Colonel Hoffman, of   , commanding, and the
Thirty-fifth New York Volunteers, Colonel Lord,
of   , commanding. The Twenty-first
Regiment had one of the finest bands in the army, and
its camp was so near ours that we got the benefit of its
music as fully as though it were our own band. This

regiment introduced a novel feature into the celebration of New Year's day. The officers all abdicated for the day, and the men elected their successors, from colonel down. Corporal Colton, of Buffalo, was chosen colonel *pro tempore*. His first act of authority was to place the line officers on guard around the camp. At dress parade, which was commanded by the corporal-colonel (and well commanded too), Colonel Rogers and his field and staff officers were in the ranks, doing duty as privates.

Wednesday evening, January eighth, the head-quarter mess of the Twentieth gave a dinner to General Wadsworth, Colonel Rogers, and a few other officers, which was a very enjoyable affair.

On the sixteenth of January the men had the pleasure of exchanging their old-fashioned arms for Austrian rifled muskets, and they were very proud of their new weapons. It was found that they were much more accurate in firing than the discarded pieces were, and the men took great pleasure in practicing the firings, and, as a regiment, became very good marksmen.

On the second of February, while the Twentieth was on picket, a solitary horseman (like one of James') was seen approaching the line from the enemy's side, waving a white flag. The peaceful emblem was recognized, and the bearer allowed to approach. He proved to be Lieutenant-Colonel Harrison, of the Second Va. Cavalry, and the bearer of a sealed communication to General McClellan from General Johnson, which he desired to present in person. He was kept outside the picket line until General McClellan could be heard from, and then an officer of General McDowell's staff, specially detailed therefor, received the communication and conveyed it to General McClellan; Colonel Harrison, meantime, being excluded from our lines, but remaining at a house a few hundred yards in front, under cover of his flag, for several days, until a reply was received. It was said that a Cabinet Council was convened to consider the matter contained in the flag-of-truce letter ; how that may have been I do not know, but certain it is, that Colonel Harrison had to wait several days for a reply The Washington correspondent of the *New York Herald* wrote to his paper that the flag-of-truce letter was from Jeff. Davis himself, and that it announced to Mr. Lincoln the resolve of the Confederate authorities to execute Colonels Lee, Corcoran, Wilcox and other Federal prisoners, then in the hands of the rebels, if the Federal Government allowed certain rebel bridge-burners to be hung, as was likely to happen, under orders of General Halleck. The *Washington Star* said this was the real subject of the communication. Well, the hangings did not take place on either side. Our Government seemed to be of Greeley's opinion, that the worst use you can put a man to is to hang him. Yet, we sometimes find men to whom nothing else in life seems so becoming as this mode of ending it. The war developed many such characters ; and, writing now, fourteen years after its close, and while an extra session of Congress is sweltering under the rays of a June sun, I feel constrained to say that a few hempen lessons, designed to make treason " odious," would have been beneficial to the tone of public sentiment in some parts of our beloved country.

At midnight on the third of February, a lively fusilade broke out along the picket line, in front of Dulan's, where a portion of I Company was stationed, and the reserves were ordered up, but the attack died out, as so many others had, without any other consequences than a little extra excitement, and the waste of a few rounds of ammunition.

During the latter part of January and the beginning of February, our camp was enlivened and honored by the visits of sundry friends from Kingston ; among them were Mrs. Gates, wife of the Lieutenant-Colonel, Mr.

Elijah Dubois and wife, and Mr. and Mrs. William B.
Fitch. Mrs. George W Pratt visited Washington
about the same time, but in consequence of the badness
of the roads did not get over to the regiment.

A very pleasant episode occurred about this time, it
being the presentation of a sword to Captain Van Rensselaer, of B Co., by his command. It was an entire
surprise to the captain, and he was quite overcome by
this merited but unexpected testimonial of the esteem
in which he was held by his company. The surprise,
added to the captain's well-known modesty, rendered
him almost speechless, and it was some time before he
could command words in which to express his emotion.

HALLELUJAH! The army is in motion! A thousand
bands peal out their joyous notes upon the resonant air,
this glorious March morning. Ten thousand starry banners reflect the light of the early morning sun. A hundred thousand men, armed in the cause of justice, good
government, humanity, have turned their faces toward
the west, and are moving upon the rebel stronghold of
Manassas. A thousand cannon glitter in their untarnish-
ed brilliancy Ten thousand horsemen clatter over roads
and fields, ready to try their maiden sabres upon the
boastful Southern cavalry The army is launched at
last upon its terrible mission. Is it to be like a thunder-
bolt in the grasp of Jove, or a mighty engine in a hand
too puny for so great a charge ?

The sun of Austerlitz was not more gloriously beautiful than the unobscured orb of day which greeted the
thousand banners of the Union army, as they expanded
in the early morning light.

Here the eye might rest for miles upon a line of
marching troops, whose neat uniforms and burnished
arms—whose steady step and well-closed files denoted
the thoroughly drilled and self-reliant soldier; while
above their ranks, the flag we love. "As it catches the

gleam of the morning's first beam," floats out on the breeze, filling the air with pictures of rarest beauty.

There again, in the distance, winds another and still another column, of which you get but now and then a glimpse. Sometimes their banners only can be seen moving through the air, as though we were supported on the right hand and on the left by an invisible host arrayed under the ensign of freedom.

Have you ever seen your country's flag thrown out against the sky, with only the blue ether for a background? Pencil or painter never wrought so beautiful a picture! Oh, how your heart has thrilled with patriotic pride as you watched its graceful dalliance with the winds of heaven, and thought how, on every sea, in every port where commerce finds its way; wherever civilization has made a home, and human freedom has an aspiration, that ensign is welcomed and beloved.

Have you ever seen that flag wreathed with the smoke of battle? Oh, then, what sublime eloquence glows in every star and speaks in every stripe! It invokes you by all the memories of the past to maintain the heritage its thirteen colonies bequeathed to you, through sufferings unspeakable. Its constellation of States tells of your wonderful growth as a nation, and your glorious destiny as a people; while through the sulphurous clouds shine out, as though written by the finger of Omnipotence, "In this symbol is the world's last best hope of *civil* and *religious* liberty!" Thus, onward moves the army of the Potomac, followed by the nation's hopes and prayers. Annandale and Fairfax Court House are passed. The rifle-pits and breastworks around the latter place are the first exhibitions we have of the digging propensity of the enemy. But he does not stay to defend his lines. Our advanced guard follows close upon the heels of his retiring outposts, until the Heights of Centreville rise before us, and we find its elaborate fortifications bristling with *wooden guns!*

CHAPTER XI.

THE day after the army drew up before Centreville,
Generals McClellan and McDowell, with their staffs and
two thousand cavalry as an escort, and a number of
field and staff officers anxious to see the famous field
of Bull Run, where General McDowell had been defeated eight months before, set out for Manassas Junction,
seven miles to the westward.

From the heights of Centreville the view south and
east is almost unlimited, while to the northward it is
bounded by the Bull Run mountains, which seem to lift
their rugged peaks into the bending heavens in the
dim and hazy distance. Westward, and enveloping
Manassas Junction, dense forests mask the country
lying beyond, and over which the rebel army had recently retreated.

Centreville is a hamlet of a half dozen houses, planted upon the most southerly of a succession of bold
ridges, which roll and swell, in ever-increasing proportions, until they are dwarfed and lost in the majestic
range that meets the horizon in the north.

The sky was cloudless, and the day was warm and
balmy as a day in May. The cavalcade that clattered

down the Centreville road towards Bull Run, at noon,
was such as never before, or since, awoke the echoes of
that lonely way General McClellan was followed by a
numerous staff, embracing, as it did, the officers regularly assigned to him, not only, but also many volunteer staff officers—native and foreign—among the latter
of whom was the Prince de Joinville, who sought to
learn the art of war, or prepare to write its history, by
actual experience in the field. General McDowell had
a less numerous staff, but mingled with the members of
it were many officers of the army, desirous of availing
themselves of the opportunity to visit the scene of the
first great battle of the war. All were richly uniformed
and superbly mounted. Add to these an escort of two
thousand fine cavalry, and a grander pageant is seldom
seen.

Taking the road leading southerly from Centreville, our course led us to Bull Run, at Blackburn's Ford,
three miles away For most of this distance, on the
left side of the road, the ground was covered with huts,
tents and forts, which a few hours before were occupied
by rebel troops, but now no living creature moved
within them—no sign of life within their walls—no curious faces gazing from their doors or windows, as the
glittering cavalcade swept by, with bugle notes and
cheerful voices floating away on the soft spring winds.

These huts or cabins were constructed by rebel soldiers and were very comfortable tenements. They were
made of logs, nicely fitted at the corners, and the inter-
stices stopped with clay The roofs were of boards or
shingles, and the more pretentious huts were floored,
and furnished with windows. The Bull Run battle-
field, west of the river, was covered with huts of this
description, composing, in fact, a city, capable of
housing a population estimated at 50,000 to 70,000 inhabitants. These houses were arranged in regular
blocks or rows, with walks or streets between, and with

bunks for the accommodation of from three to five men each. We were constrained to confess that the rebels had beaten us in the matter of hut-building.

A mile or two to the right of the road we were pursuing, was observed an immense flock of vultures hovering in the air, alarmed, apparently, by the bugle blasts, and the roar of our fast-riding column. Beneath them had been a camp of rebel cavalry, and the carcasses of near two hundred horses offered a bounteous banquet to these foul birds.

Most of the details above given were learned by subsequent inspection of the country Now we could only note exterior things. Sweeping on down the road we pass the stone cottage, which became a hospital after McDowell's defeat ; pass the point where his army was encamped on the 20th of July, and reach Blackburn's Ford at Bull Run, where Richardson's column encountered the enemy on the 18th of July. Near by, but on the rebel side of the then battle-field, stands the " Butler House," wherein General Beauregard was taking his dinner when Lieutenant Babbitt, of Tyler's Artillery, sent a shell through the building, and so near the head of the Confederate chieftian that he abandoned the table without waiting for dessert. A very slight depression of the cannon would have ended the diner with equal abruptness, and at the same time given Beauregard his *desert*.

Fording Bull Run, the cavalcade sped on, and soon reached the Plains of Manassas. The country hereabout is very level. The town or hamlet at the railroad station had no reputation before the war. It is twenty-seven and a-half miles from Alexandria, *via* the Orange and Alexandria Railroad, and is the point at which the Manassas Gap Railroad taps the former road, hence, " Manassas Junction ;" it is twenty-eight miles from Washington, as the crow flies.

As we reached the plain and approached the Junction, signs of the hasty retreat of an army from its winter quarters were visible on every hand. We came upon a large quantity of artillery harness and blankets, and like stores ; yonder to the left stand a multitude of tents, sufficient to accommodate an entire division. To the westward dense clouds of smoke hang over the Junction, and all the way, as we approach it, signs of ruin and desolation multiply

Arriving at the Junction, we found a sight simply indescribable. The railroad machine shops, the station houses, the rebel quartermaster and commissary buildings ; every thing, in fact, that could burn had been burned, or was then burning. On the railroad track was a wrecked locomotive, and near it the smouldering remains of a train of freight cars. A little farther on, and alongside the track, were hundreds of barrels of flour, vinegar, molasses, pork and beef, the barrels headless, and their recent contents strewn over the ground. On the right hand and on the left the ground was littered with clothing, cooking utensils, broken guns, and hundreds of formidable dirks. These weapons had blades about ten inches long, and two inches wide at the middle ; both edges were sharpened, and the knife was firmly set in a wooden handle, which with the blade, would weigh three pounds. I brought one of them away, and used it for many years to trim my fruit trees ; it would cut like a razor, and hold its edge under the severest treatment.

A car, standing on the track, and which had escaped the conflagration, contained a printing press, types, &c., and paper and printers' supplies. It had been used for printing military orders and other printing required in an army.

The questions suggest themselves—why did the rebels abandon thousands of dollars worth of canvas tents ? Why destroy such quantities of military stores ? Why should they have wrecked a locomotive and burned their cars, when they had but to get up steam and move safely away? Why, if destruction was the order, were the thousands of comfortable huts left intact?

The retreat of the rebel army began some days before McClellan's advance was inaugurated, and was conducted leisurely, and would have so continued, if the enemy had not taken alarm by the appearance of our cavalry, near Manassas, on the evening of the tenth. This apparition surprised the rear-guard, and in the panic which ensued, the torch was applied to the buildings and cars nearest at hand, and havoc was made of whatever could be readily destroyed at the Junction. There was no time to remove or fire the distant tents or the more numerous huts.

A native of that locality, who had escaped conscription, said that General Joe Johnson gave orders not to destroy anything, as he intended to return very soon. This appears to have been the expectation of an occupant of one of the huts, who thus expresses his intentions in a notice left in his quarters : "To the gentlemen of the North, the champions of freedom, we abandon these quarters to you, expecting to return in a month or two. Assure yourselves they are not a gift, but merely lent, with the Scriptural injunction, 'occupy till I come.' We feel constrained to burn our wearing apparel, with the exception of what will be found left as legacies—our beds and comforts only—for fear of acting treasonably, for, by leaving them, we would be giving aid and comfort to the enemy. Look out for another Manassas when we meet again. Yours, very truly, a retired but not cowed adversary. Crescent Blues, Louisiana Volunteers, for the war."

So I conclude from all the facts and circumstances that General Johnson, who had succeeded Beauregard in command, designed to remove the portable property, and to leave the buildings for future occupation, when

the rebel troops should return, as he believed they
would. But his subordinates became panicky when our
cavalry was reported to be approaching, and the results
above described ensued.

From Manassas Junction we could trace the lines of
retreat over the Manassas Gap, and Orange and Alexandria Railroads, and the contiguous wagon roads, by
the columns of smoke ascending from burning bridges.
But the pursuit of the flying foe was not the object of
this expedition, and after devoting a half hour to an inspection of the devastated Junction, the chieftains turned their horses' heads to the north; the bugles sounded forward, and we were sweeping down upon the field
where the first great trial of martial prowess between
North and South took place.

There was much in the circumstances of the occasion
to give it a dramatic character. Signs of the fierce
conflict soon became visible on every hand. Trees per-
forated by bullets, and felled by cannon balls and shells,
breast-works and rifle-pits, houses (of which there were
but four or five) rent by artillery missiles, and here and
there long, narrow mounds, indicating the blended resting places of thousands of the battle's victims. But no
halt was made to note these things; they were but the
common incidents of a field of battle. On thundered
the gorgeous cavalcade to the central point in the field;
where, drawing rein near a squalid shanty, then occupied by a negro family, and from whence the country
along the valley of Bull Run, from Sudley's Mills at the
north, where Hunter crossed the stream to Blackburn's
Ford at the south, was exposed to view, the two generals
took a position in front, and a little apart from their
staffs, while the escort drew out, as a living wall along
the slope some distance in the rear. All eyes were fixed
upon the two men sitting upon their magnificent horses
in the extreme front; McClellan to the right, McDowell
on his left. Both in the May of manhood. Both hand-

some men in face and figure. McDowell the larger of
the two, and McClellan's senior by a few years. Both
had graduated from West Point, and the art of war had
been the study of their earlier years, while now they sat
side by side upon a field, where the senior had applied
that art in practice, and had been foiled by another
graduate of the same school. He was now here to rehearse to his junior in years, but his senior in rank, the
story of that fateful July day, when he was driven in
disastrous flight from this ill-omened field. *Then* and
thereafter, till this younger man was called from the
West, McDowell was chief of the Union troops, west of
the Potomac. *Now*, he was subordinated to the comrade sitting by his side, and had been brought to this
scene of his misfortune, to have probed anew the spirit-
wounds of eight months ago.

A few minutes of silence while the eye took in the
landscape, and then, in answer to a question from Mc-
Clellan, McDowell narrated the prominent events of the
day. He seemed to make no attempt at self-vindication, but confined himself to a statement of the positions
and movements of the troops on each side, and describing the ebb and flow of the battle, at different points
and times. There, two miles left of us, at Sudley's
Mills, Hunter's division crossed at six o'clock in the
morning of the twenty-first of July. There on a hill
near the Henry House was posted Ricketts' battery,
and just over the swell of ground to the northeast of us,
the rebels charged down upon and captured it, together
with its wounded commander. There was the division
of Tyler, and yonder Heintzelman's. All along the line
we were pressing the enemy back, and victory seemed
ready to perch upon our banners, when suddenly and
unexpectedly to the Union commander, General Joseph
Johnson appeared upon the scene with 10,000 fresh
troops, which Patterson had suffered to evade him, and
which, at a critical moment, swooped down upon the

12

right flank of the exhausted, but until then confident
and nearly triumphant Unionists. Beauregard's wavering line, reanimated by Johnson's shouting legions,
rallied for a final effort, and vigorously assailed the
Federals in front, while Johnson's men overwhelmed
their right, and the wreath of victory was snatched from
McDowell's grasp.

McClellan listened to the narrative of his predecessor without a word of comment, and at its conclusion
turned toward his staff, and saying: "Gentlemen, we
will now return to quarters," put spurs to his horse.
Again the bugles blared out their signals; the escort
fell into line, and the gay cortege crossed the battle-
field, forded Bull Run, near the blown-up stone bridge,
and from thence by the Warrenton Turnpike, through
Centreville, to quarters with the army.

It is scarcely possible that General McDowell could
have gone over the history of these events, under the
circumstances in which he was placed, without a sense
of painful humiliation; and that feeling must have been
increased by the way in which it was received by
General McClellan. Almost any other man, in McClellan's place, would have sought to mollify this pain by a
word of friendly comment here and there, but the superseded general was left to draw his own conclusions as
to the views of his successor upon the subject which
had been the theme of his painful narrative.

It was remarked above, that McDowell made no attempt at self-vindication; and, it may be added, that
he never did, either as to Bull Run or other events in
his career as a soldier. He despised the methods by
which many officers magnified their exploits and explained away their failures. Charged with disloyalty,
when a truer man never wore the Federal uniform;
with incompetency, when he had few superiors in the
army; with indolence, when there was scarcely his equal
for energy and industry; with intoxication, when he

never touched a glass of wine in his life; with cowardice, when he did not know what fear was—yet he never sought to vindicate himself against these accusations, except in so far as he should do it by a steady, untiring, unswerving devotion to his duty as an officer in his country's army, in a time of great trial and danger.

Amid the passions and prejudices engendered by a great war, injustice is often done to the most meritorious participants; and it not unfrequently happens, that officers of inferior merit, who have industriously blown their own trumpets, or caused them to be blown by newspaper reporters, have caught, and for a time retained, the popular acclaim; but by and by, as the historian gathers up the scattered and diverse threads that make up the story of the time, the pretender is relegated to his proper sphere, and true manhood is given its just place on the enduring page of authentic and accepted history That General McDowell will occupy an enviable place in the record which shall tell the story of "the great rebellion" to future ages, does not admit of a doubt.

In December, 1861, McDowell was examined by the Congressional Committee on the Conduct of the War, and was asked, among other things, what was the condition of the division he then commanded in the army of the Potomac. He answered, "The men are excellent men; I do not suppose there are better men in the world." This answer reveals one of the traits of McDowell's character; he believed in the manhood—in the blood of his race, and he stood up for the men under his command. When asked how his division was in point of discipline, he said: "The discipline has an exterior which is good, but an interior which is bad." The committee naturally asked the general to explain this, and his answer gives the secret cause of half the disasters to the Federal arms during the war. He said: "I think discipline consists in an implicit

obedience, not outwardly alone, but inwardly—that implicit reliance and confidence that must exist on the
part of the commanded towards the commander.   I
think our deficiency is in the quality of our officers : I
do not think our officers stand towards the men in the
relations that officers should occupy towards men whom
they are to put into battle and hold up to their work,
and keep them from spreading or doubling their ranks,
or falling back to the rear, or breaking ranks.   I think
that in the battle in which I was engaged last summer,
that thing developed itself in a very remarkable manner, and it became very evident to both officers and
men." A truer definition of discipline, and a more
striking and concise statement of the consequences of a
lack of it have rarely been given.   It was the want of
this kind of discipline, extending from the enlisted men
up through all the grades to the General-in-chief, that
lost us Fredericksburg and Chancellorsville.   It was the
want of this kind of discipline in our forces that so
often disappointed the reasonable expectations of the
country   Men of different regiments averaged about
alike in the quality of courage and intelligence ; and it
was owing to the presence or absence among them of
this kind of discipline that distinguished one regiment
from another in its steadiness and persistency under
fire.   Without this kind of discipline, no army can be
reliable in a great emergency,

UNTIL the fifteenth of March, the army, or at all
events, the portion of it lying nearest to Centreville, remained quietly in its camp, awaiting orders.   The
Twentieth Regiment occupied a pine grove on the north
side of the Warrenton Turnpike, and about two miles
east of Centreville.

During this period the road was swarming with
civilians who came out from Washington to see the Bull
Run battle-field.   Most of them came to gratify a very
natural curiosity ; some of them to search among the
dead for the remains of friends to whom they wished to
give the rites of a Christian burial among their kin.   If
passes were required at all, in order to go out to the
army from Washington, the demand for them must have
kept several officers very busy.   Indeed, soldiers and
civilians seemed to regard the occasion as a pleasure expedition—a sort of holiday recreation.   No one seemed
to feel that this march of the Grand Army of the Potomac was the beginning of a series of movements which,
in its progress and results, would consign thirty thous-
and of its members to graves and hospitals, within the
next four months.   Men talked and acted as though
they believed the war was substantially over ; why,

said they, the enemy has run away: and if they dared
not stay to fight us behind their strong works at Centreville, which they spent eight months in constructing,
it stands to reason they will never dare to meet this
army anywhere.   So thousands comforted and deluded
themselves.

It was a source of much amusement to officers and
men to watch the flowing and receding human current,
moving past the camp.   All kinds of vehicles were represented, from the pretentious coach to the dilapidated
sulky.   Men on horseback and men on mules vied with
each other for the first occupation of the Centreville fortifications, as though each was a storming party and
ambitious to plant his banner foremost on the enemy's
works, and spike his wooden guns. And plodding wear-
ily along were hundreds of footmen who were unable
to procure any sort of conveyance, and became for the
nonce *tramps*.   Among the latter class were Messrs. Ford
and Baker, of Oneonta, N. Y., both of them gentlemen
of large wealth, and whom I had known many years before.   My surprise at seeing them *there* and on *foot* was
very great, but they said they were a little late in their
arrival at Washington, and a horse and wagon were not
to be had for love or money   As they had set out to
visit Bull Run, and it was uncertain what moment the
army might be withdrawn, they resolved to do what the
soldiers had done—march—and here they were.

The returning pilgrims were generally encumbered
with mementos from the battle-field, which, doubtless,
were shown with vivid narratives of the journey to
wondering and admiring friends at home.   So, for three
days, the home-guard passed and repassed in review, as
it were, before the army, while thousands were turned
back in bitter disappointment, as they met the head of
the armed column on its retrograde march.

Some time subsequent to this it was found necessary
to establish and enforce very strict regulations in re-

gard to visits of civilians to the army, especially on the eve of battle, or any important movement. And these, of all others, were just the occasions when men desired most to go, and they would waste their own and the time of the officials in importuning for passes. Mr. Raymond, in his life of Lincoln, tells a very good story in this connection. Judge Baldwin, of California, being in Washington, called one day on General Halleck, and presuming upon a familiar acquaintance in California a few years before, solicited a pass to go into Virginia to see his brother. "We have been deceived too often," said General H., "and I regret I can't grant it." Judge B. then went to Secretary Stanton, and met a refusal. Finally he obtained an interview with President Lincoln, and stated his case. "Have you applied to General Halleck?" inquired the President. "Yes, and met with a flat refusal," said the indignant Judge. "Then you must see Stanton," continued the President. "I have, and with the same result," was the reply "Well, then," said Mr. Lincoln, with a smile, "I can do nothing, for you must know *that I have very little influence with this administration.*"

Opposite the pine grove where the Twentieth lay lived a Mr. Boddy, who professed to be a Unionist. He said Beauregard sent out patrols just before McDowell's advance, last July, and they seized all the able-bodied men they could find, and took them to the rebel headquarters, where they were called upon to elect between taking arms and going into the ranks, or being sent prisoners to Richmond. Boddy chose the latter alternative, and was sent some three miles to the rear where he was kept with a number of other prisoners, until after the battle of July 21st, when they let him go. He said that crowds of Beauregard's men were passing the place where he was, in full retreat, and that it was said they were beaten. But that soon word passed along that General Johnson had arrived on the field, and then the retreat was checked and the men seemed eager to get back into the fight.

He also stated that the county militia, to which he belonged, had been ordered to assemble at Centreville on the tenth of March, but for what purpose he did not know. The militia, however, seemed to have waived their claim in favor of Uncle Sam's soldiers, for none of them put in an appearance, except Boddy, still, they must have gone somewhere, for Boddy was the only native, able to bear arms, who could be found for miles around.

On the fourteenth of March, Lieutenant-Colonel Gates and Captain Tuthill, Assistant-Surgeon of the regiment, set out for Bull Run on horseback, while two hundred and twenty-two line officers and men of the regiment, who desired to see the field, all under the command of Captain J. R. Tappen, began their march for the same place; the Captain was to report to Colonel Gates at the Francis Lewis House on the field. The march began late in the day, and the intention was to arrive on the ground in the evening, bivouac for the night, and examine the country the next forenoon, and return to camp in time for dress parade.

When the detachment arrived, the evening had become very dark and a steady rain was falling. The men were told to seek shelter in the rebel huts about the locality, and the officers were invited to accept headquarters' hospitality in the Lewis House. The negro family referred to in Chapter XI. had been engaged to furnish supper for the occasion, and with bacon, hoe-cake and coffee, we felt our lot was, for that night at least, cast in a pleasant place. The Lewis House, which had long been deserted by its owners and occupied as rebel headquarters by Beauregard and Johnson, was a spacious building, with large rooms above and below, and vast fireplaces; into these were piled cartloads of wood, and roaring fires, regardless of insurances, soon gave us warmth and light, while our savory supper smoked upon the improvised table. The boisterous March winds beat like ocean billows against the great barn-like house, while the rain-drops dashed themselves into spray against the window-panes. But all within was cheery and content—the sounds of elemental strife without enhancing the sense of comfort of our little party, basking in the glow of our generous fire. Here and there, through the darkness, we could detect the fitful glimmer of scattered lights, indicating the localities of some of our men. But they seemed in the deceptive gloaming wonderfully distant and far apart.

I had a sort of foreboding that something disagreeable would happen before morning. The situation seemed too pleasant and comfortable to endure till daylight. The first event that interrupted our enjoyment occurred about midnight, when Doctor Tuthill was suddenly seized with severe and painful illness, that put an untimely end to our jollity, and demanded our constant ministrations. We were for a while apprehensive he had been poisoned, and thought of arresting the negroes who had furnished our supper as the guilty parties. But as each one of us had partaken of each dish equally with the doctor, and no one else was affected, we abandoned this theory, and awaited results, which sometimes threatened dissolution.

In the midst of the excitement and anxiety caused by Dr. Tuthill's illness, and at about two o'clock in the morning, the corporal of the guard ushered into the room an orderly, covered with mud and dripping with water, who had ridden out, post haste, from Centreville, with an order to Colonel Gates to return with the 20th Detachment forthwith, as the brigade was under orders to march at daylight. The orderly had reached the house without much difficulty, because its location on high ground with its windows all aglow made it an unerring beacon. But to go out into the thick darkness and arouse two hundred and odd tired and sleepy men, dispersed in squads of three and five, over a mile square of country that was *terra incognita* to us, was quite another affair. But it had somehow to be done, and Captain Tappen and his line officers with the head-quarters guard set about it. A bugler, whom we chanced to have with us, sounded the *reveille*, but the the winds made sport of his feeble blast, and the notes floated away unheard on the boisterous air. It was manifest to the officers at the Lewis House, that no bugle call less commanding than Gabriel's could out-ring the gale and penetrate the log huts, where their tired men were enjoying nature's sweet restorer, and whose lights were long since extinguished. So it became necessary to grope about over stumps and logs, through ditches and quagmires, from hut to hut, and awaken the dreaming soldiers. But the searchers rapidly increased in numbers, and in an hour from the time the order was received, the detachment was drawn up in line in front of the Lewis House, ready to set out on its march for camp, locating as best we could the position of the stone bridge, with reference to our starting-point, and leaving rousing fires behind. We struck Bull Run a short distance below the bridge-site. The stream had become much swollen since we crossed it a few hours before, and the water was now deep and the current impetuous. But slinging their guns and cartridge-boxes over their shoulders, the men forded the river, and soon were striding down the Warrenton Turnpike, without having had the opportunity of seeing the battle-field, which they had come so far to inspect. But five months later most of them visited it again, coming upon it from the opposite direction. A hundred thousand armed men then covered the ridges and filled the val-lies, and swarmed in the woods. Then as now a storm swept over the fields, and thick clouds hung in the quivering air. The clouds were battle's pall, and the storm was lead and iron.

We had been obliged to leave Doctor Tuthill at the Lewis House, in care of two attendants, and he was able to rejoin the regiment in a few days. We reached the camp in time to permit the men to breakfast, and take their places in the ranks when the brigade marched. The rain poured down incessantly all day long, and the roads became like beds of mortar ; but onward we went with scarcely a halt, until we reached "Three Mile Run," near Alexandria. If the Confederates had been marching upon the Capital, we could not have been hurried over the road any faster. McClellan probably wanted to try our speed and bottom—that is the only apparent motive for the Centreville expedition. The march of the regiment was 17 miles, and that of Captain Tappen's detachment about 25 miles ; which, considering the condition of road and weather, was a good day's work. How much farther we should have been required to go no one can tell ; but the rain now proved our benefactor, in that it had so swollen "Three Mile Run " when we reached it that it was impossible to cross, and *we had* to stop. I wore, on this occasion, a pair of high top boots over my trowsers—indeed, my trowsers would *not* go over my boot-legs. The consequence was, that I carried about a gallon of water in each boot-leg most of the day, and when the opportunity offered, some twenty-four hours later, to detach those boots from my person, it required the united efforts of three able-bodied men to separate us. I never afterward carried water in that way

As we were bridging "Three Mile Run " next morning, preparatory to crossing and proceeding to Alexandria, an order came directing us to our old quarters at Upton's Hill, whither we proceeded, and where officers and men resumed the huts they had taken leave of six days before. On the 18th of March, the regiment left

Upton's Hill, and moving towards Alexandria about four miles, went into camp two miles south of Bailey's Cross Roads, with a view to being nearer to the shipping-point when its turn came to embark for the Peninsula. But its turn never came.

We remained in these quarters until the fourth day of April. During this time our camp swarmed with civilian visitors. Among them were Mrs. Pratt, wife of the Colonel, and Mrs. Major Miller, who were under escort of Hon. Horatio Seymour, Ex-Governor of New York.

My old friends Messrs. Fordyce L. Laflin, and his cousin Addison H. Laflin, Captain Bouck, son of Ex-Governor Bouck, and General Danforth, were among my guests. The advance to and return from Centreville, seemed to be regarded as very creditable exploits—the next best thing to an overwhelming victory Very few people were aware of the fact, that General McClellan knew the Confederates were evacuating Centreville, before he put his army in motion towards it.

The embarkation of the army at Alexandria was an interesting and herculean operation. It occupied about thirty days, and drew an immense body of spectators— soldier and civilian—who never tired of watching the strange spectacle. Troops were marching in steady streams on board of vessels at different wharfs, while at others, wagons, batteries, and all the supplies and *impedimenta* of a great army, were being hurried aboard ship. Including the troops shipped from Perryville, on the Susquehanna, and from Washington, there were 121,000 men, 14,592 animals, 1,150 wagons, 44 batteries, 74 ambulances, besides pontoon bridges, telegraph materials and enormous quantities of equipage required for such an army.

To transport this multitude of men, animals and property, there were used 113 steamers, for which the Government paid $212.10 each per day ; 188 schooners, at

$24.45 per day, and 88 barges at $14.27 per day ; aggregating for water transportation, $30,158.66 per day, and amounting, with cost of fuel, to over a million dollars to transfer the army from Alexandria to Fort Monroe.

On the 13th of March, the army was organized into four *corps d'arme*, in pursuance of an order from the President.   The 1st corps was commanded by General McDowell, and consisted of three divisions, commanded respectively by Generals King, McCall and Franklin. The 20th Regiment was in Patrick's Brigade of King's Division.   The other regiments of this brigade were the 21st N Y V., Colonel Rogers ; 23d N. Y V., Colonel Hoffman, and 35th N. Y V., Colonel Lord.

In McClellan's plans for the Peninsula campaign, was included a flank movement of McDowell's corps, and to the derangement of such plans by the retention of this corps in front of Washington, he has chiefly attributed the miscarriage of the Peninsula enterprise.   McDowell's corps was to be the last to embark and was to land in rear of Gloucester Point, thus turning York town and opening up the York river.   In view of the fact that the navy declined to put their heavily armed war vessels in range of the rebel batteries at Yorktown and Gloucester Point, it is clear that the turning movement must have been directed from the Rappahannock or Severn.   And the corps would, in either case, be compelled to cross a broad and deep river, in face of the enemy.   There was no concealment of the general plan of campaign, and it was probably quite as well known in Richmond as it was in Washington.   The share assigned to McDowell's corps, was discussed by officers of all grades, a fortnight before the time for the expected embarkation of the corps ; but West Point, at the head of the river, was understood to be the first objective.   To reach it would have required a march of thirty miles, from either the Severn or Rappahannock ; and having reached it, the Mattapony and Pamunky rivers obstruct the march and could only be crossed by bridging. West Point is connected with Richmond by rail, from which city it is but forty miles distant, and the entire peninsula from Yorktown to Richmond, was in the hands of the rebels, with a force, estimated by General McClellan, on the 7th of April, "not less than 100,000 men." How, under these circumstances, McDowell's corps of less than 25,000 men could have accomplished the role laid out for it, while McClellan's army of 100,000 was held in check by Magruder, with 12,000 men behind the works at Yorktown, is not so clear.

But the experiment was not tried, and we can only speculate upon the probable consequences of an attempt to carry it out. On the fourth of April, the Adjutant-General of the army telegraphed to General McClellan, who was then at Fort Monroe, as follows: "By direction of the President, General McDowell's army corps has been detached from the force under your immediate command, and the general is ordered to report to the Secretary of War. Letter by mail."

CHAPTER XIII.

WHILE we were lying at Centreville, General Wadsworth was appointed Military Governor of Washington,
and took leave of the brigade. Soon thereafter General M. R. Patrick was appointed his successor, and
assumed command after the brigade returned to Upton's
Hill. General Patrick did not win the affections of his
troops so easily as did his predecessor; indeed, he
made no effort in that direction. He was about the age of
General Wadsworth, but of a more slender figure and of
a sharp and rather stern face. His head was bald with a
rim of gray hair around the base, and he wore his beard
full and long. I remember well the first time I saw him
—he came strolling into our camp on foot, with a Mexican blanket hanging over his shoulders and enveloping
his form—his head passing through a hole in the centre
of this odd garment. The "boys" were amused by
the quaint costume of their unknown visitor. He said
nothing to anybody, but walked about as though he
were intent upon "spying out the barrenness of the"
camp. The next we knew of him he rode into our
midst in the uniform of a Brigadier-General, mounted
on a magnificent horse, accompanied by his staff, and
assumed command of the brigade. The aforesaid

191

"boys" looked at him, and said one to another, "why, that is the old fellow who was skirmishing around here the other day in a horse blanket. Is *he* to boss this brigade? He looks as though he could bite the head off a tenpenny nail, and would like to do it. Well, well, we'll miss Uncle Wadsworth, you bet." And they— we, rather—*did* "miss Uncle Wadsworth" for a while.

General Patrick was a graduate of West Point, and had spent the better part of his life in the regular army. He had seen service in Mexico, and, I think, on the plains among the Indians. He was a thorough soldier, and he exercised the authority of his grade with the inflexible severity of an old army officer, whose educa- tion and habits of life, for fifty years, had made him a thorough disciplinarian and a stickler for every point of military etiquette and army regulations, in so far as they were deemed conducive to the well-being and effi- ciency of the troops under his command. He was by no means a martinet, but he believed the regulations of the army were wise rules for the government of troops, and that their enforcement was necessary for the pre- servation of that gradation of authority and that main- tenance of discipline, without which an army becomes a mob. He was quick to detect, and stern in the pun- ishment of any wilful breach of these regulations, and officers and men alike were not affectionately disposed towards him. He did not care—or, at least, did not ap- pear to care. Yet, when I came to know the General better, I believed that during all the weeks of his early command of the brigade, when his hand seemed to be really against us all, he was longing in his heart for the sympathy, respect and love of his officers and men. Well, if he was, he consoled himself with a well-ground- ed faith that these sentiments would grow up in the course of time, and he did not have long to wait for them.

The benefit of General Patrick's thorough system

with his command was appreciated by all, when the real business of the war came to demand the exercise of those qualities which make men soldiers, and inspire them with a consciousness of the strength the organization gives them, either for offense or defence. The power of resistance or the impact and persistency of an attack, by an army, depends in a wonderful degree upon the faith the men have in their officers and in each other, and their dependence upon the discipline which has cemented them together as one man, and yet enables them to execute any manœuvre required to make their arms most effective. It is this discipline and this conscious strength which makes a hundred well-drilled men superior to an armed mob of a thousand. As we more and more appreciated these facts, we more and more appreciated our Brigade-commander, and, at length, there was probably no general officer in the army who was held in higher esteem by the officers and men under his command, than General Patrick was by his brigade—and as for the Twentieth, it idolized the General, and I believe he had a very good opinion of it. At all events, he writes me this letter :

MAULIUS, N. Y., 23d November, 1878.

MY DEAR GENERAL :

I am heartily glad to learn that you are preparing a history of the services rendered by the "Twentieth New York" during the late Civil War. Justice to the regiment demands that such a history be made up, from its always well-kept records, and from the documentary testimony now available from many other sources. As a rule every regiment in the Army of Potomac was attached to some brigade, of which it became an integral part of the brigade treasure, jealously guarded by Brigade, Division and Corps Commanders. Every act of heroism, every deed of gallantry was honorably mentioned, and promotion urged as the reward, by these several Commanding Generals.

The part played by that Old Brigade to which the Twentieth belonged, during the Pope Campaign, was not, certainly, less prominent than that of any brigade of Pope's Army ; but while his report as published, embodies the reports of all other Brigade-Commanders, mine alone was suppressed. A glance at the revelations made before the Fitz-John

13

Porter Board, as to the operations of my brigade at Groveton, on the 29th
and 30th of August, '62, may give the reasons for its suppression.

From the bloody and disastrous field of Groveton, was borne away
the pure and chivalrous commander of your regiment to yield up his
young and joyous life upon the altar of his country. On that field, too,
were left—I know not how many—of your gallant dead, nor how many
more were carried away to linger and die of wounds that day received.

During the Maryland Campaign that followed, the regiment under
your own command added to its reputation already established on the
crest of South Mountain and the field of Antietam ; its brilliant record
for that year, closing up with the battles around Fredericksburg, 13th and
15th December.

As Provost-Marshal-General of the Army of Potomac, from the battle of Antietam, it was absolutely indispensable that I should have troops
around me on whom I could rely. Regiment after regiment was assigned
to me, only to make further changes needful, until in early January of '63,
my request to have my Old Brigade assigned to my department was
granted, and from that hour I felt that I had those around me who could
be trusted.

In less than six months afterward the other regiments of that famous
Old Brigade having been discharged by expiration of two years' service,
the Twentieth alone remained, charged with difficult, laborious and responsible duties, increasing in magnitude and importance up to the close
of the war. Although the Provost troops were not, on ordinary occasions, in line of battle, yet, in every time of peril, from Gettysburg to
Petersburg, the hasty call on me was, "Put in your Twentieth "—and
"put in" it was; and history tells the story. It records the heroic conduct of the 20th N. Y. and 151st Pa.--a demi-brigade under your own
command—in resisting the main attack of Pickett's famous division, six
times your own number, for three hours, holding ground against nearly
100 guns, and eventually forcing the enemy from the field, but with the
loss of Corbin and Baldwin, and Brankstone, and many others of your
best and bravest.

And history too records the fact, that when the call was made, for the
last time, to "Put in the Twentieth," it did go in, and go through, and
planted the Stars and Stripes above the captured city of Petersburg.

But, with the passing away of every emergency that called the regiment into line of battle, it was relieved, with the thanks of its temporary
Commanding General, and returned to its normal duties in my
Department. Belonging to no corps, but "put in" whenever and
wherever necessity demanded, its services were not recognized and honored as were the services of other regiments permanently attached to the
corps in which the Twentieth might be temporarily fighting.

If, however, the laurels earned by this regiment were sometimes
placed on other brows, there were garlands gathered by the Twentieth on
fields that were all its own. To watch over the discipline and interior

economy of a great army, to check abuses, to carry out instructions of the most difficult and delicate character, when to shut the eye to evil practices would ensure the most liberal rewards, this was a service that tested the courage more thoroughly than to grapple with an armed foe on the battle-field.

Daily brought in contact with citizens of the Confederacy and their families, to the credit of both officers and men be it recorded, that their treatment of non-combatants in the invaded States was governed by that law which required them to do unto these people what, under like circumstances, they would consider just to themselves and their families, were their own homes invaded. The conviction, that both officers and men endeavored to act justly and kindly, as well as with firmness and decision, early forced itself upon these rebellious people, and elicited in them a disposition to yield, without strife, to requirements that, otherwise, would have involved force and violent collisions. To this day the 20th N. Y. is held in grateful remembrance by the inhabitants of Northern and Middle Virginia.

If the duties devolving upon the regiment in '63, '64, and '65 were unique and peculiar, the personal relations that came to exist between the regiment and myself were not less so. If, at the first, there was no kind feeling towards the Brigade-Commander, it was not long before good sense, reason and experience placed a different estimate upon what had been regarded as the iron rule of a heartless despot. Pride in exceptional discipline and trustworthiness took the place of discontent, and the baptism of fire purged away all bitterness. In after-times, when countless regiments were, from time to time, assigned to me, the rank and file of the Twentieth seemed to share with their officers in the feeling, that somehow, *they* were the legitimate and special custodians of the reputation of the Provost-Marshal-General's Department, and the honor of its chief.

While in the other regiments little material was afforded that could be used with safety in my department, in the Twentieth there was a sentiment of personal, almost filial obligation, in carrying out my wishes.

It would be strange, if such long-continued faithfulness and loyalty should not have given birth to a responsive feeling on my part—that this particular regiment became almost a part of my military family, and that the welfare of its members became a matter of deep personal interest. With the fall of the Confederacy, in accordance with the promise of the President, the regiment was ordered to follow me to Richmond, and it was in the conquered capital of the Rebel Confederacy, with which we had been four years at war, that our war services were fitly ended.

Since I rode down the front of that veteran regiment on Sunday evening, the 11th of June, 1865, and our last good-bye was said, I have never buckled on the old sword, but it hangs against the wall, to rust in its scabbard, I trust, forever.

Of the many troops that, at different times, served under my command, I have never met, nor kept up an acquaintance with any, save the

Twentieth, since the close of the war. This may be accounted for, in part, from the militia organization of the Twentieth, as State troops, instead of simple volunteers, who disbanded at the expiration of their term of service, but mainly, because I have always felt it to be both duty and pleasure, to meet those with whom I was so long associated in the days of darkness, and to whose personal kind feeling I was largely indebted for the carrying out of a system, which entrusted to most others, would have been sure of failure.

I have written more than I thought to have done when I sat down, and will only add, that I am sure, with the abundant material at your disposal, it will be a labor both of duty and of love to enshrine the services of the regiment you so long and worthily commanded, in a volume that will be handed down, with just pride, to coming generations of those whose fathers served in the "Twentieth New York" during the War of the Great Rebellion.

Very sincerely, General,
I remain yours, as ever,
M. R. PATRICK.

GENERAL THEODORE B. GATES,
    371 Fulton Street,
        Brooklyn, N. Y.

Accompanying the foregoing letter was a brief one, of a personal character, and which the General did not expect to see in print, but as it relates to himself and refers to his health and feelings, I know his old comrades of the Twentieth will be glad to read it, and I therefore take the liberty to insert it.

MAULIUS, November 23, 1878.

My Dear General:

I did not mean, when I dropped you a postal, acknowledging your letter of 26th September, that it would be the last of November before I should reply to it. Although I am not often rigidly confined to my room, I am much broken of late, and this season, especially. When I was East in July, I came home sick and was not about much, until September. About the 8th or 9th of October, I was called suddenly to Albany, to attend the funeral of a friend, (the mother of Prentiss, who was on my staff in '64). Being there, I concluded to go down the river to Rhinebeck, Kingston, and New York, but while staying a few days with the family in Albany, I was taken suddenly and strangely ill, and after waiting there three or four days, finding myself no better, came back home. Have only got to work again within the week, and am unloading my table as fast as possible. Some days I am unable to control my hand to write. Most of my troubles arise from rheumatism, which has saturated my whole system, and develops itself in all sorts of strange and uncomfortable ways. And now for the gist of your letter. I sat down this morning to block out something to be used in the work you are preparing; but when I endeavored to *think*, so many recollections crowded up before me, that I found it would be easier to write a pamphlet than a page, so full were the years of incident. I was unwilling, however, to say nothing; neither my sense of justice to the right, nor the courtesy due to yourself would allow that. So I have just written you a letter without delay, but which expresses my opinions in somewhat general terms. I am not at all certain that it is quite what ought to appear in your book, and I beg of you, if after reading it you should think, as others will, that it were better left out, do so, without a moment's hesitation—it don't suit me at all. You speak of a photograph—E. B. Townsend, formerly a Lieutenant of 20th, now in Washington, sent a photograph of me to my daughter, a few months ago, that the family think is the best they have seen. I don't remember, but think it must be one of Gardiner's—I'll write Townsend for one. In January '77, I rang at your door, but you and madame were both in Kingston (I think). I was in Brooklyn again, in February last, but made no calls. Can't say whether I go down this winter. With kind regards to Mrs. Gates, I remain,

Yours sincerely,
M. R. PATRICK.

GENERAL GATES, Brooklyn.

On the fourth of April, 1862, the first corps of the Army of the Potomac struck tents, and again turned its face toward the setting sun. The brigade, in which was the Twentieth, consisted of the regiments already named as composing it, while the division was commanded by General King. General McDowell commanded the corps.

We marched at four o'clock in the afternoon, and bivouacked at seven, two miles south of Annandale, having marched only about six miles. When we halted, I found myself near a quaint, old-fashioned road-side inn ; from a pole in front of which was suspended a weather-beaten, creaking sign, bearing the name of William Gooding, which the elements had failed utterly to obliterate. For sixty years this hostelry had been known as " William Gooding's tavern," and he, or some member of his family, had, during that long period of time,

offered "entertainment for man and beast," at the
same board and in the same stalls—never changing ;
never adding a rood of land to their possessions ; never
enlarging or improving buildings or lands, scarcely
restoring a shingle or board to exclude the elements.
What the tavern and stable were in the beginning, they
are now, " the natural wear and tear thereof, and damage by the elements excepted," the Gooding establishment is a type of Virginia conservatism, as it manifests
itself in the rural districts.

Passing through Fairfax Court House, Centreville,
Manassas Junction, where we struck the Orange and
Alexandria Railroad track, we went into camp at a railroad station called " Bristoe," at two o'clock, P. M., on
the sixth of April. We had marched thirty-eight
miles.

The next day a terrible storm of rain, snow and
sleet, set in, and continued for sixty hours. The only
protection the men had from this bitter storm, were the
wretched, brown paper affairs, called "tents *d'abri,*"
the only earthly use of which are to arrest the fall of a
gentle dew. The officers fared but little better than the
men, and the horses suffered fearfully. There were no
buildings into which either man or beast could take
refuge, and it only remained to us to endure—hoping for
a speedy change. The people who had lived there-
about said they had never had such a storm before at
that season of the year, and they insinuated that it was
a judgment upon the "invading Yanks."

Soon after taking command of the brigade, General
Patrick introduced the practice of having prayers at his
headquarters, when in camp, conducted by some one of
the several chaplains of the brigade. The chaplain of
the Twentieth thus describes the situation in which he
found the General, when he went to his quarters, during
the storm at Bristoe, to conduct the evening service :

" I found the General sitting before his tent, wrapped in his india-rubber robe, his feet resting on a log, and striving to get some warmth from a fire of logs, which was struggling with the storm for its very existence. He was far from well, but received me cordially, expressing his gratification that 1 had ventured to come half a mile through such a storm for such a purpose. He feared, however, that his usual attendance of officers would be missing, which proved true, for on the sounding of the bugle none came, and a chapter was read and a prayer offered in his tent, with none present but ourselves."

While tarrying at this place three or four of our officers rode off some miles to the house of a Mr. Marcellus, who was the prominent man of that section of country. He stood at the gate in front of his house when the officers came up, and received them with an air of unmitigated disdain. While they were transacting their business with him, he did not ask them to dismount. After this was over, one of them inquired if he could not accommodate them with something to eat?

He then very reluctantly invited them to dismount and walk into the house. The parlor was a pleasant room, uncarpeted and plainly furnished, and contained a book case with a very good selection of rather ancient literature.

Leaving the officers here some little time, Mr. Marcellus announced dinner in an adjoining room. There they found a table spread with a dish of cold baked beans, a few slices of fat pork, and a plate of corn bread. After partaking of these substantials, they returned to the parlor, whither Mr. Marcellus had gone immediately after showing them to the table, and one of the party offered him the contents of a pocket flask. It was politely accepted. and under its mollifying influence our host's austerity yielded to a more genial mood and a more benign manner.

He took the trouble to produce and exhibit an old-
fashioned silver-mounted horse-pistol, which he said
was one of a pair General Washington carried, and
which had somehow become an heir-loom in the Marcellus family He professed to regard it with great veneration, and had concealed it on the approach of the
Northern vandals ; but a little good bourbon had removed all his fears and inspired him with unreserved
confidence in his visitors.

As his unbidden guests were about to depart, one of
them, considering that their entertainment, such as it
was, had been very reluctantly furnished, hinted as
delicately as he could, that they would like to make
some compensation for it. This was too much for the
blood of one of the first five families ! Straightening his
tall form and putting on an air of insulted dignity, he
exclaimed : "*Sir, I am a Virginian !*" Of course, an
adequate apology was tendered, and the parties separated on the best of terms.

This incident is related merely to show the inordin-
ate conceit of these lords of the South. It was this
overweening vanity—this self-ascribed superiority and
importance, which manifested itself in such expressions,
as " Sir, I am a Virginian ;" "Sir, I am a South Caro-
linian," that did so much to engender a disdain for
the non-slave-holding portions of the country

A reasonable degree of State pride is certainly allow-
able, but to suppose that the accident of birth or the
circumstance of residence in any particular State con-
fers superior virtues and dignity, was the antiquated
notion of an arrogant aristocracy

To appreciate the absurdity of this fond conceit,
imagine, if you can, a citizen of one of our rich and
growing Western States, under like circumstances,
clothing himself with an oppressive weight of dignity,
and exclaiming to his startled guest : "*Sir, I am a
Mich-i-gander !*"

No ! Let us not glory in that we are citizens of an Eastern, Western, Northern or Southern State, for all are equal under the Constitution and Laws. But let us glory rather in the inestimable civil and religious privileges which we enjoy, as *American* citizens.

Another, and a much more numerous class, with which a longer sojourn in the State brought us in contact, was what was known in the South as "poor white-trash," and probably this term describes the despised people to whom it was applied, as well as any English words can. There are nowhere else in this country, a people who can be likened to these pitiable specimens of degraded humanity

In the North, the poorest and most ignorant of our population have some sentiment of manliness and independence—some enterprise and thrift.

But these poor creatures were the veriest slaves of a race of slaves, and possessed no sentiment above the instincts of the brute.

Dwelling in miserable kennels and sustaining a bare existence by the fitful tillage of a few acres of worn out land—the property of some neighboring planter—they came and went at the beck or nod of their imperious landlords, and were as obedient to their commands as the colored slave, who felt it a degradation to associate with these dependent whites.

Grown up themselves, and their children growing up in the most abject ignorance—mentally, morally and physically debased by their condition and habits of life —excluded from intercourse with the planters around them, and barely tolerated by the slaves, they were the dupes of the nearest demagogue and the willing tools of their task-masters.

Ignorant of the simplest forms of intelligible expression, they had an idiom constructed of negro dialect and words of unknown derivation. If you asked one of them the name of his country or township, it was an

even chance he could not tell you. If you inquired the
distance to the nearest planter's, and he ventured upon
the intellectual effort to inform you, it would be executed by a combination something like "*two rises and
a right smart level*," or, "*three sights and a go-by. I
reckon*."   He "*totes*" your baggage and "*carries*"
your horse to water.

It was such men who made up the great mass of the
rebel army, and who knew no more of the cause or purpose of the war, than they did of the planetary system.
If light ever breaks in upon their clouded perceptions,
they will realize that it was not the blacks alone who
were emancipated by the failure of their master's rebellion.

CHAPTER XIV

WE were lying west of, and but four miles from Manassas Junction. The Orange and Alexandria Railroad had been repaired, and supplies were sent to the corps by rail. The storm was succeeded by warm and beautiful weather, which soon dispelled the feelings of discontent and discomfort which for sixty hours had made several thousand men and several hundred horses very miserable indeed. The ground dried rapidly, and in a few hours after, the snow and hail had disappeared. Officers were in the saddle, giving themselves and their animals a little agreeable exercise, and inspecting their surroundings.

Manassas Junction was a favorite resort, because it had already become historical, as rebel headquarters for nearly a year, and there were still many evidences lingering about it of the occupation and destructive proclivities of Johnson's army. And, in the vicinity of

203

the Junction, there were also abundant evidences of the fearful mortality, especially among the troops from the more southerly portion of the Confederacy, which had prevailed during the preceding winter. In one lot we discovered seventy-four graves, with plain wooden head-boards, the inscriptions on which showed that they had died of disease, and not in battle, and most of them had belonged to the 10th Alabama regiment. The period covered by these interments was less than three months.

During the nine days the brigade remained at Bris-toe, we revisited Bull Run battlefield, and gave it a more leisurely inspection than we had been able to on former occasions. But there is little to be added to what has been already said of that famous field. The rebels had done an immense amount of work in build-ing huts, stables and corduroy roads. Their cabins were comfortable, but their arrangements for fires and cooking seemed to have been very inadequate. In one hut was this attempt at practical versification:

> "To this cabin there is a door,
> To this cabin there is a floor ;
> So coming in please scrape your feet,
> And closing the door there'll be some heat."

On the plateau, heretofore described, where the rebels made their final stand on the 21st of July, and upon the identical spot where he is said to have fallen, a small marble shaft had been erected to the memory of the Confederate Colonel, Francis S. Bartow, and en-graved upon it are the last words he uttered : "They have killed me, boys, but never give up the fight." They remind one of Bainbridge's dying exclamation : "Never give up the ship." It is only a heroic spirit, that can thus, in the agonies of death, forget self, and as the soul is rending its mortal tenement, devote its last earthly thought to the cause for which the body dies.

On the tenth of April, news was received in camp of the capture of Island No. 10; of a Federal victory at Corinth, and that McClellan was driving the enemy before him at Yorktown. The following Sunday morning, after inspection, prayers were offered before the troops, in thanksgiving for recent victories to the Union arms, and all seemed to unite devoutly in the solemn ceremony.

The notion used to be very prevalent that the soldiers were prone to profanity, dissipation and wickedness of all sorts, and not much given to prayer.

I suppose that opinion still prevails. But I utterly and entirely dissent from it. Necessarily, in a large army, there will be men of bad character, and there will also be weak men who may be corrupted by the bad. This is true of all times and places. But the tendency of military life, in *well* organized and *properly* disciplined troops, is the reverse of evil. It teaches men "Cleanliness which is next to Godliness." It imbues them with self-respect and a regard for law and order. It gives them a sense of the dignity of manhood, and of their just relations to their fellow men.

While some men were morally ruined by their connection with the army, a great many more, morally ruined men, were regenerated and made good citizens, in the same great school.

Officers, who have a just conception of the duties and obligations they owe their men, will look after their moral as well as their physical condition; and I find an order issued by Colonel Pratt on the 12th of May, 1861, which is so admirable that I quote it: "General Orders No. 36. The Colonel commanding, reminds the officers and soldiers of the 20th Regiment, that no one can expect the favor of the God of battles, who habitually takes His name in vain. Profanity in any man is among the worst of vices ; in the soldier, who is subject to especial hazard, it is casting away the help of the only arm that can give victory

" The Colonel commanding therefore hopes that he shall hear of no cases of profanity, which require the severe notice of military law "

The Articles of War, which constitute the military law, prohibit profanity and drunkenness, and are, in fact, a thorough moral code.

In a letter written from my camp in 1864, after three years' experience of army life, I said ; "it is doubtless true that military camps contain much wickedness, but it does not follow, necessarily, that every one who belongs to them, is sinful beyond the ordinary degree of human weakness. Such camps contain all sorts and conditions of men ; good, bad and indifferent. But I do not believe these people are any worse in the *army*, than they would be anywhere else. In fact, I do not think there are half so many temptations to err, in the army, as there are in Kingston or Saugerties, or any other little village in your county I do not think the men of my command, who may be so fortunate as to live to get home, will be any worse *citizens*, because they have been *soldiers*. "

That opinion has been strengthened by subsequent observations.

Men are too ready to believe evil of their fellow-men. It is a pitiable human infirmity. And it was fashionable to charge officers, especially if they were unsuccessful, with drunkenness. This charge was brought against McDowell, after the first Bull Run, when in fact he never touched a glass of wine in his life. He is, and always has been, a total abstainer. He drinks neither wine, tea or coffee.

The corps of military critics and self-constituted mentors was very large during the war, and they pronounced Sherman crazy and Grant habitually drunk.

One of them complained to the President of Grant's

supposed inebriety   Mr. Lincoln asked the grumbler if
he knew what kind of liquor Grant drank.   "No," said
he : "why do you ask?"   "Because," said the President, " I would like to send some of the same brand to
the other Generals."

Accompanied by the Regimental Surgeon and Adju
tant, we paid a visit to the residence of the Rev. Dr.
Balch; a learned and distinguished divine of that
neighborhood, and were invited to remain to tea.   The
doctor's house was some six miles from camp, and it
was the best furnished house, and seemed more like a
comfortable Northern home, than any other country
house we saw in the State.   His family consisted of a
grown-up son and daughter, and a young lady from
Washington was a guest in his house, at the time of our
visit.   It was evident from the manner of the young
man that he had been in the army, and he was then
probably at home on furlough.   Both young ladies
played the piano, and the parlor contained a very good
instrument.   The entire household were bitter secessionists, and had no hesitation in expressing their sentiments.   They differed from most other rebels one met
in this, that while they detested the cause which brought
you into their State, their intelligence enabled them to
distinguish between the cause and the individuals, who,
as officers of the Federal Government, were acting in the
line of their duty, in endeavoring, by proper means, to
sustain the cause.   If it were not some such reasoning
as this, then it was their superior refinement which
secured for us very courteous treatment, in so far as
we were personally concerned.

Dr. Balch, however, inveighed against the administration in as strong language as was permissible to one of his
calling, and totally unrestrained by our presence.   Mr.
Green, of Greenwich, a friend of the doctor's, had then
recently been sent to Fort Lafayette for some act of disloyalty, and the doctor was greatly incensed there-

at, and declared that the Federal Government had become the most arbitrary and tyrannical Government on
earth—that a citizen could no longer express his honest
convictions upon political matters without being arrested and immured in a Northern fort, subject to the
caprice of some civil or military officer of the Government. We told Mr. Balch, that if he really believed
what he said, he was either a very bold man or he
wanted to become a martyr to the Confederate cause.
That he had charged the officers of the Federal Government with arresting citizens for distasteful political
utterances, and that he, nevertheless, had not hesitated,
in presence of three officers of the Government, to de-
nounce that Government in the strongest language a
minister of the gospel could venture to use.   That if the
policy of the Government was such as he had asserted
it to be, it was evidently our duty to arrest him and
take him to camp with us, but we did not believe he
himself expected any such result, and we did not understand that the Government required us to arrest men
for talking treason in a treason-saturated State.

When we left Dr. Balch's house, evening had set in
and it was very dark.   Our route thither had been very
circuitous, and we had to guess as to the direction to
camp.   Roads there were none, and after riding through
fields and woods for an hour, we confessed to each other
that we did not know in which direction the camp lay
We finally told our comrades that we would give our
horse the rein and let him take his own course, believing
his instinct would guide him aright.   The surgeon had
little faith in brute instinct, but the experiment was
tried, and at midnight our horses drew up in front of
our quarters.

On the 18th of April, our brigade moved seven miles
farther west, and encamped at Catlett's Station—consisting of a shed and a station-house, both in a state of
mournful dilapidation.   The next morning at six o'clock

we faced toward the south, and set out for the Rappahannock River. The first night out, we halted some time after dark, in a furious rain storm and in impenitrable darkness. We marched twenty miles, much of the way over a road ankle-deep with mud. The men were very tired, and dropped on the saturated ground, when the order to halt for the night reached them, and went to sleep supperless.

Perhaps there are pedestrians, "go as you please," who may peruse these pages, and who regard twenty miles, even over a muddy road, an easy day's work. Very well! Let them put the equipments of a soldier on their backs : rifle, bayonet, sixty rounds ammunition, haversack, knapsack, overcoat, blanket, section of tent *d'abri*, say 40 pounds, and *then* see how they feel at the end of twenty miles—*if they get there.*

The next day, after a march of 14 miles, during the latter part of which our advance was skirmishing with the rebel cavalry, we entered Falmouth, a village on the north side of the Rappahannock River, at the head of navigation, and opposite the city of Fredericksburg.

There were three bridges, one railroad bridge and two others, uniting Falmouth and Fredericksburg. These the enemy had saturated with oil and kerosene, and having fled across, burned them, and thus checked our advance.

They also burned a number of vessels lying in the harbor, including the steamer St. Nicholas, which they had captured some little time before, by a neat ruse. A number of passengers went on board, as she was about sailing from Baltimore, among whom was a person in woman's apparel, addressed by the others as Miss Thomas. When the steamer reached Chesapeake Bay, Miss Thomas suddenly shed her feminine garments and revealed herself—if I may keep up the assumed gender, as a Confederate officer, and with her fellow passengers,

14

who were in the plot, overpowered the crew and seized the steamer, and ran her up to Fredericksburg.

Some days elapsed before we were able to cross the river and enter the ancient city, whose church-spires and dingy houses lay so invitingly before us—so near and yet so far. But when the pontoons arrived, and a bridge was thrown across the river, we took possession of the town without opposition—the enemy falling back to the valley of the Mattepony

The city seemed at first nearly deserted, and there were really very few able-bodied men among its then inhabitants. As a rule, the men we met received us with cold civility, while the women secluded themselves in their closed houses.

Rebels, as they were, against the government he, of all men, had done most to institute, these Fredericksburgers professed great veneration for the memory of Washington, and claimed a special ownership in the glory of his name and reputation. Although born at Bridges Creek, near the mouth of the Rappahannock, young Washington soon thereafter became a resident of Stafford County, opposite Fredericksburg, whither his father removed while George was an infant. The 20th encamped upon the Washington farm. The new homestead overlooked the river and the city, and here the future commander of the Continental armies and the first President of the Republic, grew to manhood ; well may the city be proud of this distinction, but how much more consistent would have been its pride, if it had stood fast by the principles which Washington himself declared, and by the government which he created !

Washington became a member of Fredericksburg Lodge, number Four, F & A. M., November 4, 1752, and was raised August 4, 1753, and subsequently became Master of the lodge. A very fair portrait of him is suspended on the wall of the lodge-room, and the jewels used in his initiation and the regalia he wore, as Master, are sacredly preserved.   In 1848 the lodge procured Hiram Powers to make a statue of Washington, at a cost of $5,000, which it designed to place in its hall.   This location, on account of weight and size, was found impracticable, and Virginia-like, no other recourse has been devised, and the statue remains in its case to this day.

In 1798, while Washington was in retirement at Mount Vernon, and in the sixty-sixth year of his age, trouble sprung up between this Government and the French Directory, and war seemed imminent.   President Adams appointed General Washington, Commander-in-chief of the American army—to be created ; and the Grand Lodge of Maryland sent him a congratulatory letter upon his appointment.   His reply thereto is preserved by the Fredericksburg Lodge.   He writes from Elkton, the capitol of Cecil County, Maryland, where, doubtless, his new duties had called him.   It will be seen that he reaffirms his faith in the Order of F. and A. M., and exhibits a devotion to the Government which his Fredericksburg admirers would have done well to imitate.

" *To the Right Worshipful Grand Lodge of Free Masons, of the State of Maryland :*

GENTLEMEN AND BROTHERS:

Your obliging and affectionate letter, together with a copy of the Constitutions of Masonry, have been put into my hands by your Grand Master, for which I pray you accept my best thanks.

So far as I am acquainted with the principles and doctrines of Free Masonry, I conceive it to be founded in benevolence, and to be exercised only for the good of mankind.   I cannot therefore, upon this ground, withhold my approbation of it.

While I offer my grateful acknowledgments for your congratulations on my late appointment, and for the favorable sentiments you are pleased to express of my conduct, permit me to observe, that at this important and critical moment, when high and repeated indignities have been offered to the Government of our country, and when the property of our citizens is plundered without a prospect of redress, I conceive it to be the indispensable duty of every American, let his situation and circumstances in life be what they may, to come forward to support the Government of his choice, and to give all the aid in his power toward maintaining that *independence* which we have so dearly purchased; and under this impression, I did not hesitate to lay aside all personal considerations and accept my appointment.

I pray you to be assured that I receive with gratitude your kind wishes for my health and happiness, and reciprocate them with sincerity.

I am, gentlemen and brothers,

Very respectfully,

Your most obedient servant,

G. WASHINGTON.

ELKTON, November 8th, 1798.

In the cemetery just back of the city of Fredericksburg, is an unfinished marble monument; around the base of an incomplete column some eight feet high lie the marble blocks once designed for finishing the structure; that column rests upon the grave of Washington's mother, and its curious history is thus briefly told.

A Southern gentleman of wealth and high social position became enamoured of a beautiful, self-willed, imperious, unscrupulous lady of Fredericksburg, who, with no affection for him, yet told him, if he would erect a certain designed kind of monument over the neglected grave of Mary Washington, she would become his wife.

With all the eagerness love could inspire, he set about his task. Marble from Italy, and cunning workmen from all parts of the country were soon upon the ground, and block after block assumed its place, until the impatient lover was beginning to count the days when the last stone should be lifted to its position, and this monument to the dead should also mark the period from which was to be dated the bliss of its devoted builder.

But alas, the familiar aphorism, that true love never runs smooth, was doomed to an exceptionally cruel illustration in the case before us. While the daydreams of the fond swain were making even this graveyard a paradise to the unsuspecting lover, the object of his adoration was quietly wedded to another, and was on her way to a distant part of the State before her dupe awoke from the stupor into which he was thrown by this sudden unvailing of his destiny.

Since then, and that was many years ago, no chisel has rung upon the marble, nor has another block been added to the pile. Rebel soldiers had used the monument as a target, and defaced it with their sacrilegious musketry, bruising it—as the heart of its builder had been bruised—and just as wantonly.

The Valley of the Rappahannock, in the neighborhood of Fredericksburg, is very beautiful. It is only some three miles in width, but is perfectly level and the soil is exceedingly rich. It is shut in by high hills on the north and south, running parallel with the river. The city lies at the upper end of this valley and stretches back from the river to Marye's Hill. The railroad, from Acquia Creek to Richmond, crosses the river at the lower end of the town, skirts the valley for two miles, and then finds its way southward, through an opening in the hills, near Hamilton's house, where Franklin was ordered to penetrate the rebel line, at the battle of Fredericksburg.

For months and months, at different times during the war, hostile armies occupied opposite sides of the river, and Rebel and Federal cannon frowned from numberless batteries along both ranges of hills—so planted as to command the river, Fredericksburg and the valley below.

Much of the time, these armies were merely watching each other, while plans were being matured for future operations. During such periods, though cannon would occasionally echo through the valley, and a random shot or shell drop or burst along the lines, the men would come down to the opposite banks of the river and talk with each other across the stream.

One of the distinguishing characteristics of the

Union army, was its numerous bands of music, while
the Confederates had scarcely any. The boys in butter-
nut, however, seemed as fond of music as their adversaries in blue were, and would often gather at the
brink, on their side of the river, to hear our bands.
Such an incident is very prettily expressed in the following lines, entitled " Music in Camp. "

1. " Two armies covered hill and plain,
    Where Rappahannock's waters
 Ran, deeply crimsoned with the stain
    Of battle's recent slaughters.

2. The summer clouds lay pitched like tents
    In meads of heavenly azure ;
 And each dread gun of the elements,
    Slept in its hid embrasure.

3. The breeze so softly blew, it made
    No forest-leaf to quiver,
 And the smoke of the random cannonade
    Rolled slowly from the river.

4. And now, where circling hills looked down
    With cannon grimly planted,
 O'er listless camp and silent town
    The golden sunset slanted.

5. When on the fervid air there came
    A strain, now rich, now tender,
 The music seemed *itself aflame*,
    With day's departing splendor.

6. A Federal band, which eve and morn,
    Played measures brave and nimble,
 Had just struck up with flute and horn,
    And lively clash of cymbal.

7. Down flocked the soldiers to the banks,
    'Till margined by its pebbles,
 One wooded shore was blue with " Yanks, "
    And one was gray with " Rebels. "

8. Then all was still : and then the band,
    With movement light and tricksy,
 Made stream and forest, hill and strand,
    Reverberate with " Dixie. "

9. The conscious stream, with burnished glow,
    Went proudly o'er its pebbles,
 But *thrilled* throughout its deepest flow
    With *yelling* of the Rebels.

10. Again a pause---and *then*, again,
     The trumpet pealed sonorous,
   And " *Yankee Doodle*" was the tune
     To which the shore gave chorus.

11. The laughing ripples shoreward flew
     To kiss the shining pebbles,
   Loud shrieked the swarming boys in blue,
     Defiance to the rebels.

12. And yet once more the bugle sang
     Above the stormy riot ;
   No shout upon the evening rang;
     There reigned a holy quiet.

13. The sad, slow stream, its noiseless flood
     Poured o'er the glistening pebbles;
   All silent, now, the Yankees stood,
     All silent stood the rebels.

14. No unresponsive soul had heard
     That plaintive note's appealing,
   So deeply " *Home, sweet Home* " had stirred
     The hidden founts of feeling.

15. Of blue or gray, the soldier sees,
     As by the wand of Fairy,
   The cottage 'neath the live oak trees,
     The cabin by the prairie.

16. Or cold or warm, his native skies,
     Bend in their beauty o'er him
   Seen through the tear mist, in his eyes,
     His loved ones stand before him.

17. As fades the iris after rain
     In April's tearful weather,
   The vision *vanished*, as the strain
     And daylight, died together.

18. But memory, waked by music's art,
     Expressed in simplest numbers
   Subdued the sternest Yankee's heart,
     Made light the rebel's slumbers.

19. And fair the form of music shines,
     That bright celestial creature,
   Who still 'mid war's embattled lines,
     Gave this one touch of nature. "

CHAPTER XV

THE rebel forces encountered on our way to Falmouth, consisted of one regiment of infantry, one of
cavalry, and a light battery, all under command of General Field.   Our advance was led by General Augur's
brigade, with Kilpatrick, then Lieutenant-Colonel of the
" Harris Light Cavalry," and commanding the regiment, at the front.   General Augur himself, with a section of artillery and the " Brooklyn Fourteenth " infantry, kept close on the heels of the cavalry ; the 14th entering Falmouth after a wonderful march, without having left a single straggler behind.   The loss in the cavalry was twenty-five men killed and wounded, and a
number of horses.

The arrival of the Union troops was a surprise to the good people of Fredericksburg. They had profited by the war up to this time, and did not expect a visitation by Federal troops in a long time, if ever. Fredericksburg had an air of business in its streets and warehouses, and in the conversation and manner of its men, that could be found nowhere else in the State, except in Richmond itself. Its society was aristocratic, after the model of aristocracy in the days of the Revolution. Confederate officers were exceedingly popular in Fredericksburg, and the city swarmed with them after the first battle of Bull Run. Every one was a hero, and nightly crowned with laurels. Nothing was too good for them, and every door opened at their approach, and fair women contended with each other for precedence in doing them honor. It was a grievous humiliation to these over-confident Secessionists, to see the gray uniforms of the Confederacy fade away in the dim distance and the blue of the Union troops take their place. They did not hesitate to censure General Field for giving way before us, and insinuated that he was not as brave as Hector. But it did no good : we were there, and they made up their minds to make the best of the situation.

General Robert H. Anderson, a graduate of West Point, was lying a few miles south of Fredericksburg, with a considerable force of Rebel troops, to which body the command of General Field belonged, and to which it returned after its futile attempt to retard McDowell's march. It strikes a cursory observer of current events as a singular fact, that this General Anderson is, at this present writing, (June, 1879,) one of the Board of Visitors attending the examination of West Point cadets, appointed by the President of the United States. "To err is human—to forgive, Divine." There has been lots of humanity and divinity in this view of those qualities, in this country, during the last eighteen years. A

Herald reporter interviewed General Anderson, and drew from him some interesting statements about the Academy, the war, and Georgia politics :

" It is twenty-two years ago," said he, " since I graduated here, but there was some difference in the studies then and now. There was an examination in gunnery but none in ordnance, that being an addition since my time; and no wonder, for gunnery has undergone a complete revolution. Why, the largest pieces we ever saw were ten-inch, and besides all the new-fangled ideas in ordnance, rifled shells and oblong shots that go through iron and stone like a knife, were then unknown. Why, at the breaking out of the war as good an artillery officer as General Lee was satisfied Fort Pulaski was safe from Gilmore's guns at a mile distance, but three and four miles was nothing impossible to Gilmore's artillery Another study they have here now is much more extensive than it was over twenty years ago, and that is law. We merely studied principles of international law, but now there is enough taught to set a man up in business as a lawyer ; besides, they have what is called a judge-advocate, whose business is all law. In old times an officer, when the occasion called for it, was detailed to attend to the necessary legal business, and that over, he returned to his army duties."

" What graduates in your class became distinguished in the Confederate army ?"

" Well, several of them were killed early in the war, who promised to be brilliant. There were Generals Strong and Putnam, besides Marmaduke, who was well known, and Kirby Smith."

" Do you recognize any old comrades here ?"

" Only a few who are instructors or professors."

" How do you get on with the Union officers ?"

" Very well. As Bishop Beckwith said of the Episcopal Church in the late struggle, 'We cherish no animosities between brethren,' and so with the men of West Point. Though on opposite sides, they were ever ready to clasp hands, and no set of men ever left a college or institution of this kind who cherish such ardent friendships for each other as the graduating class of West Point. Theirs is more than a masonic tie, and many illustrations of its strength and fervor were shown during the late war."

"What else do you find changed here, General ?"

"Well, all the changes I have noted are for the better. The quality of the food is greatly improved, and not alone that, but the cadets are charged less for it than in my time. It was a good idea to take the supplying away from a civilian and give it to an officer like the one who has charge of it at present—Commissary Mills. Another thing to be commended is the superintendency of General Schofield. He is managing this Academy with great tact and wisdom. In place of using repressive measures, he has trusted the honor of the boys, and he has never been deceived. He allows them to go boating on the river up and down, and several other small indulgences that in no way interfere with the strict discharge of duty, and yet the boys' lives are all the brighter and more cheerful."

"How is your State of Georgia getting on ?"

"Georgia is going forward to a prosperous destiny. Every town of any consequence in the State is increasing in wealth and size. The colored people have turned round to steady work, and the whole population has but one object in view, the material advancement of the State."

"You don't bother much with politics ?"

"Not much. Don't even vote."

"What do you think of Tilden's chances in the South ?"

"I don't think much of them   A much stronger

man than Tilden would be General Hancock, but the
southern people are far less anxious about political
matters than you would ever imagine, to judge by the
newspapers.''

On the night of the twenty-first of April, and while
we were still lying on the north side of the Rappahannock, trains of cars were heard coming into Fredericksburg, from the direction of Richmond, in rapid succession, and it was believed at corps headquarters that
the rebels were concentrating troops with the view to
attack McDowell.   Orders were issued putting brigade
commanders on their guard, and the troops were prepared for battle. Most of the heavy artillery of the
corps had been planted on Stafford Heights, overlooking Fredericksburg, on our arrival, and the infantry was
now posted so as to cover any point where it was
thought the enemy might attempt to cross the river.
The enemy's pickets had been visible, along the hills in
rear of Fredericksburg, from the day of our advent at
Falmouth, and the Confederate authorities doubtless
knew our strength and position.   It would have been a
brilliant *coup de main* to have swooped down upon Mc-
Dowell, and gobbled him up before McClellan could
have learned that such an enterprise was on foot.   But
it did not strike me as very probable that the wily adversary would advise us of his design, by rumbling a
dozen trains of cars into Fredericksburg under our very
noses, or that he would attack, if at all, from that direction, and with a river to be crossed, under fire of all
arms.   What he would have accomplished by moving a
large body to our right, under some such leader as
Jackson, I do not know, but certain I am that McDowell
would have given a good account of himself.   But the
cars came and went all through the night, and they
were probably removing rebel stores from the city

On our march from Catlett's Station to Falmouth,
and in and about the latter place, the '' peculiar institu-

tion," manifested its presence in groups of negroes along the wayside, and at the doors and windows of every house we passed. Girls, especially, were numerous about the dwellings, giving one the impression that the hive had swarmed. We were struck by the variety of colors presented by these scions of Africa, ranging, as they did, from a glistening ebony to a white, hardly distinguishable from the Anglo-Saxon hue. The latter complexions often accompanied with blue eyes, and hair more curly than kinky. The anomaly could only be accounted for by assuming that the climate had different effects upon different temperatures—bleaching some, while the blackness of others was what the merchant would call a "fixed color."

Among the killed, in one of the skirmishes between Catlett's and Falmouth, was Lieutenant Decker, of the Harris Cavalry. I got the impression, at the time, that he belonged to, or was connected with an Ulster County family of that name.

Falmouth was an insignificant village, lying along the river's bank, at the foot of Stafford Heights, in Stafford County, and, with few exceptions, its buildings were in that state of dilapidation common to old southern towns. Painting, repairing, or any attempt to keep houses or grounds in neatness and order, seemed never to have been thought of. "Time's erasive fingers" have left their indelible marks on every village in the South, and decay is accepted in perfect contentment, and without an effort to arrest it. Nearly every dwelling-house south of the Potomac is disfigured by a huge chimney, often constructed of rough stone, standing against one end of the building, from which capacious fire-places open into the house. It is said they build the chimney first, and then *lean* the house against it, but I cannot vouch for the truth of this statement, as I never saw a dwelling—except soldier's—in process of construction, in the South.

It will have been observed that localities have been
designated, in this volume, by the names of individuals
in the possessive case, as a rule, and it may be well to
remind the reader that the Territorial division of the
Old Dominion does not include townships.   Therefore
it is we find places bearing such names as "Upton's
Hill," "Fall's Church," "Catlett's Station," "Spotted
Tavern," where we bivouacked the first night out from
Catlett's; "Piney Branch Church," where the hero
Sedgwick was killed.   Falmouth was named after an
individual, and its neighbor, Fredericksburg, was so
called in honor of Prince Frederick, father of England's
George the Third.

There were, however, a few fine and well-kept places
in the vicinity of Falmouth.   One of them was the property of a Mr. Phillips, who was reputed to be a Union
man at heart, but constrained by his surroundings to
act with the Secessionists.   He owned a large plantation
on the Stafford Plains, two miles from Falmouth, upon
a well-chosen site, on which stood an elegant mansion,
designed and constructed with a view to beauty and domestic comfort.   The rooms were numerous, spacious
and pleasant, and reminded one of the better class of
country houses, on the banks of the Hudson.   The
house was subsequently burned, whether by accident or
design, I do not know.   About opposite to the central
part of Fredericksburg, and a few hundred feet from
the river, was an old brick mansion, known as the
"Lacy House," from its owner.   Lacy was a rebel
from choice, and ranked as Major in the Confederate army.   His house was very large, with no attempt at exterior ornamentation ; within, however, wealth and art
had left abundant evidence of their profuse employment to make the dwelling a fit abode for the most refined and esthetic inhabitants.   The grounds descended
to the river in terraces, and the house and its surroundings could not well be surpassed for beauty, elegance and

comfort. The property came to Lacy through Judge ————Coulter, who formerly owned and lived upon it. He, dying, left it to his widow, who also died about 1857 She left a will, manumitting her slaves, some eighty-five in number. The Courts of Virginia held that this provision of the will contravened the laws of the State, and they annulled it. Lacy, a relative of Mrs. Coulter, succeeded to the estate, and entered upon the enjoyment of the blessings which are vouchsafed to the owner of eighty-five human beings—black and white —more or less. General McDowell established his headquarters at the Lacy house, and General King fixed his at the Phillips house.

While lying at Falmouth, General Wadsworth and staff surprised his old brigade by riding into its camp, and there was a rush of officers and men to greet their former commander. His kind face lighted up with more than its usual benignity, as he saw how universal and genuine was the esteem in which his old command held him.

On the fifth of May, a pontoon bridge was completed across the Rappahannock, from in front of the Lacy house, and at five o'clock in the afternoon three companies of the Twentieth Regiment, two of the Twenty-third, and one of the Thirty-fifth, all under command of Lieutenant-Colonel Gates, of the Twentieth, crossed the river and took possession of the city, without opposition.

The city is in Spottsylvania County, seventy miles south of Washington, and sixty miles north of Richmond. The "Richmond, Fredericksburg and Potomac Railroad" passes through the easterly end of the city, crosses the Rappahannock, and terminates at Aquia Creek, on the Potomac River, eight miles north of Fredericksburg ; from thence to Washington the journey is by steamboat. It is the most direct route between Washington and Richmond. The population of

Fredericksburg in 1862, was about 5,000, a large proportion of whom were negroes. The Court House and County offices were located here, and the usual division in religious views was represented by five churches of different denominations, one Baptist, one Episcopalian, one Methodist, one Presbyterian and one Reformed Baptist. The city boasted three newspapers, embracing a daily, a semi-weekly, and a weekly It contained an orphan asylum, two seminaries, and two banks. The Falls of the Rappahannock, a mile above the city, afford excellent water-power, which is employed for milling purposes of various kinds. The Rappahannock is navigable up to Fredericksburg, a distance of one hundred and ten miles from the Chesapeake, into which it empties at Windmill Point. Its course is nearly parallel with that of the Potomac. Prior to the war, Fredericksburg did a flourishing trade in the export of grain, flour and tobacco, the aggregate often exceeding $4,000,-000 per annum.

Several thousand bushels of Confederate corn was found in the city, which the rebels had been unable to remove, and it was found quite useful to the Federal troops. Various kinds of property—army material—was discovered about the city, from time to time, and confiscated.

On the tenth of May the residue of the Twentieth entered the city, and, passing through, encamped along the telegraph road to Richmond, about a mile and a half beyond Fredericksburg. The other regiments of the brigade encamped in the same neighborhood, and General Patrick was placed in command of the city, with headquarters in the building formerly "The Bank of Virginia," and which showed evidences of a very hurried departure by its late occupants.

By the twentieth of May, the army had repaired the railroad from Aquia Creek to Fredericksburg, including the re-building of the trestle bridge, over the Potomac

Run, and the bridge across the Rappahannock at Fredericksburg. The work was done with astonishing rapidity, and the bridges were splendid specimens of engineering and mechanical skill. The restoration of this road enabled the Government to supply McDowell's corps with very little hauling, and in the event of its moving toward Richmond, or of McClellan's army swinging around between Richmond and Fredericksburg, this road could feed either or both, with ease and economy

On Sunday afternoon, May the eleventh, Major Duffie, with a squadron of the Harris Cavalry, and accompanied by the Lieutenant-Colonel of the Twentieth, made a reconnoissance down the Bowling Green Road, and about four miles below Fredericksburg, surprised and captured a picket post of one officer and eleven men, together with three horses and their accoutrements. The picket was posted at the edge of an extensive forest, within which, as we soon discovered, was a strong body of Anderson's infantry and cavalry The news of the capture of the picket was speedily conveyed to these troops, and they at once set out to re-capture their men, and punish the captors for their temerity. A large party of cavalry, followed by a strong infantry force, was now seen rapidly advancing through the woods and up the road, and quite too numerous to justify Major Duffie in engaging them. It was resolved, however, to carry our prisoners into camp at all hazards, and, mounting some of them, the others were sent to the front, and the retrograde movement began. At the same time a messenger was dispatched to headquarters, to inform General Patrick of impending danger. The brigade was immediately put under arms, and advanced down the road to the succor of the scouting party, whom it received into its friendly embrace before the pursuers could do it any harm. A few shots were exchanged, but the only loss on our side was one horse

15

killed. The enemy withdrew, and our troops returned to their camps. As we were still quite new to warfare, the incident was very enlivening, and gave the men something to talk and write about.

From the time we entered Fredericksburg, we had maintained a picket line around the city, starting from the river, above the falls, running along the plateau in rear of the town, crossing the plank road, telegraph road, and all other approaches to the city, and terminating on the river below the town. This picket line was manned by details from all the regiments of the brigade, with a field officer to command it. About nine o'clock in the evening of the day on which the affair narrated in the above paragraph, took place, musketry opened on the picket line, and the brigade was again put under arms, but the firing ceased, and quiet resumed its dominion along the line, and in the out-lying camps. Tattoo (a drum beat, giving notice to soldiers to repair to their quarters or tents) had been beaten and taps (a like signal to put out lights) had been sounded, when a noise like the rumbling of a gun-carriage was heard in the direction of the river, beyond which the bulk of our corps lay Gathering volume as it moved along the streets of the canvas city, on Stafford Heights, it took on form and expression, and reached our camps on the opposite side of the river, in a succession of exultant cheers, such as Union soldiers alone could give. This was the third startling event of the day, and the most mysterious one of all. Had McClellan captured Richmond? Had the Confederates confessed their sins and asked to be taken back into the family mansion? Or what *had* happened to justify such a breach of military decorum, as to be cheering after taps? At length our curiosity was relieved, and we sent back to the boys on the other side as hearty a cheer as thirty-five hundred pairs of sound lungs and glad throats could give, and all because the enemy had evacuated Norfolk, and blown up the monster Merrimac. Then we went to bed, and saw in our dreams the horrid fabric of the Confederacy scattered like the fragments of an exploded shell, glowing with a lurid glare for one single moment, as the flame that destroyed it lighted it up, as though it would make its ending a spectacle that should stand as a warning to future ages, *then* dropping into gloom and darkness while the bright rays of a newly risen sun reveal the beautiful ensign of the Republic, floating over every fort, and recognized as the symbol of undisputed authority in every part of our domain.

On Sunday, the eighteenth of May, we attended St. George's Protestant Episcopal Church. The Rector was the Reverend Alfred M. Randolph, a sincere Secessionist. He omitted the prayer for the President of the United States, and it was the first and only time we ever knew it to be omitted from the service of the Church. Mr. Randolph did not pray for the President of the Confederate States, an omission which, I have no doubt, was owing to the presence of U. S. officers in his church, and Federal troops in his city

Sunday seemed to be our day for events—it was so all through the war. On this particular Sunday the sensation was produced by the arrival from the picket line, under guard, of course, of an officer in Confederate uniform, who gave his title and name as Captain Worthington, A. D. C. to General Anderson. He was the bearer of a letter from General Anderson to General McDowell, and wished to deliver the missive in person. General Patrick directed Lieutenant-Colonel Gates to inform General McDowell, who was at his headquarters in the Lacy House, of the circumstance. Colonel Gates rode across the river and reported to General McDowell what had transpired on the other side, and informed him that the bearer of the flag wished to be conducted to his quarters. Learning that the officers on the picket line had sent this Confederate inside, and even into the heart of Fredericksburg, without blindfolding him, Mc-Dowell became very angry, and it was not entirely agreeable to be in his presence when he was in such a mood. He ordered that the man be sent back immediately, and that any communication he might have for him, be left with General Patrick.

I was reminded of this incident by one of General McDowell's answers to Mr. Choat, General Fitz-John Porter's counsel in the recent re-hearing of his case, before a Board of army officers. McDowell is a bluff and somewhat irascible man, and strangers might think him angry when, in fact, he is in the best of humor. He has some of the peculiarities of the late Judge William B. Wright, in that respect. But when he is downright angry, no one in his presence can possibly be deluded with the notion that he is in an amiable mood. Mr. Choat mistook the General's manner for anger, and asked him why he was angry "Angry," replied General McDowell, "Sir, you don't know what it is to see me angry." No, indeed ; if Choat had seen the General real angry, he would not have stayed to ask him what it was about.

On the night of the twentieth of May, the picket lines of the Twentieth, covering the plank road, were pushed forward to the toll-gate, driving the Rebel pickets down through the valley between the toll-gate and New Salem Church. Provoked by this little aggression, they thereafter kept up a lively firing wherever the head of one of our men could be seen apparently within range. This circumstance came very near proving a serious matter for a couple of Ulster County gentlemen who were making the Twentieth a brief visit at that time, and who rode out to the front with Colonel Gates. The gentlemen were Honorable John B. Steele and Mr. Jansen Hasbrouck. As the party rode into the enclosure covering the toll-gate, the

Rebel sharp-shooters opened a brisk fire, and the bullets rattled around us in a lively and suggestive manner. The civilians manifested the utmost coolness, but they deemed it a duty they owed their families and friends to get out of range as soon as they could, with due regard to the dignity that ought to accompany the movement. Mr. Steele remarked that he was not at all afraid, and, on the whole, perhaps had rather be shot than not, but he could easily imagine the uncomplimentary remarks such an event would call forth from his more judicious acquaintances, to the effect that "it served him right;" "what was he, a civilian and Member of Congress, doing on the picket line? He might have known he would be shot, and he ought to have been, for going there." The probability of some such observations being indulged in, in the event of either gentleman being hit, and the considerations first above suggested, induced Messrs. Steele and Hasbrouck to fall back, in good order, however, to a point where the gate-house covered them from the observation of the particular party of rebel riflemen whose fire they had drawn, and who seemed to be concealed in a clump of woods on the hillside in front of New Salem Church. Mr. Hasbrouck was determined to carry home a memento of his first experience under fire, and he obtained one of the bullets which had struck the building near him, and only partially imbedded itself in the wood. Mr. Hasbrouck thought he had rather take the trouble to cut it out of the wood and carry it home in his pocket, than to have it "imbedded" in his flesh and carry it home in that way. I have no doubt Mr. Hasbrouck has preserved that bullet to this day

On the twenty-third of May, his Excellency, President Lincoln, visited the troops at Falmouth and Fredericksburg, and had a sort of informal review. He was mounted on a horse that, at first sight, seemed a mere pony, whose belly was very near the ground. A horse ridden by Mr. Lincoln always appeared so to the casual observer ; but on inspection it would be found that his horse was of the medium size, and the deceptive impression was produced by reason of the spare figure and long limbs of the rider, whose feet seemed to sweep dangerously near the ground, even when mounted on a horse fourteen and a half hands high. We supposed the President's visit to Fredericksburg foreshadowed some movement of the first corps. Two days later, orders were issued for the corps to march to Catlett's Station, and the commands of Generals Shields and Ord proceeded, but the order, so far as the first division was concerned, was countermanded, and the other brigades of the division were ordered to join the first on the south side of the river.

On Monday, the twenty-sixth of May, the first division struck camp, and, facing Richmond-ward, set out at half-past two P.M. over the so-called "Telegraph Road," towards the Rebel Capital, halting for the night at Massaponix Creek, six miles south of Fredericksburg. The march was tardy and hesitating, as though it was considered of doubtful expediency, or as liable to attack. It seemed to me as though it were a "waiting march ;" a movement which was half real and half a feint, with an expectation that an event or an order would intervene to determine which character the movement would finally assume. General Anderson's men had evidently been disturbed by our advance, and we occupied, on the night of the 26th, ground that they had just abandoned. Companies C, Captain Tappen, and G, Captain Hendricks, under command of Major Hardenburgh, did picket duty through the night.

CHAPTER XVI

FOR sixty hours we remained at Massaponix Creek,
waiting for some event or order to determine our future
movements. What had become of General Anderson?
All around us were the abandoned sites of numerous
Confederate camps, and his force must have been large
enough to make McDowell's position, with his diminished members, dangerous. But no enemy appeared to disturb our quiet in the valley of the Massaponix. Indeed,
on the afternoon of the second day of our sojourn, Colonel Lord, of the 35th Regiment, and Colonel Pratt, Lieutenant-Colonel Gates, and Major Loughran, of the 20th,
rode to Massaponix church, three miles farther to the
front, without encountering a Confederate soldier. For
some reason we were being let severely alone, and we
did not know, at the time, why

On the 29th of May, the division faced to the north
and retraced its steps to Fredericksburg, and, crossing
the river, the head of the column took the direction of
Catlett's Station, from which we had advanced to Fredericksburg something over a month before. The cause
of this retrograde movement was the raid of Stonewall

231

Jackson down the Shenandoah Valley, the capture of Milroy, the retreat of Banks, and the possible danger of the Federal Capital.

Twenty-six days later, the regiment went into camp upon the ground it first occupied, opposite Fredericksburg. In the interim, it had marched over a hundred miles, and the outward march, to Hay Market, near Thoroughfare Gap, was a forced march, and a very fatiguing one. The weather was excessively warm and sultry, with frequent rains, which seemed to have no other effect than spoiling the roads, soaking the men and driving the heat of the earth up into the atmosphere, making it hotter than it was before. In this march the men of the first corps proved the superiority of human over brute endurance. The best horses gave out under the heat and fatigue of the journey, while the boys tightened cartridge-belts and knapsacks, and marched from early morning until late at night, without a murmur.

It is wonderful how much severe treatment the delicate mechanism of the human system will bear, and yet be none the worse for. What we are apt to regard as privations and injurious exposures, the thought of which strikes terror to the indolent and luxurious, are, after all, more conducive to robust health and manly development than the lives of ease and sumptuousness so many lead, and so many others sigh for.

True, one would not, ordinarily, choose army rations in preference to the savory viands and tempting delicacies that grace the table of the epicure. Yet I do not doubt the superior wholesomeness of the soldier's bill of fare.

Neither is it natural that we should be indifferent to the comforts of a cozy apartment and a spring mattress. And yet, the time soon comes, when the weary soldier finds dear mother earth as soft as eider-down; and wrapping himself in his blanket, with a saddle or stone for a pillow, says his orisons, and then, languidly seeking to trace some constellation in the pictured vault above, the stars are transformed into faces of loved ones far away, and slumber steals upon him laden with pleasant visions of home.

But, ah! if the windows of heaven are open, and the rain invades his spacious chamber, he experiences the truth that "night and storm and darkness are wondrous strong," but fails to discover in them that *beauty* which the poet says is "like the light of a dark eye in woman."

But the night is not always spent in slumber. Often through its long hours, "Tramp, tramp, tramp, the boys are marching," guided, perhaps, by some "intelligent contraband," or some less reliable specimen of "poor white trash," who, closely watched by a file of soldiers, or mounted between two cavalrymen, is made to do unwilling service in his country's cause.

While lying in our Stafford Heights camp after our return, we were visited by Messrs. Erastus Cooke and Jacob Hardenburgh, of Kingston, who spent several days with the regiment, in which they had hosts of friends. Colonel Zadock Pratt also paid us a visit at this time.

At daylight, on the 28th of July, the regiment again entered Fredericksburg, and the four right companies, A, Captain James Smith ; C, Captain J. Rudolph Tappen ; H, Captain Abram S. Smith ; and K, Captain Ambrose N. Baldwin, all under command of Lieutenant-Colonel Gates, marched to the vicinity of the Stanbury House, in the upper part of the city, to cover the plank road and the adjacent country ; while Colonel Pratt, with the residue of the regiment, took post near Fennihoe's House, at the lower suburb of the town. A cordon of sentinels was again thrown around the city, and thus things continued until the fourth of August, when the detachment under Colonel Gates joined the main

body of the regiment, under Colonel Pratt. On the
sixth of August, Colonel Pratt with companies A, E,
K, I and C, of the Twentieth, and two companies of
the 23d, and a section of artillery, made a reconnoissance down the Bowling Green Road, returning to
camp at three o'clock next morning, without having
fallen in with the enemy

On the eighth of August, the rebels captured thirteen of our wagons and a number of men of Gibbon's
and Hatch's brigades, at Massaponix Creek, on the
Telegraph Road. Thereupon, Colonel Pratt, in command
of companies D and B, of the Twentieth, six companies
of the 23d, four companies of Third Indiana Cavalry,
and a section of the First N H. Battery, marched on a
reconnoissance and foraging expedition, at 7 P. M., to
Round Oak Church, southeast of Fredericksburg, while
at the same time Lieutenant-Colonel Gates, with four
companies of the 20th, marched up the Telegraph Road
to Massaponix Creek, the bridge over which the Confederate guard fired, and then fled, as the Federal troops
approached.   Colonel Gates then marched across the
country to the Bowling Green Road, where he joined
Colonel Pratt, and the entire force returned to camp at
half-past three o'clock next morning, bringing in two
prisoners, twenty-five mules, thirty horses, and fifty
head of cattle.

While the unimportant events narrated in this
chapter were just sufficiently interesting to save us
from *ennui*, affairs were culminating on the upper Rapidan that soon involved the Twentieth in the more terrible and destructive scenes of war.

The Peninsular campaign had ended, and the shattered army of the Potomac was making its way back to
Aquia Creek, Alexandria and Washington.   General
John Pope, with the army of Virginia, composed of the
first, second and third army corps, commanded respectively by Generals McDowell, Banks and Siegel, had

been thrown forward along the line of the Rapidan, to create a diversion in favor of McClellan, and facilitate thereby the withdrawal of the latter's army from Harrison's Landing. King's division of the first corps composed a part of the forces subject to Pope's orders, but it had been left at Fredericksburg, because it menaced Richmond, and at the same time covered Aquia Creek, where some portion of McClellan's army was expected to land.

The Government counted upon rapidly re-enforcing Pope from the army of the Potomac, and designed to hold the line of the Rappahannock, if possible, because it was a constant menace to Richmond, and covered Washington. An army stationed along that river could be supplied by two lines of railroads. These roads had been put in order at great expense, and, in every point of view it was important that the position should be retained. The miscarriage of the Union cause on the Peninsula had discouraged the friends of the Government, at home and abroad, and to have the Federal forces between Washington and Richmond forced back into the works along the Potomac, would be a great humiliation, and might seriously affect our relations with European powers.

General Halleck, therefore, who had been appointed General-in-chief, had ordered Pope to hold on to Fredericksburg, and to reach out with his left and keep up his communications with General King, and guard all the passes of the river. Pope was required, at the same time, to cover the front of Washington, to guard the Valley of the Shenandoah, and so to operate upon the enemy's lines of communication, to the west and northwest, that he would be compelled to make large drafts upon his army at Richmond, and thereby be disabled from making any serious demonstration against the army of the Potomac, while withdrawing from the Peninsula.

In carrying out these objects, General King had sent out his cavalry to operate on the line of the Virginia Central Railroad, which connects Richmond with the Valley of the Shenandoah, and it had torn up the road at several points and on several occasions. General Banks sent forward all his cavalry, supported by a brigade of infantry, about the tenth of July, and took possession of Culpepper Court House, and on the 17th of July this force had advanced to Madison Court House, west of Robertson's River.

On the 16th of July Jackson's division of the Confederate army occupied Gordonsville, and checked any further movement of the Federals in that direction. It was the advance guard of the entire Confederate army, flushed with its triumph over McClellan.

Pope's army was now located along the Hedgeman and Rappahannock Rivers, with his right thrown forward to Little Washington and Sperryville, at the foot of the Blue ridge, while Hatch lay at Madison Court House. But the imminence of the danger that soon threatened him induced a concentration of his forces, and on the 7th of August Banks was directed to move down the turnpike toward Culpepper, as far as Hazel River. Rickett's division was ordered to Culpepper Court House. Siegel was directed to post a brigade of infantry and a battery of artillery at the point where the road from Madison Court House to Sperryville crosses Robertson's River, as a support to Buford's cavalry, and push on with the balance of his corps to Culpepper Court House. King's division was ordered to march from Fredericksburg on the ninth, for the same destination. The front of the army was covered by the cavalry along the line of the Rapidan, from the Blue Ridge to the forks of the Rappahannock, above Fredericksburg. The force thus brought within supporting distance, excluding King's division, which was yet at Fredericksburg, numbered about 28,000 men.

On the eighth of August, the enemy began to press the cavalry of General Bayard, who was posted at Rapidan Station, where the Orange and Alexandria Railroad crosses the river, with pickets extending eastward to Raccoon Ford, and he was compelled to fall back, slowly, before superior forces. At the same time the enemy advanced in heavy force against General Buford, who was stationed at Madison Court House. Crawford's brigade of Banks' corps was dispatched towards Cedar Mountain, about midway between Culpepper Court House and the Rapidan, to support General Bayard, who was falling back in that direction. Banks and Siegel were both directed to move at once to Culpepper. On the morning of the ninth, General Banks' entire corps joined Crawford's brigade near Cedar Mountain. Siegel had delayed his march from Sperryville, while he sent a messenger to General Pope to inquire "what road he should march over." Banks' corps was only about 8,000 strong, and it was not General Pope's design that he should bring on an engagement. Ricketts' division of McDowell's corps still lay at the point where the road from Madison Court House to Culpepper intersects the road from Culpepper to Cedar Mountain, because it might be one of the routes by which the enemy would advance, and it was within easy supporting distance of the forces at Culpepper or Cedar Mountain. On the same day Buford found the enemy in heavy force in his front, on both flanks, and partly on his left rear, and he was obliged to retire in the direction of Sperryville.

Artillery firing opened, on the morning of the ninth, between General Banks and the Confederates, whose guns were posted in the woods along the Rapidan, while Banks' were in strong positions at Cedar Mountain. The enemy's tactics led General Banks to believe that they were not in force in his front, and late in the day he resolved to advance and attack them, and, if possible, win a victory before they could be reinforced.

He accordingly threw forward his whole corps into action, and in doing so was obliged to cross a broad, open plain, which, as it proved, the enemy had so posted guns as to sweep every foot of apparently in anticipation of just such a manœuvre as Banks executed. Nevertheless, the Federals pushed boldly on through this unlooked-for artillery fire, and assaulted the enemy with great fury and determination. They found him in superior numbers, and strongly posted and sheltered by woods and ridges. His musketry fire became very destructive as our men came within range, and, after a struggle of an hour and a half, during which the second corps had displayed the utmost gallantry and resolution, they were gradually driven back to their former position, where Rickett's division had then just arrived and joined in the action. The enemy had followed Banks with great caution, and seemed reluctant to emerge into the open ground, yet he did leave his cover in hopes of making his victory more complete, but was driven back by the batteries of Ricketts' division, with considerable loss. The artillery firing was kept up until midnight.

Banks was deluded, as our Generals often were, by the wily tactics of the enemy, whereby they were led to believe that the Confederates were weak and intimidated by our superior force, and only anxious to make us believe they were strong to cover their escape from a perilous position. It seemed impossible for our Generals to believe this was craft. It was always so well acted that it seemed real, and the delusions produced by it cost the Federals a great many lives. Our loss in this battle, in killed, wounded and prisoners, was about 1,800 men. Among the wounded were Generals Geary, Augur and Carroll, and General Prince was captured. This battle was fought in violation of General Pope's orders, and was a useless waste of life, in that it produced no appreciable effect upon impending events, but rather operated to defeat the purposes of Pope, by prematurely developing his position and resources, and inducing greater caution on the part of the enemy

Pope estimated that with King's division, his force would barely equal that of the enemy in his immediate front, and he resolved to attack him, as soon as King should come up.

King marched from Fredericksburg at five P.M., on the ninth, at the hour when Banks was moving to the attack, but without any information of the impending battle. He knew, however, that he was wanted at Culpepper, and he marched until ten o'clock that night, and reached Pope's headquarters at midnight on the eleventh. Pope resolved to fall upon Jackson the next morning at daylight, but a reconnoisance revealed the fact that he had, during the night of the eleventh, fallen back in the direction of Gordonsville, leaving many of his dead unburied, and his wounded on the field and along the road from Cedar Mountain to Orange Court House. The cavalry, under Generals Buford and Bayard, pursued the enemy to the Rapidan, capturing many stragglers, and then resumed their picket line along the Rapidan, from the Blue Ridge to Raccoon Ford. So neither party seemed to have gained any permanent advantage by the sharp battle of the ninth. Certainly none commensurate with the loss of life.

By the eighteenth of August, it became manifest to General Pope that his advanced position, with his his small force, was untenable in the face of the rapidly mustering forces of the enemy General J E. B. Stuart's Adjutant-General was captured on the 17th, near Louisa Court House, and on his person was found an autograph letter from General Lee to Jackson, outlining the campaign he proposed, and showing the position and force of the Confederate army closing in around Pope.

General Reno, with 8,000 men from Burnside's corps,

had joined Pope on the fourteenth of August, and he had made a demonstration as if to advance, by throwing his whole force in the direction of the Rapidan, with Sigel on the right, at Robertson's River, McDowell in the centre, at Cedar Mountain, and Reno on the left, near Raccoon Ford. Banks' corps, badly cut up, and some of his regiments without a commissioned officer, lying in the rear.

But this was only a move in the game of bluff, and it could not deceive the enemy long, if it should have that effect for a moment. So, on the morning of the eighteenth, the trains were ordered to the rear, and the several corps of the little army were directed to retire, after the trains were well out of the way, and, crossing at different points, take position on the left bank of the Rappahannock. Reno was to cross at Kelly's or Barnett's Ford, Banks and McDowell at Rappahannock Station, and Sigel at Warrenton Sulphur Springs.

The "Twentieth" moved, with its brigade, through Culpepper Court House and Brandy Station, and dropped down in the road, for a few hours' sleep, at midnight, three miles west of Rappahannock Station, where we were to cross the river. Our brigade was the rear guard of the infantry, but in rear of us was a body of cavalry, one regiment of which was the Harris Light Cavalry, under command of Lieut.-Colonel Judson Kilpatrick. When near the station, on the morning of the 20th, Kilpatrick charged a stone wall, behind which was a body of Confederate riflemen, or dismounted cavalrymen, who emptied many of the saddles of the Harris Light Cavalry as they charged up to the wall, and retired from it, as they were forced to do, and as their commanding officer ought to have known they must do. It was another example of bad judgment and profligacy of human life. Kilpatrick was the first of his command to cross the bridge at Rappahannock Station, and while sitting on his horse, on the bridge, two men of his regiment rode up from the direction of the enemy. Their Colonel halted them and asked where the rest of the regiment was. They could give no satisfactory information, and Kilpatrick gave them a cordial damning, apparently because there were not more of them, and rode to the east side of the bridge. The matter was really very simple of explanation, and probably those two enlisted men understood it perfectly, but did not dare to speak of it, except in whispers, to each other. "Somebody had blundered," and the result was loss of lives, and disintegration of a fine regiment of cavalry.*

A great many negroes accompanied the Union army in its retreat, and some of them manifested the most extravagant and ludicrous joy when they got across the river. One party of them approached the ford a few rods below the bridge, where the water was two or three feet deep, with an ox-team drawing a wagon, filled with their worldly goods, and on top of these were three wenches, and a perfect swarm of ebony children.

When they reached the bank of the river the oxen refused to go down into the water, and whipping and coaxing were of no avail.

The black figures kept their places, waiting the better mood of their cattle. But suddenly the angry rattle of musketry in the woods near by, suggested, even to their obtuse intellects, that they should not stand upon the order of their going, but *go at once.* Quick as thought those black mothers siezed their youngest children, and, followed by the others, sprung to the ground, looking, in their descent, like fragments of night, dropping from the sky, and dashed through the water.

As they ascended the opposite bank, the matron of the party clasped her hands, and, looking up to heaven, exclaimed : " Bress de Lord—we'se on dis side ob Jo'don !"

---

* See note 1.

THE position of Pope's army on the morning of the 20th
of August, was along the east bank of the Rappahannock, with its left at Kelly's Ford and its right about
three miles above Rappahannock Station, whither Sigel
had marched after crossing the Hedgeman, at the
Sulphur Springs, until he connected with McDowell's
right.   The enemy's advance pushed up to Kelly's Ford
and Rappahannock Station, almost immediately after
the Federal troops had crossed and drove in our pickets.
But finding the army in position on the opposite side of
the river, they retired out of range, awaiting the arrival
of the main body of their army.

The 21st of August opened with artillery fire along
the river, for a distance of seven or eight miles, and
several attempts were made by the enemy to cross, but
they were each time repulsed.   The same tactics were
continued through the next day   The Twentieth Regiment was engaged during this time in supporting Cap-

tain Reynolds' Battery L, First New York Artillery, and on picket along the river, and was under artillery fire most of the time.

Having felt our lines at every ford from Kelly's to Sigel's right, probably as feints, rather than with any design to force a crossing, the enemy began on the 22d to move slowly up the river, with the intention of turning Pope's right. This General was constrained by his orders from General Halleck to maintain his communications with Falmouth, to facilitate the junction with him of troops landing at Aquia Creek, and for the other reasons hereinbefore mentioned. His left was thereby tied as it were to the lower fords of the Rappahannock, and to extend farther to his right was to weaken his line to a dangerous degree. He represented this condition of things to Halleck, but the latter could not bring himself to contemplate the abandonment of Aquia Creek and Fredericksburg, except in the very last emergency, and he directed Pope to hold on, and promised reenforcements from the Army of the Potomac in a day or two, which would enable him to maintain his line and have a force sufficient for any required movement. On the 21st he telegraphed Pope : " Dispute every inch of ground, and fight like the devil, till we can re-enforce you. Forty-eight hours more and we can make you strong enough." But the promised re-enforcements did not come. The Army of the Potomac moved slowly toward this new field of operations, and General Halleck and the President exhausted all their powers of persuation and commands to accelerate its movements, without avail.

Sigel, who apprehended his right would be turned, proposed to withdraw from his position, but this Pope forbade, and directed him to stand firm, but not to attempt to interfere with any effort the enemy might make to cross the Hedgeman above his right at Sulphur Springs. Pope then purposed to allow a considerable force of the Confederates to pass the river at the point indicated, and to suddenly mass a portion of his forces and fall upon their flank, as they should move toward Warrenton, which was supposed to be their first objective. The cavalry was watching the movements of the enemy at and above Sulphur Springs. General Lee himself was at Culpepper on the night of the 21st, and it was evident that his whole army was confronting Pope.

On the night of the 22d, Pope's information of the movements and position of the enemy induced him to contemplate an immediate withdrawal behind Cedar Run, or the massing of his entire army, re-crossing the Rappahannock, and attacking the flank and rear of the Confederates. Halleck assented to this latter plan, and Pope arranged to carry it into execution as soon as Lee had thrown a sufficient number of his troops across the upper fords of the Hedgeman to give reasonable hopes of success. It was a soldierly conception, and if carried out with judgment and spirit, would have been successful, and would have changed the entire aspect and results of the campaign. Lee's army was now stretched out from the forks of the Rappahannock to Waterloo Bridge, and necessarily exposed a long flank to its adversary, and much time would be required to concentrate a sufficient body to resist such an assault as Pope contemplated. Pope intended to strike his blow on the 24th.

Therefore, on the twenty-third, McDowell's corps marched to Warrenton, through a tremendous rainstorm, and the "Twentieth" bivouacked in the streets of Warrenton that night, after a march of twelve miles. The next day we marched two miles toward the Springs and encamped. The following morning we broke camp at six o'clock, and marched to the White Sulphur Springs, seven miles west of Warrenton. The Springs is a fashionable summer resort, with a large and fine hotel and a number of cottages, with grounds handsomely arranged and laid out. As we approached the Springs, a battery, posted near a large yellow house on the opposite side of the river (the Hedgeman river flows within a few hundred feet of the Springs), opened upon our column, and at the same moment a brisk musketry fire was delivered upon General Patrick and staff, who had ridden to the Hedgeman to water their horses, unsuspecting the presence of a foe. C Company, Captain Tappen, was at once deployed as skirmishers, and advancing through the grounds surrounding the Springs, they got into the tall grass along the Hedgeman, where the rebel infantrymen were concealed, and soon drove them from cover and forced them to retreat, leaving Captain Tappen in possession of the ground. At a later hour of the day Colonel Pratt was ordered to move across an open field, almost under the guns of the rebel battery, which still maintained its fire, and take up a position on a hill to our left and front. The regiment moved down the road by wings, the right under command of Colonel Pratt, and the left under Lieutenant-Colonel Gates. Reaching the vicinity of the Hedgeman, they filed to the left into a by-road, and moving up that a few hundred yards filed to the right into an open field. As each wing entered the field it formed line of battle—on the right by file—to present a narrower mark to the rebel artillerists, who were now directing their guns exclusively at the Twentieth. Our movements were so rapid they could not get range of us, and we reached the position we were directed to occupy without casualty Infantry skirmishing continued through the day, and we had a few men wounded. We remained in this position during the night.

The next day the streams began to experience the effect of the heavy rains, and before night they had risen six feet. Both the Hedgeman and the Rappahannock were fordable at several different places from

Kelly's to the Blue Ridge, in ordinary August weather, but now both were impassable, except by the bridge at Rappahannock Station. So, the strategy on which so many hopes had been grounded came to naught, and it was necessary to recast a plan of campaign to meet the changed circumstances, and to utilize, if possible, the unlooked-for flood.

It was believed at headquarters that a considerable body of the enemy was on the left side of the river, and Pope resolved to attack them before the subsidence of the water should allow them to retreat or to be re-enforced. The Federals were posted on the night of the 24th as follows: Ricketts' division of McDowell's corps, on the road from Warrenton to Waterloo Bridge, and about four miles west of Waterloo; King's division, between Warrenton and Sulphur Springs; Sigel's corps, near the Rappahannock, with his advance at Waterloo, and his rear in the direction of Sulphur Springs; in his rear and immediately in contact with him, was Banks' corps; while Reno was lying east, and very near the Springs.

But it was found that the enemy had not exposed himself to this peril. He certainly was not on the left side of the river, and *where* he was, became, for a time, the leading question. No fact could more forcibly convey an idea of the topography of the country in which these military operations were being carried on, than that each army was often in ignorance of the position of the other, although they were manœuvering within a few miles of each other. On the 25th, General Sigel insists that the main force of the enemy is advancing on Waterloo Bridge, where he is stationed, and he wants 20-pound Parrott guns at once. Pope orders Sigel to ford the river in the morning, at daylight, and find out what is in front of him. Pope does not believe there is any enemy in force there, but thinks they have gone to the west and northwest. McDowell telegraphs Pope:

" What is the enemy's purpose—it is not easy to discover. Some have thought that he means to march
around our right through Rectortown to Washington.
Others think that he intends going down the Shenan·
doah, either through Thornton's or Chester Gap.
Others that it was his object to throw his trains around
into the valley, to draw his supplies from that direction, and have his front looking to the east rather than
to the north. It is also thought that while a portion of
his force has marched up the immediate right bank of
the Rappahannock, a large portion has gone through
Culpepper, up the Sperryville road. Colonel Clark,
General Banks' Aide-de-Camp, telegraphs, August 26th,
that a deserter has come in and reports Longstreet's
corps, embracing Anderson's, Jones', Kemper's, Whit-
ney's and Evans' divisions, in the woods back of Waterloo Bridge. This seems to sustain Sigel's opinion. He
also reported Hill's division at Jefferson (opposite
Sulphur Springs, and about two miles from the river),
and that Jackson's corps was somewhere above Longstreet's." On the same day a negro reports to General
Buford that the head of the enemy's column was at
White Plains at noon of that day. When it is remembered that White Plains is on the Manassas Gap Railroad, and north of Bull Run Mountains, the conflicting
and distracting nature of these reports will be appreciated.

While this uncertainty as to the position and purpose of his adversary hampered Pope's movements,
Lee was executing his pre-arranged plan, with the
directness that distinguished his campaigns. His purpose was to sever Pope's communications with Washington, destroy the railroad behind him, and taking
position on his flank, compel him to fight a battle under
circumstances favorable to the Confederates.

The negro told the truth. Jackson did in fact pass
through White Plains on the 26th, and struck the rail-

road in rear of Pope, at Kettle Run, destroying it and the telegraph. Pope at once appreciated the situation, and determined his course. He resolved to abandon the line of the Rappahannock, and throw his whole force in the direction of Gainesville and Manassas Junction, and endeavor to crush the body of Confederates which had separated themselves so far from their main army.

Just one week had elapsed since the retreat of Pope began, and his troops had been in march, more or less, day and night ever since, and much of the time under fire. Several sharp skirmishes had taken place between detached bodies of infantry and cavalry, and artillery duels had been continuous. These, of course, were the picket-line contests, and failed to reveal to either side what was transpiring behind the lines. But this continuous work in August weather had told tremendously upon the men, and the sick-list was large, while the killed and wounded had run up to a large number. Pope had up to this time, however, been re-enforced by General Reynolds, with 2,500 men of the Pennsylvania reserves, and by General Kearney, with 4,500 men. On the morning of the 27th, Pope estimated his effective force as follows: Sigel's corps, nine thousand; Banks' corps, five thousand; McDowell's corps, including Reynolds' division, fifteen thousand five hundred; Reno's corps, seven thousand; the corps of Heintzelman and Porter (which had recently moved up the line of the Orange & Alexandria Railroad to the vicinity of Warrenton Junction, but had not participated in the movements of the residue of the army), about eighteen thousand men, making a total of fifty-four thousand five hundred men. The cavalry was about four thousand strong on paper, but there were scarcely five hundred men fit for duty.

Jackson moved down the Orange & Alexandria Railroad to Manassas Junction, where he found a mile of cars on the track filled with supplies for Pope's army;

these he destroyed, and wrecked everything at the Junction, and then marched across Bull Run and halted at Centreville, as though to await developments from this coign of vantage, where he could not be approached without due notice, and where he could fight with position in his favor, or from whence he could retreat in any direction.

Pope surmised what Jackson's course would be, and he issued orders designed to cut off his retreat, and bring him to battle. McDowell, with his own and Sigel's corps, and Reynolds' division, was ordered to march down the Warrenton Turnpike to Gainesville, reaching that point, if possible, on the night of the 27th. (Gainesville is the point where the Warrenton and Centreville Turnpike crosses the Manassas Gap Railroad, and its occupation, by a sufficient force, would effectually close the road by which Jackson could march toward the head of Lee's approaching but still distant army) Heintzleman and Reno were to march to Catlett's Station, and thence to Greenwich, reaching there the night of the 27th, or early next morning. (Greenwich is in the angle formed by the Orange & Alexandria and the Manassas Gap Railroad, and about midway between them. A road runs northerly from it through Hay Market, west of Gainesville, and intersects the road from Centreville to Aldie.) Porter was to remain at Warrenton Junction until Banks reached that place, and was then to push forward in the direction of Greenwich and Gainesville. Banks was ordered to retire along the railroad, moving trains back toward Manassas, rebuilding bridges where necessary, and in case the enemy should attack and be too strong for him, to destroy locomotives, cars and stores, and unite himself with Porter.

These dispositions of Pope's army were judicious, and if his plans had been carried out, it seems hardly possible that Jackson could have escaped. He was two days' march in advance of Lee's main body, or of any considerable supports. The Bull Run mountains lay between him and his Confederates, and the only practicable passes for an army, large or small, were Thoroughfare and Aldie, the former of which was to be barricaded by McDowell's force, and the latter was too remote, and carried him still farther from his supports. To pass around Pope's right would necessitate a very great detour, and throw him utterly out of connection with Lee, and place Pope between the two forces of the Confederates, at liberty to strike either way

Jackson saw the Federal army gathering around him on the 27th, and Ewell's division was struck by General Hooker, near Bristow Station, whither the former had been sent on a reconnoissance, and a sharp engagement ensued, in which Ewell was driven back along the railroad, but as darkness came on posted himself along the banks of Broad Run, and checked pursuit. The loss was about three hundred killed and wounded, on each side ; Ewell left his dead and many of his wounded, and much of his baggage on the field of battle.

Patrick's brigade marched with its division from Sulphur Springs, at twelve o'clock on the twenty-seventh, and reached the vicinity of Gainesville at midnight, as did also the residue of McDowell's command. Reno and a portion of Heintzleman's corps arrived at Greenwich on time. At dusk on the same evening Pope sent an order to Porter to march at one o'clock that night to Bristow, arriving there at daylight next morning (28th), to re-enforce Hooker, and co-operate in the contemplated attack on Jackson in the morning.

This was one of the orders in a series of three for the alleged disobedience of the last of which Porter was cashiered, and whose case is now before Congress upon the report of a Board of Officers, before whom he had a rehearing. It may be of sufficient interest to the general reader to warrant its reproduction. It is as follows:

HEADQUARTERS ARMY OF VIRGINIA, }
BRISTOW STATION, Aug. 27, 1862, 6:30 P.M. }

GENERAL : The major-general commanding directs that you start at one o'clock to-night, and come forward with your whole corps, or such part of it as is with you, so as to be here by daylight to-morrow morning. Hooker has had a very severe action with the enemy, with a loss of about three hundred killed and wounded. The enemy has been driven back, but is retiring along the railroad. We must drive him from Manassas, and clear the country between that place and Gainesville, where McDowell is. * * * It is necessary on all accounts that you should be here by daylight. I send an officer with this dispatch, who will conduct you to this place. * * *

By command of General Pope.

GEORGE D. RUGGLES,
Colonel and Chief of Staff

MAJOR-GENERAL F J. PORTER, Warrenton Junction :

The distance from Bristow Station to Warrenton Junction is about seven miles, and the road, in dry weather, is a very good one. Porter, however, did not arrive at Bristow until half-past ten.

On the night of the 27th it was discovered that Jackson had moved from Centreville to Manassas Junction, and thereupon McDowell was ordered to push on, with his own and Sigel's and Reynolds' commands, from Gainesville along the Manassas Gap Railroad to Manassas Junction—the distance being about eight miles. At the same time, Reno, Porter, Kearney and Hooker, were ordered to the same destination. Ewell had, in the meantime, fallen back and joined Jackson at Manassas Junction.

Jackson's force numbered about 30,000 men, and was composed of the best material in Lee's army   It had undergone a severe march since the 20th of the month, but for two days most of it had been resting, and was tolerably fresh. It was a dangerous army to attack, except with superior numbers, or from a very advantageous position. Jackson determined to get nearer his supports, and, about three o'clock on the morning of the 28th, he commenced to evacuate Manassas Junction, via the Centreville and Sudley Springs Roads ; each of which intersect the Warrenton Turnpike. Jackson himself rode out of Manassas Junction, with the rear of his army, at eleven o'clock on the 28th, and an hour afterward, Pope, at the head of Kearney's and Reno's troops, entered the place. Hooker, Kearney and Reno pushed on in the direction of Centreville. McDowell was now ordered to recall his forces, moving toward Manassas Junction, and to march down the turnpike toward Centreville, thus confronting Jackson, if he should attempt to reach Thoroughfare Gap. McDowell, in the meantime, and without Pope's knowledge, had sent Ricketts' division, of his corps, toward Thoroughfare Gap, to obstruct the approach of any Confederate forces—a disposition which seems to have been judicious, but it seriously weakened him in the operations he was now called upon to perform.

These shifting circumstances had necessitated a frequent change of tactics upon the part of the Union commander, and the afternoon of the twenty-eighth was well advanced when Kearney came up with the rear of the Confederates, as they were withdrawing from Centreville. Jackson now had Kearney, Hooker and Reno, in his rear, at Centreville ; McDowell, Sigel and Reynolds in his front, and advancing upon him ; Heintzleman, Banks and Porter covering the ways of egress between the forces in front and rear on one side, and the Bull Run mountains shutting him in on the other. His situation seemed to be desperate, except, perhaps, to himself.

McDowell's corps moved cautiously down the Centre-ville Turnpike until the head of column was about two miles west of Gainesville, and near the hamlet called Groveton, when it was halted. It was then near six o'clock of a beautiful August afternoon. The country on the southerly side of the turnpike was densely wooded ; on the opposite side, for the distance of a mile from the road, there were cleared fields, which ended in heavy woods among the foot-hills of Bull Run Mountain. At a point in front of these woods, and about opposite the head of McDowell's column, were seen three horsemen, apparently observing the movement of the Federal troops. Field-glasses soon enabled us to determine the character of these spectators, and after they had spent a few minutes in the inspection of our forces, they disappeared in the woods. Five minutes later a battery dashed out from the forest, and, unlimbering, opened fire upon the flank of the Union column. Gibbon's brigade, of King's division, was in the advance, and it and Doubleday's brigade, of the same division, were thrown into the field on our left, deployed into line, and advanced to attack the hidden foe. The Twentieth Regiment was thrown into the woods on the right of the road, where an ambush was suspected, and marching some distance through these woods, and finding no enemy, was recalled and posted in support of Gibbon and Doubleday The enemy advanced his infantry to meet the attack of the Federal troops, and for two hours, and until after dark, the fighting was exceedingly severe. The Federals maintained their ground until darkness put an end to the combat.

News of this battle reached Pope, at Centreville, about ten o'clock that night, and he sent word to Mc-Dowell and King to hold the ground, at all hazards, and prevent the retreat of Jackson to the west, and that at

daylight our whole force from Centreville and Manassas Junction would be up, ready to fall upon the encompassed foe.   Kearney was ordered to march from
Centreville that night at one o'clock, drive in the pickets
of the enemy and keep closely in contact with him
during the night, and at daylight to assault vigorously
Hooker and Reno were ordered to follow Kearney.
Other troops had orders conforming their movements to
this new plan.   These arrangements were all disconcert-
ed, however, by the unauthorized withdrawal of King's
division, in the course of the night, towards Manassas
Junction.   It was a most ill-advised and unfortunate
movement.   There is hardly room to harbor the shadow
of a doubt, but that Jackson would have been overwhelmed in the morning, if King had stood fast and
the other commanders had obeyed the orders that Pope
issued on the night of the twenty-eighth.   McDowell's
corps had been divided, and he himself was not present
with King's division, otherwise different results would
have ensued.   King—as loyal a man as ever lived, and
full of the noblest instincts ; popular with officers and
men, and beloved by those who knew him well— was
overcome by the tremendous responsibilities in which
he found himself placed.   The loss in one of his brigades had been terrible ; the fighting after dark was a
grand and thrilling spectacle ; dead and wounded covered the field, and the moans of the sufferers filled the
night air ; the implements of the surgeons were being
plied around division headquarters, and some of the
best officers of the division were lying dead on the field,
or writhing in the agony of mortal hurts.   The morning
would bring a renewal of the carnage, and King could
endure no more, and at midnight he marched for Manassas Junction, thus uncovering the way for Jackson to
escape or to be re-enforced.

CHAPTER XVIII

POPE was reluctant to abandon the scheme he had ar
ranged, and which had seemed to promise so well, for
the capture or destruction of Jackson's corps. He
therefore, at daylight, on the morning of the 29th, sent
orders to Sigel and Reynolds, who were yet in the
neighborhood of Groveton, to attack the enemy as soon
as it was light enough to see, and bring him to a stand,
if it were possible to do so. Heintzleman, Hooker,
Kearney and Reno were ordered to advance from Centreville at the earliest dawn, and attack in flank and
rear. Porter was ordered to move with his own corps
and King's division of McDowell's corps from Manassas
Junction to Gainesville, and participate in the attack.

Sigel attacked the enemy at daylight, a mile or two
east of Groveton, and was soon joined by the divisions

255

of Hooker and Kearney. Their onset forced Jackson's
left back nearly two miles to the neighborhood of Sudley Springs, where he struck the line of an old railroad
embankment, running nearly north and south, and
which constituted an admirable breastwork. Forming
his line behind this, he was able to resist the attacks of
the Federal troops. This railroad grade leads from
Gainesville in the direction of Leesburg, and was just
adapted to Jackson's wants, both as to position and
form. It, together with the dense woods through which
it was constructed, afforded his men excellent shelter.
The railroad embankment runs obliquely to the Warrenton turnpike, and intersects it near Gainesville. Here
rested the Confederate right, commanding the turnpike,
the Manassas Gap railroad, and the debouch from
Thoroughfare Gap.

Confronting this line were Heintzleman on the right
and west of the Sudley Springs road ; on his left Sigel,
who extended across the turnpike, and on his left Reynolds. Reno came on the ground in the course of the
forenoon, and a portion of his troops were put into action, while the remainder were held in reserve. Severe
skirmishes occurred at different points along this line
throughout the day, and losses on both sides were
heavy, although no general engagement took place.

It was ten o'clock, on the morning of the 29th, when
Porter's corps moved from Manassas Junction toward
Gainesville. King's division fell in at the rear, and proceeded about three miles, when Gen. McDowell directed
the division to file to the right ; and, crossing a portion
of the old Bull Run battle-field, the division struck the
Sudley Springs road ; and, advancing to near the Warrenton turnpike, were posted in line of battle on the
left of the road. General Pope says, in his official
report :

"By this time General McDowell had arrived on the
field, and I pushed his corps immediately to the front,

along the Warrenton Turnpike, with orders to fall upon the enemy, who was retreating toward the pike from the direction of Sudley Springs. The attack along the turnpike was made by King's division at about sunset; but by that time the advance of the main body of the enemy, under Longstreet, had begun to reach the field, and King's division encountered a stubborn and determined resistance at a point about three-fourths of a mile in front of our line of battle."

It was on the march from Manassas back towards Gainesville, that the incident narrated in the following letter occurred :

"HEADQUARTERS 20TH REGIMENT, N Y S. M.,
"SHARPSBURG, MD., Sept. 24, 1862.

"COLONEL HENDRICKS, Rondout, N Y

"*My Dear Sir :*—I was painfully shocked yesterday by receiving information of the death of your son, Captain J. T. Hendricks, of this regiment.

"I had formed a very warm attachment to him, and regarded him as one of our best and most promising officers. He was always anxious to do his duty to the uttermost, and was accounted one of the most thorough read and best drilled officers of the regiment, insomuch that whilst I was in temporary command last spring, I assigned to him the duty of drilling and instructing the non-commissioned officers.

"Our march from Fredericksburg to Cedar Mountain, and our retreat thence to Manassas, was too much for his physical endurance, and he broke down under it. He was sent to the hospital a few days before the battle of Manassas, and I hoped he was comfortably provided for, and would soon rejoin us with health restored. You may imagine my surprise when, on the morning of the battle, Captain Hendricks rejoined the regiment. I had not 'ime to inquire particularly where he had come from ; but it seemed he had walked some miles to

17

join us, and he was completely worn out. The reason he gave me for leaving his sick-bed and coming into the field was, that he understood there was to be a battle in which our regiment would be engaged, and he could not bear the thought of his company going into the action without him. It soon became evident, however, that Captain Hendricks was too ill to keep his feet ; and he was put into an ambulance ; and, after following the movements of the regiment for a time, was sent to the rear and thence to Washington.

"After the regiment crossed the Potomac, I went to Washington and saw the Captain in the hospital. He was well cared for, as I learned from himself and one of the volunteer nurses, who seemed very much interested in him. I left him expressing the hope that I should see him with the regiment again.

"I know he would have preferred to die on the field at the head of his company, but it was ordered otherwise ; and I feel that in his death I have lost the support of an ardent and gallant officer, and the society of an accomplished and amiable gentleman.

  * * * * * *

    "Truly yours,

      "THEODORE B. GATES,

       "*Colonel Commanding.*"

Porter was expected to attack the enemy's right near Gainesville ; but, up to half-past four o'clock, he had not delivered the meditated blow Pope then sent him the famous order, the alleged disobedience of which subjected Porter to a trial, and resulted in his being cashiered. The order was as follows :

"HEADQUARTERS IN THE FIELD,
"August 29, 4:30 P. M.

"MAJOR-GENERAL PORTER:

"Your line of march brings you in on the enemy's right flank. I desire you to push forward into action at once on the enemy's flank, and, if possible, on his rear, keeping your right in communication with General Reynolds. The enemy is massed in the woods in front of us, but can be shelled out as soon as you engage their flank. Keep heavy reserves, and use your batteries, keeping well closed to your right all the time. In case you are obliged to fall back, do so to your right and rear, so as to keep you in close communication with the right wing."

Pope supposed Porter would strike the enemy within an hour; and to distract his attention and hold his forces on his left, he ordered Heintzleman and Reno to attack. They did so at half-past five, and doubled the left of the Confederate line back toward its centre; and, in the end, held the scene of the conflict, with the enemy's dead and wounded. It was the effect of this gallant assault, probably, that induced Pope to believe the enemy were "retreating toward the pike," when he ordered McDowell to attack.

Porter did not fire a gun. With the freshest, finest corps in the army, he lay all the afternoon within smelling distance of the smoke of the battle-field, knew his fellow soldiers were engaged in a doubtful struggle for victory over an able chieftain; that Pope was expecting every moment to hear the thunder of his cannon on the enemy's right, and that the issues of the fight might depend upon his action—yet Porter did not fire a gun!

Porter had disobeyed the order of August 27th, requiring him to be at Bristoe at daylight next morning; he disobeyed the order of August 29, 3 A.M., requiring him to move at the first dawn of day; and now he had disobeyed this order, given in the very heat of battle, and lay upon his arms without firing a gun, while the conflict was raging within cannon shot of him.

Fitz-John Porter should have been tried by drum-head court-martial ; and, if these charges were established, he should have been shot within forty-eight hours thereafter. The example would have been worth a hundred thousand men to the Union cause—it would have saved the lives of a hundred thousand men. Disregard of orders was the crying evil in the Federal army throughout the war until Grant took command. Campaigns miscarried, and battles were lost, because subordinates assumed the responsibility of disobeying the orders of their superiors, and acting on their own judgments. War can never be successfully carried on on any such principle as this, except at great sacrifice, and the Federals experienced it to a lamentable degree. There were a dozen notable instances of it in this campaign ; and they implicate Banks, Sigel, King, and Porter ; but Porter's offence overshadowed the others, and was repeated again and again. In the case of General Banks, his disobedience was of that quality that wins forgiveness, because it was on the side of gallantry and in the pursuit of victory ; but Porter's was of that base character that offers no redeeming features, and is explainable upon but one of two theories—cowardice or disloyalty It matters not whether it was provoked by disrespect of Pope, and was designed to subject him to the ignominy of defeat ; for on that field disloyalty to Pope was disloyalty to the Government, and it was "aid and comfort" to the enemy.

Porter and his apologists seek to excuse his failure to attack upon the ground, in the first place, that the order of 4:30 did not reach him until 6:30. Assuming this to be so, although on Pope's side it is claimed that Porter received it much earlier ; still, it left an hour and a half of daylight, and if Porter was in the position he was supposed to occupy, he had time to strike an effective blow before it became too dark for troops to manœuvre. Another reason urged in extenuation of Porter's delinquency is, that Longstreet was in front of him, and therefore the proposed movement was hazardous ; that it would involve a battle with other forces than those Pope supposed to occupy the right of the enemy's line. This is equivalent to saying, that "because the enemy had increased in numbers, and an attack was therefore more dangerous, the freshest and best corps of the army should lie idly by, and leave its comrades to meet and bear the whole brunt of the battle." The moral effect of a vigorous attack by Porter, even if unsuccessful, would have stimulated and aided the Union troops engaged on his right ; and would, in an equal degree, have discouraged and demoralized the Confederates, and the results would more than have neutralized any losses which he might have sustained.

Longstreet says the head of his column reached the field about eleven o'clock on the morning of the 29th, and his last division (Anderson's, of three brigades) did not arrive until after dark. These troops had marched, almost continuously for twenty-four hours, through heat and dust, and were not in a condition to make a long or vigorous fight, and Porter graciously allowed them a resting spell. They were quite fresh in the morning.

But *why* should it have been necessary to send an order to Porter to attack at 4:30 ? At three o'clock that morning Pope had notified him of the imminence of a battle, and the importance of his putting in his corps. Why should he have loitered all day in the rear? He was a West Pointer, and a regular army officer, and why should he have needed an order *at all* to put his splendid corps into action ? The business there was *fighting*, and Pope's orders were, practically, "Fight, fight, fight." But again, why *wait for orders ?* Porter ought to have been familiar with the only maxim applicable in such a case, "March toward the sound of the cannon."

Assuming that Porter was not influenced by so grovelling an instinct as cowardice, it may be asked, "What motive could have induced him to disobey orders, stay out of the fight, and risk the sacrifice of the Union army?" Let us see if the following facts throw any light upon this question :

Pope's orders on taking command of the Army of Virginia contained some expressions that McClellan and nis friends regarded as reflections on the cautious policy of that officer. Moreover, Pope had suggested to the Administration the appointment of a General-in-Chief, and was, therefore, to some extent, responsible for the displacement of McClellan and the appointment of General Halleck.

So it came to pass, that General McClellan, who was watching the proceedings at the capital in his rear quite as closely as he was the Confederate army lying between him and the rebel capital in his front, imagined that Pope was his rival, and was gaining an ascendancy over him in the favor of the Administration. A great victory by Pope would assure that ascendancy, and perpetuate that influence. The loss of an army, or a year's prolongation of the war, were evils less to be dreaded, in the judgment of the select McClellan coterie, than the obscuration of the brilliant military luminary who commanded the Army of the Potomac.

The Seven Days' battles had been fought, and McClellan had been hurled back from the gates of Richmond, and, when Pope's campaign began, lay behind entrenchments thirty miles from the city. Pope had taken command of the newly organized "Army of Virginia," and advanced to Culpepper Court House. His army was less than 50,000 men. McClellan's yet numbered 85,000. The Confederate army, flushed with victory over McClellan, lay between him and Pope, ready to strike in either direction. McClellan would not co-operate with Pope, and declined Pope's offer of conference and mutual support. In those untoward circumstances, Pope asked the Administration to relieve him of command in Virginia : or, declining that, to appoint a General-in-Chief, who would be the superior of both himself and McClellan, and who could direct *all* military operations.

As McClellan was disinclined to advance without re-enforcements that would strip Washington of an adequate defence, the Administration resolved to recall the Army of the Potomac from the Peninsula ; and, on the 3d of August, 1862, General Halleck telegraphed McClellan to withdraw to Aquia Creek, and directed him to take *immediate* measures therefor.

To receive an order and *obey* it, without question or evasion, was not in the nature of General McClellan ; and, in answer to this dispatch, he wished to know, among other things, " the intention of the Government in regard to this army." The army had now been lying in camp something over a month, and its commander had reported it in fine condition and eager for battle ; but he himself seemed to have no use for it. The President sententiously declared, a few months before, that " If General McClellan had no use for the army, he would like to borrow it." And, possibly, McClellan thought Mr. Lincoln had some such design now.

Notwithstanding the fact, that the order of August 3d required *immediate* obedience, and that the telegraph wires were kept hot with orders and urgent appeals for expedition, it was not until the 14th of the month that McClellan was able to announce to the General-in-Chief that " the movement has commenced."

McClellan had placed himself as far as possible from Pope's army, and refusing all overtures for co-operation, it only remained for the Administration to

load the army on shipboard again, and bring it back—
if McClellan would allow it.   I shall not discuss the
policy of a union of the two armies, at or near Fredericksburg, by marching towards each other across the
country, because the position that McClellan took up,
after Fair Oaks, rendered such an undertaking difficult.

On the 9th of August, Halleck telegraphed McClellan: "I am of opinion that the enemy is massing his
forces in front of Generals Pope and Burnside, and that
he expects to crush them and move forward to the
Potomac.   You must send re-enforcements instantly to
Aquia Creek.   Considering the amount of transportation at your disposal, your delay is not satisfactory ;
you must move with all possible celerity "

McClellan, as has already been said, had about
85,000 men at this time, who had been in camp along
the James River, thirty miles below Richmond, since
the beginning of July   Yet he seems to have been utterly ignorant of the position and movements of the
enemy in front of him, and was content to rely upon
telegrams from Washington for information of his ad
versary's operations.

The fact was, that Lee sent Jackson north with two
divisions of the army on the 13th of July, and on the
27th he was followed by A. P Hill's division.   On the
very day the above dispatch was sent to McClellan,
Jackson, with these three divisions of Lee's army   attacked Pope's advance, at Cedar Mountain, near Culpepper, and the severe battle heretofore described
ensued.

On the 10th of August, McClellan was informed
that the enemy was crossing the Rapidan in large force,
and that they were then fighting Pope.   In this telegram General Halleck charges McClellan with unnecessary delay in complying with former orders, looking to
the withdrawal of the Army of the Potomac from the
Peninsula, and says: "There must be no further delay

in your movements; that which has already occurred was entirely unexpected, and must be satisfactorily explained ; let not a moment be lost. * * *"

On the 12th, Halleck telegraphs McClellan : "There has been, and is, the most urgent necessity for dispatch, and not a single moment must be lost in getting troops in front of Washington." So it goes on, day by day, and McClellan is still on the Peninsula. Lee's forces have turned their faces to the north, and are marching toward the Rapidan, while McClellan is daily apprehensive of an attack by "overwhelming numbers," and dare not send his army away, except in small detachments, and in the most dilatory and cautious manner.

On the 21st, Halleck telegraphed McClellan that Burnside and Pope were hard pushed, and required aid as rapidly as he could send it, and asked him to come himself as soon as he could. He adds : "By all means see that the troops sent have plenty of ammunition. We have no time here to supply them. Moreover, they may have to fight as soon as they land."

McClellan answered this dispatch on the same day, and said he would *try* and get some of Franklin's troops aboard that night : he had sent ammunition forward, and hoped to get off himself the next day ; says he has ample supplies of ammunition for infantry and artillery, and he would have it up in time. On the *twenty-third*, 1.30 P.M., McClellan telegraphs Halleck *from Fortress Monroe*, as follows : "Franklin's corps has started. I shall start for Aquia in about half an hour." On the 24th, he telegraphs that he is at Aquia. In another dispatch, on the same day, he wants to know what his "command and position are to be."

General Halleck telegraphed McClellan on the 26th to come to Alexandria, some six miles from Washington, and between which places their subsequent telegraphic correspondence was carried on. On the 27th, Halleck informs McClellan that a general battle is imminent, and says, "Franklin's corps (now at Alexandria) should move out by forced marches. * * *" McClellan replies, "I have sent orders to Franklin to prepare to march at once," and that he had directed him to come to his headquarters to *talk about transportation*. This was very suspicious, and looked like the Peninsula tactics over again. If Franklin was going to do any good he had to *go at once*. Halleck replied at 12 M., "Franklin's corps should move out by forced marches, carrying with them four days' provisions, and to be supplied, as far as possible, by railroad."

At 1.25 P.M. McClellan telegraphs to know whether it "would not be advisable to throw the mass of Sumner's corps here, *to move with Franklin*." He thinks a disaster would leave troops on the lower Rappahannock in danger, and that they would do better service in front of Washington. This was evidently designed to frighten the Administration, as to the safety of Washington, and induce a countermand of the order for Franklin to march, or a suspension of the order until Sumner could be brought up—either course preventing Franklin aiding Pope. At 1.40 P.M. General McClellan telegraphs Halleck, that he learns that heavy firing has been heard that morning in the direction of Centreville, and wants to know if the works (around Washington) are finished and ready for defence. Assuming that Pope would be beaten, and designed to excite fears for the safety of the Capital. At 1.50 P.M. he telegraphs that "*Franklin's artillery has no horses, except for four guns without caissons. I can pick up no cavalry. In view of these facts, will it not be well to push Sumner's corps here by water as rapidly as possible*, to make immediate arrangements for placing the works in front of Washington in an efficient condition of defence ? * * Can Franklin, without his artillery or cavalry, effect any useful purpose in front ?" * * So suggestions and equivocations continue through the day and evening, and Franklin does not move.

On the morning of the 28th, Halleck adopts new tactics, and writes to Franklin that he parted with McClellan at two o'clock that morning, and that it was understood Franklin was to move to-day That if he had not received McClellan's order he should act on this.   At 1.05 p.m. McClellan telegraphs Halleck, that "The moment Franklin can be started with a reasonable amount of artillery he shall go." And he thinks the enemy so strong "as to make it necessary for us to move in force." To this Halleck replies that, "Not a moment must be lost in pushing as large a force as possible towards Manassas, so as to communicate with Pope before the enemy is re-enforced." At 7.30 p.m. General McClellan telegraphs to Halleck, "General Franklin is with me here (Alexandria). * * * *We are not yet in a condition to move; may be by to-morrow morning.*" And he again proceeds to urge the garrisoning of the works in front of Washington. In answer to a dispatch from Halleck, he telegraphs him at 6.15 p.m., "*Neither Franklin's nor Sumner's corps is now in condition to move or fight a battle.* It would be sacrifice to send them out now. * * I repeat that I will lose no time in preparing the troops now here for the field ; and that whatever orders you may give, *after hearing what I have to say*, will be carried out." Extraordinary condescension ! For nearly two days the General-in-Chief had been ordering and pleading that his subordinate would dispatch General Franklin to the assistance of his brother officer, known to be engaged with Lee's entire army, and upon the issue of the pending battles incalculable results were known to depend, and now, at the last moment, Halleck is told that neither Franklin nor Sumner can move. Neither of these corps had fired a gun since the first day of July. They had come up leisurely from Harrison's Landing—

most of the way by transports, and now, in this great emergency, were unfit for service, in the judgment of General McClellan.

It was a most discouraging business to attempt to get McClellan to throw any of his army towards Manassas, but Halleck persevered, and at 8.40 P.M., telegraphed, "There must be no further delay in moving Franklin's corps towards Manassas. They must go tomorrow morning, ready or not ready." McClellan answers this peremptory order, by a long telegram, in which he reiterates the statement as to want of horses, &c., but says, "Franklin has been ordered to march at six o'clock to-morrow morning." He then informed Halleck that he has learned that the enemy " with 120,000 *men*, intend advancing on the forts at Arlington and Chain Bridge, with a view to attacking Washington and Baltimore." McClellan seems to have assumed from the first that Pope was to be overcome, and he talks as though no other result were possible. With an army only half as large as the one with which McClellan had made the Peninsula Campaign, and confronted, as he was, by the army which had vanquished McClellan, it was but natural the latter should expect a similar misfortune to befall Pope. Did he wish it? McClellan foresaw that a victory for Pope would place him at the head of the army ; that Pope's defeat, and the advance of the Confederate army toward Washington, would force the Government to have recourse to himself, and would result in his restoration to power, if not in his reinvestment with authority, as General-in-Chief. It is hazarding nothing to say, in the light of known facts, that an immediate and cordial co-operation of General McClellan's army would have changed the defeat of the second Bull Run into a victory for the Union arms.

Franklin did really set out on the morning of the 29th of August. But McClellan was continually telegraphing Halleck to induce him to allow a suspension of the movement. At 12.08 P.M. he asks, "Do you wish the movement of Franklin's corps to continue ?" Again : "Franklin has but forty rounds of ammunition, and no wagons to move more. I do not think Franklin is in a condition to accomplish much, if he meets strong opposition. I should not have moved him but for your pressing orders of last night." Again, at 12.50 P.M. : "Franklin has only between 10,000 and 11,000 ready for duty. How far do you wish this force to advance ?" At 1.45 he telegraphs that he thinks Franklin ought not to go beyond Anandale. Halleck replies that he wants him to go far enough to find out something about the enemy, and adds, "Our people *must* move more actively and find out where the enemy is. I am tired of guesses." Franklin had gone but six miles.

President Lincoln, now, at 2.40 P.M., telegraphs to McClellan for news, and in reply McClellan gives what news he has, which is very meagre, and then adds : " I am clear one of two courses should be adopted ; first, to concentrate all our available forces to open communication with Pope ; second, to *leave Pope to get out of his scrape*, and at once to use all our means to make the capital perfectly safe." Then comes the key to all this diplomacy : "Tell me what you wish me to do, and I will do all in my power to accomplish it. *I wish to know what my orders and authority are.*"

At 7.50 P.M. of the 29th, Halleck telegraphs McClellan : " I have just been told Franklin's corps stopped at Anandale, and that he was this evening in Alexandria. This is all contrary to my orders." McClellan replies that *he did not think it safe* for Franklin to go beyond Anandale, until he knew what was at Vienna. That he is responsible for the halting of the corps and Franklin's presence in Alexandria, *but did not suppose it was contrary to orders.* He then adds : "Please give *distinct* orders in reference to Franklin's

movements *to-morrow.*" As though McClellan misun-
derstood the wishes of the General-in-Chief. As though
he did not know, even without orders, that Franklin's
place was at the front. As though he and his subordinates did not know it was treason to their Government,
and to their brother soldiers in the field, to hold the
splendid troops of Franklin in the leash, almost in
sound of the cannon, while a three days' battle was
raging but a few miles away.

Franklin did finally advance, but reached Centreville
only in time to meet Pope's retreating army, on the
evening of the 30th day of August, twenty-seven days
after McClellan had been ordered to withdraw from the
Peninsula, and four days after he had been directed to
send Franklin from Alexandria to the battle, a little
more than a day's march away, and with railroad communication to within six miles of the battle-field.

The foregoing narrative can leave no doubt upon
any unprejudiced mind, that McClellan was resolved
not to aid Pope, if he could help it, and save his own
position in the army In this unworthy purpose, Mc-
Clellan had the sympathy of a certain set of his corps
and division commanders, and Fitz-John Porter belonged to that set.

THE brunt of the attack by King's division, on the
evening of the 29th, was borne by Hatch's brigade,
which suffered severely. The enemy were found strongly posted in the edge of the woods, and their artillery
and musketry fire was murderous to the Union troops,
who had to cross a broad, open field from the Federal
line up to the very muzzle of the rebel guns. The repulse was so severe and the position so exposed that it
was impossible to remove our wounded, and they lay
all that night and through the next day, between the
lines and in view of both sides, unable to help themselves and beyond the help of their comrades. The
poor fellows would signal for aid during the 30th, but
it would have been death to approach them from our
side. The twenty-four hours during which they lay on
the field, suffering from wounds and dying of thirst,
with the roar of battle in their ears and shells rushing
over and bursting around them, must have seemed an
eternity of misery The red trousers of the Brooklyn
Fourteenth were conspicuous among the dead and
wounded.

It was late in the evening when the division of King
got back into its position in line of battle ; the night
had become excessively dark, and the utmost difficulty
was experienced in finding our way While pausing

for a subdued conference, for we were at last in doubt whether we were approaching our own line or the enemy's, a body of cavalry dashed by the front of Patrick's brigade, discharging their carbines as they passed the right of the brigade, and shooting Lieutenant Bouvier, one of General Patrick's aids, through the body It was not known whether the fire was from friend or foe, and therefore it was not returned. General Patrick ordered the brigade to lie down, and Lieutenant-Colonel Gates went forward to find our line of battle ; he came upon the line in front of the Ohio brigade of General McLean, whom he chanced to know. The General had heard the movement of troops in his front and the rush and fire of the cavalry. He did not understand it, but as we were approaching him from the direction of the enemy, he had put his brigade under arms, and they were now drawn up, ready for battle. The situation was explained, our place in line found, a little to the left of General McLean, and the brigade marched into it at eleven o'clock.

Pope's losses on the 29th were very large ; probably not less than 7,500 killed and wounded. Generals Hooker and Kearney, who went over the battle-field from whence the enemy had been driven on our right, estimated the Confederate loss at least two to one of the Federals.

During the night of the 29th, and up to ten o'clock of the morning of the 30th, the impression was prevalent at several corps and division headquarters of the Union army, that the Confederates were retreating. On the evening of the 29th, Generals McDowell and Heintzleman reconnoitred the positions held by the enemy's left during the day, and they found they had been evacuated, and there was every indication that he was retreating in the direction of Gainesville. Paroled Union prisoners, who came into our lines on the morning of 30th, confirmed the impression of a retreat, and

General Pope, himself, became persuaded that the enemy was withdrawing.

These indications of a retreat existed, but they were misinterpreted by the Federal officers. Jackson had shortened his line towards his right, whereby McDowell and Heintzleman were misled, and Longstreet, who had made a strong reconnoissance at dark, on the evening of the 29th, withdrew his forces a half mile to the rear after midnight, and the Confederate line of battle for the next day was then established.

The 29th had been warm and sultry ; the Federal troops had been marching or fighting from early in the morning—some of them having marched nearly all of the preceding night. The skirmishes along the lines had been kept up until late in the evening, and very little rest or sleep was obtained during the night. They had had little to eat for the two previous days, and no opportunity to build fires and make coffee. The result was, that on the morning of the thirtieth the Federals were not in a condition for the most active and efficient service. The "Twentieth" had been without a full ration since the morning of the twenty-eighth.

The destruction of the cars and contents, at Manassas Junction, had produced an unlooked-for deficiency in supplies for man and beast, and General Pope telegraphed to General Halleck, on the twenty-eighth, for rations and forage. General Halleck directed General McClellan to forward the required articles, from Alexandria, where the stores were abundant, and at daylight on the 30th, General Pope received a note from General Franklin, written by direction of General McClellan, of which the following is a copy :

August 29, 1862, 8 P. M.

To the Commanding Officer at Centreville :

I have been instructed by General McClellan to inform you that he will have all the available wagons at
Alexandria, loaded with rations for your troops, and
all of the cars, also, as soon as you will send in a cavalry escort to Alexandria as a guard to the train.

Respectfully,

W B. FRANKLIN,
Maj.-Gen., Commanding Sixth Corps.

To comment upon this letter would be a work of
supererogation ; yet I cannot forbear a word. Pope's
army was in front of an enemy by which McClellan's
had been beaten on the Peninsula, a few weeks before.
Nine days of battle, skirmishes and marches had just
taken place, and the cavalry had been reduced to less
than a regiment of effective men. Eighty-five thousand
Confederates were closing in around Pope's army of
less than fifty thousand men. Alexandria was swarming with troops of all arms, fresh and well fed, and yet,
before General McClellan would send the supplies
necessary to feed the army at the front, he required
" the commanding officer," whose name he seemed not
to know, to detach a force of cavalry from his army, to
act as escort to a *railroad train.*

Ricketts' division, which we left at Thoroughfare
Gap on the twenty-eighth, had failed to accomplish the
purpose McDowell had in view in sending it there, pri-
marily, because it reached the objective point too late.
Ricketts found, on approaching the Gap, that the
enemy had already taken up strong positions in the
narrow pass, and occupied the crowning heights ; but
he pushed boldly on, and engaged them in an action
which continued until dark ; meantime, finding this
obstinate obstruction at Thoroughfare, the enemy threw

a large body of his forces through the mountain, at the more difficult pass of Hopewell Gap, three miles east of Thoroughfare, which was unguarded, and through which his legions poured. This movement turned Ricketts' right, and he was forced to retire from Thoroughfare, but was unable to rejoin his corps until the evening of the twenty-ninth.

During the morning of the thirtieth, each army appeared to be waiting for its opponent to take the initiative, and with the exception of artillery firing, and an occasional infantry skirmish, quiet prevailed along the lines. About ten o'clock Patrick's brigade was marched to the right, and posted in a piece of woods, in support of Sigel. Here the brigade remained, under artillery fire, until about two P.M., when it was ordered to return to its position on the left, preparatory to its participation in a contemplated attack upon the enemy's position. As Patrick's brigade moved down the line, from right to left, the manifestations of exultation over the supposed flight of the enemy were very conspicuous. The writer distinctly remembers encountering several general officers who declared in exultant tones that the enemy was in full flight. Our stretcher-bearers were marching in rear of their several regiments, with stretchers in hand, and we were subjected to some derision because we were prepared to remove our (possible) wounded from the field to which we were marching. General Warren, especially, ridiculed the idea of such preparations, and asserted that we would not get near enough to the enemy to exchange shots with them. All these predictions proved groundless. The enemy was not only *not* retreating, but seemed to have no intention of doing so.

About two o'clock in the afternoon, Pope determined to deliver a blow along the enemy's front and flank, which he believed would accelerate his flight and crown

the operations of the Union army with the laurels of
victory

Reaching the vicinity of Groveton, Patrick's brigade
was formed for the attack, in two lines. The first line
was composed of the Twenty-first New York Volunteers on the right, and Thirty-fifth New York on the
left. Second line, Twentieth New York State Militia
on the right, and the Twenty-third New York Volunteers on the left. It was after three o'clock when the
order was given to advance. The two lines moved forward through an open field to the woods, in which the
enemy was known to have been swarming the night before, but who now gave no sign of his presence. As we
entered the woods, we found the Fourteenth Brooklyn
and the Thirtieth New York Volunteers, Colonel Fris-
bie, formed on our right. The line was extended towards the left by General Porter's corps, which now,
for the first time, came into action. The enemy allowed
us to advance two hundred yards into the woods, without giving us a shot ; then, when our lines had reached
a point within blank range of the railroad embankment
heretofore mentioned, they opened a murderous fire,
apparently in the very face of our men, from behind
the embankment. The first line melted away under
this destructive fire, and the second line then received
the full force of the leaden tornado ; the enemy's artillery, posted on high ground in rear of his infantry line,
and at openings at various points, opened their fire, and
shot and shell came crashing through the woods, cutting down trees and men alike. It was impossible for
the Union troops to do any very effective work upon
their adversaries, by reason of the admirable protection
afforded to them by the railroad embankment, unless
they could carry this line by a charge. This was attempted, but the fire was too heavy for men to endure,
and they were forced to fall back. If the ground in
front had been open between our line and the embank-

ment, the Federals could have cleared it in a rush, before the Confederates could have delivered more than one or two rounds; but the trees, the lower limbs of which had been cut off so that the Union line was clearly distinguishable to the Confederates lying along the embankment, from the breasts of the men downwards, had the higher branches remaining, and the Federals could not see twenty feet before them, except they stooped so low as to render it difficult to use their arms.

A second and a third time they tried to reach the hidden foe, but they were each time repulsed with heavy loss. When they had been driven back a third time, and while standing in line of battle, irresolute whether to make one more attempt to penetrate the thicket and reach the enemy, whose shots were still rattling around them, an aide of General Porter appeared upon the scene, with an order for the troops to retire. They withdrew leisurely and in perfect order, but with the brigades and regiments somewhat separated by the march through the woods and the several movements which took place among the dense trees. The enemy followed the retiring Federals, but when they reached the open country they were met by so destructive a fire of artillery and musketry that they threw themselves flat upon the ground. Our gunners soon got range of them, and they were forced to arise and escape to their cover in the woods, which they did with heavy loss. This, practically, was the end of the second battle of Bull Run, and the last rays of that August sunset shone upon a weary, battle-stained and discomfited army emerging from the woods and filing in sullen silence across the bridges and through the fords of fatal Bull Run. There were thousands of brave fellows missing from the ranks, who never would answer at roll-call again. They had fought their last fight, and had paid the highest price man can pay for his country; other thousands lay wounded and helpless in the fields and woods where the combat had raged, and darkness fell like a pall upon the scene of carnage, and the dead and wounded had possession of the field.

It was in this fight in the woods, where Colonel Pratt received his death-wound. Colonel Pratt proposed to take charge of the left wing of the regiment, and directed the Lieutenant-Colonel to look after the right. With this hurried interview we separated, and I never saw the Colonel afterwards. He was wounded early in the battle, and was taken from the field and removed to Washington, and from thence to Albany, where he died on the eleventh of September following.

The Twentieth retired leisurely toward Bull Run, and at the crossing of that stream at the Stone Bridge, they had the good fortune to find a commissary engaged in the business of issuing fresh meat. He was persuaded to extend his attentions to the Twentieth, although he belonged to Franklin's corps. It was the first fresh meat we had had in a week, and the first mouthful we had eaten during the day The retreating army was ordered to rendezvous at Centreville, but the roads were crowded with men, artillery, and cavalry, rendering marching very difficult and tedious ; therefore, after crossing Cub Run, three miles west of Centreville, the Twentieth filed to the left, and, marching a few hundred yards up the stream, bivouacked, and remained there until daylight, and then proceeded to Centreville and joined the brigade.

CHAPTER XX

SUNDAY, the thirty-first of August, was a rainy and
sultry day. The army was utterly worn out, and, fortunately for us, the enemy was in a condition but very
little better. Pope made his disposition to repel any
attack that Lee might make on him by posting his
troops at the most defensible points around Centreville.
Porter was assigned to the intrenchments on the north,
or right ; Franklin was posted on his left, and in rear,
between Porter and Franklin, Heintzleman's corps was
stationed ; while Sigel held the works on the south side
of the town, with Reno on the left and rear. Banks
was posted on the easterly side of Bull Run, and in disposition to cover the left flank of the army and the railroad bridge across that stream. Sumner, who arrived
that day, was stationed between Centreville and Chantilly ; while McDowell occupied the road from Centreville to Fairfax Court House.

The enemy's cavalry appeared in considerable force,
in front of our advance, at Cub Run, on the morning of
the thirty-first, but made no attempt to cross. A little
artillery firing took place, but there was no fighting
during the day. Officers were engaged in ascertaining
their losses and reorganizing and supplying their commands with rations and ammunition.

Pope's army, at Centreville, on the morning of the

279

first of September, embraced McDowell's corps of 10,000 ;
Sigel's corps of about 7,000 ; Heintzleman's corps of
about 6,000 ; Reno's, 6,000 ; Banks', 5,000 ; Sumner's
(just arrived), 11,000 ; Porter's, 10,000 ; and Franklin's
(came up on the evening of 30th), 8,000—making a total
of 63,000 men—a larger army, by ten thousand, than
Pope fought the battle of the thirtieth with. In view
of this fact, it may be asked : " Why did not General
Pope renew the fight after these re-enforcements had
joined him. The enemy's force was greatly reduced
and exhausted by the battles and marches which it had
undergone within the last ten days, and was there not
ground for a reasonable hope of success, if Pope had
forced the enemy to renew the battle on the second or
third of September ? "

Pope's experience with the commanders of some of
the newly arrived troops did not encourage him to hope
for a cordial and efficient support from these Peninsula
veterans. Of Generals Heintzleman, Hooker, Kearney
and Reynolds he speaks in the highest terms ; but in a
letter to General Halleck, written from Centreville, September 1, he thus speaks of certain other officers of the
Army of the Potomac : " I think it my duty to call your
attention to the unsoldierly and dangerous conduct of
many brigade and some division commanders of the
forces sent here from the Peninsula. Every word and act
and intention is discouraging, and calculated to break
down the spirits of the men and to produce disaster. One
commander of a corps, who was ordered to march from
Manassas Junction to join me near Groveton, although
he was only five miles distant, failed to get up at all ; and
worse still, fell back to Manassas without a fight, and
in plain hearing, at less than three miles distance, of a
furious battle which raged all day   It was only in consequence of peremptory orders that he joined me the
next day. One of his brigades, the Brigadier-General of
which professed to be looking for his division, abso-

lutely remained all day at Centreville, in plain view of
the battle, and made no attempt to join. What ren-
ders the whole matter worse, these are both officers of
the regular army, who do not hold back from ignorance
or fear. Their constant talk, indulged in publicly and in
promiscuous company, is that ' the Army of the Potomac will not fight ;' that they are demoralized by withdrawal from the Peninsula, &c. When such example
is set by officers of high rank, the influence is very bad
among those in subordinate stations. You have hardly
an idea of the demoralization among the officers of high
rank in the Potomac army, arising, in all instances,
from personal feeling in relation to changes of Commander-in-Chief and others. These men are mere tools
or parasites, but their example is producing, and must
necessarily produce, very disastrous results. You
should know these things, as you alone can stop it. Its
source is beyond my reach, though its effects are very
perceptible and very dangerous."

Pope's army was re-victualed and given a much-
needed day's rest at Centreville. Its numbers and attitude, and the naturally strong position it occupied, admonished the Confederate leader of the impolicy of an
attack. But during the day and night of the thirty-
first, Lee dispatched Jackson, by a broad detour around
Pope's right, with orders to strike the Little River
Turnpike, and again cut his communications near Fairfax Court House. It was a repetition of the strategy of
the preceding week, but it lacked the energy and dash
which characterized its predecessor. The campaign had
told upon the physique of the Confederates, and had
greatly subdued their ardor. Moreover, their losses
had been very heavy, and they had no expectation of
re-enforcements, while they were aware their adversary
had already been considerably strengthened, and they
knew not how formidable his army might become
before they could bring him to battle.

General Lee was not remarkable for his tenacity in pursuit after his opponent had once been brought to bay and had delivered battle. His energy for offensive operations seemed to expend itself in the crisis of a great combat. Indeed, there were no instances on either side on which a pursuit of the defeated army was pressed with vigor and persistency, looking to the capture or destruction of the fleeing foe, except in Grant's pursuit of Lee, after the evacuation of Petersburg.

To check this flank movement, and to protect his communications, Pope threw a portion of his troops into Fairfax Court House, and Patrick's Brigade was ordered out on the Little River Turnpike, towards Germantown, about two miles northwest of Fairfax Court House, and near the road running from the Little River Pike to Flint Hill.

The brigade marched from Centreville at three o'clock on the morning of September 1st. It had rained the preceding day and night, and the roads were heavy We reached Fairfax Court House, seven miles from Centreville, soon after daylight, and halted for breakfast. This over, we were ordered to return to Centreville, and had marched two miles in that direction, when the head of the column encountered General Joe Hooker, who had been assigned to the command in that locality, and who ordered the brigade to face about and return to Fairfax Court House ; reaching which place once more, we were directed to the position, on the Pike, above mentioned.

We found the point of intersection of the Flint Hill Road with the Little River Turnpike very well fortified by earth-works, thrown up by the Confederates during their occupation of the place the preceding winter, and Patrick's Brigade took possession of them, and remained in them until about three o'clock in the afternoon. At that hour General Patrick said to Lieutenant-Colonel Gates, "General Hooker has sent an order for one of my best regiments to report to him, at once, on the Little River Turnpike, and I am going to send you." The Twentieth fell in and marched up the Turnpike about a mile, where General Hooker and staff and a squadron of cavalry were found watching the movements of the enemy, who had appeared on the road and in the fields, at the edge of a piece of woods, a mile farther up the pike, and who were planting a battery behind a ridge, near the woods. The ground they occupied was considerably higher than that where General Hooker was, and from thence fell away in their rear, enabling them, by the aid of the woods, to conceal their strength. Opposite Hooker, on the south side of the pike, was an open woods extending westwardly, in the direction of this Confederate force, a half mile, and beyond that the country was cleared up to the woods occupied by the enemy General Hooker directed Colonel Gates to enter the woods near him and march rapidly to the west edge and take position there, and "hold it at all hazards."

The regiment was certainly not formidable in point of numbers, and Colonel Gates' countenance must have expressed as much, for General Hooker remarked, in answer to a look, "Oh, I will support you; I will support you." The regiment moved as fast as possible through the woods, and approaching the farther side, found the enemy's skirmishers advancing rapidly, and within 150 yards of the woods, the cover of which they wished to gain. The Twentieth, with the exception of a small reserve from each company, was at once deployed as skirmishers, and extended, as far as practicable, along the edge of the woods, giving the appearance of a large force. They opened fire at once on the approaching enemy, and compelled them to fall back. But taking advantage of the inequalities of the ground, and seeking cover wherever they could, they kept up a steady fire for two hours. Meantime, a mountain howitzer was brought forward, supported by a body of cavalry, to within range of the woods, and opened a vigorous fire with grape and canister. A small party of sharpshooters from the regiment was sent across the pike into a corn-field, from whence they picked off some of the gunners and its supports, and the piece was withdrawn. Soon, however, the enemy opened upon the regiment with shot and shell from their guns on top of the hill spoken of above, and thoroughly shelled the woods, but their infantry found, whenever they essayed to advance, that the fire from the woods was as vigorous as ever; and about five o'clock they fell back out of range, and their artillery fire ceased. Almost immediately thereafter heavy artillery and musketry firing opened in the woods in front of us, and apparently well over towards the Centreville Road. This combat was very severe, and continued until dark. The Union troops engaged were the forces of Generals Hooker, McDowell, Reno, Stevens and Kearney, the two latter of whom were killed. In the midst of this fight a furious thunderstorm took place, and earth and heaven seemed engaged in a fearful Titanic battle. Darkness put an end to this engagement—the storm in the heavens passed away, and the fierce human struggle in the dense woods ceased ; quiet reigned on the earth, and the stars glimmered in the blue vault above, invoking peace and good among men.

At ten o'clock we were relieved by the Ninetieth Pennsylvania Volunteers, Colonel Lislie, and returned to the brigade, whither a report had preceded us that the regiment was nearly annihilated, the commanding and most of the other officers killed. Colonel Gates aroused General Patrick's Adjutant-General from a sound sleep to report his return and to inquire for orders. Rubbing his eyes a minute, and staring at his interlocutor as though he would assure himself of the identity of the person, he finally ejaculated: "Why,

Colonel, is it really you? I was never more surprised in
my life. We had a positive report of your death four
hours ago, and we had all given you up as lost. I am
very glad to see you alive." "Well, Captain, the report did not seem to have made you very unhappy, for
I must confess you were the soundest asleep man I have
seen in three months. One would not have supposed
you had the slightest concern about anything or anybody from the childlike slumber in which I found you
five minutes ago." "Colonel, the fact is one can't
afford to make himself sleeplessly miserable over the
casualties that befall his friends in such scenes as we
are passing through. Friends and acquaintances are
dropping all around us, and we have come to regard it
as the natural and inevitable fate of soldiers. We murmur a regret, and in the hurry and excitement of the
next hour almost forget that they ever lived." This
was not very consoling, but it was a true expression of
the effect produced upon the emotional part of ones'
nature by participating in scenes of carnage and savage
warfare.

Lee's turning movement proved abortive, and his
forces were driven back with heavy loss. But Pope
considered it advisable, for the reasons mentioned in
the foregoing extract from his letter to General Halleck,
that the army should be drawn back to the entrenchments in front of Washington, and at twelve o'clock of
the second of September the movement began. The
Twentieth left Fairfax Court House at two o'clock P.M.,
and bivouacked at ten, a few miles from Upton's Hill.
The next morning we marched into our old camp, on
the Hill, and settled down like a family who had made
a long, fatiguing and disastrous journey, and had once
more arrived at home, with numbers so greatly diminished that they found their old quarters too large for
them, and two hundred and three names on the roll
against which was written "killed" or "wounded."

CHAPTER XXI.

OUR sojourn in the old quarters was restless and
brief. On the day following our return to them, we
were ordered to the front to repel a party of rebels who
had appeared at Bassett's Hill, and whose artillery had
driven in our cavalry out-posts. The enemy withdrew
without hazarding a brush with our infantry, and the
"Twentieth" remained out on the picket-line during
the night and part of the next day

At ten o'clock on Saturday night, the sixth of September, we received orders to march forthwith, and the
regiment was soon in line awaiting the final command to
move. Not receiving it for half an hour, arms were stacked, and the men lay down beside their muskets, while the
officers sauntered along the line, wondering how long
they were to wait and where they were to go. At two
o'clock in the morning the order came, and the familiar

cry "fall in!" aroused the sleepers, and in a few minutes we bade a final farewell to Upton's Hill, and, facing toward the eastern horizon, where there was yet no
sign of the morning sun, marched over the road we first
traversed in the Old Dominion, as far as Ball's Cross
Roads, and from thence, *via* Aqueduct Bridge, across
the Potomac to Georgetown, down Pennsylvania Avenue
through Washington to Seventh street, and filing into
that street as the sun began to show itself in the east,
we soon left the " City of magnificent distances " behind
us.   And at five o'clock that afternoon, about fifty officers and men of the regiment found themselves together
at Leesboro, in Maryland, at which point we were
ordered to halt for the night.

The distance marched by the "Twentieth" was
only sixteen miles.   It had on several former occasions,
and did, often afterwards, make nearly twice that distance in the same number of hours, and every man answered to his name at roll-call at the end of the march.
But here was an almost total disruption of a regiment
which prided itself somewhat upon being able to make
long marches and hold together to the end.   Probably
no other troops marched an equal number of consecu-
tive miles, in such an impenetrable cloud of dust as enveloped and blinded and suffocated the First and Ninth
Corps of the Army of the Potomac on that memorable
and distressing occasion.   Certainly they never before
or afterwards had anything like so terrible an experience.   There had been no rain for a long time ; the road
was broad and the surface was covered with a fine flour-
like dust, ankle deep ; the day was excessively warm
and the air utterly stagnant ; for miles this road was
crowded with marching men, with horses, army wagons,
gun carriages, caissons, ambulances, and all the *impedimenta* of an army, which completely filled it from side
to side.   For a time officers attempted to keep their respective commands together, but it finally became im-

possible even to recognize one's own comrades, so dense
was the cloud of dust, and so dust-covered were officers
and men. So, companies and regiments became disin-
tegrated, and the fragments struggled on as best they
could, and found their regimental and company headquarters during the night, but it made a terribly severe
day's work for the troops. The "Twentieth" had men
enough present at the finish to make several stacks of
arms, and its silk and satin colors floated near the out-
spread blanket whereon was Regimental Headquarters.
We plumed ourselves upon these facts when we learned
from several other regimental commanders. that they
halted at night without their colors, and without men
enough present to form a stack of arms.

The march of the First Corps was sudden, and to
most of us unexpected. Where Lee was or what doing,
was unknown in our army except at and very near the
head of it, and it was generally supposed that we would
be given a breathing time and undergo a partial reorganization. Relying too confidently upon these expectations, many officers had sent for their families to come
to Washington, hoping to have a brief reunion with
loved ones from home before another campaign began.
Some were able to arrest the family movement by letter
or telegram, but in numerous other instances wives and
children were hurrying on to Washington, while the
husbands and fathers were launching forth on the Maryland campaign. The latter was our case, and wife and
child arrived in Washington the day after the regiment
marched through the city

The successes of General Lee in the recent operations
against the Army of the Potomac on the peninsula, and
against Pope's army at Bull Run, had induced the Confederate commander to cross the Potomac and plant his
army upon the soil of Maryland. This strategy was
expected to develop the disloyal sentiment of that
State and greatly augment the rebel army. It was one

of the delusions under which the South labored, that the State was ready to throw itself into the Confederate cause, the moment it saw an opportunity to deliver itself from the dominion of the Federal Government. The presence of a large and victorious Confederate army, certainly seemed to offer such an opportunity, but to the surprise and chagrin of General Lee, the people received him with great coolness, and there were no recruits for the invading army General Lee issued a proclamation to the people, assuring them the time had come for "the recovery of their liberties," but it was of no avail. They did not seem to appreciate the boon offered them, and they remained quietly at home or fled from the routes of his advancing columns.

General Lee seems to have supposed that the Federal Government had treated the people of Maryland with tyrannical severity, and that they were ready to rise in arms ; and that the Federal Government, conscious of its misdeeds towards this people, and having, therefore, to expect a revolt, so soon as they should be encouraged thereunto by the presence of the Confederate army, would feel constrained to retain the Union forces around the capital to protect it from this new and formidable danger. At all events, this only can be the meaning of General Lee's statement rendered to his government, as to the motives underlying this invasion. He says : "The condition of Maryland encouraged the belief that the presence of our army, however inferior to that of the enemy, would induce the Washington Government to retain all its available force to provide against contingencies which its course towards the people of that State gave it reason to apprehend."

The refugees from Baltimore had sung "My Maryland " in the streets of Richmond for months, and represented to Davis and Lee that all that the people of that State required to induce them to join the Confederacy, was the presence of a Confederate army within their bounds. Now they had it ; and behold, they seemed only anxious to get rid of it at the earliest moment ! Perhaps the external condition of the Confederate troops had something to do with the coolness of their reception. A host likes to see his guests in apparel becoming the individuals and honorable to the entertainer ; but here was a swarm of ragged and bare-footed veterans, whose filth and repulsive tatters bespoke the poverty of the Quartermaster's department, and the total absence of the habit of ablution. General Lee says in his Report of the Army of Northern Virginia (Vol. I, page 27) : " Thousands of the troops were destitute of shoes." General Jones, who commanded a division, says : " Never had the army been so dirty, ragged, and ill provided for, as on this march." (*Ibid.*, Vol. II, page 221). It was this army of *tatter-de-malions* that the Union forces had to come out to meet, regardless of the danger of an uprising in Maryland.

Lee's army had crossed the Potomac between the fourth and seventh of September, by the fords near Leesburg, and encamped in the country around Frederick. Lying in rear of Lee's army, and on his line of communication, by way of Shenandoah Valley, with Richmond, was a Union force of about nine thousand men, under Colonel D. H. Miles, at Harper's Ferry ; while Martinsburg and Winchester were held by a force of twenty-five hundred Federals, under General White. Lee desired unobstructed 'access to the Shenandoah Valley, and he supposed his movement on Frederick would induce the Federals to withdraw ("It had been supposed that the advance on Frederick would lead to the evacuation of Martinsburg and Harper's Ferry, thus opening the line of communication through the valley." Lee's Report Army Northern Virginia, Vol. I, p. 28). Besides the fact that these Union forces lay across Lee's most desirable line of communication with his base, they also constituted a continuous menace to

his rear and flank, and, in case of a reverse, might become a very dangerous factor in the situation of the
Confederate army.

Lee, therefore, determined to disperse or capture
these forces before he should be drawn into a general
battle with the Army of the Potomac. The Order of
General Lee, directing the movements of the troops detached for these purposes, is so characteristic of the
man, and such a revelation of the government and system that prevailed in this ragged army, that I venture
to insert it in full. It will be seen that the route of
march is designated, the time of arrival, the work to be
done, and the return to the army. This Order fell into
the hands of General McClellan on the thirteenth of
September, and while it was in process of execution.

" Special Orders No. 191.   )
"HEADQUARTERS ARMY OF NORTHERN VIRGINIA, }
                 " September 9th, 1862.)

"The army will resume its march to-morrow, taking
the Hagerstown road. General Jackson's command will
form the advance, and, after passing Middletown, with
such portion as he may select, take the route towards
Sharpsburg, cross the Potomac at the most convenient
point, and, by Friday night (the twelfth,) take possession of the Baltimore and Ohio Railroad, capture such of
the enemy as may be at Martinsburg, and intercept
such as may attempt to escape from Harper's Ferry

"General Longstreet's command will pursue the
same road as far as Boonsboro', where it will halt with
the reserve supply and baggage trains of the army.

"General M'Laws, with his own division and that of
General R. H. Anderson, will follow General Longstreet ; on reaching Middletown, he will take the route
to Harper's Ferry, and, by Friday morning, possess
himself of the Maryland Heights, and endeavor to capture the enemy at Harper's Ferry and vicinity.

"General Walker with his division, after accomplishing the object in which he is now engaged, will cross the Potomac at Cheek's Ford, ascend its right bank to Lovettsville, take possession of Loudon Heights, if practicable, by Friday morning ; Keys' Ford on his left, and the road between the end of the mountain and the Potomac on his right. He will, as far as practicable, co-operate with General M'Laws and General Jackson in intercepting the retreat of the enemy.

"General D. H. Hill's division will form the rear guard of the army, pursuing the road taken by the main body. The reserve artillery, ordnance and supply trains, &c., will precede General Hill.

"General Stuart will detach a squadron of cavalry to accompany the commands of Generals Longstreet, Jackson and M'Laws, and, with the main body of the cavalry, will cover the route of the army, and bring up all stragglers that may have been left behind.

"The commands of Generals Jackson, M'Laws and Walker, after accomplishing the objects for which they have been detached, will join the main body of the army at Boonsboro' or Hagerstown.

"Each regiment on the march will habitually carry its axes in the regimental ordnance wagons, for use of the men at their encampments to procure wood, &c.

"By command of GENERAL R. E. LEE.
"R. H. CHILTON,
"Assistant-Adjutant-General."

Pope's army and Burnside's corps had been consolidated with the Army of the Potomac immediately after the termination of Pope's campaign, and General McClellan had been assigned to the command. This army now numbered eighty-seven thousand one hundred and sixty-four men of all arms, exclusive of the corps of General Porter, which remained in Washington until the twelfth. McClellan's advance was made over five nearly parallel roads, which enabled him to cover both Washington and Baltimore from any movement down the east side of the Potomac. The army had been divided into wings; the right consisted of the First Corps, under General Hooker, and on his right the Ninth Corps under General Reno. This wing was commanded by General Burnside. The centre was composed of the Twelfth Corps under General Williams, and the Second Corps, Sumner's; the latter commanding the centre. The left wing consisted of the Sixth Corps and Couch's division of the Fourth Corps, and Syke's division of the Fifth Corps. General Pleasonton was in command of the cavalry, and covered the front of the army. General King's old division remained in the First Corps, but was now commanded by General Hatch, while General Patrick continued to command his brigade. Our army designation was: "First Brigade, First Division, First Army Corps."

From the night of the sixth of September, when we reached Leesboro, up to the morning of the fourteenth, we had made five short marches, aggregating forty-six miles, and for thirty-six hours we had been in bivouac on the banks of the Monocacy, near where the turnpike road from Frederick to Baltimore crosses the river. The pretty city of Frederick lay before us, across the river, "green-walled by the hills of Maryland."

The scenery from our bivouac was magnificent; the broad, rich plain through which the Monocacy flows was covered with troops and gorgeous with banners and all the paraphernalia of a mighty army. Beyond, and at the foot of the pine-covered mountain, Frederick lay; yesterday the sport of a rebel army, to-day, out-peopled by the encompassing Federal troops.

" Round about them orchards sweep,
  Apple and peach-trees, fruited deep ;
  Fair as a garden of the Lord,
  To the eyes of the famished rebel horde.

" On that pleasant day of the early Fall,
  When Lee marched over the mountain wall—
  Over the mountains winding down,
  Horse and foot into Frederick town,
  Forty flags! with their silvery stars;
  Forty flags! with their crimson bars
  Flapped in the morning wind; the sun
  Of noon looked down and saw not one."

Pleasonton's troopers struck the rebel rear-guard, as it was leaving Frederick on the afternoon of the twelfth, and skirmished with them all the way to South Mountain. We could distinctly hear the artillery, and, occasionally, volleys of musketry On Sunday morning the fourteenth, reveille was sounded at three o'clock, and at early daylight we resumed our march northward, passing through Frederick and Middletown, and reaching Catoctin Creek, which flows through the valley east of South Mountain about noon. The residue of the army was in position, then or soon after, along this valley

South Mountain is the name given to the mountain range on the north side of the Potomac, while the corresponding range on the south side is called Blue Ridge, the river having severed the range, in its way to the ocean.

South Mountain, covering the front of the army, was about a thousand feet in height, and its general direction from northeast to southwest. The national road from Frederick to Hagerstown crosses it nearly at right angles through Turner's Gap, a depression which is some four hundred feet in depth. On the north side of the road, the mountain is divided longitudinally into two crests by a narrow valley, which, although deep at the pass, becomes a slight depression a mile to the north. There are two country roads, one to the right and one to the left of the turnpike, which conduct to the two crests spoken of. The road on the right of the turnpike is called the " Old Hagerstown Road," and passes up a ravine about a mile from the turnpike, and then bending to the left over and along the first crest, enters the turnpike at the Mountain House, near the summit of the pass. The road on the left of the turnpike is called the " Old Sharpsburg Road," and is about a half a mile south of and parallel to the turnpike, until it reaches the crest of the mountain, when it bends to the left. Five miles south of Turner's Gap is Crampton's Gap, with a road leading through it from Burkittsville. In Pleasant Valley, west of the mountain range, are situated the villages of Boonsborough, Rohersville and Brownsville. Pleasant Valley is bounded westerly by Maryland Heights, which, starting from the Potomac, run northerly, nearly parallel with South Mountain, and terminate at Rohersville.

The right wing of the army drew up in front of Turner's Gap at noon, on the fourteenth of September, and found the enemy in possession of the pass, with artillery planted to command the turnpike and the plain at the foot of the mountain. Gibson's, and afterwards Benjamin's batteries, of Reno's corps, were placed in position on a high point of ground south of the turnpike, from whence they had a direct fire on the enemy's guns in the gap. The first brigade of Cox's division was sent up the " Old Sharpsburg Road," to gain the crest on that side, but the enemy were found in possession of it in strong force. The entire division of General Cox was then ordered to assault the position. At the same time, the Thirty-fifth New York Volunteers and the "Twentieth," (Patrick's brigade) were sent up the mountain side, on the right of the turnpike, to ascertain if the enemy occupied the ground, and to check any flank movement from that direction against Cox. After a severe struggle of an hour's duration, in which the losses on both sides were large, Cox's division carried the crest, and in spite of desperate efforts by the enemy to prevent it, established itself in this strong position.

The Thirty-fifth and Twentieth then rejoined their brigade, which, about two o'clock, was moved north, along the foot of the mountain about a mile and a half from the turnpike. The enemy opened a battery from the mountain side upon our column, and Cooper's battery "B," 1st Pennsylvania artillery, was placed in position, and for a while replied, but as its fire finally endangered our own troops as they advanced up the mountain, it was discontinued. The right wing of the army, excepting Gibbon's brigade, which was detached for the purpose of making a demonstration against the enemy's centre on the turnpike, and Ricketts' division which was held in reserve, now advanced up the mountain side, in line of battle, with a strong skirmish-line in advance.

The general order of battle in the attempt to carry the crest on the left of the Old Hagerstown Road, was for two regiments of Patrick's brigade to precede the main body, deployed as skirmishers, and supported by the two remaining regiments of the same brigade ; these to be followed by Phelps' brigade, two hundred paces in the rear, and this in turn to be followed by Doubleday's brigade, with the same interval. General Patrick deployed the 21st New York, under Colonel Rogers, as skirmishers, on the right, and the 35th New York, under Colonel Lord, on the left, supporting the former with the 20th N Y S. M., under Colonel Gates, and the latter with the 23d New York, Colonel Hoffman. General Patrick rode to the front with his skirmishers, drew the fire of the enemy, and developed their position.

The enemy opened a brisk musketry fire as the Union lines approached the summit of the mountain, but most

of their shot went over the heads of our men, doing execution only in the branches of the trees, among which
they rattled like hail stones. The enemy was found
posted behind a fence, near the summit of the mountain, running nearly north and south. The woods
through which the Union troops had made their advance
up the mountain side terminated at this fence, and beyond it was a cornfield full of rocky ledges, on some of
the higher of which the Confederates had planted cannon.

The Union troops pressed on until within fifty paces
of the fence, when the fire became very rapid on both
sides, but the Confederates still fired too high, and at
least 80 per cent. of their shot flew harmlessly over the
heads of the Federals. The trunks of the trees, among
which they were standing, received a large proportion
of the remaining 20 per cent., and the result was that
casualties were not large among the Union troops. On
the other hand, the Federal fire was very fatal to the
Confederates, notwithstanding the fact that they were
protected to some extent by a fence. The relative positions of the contending parties, would seem to give the
Confederates a great advantage, but a study of this battle, and of that of Lookout Mountain, Missionary
Ridge, and other instances in which the attacking party
ascended a steep mountain side, seem to prove that the
percentage of killed and wounded is much greater among
the troops stationed on the high ground than among
their assailants. The fact is, that unless troops have
been especially drilled in firing down the face of a mountain, they are sure to fire ninety per cent. of their shots
too high. Indeed, this is the fault of the best drilled
troops, as well as of tyros, on the most favorable ground
—they fire too high.

Some singular and interesting statistics have been
gathered, principally in Europe, to show the great waste
of ammunition that takes place in battle. The percent-

age of men disabled is astonishingly out of proportion
to the number of cartridges fired. It has been estimated
that from 3,000 to 10,000 balls were fired in European
armies to place one man *hors de combat.* Improved
fire-arms have somewhat diminished this gross disproportion between ammunition expended and results produced. But the best breech-loader or needle-gun ever
made will hurt nobody if it be fired at an angle of 45
degrees over the head of the man it is designed to hit.
Another curious fact in regard to the non-effectiveness
of arms, but from a very different cause, is that men
will put cartridge after cartridge into their guns, without firing one out of them. This is the result of inadequate drilling, nervousness or excitement. Men go into
battle feeling that the more ammunition they consume
the greater the chances of victory, and they load and
fire with the utmost rapidity—or continue to load without firing at all ; simply going through the motions and
supposing they have fired, but never having cocked their
guns or capped them. Of course, one shot deliberately
and effectively fired, would have contributed more
toward a victory than all this noise and wasted ammunition.

There were picked up on the battlefield of Gettysburg, 27,574 muskets, Union and Confederate, of which
24,000 were loaded. 12,000 contained two loads each,
and 6,000 were charged with from three to ten loads
each. One musket contained 23 loads, each charge
properly inserted. Oftentimes the cartridges were put
in the guns without being first broken, and sometimes
they were inserted wrong end first. But to return to
South Mountain :

The Confederate divisions of D. H. Hill and Longstreet were in possession of the position which the First
and Ninth corps essayed to carry, and they were composed of some of the best troops of Lee's army   Their
position was an exceedingly strong one, and they fought

until dark with great resolution. The fence along the east side of the cornfield had afforded the rebels an admirable cover, and they held on to it until nearly dark, when the Federals carried it by a gallant charge, capturing at the same time a number of prisoners. The ground along the inside of the fence was covered with rebel dead and wounded, and it was a matter of surprise to the Federals that their fire should have been so destructive, against an enemy seemingly so well protected. With the capture of the fence, the fighting practically ceased on this part of the field, and darkness prevented a further advance over such ground as lay in front of us. The enemy made an attempt to turn our left, but was repulsed, and the troops composed themselves for a little rest, after their hard day's work—ready, however, for battle, if the enemy should attempt to recover the position during the night.

While these events were transpiring on the right, there had, by no means, been inactivity or cessation of battle at the centre. General Wilcox's division was ordered to move up the Old Sharpsburg Road and take position to its right, overlooking the turnpike. While proceeding to execute this order, and when in the act of deploying to the right of the road, the enemy suddenly opened upon them at one hundred and fifty yards, with a battery which enfiladed the road at this point, and caused a temporary panic, in which a Union battery was nearly lost. Order, however, was soon restored, and the division formed line on the right of General Cox, already in position. The troops, however, were exposed to the fire of a battery in front, not only, but also to the batteries on the other side of the turnpike, and their loss was very heavy. The divisions of Generals Sturgis and Rodman were ordered to the support of Wilcox and Cox, and this entire force was ordered to move upon the enemy's position as soon as the First Corps was well advanced up the mountain, on the opposite side of the turnpike. This order was executed with enthusiasm and success. The enemy made a desperate resistance, charging our lines with fierceness, but they were everywhere routed, leaving the field covered with their dead and wounded. Here also, a last effort was made by the enemy to recover their lost ground, and about seven o'clock they made a furious assault along Sturgis' and a part of Cox's front. A lively fire was kept up until nearly nine o'clock, the enemy making several charges, but they were repulsed with great slaughter and finally compelled to withdraw. In connection with these movements on the right and left of the turnpike, General Gibbons' brigade had advanced up the turnpike itself. With one of his regiments deployed as skirmishers, stretching out on each side of the turnpike, and followed by the other regiments of the brigade in double column, they advanced steadily under a heavy fire. The enemy held stubbornly on to their position, but Gibbons constantly gained ground, until, finally, with this severe pressure on their front and the success of the Federals on their right and left, the Confederate centre gave way, and at nine o'clock on the evening of the fourteenth of September, the Federals were in possession of Turner's Gap and of the crests above it, dominating the turnpike. It was not believed the enemy would invite a renewal of the conflict on this ground.

The night of the fourteenth was exceedingly cold on the mountain top, and the officers and men of the "Twentieth" suffered severely in consequence. Overcoats and blankets had been left at the foot of the mountain when the ascent began, and they could not now be obtained nor could fire be allowed ; so, we huddled together and shivered through the night. As was expected, daylight showed that the enemy had retreated, leaving their dead and many of their wounded upon the field.

The divisions of Hill and Longstreet numbered about

thirty thousand men, and the Federal force opposed to them did not much exceed that number. The Federals captured about fifteen hundred prisoners, and the Confederate loss in killed and wounded was evidently much greater than ours, and a very large percentage of their killed were shot in the head. The Union loss was three hundred and twelve killed, twelve hundred and thirty-four wounded, and twenty-two missing. Among the Union killed was General Reno, and among the Confederates General Garland. In the afternoon of the fifteenth, the President telegraphed General McClellan as follows: "Your dispatch of to-day received. God bless you, and all with you. Destroy the rebel army if possible."

The victory of South Mountain was one of the most brilliant achievements of the Federals during the war. It involved very little strategy, but that little was bold and was carried out with energy and courage. The enemy had chosen his position, and it was an exceptionally strong one. The army before him he had recently beaten on the Peninsula and at Bull Run, under circumstances apparently much less favorable to him. But the position itself was misleading, as has already been shown, and the advantage of position, therefore, was only apparent. There were no manœuvres on the Union side, and no surprises of the enemy It was a victory won by square open fighting, where boldness, endurance and accuracy of fire won the day.

IT will have been observed that the movement of the
army from Washington to the line of the Monocacy,
was very gradual—very tardy Perhaps the responsibility for this was about equally divided between Halleck and McClellan. But it was the latter's business to
find out the position and design of the enemy, and to
manœuvre his army accordingly The means taken to
this end seem to have been utterly inadequate, and,
until Lee's order for the march on Harper's Ferry fell
into General McClellan's hands, he knew very little of
the location or movements of the Confederates. Nine-
tenths of the population of the western part of Maryland were loyal—McClellan had the Potomac river on
his left, which could be crossed by an army only at certain well-known points, and it seems as though it ought
to have been possible to procure speedy and accurate
information of the enemy's passage of that stream, and
the direction of his march after he threw his army into
Maryland.

As stated in the preceding chapter, Lee crossed the
Potomac between the fourth and seventh of September,
and drew up his forces around Frederick. The several
corps of the Army of the Potomac were on the latter day lying in divisions and brigades at Leesburg,
Rockville, Tenallytown, Offut's Cross Roads, Brook-

ville, Middleburg, Darnstown and at the Mouth of Seneca—the nearest within less than a day and the most remote not more than two days' march from Frederick. McClellan "supposed it would be necessary to force the line of the Monocacy," (Report of Army cf Potomac, p. 186,) and his dilatory movements gave the enemy abundant opportunity to compel him to fight his way across that stream, if they had chosen to do so. The river is a broad and deep one, and its passage in face of such an army as Lee commanded would have been difficult, if not impossible.

But McClellan's plans were yet unformed, and as late as eight o'clock, on the evening of the eighth of September, twenty-four hours after Lee had crossed, and when his entire army was advancing on Frederick, he telegraphed to General Halleck : ''I am by no means satisfied yet that the enemy have crossed the river (Potomac) in any large force.'' The positions of the Federal Army remained practically unchanged on the tenth, waiting for the enemy to develop himself or for General McClellan to mature a plan of campaign, and on this day he changed his views as to the locality of the enemy and telegraphed to the President as follows : ''The statements I get regarding the enemy's forces that have crossed to this side (Maryland), range from 80,000 to 150,000.'' This put a very different aspect on the situation of affairs, and if General Lee really had anywhere near the larger number of men given, he was numerically much stronger than McClellan; and if he had anywhere near the lesser number his losses must have been extraordinary and unaccountable, for he states that he fought the battle of Antietam ''with less than forty thousand men on our side.'' (Reports of Army of Northern Virginia, page 35.)

These exaggerated stories of the strength of the Confederates drove McClellan to his cautious and dilatory policy, and he began to call for re-enforcements. On the eleventh he telegraphed General Halleck that evidence from various sources goes to prove that "almost the entire rebel army in Virginia, amounting to not less than 120,000 men, is in the vicinity of Frederick." " * * They are probably aware that their forces are numerically superior to ours, by at least twenty-five per cent." (Report on Conduct of the War, Part 1, page 479.) General McClellan then asks that one or two of the three Army Corps opposite Washington be sent to him, and that Colonel Miles, commanding the garrison at Harper's Ferry also be directed to join him. At three o'clock and forty-five minutes, the same afternoon, he telegraphed to have the "Corps of Porter, Heintzleman and Sigel, and all the other old troops" sent to him. As to Colonel Miles, General Halleck replied : " There is no way for Colonel Miles to join you at present. The only chance is to defend his works until you can open a communication with him. When you do so he will be subject to your orders." Lee's army of 150,000 men, more or less, was between McClellan and Miles' 9,000 men, and if the former could not reach Miles, the latter could hardly have been expected to be able to reach McClellan.

To the residue of the dispatch the President responded the same day, and among other things said : " If Porter, Heintzleman and Sigel were sent to you it would strip everything from the other side of the river, because the new troops have been distributed among them ; as I understand it, Porter reports himself 21,000 strong. * * He is ordered to-night to join you as quickly as possible. I am for sending you all that can by spared, and I hope others can follow Porter very soon." On the 12th Halleck telegraphed McClellan : " Is it not possible to open communication with Harper's Ferry so that Colonel Miles' forces can co-operate with yours ?"

McClellan forbore to employ the tactics that a bold

and confident commander would have resorted to, under the circumstances in which he found himself placed. Such a commander would have pushed forward his left and interposed between Lee and his line of communication with his base, and his line of retreat in case of disaster. This would have been the initial object of the campaign for the reasons given, and it would have been the proper policy, also, in view of the position of Miles and White, whose forces should have been saved.

From the time McClellan possessed himself of Lee's Order he knew what his adversary's immediate tactics were, and he should have manœuvred to support the garrison at Harper's Ferry, not only, but to destroy the forces detached to operate against it—or he should have moved rapidly against Lee, himself, and overwhelmed him before the large force moving against Miles could succor him. Something more than energy was demanded of the Federal commander, by the circumstances of the case. There was needed boldness, dash, impetuousity —a rapid concentration of his forces on his left and a resistless assault of the passes of the mountain at Crampton's and at the Potomac itself. Crampton's Pass is but six miles south of Turner's, and debouches into Pleasant Valley, five miles from Maryland Heights, opposite Harper's Ferry In the pre-arranged order of march, the left wing of the Federal Army, under Franklin, was to cross South Mountain at Crampton's. On the evening of the thirteenth, McClellan communicated to Franklin the substance of Lee's Order, and urged him to "seize the pass if not occupied by the enemy in force." If so occupied he was directed to make his preparations for attack and commence it a half an hour after he hears severe firing at Turner's.

The rebel General McLaws, who commanded one of the divisions detached against Miles, learning of the approach of the Union forces to Crampton's, and at once appreciating the danger of allowing this force to get in his rear, sent back General Cobb, with three brigades, with orders to hold Crampton's Pass until the work at Harper's Ferry should be completed, "even if he lost his last man in doing it." (Reports of Army of Northern Virginia, Vol. II., Page 165.)

As late as two o'clock on the afternoon of the fourteenth, Franklin was held in check at Burkettsville, a hamlet at the foot of the mountain. At that hour McClellan telegraphed him: "Mass your troops and carry Burkettsville at any cost." Franklin attacked, and after a fight of three hours' duration, drove the enemy out of Burkettsville, and following closely up the mountain, dislodged them from one point after another, until he gained the crest of the mountain, and the Confederates fled down the other side. On the evening of that day, Franklin's advance was in Pleasant Valley. Franklin's loss was one hundred and fifteen killed and four hundred and sixteen wounded. He captured four hundred prisoners, seven hundred stand of arms, one piece of artillery and three colors. The enemy's loss in killed and wounded was about equal to Franklin's.

At 8:50 on the morning of the fifteenth, Franklin telegraphed McClellan from Pleasant Valley: "The enemy is drawn up in line of battle about two miles to our front, one brigade in sight." Two hours later, he telegraphs again from the same place, that the enemy in front outnumber him two to one; "it will, of course, not answer to pursue (?) the enemy under these circumstances." But the crisis, so far as Miles was concerned, had passed. He surrendered into the hands of the enemy at eight o'clock that morning, 11,583 men, 73 pieces of artillery, 13,000 small arms and large quantities of ammunition and other stores. Colonel Miles himself was killed by a rebel shot, after the white flag had been run up.

It was not too late for McClellan to revenge this unfortunate result of timid generalship. Lee's army was divided, and he lay between the widely separated forces with nearly his entire army. On losing Turner's Gap, on the night of the fourteenth, Lee had withdrawn the shattered troops of Hill and Longstreet, across Pleasant Valley, over the next dividing ridge, and halted in the valley of the Antietam. McClellan moved into Pleasant Valley on the morning of the fifteenth, seven miles north of the position occupied by Franklin, and with an aggregate of not less than eighty-five thousand men, exultant over their recent victories, in the mountain passes. The army would have cordially seconded any bold and dashing tactics of its leader, but he was hampered by his cautious policy and his apprehensions of Lee's "overwhelming numbers." He had telegraphed to Franklin on the thirteenth, "My general idea is to cut the enemy in two and beat him in detail." But when the enemy himself had presented the first condition to him voluntarily, he would not avail himself of the opportunity

So General Franklin was ordered to remain where he was, "to *watch* the large force in front of him, and protect our left and rear *until the night of the sixteenth*, (thirty-six hours,) when he was ordered to join the main body of the army at Keedysville. It came to pass, of course, that while Franklin waited, the rebel troops (McLaws' division) he was set to "watch" skillfully withdrew, being really greatly inferior to Franklin in numbers, and, anxious to avoid a battle, repassed the Potomac at Harper's Ferry, and by a wide detour struck the river again at Shepardstown, crossed to the Maryland side once more, and rejoined Lee at Sharpsburg, in time to participate in the battle of Antietam. So, also, with regard to the entire force which Lee sent on this perilous expedition—every regiment was back and in line of battle on the seventeenth of September.

CHAPTER XXIII

THE fifteenth of September was a clear, cool and
breezy day Patrick's brigade moved down from the
mountain top to the turnpike, and halting by the road-
side, prepared and ate its frugal breakfast.   The enemy
had disappeared from our front, and McClellan had begun the pursuit at an early hour.   He telegraphed to
Halleck at eight A.M., "I have just learned from General Hooker in the advance—who states that the information is perfectly reliable—that the enemy is making for
the river in a perfect panic ; and General Lee stated last
night publicly that he must admit they had been
shockingly whipped.   I am hurrying everything forward to endeavor to press their retreat to the utmost."

General McClellan knew that only D. H. Hill and
Longstreet had been in front of his right wing, and that
they were now retiring towards the Potomac, in the

direction of Sharpsburg. He knew equally well that the strong divisions of McLaws, Anderson, Walker, A. P Hill and Stonewall Jackson were at Harper's Ferry or its vicinity ; a full day's march away   Now seemed the auspicious opportunity to crush the divisions of D. H. Hill and Longstreet, before the absent divisions could come up. And to secure this result expedition was necessary, and such positioning of the Federal army as would compel Lee to fight at once, or force him to separate himself farther and farther from his detached divisions.

Pleasonton's cavalry led the advance and overtook the enemy's rear guard at Boonsborough, where a brisk skirmish occurred, resulting in the defeat of the rebels with a loss of a number killed and wounded, and two hundred and fifty prisoners and two guns. Richardson's division of Sumner's corps followed Pleasonton, and after a march of about ten miles, descried the enemy in possession of the hill on the west side of Antietam Creek, and in front of the little village of Sharpsburg. Richardson deployed on the right of the road from Keedysville to Sharpsburg, and on the east side of the creek. Sykes, with his division of regulars, arrived soon after, and deployed on the left of the road. The afternoon was now well spent.

To have moved the right wing of McClellan's army from Turner's Gap to the Antietam in time to have attacked Lee in the afternoon of the fifteenth, does not seem an impossible exploit, and when such great advantages were offered to the Union commander by making battle before the Rebel detachments could join their chief, the utmost celerity was demanded.   Franklin had telegraphed McClellan that firing ceased at Harper's Ferry at eight o'clock that morning, and the deductions were either that Miles had surrendered or that Lee had recalled his troops. In either event they would be on their return, and would increase the strength of the

Rebel army a hundred per cent. within twenty-four hours.

In his report of the battle, McClellan says : " It had been hoped to engage the enemy during the fifteenth ;" but, "after a rapid examination of the position, I found it was too late to attack that day, and at once directed the placing of the batteries in position in the centre, and indicated the bivouacs for the different corps, massing them near and on both sides of the Sharpsburg turnpike. The corps were not all in their positions until next morning after sunrise."

Patrick's brigade marched through Boonsborough on the fifteenth, and bivouacked, supperless, about three miles beyond. Marching next morning at six o'clock, we reached the circle of hills on the east side of the Antietam, a little after seven. The position taken by Patrick's brigade proved to be in range of the enemy's batteries, and the brigade was withdrawn to a ridge which protected it from the guns.

At any time before twelve o'clock on the sixteenth, McClellan could have hurled 60,000 troops against less than half their number. Jackson had rejoined Lee that morning after an exhausting march, but he had left A. P Hill to receive the surrender of Harper's Ferry, and McLaws, with his own and Anderson's division, was still in front of Franklin, in Pleasant Valley, and did not reach Lee until the morning of the seventeenth. Walker arrived about noon of the sixteenth ; so it will be seen that Lee was allowed time to gather together the scattered divisions of his army (excepting only A. P Hill,) before McClellan delivered battle.

The position of Patrick's brigade was changed a number of times during the day, and about three o'clock in the afternoon, it was moved to the right of the Union line, and, fording the creek, advanced up the slope on the west side, through the fields for the distance of a mile under a heavy fire of shell and solid shot, to a piece of woods on the Williamsport road, where it formed line of battle, and where it lay on its arms during the night.

There are four stone bridges that span Antietam Creek in the vicinity of the battle-field—the most northerly one on the Keedysville and Williamsport road ; the next on the Keedysville and Sharpsburg Turnpike ; the third about a mile below the second, on the Rohrersville and Sharpsburg road, and the fourth near the mouth of the creek on the road leading from Harper's Ferry to Sharpsburg, some three miles below the third bridge. The stream is sluggish, with few and difficult fords.

Sharpsburg occupies a high point of ground about a mile east of the Potomac, and a little less than a mile west of Antietam Creek. The Potomac is very serpentine in the vicinity of Sharpsburg, and immediately opposite that place makes a sharp bend to the east. Two miles north of Sharpsburg, and at an equal distance south of it, the river again diverges from its generally southerly course and runs nearly east, a distance of a mile and a half. It then turns abruptly to the westward, flows back to the line of its general direction, and pursues its course southerly   A cord drawn from the easterly point of the bend above Sharpsburg to the bank of the river at the bend below, would intersect the village, and would be about five miles long. The Antietam flows into the Potomac three miles south of Sharpsburg, and is not fordable below bridge number four. The Baltimore & Ohio Canal is constructed along the east bank of the Potomac, rendering access to the river difficult, except in the few localities where the canal is bridged. The ground rises by a steep ascent from the Potomac, about seventy-five feet, and thence easterly, the surface is broken into ridges running parallel with the river, until the high ground breaks away into the valley of the Antietam.

It was in this *cul-de-sac* and behind these ridges, stretching through Sharpsburg and a mile below and two miles above it, that Lee had posted his army, to meet the onset of his old adversary   Longstreet's corps on the right, crossing the Boonsborough and Rohrers- ville roads, and extending across the front of Sharps- burg. On his left were the corps of D. H. Hill, Hood and Jackson, in the order named, and terminating the line in a woods on the road from Sharpstown to Hagerstown, with one brigade across this road. The left of the line curved to the rear and towards the Potomac ; and here was posted Stuart's cavalry Near- ly opposite the Confederate centre was a ford somewhat difficult of access, by reason of the precipitous descent of the river bank, but quite practicable for all arms, when reached.

It will be seen at a glance, that this was a strong po- sition, and Lee evidently expected to be able to hold it until he should choose to retire. That he contemplated anything beyond this, except in the event of some oc- currence not within the scope of probable chances, is manifest from all the circumstances.

Whatever may have been the original design of the Confederate commander in entering Maryland, he evi- dently had no intention of taking the aggressive against the Army of the Potomac.   He had been grievously disappointed in finding an utter lack of sympathy with the secession cause in Maryland. He had supposed that thousands would eagerly flock to his standard, and that the Federal Capital would be suddenly encom- passed by swarms of armed and revengeful enemies, whose threatening attitude would demand all the re- sources of the Government. But when it was discovered that these expectations were utterly groundless, and Lee found the Army of the Potomac launched against him, largely augmented in numbers, while his own army was dwindling away by straggling, a safe and honorable withdrawal was the utmost the Confederate chieftain hoped for.

[That the Confederate soldiers took advantage of their presence in a loyal State to escape from the Confederate army, is shown by official records. It is probable Lee's army lost more men by straggling than by battle. In Lee's Report, page 35, he says: "The arduous service in which our troops had been engaged, their great privations of rest and food, and the long marches without shoes over mountain roads, had greatly reduced our ranks before the action began. These causes had compelled *thousands* of brave men to absent themselves, and many more had done so from unworthy motives. This great battle was fought by less than forty thousand men on our side." Of the same condition of things General Hill says: "Had all our stragglers been up, McClellan's army would have been completely crushed or annihilated. *Thousands* of thieving poltroons had kept away from sheer cowardice. The straggler is generally a thief and always a coward, lost to all sense of shame; he can only be kept in the ranks by a strict and sanguinary discipline."—Reports of Maryland Campaign, Vol. II, page 119.]

The garrison at Harper's Ferry, with its rich spoils, afforded Lee the opportunity of giving his venture the appearance of success, and to grace his return to Virginia with a prisoner-list a quarter as large as his entire army ; with a long train of captured cannon, and with a hundred wagon loads of small arms, and other war *materiel*. Lee had not even intended to dispute the passage of South Mountain, but had ordered the Harper's Ferry detachments to meet him at Boonsboro' or Hagerstown. And, doubtless, those detachments would have been able to rejoin their chief, leisurely, at either of those places, except for the chance which placed a copy of Lee's Order in McClellan's hands. Then the latter displayed so much unexpected energy that Lee was obliged to make the fight at South Mountain to give time for the reduction of Harper's Ferry. To make this fight he had to countermarch Hill's division from Boonsboro' and Longstreet's from Hagerstown. McLaws held Franklin in check at Crampton's Pass, where Lee had made no provision for defending it, by throwing a brigade from his division into it, on his way to the Ferry Six hours earlier or twenty-four hours later, McClellan would have found both passes unoccupied. But as Lee had to fight to give time to the expedition moving against Miles, so now he had to fight again, to enable him to withdraw his army across the Potomac.

We have said that Lee's position was a strong one, but we must add that it was a dangerous one for an army not entirely sure of being able to hold it. It could move by neither flank. Its right was obstructed by Antietam river and its left by the Potomac. While the streams covered and protected its flanks they also limited its capacity for manœuvring. Its movements were restricted to its front and rear, and parallel to its line of battle, within these narrow confines. To advance, the Confederates must march through or over the Army of the Potomac ; to retire, they must mass on their centre, and depend upon a solitary narrow ford, at the foot of a steep hill, where an overturned army wagon or a disabled gun carriage, might at any moment interrupt the march.

On the afternoon of the 16th, General McClellan began to arrange his line of battle, and Hooker was ordered to cross the Antietam at bridge number one and at a contiguous ford, and to attack, and, if possible, turn the enemy's left. Hooker's division commanders now were Doubleday, First Division (the Twentieth's), and Meade and Ricketts, Second and Third Divisions. Two of these officers subsequently commanded the Army of the Potomac—one leading it to defeat at Chancellorsville and the other to victory at Gettysburg.

In the passage of the stream, Patrick's brigade took the ford, and emerging from the water, formed line in the fields on the enemy's side and moved forward toward the front and left flank. The ground over which he advanced was of very uneven surface and covered with grass and corn, and here and there a fence.

Hooker, mounted upon a magnificent white horse, and riding at the head of his corps, was the most conspicuous object on the field. As we began to ascend the hill toward the rebel position, their batteries opened upon us with shot and shell in the most vigorous manner. The corps pushed on, however, and soon began to feel the fire of a strong line of skirmishers, concealed behind ridges and fences and wherever they could find cover. Hooker's skirmish line routed these sharpshooters, and as they fell back the corps pressed forward and became engaged with some troops thrown forward on the enemy's left, and who were holding a piece of woods near I. Miller's house. After a brisk but brief engagement these Confederates were driven out of the woods and back upon their line, and Hooker's men rested upon their arms during the night upon the ground thus won. It was after dark when this affair was over.

During the night Mansfield's (Twelfth corps) crossed the Antietam at the same points at which Hooker had crossed, and bivouacked on the farm of J. Poffenberger, about a mile in rear of the First Corps. The Second Corps was to be held in readiness to support Hooker and Mansfield. Porter's Corps lay along the turnpike in front of bridge Number 2, Burnside's Ninth Corps was on the Rohrersville and Sharpsburg roads, in front of bridge Number 3. General Franklin was still in Pleasant Valley.

General McClellan's plan of battle was, to attack the enemy's left with the corps of Hooker and Mansfield, supported by Sumner's ; and, when matters looked favorable there, to move the corps of Burnside against the enemy's extreme right ; *this* movement being successful, to attack the centre. (McClellan's Report, page 201.) This plan was radically faulty, in that it allowed the Confederate commander to employ his main body against any assaulted point. Lee held the interior line and the movement of his troops from point to point could be made without being seen from the Federal lines, of which circumstance he availed himself

during the battle. The plan, bad as it was, was faulty
in the mode in which it was sought to be executed.
The movement of the right wing across the Antietam,
in the afternoon of the sixteenth, was an ostentatious
notice to Lee of his adversary's purpose, and given at a
time that enabled Lee to employ eight or ten hours in
preparing to meet it. Indeed, while Hooker was moving into position, Lee had thrown two of Hood's brigades into the piece of woods spoken of above, and
which force Hooker encountered, and met in it sufficient
opposition to delay him for the night, without being
able to molest the true Confederate line of battle at all.

At daylight, on the seventeenth, Hooker's corps was
under arms, and, as the gray light of the Autumn
morning lit up the scene sufficiently to enable the
troops to move without difficulty, they advanced to the
attack. The Confederate left had been slightly refreshed
during the night, and now occupied a piece of woods
on the west side of the Hagerstown road, at the margin
of which stands the Dunker Church. A strong picket
line, however, was posted considerably in front of this
position, and disputed the Federal advance with great
tenacity The piece of woods in which the enemy's left
was posted (Jackson's corps,) was traversed by out-
cropping ledges of rock, making impervious breastworks, while several hundred yards to the right and
rear was a hill which commanded the debouch of the
woods, and in the fields between was a long line of
stone fences, continued by breastworks of rails, which
covered the rebel infantry from our musketry. The
woods formed a screen behind which the movements of
the enemy were concealed from observation, and masked
his batteries on the hill.

By a strange oversight of both Union and Confederate commanders, a high point of ground lying a little
beyond the Confederate left, and which was the key-
point of the entire field, had been neglected by both

sides. A battery planted there would have made the position of either hostile force utterly untenable. On the 18th, General McClellan's attention was called to this commanding point, and it was *proposed* to seize it; but it was not done; and as the battle was not renewed, it was no longer of consequence.

Hooker's corps went into the fight about eighteen thousand strong. His line was formed with Doubleday's division on the right, Mead's in the centre, and Ricketts' on the left. The route of march of the "Twentieth" was across the fields, and through the woods on the left of the road on which the Dunker Church stands, until it reached the farther side of an orchard, in front of which, and but a few rods off, was a cornfield, with cornstalks standing higher than a man's head. From this cornfield we encountered a perfect hailstorm of shot from small arms; while the hidden guns of the enemy, on the hill back of the woods, dropped their shell in our way with wonderful accuracy.

Just across the road leading to Sharpsburg, and a little in front of our line, two sections of Battery B, Captain Campbell, were stationed, between some stacks of straw and a barn, and the enemy's sharpshooters had crept up until they had gotten within range, and were picking off the horses and gunners. The brigade was faced by the right flank, and moved across the road, in rear of Campbell's battery, and after marching into the field near the woods, covering Jackson's position, the "Twentieth" was detached and sent back to support Captain Campbell's battery, against which the enemy were seen to be advancing in considerable force. Returning at "double-quick," the right wing formed near the guns, while the left wing under Major Hardenburgh, advanced down the field, along the road side, behind the fences of which and in the cornfield on the opposite side the enemy were posted, and from whence they

commanded the position of the battery ; they had also
taken possession of a hollow piece of ground just in
front of the guns. Major Hardenburgh pushed forward,
under a hot fire, driving the enemy from their cover,
and clearing the ground and the edge of the cornfield on
our left. The Sixth Wisconsin, which had advanced
into the cornfield on Major Hardenburgh's left, was
very roughly handled by the enemy in its front, and
was thrown into disorder and forced to retire. Its
color-bearer was shot down, and its colors left on the
field. Major Hardenburgh covered the retreat of the
Wisconsin regiment, and brought off its colors. He also
captured and brought off a Confederate battle-flag, the
bearer of it having been shot down by private Isaac
Thomas of G company. The enemy were soon re-
enforced ; and, advancing upon Major Hardenburgh in
overwhelming numbers, he was obliged to fall back,
which he did deliberately, delivering his fire as rapidly
as the men could load, while the battery and the right
wing opened upon the advancing rebels, who seemed
resolved to take the guns.

Hardenburgh joined the right wing, and the regiment poured a steady fire into the brave fellows, whose
courage and resolution won our admiration, although
displayed in so bad a cause. For a time they drove the
gunners from their pieces, but they could not endure
the withering fire of the regiment at close quarters, and
they fell back under cover of the ridge, a few hundred
yards in front of our position. But it was only for a
brief breathing spell—the battery was the nearest one
to their line of battle, and had done splendid execution,
and Jackson had ordered its capture. Re-enforced and
reorganized, on they came again, rising the knoll and
coming over the open field in splendid order ; delivering
their fire as they advanced, and receiving that of their
adversaries without wavering, they gave one of the
finest exhibitions of manhood and pluck ever seen on

any battle-field. Captain Campbell had double-shotted his guns—in fact, filled them to the muzzle with grape and canister, and reserving his fire until the Confederate line was within fifty feet of him, he gave the word to *fire!* and the guns were discharged almost in the faces of the foe The havoc was frightful. Their ranks were torn to pieces. The "Twentieth" on the instant poured in a deadly volley, and then sprang forward with the bayonet. The remnant of the rebel line broke and fled, leaving the ground covered with their dead and wounded. No further attempt was made against this position ; and this practically ended the "Twentieth's" participation in the fight, although it remained in line of battle and under fire most of the day.

The "Twentieth" went into action with one hundred and thirty-five officers and men ; and lost, in killed and wounded, forty-nine, or over 34 per centum.

On the right of the field, in which the scenes just described took place, Jackson had thrown forward Ewell's division to meet Hooker's onset, while his own was held in reserve in the woods, on the west side of the Hagerstown Road. A desperate contest, of an hour's duration, was maintained by this rebel division, against largely superior numbers. This was part of the expeditionary force which returned from Harper's Ferry the preceding night, and they now fought like very devils. Lawton, who commanded the division, was borne from the field wounded ; Colonel Douglass, who commanded Lawton's brigade, was killed ; and the brigade sustained a loss of five hundred and fifty-four killed and wounded, out of one thousand one hundred and fifty ; losing five regimental commanders out of six. Hayes' brigade sustained a loss of three hundred and twenty-three out of five hundred and fifty, including every regimental commander and every staff officer ; Colonel Walker and one of his staff had been disabled, and the brigade he commanded sustained a loss of two hundred and twenty-

eight out of less than seven hundred present, including
three out of four regimental commanders. (Report of
the Army of Northern Virginia, vol. II., pp. 190, 191).
The residue of this division was finally driven in disorder, across the fields and into the woods occupied by
the "Stonewall" division.

The Union batteries on the east bank of the Antietam, as well as those immediately in front, had gotten
range of Jackson's lines, and were doing considerable
execution. Meade's division now attempted to seize the
Hagerstown Road and the woods in which Jackson lay,
who, meantime, had been re-enforced by two divisions
under Hood, while his right, which had been "in air,"
was now connected with Hill. Meade met a severe fire
from this strong Confederate line, and after a gallant
attempt to carry it was forced back in some disorder, to
the east side of the road.

About the time of Meade's advance, Ricketts became
hotly engaged on the left of Meade and with the division
of Hill, which had closed up on Jackson's right.
Doubleday's division, except the "Twentieth," which
was supporting Campbell's battery, was holding the
ground first seized in the morning on the right, but was
unable to dislodge the enemy in front.

Hooker, whose corps had thus far been alone engaged, now ordered up Mansfield's corps, which had been
assigned as his support, and which was required to relieve a portion of the First corps, whose loss had been
very heavy and whose ammunition was nearly expended. While deploying his corps, General Mansfield fell
mortally wounded, and the command devolved on General Williams. General Crawford, with his own and
Green's brigade, moved rapidly across the open field,
and made a lodgment in the woods west of the Hagerstown Road, while the left of the division pressed forward as far as the Dunker Church. These movements
were attended with heavy losses, and it was found im-

possible to dislodge the enemy from their strong positions in the woods, while their fire was telling fearfully on the exposed Union line.

About nine o'clock, Hooker was wounded and carried from the field. Sumner, who had been ordered forward to support the attack on the right, arrived about the same time, and assumed command on that scene of action. Thus far, the fighting had been on the Union right and the Confederate left. Four corps of the Union army had been spectators of a terrible conflict for four hours, without firing a gun, or even making a demonstration to prevent the Confederates on their right and centre from detaching largely to support their left. General Sumner afterwards said : " I have always believed, that instead of sending these troops into the action in driblets, had General McClellan authorized me to march these forty thousand on the left flank of the enemy, we could not have failed to throw them right back in front of the other divisions of our army on the left." (Reports on the Conduct of the War, vol. I., p. 368).

Sumner threw Sedgwick's division across the open field, over which the battle had advanced and receded all the morning, and into the woods beyond—where Crawford had been fighting—and, driving the exhausted Confederates before him, got possession of the coveted woods around the Dunker Church. French's division closed up on the left of Sedgwick, and Richardson's division on French's left. Prospects of a Federal victory were brightening, and the troops of Jackson and Hood, who had borne the heat and burden of the rebel battle, were retiring in disorder. The left of the Confederate line had been borne back until it was almost perpendicular to the position it occupied when the battle opened. At this auspicious moment, the divisions of of McLaws and Walker, just returned from Harper's Ferry, were hurled upon Sedgwick's division. Jack-

son's and Hood's men, reanimated by these fresh ar-
rivals, rallied again, and their united onset swept Sedgwick back out of the woods, across the open field and to
the east side of the road, the position from whence
Hooker had opened the fight in the morning. The Confederates made no pursuit beyond the road, but retired
to the position held by Jackson in the morning—apparently contented to hold their own ground.

Meantime, French had advanced against the Confederate division of D. H. Hill, and drove it back in disorder to a sunken farm road, running easterly from the
Sharpsburg Road, and some two feet below the surface
of the adjacent land. In this the Confederates rallied
and made a stand. It proved to be the most horrible
death-trap men ever entered. French and Richardson
were now both advancing against this line, and Thomas
Francis Meagher, who commanded one of the brigades
of Richardson's division, got possession of a crest overlooking the sunken road, and opened a murderous fire
upon the unfortunate men who had rashly taken refuge
in it. The Confederates fought desperately and inflicted heavy loss on Meagher, but they, themselves,
were being slaughtered. Meagher's ammunition being
nearly expended, Caldwell, who commanded another of
Richardson's brigades, came to his relief. Meagher
broke by companies to the rear, and Caldwell by companies to the front, and there was scarcely a moment's
cessation of the Union fire. The rebels were re-enforced
by General Anderson, and efforts were made to flank
the Union forces, but they were defeated by the
manœuvres of Colonel Gross of the Fifth New Hampshire, and by Brook, French and Barlow—the latter of
whom captured three hundred prisoners and two colors.
The Federals now advanced and carried the sunken
road, and captured a large number of prisoners. The
road itself was a sickening sight, filled as it was with
rebel dead and wounded.

Three corps of the Army of the Potomac had not yet
participated in the battle. The three which had been
engaged were now resting on their arms, and there was
a lull in the conflict. Burnside still lay on the east
side of the Antietam ; Porter, with fifteen thousand
men, was on the same side of the river, and opposite
the Union centre; Franklin, with the divisions of
Slocum and W. F Smith, arrived about one o'clock.
Soon after one Burnside put his columns in motion, and
carried the bridge in his front and crossed the river.
Pushing on for the high ground in front of him he
drove the enemy back and captured a battery, which
had been doing serious execution on the Union troops.
At this juncture, the Unionists experienced another of
the bitter fruits of the tardiness of the Federal commander. Just as Burnside had obtained a foot-hold on
the west side of the river, and had won his initial point,
the division of A. P Hill, which Jackson had left behind to receive the surrender of Harper's Ferry, arrived
upon the field, and throwing his troops into the conflict,
Burnside was driven back, the battery recaptured and
Burnside forced to take shelter under the bluff near the
Antietam. Here, as on the right, the Confederates made
no attempt to penetrate the Union lines, being content to
hold their own ground. There can be no doubt but that
this policy was dictated by the inferior numbers of the
rebel army, and the desperate situation in which they
would have been placed by a defeat.

The repulse of Burnside concluded the battle of Antietam. When the last shot had been fired neither party
could claim a victory. The Confederates had stood
upon the defensive from the beginning, and the Federals had gained no vital point anywhere on their line.
The two armies held, substantially, the same ground
they occupied at the beginning of the battle. Another
day, and greater concert of action, were necessary to
such a result as would justify the Union commander in

claiming a victory.   He was strong enough, even yet, to
crush the enemy, if he would but hurl his whole army
upon him, and forbear frittering away his strength by
fighting in "driblets."   McClellan was too thoughtful
of reverse—too apprehensive of disaster—too timid for
a successful commander.   He impaired his effective
force by holding half his army in reserve to cover his
retreat in case of disaster.   His apprehensions magnified his adversary's numbers until he credited him with
two men for every one he had in the field.   Under a
really able and bold leader of the Union army, General
Lee never could have escaped from the position he had
put his forces in at Antietam.   But, if the Federal Commander-in-Chief had been distinguished for such qualities, it is not likely Lee would have put his forces in
that situation.

CHAPTER XXIV

THE morning of the eighteenth found the two armies
occupying the same positions they held at the conclusion of the battle, the evening before. The interval between the picket lines was the narrow strip of ground
over which the contending forces had fought, and it
was covered with the dead and wounded of both armies.
Some attempts were made by the officers of the " Twentieth " to remove their wounded, but the moment they
exposed themselves on the field, the hissing of musket
balls around them admonished them of the dangerous
enterprise upon which they had entered, and they were
obliged to abandon the undertaking.

The circumstances referred to in the following ex-
cerpt from the Baltimore *American* of Sept. 23d, 1862,
and in the statement following it, will be remembered by
the veterans of the " Ulster Guard."

" Passing back again through the woods two Rebel
Colonels and one Brigadier were found on the ground,
and interspersed with the multitudes of their fallen were
so many of those in the National uniform that at a
glance one might see how fearful was the cost of the victory. Upon one dead body was found a large black dog,

dead also from some chance shot which had struck him whilst stretched upon his master's corpse caressingly, his fore-paws across the man's breast. Ride where one might for a space of perhaps a mile and a half in width in places, and four or five miles in length, the dead were on every side, interspersed with the arms that had fallen from their hands. Shattered cannon wheels and caissons, and enormous quantities of round shot and conical shell gave more evidence of the deadly storm that had come with destruction in its track.''

''MR. EDITOR:—In a communication on the recent battle near Sharpsburg, published in the Baltimore *American* of the 23d of September, is the above paragraph.

''The dog referred to was a voluntary *attache* of the Twentieth Regiment, and had passed through one battle with us unharmed, previous to that in which he lost his life. He was a beautiful Newfoundland, and joined the regiment on its march somewhere this side of Frederick, and remained with it up to the time of his death on the Sharpsburg battle-field.

''I noticed him particularly in the battle of South Mountain, where, standing with the men, he seemed indifferent alike to the whistling of the enemies' bullets around him, and to the rattle of our own arms. He came on with us, and his fidelity to his new friends cost him his life on Wednesday. I saw him early in the action, apparently an unconcerned spectator of the combat. Later in the day, when I again observed him, he was lying upon the ground, somewhat to the left of the regiment and near the body of W J. Pollock, of Co. H. Man and beast were both dead.

''I doubt not the dog had received his food of Pollock while with us, and was with him when he fell, or subsequently placed himself by his side and remained there until shot. The incident made a very strong impression

on me, but I had not expected to see it gain so much
notoriety

" The poor beast is buried, and I don't know but he
deserves an epitaph."

We expected the incomplete battle would be renewed
on the morning of the eighteenth. But hour after hour
wore away and still the Union army lay quietly on its
arms. General McClellan was waiting for re-enforcements and Lee had no intention of assuming the offensive. His army had been seriously crippled by the severe fighting of the seventeenth, and his losses amounted
to over eight thousand men. Although McClellan's ex-
ceeded this number by four thousand, the impairment
of the Confederate army was relatively greater than that
of the Federals, and the disproportion in numbers between the two armies was decidedly in favor of the
Unionists.

But more than this ; General McClellan was re-enforced on the morning of the eighteenth by the divisions
of Couch and Humphrey, numbering about fourteen
thousand men. Yet McClellan thought best to wait until the troops were rested, the supply trains brought up,
etc., and he resolved to renew the battle on the nineteenth. With a perverseness that was entirely unexpected in so courteous a man as General Lee, he went
away on the night of the eighteenth, and when the next
morning dawned upon the Union army there was no foe
in its front. The facility with which the rebel army
could retire into Virginia, if unmolested, has been heretofore shown, and General McClellan says in his Report,
page 212, "as their line was but a short distance from
the river, the evacuation presented but little difficulty,
and was effected before daylight." Why it should
have been expected that they would stay there before
this growing Union army, to be attacked at its pleasure,
is a problem we are not equal to the solution of.

General McClellan gives his losses in this battle at

12,469, of whom 2,010 were killed ; 9,416 wounded and
1,043 missing.   Lee omits to state his losses in his report of this campaign, but his division commanders give
their losses severally and they make an aggregate of
13,533. This covers the entire period of two weeks
which was the duration of the Maryland campaign. If
the Harper's Ferry garrison is put into the account it
will be seen that this invasion, though a failure as to its
prime object, depleted the Union army at the rate of
two to every one Confederate.

On the nineteenth of September, General McClellan
telegraphed to General Halleck :   "I have the honor to
report that Maryland is entirely freed from the presence
of the enemy, who has been driven across the Potomac.
No fears need now be entertained for the safety of
Pennsylvania. I shall at once occupy Harper's Ferry."
And this was "the lame and impotent conclusion" at
which the Federal commander had arrived. It was not
strictly true to say that Lee had "been *driven* across
the Potomac," for the fact was, that the force that had
been brought to bear against him retarded rather than
expedited his movement in that direction. Two divisions of his army had been badly whipped at Turner's
Gap and a brigade had been defeated at Crampton's,
but these battles were fought by the Confederates to
gain time for the completion of the operations against
Harper's Ferry, as has heretofore been shown, and the
battle of Antietam was the result of the voluntary delay of the bulk of the rebel army, to cover those operations. Antietam was a drawn battle, and on the morning of the eighteenth of September, neither McClellan
or Lee could claim a victory   Did the fact that the two
armies spent the next day in looking at each other and
that on the following night, Lee carried out his original
design, and withdrew into Virginia, convert the drawn
battle into a victory ? We rode over the field early on the
morning of the nineteenth, and down to the ford across

which the Confederates had retired, and there was no
sign of haste or confusion visible, anywhere. They had
carried off all their artillery, wagons, stores and property of every description—in fact had made as clean a
removal as though no opposing force was within a hundred miles of them. They left their badly wounded for
the Union surgeons to take care of, because they themselves would only be encumbered by them, and they
knew they would fall into good hands. They also left
the small arms of their men which had been dropped
upon the battle-field, because to attempt to gather them
would have been impracticable.

Neither was it strictly true that "Maryland is entirely freed from the presence of the enemy;" for at that
very moment the Rebel General Stuart, with four thousand cavalry and six pieces of artillery was at Williamsport, and General McClellan had sent General Couch in
pursuit of him.

Neither was it strictly true, as events proved, that
"no fears need now be entertained for the safety of
Pennsylvania." For on the tenth of October, this same
Stuart, with 1,800 cavalry, again crossed the Potomac
above Williamsport and raided into Pennsylvania—entered Chambersburg, in that State, destroyed a large
amount of Government property, seized and paroled
275 sick and wounded soldiers, whom he found in hospital there, burned the railroad depot, machine shops
and several trains of loaded cars ; destroyed 5,000 muskets and large amounts of army clothing, and then, riding around McClellan's army, returned into Virginia
via White's Ford, below Harper's Ferry, without the
loss of a man.

On the nineteenth of September, at dark, General
Griffin with his own and Barnes' brigade of Porter's
corps, crossed the Potomac at the ford through which
the Confederates had passed and gallantly attacked and
carried the bluff on the Virginia side, where Lee had

posted eight batteries supported by six hundred infantry under Pendleton. Four guns and a number of
prisoners were captured. Encouraged by this success,
a reconnoissance in force was made next morning by a
portion of Porter's corps, who proceeded about a mile
from the ford, when they were ambushed by D. P Hill's
division, and after a brief struggle were driven in confusion into the river, losing a large number in killed
and wounded and two hundred prisoners.

General Lee posted his army in the vicinity of
Bunker Hill and Winchester, Virginia, and awaited the
movements of his adversary   McClellan was loth to resume the offensive. In a dispatch to General Halleck,
dated the twenty-seventh of September, he says : '' My
present purpose is to hold the army about as it is now,
rendering Harper's Ferry secure and watching the river
closely, intending to attack the enemy *should he attempt to cross to this side.*'' (McClellan's Report, page
217.)

General McClellan seems to have had little confidence
in his army, notwithstanding the splendid fighting portions of it did at Turner's Gap and at Antietam. He
explains his inactivity after the latter battle by the
statement that ''the greater part of all the available
troops were suffering under the disheartening influences
of the serious defeat they had encountered during the
brief and unfortunate campaign of General Pope.''
Now when it is remembered that the residue of the army
must have been suffering under the disheartening influences of even more serious defeats that they had encountered during the somewhat longer but quite as unfortunate campaign of General McClellan on the Peninsula,
which he seems to have overlooked, it is not wonderful
that '' they had lost something of that *'esprit du corps'*
which is indispensable to the efficiency of an army ''
(*Id.* p. 215.)

It must strike one as a little inconsistent that General McClellan should have employed the demoralized troops from Pope's army to bear the heat and burden of the battles of Turner's Gap and Antietam. The reader will have observed that most of the fighting on both fields was done by troops who had served in Pope's " brief and unfortunate campaign.'' In these two battles, Hooker's corps (formerly McDowell's,) lost 2,209 ; second corps lost 5,209 : Banks' corps lost 1,743, making a total of 9,571 out of a grand total of 12,469. The residue of losses is made up as follows: F J. Porter's corps, including the artillery reserve, 130, of whom 20 only were killed (these casualities were all from artillery fire ; Porter was not in range of small arms) ; Burnside's corps, 2,293 ; Couch's division, 9, and Pleasanton's cavalry, 23.

The Federal army remained in the vicinity of Sharpsburg until the twenty-sixth of October, when it commenced the passage of the Potomac at Berlin. During this long interval, General McClellan was calling upon the Government for re-enforcements, horses, clothing, shoes and other supplies, and the correspondence between him and General Halleck often assumed an unfriendly ~or ironical tone. On the sixth of October, Halleck telegraphed: "The President directs that you cross the Potomac and give battle to the enemy, or drive him South. Your army must move now, while the roads are good." But McClellan did not go. On the 21st he telegraphed Halleck that he had been making every exertion to get the army supplied with clothing, which was now nearly accomplished, and he wished to know "whether the President desires me to march on the enemy at once, or await the reception of new horses." To this Halleck replies : " He (the President,) directs me to say he has no change to make in his Order of the sixth instant. If you have not been and are not now in a condition to obey it, you will be able to show want of ability " On the twenty-fifth, McClellan sent a long dispatch to Halleck on the subject of guarding the line of the Potomac after he should have crossed, and among other propositions suggested : "It has long appeared to me that the best way of covering this line would be by occupying Front Royal, Strasburg, Wardensville and Moorefield," and finally proceeds to say : "An important element in the solution of this problem is the fact that a great portion of Bragg's army is probably now at liberty to unite itself with Lee's command." Halleck replies to this on the next day, and in conclusion says : "Moreover, I think it will be time enough to decide upon fortifying Front Royal, Strasburg, Wardensville and Moorefield, when the enemy is driven south of them and they come into our possession.

"I do not think that we need have any immediate fear of Bragg's army You are within twenty miles of Lee's, while Bragg is distant about four hundred miles." This dispatch was signed by Halleck, but it sounds very much like Lincoln.

There is no doubt but that the Army of the Potomac was pretty well worn out after the battle of Antietam, but probably, much less so than the rebels were, who had done more marching and quite as much fighting. There is no doubt but that the Federal army would have looked better on parade with new uniforms, but it was luxuriously clothed compared with its ragged adversaries. Its supplies of food and forage were abundant, while the Confederates were often suffering from want of food. But the systems in the two armies were entirely different—and continued to be so throughout the war. The Confederates marched and fought without regard to the question of food or clothing. If their ammunition boxes were full and their muskets bright, they considered themselves fit for duty They moved in " light marching order," and were not encumbered with long trains of wagons. Their surprising marches, especially some of Jackson's, could never have been made with the *impedimenta* that loaded down the Union armies. There is no example of such vast armies as the Federal Government had in the field with such unfailing and bountiful supplies of food and clothing. If we could have adopted the Confederate system, probably a necessity in their case, we would have whipped them in half the time it took to do it in our way

McClellan's army now numbered 110,000 men, fresh and well clothed, and on the second of November were all across the Potomac and moving unopposed down the east side of the Blue Ridge, while the Confederates made a corresponding movement on the opposite side of the mountain. But the long delay had aggravated the dissatisfaction felt with regard to McClellan at the Capital, and on the night of the seventh of November, General Buckingham arrived at Warrenton and delivered the following order to McClellan :

GENERAL ORDERS No. 182.

War Department, Adjutant-General's Office.

WASHINGTON, November 5, 1862.

By the direction of the President of the United States, it is ordered that Major-General McClellan be relieved from the command of the Army of the Potomac, and that Major-General Burnside take the command of that army. By order of the Secretary of War.

E. D. TOWNSEND,
Assistant-Adjutant-General.

McClellan read the Order, and turning to Burnside, who chanced to be present, said : " Well, Burnside, you are to command the army "

Burnside was overcome with astonishment. He subsequently stated before the Committee on the Conduct of the War, what his feelings were on the occasion. He said : " After getting over my surprise, the shock, etc., I told General Buckingham that it was a matter that required very serious thought; that I did not want the command; that it had been offered to me twice before, and I did not feel that I could take it. I told my staff what my views were with reference to my ability to exercise such a command, which views were those I had always unreservedly expressed—that I was not competent to command such an army as this." A very candid and just estimate of himself. The next day McClellan took final leave of the army, with very general regret on the part of officers and men, and Burnside assumed command.

On the twentieth of September, and while lying near Sharpsburg, we received the news of the death of Colonel Pratt, and the following Order was issued:

HEADQ'RS ULSTER GUARD, TWENTIETH REG'T,
N Y. S. M.
Near Sharpsburg, Va., September 20, 1862.
GENERAL ORDERS No. 47.

It is with feelings of profound sorrow that the Lieutenant-Colonel commanding announces to the "Ulster Guard" the death of its late worthy and honored commander, Colonel George W. Pratt.

While gallantly encouraging his officers and men in the final hour of the fearful combat at Manassas, on the 30th of August last, he was shot down and borne from the field. Though conscious of the serious character of his wounds, he maintained his habitual serenity and cheerfulness, and, forgetting self, seemed only concerned for the safety of his command and the issue of the battle in which he had borne so noble, and, as it proved, so costly a part.

He was removed to Washington, and from thence to Albany, N. Y., where he was surrounded by his kindred and friends. Death terminated his career of usefulness and promise on the 11th inst. Though cut down in the spring of his manhood, he has not lived in vain.

Born to wealth, and growing up in affluence, he spurned the ease and indolence which too often beguile fortune's favorites, and with an earnest energy and tireless industry, he sought to win for himself a name honorable in the highest walks of life.   How well he succeeded, the general and deep sorrow for his early death attest. When the present unholy war broke out, he was foremost in tendering his services to the Government ; and surrendering the comforts and enjoyments of a home unusually attractive, he became a patient, tireless and devoted laborer in behalf of the Union.   Finally he has given his life to the cause, and has died a soldier's honored death in the faithful discharge of his self-imposed duties.   We who have been so long associated with him in the camp and field ; we who have shared with him the hardships, privations, fatigues and dangers of the soldier's life ; we who have witnessed his self-denial, his dauntless courage, his ready obedience to the authority of his military superiors, and his mildness and moderation in the exercise of his own authority—we, next to those who are bereaved of husband, father, son, can best appreciate the loss sustained in the death of Colonel Pratt.   Let us emulate his example and be stimulated to increased diligence in duty, and a more entire devotion to our country and the struggle for its preservation, by the recollection of his virtues and his sacrifices.   The Lieutenant-Colonel commanding avails himself of this opportunity to express his satisfaction with the conduct of the officers and men of the regiment who participated in the marches and battles which have rendered memorable the last forty days of this campaign. Within that time you have marched upward of 170 miles, without tents or blankets, and often without food, in the burning heat of mid day and the cold dews of night, resting frequently but four hours in twenty-four, and then upon the bare ground.   There has been no murmur or complaint, no relaxation of obedience or

discipline. The battle-fields of Norman's Ford, Warrenton Springs, Groveton, Manassas, Chantilly, South
Mountain and Antietam, bear witness to your prowess
and courage. Your coolness and steady bearing under
heavy fire of artillery and musketry were equal to veterans, and entitle you to the highest praise the soldier
can earn. Let the future correspond with the past in
diligence, in discipline, in courage, and our friends will
have no cause to blush for the reputation of the "Ulster
Guard."   By order of

THEODORE B. GATES,

(Signed)   *Lieutenant-Colonel Commanding.*

A. S. Schutt, *First Lieutenant, Acting-Adjutant.*

At a meeting of the Field, Staff and Line Officers,
held in camp Sept. 23d, the following action was taken :

"Whereas, Intelligence has reached us of the death
of Colonel George W Pratt, late commander of this
regiment, who died in Albany, N Y., on the 11th inst.,
from the effects of a wound received at the battle of
Bull Run, Aug. 30th ; and whereas, the Field, Staff and
Line officers lately associated with him, deeply affected
by their bereavement, desire to give expression to the
sentiments with which a long and close intimacy caused
them to regard his high personal and professional
worth—it is therefore—

Resolved, 1. That we profoundly deplore the death
of our late commanding officer, who, by his affable and
courteous demeanor, genial spirit, frank and manly
bearing, as well toward his associates as in the performance of his duty, received in large measure the respect, confidence and affection of all who enjoyed his
acquaintance.

2d. That the early and hearty espousal of the cause
of the imperilled Commonwealth, in which our late
commanding officer entered, with all the ardor of a true
patriot and gallant soldier, and to which his best ener-

gies were consecrated, at the sacrifice of whatever makes
an affluent and refined home attractive, if need were to
lay down life itself in the service of the Government,
evinces at once the warmth and earnestness of his devotion to the interests of his afflicted country, and the serious loss these interests have sustained in the death of
such an advocate.

3. That in all the duties of a good soldier, firm without being austere—strict in discipline and yet kindly in
its execution—skillful, without ostentation, in the control and management of his regiment—not less prompt
to render obedience to those above him, than determined
to exact it from those under his command—regardful of
the personal comfort of the soldiers entrusted to his
care, ever promoting it to the utmost of his power—he
has left behind him a record at once honorable and exemplary.

4. That his bearing in the fierce battle, in which his
death-wound was received, standing with unfaltering
gallantry beside his men, cheering them on by voice and
example, while the deadly tempest was rapidly thinning
the ranks of those around him, nor ceasing his efforts
till he fell and was borne bleeding from the field, presents a shining example of the qualities by which the
true soldier should be distinguished, and must prove an
ever fragrant memory to those who honored and loved
him while living.

5. That we sincerely and deeply sympathize with
the sorrowing family of our late commander, in the irreparable loss they have sustained—that a copy of these
Resolutions be forwarded to them, and published in the
New York and Albany papers and those of Kingston
and Catskill, N. Y "

September 29.—Marched with brigade 2.30 P.M. to a
point one mile northwest of Sharpsburg, near the Potomac river, where encamped.   Distance marched, 1½
miles.

October 7.—General Patrick having been assigned to duty at General McClellan's Headquarters, as Provost-Marshal-General of the Army of the Potomac, took leave of the brigade in the following Order :

HEADQ'RS THIRD BRIGADE, FIRST DIVISION,
FIRST ARMY CORPS,
Camp Barnett, October 7, 1862.

GENERAL ORDERS, No 64.

The Brigadier-General commanding having been assigned to duty at the Headquarters of the Army of the Potomac by General Orders No. 161, of the 6th inst., hereby relinquishes to Colonel Rodgers, of the Twenty-first N Y Volunteers, the command of the brigade he received from him 7 months ago.   Only 7 months ago he assumed command ; yet the ties that bind those who, like ourselves, have shared each other's hardships and dangers, who have followed the same standard through so many battles, and gathered around it with their ranks thinned, but unbroken, when the combat was over—such ties *cannot* be broken by the Order that relieves your General from the command.

That he must continue to take the liveliest interest in the welfare of a brigade that has never failed in the hour of peril, whether in daylight or darkness, to honor his every command, no one can doubt ; and he trusts that both officers and men will touch lightly upon his faults, in the full conviction that, as their commander, he has endeavored to discharge his duties to them, to his country and his God.   He leaves you with fervent wishes for your prosperity, and the earnest hope that an honorable peace may soon be won, so that we may once more return to our loved homes by the broad rivers and lakes of the Empire State.

By order of   GENERAL PATRICK.

General Gabriel Paul, an accomplished and gallant officer, who subsequently lost both eyes by a gun-shot wound at Gettysburg, was assigned to the command of the brigade, and retained the command at the time the regiment was transferred to General Patrick's provisional brigade, January 7, 1863.

CHAPTER XXV

WHEN General Burnside was placed in command of the
Army of the Potomac the administration and the loyal
people of the country were impatient of the long delay
that had followed the battle of Antietam. They were
likewise dissatisfied with the results of that battle, and
the escape of the Confederate army with the trophies
of Harper's Ferry and the plunder of Chambersburg.
Lee had lain during these five weeks of inactivity within a few miles of McClellan's army, but no attempt had
been made by the latter to disturb his repose. It was
well known that the Confederates had left Maryland in
a wretched plight, in so far as shoes, clothing, and supplies were concerned, and that they were greatly inferior
in number to the Union Army. It was thought by the
President and his advisers and by the country generally
to be a favorable time to strike a telling blow at this
audacious foe.

Burnside knew he was expected to do what McClellan had failed to do, and that whatever he did must be done quickly. It was on the seventh of November, and a furious snow-storm was prevailing, when General Buckingham rode into camp with the Order assigning Burnside to the command. The season for active operations was near its close. To go into winter quarters without a battle was the last thing to be thought of. In twelve hours the snow had disappeared, the ground was dry, the roads were in splendid condition and the air was as balmy as though it had never floated a snow-flake.

Lee had moved up the Shenandoah Valley, the great highway of rebel armies, keeping opposite the Army of the Potomac, and separated from it by the Blue Ridge, some of the passes of which were occupied by the Federals and others by the Confederates.

Burnside had given higher promise of energy and capacity than any other of the corps commanders of the army. He had the prestige of a successful campaign in North Carolina, and the country confided in his earnest and indefatigable energy and unquestionable patriotism. In short he seemed the fittest man to succeed McClellan if McClellan were to have a successor, and was accepted by the army with more satisfaction than any other man who could have been named.

In view of the relative positions and conditions of the two armies, and of the public expectations (if these may be taken into account in such momentous affairs), Burnside should have made it his instant business to find the rebel army and fight it. He knew where to look for it and two days' march would have brought Lee to battle or compelled him to flee. Moving by his left upon Gordensville he might have placed himself between Lee and Richmond and compelled him to fight to recover his communications and open his way to his base. Instead of this, Burnside spent ten days at Warrenton, deliberating and reorganizing the army. He formed the six

corps into three grand divisions ; the right composed of
the Second corps, under General Couch, and the Ninth
corps, under Gen. Wilcox ; Gen. Sumner commanding.
The centre grand division was made up of the Third corps,
under General Stoneman, and the Fifth corps, under Gen.
Butterfield ; Gen. Hooker commanding. The left grand
division consisted of the First corps, under Gen. Reynolds, and the Sixth corps, under Gen. W F Smith ;
General Franklin commanding. He then made a feint
towards Gordonsville, but facing suddenly to the left,
moved across the country to the Rappahannock, opposite Fredericksburg. The degree of rapidity with which
this march was conducted was not calculated to accomplish the purpose Burnside had in view. It was not
remarkable for its celerity.

General Burnside had expected to reach and cross
the Rappahannock and occupy the vantage ground in
rear of Fredericksburg before Lee could get into that
vicinity. But he miscalculated the watchfulness and
fleet-footedness of the rebel army. Stuart's troopers
rode into Warrenton as the rear of Burnside's army
marched out. Lee moved down the south bank of the
river as his adversary went down on the north side, and
when our advance under Sumner reached Falmouth and
attemped to cross the river to Fredericksburg, he
found the enemy there to oppose him, and was repulsed. The bridges having been again burned, pontoons were necessary for a speedy and general crossing,
and these Burnside supposed General Halleck would
have on the ground against his arrival, and Halleck
supposed General Burnside would himself attend to it ;
so there were no pontoons present, and before they did
arrive Lee's entire army was in position on the Fredericksburg Heights.

Thus had Burnside's first move utterly miscarried.
Instead of treating the rebel army as his objective he
manœuvred as though the rebel capital were the real

objective, and instead of posting himself on Lee's line
and compelling him to fight on ground of Burnside's
choosing, he had given Lee the option of this choice and
now found him lying across his path, from whence only
a desperate and disadvantageous battle could displace
him.

It has been stated by some writers that this manœuvre was ordered from Washington, but in making
his report upon the battle which followed, General
Burnside says : "The fact that I decided to move from
Warrenton on to this line rather against the opinion of
the President, Secretary of War and yourself, (General
Halleck) and that you have left the whole movement in
my hands, without giving me orders, makes me the
more responsible."

Considering the strong position that Lee occupied, it
would have been deemed judicious by most commanders
to have recourse to such tactics as should neutralize this
advantage as far as possible, and there seems to have
been no insuperable difficulty in a movement by his
right, which, if skillfully planned and conducted, gave
reasonable hopes of success.   The enemy were closely
watching the river above and below Fredericksburg, it
is true, but no more so than they were at Fredericksburg itself, and here the bulk of their army was posted
and they had now constructed formidable fortifications.
Moreover, their position in rear of Fredericksburg was
naturally very strong, and after crossing the river, Burnside's charging columns would have a difficult canal to
pass, running parallel with the rebel works and much
of the way within range of their small arms.

But Burnside supposed the enemy would anticipate
a flank movement, and that they would hardly expect
the boldness of an attack in front, and he resolved to
make it.   It is said to be bad policy in war to do what
your enemy anticipates, but it does not follow that it is

always good policy to do what he least expects you
will do.

The bluffs on the Stafford side of the river approach
so near it, opposite Fredericksburg, that artillery posted
on the heights, afford a good cover for troops attempting to cross, and effectually sweep the broad plain on
the other side. Lee, therefore, resolved not to oppose
the passage of the stream but to make his fight from
behind his fortifications when Burnside should seek to
advance. This, however, did not inhibit a very stubborn opposition on the part of rebel sharp-shooters
who had concealed themselves in the buildings along
the river in the city of Fredericksburg, and whose
rifles commanded the stream where it was proposed to
lay the upper pontoon.

Nearly four weeks had now passed since Burnside
set his columns in motion from Warrenton, and on the
night of the tenth of December, one hundred and forty-
seven heavy cannon were planted on Stafford heights,
the army was moved near the river and the pontoon
trains were drawn to the points where it was intended
to lay the bridges—three directly opposite the city, and
two a couple miles below.

The left Grand Division, under Franklin, forty thousand strong, was to cross at the lower bridges, while
Sumner's Grand Division of the Second and Ninth
Corps were to cross over the upper bridges. Hooker,
with the centre Grand Division, was to remain in reserve.

Before daylight on the eleventh, the engineer corps
began the work of laying the bridges. The work progressed almost uninterruptedly at the lower crossings,
but at the upper the artificers were instantly fired upon
by the watchful sharpshooters, concealed along the
Fredericksburg side of the river. As the report of the
small arms rung out upon the morning air, two cannon
shots boomed from the heights back of Fredericksburg

—signal guns, to summon the Confederate host to the lines of defense. Longstreet says, in his report of the battle : " At three o'clock our signal guns gave notice of the enemy's approach. The troops being at their different camp grounds, were formed immediately, and marched to their positions along the line." Meantime a dense fog filled the valley, but the rifle-bullets sped through it on their deadly errand, and it was found impossible to proceed with the work.

So time went on until ten o'clock ; then Burnside gave the order to train the batteries on the town and batter it down. For an hour an iron storm poured upon the city, and seven thousand three hundred and fifty cannon balls and shells were hurled into its streets and buildings. The city was still enveloped in fog, and the effect of this terrific bombardment could not be seen, but here and there dense columns of smoke rose above the mist-hidden town, showing that conflagrations had broken out. When, soon after eleven o'clock, the fog rolled away, the city was seen to be on fire at a number of points ; but the buildings along the river's brink still stood, and gave cover to the riflemen, whose unerring bullets bade defiance to all attempts to lay the bridges. Some progress had been made, but the nearer the bridge builders approached the farther shore, the more deadly became the fire. The Fifty-seventh New York, Lieutenant-Colonel Chapman, and the Sixty-sixth New York, Lieutenant-Colonel Bull, who were posted along the river bank to cover the working party, lost one hundred and fifty men in a short space of time.

The afternoon had now been reached and no further progress could be made. The enemy, whose fatal fire was thinning the ranks of the exposed Federals, could not be seen, and the pontooners were exposed to certain slaughter if they proceeded with their work. In this emergency General Hunt, Chief of Artillery, proposed that a party should be sent across the river in the open pontoon boats, and capture or disperse the hidden foe. It was a perilous undertaking, and one upon which an officer would hesitate to order his men. Volunteers were called for, and the Seventh Michigan and the Nineteenth and Twentieth Massachusetts regiments of Howard's division, offered themselves for the desperate service. Rushing to the bank of the river, they opened a rapid fire upon the opposite shore to force the rebels to keep their cover, while the rubber pontoon boats were being launched. Filling a number of these they were rapidly rowed across the stream, other boats swiftly following, and dashing up the opposite bank, they charged into the town, capturing upwards of a hundred rebels and putting the others to flight. Our gallant fellows then took possession of the south shore of the river, and the bridges were finished without further molestation.

Howard's division of Couch's corps crossed to Fredericksburg that evening, and met a strong skirmish line of the enemy in the streets of the city, which it forced back toward the rear of the town. The next morning the city, valley and river were again enveloped in a dense fog, under cover of which the Ninth Corps crossed to Fredericksburg, and a portion of Franklin's Grand Division passed over at the lower bridges.

Another cold December night ; another fog-curtained morning, and yet we were not ready for the impending battle. Four additional pontoon bridges were laid to facilitate the withdrawal of the army, in case of disaster, and the day was consumed in reconnoitring the Confederate position.

Lee's army was now eighty thousand strong, divided into two divisions, Stonewall Jackson commanding the right and Longstreet the left. The bluff on which the main body of the Confederate army was posted, starts from the river above the city, and curving towards the south, sweeps around the rear of the town and leaves a plain below the city and between the base of the bluff and the river, two miles wide ; then bending northerly it approaches within a half mile of the river at Massaponix Creek. Near this latter point the rebel right was posted under charge of D. H. Hill. On the plain below was Stuart's cavalry. The Richmond and Fredericksburg Railroad runs over the plain and then passes south through a gap in the bluff near Massaponix creek. Across this plain and parallel with the river runs a broad wagon road known as the " Bowling Green " road. Another wagon road, starting from the lower part of the city and running directly south, ascends the bluff, passes through the Confederate line and continues to Richmond. This is known as the " Telegraph Road." Still another highway leaves from the upper part of the town, climbs the hill near where the Confederate left was posted and conducts to Orange Court House ; this is a plank road.

While the Federals were preparing to assault this strong position, the enemy had by no means been idle. Every art that engineering skill could resort to was employed to make the line of works behind which Lee had taken stand, impregnable. Three hundred cannon had been mounted in battery, and their fire would sweep almost every foot of ground on the plain below. The Union guns on Stafford Heights were too remote to do execution on the Confederate batteries, and proved of little use in the battle which ensued—indeed, they inflicted damage upon our own troops as they advanced, and Burnside ordered them to cease firing.

Another foggy morning ushered in the thirteenth of December, which was to see the encounter between these two mighty forces. The attack was to have been made early, but the thick mist compelled a delay until near ten o'clock. Then, as the rays of the sun began to penetrate the dank air, the plain far below Fredericksburg was seen alive with marching troops, whose arms

gleamed like burnished steel as they met the light of
the December sun.　Meade's division was advancing to
attack the rebel right.　They had not proceeded far before they were forced to halt and turn their attention to
Stuart, on their left, whose batteries were raking their
columns.　Some time was spent in silencing this flank
fire, and then Meade pushed on toward the woods, near
where the railroad strikes the bluff.　Meade's front was
covered by a cloud of skirmishers, and his batteries continuously shelled the woods and heights toward which
they were advancing.　But the rebel works were as silent as though they were deserted, until the Federals
had reached within point blank range, when they burst
forth with a murderous fire of grape, canister and musketry　By no means daunted, the Federals rushed on,
compelling the enemy to hastily withdraw three batteries they had stationed on the north side of the railroad.
Striking the Confederate brigade of Lane, in the edge of
the woods, it was driven back in confusion upon Greggs'
brigade, in its rear.　The right of Archer's brigade next
felt the shock, and was crushed by the on-coming Federals, who captured some two hundred prisoners, and a
number of battle flags.　No halt was made, but advancing up the crest of the hill, the assailants reached the
second line, posted in a military road on the plateau,
and held at this point by Greggs' brigade of South
Carolinians.　They poured a withering fire into the very
faces of Meade's men, and checked their advance.
Rebel re-enforcements hurried to the endangered line,
and after a fierce struggle, Meade was thrust back with
the loss of 1,760 men, in killed, wounded and prisoners,
out of a total of six thousand engaged.　As Meade fell
back, General Gibbon formed on his right, and Birney
on his left, covering his retreat, and checking the rebel
advance.　Sickles' division of Hooker's corps advanced
to the front and relieved Gibbon.

Here was another lamentable instance among the

many on our side, in which a mere fragment of the army was delegated to do the work that should have been committed to thrice their numbers. And when we consider the partial success which Meade secured with his six thousand men, while thirty odd thousand were standing behind him, it seems as though it would have been possible to have absolutely crushed the rebel right, and to have completely turned their line. Franklin, who commanded our left grand division, excuses himself for making the assault with so small a force, upon the ground that his orders were to advance but one division. Burnside's instructions to him were, "keep your whole command in position for a rapid movement down the old Richmond road, and you will send out a division, at least, to pass below Smithfield, to seize, if possible, the heights near Captain Hamilton's, on this side of the Massaponix, taking care to keep it well supported, and its line of retreat open." He also informed Franklin that a simultaneous attack would be made on the enemy's extreme left, and adds: "Holding these heights, (on the enemy's left) and the heights near Captain Hamilton's, will, I hope, compel the enemy to evacuate the whole ridge between these two points." It was apparent then that these two attacks were to be the key points of the battle, and, while it must be admitted that Burnside's order was less definite and imperative than it should have been, yet it revealed to Franklin the nature, object and scope of the work intrusted to him ; and a General capable to command, loyal to his chief, and with zeal in the cause, would have thrown twenty, instead of six thousand, upon this pivotal point.

While the events above narrated were transpiring on our extreme left, a similar and quite as harrowing a scene was enacted on our extreme right. General French's division of the second corps was assigned to carry the works on the rebel left. Hancock's division

was to support the movement. French moved out of
the town by the plank and telegraph roads, and crossing the canal, deployed his columns on the terrace below Marey's Hill. All this while the rebel artillery
ploughed through our ranks. Longstreet says : "This
fire was very destructive and demoralizing in its effects,
and frequently made gaps in the enemy's ranks that
could be seen at the distance of a mile." When
French's melting lines came under the infantry fire,
they met such a deluge of lead that one-half their numbers fell before the first blast. It was more than the
bravest men could endure, and they fell back out of
range of this desolating fire.

Hancock now pushed to the front, joined by a portion of French's division, and met the same destructive
reception. A brief struggle for the wall and bank from
behind which this fiery storm came, and he, like French,
was forced to fall back with a loss of over two thousand
men, out of a force of five thousand and six. The divisions of Howard, Sturgis and Getty, advanced to the
support of French and Franklin, and joined in the attacks, but the utmost the Unionists could do, was to
hold a line south of the canal, out of musket range, and
somewhat protected from artillery by the conformation
of the ground.

Burnside would not yet forego this desperate undertaking. Hooker was now ordered to cross the river with
a portion of his grand division, and storm the heights
where French and Hancock had destroyed two divisions. Couch had been battering the enemy's works
with a dozen cannon, planted within one hundred and
fifty yards, to make a breach through which an assaulting column could pass, but made no perceptible impression. Hooker sent Humphrey's division upon the forlorn assault of these cannon-proof works. The men
were to rely upon the bayonet exclusively They moved forward with great gallantry and celerity, and reach-

ed the extreme limit to which their predecessors had attained, and then were swept back by the same overwhelming, resistless leaden sirocco, leaving seventeen hundred out of four thousand who had advanced, dead or wounded, upon the field.

Our losses in this day's battles amounted to thirteen thousand seven hundred and seventy-one men. The rebel loss was between five and six thousand. The withdrawal of the Union army was very skillfully and successfully accomplished on the night of the fifteenth of December.

Night now interposed before another sacrifice could be arranged, and although General Burnside was intent upon renewing the costly experiment of dashing his army to pieces on the following day, he was finally prevailed upon to desist. His own statement on this point, made before the committee on the conduct of the war, is interesting and pathetic. He says:

"The two attacks were made and we were repulsed; still holding a portion of the ground we had fought upon, but not our extreme advance.

"That night I went all over the field on our right; in fact I was with the officers and men until nearly daylight. I found the feeling to be rather against an attack the next morning; in fact, it was decidedly against it.

"I returned to my headquarters, and, after conversation with General Sumner, told him that I wanted him to order the Ninth Army Corps—which was the corps I originally commanded—to form the next morning a column of attack, by regiments. It consisted of some eighteen old regiments and some new ones. and I desired the column to make a direct attack upon the enemy's works. I thought that these regiments, by coming quickly up after each other, would be able to carry the stone wall and the batteries in front, forcing the enemy into their next line, and by going in with

them they would not be able to fire upon us to any
great extent. I left General Sumner with that understanding, and directed him to give the order.

" The next morning, just before the column started,
General Sumner came to me and said : ' General, I
hope you will desist from this attack ; I do not know of
any general officer who approves of it, and I think it
will prove disastrous to the army.' Advice of that
kind from General Sumner, who had always been in
favor of an advance whenever it was possible, caused
me to hesitate. I kept the column of attack formed and
sent over for the division and corps commanders, and
consulted with them. They unanimously voted against
the attack. I then went over to see the other officers of
the command on the other side, and found that the
same impression prevailed among them. I then sent
for General Franklin, who was on the left, and he was
of exactly the same opinion. This caused me to decide
that I ought not to make the attack I had contemplated.
And besides, inasmuch as the President of the United
States had told me not to be in haste in making this attack ; that he would give me all the support that he
could, but he did not want the Army of the Potomac
destroyed, I felt that I could not take the responsibility
of ordering the attack, notwithstanding my own belief
at the time, that the works of the enemy could be
carried." For the part performed by the "Ulster
Guard" during these operations, see Chronolog. Hist.

It is truer of military operations than of anything
else that "nothing succeeds like success," and nothing
extinguishes a General's popularity and the confidence
of his army in his ability, like failure. Explanations
and excuses are not accepted ; the delinquencies of subordinates are not taken into the account. The commanding general who planned and ordered the abortive
campaign must bear the responsibility for its failure.
No one understood this better than Burnside himself,

and when asked if Franklin's inefficient attack was not
the real cause of the failure, he at once replied : " No !
I understood perfectly well that when the General commanding an Army meets with disaster, he alone is responsible ; and I will not attempt to shift that responsibility upon any one else." The Corps and Grand Division commanders had, from the first, been opposed
to Burnside's plan of assault, and they had generally
remonstrated against his proposed renewal of the battle. To what they regarded as bad judgment in the beginning, was now added the quality of rashness ; and
to their want of confidence in his military sagacity was
now added an apprehension that he might undertake
some desperate exploit to retrieve his waning reputation.

So it came to pass that when Burnside was about to
set the army in motion on another campaign, on the
last day but one in December, the President countermanded it by telegraph. Burnside repaired to Washington, where he learned that certain of his subordinates—Generals John Newton and John Cochrane—had
visited the President and represented the condition of
things in the Army in such a light that the President
felt constrained to suspend the contemplated enterprise. Now, for the first, the purport of these clandes-
tine communications were imparted by the President
to General Halleck and the Secretary of War ; and the
result was an adherence to the decision at which the
President had arrived.

The movement designed by Burnside was a feint
above Fredericksburg, and an actual crossing seven
miles below, with a co-operating cavalry raid in rear of
the Confederate Army　Chafing under the mortification of the Fredericksburg repulse and indignant at the
unofficer-like conduct of some of his subordinates—conscious that his camp was full of croakers of high rank,
and that faith in his capacity was growing less and less

as time went on, he resolved to make one more effort for
his own reputation and his country's cause. He believed
a great victory was yet possible before the storms of the
later winter should render the roads impassable. His
movement by the left had been prohibited by the President. On the twentieth of January he set his columns
in motion by the right, with a view to cross the main
body of the army at Banks' Ford, four miles above
Fredericksburg, while making feints below the city, and
at several fords above. New roads had been cut to the
river at various points, and cavalry demonstrations made
to mislead the foe, whose pickets lined the south side
of the stream. The weather was mild for the season,
and the roads were excellent. The grand divisions of
Hooker and Franklin marched up the river by parallel
roads and on the night of the twentieth bivouacked
in the woods near the ford. Couch's Corps moved down
the stream as though to cross near the Sedden House.
Sigel, with a reserve Corps, guarded the line of the river
between the right and left wings of the Army, and kept
open their communications. The enterprise was of decidedly better promise than the direct attack on Fredericksburg ; and if the weather had continued favorable there was but one element that added to the danger of the ordinary chances of war, and that was the
want of confidence in the commanding-general. The
morale of the Army was seriously impaired, and it
obeyed by compulsion of military law, and not freely
or from choice.

Banks' Ford was at this time only a ford in name,
and the crossing was to be by pontoon bridges. The
pontoons were on the ground, and the artillery ready
to be placed in position to cover the crossing, and the
morrow was to see the Army again on the Richmond
side of the Rappahannock. Night had set in ; the
clouds began to gather, and one by one the stars went
out and thick darkness reigned. At ten o'clock the

flood-gates of Heaven were rent asunder, and such a
storm as that region had not known for years, burst
over the Army. Through wind and lightning and driving sleet and snow and rain, the men worked on, hour
after hour, in getting the guns up the heights and placing them in position, and drawing the pontoons to the
river's brink. And every hour the ground beneath
their feet was becoming more and more incapable of
sustaining their weight, until finally every foot of territory had become a quagmire. Morning found the
Army in this deplorable condition, with the Commander still resolute in his purpose to proceed. But
now it was found impossible to bring forward the artillery and ammunition wagons—all were stalled in the
mud ; the supply trains were immovable ; horses and
mules sunk into the fathomless muck up to their
bodies. Ropes were attached to the vehicles, and long
lines of men added their strength to that of the floundering beasts ; but it could not be—the advance was at
an end. With the utmost difficulty and in a state of
demoralization that has no parallel in the history of
the Army of the Potomac, the old camps were finally
reached, and the "Mud Campaign" was at an end.
So also, was General Burnside's usefulness as Commander of the Army

Burnside could not but feel that he was the victim
of "the slings and arrows of outrageous fortune," and
the jealousy of some of his subordinates. Against the
former there was no redress, but as to the latter he resolved to retaliate ; and prepared " General Order No.
8," whereby Major-General Hooker, Brigadier-Generals
W T. H. Brooks and John Newton were named for ig-
nominious dismissal from the service, and Major-Generals W B. Franklin and W. F Smith, and Brigadier-
Generals John Cochrane and Edward Ferrero and Lieutenant-Colonel J. H. Taylor, were relieved from duty
with the Army   Before promulgating this Order, Gen-

eral Burnside was persuaded to submit it to the President, who, after consultation with his Cabinet, decided to relieve General Burnside, instead of approving the Order ; and, on the twenty-eighth of January an Order was issued by the Secretary of War relieving Burnside from the command, "At his own request;" and Hooker, whom he had proposed to " ignominiously dismiss," became his successor. The same Order relieved General Sumner, at his own request, and also General Franklin, without assigning any reason therefor.

CHAPTER XXVI

THE winter of 1862-3 proved a very disastrous one for
the Army of the Potomac, and its misfortunes imparted
a gloom to the prospects of the Federal cause which
was felt throughout the loyal portion of the country no
less than in the army itself. It seemed impossible for
the Administration to find a competent commander for
that unfortunate army "Failure!" had been written
against the name of every man who had been placed at
its head. Would such be the record of the dashing
soldier to whose hands the baton had now been transferred?

During this winter the rebel cavalry amused itself by
riding "rough-shod" over the country in rear of the
Federal Army, capturing small parties of Union soldiers, carrying off horses and wagons, burning railroad
bridges, and destroying army supplies, in all directions.
Desertions from the Union Army were reported to be at
the rate of two hundred a day, and there seemed to be
no way to stop them. Citizens despairing of success,
and regarding the Army of the Potomac as consigned to
slaughter, aided their relatives to escape from it by
every means in their power—chief among which was
smuggling civilians' clothes to them; and, arrayed in

these, their escape was not difficult. General Hooker testified before the Committee on the Conduct of the War, that the rolls showed 2,922 officers and 81,964 men absent from the army, a large proportion of whom could not be accounted for. This aggregate must have included all absentees from the first organization of their commands. It is not unlikely that many of them had been killed or captured on the Peninsula and in Pope's campaign, and not accounted for, while many others may have been in hospital. The effect of "General Order No. 162, A. of P., 1862," was to place men in the attitude of deserters who might be dead on the battle-field, or prisoners, or in hospital. After such marches and battles as those on the Peninsula and in Pope's campaign, it was not always possible to account for every man, and a number of men were dropped from the rolls of the "Ulster Guard," under that Order, who subsequently reported, and whose absence was the result of sickness or capture.

Hooker was the army's *beau-ideal* of a soldier in all physical qualities, and he soon made a very perceptible improvement in the *morale* of his command. He visited all portions of the army, and infused a good deal of his own confident spirit into his officers and men. Desertions ceased, and the army began to grow as recruits came forward, and when the season for active operations arrived, Hooker found himself at the head of one of the finest armies the Government had ever put in the field. In infantry it numbered one hundred thousand men; in artillery ten thousand, and its cavalry was thirteen thousand strong. All arms were in the very best condition of spirits, and in complete preparation for the coming campaign. Confidence and an eagerness for the fray had taken the place of hopelessness, and a desire to escape the service—the rank and file had come to believe in their new commander.

Hooker designed to open the campaign about the

middle of April, and on the thirteenth he despatched
the cavalry under General Stoneman, to proceed up the
Rappahannock, cross the river above the rebel picket-
line, and sweep down in rear of Lee's army When
this movement began to make itself felt, the infantry
columns were to cross the river and turn the Confederate position. Soon after the cavalry set out, a heavy
storm came on, rendering the river impassable, and the
movements were suspended.

Two weeks elapsed before the water and roads were
in a condition to justify a renewal of operations. Then,
on Monday, April twenty-seventh, the 11th Corps, under General Howard ; the 12th, under General Slocum ;
and later on the same day, the 5th Corps, under General
Meade, left their camps on the right of our line, and set
out for Kelly's Ford, on the Rappahannock, seventeen
miles above Fredericksburg. Two divisions of the 2d
Corps, General Couch, were to march at sunrise on the
28th, to the vicinity of Banks' Ford, four miles above
Fredericksburg, and from these, one brigade and one
battery were to be sent to United States Ford, eight
miles above Fredericksburg. These two divisions were
not to show themselves along the river bank. The
Third Division of this Corps was to remain in camp at
Falmouth, and picket the river along that line, and be
in readiness to repel any attempt of the enemy to cross.
The 1st Corps, General Reynolds ; the 3d, General
Sickles ; and the 6th, General Sedgwick, were to take
positions to cross the river below Fredericksburg—the
6th Corps, at what was called Franklin's crossing, being
the point at which General Franklin crossed at the
battle of Fredericksburg, and the 1st Corps at Pollock's
Mills, a short distance below. The 3d Corps was to be
ready to cross at either point in support of the 1st or
6th, as might become necessary The cavalry was to
cover the right flank of the corps assigned to cross the

river at Kelly's Ford, and to raid on Lee's communications with Richmond.

When these operations were inaugurated, and during their continuance, the Confederate Army numbered less than fifty thousand men. Two divisions of Longstreet's Corps were at Suffolk, and did not return until after the battles of Chancellorsville. Walter H. Taylor, Lee's Assistant-Adjutant-General, gives the strength of the Rebel Army at this time as follows : Anderson and McLaws' commands, 13,000 ; Jackson's, including the divisions of A. P Hill, Rhodes (late D. H. Hill's) and Trimble, 21,000 ; Early, 6,000 ; and cavalry and artillery, 7,000. Hooker appreciated his own superiority of numbers, and in his orders to General Slocum, who, as senior officer, had command of his own and the 11th Corps, he said : "You will have nearly 40,000 men, which is more than he (Lee) can spare to send against you." It could have been only in view of the very great disparity in numbers that Hooker adopted what are ordinarily considered rash and unjustifiable tactics, by dividing his army into two nearly equal parts, and then separating the right and left wings by at least a day's march, with a difficult and capricious river between them. He was liable to be whipped in detail, and the result proved that it was within the compass of possibilities for Lee to have fallen upon either wing and defeated it before it could be supported by the other. But Lee was in doubt as to Hooker's real purpose, and the disposition he had made of his army until the morning of May first, and by that time General Hooker had re-enforced his right wing by ordering up the Third Corps, and the two divisions of the Second Corps, which had been lying near Banks' and United States Fords. This left the First Corps, General Reynolds, and the Sixth, General Sedgwick, below Fredericksburg, while one division of the 2d Corps remained in its camp at Falmouth.

The corps dispatched to the extreme right crossed

the Rappahannock and Rapidan, and then facing to
the south-eastward, marched down the right bank of
the latter river, over such roads as could be found, and
on Thursday, the 30th, arrived at Chancellorsville,
which was designated as the rendezvous.   *Why* it
should have been, it is difficult to tell. Probably, in
the first instance, because the place had a name, and
its geographical position was known with reasonable
accuracy   It was about the worst position to manœuvre
civilized troops in that could be found on this continent.
The locality is known as "The Wilderness," and is an
almost unbroken expanse of dense thicket, with only
here and there a human habitation. The far-famed
Chancellorsville itself consisted of a solitary house and
a few out-buildings, and was used as a hostelry   The
plank road from Fredericksburg to Orange Court-House
passes this tavern ; and a number of obscure wood roads
converge upon the same point. The distance to Fredericksburg is about 11 miles, *via* the plank road, which
runs nearly parallel with the Rappahannock, and at
Chancellorsville is about four miles south of the river.
There is a dirt-road running from Chancellorsville,
nearly parallel to the plank road, and uniting with it
about six miles east of the latter place, and near Tabernacle Church. Still another road leads to Banks' Ford,
about four miles above Fredericksburg, and whither a
part of the Second Corps had been ordered. Somewhat
less than three miles to the eastward of Chancellorsville
the "Wilderness" terminates ; and the country from
thence to Fredericksburg is rolling, and generally
cleared, and presents no unusual obstacles to the manœuvre of large bodies of troops of all arms.

General Hooker himself gave the Committee on the
Conduct of the War the following description of the
place called Chancellorsville : "Much of that region
was swampy at the time, and a great deal of it covered
with undergrowth, and is impenetrable even to infantry.

I directed General Slocum to send a force through this forest in his front, and he reported to me that he could not do it." Hooker halted three corps of his army in this tangled thicket about noon of the thirtieth day of April, and signalized the occasion by issuing a congratulatory Order upon their successful crossing of the rivers, and declared therein "that the operations of the last three days have determined that our enemy must either ingloriously fly, or come out from behind his defences and give us battle on our own ground, where certain destruction awaits him. The operations of the Fifth, Eleventh and Twelfth Corps have been a succession of splendid achievements."

Now these operations had really been remarkably successful. They had been planned with judgment, and executed with great skill. But their value to the Union Commander depended upon the use he would make of this initial triumph over his adversary It was but the first step in what needs must be a series of operations, having as their main object the destruction of the Rebel army   To pause here was to surrender all advantage supposed to have been gained by the secrecy and celerity of the preceding operations ; and, as a turning movement, it would have no especial effect, because it would give the enemy time to select and fortify another position, keeping himself constantly between Hooker and Richmond. Lee had never yet made any serious opposition to the various crossings of the Rappahannock by the Army of the Potomac, nor did he to the crossing of the Monocacy, in the Maryland campaign ; and Hooker knew that the tactics of the Confederate chieftain was rather to allow the army to cross, and fight it afterwards. Therefore, he could not reasonably argue that Lee would be greatly alarmed on learning that he was actually across the river, and waiting in the "Wilderness" for the Confederate Army to attack him.

I think it is fair to conclude, from all the facts and circumstances, that Hooker had in view but two contingencies when he began his campaign. The first was a battle at the river crossing, in which event he would fight as circumstances dictated, and be governed by the result ; the second was, that Lee *must* retreat, if the Union Army were successfully transferred to the south side of the stream and threatened his flank and rear. The pursuit was left to be directed at the proper time and in the proper way Hooker really had no idea that Lee would " come out from behind his defences and give him battle." He did not believe his forces would justify such tactics ; but he supposed his adversary would have recourse to the other horn of the dilemma, and "ingloriously fly " That he did not do this was a great surprise to the Union Commander, and it left him without further plans of immediate operations. The halting of his army in the " Wilderness," and his telegram to General Sedgwick on the thirtieth, show that he did not propose to fight so much as to manœuvre. He telegraphed to Sedgwick, below Fredericksburg : " Make a demonstration on the enemy's lines in the direction of Hamilton's Crossing at one o'clock, the object being simply to ascertain whether or not the enemy continues to hug his defences in full force ; and, if he should have abandoned them, to take possession of his works and the commanding ground in their vicinity * * * * This demonstration will be made for no other purpose than that stated." Indeed, General Hooker himself testified before the Committee on the Conduct of the War, speaking of his later order to Sedgwick to attack : "When I gave the order to General Sedgwick, I expected that Lee would be whipped by manœuvre. I supposed he would be compelled to march off on the same line that Jackson had. He would have been thrown on the Culpepper and Gordonsville Road, placing me fifty or sixty miles nearer Richmond than himself." So fully persuaded had Hooker been from the first that Lee would retreat if he found his powerful opponent across the river, that he could not divest his mind of that idea and direct his thoughts to the necessity of providing for a different contingency I believe the disaster at Chancellorsville was owing to this preconceived and fatal notion. The enemy was to be whipped by manoeuvre and not by battle. In this view of the purposes of the campaign, Hooker's congratulatory Order on the successful crossing of the rivers, and his halting in the "Wilderness," seem consistent with the object in view. But, under the circumstances in which the Federal commander was placed, he should have looked for more decisive results than could be hoped for from a campaign of manoeuvres.

Two brigades of Anderson's division had been posted at Ely's and Banks' Fords, and as the Federals advanced, they fell back towards Fredericksburg. The other brigade of the same division was sent forward to support them, and they united at Tabernacle Church, on the Fredericksburg and Orange Court-House Plank Road, and about mid-way between the former place and Chancellorsville, two or three miles beyond the boundary of the "Wilderness."

While these events were transpiring on the right, the First and Sixth corps had crossed the Rappahannock below Fredericksburg as directed, and General Sedgwick had made the demonstration required by General Hooker's order of the Thirtieth, and found that the enemy continued "to hug his defences." The Sixth Corps was 22,000 strong, and the First and Third Corps contained about 35,000 men. (Sedgwick's testimony before the Committee on the Conduct of the War). But as has been already said, the Third Corps was ordered to the right on the Thirtieth, and two days later the First Corps was also called from the left to the right. This left General Sedgwick's Corps alone on the south

side of the river below Fredericksburg, and Gibbons'
division of the Second Corps on the north side, opposite
that town.

Lee, standing on the heights in rear of Fredericksburg, tried to read his adversary's designs in the movements of his troops. The corps on the right had
marched in the night, and from positions beyond the
reach of his observation, yet his vigilant vedettes and
fleet couriers had conveyed the news to him of large
bodies of Union troops crossing at the fords above Fredericksburg, and the problem for the Confederate commander to solve was, "Where is the blow to fall !
Which is the feint and which the real menace ?" He
saw three corps of 57,000 men prepare to cross the river
below the city, while a division remained in its camp
directly opposite. Here at his feet as it were, was an
army out-numbering the Confederate array at his back,
while messenger after messenger reported swarming
thousands moving towards his left and rear. General
Hooker believed this threatening aspect would induce
his wily antagonist to "ingloriously fly ;" but he stood
and studied the moves of his opponent, and calculated
the chances of the great game about being played, upon
which depended the lives of thousands of human beings,
and, perhaps, the destiny of a nation. He saw Sedgwick and Reynolds cross the river on the twenty-ninth,
and draw up their forces on the plain below the city
and almost under his guns, and yet he "hugged his defences." The next afternoon he stood and saw Sedgwick's demonstration against his right, and sent Stonewall Jackson to meet it. Closely scrutinizing these
operations, with practiced eye, he determined the important question on which his mind had been intent for
three days, and he said to himself, "This movement on
my right is a *ruse de guerre*, the real danger is on the
other flank and in my rear." He immediately recalled
Jackson, and sent him to re-enforce Anderson at Taber-

nacle Church. That night, Lee put Early with 6,000
men in charge of the rebel works at Fredericksburg, and
then proceeded with the residue of his army, (M'Law's
division) to re-enforce Jackson and Anderson at Tabernacle Church.

Thus matters stood on the morning of the first of
May—Hooker at Chancellorsville, with the 3d, 5th, 11th,
12th and two divisions of the 2d Corps, present, or within
supporting distance ; an aggregate strength of about 60,-
000 men. Sedgwick and Reynolds below Fredericksburg.
and Gibbon within supporting distance, with a combined strength of about 39,000 men. The Union cavalry swinging around the rebel army's left. Lee at
Tabernacle Church, half way between Fredericksburg
and Chancellorsville, with about 36,000 infantry and
artillery ; Early's division, augmented by Barksdale's
brigade, holding the Confederate line at Fredericksburg,
and the rebel cavalry scouting on Hooker's right flank.

Manifestly, Hooker had sacrificed the opportunity of
compelling Lee to " give us battle on our own ground,"
unless, indeed, that ground was the " Wilderness," and
we cannot do General Hooker's judgment the injustice
to believe that he deliberately meditated making that
his battle-field. His own description of it, shows that
he knew it was not the place to fight a battle on, and,
moreover, he stated on the same occasion from which
we have already quoted him, that " I could not find out
anything about that country, except I knew that it was
called the Wilderness. I could find out nothing about
roads there, either before I crossed the river or afterwards." Then one is constrained to inquire : " Why
spend twenty-four hours there when a march of an hour
will bring the heads of your columns ' out of the Wilderness,' and enable you to deploy in an open country with
a conformation just adapted to your purposes ?" Was
Hooker afraid he would *intercept* Lee in his " inglorious flight," if he threw his columns across the road over

which Jackson marched ? If Sedgwick crowded Lee off
the Bowling Green and Telegraph roads, then he must
needs fly over the road leading to Orange Court House,
and Hooker's advance would obstruct that highway.
It was to be a campaign of manœuvres and not of battles. Hooker had determined to capture Richmond by
forcing Lee on a line of retreat to his Capital fifty or
sixty miles farther than Hooker himself would have to
go to reach the same goal. With Richmond in Hooker's possession and Lee's army cut off from aid or supplies, its capture or dispersion would next be in order.
But the defect in this strategy consisted in its being pre-
dicated upon unreal premises, and when the pivotal
condition failed, the entire scheme mis-carried. Not
that it necessarily need to have done so, but either because Hooker lacked resources in an unlooked-for emergency, or because he *would* believe that what he had
expected *must* ensue ; it did grievously miscarry. So
he tarried in the Wilderness.

But Sedgwick's demonstration on the afternoon of
the thirtieth had failed to relax the rebel embrace of
his works, and no signs of flight manifested themselves.
With but eight days' rations when his march began
four days ago, Hooker could not wait forever for Lee to
decamp. Sixty thousand Union soldiers could scarcely
have been maintained upon the supply of locusts and
wild honey to be found in the Wilderness of Chancellorsville. Therefore, about nine o'clock on the morning of
May first, General Hooker did what he should have
done some hours before—he ordered his columns to advance into the open country Syke's division of the
Fifth corps led the way over the Dirt road, between the
Plank and River road, and was followed by a division
of the Second corps ; the other two divisions of the
Fifth corps were to march over the River road. The
Third corps was ordered to mass on the road to United
States Ford, and about a mile from Chancellorsville ;

practically in reserve; the Twelfth corps was to move down the Plank road until the head of the column was near Tabernacle Church; the Eleventh corps was to mass on the Plank road a mile in rear of the Twelfth. These several movements were ordered to be completed by two o'clock. "After the movement commences, headquarters will be at Tabernacle Church." Evidently, Hooker knew very little as to what was going on in his near front. He had no idea that at the moment he issued that order, Lee's headquarters were even then " at Tabernacle Church."

What ensued upon this late attempt to disengage the Federal Army from the folds of the Wilderness is told by General Hooker in his examination before the Committee on the Conduct of the War, in the following words:

"Two roads lead from Chancellorsville to Fredericksburg, which intersect about four miles from Chancellorsville, in the direction in which we were marching. It was at this point that the enemy had established his main force, his right reaching to the south of the Plank road, and his left resting on the Rappahannock.

"The ground in our vicinity was broken and covered with dense forests, much of which were impenetrable to infantry. The ravines to the north of the road were deep, and their general direction was at right angles to the Rappahannock, affording the enemy a formidable position behind each of them. Here was the enemy's entire army, with the exception, as I have already stated, of Early's division and Barksdale's brigade, making a force of about 8,000 men, which had been left to hold the line from below Hamilton's crossing to the heights above Fredericksburg, a distance of between five and six miles. They had left one entire brigade to guard their depot at Hamilton's crossing; and two regiments, the 18th and 21st Mississippi, to defend Fredericksburg.

"The 12th Corps had been ordered to advance on the Plank road, to be followed by the 11th Corps ; the 5th Corps had been ordered to advance on the road nearest the river, to be followed by the 2d Corps. They had proceeded but a short distance when the head of the column emerged from the heavy forest and discovered the enemy to be advancing in line of battle. Nearly all of the 12th Corps had emerged from the forest at that moment, but, as the passage-way through the forest was narrow, I was satisfied that I could not throw troops through it fast enough to resist the advance of General Lee, and was apprehensive of being whipped in detail.

" Accordingly, instructions were given for the troops in advance to return and establish themselves on the the line they had just left, and to hold themselves in readiness to receive the enemy In the execution of this order a part of the 12th Corps and one division of the 5th Corps had a skirmish with the enemy, but returned and established themselves on the line in good order. The enemy continued his advance, and upon reaching the forest, with a contracted front, fell upon the 12th and 2d Corps, but were promptly and easily repulsed. Nothing more transpired that night, except perhaps some random firing among the pickets."

Now, did Hooker believe that Lee meant to fight him in the woods, or that his movement was the looked-for retreat ? Even on the following day, while Jackson's column was passing across Hooker's front to make the attack on his right, Hooker believed the inevitable retreat was in progress, and sent word to Sedgwick : "We know the enemy is flying, trying to save his trains ; two of Sickles' divisions are among them."

It is scarcely possible to conceive of a more "inglorious" retrograde than that described in General Hooker's statement, and it presents a most striking contrast to his congratulatory Order of the day before. The re-

24

call went far to dispirit the army, because it tended to prove either that General Hooker's policy was unformed or vacillating, or that he was surprised by meeting the enemy and was afraid to fight him. Several of the corps and division commanders endeavored to induce Hooker to revoke the order recalling the troops to Chancellorsville. The left column under Griffin and Humphreys had nearly reached Banks' Ford, the possession of which would have shortened the line of communication between Hooker and Sedgwick by twelve miles. The centre column under Sykes had obtained possession, after a spirited skirmish between the advance guards of the two armies, of a commanding ridge that runs across the roads over which Hooker's forces were advancing, and of which Couch says in his report: "The ground on which I had posted Hancock in support of Sykes, was about one and a half miles from Chancellorsville, *and commanded it.* Upon receiving orders from General Hooker to come in, I sent Major Burt to him urging that, on account of the great advantages of that position, it should be held at all hazards. The reply was, to return at once." General Slocum's column on the right had met no resistance, and was well advanced into the open country, and it seems as though the debouche from the Wilderness was secured by the movements and positions of the leading divisions of the Union Army. Generals Warren and Humphreys besought Hooker to hold on to these positions (Reports of these officers), but he only reiterated the order to fall back.

General Hooker having brought his forces back into the Wilderness, with the enemy following closely the retiring Unionists, formed his line of battle; with his left resting near the river road, and a little north of east from Chancellorsville, from thence in a westerly direction it ran to the Fredericksburg and Orange Court House plank road, which it struck and crossed a few hundred yards east of Chancellorsville, and then ran westerly along the south side of that road, about three miles, when it turned sharply towards the rear of the line, and stretched back across what is known as "The Old Turnpike," forming a defensive crotchet to this flank. The line was about five miles long. Near where it intersected the plank road, and a few hundred yards in rear of the line, was a clearing of about an acre of ground, whereon stood the Chancellor House and its appendages. This house General Hooker used as head-quarters, and the cleared ground around it was covered with army wagons, horses, &c. Posted along our line of battle, from left to right, and in the order named, were Meade's Fifth Corps, one division of the Second Corps, Slocum's Twelfth Corps, one division of the Third Corps, with Howard's Eleventh Corps on the right. The residue of the army was held in reserve. These movements and operations consumed Friday, the first day of May.

On Saturday morning the force of General Couch's reasoning of the day before was made manifest by the thorough shelling which the Confederates gave the open space around the Chancellor House, from guns which they had posted on the ridge which Couch had carried on Friday, and which he had urged Hooker to retain possession of. At an early hour the enemy's skirmish-line advanced, and began to feel the Federal position from the river road up to the Chancellor House, and for some distance along the plank road, as though seeking for a weak spot in Hooker's armor. These offensive demonstrations were continued, at intervals, through the day, but no general attack was made on these parts of the lines. These operations were de-signed only to occupy Hooker's attention, while the vital blow was preparing to be struck at the extreme right.

STARTING from near Tabernacle Church, at about the
time Lee's skirmishers approached Hooker's lines,
Stonewall Jackson began his march with 22,000 men,
for the right flank of the Union line. This march
would be for three miles nearly parallel with Hooker's
front, and was a most perilous one to make before a
watchful and energetic opponent. It likewise left Lee
himself in a position of great danger, if the movement
of Jackson should be discovered, and advantage of his
absence taken to attack Lee, with his force reduced to
about 13,000 men. But after Hooker had been so
easily forced to abandon the open country, and take
cover in the Wilderness, Lee seems to have had no apprehension that he would assume the aggressive.

Jackson moved over the dirt road until nearly opposite Chancellorsville, when he filed to the left into an
obscure road running nearly west, called "The Old
Mine Road." Fitz-Lee's cavalry was deployed on
Jackson's right flank to mask the movement. At the
"Furnace," on the Old Mine Road, Jackson detached
the Twenty-third Georgia to guard a forest road leading from the "Furnace" to Chancellorsville, and by
way of which his rear was liable to attack.

The condition of the country was exceedingly favorable to the success of such an enterprise as Jackson
had undertaken, and his reputation for such bold ex-

ploits should have put his adversary on' his guard
against him. His guides were familiar with the roads
and paths through the forest, while to the Unionists it
was a *terra incognita*. But it was ground of our own
choosing, and we have no business to find fault with it.

While Jackson's column was passing the "Furnace," it was observed by the Union pickets, and the
fact that a large body of Confederates were moving towards the Federal right was duly reported to Headquarters. Birney's Division of Sickles' Corps was at
this time posted well to the front of the Union line,
and nearly opposite the point where the Eleventh and
Twelfth Corps joined. Upon Sickles' suggestion,
Hooker directed that Birney's Division should be still
farther advanced, in order to discover the strength and
purpose of the enemy's movement. A second division
of Sickles' Corps was thrown forward to support Birney. Birney reached the road over which Jackson was
marching, in time to strike the rear of his column and
capture a few prisoners, and the Twenty-third Georgia,
left at the "Furnace," was captured *en masse*. Sickles
regarded the operations in which he was engaged, sufficiently important to justify his calling upon General
Hooker for re-enforcements, and the latter ordered
Pleasonton's Cavalry and a brigade of infantry from
each of the two right Corps (Eleventh and Twelfth) to
report to General Sickles.

General Hooker states in his examination before the
Committee on the Conduct of the War (page 126), that
this movement of Jackson was reported at his Headquarters as early as half-past nine in the morning, and
that he directed two divisions of the Third Corps to *follow up* the movement   "This order was promptly executed, but the two divisions did not reach the line of
the enemy's flank movement until after the main column
had passed, still in season to capture nearly a regiment
of its rear guard, and they were ordered to *follow up*

the enemy's column that had passed off to our right.
I learned from the prisoners that this column was
Jackson's Corps, numbering about 25,000 men. His
route had been over a by-road through the forest, diagonally across my front, and approaching within two or
three miles of the right of the Eleventh Corps."

Whether it was good generalship in view of the information thus obtained of the strength and direction of
this hostile body, to be content with giving orders to
"follow it up," admits of serious doubt. Birney was too
late to do more than to strike the rear guard, while the
main column pushed on to its destination. Jackson's
object ought to have been apparent to General Hooker,
and something more should have been done than to follow him up, unless such following up could have brought
him to a stand and forced him to accept battle under
circumstances less favorable to him than they would be
at the right of the Union Army, whither he was evidently going. But that he had not been arrested in his
march—that, in fact, he had strided on, regardless of
the turmoil of battle in his rear was manifest, and yet
General Hooker seems to have taken no steps to meet
the impending onset. Instead of doing so, he weakened
his right flank by sending two brigades from it to Sickles.
The next he hears from Jackson's column is the outburst of battle on the right, at six in the evening. If
the two divisions of Sickles' Corps, which had been thus
thrown to the front, had been at once recalled, and, with
the other reserves of the army, had been posted on the
right, to support the threatened flank, the result of Jackson's attack ought to have been the very reverse of what
it was.

Jackson, meantime pushed on, and reaching the
Brock Road, turned the head of his column to the right,
and marching in a northerly direction, crossed the plank
road, and bending to the eastward, crossed the old turnpike about a mile beyond the right of Hooker's line.

Here he halted and prepared his column for the assault. His design was to swing his left around the right flank and strike the rear of the Eleventh Corps, and at the same time deliver a furious attack along its front.

General Devens' Division of the Eleventh Corps occupied the extreme right of the Union line, and the two right regiments were formed so as to present nearly a right angle to the general course of the Federal position—in military parlance they were "refused," so as to present a front to any force moving upon the works from the westward. But there were no natural obstacles on this flank upon which to rest it—it was "in air." There were no reserves to the right division, except two regiments, and nearly the whole of the Eleventh and Twelfth Corps were posted on the line.

Jackson's attack was made with his usual impetuosity, at about six o'clock in the evening, and the force of the blow fell upon General Devens' Division, and at first principally upon the two regiments which were "refused." Devens at once ordered up his two reserve regiments and made a stubborn fight against absolutely overwhelming odds. His entire division consisted of but two brigades, numbering less than four thousand men, and against these was being hurled, with all the energy of their enthusiastic leader, and with all the *elan* inspired by the initial success of preceding operations, 22,000 men. Unless this flank was supported, and that soon, there was but one result to be anticipated—the right would inevitably be crushed. Two divisions of the army constituting a part of its reserves, were floundering in the thicket two or three miles in front of the line, supposed to be "following up" this movement, and liable to be cut off by the advance of Jackson's column; the residue of the reserves were posted near the Chancellor House, and too remote to be of any avail. The situation could scarcely have been worse if planned with a view to facilitate the operations of the assaulting column.

Devens made the best disposition he could of his own
division to meet the rebel on-set, and when the attack had fully developed, and he saw the purpose of the
Confederate commander to be the disruption of our right
and an advance down the old turnpike, sweeping the
rear of the Federal line, he at once sent an aide to General
Schurz, commanding the next division on his left, in-
forming him of the character of the attack, and sug-
gesting that he change front across the road.   This was
done by one of General Schurz's brigades, that of General Schimmelfennig, who changed front to the west,
and nearly perpendicular to the established line.

Jackson's attack on Devens' "refused" wing was
made by a column of battalions *en masse*, while heavy
lines enveloped his extreme right, and extended across
his front to the left.   Pushing the left of his line around
Devens' right, Jackson opened a heavy fire upon the
flank and rear of the Federals.   No troops can long be
held to their work under such circumstances, and after
a very determined resistance upon the part of officers
and men, the division gave way and retired in confusion.
General Schimmelfennig's Brigade were next encountered by the exultant and yelling Rebels, and their
advance was checked for nearly an hour.   General Devens succeeded in re-forming a portion of his division
at this point, and contributed in retarding the advance
of the foe.   Meantime, General Howard had directed
General Steinwehr, who commanded his third division,
to change front, which was accomplished in time to receive the enemy's attack, but he could only offer a temporary resistance to the masses brought against him,
and was compelled to fall back.   General Howard personally directed the operations of his Corps from the
time the right gave way, and displayed great coolness
and gallantry on the field.   Of General Devens, General
Howard said : " Your own conduct was noble and self-
sacrificing in the extreme.   More than an hour after the

attack, I saw you still rallying men, forming lines to resist the enemy's attack, though suffering from a severe
and painful wound received early in the action." General Devens had received a painful wound in the foot
early in the action, but he continued in command until
the battle was over, and remained on the field in an ambulance during that night and the next day

About the time Jackson burst upon the right of
Hooker's line, Lee, with his 13,000 men made a determined attack upon the front of the left and centre,
held by the Corps of Couch and Slocum. The attack
was in aid of Jackson's operations rather than with any
expectation of carrying the works. The resistance of
the Eleventh Corps had delayed Jackson nearly two
hours and it was now growing dark, but the Confederates were still advancing down the line with the prospect of sweeping the entire Federal Army out of its
works. The utmost confusion reigned within the lines
of the Unionists ; the noise of battle, now extending
along the front for two miles and rolling up from the
right with increasing volume, as position after position
was gained by the exultant rebels, swept in threatening thunders over the Headquarters of General Hooker
at the Chancellor House. Flying men, riderless horses,
caissons with and without drivers, artillery carriages,
army wagons, all crowded and struggled over the narrow road, seeking to escape the shot and shell that
rained around them and the swarming hordes that came
yelling in their rear.

Hooker now appeared in person upon the scene and
riding to the head of his old division, then commanded
by General Berry, which with a brigade of the Second
Corps had been held in reserve near Headquarters,
double-quicked them in the direction of the approaching rebels and ordered Berry to seize and hold, if possible, a point of high ground a little to the right of the
Twelfth Corps, and which had constituted a part of the

line of the Eleventh. It was a commanding position
and its possession by the enemy would endanger the
residue of the line. Hooker shouted to Berry above the
roar of battle : "Throw your men into the breach—receive the enemy on your bayonets—don't fire a shot—
they can't see you!" (N Y *Times*, May 5, 1863.)
Berry advanced some three-quarters of a mile and finding that the enemy were already in possession of the
coveted point, he halted and formed line of battle across
the road.

General Pleasonton, who had been acting in support
of General Sickles' movement against Jackson's marching column, in the afternoon, opportunely returned to
the lines at this moment and at once comprehended the
situation and saw that immediate and effective action
was necessary to prevent a stampede of the entire army
He had but two regiments of cavalry with him and one
battery of horse artillery. The woods on Pleasonton's left were filled with Confederates who were rapidly advancing, and it was necessary that they should
be brought to a halt. It was a most unpromising place
for a cavalry charge, but Pleasonton had no other
forces to employ and what was required was immediate
action. Turning to Major Keenan, commanding the
Eighth Pennsylvania regiment, he said : " Major, you
must charge in these woods with your regiment and
hold the rebels until I can get some of these guns into
position. You must do it at all cost." The Major replied : " General, I will do it." He made the charge in
gallant style and fell dead at the head of his regiment.
Pleasonton says: "I mentioned, (selected) the Major,
because I knew his character so well ; that he was the
man for the occasion. He replied to me with a smile on
his face, although it was almost certain death, "General, I will do it." Major Keenan's charge surprised
and alarmed the rebels and brought them to a temporary halt. Pleasonton availed himself of the opportu-

nity to put his battery in position, unlimber and double shot it with canister. Gathering the passing and abandoned guns, he soon had twenty-two cannon in position and each one double shotted. Soon a blaze of fire burst out of the woods in front of Pleasonton, and a multitude of the enemy came charging upon the guns. Pleasonton had cautioned his gunners not to fire until he gave the command and to aim their pieces at the ground-line of the parapet lately occupied by the Eleventh Corps. A moment later and the command " *Fire !*" rang out, and twenty-two cannon, filled almost to the muzzles with canister, hurled their deadly missiles into the charging throng. The discharge swept their ranks away—it seemed to blow them, bodily, over the parapet. They several times returned to the assault only to be met by the same consuming fire, and they abandoned the attempt to make any farther progress for the night. This was one of the most soldier-like and gallant exploits of that fatal day, and but for it the enemy might, and probably would, have swept on until they had taken our entire line in reverse. To no man more than to General Pleasonton is due the credit of having saved the Army from utter rout.

At midnight Ward's Brigade of Birney's division, under orders from General Sickles, made a successful attack upon the Confederates and drove them back across the Union line of works and reoccupied General Howard's rifle-pits, and recovered several pieces of artillery and some caissons which had been abandoned during the day Thus, the final success of the day's operations was with the Union Army.

The bold and tireless enthusiast who directed and inspired the column which smote Hooker's right, had himself been stricken down, in the moment of his first success, by the fire of his over-zealous followers. With the religious faith and formal severity of a Puritan, and with the sincerity and devotion to the Confederate cause

of a Crusader, Jackson strongly impressed his officers
and men with the faith that animated himself in his
invincibility and in the ultimate success of the cause in
which they were engaged. His brief military career had
been exceptionally striking and was surrounded with a
halo of romance which tended to magnify his martial
exploits and win the unbounded admiration of his
people. But with all his dash and enthusiasm he was
a remarkably discreet leader, and conducted his operations upon well-considered plans, and it was in the
pursuit of information upon which to guide his conduct
in the further operations against Hooker's right that he
received the wounds of which he soon after died. John
Esten Cooke, in his life of General Lee, narrates the
circumstances attending the wounding of Jackson.
"It was now between nine and ten P. M., and Jackson
rode to the front to reconnoitre. The fighting had
ceased—the moon was shining through misty clouds.
Jackson rode forward on the Chancellorsville road a
hundred yards in advance of his lines, with a few
officers, and halted to listen. Suddenly a volley from
his own infantry, was fired into his party—several of
whom fell from their horses. Wheeling to the left,
Jackson galloped into the woods to escape a second
volley In doing so, he passed in front of his men who
fired upon him, at twenty paces, and wounded him in
three places—twice in his left arm and once in his right
hand. He dropped the reins from the left hand as the
bullets passed through that arm, and seized them in his
bleeding right hand. His horse wheeled suddenly and
dashed off towards Chancellorsville. He passed beneath the limb of a pine tree which struck Jackson in
the face and tore off his cap and nearly dismounted
him. He retained his seat, however, and regained the
road, when he was met by Captain Wilbourn, one of his
staff officers." In "The Life of Stonewall Jackson, by
a Virginian," it is said that Jackson had ordered A. P

Hill to advance with his division, and to reserve his fire unless cavalry approached from the direction of the enemy, and that Jackson with his staff, rode forward to the skirmish line. That there he ordered an aide to ride back and tell Hill to press right on. Soon after giving this order, he, himself turned and rode back at a trot, followed by his staff. The little body of horsemen were mistaken for Federal Cavalry and fired upon as described. Captain Boswell was killed; Colonel Crutchfield, Chief of Artillery was wounded, and two couriers were killed. The bone of Jackson's left arm was shattered, and the chief artery severed; another ball, entering the same arm between the elbow and wrist, passed out through the palm of the hand. This writer says Jackson fell from his horse and was caught by Captain Wormly, to whom he said, "All my wounds are by my own men." This writer adds, that the fire which wounded Jackson, was responded to by the Federals who made a sudden advance; and, the Confederates falling back, their foes actually charged over Jackson's body Subsequently regaining the ground, Jackson was placed upon a litter and borne to the rear, amid a heavy fire from the Federal lines. One of the litter-bearers was shot down, and the General fell from the shoulders of the men, receiving a severe contusion, adding to the injuries of the arm, and injuring the side severely. The Federal artillery fire, he says, was terrible, and the wounded General was left for five minutes until the fire slackened, when he was placed in an ambulance and borne to the rear. He died eight days afterwards at Guineas' Station, five miles from Chancellorsville. Jackson was wounded about the time of the operations of General Pleasonton, above described, and the "terrible" artillery fire was no doubt from his guns.

CHAPTER XXVIII

GENERAL HOOKER, unlike Burnside, seeks a scape-goat
to bear the blame for the misfortunes of his army at
Chancellorsville, and the Eleventh Corps is made to
carry the burden—not only through the Wilderness, but
through every history of the campaign which has since
been written, and the foundation for this generally
accepted state of facts is the allegation of General
Hooker himself at the time of the occurrence, and repeated before the Committee on the Conduct of the War,
that "The bad conduct of the Eleventh Corps had cost
me the key of my position, and had very much embar-
rassed me by contracting my sphere of action. The
Eleventh Corps had been completely surprised and dis-
gracefully routed," and very much more to the same
effect. General Hooker says that the dispositions for
defence were inadequate on the right, and that no
pickets were on the alert to advise of the approach of
the enemy. He says, "It has been reported to me that
the Corps-commander was under the impression that
the enemy was retiring."

The fault of position of the Eleventh Corps, if there
was any, is not chargeable to the Corps-commander, for

he held the position he was assigned to. General Devens testified before the Committee that General Hooker
visited his portion of the line on Saturday morning, accompanied by General Howard, and that the latter
asked General Hooker "if the dispositions were satisfactory, and he replied that they were." General
Sickles stated, before the same Committee that he accompanied General Hooker on this occasion, and "the
condition of affairs, as it seemed to him (Hooker), and I
think to others who accompanied him, and as was reported to me by Generals Howard and Slocum, was entirely satisfactory."

As to the charge that the Eleventh Corps was surprised, it is shown by General Devens statement that
the column of Jackson was seen from the right, as it
passed over a high point of the road (near the "Furnace)" about eleven o'clock in the morning ; and that
he sent an aide, Lieutenant H. G. Davis, to report the
fact to General Howard. General Howard informed
Lieutenant Davis that he had already observed the
movement, and that it was known at General Hooker's
Headquarters. It appears from the same statement,
that the picket line of the Eleventh Corps was from
half to three-quarters of a mile beyond the line, and
that during the day they were frequently engaged with
the enemy's skirmishers. About two or three o'clock
in the afternoon, two soldiers, who had been sent out
especially to observe and report the enemy's movements, came in and stated that the enemy was massing
heavily on the Federal right. These men General Devens at once sent to General Howard, and from thence
they were sent to General Hooker's headquarters. The
skirmish line of the Eleventh Corps met the enemy's
advance well in front and resisted it with great determination, but was finally driven back upon the main
line. The right division, Devens', which General
Hooker says "was flying, panic-stricken to the rear,"

contained something less than four thousand men, and
its loss was sixteen hundred. Among them were
nearly every brigade and regimental commander, and
the division-commander himself was wounded. These
facts show that the corps did some fighting, and go far
to disprove the injurious imputations of the Commander of the Army.

If "the corps-commander was under the impression
that the enemy was retiring," (which seems hardly
probable when he was sending information to General
Hooker that he was massing on his right), he was by no
means singular, for Hooker himself believed the fact to
be so, and as late as Saturday afternoon wrote to General Sedgwick, "The General commanding directs that
General Sedgwick cross the river as soon as indications
will permit ; capture Fredericksburg, with everything
in it, and vigorously pursue the enemy. We know the
enemy is flying, trying to save his trains ; two of
Sickles' divisions are among them." (General Sedgwick's testimony before the Committee.) Did General
Sickles, too, believe this? He stated before the Committee that "The direction which the enemy's column
took, judging from what information we had of the
country, and from the maps we had, was susceptible of
two interpretations. It was, perhaps, a movement *in
retreat;* for they had a large train with them, a great
many wagons, and all arms, except cavalry, were in
large force. I forced the column to abandon the road
which they were taking, and seeing no further movement of the enemy's troops, we supposed for a time
that they had, perhaps, abandoned the operation, if it
was a movement of a column for the purpose of attack ;
or if it was a movement for a retreat, that they had
taken a more available route. A reconnoisance was
then pushed out, which resulted in ascertaining that
the movement of the enemy still continued." But
whitherward? This, General Sickles omits to state.

It is manifest that Generals Hooker and Sickles both believed this was a retreat, and that accounts for the extraordinary position of two of General Sickles' divisions when the attack was made on the right, and for the failure of General Hooker to move his supports to the imperilled flank in season.

If the "key" of the position had been wrenched from the Eleventh Corps, it had been regained by Generals Pleasonton and Sickles during the night of Saturday, and the enemy had probably suffered as much from the fighting of that day and night as the Federals had. Therefore, it would seem not to have been a good ground upon which to base a reason for the subsequent dispositions of the Army, and, least of all for the ultimate retreat.

On the morning of the second of May, General Hooker ordered General Reynolds to join him with the First Corps. This left Sedgwick with his own Corps, and General Gibbons' division of the Second Corps, less one brigade which had been ordered to Banks' Ford. After the disaster on his right Saturday night, General Hooker telegraphed to General Sedgwick to at once take up his line of march on the Chancellorsville road until he connected with the main body of the Federal army, "and you will attack and destroy any force you may fall in with on the road." In this dispatch Sedgwick was informed, "You will probably fall upon the rear of the forces commanded by General Lee, and, between you and the Major-General commanding, he expects to use him up." While this movement was going on General Gibbon was directed to take possession of Fredericksburg.

This order for General Sedgwick's advance reached him at eleven o'clock on Saturday night, about three miles below Fredericksburg, making the distance between him and Chancellorsville about fourteen miles. Before he could "take up his line of march on the

5

Chancellorsville Road," he had to carry the heights of Fredericksburg, where Early was posted with about 6,000 men, behind works that had resisted the onset of Burnside's army After removing this obstruction to his advance, he had the army of General Lee to encounter, which now held General Hooker shut up in the *penetralia* of the "Wilderness." If Hooker, with sixty thousand men, (and when Reynolds joined him he had eighty thousand) could not fight his way to Sedgwick, how could the latter with but twenty-two thousand fight his way to Hooker? If Mahomet could not go to the mountain, surely the mountain could not come to Mahomet.

At eleven o'clock on Sunday morning, the third of May, Sedgwick assaulted and carried the heights at Marie's, capturing a large number of prisoners and several guns. Sedgwick had left his position below Fredericksburg during the night, and the enemy had opposed his march all the way to Fredericksburg, and fought valiantly to hold their works there. When the heights had been carried, Sedgwick pushed on towards Chancellorsville.

But meantime, momentous events were transpiring at Chancellorsville. General Hooker had directed Generals Warren and Comstock, on Saturday night, to trace out a new line for the Federal Army to fall back upon, and before daylight it was withdrawn to this new position. At dawn the Confederates began to move upon the Union Line. J. E. B. Stuart, who had succeeded to the command of Jackson's corps, (Hill having been wounded) advanced against the right of the line now held by Sickles, a part of Slocum's corps, and French's division of Couch's corps, and which faced nearly westward, from whence Stuart's attack would come. The rest of Slocum's corps and Hancock's division of Couch's corps formed the centre and left, covering the roads from Chancellorsville to Fredericksburg. Hancock's left brigade was "refused" so as to face nearly eastward, to prevent the enemy passing to the rear of our lines. Thus the line described nearly the three sides of a hollow square, facing east, south and west.

Stuart gradually extended his right toward Lee, who had opened the action on his part of the line at the same moment Stuart's attack began. Lee's blow fell upon the centre and left of Hooker's line, and was met by the Federals with a determined front. McLaws, who confronted Hancock, was handsomely repulsed with heavy loss, but Anderson succeeded in gaining ground in front of Slocum, and finally reached out his left and met Stuart's approaching right, and the rebel army was once more united, and, by a thin line, encompassed Hooker's position. Lee had, meantime, posted thirty cannon on the elevated position, which had been abandoned on the right and enfiladed Slocum's line. He sent word of the fact to Hooker, and desired to know if any movements were being made to relieve him, or if he might expect re-enforcements and ammunition. Hooker replied that he could not make soldiers or ammunition; yet, at that very moment 30,000 men were disengaged, and so continued throughout the action.

Lee now gave the order for his whole line to advance. With wild yells and shouts of "Charge, and remember Jackson," the rebels rushed upon the Federal works. Repulsed at different points, and especially in Sickles' front, they returned to the attack again and again, until the Union line began to waver, and finally give ground. Shot and shell were now pouring as thick as hail stones around the Chancellor House, and one of the pillars of the piazza against which General Hooker was standing was shattered by a cannon ball, and the General overthrown and stunned by the concussion. A considerable interval followed, during which the Army was without a head to direct its operations or to issue an order. Reports and applications for re-enforcements came from different parts of the struggling line, but there was no one to act in the unlooked-for emergency. Sickles was making a most gallant fight on his part of the line, but the enemy were pressing him with great numbers and resolution. His ammunition was nearly exhausted, and he sent his aide, Major Tremaine, to general headquarters with a request for re-enforcements and ammunition. Tremaine found Hooker prostrate and surrounded by his staff, who supposed the General to be dead or dying, and could get no attention to his message. General Couch, next in rank to Hooker, finally assumed command, and the army was again retired toward the river, surrendering the Chancellor House and the roads to Fredericksburg. Fortunately, an interior line of works had been constructed a mile in rear of that just abandoned, in which were posted the Corps of Meade and Reynolds. The army fought its way back to these works in tolerable order, and again faced the advancing foe. Hooker's headquarters had but just been removed from the Chancellor House when its battered walls took fire, and it was burned down.

It was ten o'clock in the morning when the Confederates obtained possession of Chancellorsville. A most desperate struggle of six hours' duration had made an interval of rest desirable to each army. Moreover, the Confederates had won their triumph at a heavy cost of officers and men, and General Lee paused to re-arrange his lines and restore the formation of his troops. The works into which the Federals had now retired were in the form of a redan, with the left flank resting on the Rappahannock, and the right upon the Rapidan, which streams unite in rear of the works, and just below the point of union, is the United States Ford.

As Lee was about to renew his assault, he received information of the storming of Fredericksburg Heights and the retreat of Early, and the advance of Sedgwick's

Corps on his rear. Without a moment's hesitation, he
detached the brigades of Mahone, Kershaw, Wofford,
and Semmes, under General McLaws, to take up their
march towards Fredericksburg, and arrest the advance
of Sedgwick. Wilcox's Brigade, which had been
guarding Banks' Ford, was ordered to join these
forces, and the remnant of Early's command was directed to fall on Sedgwick's rear. While most of
Early's command had been forced off in the direction
of the Bowling Green and Telegraph roads, and were
therefore now in Sedgwick's rear, Barksdale's Brigade
had taken the Plank road and moved toward Chancellorsville. So it happened that when Barksdale reached
Salem Church, some four miles from Fredericksburg,
and opposite Banks' Ford, he met the brigade of Wilcox, up from which it had just marched. The position
for a defensive battle was all that could be desired—a
bold ridge running perpendicular to the road, with a
wooded crest and an open country in front, over which
the Federals must advance. Forming line of battle
along this ridge, they awaited the approach of Sedgwick's column, and received it with a well-directed and
steady fire. The Federals made repeated attempts to
carry this position, but they were repulsed with heavy
loss. McLaws had now arrived and assumed command
of operations, and the struggle went on until night,
without a change in the relative position of the forces.
Monday morning showed an augmentation of the rebel
strength, and attacks were now delivered along Sedgwick's flank, and hostile troops were gathering in his
rear. They had reoccupied the Fredericksburg Heights,
and while they barred his advance, they threatened to
to cut off his line of retreat. Hooker, meantime, with
the bulk of his army around him, lay quietly within his
works, while Lee, with a mere handful of men, confronted him. General Hooker stated to the Committee
that "My object in ordering General Sedgwick forward

at the time named, was to relieve me from the position
in which I found myself at Chancellorsville on the
night of the second of May " And he adds, that he
supposed such movement would induce Lee to retreat.
Never did a General have a more favorable opportunity
offered him to deal his antagonist a mortal blow than
Hooker had at this moment, at Chancellorsville. He
should have marched out of his works, dispersed the
insignificant force Lee had in hand, and pressed forward to the relief of Sedgwick. With a modicum of
generalship, and with one-half the energy he had displayed before he met the enemy, Hooker might have
destroyed the rebel army, even so late as the fourth of
May.

Impatient of this menace in his rear, and convinced
that no fight remained in Hooker, Lee sent Anderson
with three additional brigades on Monday morning, to
re-enforce the Confederates at Salem Church. It was
late in the afternoon before Anderson could get his men
in the position from which he purposed to assail Sedgwick's left, and, if possible, close up his avenue of
escape towards the river. At six o'clock the battle
burst out furiously on Sedgwick's front and left, and
until dark the fighting was of the most desperate character on both sides. The Federals had been forced to
yield ground, and the left of Sedgwick's line had been
pressed back toward the direction of Banks' Ford.
Night, fortunately, put an end to the combat, and under its cover, Sedgwick withdrew from the field, and
reaching the Rappahannock at Banks' Ford, crossed
to the north side over a pontoon bridge, which had been
laid by the Federals after the withdrawal of Wilcox.

Sedgwick having been thus disposed of, Lee recalled
his troops to Chancellorsville on Tuesday, and positioned them for the final assault on Hooker's lines, which
the Confederate commander proposed to make on Wednesday morning. Hooker dreaded the impending blow,

and summoned his corps-commanders to a council of war. They, appreciating the condition of disorganization and demoralization to which the army had been reduced by the unwisdom and vacillations of the commander, assented to the proposition to "ingloriously fly" to the north side of the Rappahannock, and that night the army regained the other bank without molestation. When the rebel skirmishers advanced at daylight next morning, they found no foe to dispute their occupation of the Federal works.

Such were the misfortunes, and such the conclusion of a campaign which opened with promising auspices of success. A superb army animated by the highest hopes, and confident of winning, at last, a victory over its obstinate adversary that should go far toward ending the rebellion, found, at the conclusion of this brief campaign, that the old fatality still overhung it, and that its fate was, to be led to useless slaughter. Once more the mournful words were written under the name of the new commander, "Unequal to his exalted position!" Silently, dispiritedly, the army returned to its old camping-ground, and sat down to reflect upon the mysterious providence which had so strangely overruled its destiny ; had so dazed and confounded the usually clear intellect of the keen-eyed and handsome soldier who had won its confidence, and whom it so recently delighted to honor.

On reaching camp, General Hooker issued an Order in which he said : "The Major-General commanding, tenders to this army his congratulations on its achievements of the last seven days. If it has not accomplished all that was expected, the reasons are well known to the army   It is sufficient to say they were of a character not to be foreseen, nor prevented by human sagacity or resources." It was entirely true that the reasons of failure were "well known to the army," and they did not tend to mitigate the chagrin and mortification that officers and men alike felt for the disgraceful failure of this campaign, but there was an almost universal non-concurrence in the statement, that the causes of failure were "of a character not to be foreseen nor prevented by human sagacity or resources." On the contrary, it was apparent that the exercise of very ordinary sagacity and the most moderate amount of resources, would have secured a glorious triumph to the Union arms.

He proceeds to speak of the withdrawal from the south side of the river in such sophistical terms as these: "In withdrawing from the south bank of the Rappahannock before delivering a general battle to our adversaries, the army has given renewed evidence of its confidence in itself and its fidelity to the principles it represents. In fighting at a disadvantage, we would have been recreant to our trust, to ourselves, our cause, and our country Profoundly loyal, and conscious of its strength, the Army of the Potomac will give or decline battle whenever its interest or its honor may demand. It will also be the guardian of its own history and its own honor." In this paragraph General Hooker seems to have forgotten the boast of seven days ago that the enemy must fight him on ground of his own choosing, or ingloriously fly.

He again refers to the successful crossing of the rivers in his advance, and to the equally successful recrossing in his retreat, and concludes with the following somewhat consolatory paragraph: "The events of the last week may swell with pride the heart of every officer and soldier of this army. We have added new lustre to its former renown. We have made long marches, crossed rivers, surprised the enemy in his entrenchments, and, wherever we have fought, have inflicted heavier blows than we have received. We have taken from the enemy 5,000 prisoners, fifteen colors; captured and brought off seven pieces of artillery;

placed *hors de combat* 18,000 of his chosen troops ; destroyed his depots filled with vast amounts of stores ; deranged his communications ; captured prisoners within the fortifications of his capital, and filled his country with fear and consternation. We have no other regret than that caused by the loss of our brave companions ; and in this we are consoled by the conviction that they have fallen in the holiest cause ever submitted to the arbitrament of battle."

The destruction of depots and derangement of communications, and capture of prisoners within the fortifications of his capital, herein claimed, are supposed to refer to the operations of the cavalry under General Stoneman. With everything in its favor, it was, probably, the most utter abortion of the war—if it were possible that there could be, then it was a more absolute failure than Hooker's. Suffice it to say, that with scarcely any opposition, the utmost Stoneman accomplished, with his splendid cavalry of ten thousand sabres, was to do a little damage to the James and Kanawha Canal, burn two or three turnpike bridges, cut a railroad in a couple of places so inefficiently that the Rebels repaired it before the clatter of the horses' hoofs had died out, captured and paroled a train-load of sick Confederates, destroyed a small quantity of stores, and—rode back ! The total loss of the cavalry corps in the operations described in this chapter was 145, most of which occurred at Chancellorsville, among the small force under Pleasonton. Hooker, when he came to understand the true state of the case, relieved Stoneman, and assigned General Pleasonton to the command. From thenceforth our cavalry was a very efficient arm of the service.

It may be interesting to compare the Order issued by General Lee with that of General Hooker, and I therefore incorporate it. He said : "With heartfelt gratification, the General commanding expresses to the Army his sense of the heroic conduct displayed by officers and men during the arduous operations in which they have just been engaged.

"Under trying vicissitudes of heat and storm, you attacked the enemy, strongly intrenched in the depths of a tangled wilderness, and again on the hills of Fredericksburg, fifteen miles distant, and by the valor that has triumphed on so many fields, forced him once more to seek safety beyond the Rappahannock While this glorious victory entitles you to the praise and gratitude of the nation, we are especially called upon to return our grateful thanks to the only giver of victory, for the signal deliverance He has wrought.

"It is, therefore, earnestly recommended that the troops unite on Sunday next, in ascribing to the Lord of Hosts the glory due His name.

"Let us not forget in our rejoicings, the brave soldiers who have fallen in defense of their country ; and, while we mourn their loss, let us resolve to emulate their noble example. The army and the country alike lament the absence for a time of one (Jackson, who was supposed not to be mortally wounded) to whose bravery, energy and skill, they are so much indebted for success."

In these operations the Union Army lost 17,197 officers and men, distributed among the different corps and arms of the service as follows : First Corps, Reynolds, 292 ; Second Corps, Couch, 2,025 ; Third Corps, Sickles, 4,039 ; Fifth Corps, Meade, 699 ; Sixth Corps, Sedgwick, 4,601 ; Eleventh Corps, Howard, 2,508 ; Twelfth Corps, Slocum, 2,883 ; Engineers, 3 ; Signal Corps, 2 ; Cavalry, 145. The loss of the enemy was nearly or quite as great as that of the Federals.

These operations proved that the Administration had not yet found the man who was destined to lead the Army of the Potomac to victory At the head of a division or a corps, Hooker had no superior ; he could quickly perceive and take advantage of circumstances which were embraced within the sweep of the eye, and fight his men as long as there was a chance of success. His bearing under fire was gallant and inspiring, and his record in the various subordinate capacities which he held is above praise, but his mental grasp was not equal to the command of an army of a hundred thousand men, and he could not take in and comprehend the various phases and demands of a battle-field extending over miles of country and the operations on which must be directed while they could not be seen. His campaign was planned upon certain assumed facts, and from these certain results were deducted, as inevitable, and when this theory proved delusive, there was an utter failure of resources to meet the changed condition of things—an intellectual obscuration ensued, which was but partially enhanced by the shock of a cannon ball. The magnitude of the situation was out of all proportion to the capacity of the Federal commander, and his mind became chaotic under the weight of its responsibilities.

CHAPTER XXIX

ELATED by the successes gained over the Army of the
Potomac during the winter and spring, and counting
upon their disheartening effects among the people of
the loyal States—knowing, moreover, that General
Hooker's army had been reduced in numbers by the
Chancellorsville Campaign about 20,000 men, and
that since that time it had undergone a further
diminution by the mustering out of some 20,000 nine
months' and two years' men, General Lee determined
to try his fortunes once more on loyal soil ; his army
was in the best spirit for such an enterprise, and, in the
language of General Longstreet, it was in a condition
"to undertake *anything*." (Swinton's Army of Potomac, p. 310.) Longstreet had returned from his fruitless operations at Suffolk, with his two divisions, and a
large number of conscripts had joined Lee's army, making its aggregate strength about ninety thousand men.
On the other hand, Hooker reported his infantry on
the thirteenth of May, at about eighty thousand men,
and on the twenty-seventh of the same month General
Pleasonton reported the effective cavalry at 4,677 horses

—a reduction of two-thirds its strength since March. Thus it had come to pass that the rebel army was numerically stronger than its opponent, and its *morale* was of the very highest order.

On the third of June McLaw's division of Longstreet's corps began its march from Fredericksburg for Culpepper Court House, and was followed next day by the corps of Ewell and Hood. The route of march of these forces was effectually screened by the hills and woods on the south side of the Rappahannock. A. P Hill's corps was retained in the works at Fredericksburg, and so displayed as to represent the presence of the entire army. But Hooker suspected that some movement was afoot across the stream, and he ordered General Howe to find out what it was. Howe crossed with his division of the Sixth Corps at " Franklin's Crossing " on the fifth of June, and made a demonstration against the right of the enemy's lines. Hill met it with such apparent confidence and force, that Howe was impressed with the belief that the whole rebel army was present, and after a little skirmishing, withdrew.

On the sixth of June Hooker learned that there was a large concentration of rebel cavalry at Culpepper, and he telegraphed General Halleck on that day, saying : " As the accumulation of the heavy rebel'force of cavalry about Culpepper may mean mischief, I am determined, if practicable, to break it up in its incipiency. I shall send all my cavalry against them, stiffened by about three thousand infantry " Therefore Hooker directed Pleasonton to look after these rebel horsemen, and "stiffened" him with the infantry brigades of General Ames of the Eleventh Corps, and General Russel of the Sixth, and two batteries. This force moved up the Rappahannock, and was to cross in two divisions at Kelly's and Beverly's Fords, some six miles apart. Buford's brigade of cavalry, supported by

Ames' infantry, crossed Beverly's Ford at daylight on the ninth of June, and was confronted by Jones's rebel cavalry brigade and a small infantry force. Jones at once charged the leading Union regiment, the Eighth New York, killing B. F Davis, its colonel, and putting the regiment to flight. The Eighth Illinois cavalry now in turn charged Jones, and forced him to fall back. Russell now came up with his infantry, and Pleasonton ordered him to attack the enemy in front while he fell on their flank with the Sixth Pennsylvania cavalry, supported by the Fifth and Sixth regulars. The combined attack was gallantly made, but two additional regiments of rebel cavalry assailed the flank of Pleasonton's flanking forces, and they were driven back with loss. It was evident that Jones was being rapidly reenforced by both infantry and cavalry, and that Pleasonton's situation was becoming critical. Gregg, who commanded his other cavalry division, which had crossed at Kelly's, arrived on the field at one o'clock,. having fought the enemy all along his route, and taken 150 prisoners. The country seemed to be full of Confederate soldiers. Late in the afternoon Pleasonton made an impetuous dash upon the foe in his front, and forced him to retire upon his reserves, and then he withdrew his own troops across the river. His loss in this days' fighting was about five hundred men. Stuart, who commanded the rebel cavalry, admitted a loss of over six hundred men and two field officers killed, and one general and two field officers wounded.

This spirited reconnoissance established the fact that a very large cavalry and infantry force was in the neighborhood of Culpepper, and indicated a movement of the entire rebel army toward some point on the Potomac. Two days after Pleasonton's fight a rebel cavalry regiment appeared at Edwards' Ferry, and dashed across the river into Maryland, dispersed the Sixth Michigan Cavalry picketing the river, burned their camp, and re-crossed into Virginia. Hooker still held on to his lines along the Rappahannock ; but he sent his sick and wounded away, and watched and waited for further information. He kept Howe's division across the river, but hostilities were not resumed.

The Valley of the Shenandoah, which had been the granary of Lee's army, and the route of its operations time and again, was now guarded by about ten thousand men under command of General R. H. Milroy, and distributed at points from Harper's Ferry up to Front Royal, a town on the north side of the Blue Ridge, and thirty-five miles southwest of the Ferry. On the seventeenth of June the patrols reported the enemy advancing in force on the Front Royal road ; and when Milroy sent out reconnoissances on the different roads leading up the Valley to find out what was going on, they encountered the enemy on every one of them. A prisoner, taken in one of the numerous skirmishes that ensued, communicated to Milroy the astounding intelligence that the corps of Ewell and Longstreet were in the vicinity, numbering about fifty thousand men. Milroy gathered his little army together at Winchester, and still seemed incredulous as to the proximity of any considerable rebel force. He believed it impossible that Lee's army could have reached his vicinity without his having received due notice of its approach from General Hooker or General Halleck ; and so he held on. During the fourteenth the enemy threw a force in Milroy's rear to cut off his retreat ; and at a late hour of the day they made a dash upon his works from the front, but were handsomely repulsed. Milroy then made a sally, but found the enemy in great force, and withdrew within his fortifications. Soon afterwards, the rebels opened a severe artillery fire, and following this Ewell's men charged and carried the Federal breastworks, on the westerly side of the city An attempt to seize the principal fort was

repulsed, and for a time the fighting ceased. Convinced now of the hopelessness of resistance. Milroy
decided to retreat, and soon after midnight spiked his
guns, and began his flight. The enemy instantly renewed their attacks, and a running fight ensued, in
which the Federals lost heavily in killed, wounded,
and prisoners. The main avenues of escape had been
closed by rebel troops, and the end of the affair was the
loss of more than half of Milroy's command ; some
thirty cannon ; two hundred and seventy odd wagons ;
and four hundred horses. This was a pretty good beginning of a second invasion—almost equal to the capture of Miles on the former occasion ; would it have a
similar sequel ?

Hooker re-called Howe, and set his army in march
northward, on the thirteenth of June. His route was
over the beaten track of the army to Centreville, and
from thence to Edwards' Ferry, which was reached by
the head of the column (Eleventh Corps) on the afternoon of the twenty-fourth of June. During this and
the next two days the infantry and artillery crossed the
Potomac at this point, and pressed on toward Middletown and Frederick. The cavalry under Pleasonton,
had marched on the left, and some portion of it was almost daily in contact with the Confederate troopers,
under Stuart. Our cavalry had now begun to show
that it could fight as well as ride, and the rebels were
worsted in most of the skirmishes in which they engaged our men.

A brigade of Rebel Cavalry, under General Jenkins,
had ridden into Chambersburg, Pa., eight days before
the Federals began to cross the Potomac, and laid hands
on all the horses and cattle they could find, and destroyed the railroad. The following day Ewell's corps
paid the same unfortunate city a visit, and, from thence
one division, Early's, was sent to York, while Johnson's was directed upon Carlisle. On the twenty-fourth

and twenty-fifth the corps of A. P Hill and Longstreet forded the Potomac at Shepherdstown and Williamsport, and the entire army of General Lee was once more on loyal soil, and on the twenty-seventh of June these two corps were also at Chambersburg. Meantime, Imboden, with a brigade of Rebel cavalry, was raiding along the line of the Baltimore and Ohio railroad, northwest of Chambersburg, effectually destroying that great line of communication between Washington and the West, and at the same time rendering useless the Chesapeake and Ohio Canal. Two days after the Army of the Potomac crossed the river, the Rebel General Stuart crossed at Seneca, below Edwards' Ferry, and moving eastward between our army and Washington, picked up a number of Union officers on their way to their commands; seized and burned a train of 187 army wagons laden with stores for the army, and rode into Winchester, Md. From thence, turning northward, he passed around the head of our army and proceeded to Carlisle. Finding that the forces of General Johnson had evacuated the place, he pushed on in the direction of Gettysburg and joined the Confederate troops gathering around that borough on the first day of July.

Thus the Confederates marauded over a great portion of western Maryland and penetrated Pennsylvania as far as the Susquehanna River, levying contributions wherever there appeared to be an ability to meet their requisitions. As an example of the summary process by which the Confederate exchequer and Commissary's and Quartermaster's departments were replenished from the town of York, the following is reproduced : "Required for the use of Early's division : 165 barrels of flour, or 28,000 pounds of baked bread ; 300 gallons of molasses ; 1,650 pounds of coffee ; 3,500 pounds of sugar ; 1,200 pounds of salt ; 32,000 pounds of fresh beef, or 21,000 pounds bacon or pork. The above articles to be delivered at the

2 6

Market House on Main street, at 4 o'clock P M. Wm.
W Thornton, Captain and A. C. S." And again :

" Required for the use of Early's command : 2,000
pairs shoes or boots ; 1,000 pairs socks : 1,000 felt hats:
one hundred thousand dollars in money   C. E. Snod-
grass, Major and Chief Q. M., Early's division.   June
28, 1865."

"Approved; and the authorities of the town of York
will furnish the above articles and the money required ;
for which certificates will be given.   J. A. Early, Maj.
Gen. Commanding." They compromised these claims
for $23,000 cash.

After Hooker entered Maryland, his army was re-enforced by about 15,000 men from the defences of Washington, and he applied to General Halleck to have General French's command of about 11,000 men, posted at
Maryland Heights, opposite Harper's Ferry, placed under his orders.   McClellan had made a similar application pending the Antietam campaign, when Colonel
Miles was holding the same post with an equal force.
Halleck was reluctant then to have the post broken up,
and Lee captured the entire garrison and all its arma-
ment and stores.   But the General-in-Chief had grown
no wiser from experience, and in answer to Hooker's application he said : " Maryland Heights has always been
regarded as an important post to be held by us, and
much expense and labor incurred in fortifying them. I
cannot approve of their abandonment, except in case of
absolute necessity "

That Halleck's reasons for retaining this considerable force at Harper's Ferry, under the circumstances,
were utterly unsound, there can hardly be two opinions.   It was even a worse infatuation than that which
possessed him in regard to Fredericksburg during
Pope's campaign.   Hooker availed himself of this re-

fusal to ask to be relieved of the command of the Army, in the following communication :

"SANDY HOOK, June 27, 1863.

"MAJOR-GENERAL H. W HALLECK,
                General-in-Chief :

" My original instructions require me to cover Harper's Ferry and Washington. I have now imposed upon me, in addition, an enemy in my front of more than my numbers. I beg to be understood, respectfully, but firmly, that I am unable to comply with this condition, with the means at my disposal, and earnestly request that I may at once be relieved from the position I occupy

" JOSEPH HOOKER,
           " *Major-General.*"

The next day Colonel Hardie arrived at General Hooker's Headquarters, then at Frederick, with an Order relieving him, and placing. General Meade in command. Hooker at once issued the following Order, which terminated his connection with the Army of the Potomac :

"HEADQUARTERS ARMY OF THE POTOMAC,
       " FREDERICK, MD., June 28, 1863.

" In conformity with the orders of the War Department, dated June 27th, 1863, I relinquish the command of the Army of the Potomac. It is transferred to Major-General George G. Meade, a brave and accomplished officer, who has nobly earned the confidence and esteem of the army on many a well-fought field. Impressed with the belief that my usefulness as the Commander of the Army of the Potomac is impaired, I part with it, yet not without the deepest emotions. The sorrow of parting with the comrades of so many

battles, is relieved by the conviction that the courage and
devotion of this army will never cease nor fail; that it
will yield to my successor, as it has to me, a willing
and hearty support. With the earnest prayer, that
the triumph of the army may bring successes worthy
of it and the nation, I bid it farewell.

" JOSEPH HOOKER,
" <i>Major-General.</i>"

General Hooker took leave of his general and staff
officers, and retired to Baltimore, where he was directed
to await orders from the Adjutant-General's office, but
venturing to Washington, three days afterwards, without leave, he was arrested, by direction of General
Halleck, but soon released. Halleck and Hooker had
no affection for one another, and the former had opposed Hooker's promotion, and had prevented his selection at the time of McClellan's removal. He did not
believe Hooker had the ability requisite for such a
command, and was no doubt pleased with the tender of
his resignation. With a juster estimate of his capacity than he had before the battle of Chancellorsville, it is
by no means improbable that General Hooker made use
of the refusal of Halleck to extend his authority over
French, to relieve himself of a command that he felt he
was unequal to. A commander who believed himself
entirely able to handle his army would not have resigned for so paltry a reason, on the eve of a battle which
presented an opportunity to wipe out the stigma of a
recent disgraceful defeat.

Meade was the very opposite of Hooker in manner
and temperament. He had none of that demonstrative
bon homme manner which characterized his predecessor
and did much to make him popular with the army,
even in spite of his evident incapacity Meade, in
civilian clothes, would have passed for a clergyman or

professor in one of our Colleges, but the army knew he was a thorough soldier, and he had the most unqualified respect of every officer and man in it. He at once issued the following modest and sensible Order:

" HEADQUARTERS ARMY OF THE POTOMAC,
June 28, 1863.

" By direction of the President of the United States, I hereby assume command of the Army of the Potomac. As a soldier, in obeying this order—an order totally unexpected and unsolicited—I have no promises or pledges to make. The country looks to this army to relieve it from the devastation and disgrace of a hostile invasion. Whatever fatigues and sacrifices we may be called upon to undergo, let us have in view constantly the magnitude of the interests involved, and let each man determine to do his duty, leaving to an all-controlling Providence the decision of the contest. It is with just diffidence that I relieve in the command of this army an eminent and accomplished soldier, whose name must ever appear conspicuous in the history of its achievements; but I rely upon the hearty support of my companions in arms to assist me in the discharge of the duties of the important trust which has been confided to me.

GEORGE G. MEADE, Maj.-Gen. Commanding."

Simultaneously with Meade's appointment, Halleck abandoned the absurd theory about Harper's Ferry, and French was placed under Meade's command, as was also General Couch, who had a force of about 20,000 militia, which had been hastily congregated at Harrisburg, the capital of Pennsylvania, and which place was threatened by the Rebel advance. On the morning of the twenty-ninth of June General Meade put his columns in motion, toward the north, to intercept the Confederate army, which was supposed to be moving towards

Harrisburg. The First and Eleventh Corps took the Emmettsburg road, and composed the left flank of the army; the Third and Twelfth Corps marched over the road leading to Taneytown; the Second was directed on Frizzleburg; the Fifth to Union and the Sixth to Windsor. These dispositions led toward the supposed route of march of the Confederate forces and at the same time covered Washington and Baltimore.

On the thirtieth of June Kilpatrick's brigade of cavalry very unexpectedly ran into a body of rebel troopers at Hanover, in Pennsylvania, and were overmatched in the encounter that ensued, but General Custer, who had passed the Point without discovering the enemy, hearing the noise of battle, returned and threw his forces into the fight and the rebels were repulsed. On the same day Meade issued an Order requesting corps and other commanders to address their troops, explaining to them the immense issues involved in the struggle. He closed with these words: " Homes, firesides and domestic altars, are involved. The army has fought well heretofore; it is believed that it will fight more desperately and braver than ever, if it is addressed in fitting terms. Corps and other commanders are authorized to order the instant death of any soldier who fails in his duty this hour."

Lee had now become apprised of the proximity of the Army of the Potomac, and he began to gather his scattered divisions around him at Gettysburg, a village of some three thousand inhabitants and the capital of Adams County, Pennsylvania. So, on the morning of the twenty-ninth of June, Hill and Longstreet began their march from Chambersburg, twenty miles west of Gettysburg, toward that town, and at the same time Ewell's corps evacuated York and countermarched for the place of general rendezvous.

Meade had no information of the movements toward a concentration of the Rebel Army at Gettysburg; and it is not probable that Lee expected the impending battle would be fought at that particular locality. The *role* that he was now playing compelled him to fight wherever the Federal army offered battle. He was a great distance from his base, and in a hostile country, and his communications were liable to be interrupted at any moment. He knew the Federal army was growing in numbers daily, and the militia were gathering in great force to oppose his progress eastward. To attempt to retire with no other achievements than the insignificant skirmishes and the inconsiderable spoils which had thus far signalized his march, would have seemed pusillanimous ; besides, the Federal army was now so near his line of retreat that it was not possible to retire without having his flank and rear exposed to almost certain attack. He must, therefore, *fight ;* and the sooner the two armies were brought into collision, the better for the Confederates. Meade could afford to wait : Lee could not. It is very probable that the rapid march of the Army of the Potomac had surprised the Confederate commander. He knew that his strategy had misled Hooker, and detained the army at Falmouth a full week after he had set all his corps but Hill's in motion for the North ; and his information seems to have been less prompt than usual as to the operations of his adversary after he began his march. This is manifest from the following statement in General Lee's report of the Gettysburg campaign : "Preparations were now made to advance upon Harrisburg ; but, on the night of the 28th, information was received from a scout that the Federal Army, having crossed the Potomac, was advancing northward, and that the head of the column had reached South Mountain. As our communications with the Potomac were thus menaced, it was resolved to prevent his further progress in that direction by concentrating our army on the east side of the mountains." General Lee had been deprived of the

source from which his information chiefly came as to
his opponent's movements, by a singular disposition of
the main body of his cavalry, under Stuart himself,
who was the brains and spirit of that arm of the Confederate service. He had been dispatched to watch
Hooker ; and, if possible, to impede his passage of the
Potomac. He was then to cross himself, and take his
proper position on the right flank of Lee's advancing
columns, presenting a barrier to the Union cavalry, and
giving information of the movements and positions of
Meade's columns. But Stuart failed, on this occasion,
to comprehend the situation ; and, having advanced to
Fairfax Court House, he faced to the northward, and
crossed the Potomac at Seneca, forty miles *below* the
point at which the Army of the Potomac had crossed,
and consequently found himself on the *right* flank of
the Union Army, and that entire army between himself
and Lee. It was in his endeavor to pass the head of
the Federal columns that he reached Hanover, and encountered Kilpatrick and Custer. He expected to find
Ewell at Carlisle, whither he went, but did not reach
that place till the first of July, and then Ewell was
drawing up his forces around the northeast side of
Gettysburg, and thither Stuart followed him.

On the night of the 30th of June, Meade issued orders
for the movement of the army on the next day. The
First, Third and Eleventh Corps constituted the left
wing of the Army—nearest the enemy—and was under
command of General Reynolds, who was directed to
move on Gettysburg. The Fifth and Twelfth Corps
were to march to Two Taverns and Hanover ; the Second
Corps, with headquarters, to Taneytown, and the Sixth
Corps to Manchester. These dispositions go far to show
that General Meade had no expectation of a general
battle at Gettysburg, for the result was to increase the
distance between some of the corps and that place.
Probably General Meade knew little or nothing about

the strategical advantage of that position ; and that the great battle which was fought there was the result of chance rather than of design upon the part of either commander.

CHAPTER XXX.

GETTYSBURG lies upon the north slope of a hill which rises in its immediate rear, some four hundred and eighty feet above the valley, just north of the town, through which flows a rivulet called "Stevens' Run." The contour of this hill is not unlike a fishing-hook, and taking this familiar figure as a guide, we will briefly describe it. Turning the apex of the convex bend so it will point due north, it will embrace "Cemetery Hill." Standing now, with your back towards Gettysburg, and your eye follow-ing the course of the hook on your left and to the south-ward, and towards its point, you find it crosses a slight depression a few hundred rods from the apex of the bend, and then begins to rise until it attains the top of "Culp's Hill," and passing that, terminates at the point, on "McAllister's Hill." The distance from on this side the hook is a little less than two miles. Along the base of this hilly ridge runs "Rock Creek," and on the east side of it, opposite "McAllister's Hill," abruptly rises another bluff, which swells into "Wolf Hill," at a short distance from the creek, and then continues in a high ridge toward the northeast, for a considerable dis-tance. Turning now to the other side of the hook, you will first observe that it is a mile longer than the left side, and is more uniform in its course, but characterized by the same general outlines. A few hundred rods from the apex of the bend is a bluff, rising higher than "Cemetery Hill," then follows a depression for a distance of half a mile, where the ridge is but twenty feet above the bed of "Stevens' Run;" then the ground rises again in a bold rocky ledge into "Little Round Top," and making another ascent culminates in "Round Top." The distance across, from point to shank, is about two and a half miles, and the circumference about five miles. Within the hook the ground is low and tolerably level, but as you approach the bend it becomes hilly, and finally rises abruptly into "Cemetery Hill." The Baltimore Pike and the Taneytown Road enter Gettysburg, through the level space within the hook, and cross it at the bend.

Retaining the same position but looking to the north, Gettysburg lies at your feet, extending from near the top of Cemetery Hill to the foot of the valley, through which flows "Stevens' Run," and which empties into Rock Creek, a mile northeast of the village. This valley curves around the point of the hill, on the slope of which the town stands, and follows the conformation of the fishing-hook until it is interrupted by the opposing ridge of Wolf Hill. Still looking to the north, right over the tops of the houses on the westerly side of Gettysburg, and about a mile from where you stand, you see a ridge on the farther side of the valley, running nearly north and south, but much lower than the Cemetery Hill. On this ridge stands the Lutheran Seminary, and the ridge itself is called "Seminary Ridge." Beyond this, at short intervals, plain ridge and valley succeed each other, until the South Mountain range terminates the scene. To the northward and to the right and left, the landscape was fair to look upon on the first day of July, 1863. Woods, rich in their summer foliage, stood as a glowing and animate frame-work around the cultivated fields and the rural village which was soon to become famous as the scene of the greatest battle of modern times. The Emmetsburg road starts from the

south side of Gettysburg, passes along the hillside west
of the cemetery, cleaves the valley diagonally in a south-
westerly course, and ascends and crosses Seminary
Ridge, at a point nearly opposite Little Round Top, and
about a mile from it. The Hagerstown road leaves the
north side of Gettysburg, and crossing the ridges in a
westerly direction, is lost to sight in the forest toward
South Mountain. Across the low ground from the
ridge, near the Seminary to Gettysburg, was built up a
dirt causeway or railroad embankment, and over which
the "Ulster Guard" marched into Gettysburg, after the
battle of the first of July.

For several days, rebel troops, both infantry and
cavalry, had visited Gettysburg, and numerous bodies
of soldiers were hovering on the north side of the town.
On the thirtieth of June, at about nine o'clock A. M., a
considerable portion of Hill's Corps approached within
half a mile of the village, and stationed pickets along
Seminary Ridge. At the end of an hour they withdrew
towards Cashtown, and an hour later General Buford
rode into Gettysburg, at the head of six thousand Federal cavalry, and passing through the town took position on the farm of Honorable E. McPherson, a mile
and a half northwestward, where he unlimbered his
guns and made his dispositions to resist an attack. One
corps of the left wing—the First—reached Marsh Creek,
four miles southwest of Gettysburg, on the afternoon
of the thirtieth, and halted there for the night. The
Eleventh was at Emmettsburg, six miles in rear of
the First. On the same night, the Rebel General Hill,
encamped his corps, 35,000 strong, a few miles north
of the point occupied by General Reynolds. Longstreet's Corps, with the exception of Pickett's division, which was still at Chambersburg, closed up in
rear of Hill. This corps was 31,000 strong, and 24,000
of these men were near at hand. Rodes' and Early's
divisions, of Ewell's Corps, numbering 19,000 men,

bivouacked at Heidlersburg, nine miles from Gettysburg, on this night. Johnson's division of this corps, 12,000 strong, was countermarching from Carlisle, and yet some distance from Gettysburg.

No one fact about the Gettysburg battle has been a subject of more controversy than that in relation to the actual numbers composing the two armies. I suspect that each side has attempted to show the opposing army greater than it really was, and at the same time to understate its own forces. This enhances the merits of the victory on the Federal computation of relative strength, and the Confederates seek to parry the discredit of defeat by exaggerating the numbers of the Unionists, while they place their own upon returns which do not include the re-enforcements that joined them after they crossed the Potomac. The system of returns adopted in the Federal Army was either defective in itself or in its execution, for it failed to give an accurate report of the strength of the army. The nearest the general-in-chief, or a corps, division or brigade commander could come to a positive statement of his command was "about" such a number. The system in the Confederate Army was even worse, or its officers were more skilful in concealing its true strength. It is probably not possible to give the exact figures of the strength of a large army from day to day, especially when it is on the march or engaged in an active campaign. Sickness, casualties from various causes, and the inevitable evil of straggling diminishes its ranks, but a very close approximation ought always to be possible. The numbers above given as the strength of the three Rebel Infantry Corps are derived from authorities strongly Federal, and I think they over-state them.

Lossing's "Pictorial History of the Civil War," Vol. III, page 59, foot-note 2, gives the figures I have quoted as the strength of these corps, and distributes them as follows: Hill's Corps—Heath's and Pender's divisions,

10,000 men each; Anderson's division, same corps, 15,000 men. Longstreet's Corps—McLaws' and Hood's divisions, 12,000 each; and Pickett's division, same corps, 7,000. Ewell's Corps—Rodes' division, 10,000; Early's, 9,000; and Ed. Johnson's, 12,000.

This would make the infantry arm of the Confederate Army 97,000 strong, which I believe to be an over-estimate, although Mr. Lossing 'is supported by other writers, and expresses substantially the views on the subject said to have been entertained by Generals Hooker and Meade.

Mr. Greeley, in his "American Conflict," Vol. II, page 371, says, the corps of Ewell and Longstreet (while marching down the Shenandoah Valley) numbered about 50,000 men. Mr. Bates, in his History of the Battle of Gettysburg, quotes General Hooker's statement, that two Union men had counted the Confederate force as it passed through Hagerstown, and that they compared notes every night. That in round numbers Lee had 91,000 infantry and 280 pieces of artillery, and that there were about 6,000 cavalry marching with that column. The body of Confederate cavalry that crossed at Seneca, General Hooker estimates at 5,000. General Meade says: "I think General Lee had about 90,000 infantry, from 4,000 to 5,000 artillery, and 10,000 cavalry." (Bates, p. 196.) Professor Jacobs (Notes on the Rebel Invasion, pages 22-3) gives Hill's Corps 35,000; Longstreet's 31,000, and Ewell's 31,000.

Mr. Swinton, in his " History of the Army of the Potomac," page 310, gives the aggregate present, 88,754; present for duty, 68,352. He says he learns from General Longstreet that when the three corps were concentrated at Chambersburg, the morning reports showed 67,000 bayonets. John Esten Cooke (Life of General Lee, page 273) says, that Lee's army numbered 68,352 bayonets, on the last day of May. 1863. But after this date, and before the battle of Gettysburg, it is certain that Lee received considerable re-enforcements. He was obliged to cover his line of communications by strong guards, and his long march and numerous skirmishes cost him a good many men. It is impossible to tell what his re-enforcements numbered, but they, no doubt, more than equaled his guards and losses on the march.

I have very conclusive evidence of the fact that some re-enforcements arrived to General Lee, *after* "the three corps" had marched from Chambersburg, and, in fact during the battle. This I have in the record kept of the marches of the 14th Virginia Regiment, by its Colonel, James M. Hodges, on the back of a pocket map of the State of Virginia, and whose regiment was in the final charge made by Pickett's division (Armistead's brigade) on the third day of July, and Colonel Hodges was killed within a hundred feet of me.

This record shows that Colonel Hodges was at Richmond in May   June 3d, he was at Hanover Junction (Fredericksburg and Richmond Railroad). June 8th, he left Hanover Junction, and crossed the Potomac on the 25th. On the 2d of July, he marched 23 miles, and "camped within three miles of Gettysburg." He was just in time to participate in the closing scenes, and he led his regiment up almost to the muzzles of the muskets of my men, through a fire that thinned his ranks at every step. No one could have displayed more courage than Colonel Hodges did. His gallantry, even in so bad a cause, won my admiration, and I desire to pay this slight tribute to his memory.

Another fact, tending to show that Richmond had been stripped of troops to augment Lee's columns, is narrated on page 289 of Mr. Cooke's "Life of Lee," as follows: "The movements of the Federal commander were probably hastened (towards Lee's line of march) by the capture, about this time, at Hagerstown, of a dispatch from President Davis to General Lee. Lee, it seems, had suggested that General Beauregard should be sent to make a demonstration in the direction of Culpepper, and by thus appearing to threaten Washington, embarrass the movements of the Northern army. To this suggestion the President is said to have replied that he had no troops to make such a movement; and the capture of this dispatch on its way to Lee probably hastened the movements of General Meade, who had thus the proof before him that Washington was in no danger. The Confederacy was thus truly unfortunate again, as in September, 1862, when a similar incident came to the relief of General McClellan.''

General Butterfield, Chief-of-Staff to Generals Hooker and Meade, testified before the Committee on the Conduct of the War that the returns of the Federal Army on the tenth of June gave the strength of the several corps as follows: First Corps, 11,350; Second, 11,361; Third, 11,898; Fifth, 10,135; Sixth, 15,408, Eleventh, 10,177; Twelfth, 7,925—giving a total of 78,255 men. Subsequently, and before the battle, the Fifth Corps was augmented by two brigades of the Pennsylvania Reserves, of about 4,000 men; the Twelfth by Lockwood's Maryland Brigade, 2,500 strong, and the First Corps, (on the 2d of July) by Stannard's Vermont Brigade, of 2,500 men, whose time had expired but who determined to stay until the battle was over. The Union cavalry mustered about 12,000 sabres, and gave Meade an army of 99,000 men on paper, excluding General French with the Maryland Heights forces, who was posted near Frederick to look after the communications. Making the usual deductions for guards, sick and stragglers (whose numbers always increased as a battle became imminent) it is supposed that Meade had on the heights of Gettysburg, after deducting the losses of the first day, only about 65,000 men. As a guide to a calculation of the numbers actually present on the battle-field, it may be stated that the First Corps was

11,350 strong on paper according to the last preceding report, whereas it is known that it went into battle on the first day of July with only 8,200 men.

It has been seen that the country adjacent to Gettysburg became very populous on the last night of June, 1863. Nearly one hundred thousand armed men were lying in the fields and woods within a few miles of the town—seventy thousand of them Confederates and thirty thousand Federals. Did either know of the proximity of the other? Mr. Swinton says the battle (of the first day) was precipitated contrary to the expectations of either army, (page 328). And this idea has generally been accepted and is probably correct, as to both Meade and Lee and the great majority of their officers.

The Brookline (Mass.) *Chronicle*, under date of February 16, 1878, published an article on the first day's battle, "from the original manuscript now in possession of a staff officer of the volunteer army, resident in Brookline," wherein this paragraph occurs:

"It was always supposed by us that Gettysburg was a mutual surprise. That it was such to the Confederates, I for one have no doubt. It so chanced that I was wounded and taken prisoner near the close of the first day's battle, and the universal feeling of disbelief that existed among the Confederates, as to what troops they had fought was amusing. They would not believe that we belonged to the Army of the Potomac, insisting that we were Pennsylvania militia in disguise. I well recollect that General Ewell was uncomfortably emphatic in his denial of our representations, and should say that it was not until near sunset that the Confederates settled down into the belief that we had been telling the truth. I have always considered that this was the reason behind Lee's official statement that the attack was not pressed that afternoon, the *enemy's force being unknown*, and it being advisable to await the arrival of the

27

rest of our troops. While they knew we had crossed
the Potomac, they had no idea we were so near."

In a speech made at Boston, Sept. 17, 1877, by General Heth, who commanded the van-guard of Hill's
corps and opened the fight on the first of July, there is
an insinuation that the battle was the result of a chance
encounter, and an admission that the stubborn fighting
of the Federals, on that day, saved the battle. He said:

"As my command, by one of those strange accidents of war, brought on accidentally this battle, I was
in a position to know that Reynolds, in sacrificing his
life, saved at that time this battle to his country."

General Longstreet, speaking through the *Grand
Army Gazette*, of December, 1877, says: "On the
morning of the 1st, General Lee and myself left his headquarters together, and had ridden three or four miles,
when we heard heavy firing along Hill's front. The firing became so heavy that General Lee left me and hurried forward to see what it meant. After attending to
some details of my march, I followed. The firing proceeded from the engagement between our advance and
Reynolds' corps, in which the Federals were repulsed.
This rencontre was totally unexpected on both sides."

General Lee, himself, says in his report of his operations in this invasion: "It had not been intended to
deliver a general battle so far from our base unless attacked; but, coming unexpectedly upon the whole Federal Army, to withdraw through the mountains, with
our extensive trains, would have been difficult and dangerous. At the same time, we were unable to await an
attack, as the country was unfavorable for collecting
supplies in the presence of the enemy, who could restrain our foraging parties by holding the mountain
passes with local and other troops. A battle had, therefore, become in a measure unavoidable; and the success
already gained gave hope of a favorable issue."

Mr. Cooke says, at page 300: "When the sound of

the engagement was first heard by Lee, he was in the rear of his troops at the headquarters which Hill had just vacated, near Cashtown, under the South Mountain. The firing was naturally supposed by him to indicate an accidental collision with some body of the enemy's cavalry, and, when intelligence reached him that Hill was engaged with the Federal infantry, the announcement occasioned him the greatest astonishment. General Meade's presence so near him was a circumstance completely unknown to Lee, and certainly was not desired by him."

So it would seem that although Lee concentrated his army on Gettysburg, he did not intend, as we have already said, to deliver a general battle at that place. There is nothing that indicates that he had any idea of the strategic value of the position on the south side of the town. He certainly made no effort to possess himself of it prior to its occupation by the Federal troops. Detachments, large or small, of the Rebel army had been in Gettysburg and the adjacent neighborhood, off and on, since the 21st of June. On the afternoon of the 26th, General Gordon's brigade of Early's division, Ewell's corps, 5,000 strong, entered the village, Early himself being with the brigade, and remaining over night. He demanded of the town council a contribution of 1,200 pounds of sugar, 600 pounds of coffee, 60 barrels of flour, 1,000 pounds of salt, 7,000 pounds of bacon, 10 barrels of whiskey, 10 barrels of onions, (whiskey and onions in equal proportions), 1,000 pairs of shoes, 500 hats ; or, in lieu thereof, $5,000 in money Messrs. Kendlehart and Buchler of the town council, informed General Early the goods demanded were not in town, and that the burrough had no funds. Early did not attempt to enforce the requisition. (Notes on the Rebel Invasion, by Prof. Jacobs, page 16.)

If Early had supposed it even possible that the two great armies would collide on this ground, he would have devoted himself to an inspection of the position, rather than to a fruitless attempt to extort goods or money out of the burrough of Gettysburg.

It was probably owing to the concentration of roads on Gettysburg that led the Confederate commander to select that as the point of combining his army, which was then dispersed to points east, north and west of that town. In addition to the roads heretofore mentioned as leading out of the village, were the Hagerstown, Chambersburg, Carlisle, Harrisburg, Bonoughtown, York and Hanover roads. These roads had been occupied by Lee's columns and raiding parties, and when his order to concentrate was issued on the 28th of June, Longstreet and Hill were at Chambersburg, twenty miles westerly of Gettysburg, while Ewell's corps was at York, thirty miles east, and Carlisle, twenty-eight miles north of Gettysburg, with Stuart's cavalry trying to work its way around the head of the Federal columns, and with detachments distributed over the country between the remote points of York and Chambersburg.

General Meade was no better informed than Lee was as to the favorable formation of the rocky ledges behind Gettysburg for a defensive battle. He testified before the Committee on the Conduct of the War, that prior to July, 1863, he had never seen the place or knew anything about it. He contemplated occupying the line of Pipe Creek whereon to receive battle, if circumstances would admit of it. That place he had seen, and knew it was a strong position. But Meade was resolved to arrest Lee's march on Harrisburg by a strong demonstration against his flank and rear, and for that purpose the left wing of the Union army was thrown well out toward Gettysburg. While Meade was probably unaware of Lee's intention to concentrate on that place, it can hardly be supposed that he was ignorant of the fact that considerable bodies of Confederate troops were in that neighborhood. There was no obstacle in the way of

communication with the town, and on the 28th of June,
General Cowpland, at the head of two regiments of
Federal cavalry, entered the village from Emmettsburg
and encamped on the north side for the night. The next
day he had a slight skirmish with rebel infantry near
Fairfield, about eight miles west of Gettysburg. The
writer, who had been ordered by General Reynolds to
join the first corps with his command, finds in his diary,
under date of June 30th, the following entry : "Marched
at four o'clock A.M. (from Lewiston) ; mustered on the
road ; halted in a grove in front of St. Mary's College
and had coffee ; marched through Emmettsburg and
joined first brigade, third division first corps, at four
P.M. ; rainy, with heavy showers ; my regiment posted in
woods along Marsh Run, to overlook approaches from
Fairfield, about five miles off—west of north—*where the
enemy are said to be six thousand strong*; General
Reynolds commands left wing of army ; General Doubleday succeeds to command of first corps; General Rowley commands the division, and Colonel Chapman Biddle (senior colonel) commands the brigade." The opening of the next day's entry is as follows: "Up at six ;
received orders last evening to have three days' rations
in haversacks." General Reynolds must certainly have
known of the proximity of large bodies of rebel troops
and of the imminence of a collision. The order requiring
the men to carry three days' provisions clearly indicated
that he anticipated fighting before the next day closed.
In his article on the "Campaign and Battle of Gettysburg," published in the *Atlantic Monthly* of July, 1876,
General Howard says, at page 52 : "Just at night (June
30) I received a note from General Reynolds requesting
me to ride up to Marsh Run and see him.   *   *
He showed me a bundle of dispatches—the information
brought to him during the day—evidence of the near-
ness, position and designs of the enemy." Reynolds
could not have known just how strong the hostile force

on his front and left was, but that he knew there was
such a force there, great or small, there can be no
doubt, and that he informed General Meade of the fact
is equally certain.

General Pleasonton testified before the Committee
on the Conduct of the War, that he had studied the
country very carefully, and that he regarded Gettysburg as the only point where the decisive battle could
be fought, and that he ordered General Buford to hold
that point to the last extremity, until the Army of the
Potomac could get there. General J. Watts De Peyster, in his Decisive Conflicts, reports a conversation
which took place between General Buford and Colonel
Thomas Devin, commanding one of Buford's brigades,
on the night of the thirtieth of June.   General De
Peyster says: " On the night of the thirtieth General
Buford spent some hours with Colonel Tom Devin, and
while commenting upon the information brought in by
Devin's scouts, remarked that the battle would be
fought at that point, and that he was afraid it would be
commenced in the morning before the infantry would
get up."   Devin did not think the enemy were so near
in any considerable force, and said he would take care
of all that would attack his front during the succeeding
twenty-four hours.   " No you wont," said Buford,
" they will attack you in the morning, and they will
come *booming*—skirmishers three deep. You will have
to fight like the devil to hold your own until supports
arrive. The enemy must know the importance of this
position, and will strain every nerve to secure it, and if
we are able to hold it we will do well."   Buford's signal officer, from whom General De Peyster gets this information, says General Buford told him to seek out
the most prominent points and watch everything ; " to
look out for camp-fires during the night and for dust in
the morning." He says Buford seemed more anxious
than he ever saw him before.

CHAPTER XXXI

BUFORD was early in the saddle on the morning of
the first of July His skirmish-line, composed of dismounted cavalrymen, extended from the west side of
the Millerstown or Hagerstown road, where it crosses
Willoughby Run, easterly, along the ridge, on the left
bank of the stream, across the Chambersburg, Mummasburg, Carlisle, and Harrisburg roads, and terminating on Rock Creek. His reserves were posted behind
the ridge, in rear of this one, and his horse artillery
was planted to cover the roads over which he momentarily expected to see the enemy advance. Soon after
nine o'clock the enemy's skirmishers came " booming "
along, over the roads and through the woods and fields,
and the rattle of musketry announced to Buford's
practiced ear, that something more than a reconnoissance and a consequent skirmish had begun. The fire
increased rapidly on both sides, and in half an hour the
Confederates had gotten some of their batteries in position and opened a brisk artillery fire. Buford's guns
now broke silence, and answered the Rebels, gun for gun.
Buford readily saw that he had a very large Confeder-

ate force in front of him, and that their superiority of numbers must, in the end, overpower him. He was naturally anxious to see the columns of Federal infantry approaching, and as time went on he turned an earnest gaze towards the south. With consummate generalship he led the enemy to believe that they were contending with infantry, and that it was in large force. They were therefore cautious, and felt their way with deliberation. But they were steadily increasing their pressure on Buford's lines, and extending towards his flanks. Help must come, and quickly, or these brave fellows will be captured or driven from the field. Buford's orders from Pleasonton were to *hold on*, to the last extremity, and Buford himself knew, as well as any one, the prize for which he was making the gallant fight. It lay behind him in the natural fortifications on the other side of Gettysburg, and Buford meant to save it for his comrades, rushing to his support.

The cupola of the Theological Seminary had been taken possession of by Buford's signal officer, and he was looking southward for the hoped-for succor. About ten o'clock he observed a cloud of dust on the Emmettsburg road, and by and by he was able to distinguish the flag of the First corps fluttering in the wind, as the fast riding cavalcade came rapidly towards the battlefield. Buford himself went into the cupola to gladden his own eyes with the sight of Reynolds' corps flag, but he had hardly attained the outlook, before the eager corps commander, now commanding the left wing, drew up his panting horse beneath the signal station, and called out to Buford, "What's the matter, John?" "The devil's to pay," replied the trooper, and came down to confer with Reynolds. Reynolds had ridden on when hearing the familiar noise of battle, with his staff and escort, directing that the First corps should hasten after him. He now asked Buford if he could hold his ground until the infantry came up, the head

of the column being a mile and a half behind.   Buford
said he thought he could.

General De Peyster, in the article heretofore referred to, thus describes the advance of the gallant old
First corps : "Spectators in the cupola of the Evan-
gelical Lutheran Theological Institute, known as the
" Seminary," and other adjacent elevated positions,
who were watching the advance of the First corps
along the Emmettsburg road and across the swale
drained by Stevens' Run, to the left of the town, spoke
of it with an enthusiastic admiration which, under the
circumstances, it is easy to conceive, since those troops
brought with them, as they believed, not only succor
but assured rescue.   They described the spectacle as
something perfectly magnificent, as the ranks double-
quicked across the interval, swept up Oak Ridge, and
deployed on its crest, their bayonets scintillating and
flashing back the rays of that bright July morning sun.
Ahead, as they dipped into the low ground along
Stevens' Run, and making the fences fly with the
strokes of their flashing axes, bounded the Pioneers of
the leading brigade, and in their track the panting but
ardent thousands of Boys in Blue."

Wadsworth's division was the first to reach the field,
with Cutler's brigade leading.   Reynolds had been on
the ground long enough for his quick military eye to
take in the situation, and he was prepared to give
Wadsworth his orders as soon as he rode up, and he
directed him to take the three right regiments (76th
and 147th N Y and 56th Pa.) to the north side of a
railroad bed running parallel with the Chambersburg
Pike and a few hundred feet north of it, and form line
of battle facing nearly west.   This disposition threw his
right well out towards the left of Devens' brigade of
cavalry, then occupying the northerly extremity of Seminary Ridge, with one regiment across the Mummasburg
road.   But there was still a wide interval between the

two brigades.   The two remaining regiments of Cutler's brigade (14th Brooklyn and 95th N Y.,) with Hall's (Maine) battery, and which was the only one that marched with the division, Reynolds himself conducted to the south side of the railroad cut where he posted the battery on the Chambersburg Pike a hundred feet in advance of the brigade line and leading the other regiments a hundred feet in advance of the guns, posted them in line of battle on the south side of the Chambersburg Pike and on the right of a little grove which crowns Seminary Ridge, a few hundred yards south of the point where the Pike crosses it.   The formation was somewhat *en echelon*, with the left regiments forward.   The official map of the battle-field, published by authority of the War Department, states the time as 10:15 A. M., when the formations were completed, from which it would appear that the cavalry had been holding the ground something over an hour.   As the infantry took their places in line the dismounted troopers along this part of the field withdrew, but Devin remained in position on the right and the cavalry skirmishers extended the line on Wadsworth's left.

The rebel force thus far on the field was Heth's division of A. P Hill's corps, which had marched down the Chambersburg Pike from its last encampment, and finding Buford in front, deployed to the right and left of the Pike, and, sending his skirmishers "booming" along over the fields and through the woods, advanced to the attack.   The official map gives this time as 9 o'clock A. M.   Meredith's brigade of Wadsworth's division arrived on the ground soon after Cutler was posted and took position on the left of his two advanced regiments.   Meredith's two right regiments rested in the edge of the grove on the top of the ridge and his line conformed to the course of the ridge.   Up to this time the enemy's demonstrations had been against the troops on and contiguous to the Chambersburg Pike—

he had not shown himself as far west as the left of
Meredith's brigade. About the time Meredith got into
position, Heth had discovered the importance of the
grove on the top and westerly slope of the ridge, which
General Doubleday says "possessed all the advantages
of a redoubt, strengthening the centre of our line, and
enfilading the enemy's columns should they advance in
the open space on either side. I deemed the extremity
of the woods, which extended to the summit of the
ridge, the key to the position." Heth sent General
Archer with his brigade to seize this bit of woods.
Archer crossed the run with his brigade and gallantly
advanced up the opposite slope. The left regiment of
Archer lapped over upon the position occupied by the
14th Brooklyn and 95th N Y., and these regiments
stubbornly resisted the rebel advance. General Reynolds riding up at the moment and at once compre-
hending the object of the enemy and appreciating the
importance of the woods, ordered Meredith's brigade
to advance through the woods at double-quick. Archer's men were already entering the woods at the foot of
the slope near the Run, and General Reynolds shouted
to Meredith's brigade "Forward, men! forward, for
God's sake, and drive those fellows out of the woods."

General Reynolds had already dispatched couriers to
Howard and Sickles, whose corps belonged to Reynolds'
left wing, urging them to hurry forward to the battle-
field. He had now assumed the task for the whole
army that Buford had already performed for the First
corps—to check the enemy's advance until the main
body of the army should arrive and take position on the
heights in rear of Gettysburg. The difficulty of the
undertaking was momentarily increasing by the constantly augmenting numbers of his opponents, but Reynolds was the last man to surrender a position he believed it vital to the success of the Union Army to hold.
Howard was on his way from Emmettsburg to the

battle-field, but Sickles' corps was lying in its camps near the same place when Reynolds' messenger arrived there.

When Reynolds had sent Meredith's brigade into the woods, with the exclamation above quoted, he drew up his horse near the edge of the grove, and at that moment the bullet of a rebel sharp-shooter pierced his brain, killing him instantly. No abler man or truer patriot fell during the war. He died in defence of his native State and within a few miles of the place of his birth. He graduated from West Point with the rank of Second Lieutenant in July, 1841, and was breveted Captain for gallant and meritorious conduct at Monterey, Mexico, in 1846, and Major for similar conduct at Buena Vista, February, 1847. At the breaking out of the rebellion he was Lieutenant-Colonel of the Fourteenth U. S. Infantry. For gallantry on the Peninsula he was breveted Colonel of his regiment and Brigadier-General U. S. A. He was captured by the enemy on the Peninsula and taken to Richmond. Having been exchanged he was given the command of a division and subsequently of the First corps, with the rank of Major-General U. S. Volunteers. As has heretofore been shown, he was commanding the left wing of the army, consisting of three corps, at the time of his fall. His death was a great loss to the army and the country, and his memory is held in reverential esteem by the officers and men who served with him, and by a grateful people, the integrity of whose government he did so much to preserve and for whose safety and honor he gave his life.

Meredith's brigade pressed on through the woods and met the enemy on the westerly slope moving cautiously toward the summit. Meredith's men opened fire upon them at once and checked their advance. Swinging his left forward, he enveloped the right flank of Archer's brigade and captured nearly fifteen hundred officers and men, including Archer, himself. This was a well conducted and most gallant achievement and inspired our men with hope and confidence along this part of the line. But farther to the right, things were not working satisfactorily.

The death of General Reynolds had wrought a change of commanders as sudden as it was unfortunate. General Abner Doubleday, a West-Pointer, and an officer of Sumter fame, was the ranking officer on the field after Reynolds fell, and was entirely competent to command. He is a man of unquestioned bravery, cool and clear-sighted on the battle-field, and handles his troops under fire with the same composure he would exhibit at a review or parade. He had ridden on in advance of the second and third divisions of the First corps, and reached the battle-field just before Reynolds fell. He immediately assumed command of the field on that event happening and personally supervised the further movements of Meredith's brigade, above described. The direction of affairs could not have fallen into better hands. His dispositions were the best possible, and he enjoyed the confidence and respect of the troops to the fullest extent. General Wadsworth succeeded to the immediate command of the First Corps, and in this instance nothing could have been better or more satisfactory   Brave, cool, zealous in the cause, and believing that the business of war is to *fight*, and beat your enemy as badly as possible ; yet his zeal was tempered with discretion, and he was careful of the lives of his men ; he never ordered them where he was not willing to lead them.* These changes resulted in advancing the commander of the First Brigade of General Doubleday's own division to the command of the division itself.   While this change was certainly not to the disadvantage of the First Brigade, which thereby fell under the command of Colonel

---

* At the crossing of the Rappahannock by his skirmishers in pontoon boats, before the bridge was laid, prior to the battle of Fredericksburg, he mounted and swam his horse over alongside the foremost boat, under the fire of the Rebel sharpshooters.

Chapman Biddle, of the One Hundred and Thirty-first Pennsylvania, and who proved himself a most gallant and capable officer ; it was detrimental to the efficiency of the division, and left the brigades to act very much upon their own discretion.

The impetus or *elan* with which Meredith's brigade had swept Archer into its net, carried them across Willoughby Run and up the bank to the top of the ridge on the west side. But this position threw them so much out of line with the troops on their right, that General Doubleday ordered them back to the ridge and grove from which they had made their gallant and successful advance.

Meantime, as has been intimated, trouble had taken place on the east side of the railroad cut, on the extreme right of the infantry line. Davis' Confederate brigade advanced against the three right regiments of Cutler, and finding the interval between him and Devens' cavalry, heretofore mentioned, swung a regiment through it, and while he pressed Cutler's front, also assailed him in flank and rear. Cutler was forced back upon Seminary Ridge, with heavy loss. This left Hall's battery on the Pike with its right wholly uncovered. The enemy seeing the exposed condition of this battery, dispatched the Second and Forty-second Mississippi regiments to capture it. The two regiments, with full numbers, charged up the railroad bed upon the right of the battery; firing as they came and killing many of the horses and doing serious damage among the men. General Wadsworth now sent an order to Hall to withdraw his guns to the cover of Seminary Ridge, and to go into position there. He succeeded in getting all but one of his pieces away, and that having no horses to draw it he was compelled to leave. But mean time he had done fearful execution on the advancing foe, and their route of march was covered with their dead and wounded.

The Fourteenth Brooklyn and Ninety-fifth N Y

still held their position at the apex of the ridge along Willoughby Run, and were now in advance of the regiments which had driven in Hall's battery. General Doubleday, who had posted the Sixth Wisconsin in reserve on Seminary Ridge, seeing the disaster to Cutler's right and Hall's battery, now ordered it forward, and uniting it with the Fourteenth Brooklyn and Ninety-fifth New York, changed front to the east, and ordered them to charge the Mississippians, who were holding the railroad bed east of the Pike. At them they dashed, pouring a heavy fire into their ranks as they advanced. Protected somewhat by their position, the rebels made a desperate defence, and the fighting for a few minutes was very severe and deadly. Colonel Dawes, of the Sixth Wisconsin, who was on the right of our line, now threw his right platoon on to and across the railroad bed, from whence they poured an enfilading and decimating fire into the left of the Mississippians. The pressure was too much for them, and as their retreat had now become impracticable under the near and heavy fire, they surrendered to our boys, who sent them and their colors to the rear. They also recovered the gun which Hall had been forced to abandon.

These events had not occupied more than an hour from the time Wadsworth's division fired its first gun, and the advantage was with the Federals. The killed and wounded were about equal on each side, but the enemy had lost heavily in prisoners. He now manifested a desire to find out just what he had before him before exposing any more of his men to capture, and the firing dwindled down to a picket skirmish. This continued until about a quarter after eleven, when the Second and Third divisions of the First corps arrived on the field. The second division, General John C. Robinson's, was placed in reserve behind the Seminary, while the third, (Doubleday's own) now commanded by

General Rowley, was divided—the left brigade (Rowley's, now commanded by Colonel Chapman Biddle) was detached for duty on the extreme left of the Union line, while the residue of the division was posted on the ridge on Meredith's right.

The enemy had not yet developed any strength beyond Meredith's left, but the country was very favorable to cover the concentration of a large force in that direction. The road over which the third division marched, is called indifferently Hagerstown road, (Professor Jacobs and Government map); Millerstown road, (Mr. Greeley and Mr. Swinton); and Fairfield road, (Mr. Bates). Its course is northeast and southwest, and it crosses Willoughby Run and unites with the Chambersburg Pike at the edge of the village. The two roads represent two contiguous spokes of a wagon wheel— united at the hub and diverging in straight lines as they extend from it—the Chambersburg road northwest, and the Hagerstown road southwest. When Rowley's brigade reached the ridge on the west side of Willoughby Run, and in a piece of woods, it was halted and line of battle formed in the Hagerstown road, right towards Willoughby Run, the "Ulster Guard" on the left. The brigade then advanced some two or three hundred feet through the woods on the north side of the road, when it was faced by the right flank and moved through the fields towards Gettysburg, crossing Willoughby Run between the road and the house of D. Finneprock, around which Buford's dismounted cavalry were skirmishing. When the brigade reached the foot of the ridge east of Willoughby Run, it filed to the left and took position in line of battle on the slope of the ridge and nearly opposite the Seminary, facing west. Ten minutes later, the brigade was ordered to advance over the ridge, and down into the ravine through which Willoughby Run flows—the right of the brigade passing near the grove where General Reynolds fell. Along the

top of the ridge on the opposite side of the Run was a
fence, and the field beyond it was covered with grain,
affording excellent shelter for the enemy's sharp-
shooters, and the field was alive with them. In this
ravine the brigade found itself under a hot infantry fire,
and was unable to see the enemy from whom the fire
came, and did not attempt to reply to it. It is not
probable that any one knew just why the brigade was
sent down into that valley, and it was soon ordered back
over the ridge to the position from which it last marched.
The "Ulster Guard" was then directed to take position on the top of the ridge, whither it marched and
halted, remaining there in line of battle and receiving
an occasional shot from the grain-field beyond Willoughby Run. Ten minutes later, General Wadsworth
rode up to Colonel Gates, and directed him to throw a
company of his regiment into the house and out-buildings of E. Harman, in a field on the farther side of and
some thirty rods beyond the Run. Colonel Gates
detached Captain Ambrose N. Baldwin, K Company,
a most capable and courageous officer, and who was
killed two days later, to perform this duty Captain
Baldwin deployed his company as skirmishers and
after a spirited contest drove the enemy from the
buildings and took possession of them. Some time subsequently Captain Baldwin sent word that he was severely pressed and that the enemy were multiplying
around him and asked for re-enforcements. Thereupon
Colonel Gates sent Captain William H. Cunningham,
G Company, to his assistance. Captain Cunningham
fought his way to the buildings and joined Captain
Baldwin. These two companies held these buildings,
which served to cover our left flank and keep the
enemy's right in check, for over two hours. The enemy
had then surrounded the buildings on three sides and
succeeded in setting some of the out-houses on fire,
when to avoid being captured, the men were withdrawn,

and moving through a ravine southerly and covered in a measure by a small party of cavalry, they made good their escape and rejoined the regiment that evening on Cemetery Hill.*

Colonel Stone's brigade of Rowley's division was posted on the right of Meredith, as has been stated, with his right reaching across the Chambersburg Pike, nearly where Hall's battery stood, earlier in the day He had had to fight his way to this position, and he subsequently maintained it against great odds, until new developments on the right necessitated a change. The brigade was composed of Pennsylvania troops, and

---

* "Biddle (?) made a skillful disposition of his troops, sending two companies of skirmishers forward to occupy a brick house and stone barn considerably to the front of his line, who did fearful execution upon the advancing enemy, without being themselves exposed. Later in the day they were obliged to abandon this coign of vantage to escape capture, as the enemy in overwhelming numbers advanced, and the buildings were finally burned." ["The Battle of Gettysburg," by Samuel P. Bates, page 66.]

Mr. Bates is a Pennsylvanian, and he feels a just pride in the exploits of the soldiers of the Keystone State. It sent 366,107 soldiers into the field, and their bravery was conspicuous and their blood flowed like water in every great battle of the war. The reputation of the State for patriotism and for its contributions of men and money to sustain the Government is second to none, and whoever writes the history of Pennsylvania's soldiers in the War of the Rebellion can well afford to give all due credit to their brethren of other States, and yet leave room for ample praise to themselves. When General Reynolds crossed the Potomac to Edwards' Ferry, the "Ulster Guard" was occupying the left bank of the river opposite the Ferry. General Reynolds rode to the Colonel's tent and lunched with him, and, before leaving, wrote an order directing him to join the First corps with his Regiment, as soon as he should be relieved. This was on the 26th of June. When relieved, the First corps had twenty-four hours the start of the Guard, but it overtook it on the afternoon of the 30th by marching early and late, and was put into a brigade of Pennsylvanians, who were strangers to it and it to them. The next morning they went into battle together. The next afternoon the brigade was separated, and thereafter, until the fighting was over, the 151st Penn. and the "Ulster Guard" were separated from the rest of the brigade and acting as a demi-brigade under command of Colonel Gates. A few days afterwards the "Ulster Guard" was transferred from the brigade and never served with it again. It was one of the cases referred to by General Patrick (see page 194), and while the services are appreciated the identity of the Regiment is ignored. Mr. Bates says, "Colonel Chapman Biddle, of the 121st, was sent to the left to cover the Millerstown road and the left flank of the Iron Brigade." Then follows the statement first quoted. With the care that Mr. Bates has evidently taken in gathering the information upon which his book is written, he *must* have known that there was a New York regiment in Colonel Biddle's brigade and that the two companies whose work he commends were from *that* regiment. He must also have known, although the fact is of no consequence, that from the afternoon of the second day until the evening of the third, the brigade was divided and the two left Regiments were operating as a demi-brigade, under the Colonel of the New York Regiment.

was known as the " Buck-tail Brigade." Its loss was heavy.

Pender's Confederate division of Hill's corps had arrived upon the ground meantime, and the pressure upon the Union lines was momentarily growing heavier. The rattle of musketry and roar of artillery was contin uous and deafening ; and on the rebel side the volume was swelling louder and louder, as their fresh troops and hurrying batteries came into action. It was now one o'clock, and two small divisions of the First corps, and a portion of Buford's cavalry, numbering together less than nine thousand men, had held in check, at first ten, and latterly, not less than eighteen thousand Rebels, since ten o'clock.

The van of Ewell's corps, consisting of the division of Rodes, now appeared upon the field, marching in from the direction of Heidlersburg, and taking post on the high ground on the right of the Union line, a prolongation of Seminary Ridge, called Oak Hill, and overlooking the Ridges to the southward, and the vales between them. He at once planted his batteries in commanding positions on these heights, and opened an enfilading fire on the Federals. His shot and shell swept the line from the right to the extreme left, and the position had become untenable, unless those murderous guns could be silenced. His skirmishers at the same time came "booming, three deep," and a mile long, against Devens' cavalry, who still held their ground on the right ; and he found he had to "fight like the devil," as Buford had predicted. Gradually, the cavalry were pressed back toward the left and rear, although they fought desperately and made the enemy pay dearly for every foot of ground he wrested from them. Calef's battery of light guns, attached to Devens' brigade, did excellent service on this part of the line.

The Eleventh corps had now reached Gettysburg,

after a long and hurried march, and General Howard
sent his artillery forward on a trot, while the divisions
of Schurz and Barlow followed, coming upon the field
on the north side of the village, and going into position
a little to the right and rear of Deven, so as to confront
the left brigade of Rodes' division, east of the Mummasburg road, and facing north. The Federal line had
thus become crescent shaped, with the apex on the
Chambersburg Pike, and extended from the Hagerstown road on the left, where Colonel Biddle was posted,
to Rock Creek, north of Gettysburg, and a few hundred yards in front of the point where the Harrisburg
road crosses the stream. Von Gilsa's brigade of Barlow's division held the extreme right. On Barlow's
left was Schurz' division ; to his left was Wadsworth's
division ; and beyond him, Rowley's. When the divisions of the Eleventh corps got into position, the cavalry was withdrawn from the front. Along this curved
line were posted the following batteries, from right to
left : Wilkenson's 4th, U. S.; Wheeler's 12th, N Y
Independent ; Dilger's Ohio battery ; Hall's Maine;
Reynolds' N. Y., and Cooper's Pa. batteries—all four-
gun batteries except Hall's and Reynolds', which were
six guns each. The two divisions of the Eleventh
corps, which had come upon the field, numbered about
7,500 men. The remaining division of this corps, Steinwehr's, General Howard had posted on Cemetery Hill,
to hold that position, and as a nucleus around which to
rally in case of defeat, on the farther side of the town.
As General Howard ranked General Doubleday, he
took command of the field, and the latter resumed command of the First corps.

The heavy enfilading fire from Oak Hill was replied
to by as many of the Union batteries as could be brought
to bear, but the rebel guns could not be driven off or
silenced. It therefore became necessary to change the
formation of the First corps line to meet this new

menace on its right flank. Wadsworth's division was drawn back under cover of a strip of woods on Seminary Ridge, and on the north side of the railroad bed—Reynolds' battery accompanying. Stone swung his right regiments to the rear and almost perpendicular to their former position and into the Chambersburg Pike; his left regiment remained faced to the west. Biddle's brigade changed front to the right and was posted in support of Cooper's battery, which replied to the enemy's guns on Oak Hill.

Twenty minutes after the two divisions of the Eleventh corps had taken position, the Confederate division of Early (Ewell's, formerly Stonewall Jackson's corps), with three batteries, came upon the field over the Harrisburg road, striking the right of Barlow's division. This was the signal for a general advance of the enemy's infantry along the whole line. There could not have been less than 35,000 Confederates confronting the small body of Federals drawn up around the north and west side of Gettysburg. It was near two o'clock when the long, deep and closely-formed lines of rebel infantry began their advance; behind these came heavy reserves. The formation of the Union line was such that the first shock of the enemy's blow fell upon the right brigades of the First corps who occupied the apex of the crescent. At this critical moment General Doubleday discovered that there was an interval between his right and the left of the Eleventh corps (from whence the cavalry had been withdrawn), and he ordered General Baxter, of General Robinson's division (in reserve), to move up and fill it. Baxter rushed into the dangerous gap in time to meet the enemy's onset. His brigade drove back the assailants at this point and captured three battle flags and a number of prisoners. But the interval was too long for Baxter to close and the rebels began to press in between his right and the Eleventh corps. General Doubleday then dispatched

General Robinson, himself, with the remaining brigade of his division, General Paul's.* General Robinson put Paul's brigade in on the right of Baxter, before the enemy had succeeded in working through. But the gap was not yet filled and the right regiments of Paul's brigade were "refused" so as to cover his flank and at the same time extend across the Mummasburg road, while Stuart's battery, 4th U. S. artillery, was sent to his support. Cutler's brigade and then Meredith's received the onset in succession, as the rebel line swung around the crescent, and each brigade maintained its reputation for bravery and cool and effective fighting. They were losing men fast but they were taking a fearful revenge on their swarming assailants. Time and again the enemy dashed his strong lines against the thin ones of Paul, Baxter, Cutler, Stone and Meredith, and time and again was repulsed with the loss of large numbers of killed and wounded and many prisoners.

While the battle was thus raging along the First corps front, the Eleventh was furiously assailed by Rodes and Early, whose lines now united with the troops of Hill. Von Gilsa's Brigade was forced back to the Alms House, and the exultant enemy crowded such masses upon the whole division, that it was forced to give ground. General Barlow, its gallant commander, was wounded several times, and left on the field for dead. Schurz' division withstood the onset for some time, but overpowered by numbers, fell back in the

---

* General Paul was a graduate of West Point and a brave and capable officer. When General Patrick was appointed Provost-Marshal-General of the Army of the Potomac, soon after the battle of Antietam, General Paul was assigned to the command of Patrick's brigade. He continued in the command until he was wounded on the first day of July at Gettysburg, and left upon the field for dead. He, however, was only seriously wounded and lost the sight of both eyes. The writer had the pleasure of meeting General Paul at West Point some years ago, and found him in good health and spirits but totally blind. General John C. Robinson, who commanded the division, was a splendid and courageous officer, who, having passed through the fire of a dozen battles unharmed, lost a leg at Spottsylvania Court House. He has since been Lieutenant-Governor of New York, and is now the honored head of the "Grand Army of the Republic" of that State.

direction of the town. The retreat had now fairly set in, and the troops on the right were thrown into disorder. Portions of them made stands here and there, and resisted the enemy's advance, but could accomplish no permanent results. As the streets of the village were reached, the crowding and confusion increased, while the Rebel batteries played upon the dense masses packed in the narrow ways, and their infantry following closely, kept up a rapid fire, and gathered in many prisoners.

Thus the right of the Federal line, consisting of two divisions of the Eleventh corps, and nearly or quite half of the entire Union force on the field, had been swept away, and the First corps was left to fight it out alone.

CHAPTER XXXII

LONG before the Eleventh corps gave way, the right
of the enemy's lines of assault had swung around the
curve of the Union line, and struck the Federal left
near the Hagerstown road, and the roar of battle then
swept along the whole line with great fury Biddle's
Brigade was still holding the left. Cooper's battery of
four pieces was posted in the brigade line, between the
" Ulster Guard " and the 142d Pa., the brigade being
now posted on the ridge, in Front of Willoughby Run,
and in nearly the identical position it occupied just before advancing into the ravine, some hours before. In
the separation of the brigade to make an interval for
Cooper's battery, the right and left regiments were
thrown so far apart, that Colonel Biddle directed
Colonel Gates to take charge of the two regiments on
the left (121st Pa. and " Ulster Guard "), while he
looked after the two regiments on the right. The
brigade was not reunited again until it formed behind
the barricade in front of the Seminary, at about four
o'clock in the afternoon.

Mr. Bates, after describing the operations on the

right, thus speaks of the events on the left: "But the wave of battle, as it rolled southward, reached every part in turn, and the extreme Union left, where Biddle's brigade was posted, at length felt its power. A body of troops, apparently an entire division, drawn out in heavy lines, came down from the west and south, and overlapping both of Biddle's flanks, moved defiantly on. Only three small regiments were in position to receive them ; but ordering up the One Hundred and Fifty-first Pennsylvania, which had been detached for special duty, and throwing it into the gap between Meredith's and his own, and wheeling the battery into position, Biddle awaited the approach. As the enemy appeared beyond the wood, under cover of which they had formed, a torrent of death-dealing missiles leaped from the guns. Terrible rents were made ; but closing up, they came on undaunted. Never were guns better served ; and though the ground was strewn with the slain, their line seemed instantly to grow together. The infantry fire was terrific on both sides ; but the enemy, outflanking Biddle, sent a direct and a doubly destructive oblique fire, before which it seemed impossible to stand. But though the dead fell until the living could fight from behind them as from a bulwark, they stood fast as if rooted to the ground." [pp. 72-3.]

The right of the first corps had now been forced to give way, as the enemy were pouring their thousands upon its exposed flank, and brigade after brigade was swept from the field until Biddle's brigade stood alone upon the line, holding in check a whole division of Confederates. Cooper's battery, which had most gallantly breasted the storm and poured grape and canister into the foe with destructive effect, was now sent to the rear to save it from capture, and the brigade prepared to retire. The enemy were moving down the Hagerstown road, and would soon have turned our flank and taken the brigade in reverse. It was almost as dangerous to retreat as to remain, for we were now receiving a fire on both flanks as well as in front. But to remain was to be captured, and pouring a volley into the enemy as they came rushing up the slope in front, and at short range, the order to retreat was given. Anticipating that the rebels would dash forward when our retreat began, and possibly throw the troops into confusion, the Colonel of the "Ulster Guard," who was the only officer of the brigade mounted, took from his color-bearer the regimental colors, which had been presented to the regiment by the ladies of Saugerties, and hoisting them over his shoulder, called upon his men to stand by them. As he was mounted the colors became very conspicuous. The two regiments under Colonel Biddle preceded the left regiments. These regiments marched slowly and in perfect order, halting as often as they could load, and facing about and delivering their fire with so much coolness and effect that the pursuit was very tardy Seeing this, Colonel Gates returned the color to its proper custodian. The parting volley on the ridge was very destructive, and while it checked the advance for a few minutes it taught the enemy caution. We lost no prisoners, except our wounded, whom we were compelled to leave on the field, and we damaged the enemy quite as much in our retreat as he did us.

In front of the seminary (on the side toward Willoughby Run), and but a few feet from it, was a narrow strip of woods. Along the edge of this, next the seminary, was a rail and stone fence. Here Colonel Wainwright, Chief of Artillery of the First corps, had posted the batteries of Cooper, Breck, Stevens and Wilbur, and at the railroad cut to the right were the guns of Stuart. Colonel Biddle had posted his two regiments behind this fence, and when the other two arrived they were formed on his left. This line was prolonged to the right beyond the railroad bed by Meredith's brigade, which had already arrived there, and this position was held for nearly or quite half an hour, against four times the number of defenders. But to do more than to give the fleeing troops farther to the right the opportunity to escape through the town and form on the heights beyond was not expected. The repulse of the enemy's first attack on this new line was so complete and disastrous that they retired beyond the ridge and into the valley of Willoughby Run. Colonel Gates rode through the strip of woods at this time, and sat on his horse several minutes watching the right and left of the rebel line, while immediately in front there was not a Confederate to be seen except dead and wounded. Colonel Biddle, while conversing with Colonel Gates in rear of the line, during the second assault, received a musket ball wound in the scalp; the sound of the blow was distinctly heard, and both gentlemen thought the injury of a serious character. Colonel Biddle turned over the command of the brigade to Colonel Gates, as the wound was very painful, and withdrew. He returned, however, while the brigade was still in the same position, with his head bandaged, and remarking to Colonel Gates that the wound was not as bad as he had feared, resumed command of the brigade. Colonel Gates' horse received five bullet wounds while at this position. These somewhat personal matters are narrated with a view to give to the reader an idea of the nature of the defence which this brigade made, the length of time it held the enemy in check, and of the entire coolness and composure of its conduct. The retreat of the Union troops from the field of the first day's fight has generally been characterized as "disorderly," and while this is true as to a portion of them, it is unjust as to nearly the entire First corps. Even so close an observer and accurate writer as General Hancock has fallen into this error. In his controversy with General Howard as to which was entitled to most credit for posting the army on Cemetery Hill, and as to what time he himself arrived there,

General Hancock says : "I hurried to the front (Cemetery Heights), and saw our troops retreating in disorder and confusion from the town, closely followed by
the enemy"—"Galaxy," December, 1876, page 822.
General Hancock says this was "about 3:30 P. M." At
that hour the left of the First Corps certainly was
fighting on the Willoughby Run line, and had not
yielded a foot of ground. It was at least half an hour
later when it fell back to the seminary, and that position was retained for more than half an hour. The retreat from there was deliberate and orderly ; and my
diary gives the time as 5:30 when we reached Cemetery
Hill.

The enemy had been repulsed in three several attacks on our position, but he had now thrown M'Gow-
an's brigade upon our left flank, and his troops were
pushing forward on our right, threatening to cut off our
retreat. Colonel Biddle conferred with Colonel Gates
upon the subject of withdrawing the brigade, and it was
agreed that it was impracticable to remain longer. The
batteries were safely removed, with the exception of
one gun and three caissons, the horses of which being
killed, had to be abandoned. The "Ulster Guard"
marched in rear of the brigade, covering the retreat.
The enemy were then closing in on both flanks, and
pushing forward in rear, and there was not so much as
a company of Federal troops, except killed and
wounded, upon the battle-field when we left it. Reaching Cemetery Hill, we were posted along a stone wall,
overlooking the Taneytown road, and there remained
during the night, and until 11 o'clock, A. M., next day.

Mr. Swinton says, at page 334 of his "Campaigns of
the Army of the Potomac" : "The left of the First alone
drew back in some order, making a stand on Seminary
Ridge until the artillery and ambulances had been withdrawn, and then fell back behind the town." After
describing the repulse of our right, Mr. Lossing says :

"The First Corps, whose left had been held firmly by
Doubleday, now fell back.   It brought away the artillery and ambulances from Seminary Ridge."   This does
not indicate much "disorder and confusion" on that
part of the line.   Professor Jacobs says : "But though
the enemy attacked us with two men to our one, our
left was able, during the forenoon, and until three P. M.,
not only to hold its own, but to drive back the enemy
in their fearful charges."

At the risk of being charged with egotism, I take the
liberty to make some extracts from a letter of General
Doubleday's, dated September 10th, 1863.   If it reflect
any credit upon the author of this work, it reflects still
greater credit upon the officers and men he commanded,
and this is my justification for its insertion in these
pages.   Without the cordial and hearty co-operation of
my command, I could not have won the commendation
General Doubleday bestows upon me, and whatever of
compliment is expressed or implied in his letter, the
officers and men under my command are entitled to the
credit of.   General Doubleday says : " Colonel Theodore
B. Gates, of the Twentieth New York, served under me
in the recent battle of Gettysburg, as well as on several
other occasions.   The many battles in which this officer
has been engaged, his great bravery and sound military
judgment led me to place great dependence upon him.
On the first day at Gettysburg he was assigned to the
important duty of protecting the left flank of the First
corps against the heavy forces which threatened it.
His manœuvres were all excellent, and he held his position for several hours, until the right of the line gave
way and forced him to retire, which he did in good
order.   Although out-flanked by a whole brigade, he
continued, as I have said, to hold them in check, and
to fall back without disorder, to a second position on
Seminary Ridge.   There he formed his line again, and
most gallantly checked the enemy's advance, until the

corps had nearly all withdrawn. His position was that of a forlorn hope, covering the retreat of the corps and saving it from a great disaster.

"Exhausted as his command must have been, from the desperate and prolonged fighting on the first day, he, nevertheless, had an equally desperate combat on the third day, after the terrific artillery assault which preceded the final attack of the rebels on our left centre. The rebels had already penetrated Hancock's line of battle, when the two regiments, under command of Colonel Gates, attacked them furiously in front, at short pistol range, charged and drove them from the protection of the felled timber in which they were sheltered, and took a large number of prisoners. On the occasions alluded to, Colonel Gates commanded the 20th New York (his own regiment), and the 151st Pennsylvania Volunteers.

"I do not mean by these remarks to detract in any way from the great merit of the other troops who cooperated with Colonel Gates. The desperate nature of the fight is indicated by the fact that the official returns show that Colonel Gates lost considerably more than half his force."

The enemy made some desultory attempts to carry the Federal lines of Cemetery Hill in the evening, and at one or two points sharp but brief fighting ensued; but in every instance the Confederates were repulsed, and retired to the shelter of the town, or rejoined their comrades at its suburbs. If General Lee had pushed forward the forces he had in the immediate neighborhood of Gettysburg, at six o'clock in the afternoon of July 1st, and had made a vigorous and determined assault upon Cemetery Hill, it is very doubtful if the small body of Union troops then on the ground could have prevented the Confederates from obtaining possession of the strong position along Rock Creek, east of the cemetery, and which would have compelled the

Federals to abandon the ground on which they subsequently fought, and would possibly have reversed the positions of the armies in the great struggles of the next two days. But Lee had been confounded by the unexpected presence of the Army of the Potomac, and with the imperfect knowledge he then had as to the strength of the position and the numbers present to defend it, he deferred his attack.

Thus the van-guard of the Federal Army had accomplished its mission. It had met the wishes of its dead chieftain, Reynolds, and of Howard and Doubleday, Pleasonton and Buford. By an almost unexampled persistency, by steady and continuous fighting on an exposed field and against double its numbers for eight hours, it had saved the natural bulwarks in rear of Gettysburg for the occupation of the Union army, and from these bulwarks it delivered battle on the next and the succeeding day, and upon these bulwarks and the brave men who defended them, the Confederate army was dashed in vain, until decimated and demoralized, its worn and hopeless remnant, like the shadow of the grand and confident array which so lately marched across the border, sought safety and seclusion in a midnight flight.

Of the battle of the first day, Mr. Bates says: "What the result would have been had Reynolds lived, it is impossible to divine. He had scarcely marshalled his first battalions before he was slain. The chief command upon the field then devolved upon General Doubleday, which, for upwards of two hours, he continued to exercise. It was during this time, and under his immediate direction, that the chief successes of the day were achieved, a large number of prisoners and standards having been captured in successive periods of the fight, and at widely separated parts of the field. To any one who will traverse the ground held by the First Corps from ten in the morning until

after four in the afternoon will note the insignificance
in the number of its guns and of its muskets, as compared with those of the two divisions of Hill and one of
Ewell which opposed it, and will consider the triumphs
won, and how every daring attempt of the enemy to
gain the field was foiled, it must be evident that the
manœuvring of Doubleday was admirable, and that it
stamps him as a corps leader of consummate excellence.
For mark how little equality of position he enjoyed!
the opposing ridge and Oak Hill affording great advantage for the enemy's artillery ; and how his infantry
stood upon open ground, with no natural or artificial
protection except in a short distance upon his extreme
right, where was a low stone wall.   Where, in the history of the late war, is this skill and coolness of the
commander, or this stubborn bravery of the troops
matched?

*   *   *   *   *   *   *   *

"But where, during all this long day of carnage,
was the rest of the army ? Why were these two feeble
corps left from early morn until the evening shadows
began to set, to be jostled and torn without succor ?
Were there no troops within call ? Was not the very
air laden with the terrible sounds of the fray ? Was
not the clangor of the enemy's guns more persuasive
than the summons of staff officers ?

"The order of General Meade for the march of the
several corps of the army on the first would carry the
Third corps to Emmettsburg.   But General Sickles says
in his testimony, that he had reached Emmettsburg on
the night of the 30th.   This place is ten miles from Gettysburg.   The Third corps had been placed under the
command of Reynolds as the leader of the right wing of
the army, and he had sent a staff officer on the morning
of the first to summon it forward.   It had no farther to
march than had Howard's corps, and following the
course that Howard went—the by-way leading to Taney-

town road—not so great a distance. But Sickles had
that morning received the circular of Meade, indicating
the purpose to concentrate on Pipe Creek, though containing no order. It was his plain duty, therefore, to
have responded, had the message reached him, to the
call of Reynolds. But to this he seems to have paid no
attention. In his testimony Sickles says : 'I was giving my troops a little repose during that morning
Between two and three o'clock in the afternoon, I got
a dispatch from General Howard, at Gettysburg, inform-
ing me that the First and Eleventh corps had been
engaged during the day with a superior force of the
enemy, and that General Reynolds had fallen ; that he
(Howard) was in command, and was very hard pressed,
and urging me, in the most earnest terms to come to his
relief with what force I could. I of course, considered
the question very anxiously My preliminary orders in
going to Gettysburg were to go there and hold that
position with my corps, as it was regarded as a very
important flanking position, to cover our rear and line
of communication.' In this testimony Sickles ignores
the early summons of Reynolds, which a staff officer,
Captain Rosengarten, asserts was sent by an aide with
great dispatch, and immediately after Reynolds had
reached the front; but Sickles says, 'My preliminary
orders in going to Gettysburg.' Is this a misprint in
the testimony, and should it read Emmettsburg? If
Gettysburg, then to what order does he refer? General
Meade had given no such order. If Gettysburg, he
must refer to an order which he had received from Reynolds, which he disobeyed; probably allowing the circular of Meade, which had no binding effect, and which
bore that declaration in so many words on its face, to
override it. But, when, between two and three o'clock,
he received the summons of Howard, he concluded to
respond to it. Moreover, it would seem that besides the
order of Reynolds and the appeal of Howard, other

2 9

messages had reached Sickles before he decided to go to Gettysburg. An article published in the 'Rebellion Record,' Vol. VIII., page 346, contains this statement: "besides numerous reports, the following brief communication reached him (Sickles) which accidentally fell into my hands: 'July 1, Gettysburg, General Sickles: General Doubleday (First corps) says, for God's sake, come up with all speed, they are pressing us hard. H. T. Lee, lieutenant, A. D. C.'

"The Twelfth corps, according to Meade's programme, was to march from Littlestown, ten miles from Gettysburg, to Two Taverns, which would bring it within five miles of the battle-field, four and a quarter from Cemetery Hill. The march was commenced at six in the morning, and, after passing Two Taverns, a line of battle was formed. The following is from the diary of an officer who commanded a regiment in Kane's Brigade: 'July 1st, Marched at six A.M. a short distance: passing Two Taverns; formed line of battle; heavy firing in front. A report that the First and Eleventh corps are engaged with the enemy ' The enemy's Whitworth gun could have sent a bolt nearly this distance. The smoke from the field must have been plainly visible. The roar of the battle was constantly resounding. But here the corps remained idle during the whole day "

The First corps was nearly annihilated. It went into battle with 8,200 men and came out with but 2,450—5,750 killed, wounded and captured. The two divisions of the Eleventh corps which came upon the field lost little more than half their number. There were but few prisoners taken from the First corps, but a large number from the Eleventh. Over 2,500 Confederate prisoners had been taken and the field was covered with dead and wounded Rebels—and Cemetery Hill, Wolf and Culp Hills and the Round Tops were ours.

On the Left at Gettysburg.

Respectfully dedicated to the Twentieth Regiment, N. Y. S. M.

BY H. L. ABBEY.

Soldier of the picket guard,
Keeping midnight watch and ward,
While a mighty nation sleeps ;
On yon dark, beleaguered steeps—
On the heights at Fredericksburg—
Tell us how at Gettysburg,
On the left at Gettysburg,
   Valor stayed disaster ;
When the raiding Rebel crew,
Hurled upon our weary few
   Columns dense, and vaster,
Ten to one, than they who stood,
For a grateful nation's good,
   On the left, at Gettysburg,
   Beating back disaster.
   *   *   *   *

Though, before their fierce attack,
Right and centre both fell back,
Scarce three hundred Ulster men,
Linked with brawny sons of Penn,
All that day at Gettysburg—
On the left at Gettysburg—
   Held at bay the traitor.
   *   *   *   *

Ho ! watcher of our destiny
Tell us yet if liberty,
   On the Nation's forehead
Sets her crown, no longer scoffed
By the blazoned curse, that oft
   Made her name abhorred.
If the stain be cleansed away,
Not in vain upon that day,
On the left at Gettysburg,
   Fought our sons and brothers.
If the curse must still remain,
Vain their fight, our longing vain ;
   And the tears of mothers
Will not find a balm to soothe—
Marah never will be smooth—

Torn with waves of sorrow.
But the right shall rule, we know,
Lo ! the morning splendors glow
    Of the golden morrow.
Mothers' tears are pearls, that buy
Many a nation's liberty,
    Making freedom vaster.
Pray for those who vainly weep
For their darling sons, who sleep
Where they fell at Gettysburg,
On the left at Gettysburg,
    Beating back disaster.

CHAPTER XXXIII

To most of the officers and men of the Federal Army
the night of the first of July was an anxious, sleepless
and tiresome one. The worn-out troops of the First and
Eleventh corps lay upon their arms around the bend of
the fish-hook, guarding the approaches from the direction of Gettysburg. The residue of the army was in
march to join them. Would they arrive in time for the
anticipated assault in the early morning? The positions
of the Third and Twelfth corps were shown in the concluding paragraphs of the preceding chapter. The
Second corps was still at Taneytown, fourteen miles
away The Fifth corps was near Uniontown, still
farther away, and the Sixth, the largest corps in the
army, was at Manchester, thirty-four miles from the
battle-field. But by and by the sound of thousands of
hurrying feet and the rumble of batteries and caissons,
told to the anxious listeners the glad story of the in-
pouring of the Union Army. The fight to-morrow would
be a more equal combat; the repulse of to-day would
surely be avenged. These boasting rebels, who filled
the streets of Gettysburg and recounted to its terror-
stricken citizens their exploits of the day, should have

a far different tale to rehearse on the coming night.
Professor Jacobs, a citizen of Gettysburg and a spectator
of and a listener to the things and conversations he
speaks of, says : " The portion of Rodes' division
which lay down before our dwelling for the night was
greatly elated with the results of the first day's battle,
and the same may be said of the whole rebel army.
They were anxious to engage in conversation, to communicate their views and feelings, and to elicit ours.
They were boastful of themselves, of their cause, and of
the skill of their officers ; and were anxious to tell us of
the unskillful manner in which some of our officers had
conducted the fight which had just closed. When informed that General Archer and 1500 of his men had
been captured, they said : ' To-morrow we will take all
these back again ; and having already taken 5000 (!)
prisoners of you to-day, we will take the balance of
your men to-morrow.' Having been well fed, provis-
ioned and rested, and successful on this day, their confidence knew no bounds. They felt assured they should
be able, with perfect ease, to cut up our army in detail,
fatigued as it was by long marches and yet scattered,
for only two corps had as yet arrived. Resting under
this impression, they laid down joyfully on the night of
the first day."

General Meade arrived at Cemetery Hill about one
o'clock on the morning of the second of July, and as
soon as day began to break he was in the saddle, riding
over the ground and giving orders for the positioning of
his army. The Eleventh corps retained the position it
assumed on the evening of the first ; next on its right
was Wadsworth's division of the First corps, extending
into the fastness of Culp's Hill ; next to Wadsworth
was posted Slocum's Twelfth corps (excepting Geary's
division, which was stationed in the neighborhood of
Round Top, on the left) with its right resting on McAllister's Hill. On the left of Howard, and extending

along the shank of the fish-hook, was Hancock's Second corps, with its right in Zeigler's Grove and its left thrown out towards Round Top. The Third corps, Sickles, had arrived in the evening of the first and was massed in rear of the left of the Eleventh corps. The Fifth corps was placed in reserve in rear of Cemetery Hill, on its arrival, but on the afternoon of the second was moved over to the Round Tops, under circumstances hereafter narrated. The Sixth corps, Sedgwick, which left Hanover on the evening of the first and made a forced march of thirty-four miles, arrived on the field at two o'clock on the 2d, and was posted in reserve in rear of the left flank. The divisions of Doubleday, (General Meade had assigned General Newton to the command of the First corps) and Robinson were in reserve.

The road from Gettysburg to Baltimore, after passing through the Federal line at Cemetery Hill, continued southeasterly, along the rear of the right wing of the army. The Taneytown road ran through the left centre of our line, and thence along the rear of the left wing ; each road passing out between the Round Tops and McAllister's Hill. The Emmettsburg road ran close to the front of the left, until it passed Hancock's corps and then diverged to the west, and disappeared over a wooded ridge a mile and a half west of Round Top. The ground in front of the left of the Federal line sloped gently for an eighth of a mile, and then, by a gradual ascent, reached the ridge over which the Emmettsburg road passed, and which is a prolongation of Seminary Ridge. The country between the Union line and this ridge is open, cultivated land, excepting two small groves on the left, and Sherfy's peach orchard, near the Emmettsburg road, nearly opposite Little Round Top. The opposite ridge is wooded, and afforded a complete mask to the enemy's movements ; while the position of the Federal troops, at the centre and left of their line, could be distinctly seen from the ridge across the Emmettsburg road.

From early morning, until about four o'clock in the afternoon, no hostile demonstration was made. While the Federal commander was stationing his troops, the Rebel Chieftain was engaged in a like occupation, and studying the ground and waiting for his entire force to assemble. At about that hour, General Webb, Colonel Sherrill, Colonel Hardenburg and myself, were sitting on our horses near Dilger's battery, overlooking the field towards the Seminary Ridge, when we were surprised to see a heavy column of Federal troops debouch from the extreme left of our line and take its way across the open fields above described, towards the Emmettsburg road. Although no enemy could be seen in the woods beyond, no one doubted that they were swarming with Rebel troops, and planted thick with Confederate cannon. It was supposed we had taken position to fight a defensive battle ; and the initiation of an offensive, by a single corps, and that corps advancing in column in mass, almost under the guns of the enemy, without skirmishers or any apparent preparation for immediate battle, was what spectators could not comprehend.

For ten minutes the column moved steadily forward ; the spectators of this strange proceeding held their breath in suspense ; all was quiet as death, save the murmuring sound of the tramp of those misguided men, and an occasional exclamation in our lines of astonishment and dismay Colonel Sherrill, formerly an Ulster County man, suddenly exclaimed : "There it comes ;" and a moment later the woods along the ridge were wreathed in smoke, while a hundred cannon thundered on the air. The Union guns answered this Rebel outburst, and for some time the artillery maintained a furious combat. General Meade now appeared on this part of the field, and finding a battle thrust upon him

unexpectedly, had no choice but to sustain the troops
which had thus become engaged, and he ordered up re-
enforcements to support Sickles. Longstreet, who held
the right of Lee's line, and was, therefore, opposite
Sickles, was directed to move out and meet him ; while
orders were sent to Ewell to attack the right of the
Union line, and to Hill, to menace the centre ; so that
the Union commander would not dare to withdraw
troops from those positions to support the imperilled
left. If the' Third corps could be swept away, the Confederates could move upon the very key of the Union
position—Round Top : and take the Federal lines
in reverse Longstreet sent Hood against Sickles,
whose column was now deployed, with directions
to strike it near Sherfy's peach orchard, while McLaws
and Anderson were to throw their forces against Sickles'
left, and, breaking through that flank, seize the Round
Top. Troops from the Fifth and reserves of the First
Corps were sent forward to re-enforce Sickles, but the
pressure upon his left was irresistible, and after the
most desperate resistance the enemy forced his way
through, and Hood's Texans were climbing the ragged
side of Round Top, on which as yet the Federals had only
a signal station, when fortunately General Warren, the
Chief Engineer of the Army, and a soldier of quick and
correct apprehension, chanced to ride to this point of
the field, and, ascending Round Top, found it bare of
troops, and even the signal officers were rolling up their
signal colors to depart, seeing the enemy ascending the
mountain side Warren ordered them to unroll and
display their flags, and then detaching General Vincent's brigade and Hazlett's battery from Barnes' division as it was passing to the support of Sickles, succeeded in getting this force upon the mountain top while the
Confederates were ascending the more difficult face
from the opposite side. A fearful combat ensued for
the possession of the commanding point. The bayonet

and clubbed muskets were often resorted to, and for half an hour the struggle was almost unparalled. At length a gallant charge by the Twentieth Maine, Colonel Chamberlain, swept the Texans from the hill and left the coveted position in the hands of the Federals. While the struggle was going on both sides had been re-enforced, and among the Federals who had come to the aid of Vincent was General Weed, commanding the brigade of Ayre's division to which Hazlett's battery belonged, and among the dead of this sanguinary fight were Generals Weed and Vincent, and Lieutenant Hazlett.

On the plain and in the valley below, the combat was gallantly maintained on the Union side, but the left of our line was driven back upon the ridge north of Little Round Top, while the right division, Humphrey's. swung its left to the rear, still clinging with its right to the Emmettsburg road. Caldwell's division of the Second corps, now moved out to the support of Humphrey's. The left of Sickles' line having been driven in the Confederates turned in overwhelming force upon the right, while a part of Hill's corps, foregoing its menace against the centre, joined in the attack upon Humphrey and swept him back to the Union lines.

"The Confederates, elated by their successes, dashed like turbulent waves up to the base of the ridge occupied by the Nationals, fighting most desperately, and throwing themselves recklessly upon supposed weak points of their antagonist's line. In this encounter Meade led troops in person, and everywhere inspirited his men by his presence. Finally, just at sunset, a general charge was made, under the direction of Hancock, chiefly by fresh troops under General Doubleday, who had hastened to his assistance from the rear of Cemetery Hill   These, with Humphrey's shattered regiments, drove the Confederates back, and a portion of Doubleday's division, pressing up nearly to the opposite lines, recaptured four guns which had been lost. At twilight, the battle on the left and left centre had ended, when a new line was formed by the divisions of Robinson and Doubleday, and troops from the Twelfth corps brought up by General Williams who was in temporary command of it, Slocum having charge of the entire right wing."—Lossing, Vol. III, page 68.

About the time the fighting was concluded on the left, Johnson's division of Ewell's corps burst upon the Union line, at a low point between Culp's and McAllister's Hills. Some of the Federal forces had been withdrawn from this locality to aid their brethren on the left, and the watchful Confederates had noticed the fact. Just before dark the attack began with great impetuosity For two hours the conflict was carried on with heavy loss to the assailants, but ended in their getting possession of a portion of the Union works near Spangler's Spring, at the southern extremity of Culp's Hill, but the darkness now prevented the further prosecution of their enterprise, or any attempt to expel them. So, holding this breach in the Federal line, the two armies gave over their struggles for the night.

Among the troops which were ordered to the left in support of General Sickles were the 151st Pennsylvania and the "Ulster Guard," still acting as a demi-brigade, and when the fighting ceased, they found themselves in the front line and immediately on the left of the Second corps. At ten o'clock comparative quiet reigned along the lines of the two armies, and the weary men threw themselves upon the ground to sleep. I took this opportunity to walk with some of my officers over that portion of the battle-field, in our immediate front, across which the Third corps had retreated. The enemy's pursuit was pushed close up to our lines, and the dead and wounded, of both sides, mingled together and covered the ground.

Our pickets for the night—the men who watch while

the army sleeps—had been posted along the little valley I have mentioned, some six hundred yards in advance of our line of battle, and embraced a portion of the field where the combat raged fiercest in the afternoon.

The night was very dark, but the low moans of the wounded, as they broke upon the chilly air, guided us in our search. We found among them, men from almost every State—loyal and disloyal—the fierce, half barbaric Texan, side by side with the cool, unimpassioned soldier from Maine—the Georgian and New Yorker —the Mississippian and Pennsylvanian—who, a few short hours before thirsted for each others' lives, now, softened by the anguish of wounds, and still more, by the soothing spirit that pervades the night while its myriad stars are looking down upon you—all their fierce passions hushed and all their rancor gone—these wounded men sought to comfort and to cheer one another.

The stretcher-bearers, groping about for the wounded, moved noiselessly over the field, carrying their human burdens to the ambulances within our lines, and these conveyed them to the hospitals.

One, among those wounded men—an officer of the 120th N. Y. Vol.—I had known long and well. He had grown up, surrounded by every luxury a refined and cultivated mind could demand and affluence could supply. His generous impulses—his social qualities—his ready wit—his bright intelligence—had made him an universal favorite. He had but recently exchanged the cheverons on his sleeve for the Lieutenant's strap, and in the retreat of the Third corps, was one among the hundreds left upon the field, wounded beyond recovery

I can never forget his calm demeanor as he lay upon the damp earth, patiently waiting his turn to be cared for. While his young life was ebbing away, he was as composed as he could have been sitting by his mother's fireside. He was anxious only to give us no trouble, and shut up his anguish in his own breast. No external exhibition of suffering could have touched me as did his unmurmuring submission to the fate that had befallen him.

While I could imagine what he suffered—from his wound less than from the consciousness that all his life-hopes and promises were thus cruelly blighted—I could not but envy the calm resignation of Lieutenant Cockburn.

Another severely wounded officer of the 120th was Lieutenant-Colonel Cornelius D. Westbrook, of Kingston, formerly Captain of Engineers of the "Ulster Guard."

During the night, some changes were made in the positions of our forces, to meet the emergencies of the morrow, and our defences were strengthened as much as possible. A strong column of infantry and several batteries quietly moved as near as practicable to the point on our right, where the enemy had broken through, and every preparation made to drive them out.

CHAPTER XXXIV

To allow the enemy to retain his hold upon a section of the line which he had carried the night before was to give him an entering wedge with which he might possibly disrupt the entire right wing. The first thing to be done then was to expel him at any cost, and that too before he could take advantage of his position. At early dawn our artillery opened a terrific cannonade upon Johnson's men, which was kept up until half-past five, when the divisions of Williams and Geary, and the brigade of Shaler, advanced to the attack. The enemy had been greatly strengthened at this point during the night and when our guns opened at four o'clock in the morning, were themselves preparing to press on through our line and dash in between the wings of the army. The intruders made a desperate resistance, and for four hours the infantry struggle was fierce and deadly. At the end of that time Geary's division rushed upon the

462

enemy with the bayonet and drove them out of the works, and the Union line was re-established.

The following narrative of the operations of the 151st Pennsylvania and the "Ulster Guard," is taken from the official report of their commanding officer:

"About 5 P.M., on the second of July, the brigade was ordered to the left centre to support the Third corps. Two regiments only of the brigade, (the 20th N Y S. M., and the 151st Pa. Vol., the latter under command of Captain Owens), reached the front line, where they were halted on the last and lowest of the ridges running nearly north and south between the Taneytown and Emmettsburg roads. Some 350 yards on our right was a bluff, on which were standing a few trees and a battery. The trees on the westerly face of the bluff had been felled to clear a range for the guns. A rail fence stood at the foot of the bluff and extended along the ridge southerly. A little in advance and to our left, was a small grove. The ground in front descended gradually to a little valley, wet and marshy, and then by a corresponding ascent reached the Emmettsburg road and the position occupied by the enemy. Some 300 yards in rear of me was a ridge running parallel to the one I was on, but much higher. On my right was one regiment of Stannard's brigade ; on my left two others, and one in rear and partly to my left. Receiving no orders, and finding myself the senior officer of the brigade present, I assumed command of the two regiments, and in the course of the evening, constructed a breast-work of the fence heretofore mentioned, and of such other material as could be found.

"About 5 A.M., on the third, the enemy opened with artillery, and for some time kept up a brisk fire upon our position. This finally ceased, and until about 1 P.M., no further firing took place on this part of the line. During this interval the Vermont troops threw up a breast-work to my left, and about one hundred feet in advance

of my line, masked by the small grove before mentioned.
The regiment of that brigade on my right, took position
in rear of this new work, leaving the space between my
right and the bluff, on which the nearest battery was, uncovered. At one o'clock the enemy opened from his right
centre battery, which was soon followed by all his guns
on his right and centre, and the position occupied by
my command was swept by a tempest of shot and
shell from upwards of a hundred guns for nearly
two hours. Then the cannonading subsided and
the enemy's infantry debouched from the orchard
and woods on his right centre, and moved in two
lines of battle across the fields towards the position
I have described. Our skirmishers (from the Vermont
brigade) fell back before them, and sought cover behind
the breastworks on my left. The enemy came forward
rapidly, and began firing as soon as they were within
range of our men. When they had approached within
about two hundred feet of the bottom of the valley
heretofore mentioned, the troops of my command
opened a warm fire upon them. Almost immediately,
the first line faced by the left flank, and moved at a
double-quick up the valley and towards Gettysburg.
The second line followed the movement. Reaching a
position opposite the bluff, they faced to the right, and
moved forward rapidly in line of battle. Perceiving
that their purpose was to gain the bluff, 1 moved my
command by the right flank up to the foot of the bluff,
delivering our fire as we marched, and keeping between
the enemy and the object of his enterprise. He succeeded in reaching the fence at the foot of the bluff,
but with ranks broken, and his men evidently disheartened. Some succeeded in getting over the fence into
the slashing, from which and behind the fence they
kept up a murderous fire. The men were now within
quarter pistol range ; and as the fence and fallen trees
gave the enemy considerable cover, I ordered the 20th,

N. Y S. M., and the 151st Pa. Vol., to advance to the fence, which they did, cheering and in gallant style, and poured a volley into the enemy at very short range, who now completely broke, and those who did not seek to escape by flight threw down their arms. Very few of those who fled reached their own lines. Many turned, after having run several rods, and surrendered themselves. We took a large number of prisoners, and the ground in front of us was strewn with their dead and wounded. During the latter part of this struggle, and after it ceased, the enemy's batteries played upon friend and foe alike. The troops engaged with us were Pickett's division of Longstreet's corps.

" Among the killed and wounded in my immediate front was Colonel Hodges, 14th Va., and seven line officers. Two colors were left upon the ground on our front by the enemy

" This terminated the final and main attack upon our left centre. It was now nearly six o'clock, P. M., and my command was relieved by a portion of the Second corps, and withdrawn to the Taneytown road, where it remained through the night. It will thus be perceived that the two regiments I had the honor to command were either actually engaged with the enemy, or occupying a position in the front line from the beginning of the battle on the morning of July first, until its close on the evening of the third, excepting only about six hours on the second.

" My loss in killed and wounded was two-thirds of my officers and half of my men. I have no report of the casualties in the 151st Pa. Vol. They behaved with the utmost gallantry ; and their loss was very heavy."

The following letter was addressed to General Doubleday with reference to Mr. Bachelder's Map of the Battle of Gettysburg.

30

HEADQUARTERS 20th N. Y. S. M.

Brandy Station, Va., Feb. 4, 1864.

Major-General ABNER DOUBLEDAY,

U. S. Volunteers.

DEAR GENERAL—Mr. Bachelder called on me a few evenings since, and exhibited the draft of his proposed map of the Battle of Gettysburg. I was sorry to find it wholly inaccurate in the position it assigns to my command on the 3d of July. He represents my regiment and the 151st Pa. Vols., (then under my command) as lying *in rear* of General Stannard's Brigade. *The truth is the exact reverse of this.* A portion of General Stannard's brigade was lying *behind me*, and at no time was there so much as a file of his command *in front* of me, saving only his skirmishers. One regiment of his brigade constructed a breast-work in the forenoon, to my left, and perhaps one hundred feet *in advance* of me, and in rear of the little grove, but in no wise covering my line.

Then again he has the space between my right and the bluff where the severest fighting along that part of the line took place, filled up with other troops. When the enemy made his attack there was not a man between my right flank and the bluff—a distance of three hundred yards.

I therefore moved my command over this interval to the bluff when it became apparent that that was the point of assault, and *did so because there were no other troops there to defend it.*

Whether Mr. Bachelder will make the proper corrections I do not know, but I desire to put you in possession of the facts, and with that view send you herewith a report covering every movement of my command, not only on the third, but during the three days fighting, and it is accurate in every particular.

It was my misfortune to be associated during the three days with strange troops, from whom I almost immediately separated, and whose interest and preference do not require them to bestow much notice upon my command.

During the fighting on the first day the General commanding the division was hardly competent to judge correctly the condition of things, or to know what transpired on the field, (Note by General Doubleday; "This refers to General Rowley") and from the time I took position with my regiment and the 151st Pa. Vol., in the front line in the afternoon of the 2d, until after the battle on the 3d, I was the senior officer of the brigade in that part of the field.

I presume it was intended that the left of the 2d corps should fill the interval between my right and the bluff. *But they did not do it.* They were on the ridge in rear, and two or more regiments were massed behind the battery on the bluff while the fighting was taking place at the foot of the bluff in front. My Lieutenant-Colonel went to the regiment near the battery and endeavored to get them moved down to my support, *but did not succeed. After the fighting was entirely over they came down and relieved me.*

The trenches in which hundreds of the enemy's dead are now lying, on the ground where we fought, bear witness to the desperate character of the contest, not to speak of still larger numbers wounded and captured, and larger still who surrendered unharmed. I am sorry to be driven to the belief that the troops who relieved me subsequently assumed to have done the fighting at that particular point. Hoping this may not be deemed intrusive or prove annoying,

I have the honor to be, General,

Your obedient servant,

THEODORE B. GATES,

Colonel Commanding.

To this I received the following reply from General
Doubleday :

To COLONEL T. B. GATES,
      Commanding 20th N. Y. S. M.,
            3d Division 1st Army Corps,
                  Near Culpepper, Virginia.

                        WILLARD'S HOTEL,
                        WASHINGTON, D. C.,
                              February 10th, 1864.
DEAR COLONEL :

I saw Mr. Bachelder, with reference to your statement. He has removed on his picture all troops from
your front, but declines to leave the space vacant indicated by you on your right, as he considers the weight
of evidence against your claim, and says he does not
feel at liberty to disregard it.

                        Yours very truly,

                        A. DOUBLEDAY,
                              Major-Gen'l Vol.

The following letter from General Hardenburgh was
written in answer to a request for a statement of his
recollection of the positions and operations of the
Guard during the three days at Gettysburg :

                        CANAAN, CONN.,
                              Oct. 9, 1878.
GENERAL T. B. GATES :

Dear General:—I will now endeavor to answer the
letter you refer to in yours of the 23d ult., although I
confess my recollection as to details is not very clear.
My recollection is, that on the first day at Gettysburg
we held the extreme left, and Bachelder's map, which
places a Pennsylvania regiment on our left, is clearly
wrong. You will recollect one of our companies (Cun-

ningham's) was stationed at a house, way in advance of the left, which was afterwards burned by the enemy.

In regard to giving way, my recollection is this : we were on the extreme left ; the enemy's right lapped our left considerably, and when you saw them coming around our left into our rear, you gave the order to retire ; we then fell back to Seminary ridge, decently and in order, but not until we were ordered to do so. I recollect distinctly, that when we got back to the Seminary, it struck me that the whole thing would turn into a perfect rout, and that we ought to try and· make a stand and check the enemy's advance ; I went to you and spoke to you about it, and we both then went to see Colonel Biddle, who was in command of the brigade. While you were speaking to him he was hit in the head by a bullet, and he turned away and left. You then turned back, gave the order yourself to the men to halt, which they immediately did, and we made a stand then for, I should say. from 15 minutes to half an hour, and checked for a time, at least, the advance of the Rebs. I have always thought we have never got sufficient credit for that stand. It is alluded to, I believe, by *Swinton*, in his history, but nowhere else. Now, you know, the enemy never advanced his lines much beyond Seminary Hill, and you know that if he had pressed on to *Cemetery Hill*, the whole thing would have ended in a complete rout, and there would have been a skedaddle back to Washington. *Why didn't they press on ?* My idea is, and always has been, that it was because of the determined stand we made back of the Seminary.

When we fell back from the Seminary, you will recollect we could not go directly back to Gettysburg, because the enemy had again got around our left flank, but we had to make a detour around to the railroad track and then up through Gettysburg to Cemetery Hill. My recollection is, and it is quite distinct on that

point, that when we fell back from the Seminary, the
rear of the 11th Corps had passed by, and there was
nothing behind us in that direction. When we reached
Cemetery Hill, Howard and his corps were all there.
This must have been, I should think, in the neighborhood of 5 o'clock. That evening we were in line on
Cemetery Hill. The next day we moved down back of
the Hill, and remained there until the afternoon. In
the afternoon sometime we rode up on the ridge, where
we saw Colonel Sherrill, and while there, the attack on
the Third Corps was made. Seeing this, we hastened
back to the regiment, and directly an order came to
move up to the front. We took position in the front
line, and never changed it until the attack by the
enemy on the third day. I recollect that night Major
Van Rensselear and I slept in front of our line with a
stone for a pillow, and in the course of the evening our
men brought in some of the wounded of the 120th,
among them James Cockburn. I see Bachelder, on his
map, places us in a position diagonally to the line, at
an angle of about 45° We never occupied any such
position ; it is simply ridiculous. We remained in precisely the position we took up in the afternoon of the
2d, with, I think, a Pennsylvania regiment on our left.
Some time before the attack on the 3d, a brigade of
troops moved up to our rear, and remained there during
the cannonading. I understood they were nine months
men and were Vermont troops—Stannard's brigade. I
recollect them lying in our rear during the cannonading, more especially from two circumstances ; 1st, one
man was killed directly behind me, it was supposed by
a cannon ball. He was thrown over and never moved a
muscle—was stone dead. 2d, I remarked the difference
between them (new men) and ours (old soldiers) ; ours
during the cannonading were smoking and joking, while
the others lay there hugging the ground, and big drops
of perspiration stood out on their foreheads and faces.

I recollect that about noon of the third, you requested
me to go and find General Doubleday, and see if he
could not make some arrangements about getting
rations—our men had nothing to eat. I found him
over the ridge directly in our rear, under a tree with his
staff. After telling him what I came for, he told me to
say to you that he could not do anything about rations
then, that he had just received an order from General
Meade for a general attack upon the enemy at 2 o'clock
that afternoon—that he knew it was hard, but the salvation of the country depended upon the issue, and
he wished you to hold your command in readiness to
move promptly at any moment. I went back and just
as I got on the brow of the hill or ridge, a gun
was fired from the rebel lines directly in front of me,
and instantly the batteries on both sides opened and continued to "volley and thunder" for about two hours.
During this firing, as I have stated, we were lying in
the same position we first occupied the evening before
—behind, if I remember, the remains of an old rail fence.
I recollect distinctly that when we saw the rebs form
and advance, our men rose up and formed in line, and
Jersey and Binkey, who then belonged to the color
guard, mounted some stones and waved the colors towards the enemy, and shouted to them to come on. Some
of the men, in the excitement of the moment, commenced firing, but my impression is you ordered them
to reserve their fire until the enemy came closer.
While they were waiting for them to approach, they
suddenly and rapidly obliqued to the left and made a
rush for a hill covered with some brush and trees on
our right. As soon as you saw this movement you
formed the regiment by the right flank, and with it followed the movement of the enemy until you reached
this hill or mound, when you took a position on the
brow of the hill, a little obliquely to the general line,
some distance in advance of the other troops, and re-

mained in that position while the attack lasted. After the attack was over, an officer came with some troops, and said he had been ordered to occupy that position. After some parleying between you, and some hesitation on your part, you finally retired "with what was left of them—left of the six hundred." When you commenced to move to the right there were no troops on our right between us and the mound. What had become of them I don't know, but suppose they had collected on this mound and around this grove. There was a great mass of them there in perfect confusion. As the rebs advanced they kept swaying back, and I tried to get them to move up and hold their ground, but it was no use. It struck me as being, to say the least, very ridiculous. The 20th stood, firing on the brow of the hill away in their advance, and they were huddling around this point like a flock of sheep.

I recollect that we took a number of prisoners, and also about the Eagle. My recollection about this is, that some of our men saw a party taking the Eagle to headquarters, and recognized it as the Eagle off our color-lance, which was missing. They informed you of it, and you went to headquarters to see about it.

Very truly yours,

J. B. HARDENBURGH.

The circumstance of the Eagle, to which General Hardenburgh refers, was this. During the engagement in the afternoon of the 3d, the gilt eagle had been shot off the top of the color-staff of the "Ulster Guard," but it had not been missed until the regiment moved back from the line, after the battle. Then some men were sent to recover it, but were unable to find it. The next morning it was reported to me that a body of the troops who had relieved us the night before had recently marched by our bivouac in direction of General

Meade's headquarters with a rebel color and *our* Eagle. I proceeded at once to headquarters to reclaim the Eagle. I found that a conference was being held between General Meade and his corps commanders, and I could not obtain an interview Col. Sanderson informed me that a party of officers and men from the Second corps had recently paraded before headquarters and turned in as some of the trophies of their valor and victory over the enemy a rebel color and *our Eagle*. As the enemy did not carry Eagles it was self-evident that their claim was fraudulent as to that, and it probably was as to the flag, in so far as their capture was concerned. They probably picked it up from the ground in front of where we had fought, as they did the Eagle, and upon the strength of these proofs, to support the claim of their presence there and their desperate and successful bravery Mr. Bachelder gives them the place in his map, and historians give the Second corps the credit for repulsing Pickett's men at this particular point. Colonel Saunderson, who was the only staff officer of General Meade who was disengaged on the occasion of my visit to headquarters, promised me the matter should be investigated as soon as time could be found for it ; but time was never found.

The mound of which General Hardenburgh speaks was covered with Union guns, and was the highest point on our left between Cemetery Hill and Little Round Top, and its possession by the enemy would have greatly endangered our lines. With the fullest measure of praise to the gallant Vermonters, under the brave Stannard, who fought on our left, and to the men of the Second corps who really stood up to their work on the line and fought on our right, we claim for the 151st Pennsylvania and the 20th New York Militia only this, that at the point in our front line which I have described they met the onset of Pickett's attack—that they broke his line and killed and wounded a large number of his troops and that hundreds surrendered to them. That *after* the fighting was over, other troops relieved these two regiments—probably the same of which General Hardenburgh speaks, and who then set up a claim for having held the position during the battle. Whether they are the same troops whom Mr. Bachelder gives the place to on his map, I do not know. but I would be glad to see the official list of killed and wounded of this particular command at that particular time and place.

On the fourth of July General Doubleday issued the following Order :

HEADQUARTERS THIRD DIVISION, FIRST CORPS.
July 4, 1863.

GENERAL ORDERS.

The Major-General commanding the division desires to return his thanks to the Vermont Brigade, the One Hundred and Fifty-first Pennsylvania Volunteers, and the Twentieth New York State Militia, for their gallant conduct in resisting in the front line the main attack of the enemy upon this position, after sustaining a terrific fire from seventy-five to a hundred pieces of artillery He congratulates them upon contributing so essentially to the glorious, and it is to be hoped, final victory yesterday

By command of

MAJOR-GENERAL DOUBLEDAY

(Signed) EDWARD C. BAIRD,
Captain and A. A. G.

CHAPTER XXXV

IF, as General Lee says in his official report, "It became a matter of difficulty to withdraw through the
mountains with our large trains," because he found the
Army of the Potomac within a day or two days' march
of him, it would seem that the difficulty ought to have
been greatly increased after the concentration of the
Army of the Potomac in his immediate front, and after
his own army had been weakened and demoralized by a
terrible defeat. But the tardy tactics of which we have
before spoken as distinguishing both sides, characterized General Meade's operations after the battle ; and
the Confederate Army, moving off under cover of the
night of the fourth of July, reached the west side of the
Potomac with little difficulty.

The losses during the three days' fighting were very
great on both sides. General Meade reports his to have
been 2,834 killed, 13,709 wounded, and 6,643 missing—
making a grand total of 23,186. The loss among officers
of high rank was unusually large. On the Union side,
Major-General Reynolds and Brigadier-Generals Vincent, Weed and Zook were killed. Major-Generals
Sickles (losing a leg), Hancock, Doubleday, Gibbon,
Barlow, Warren, and Butterfield, and Brigadier-Gener-

als Graham, Paul (losing both eyes), Stone, Barnes and
Brooke were wounded. Field and line officers almost
without number were killed and wounded. In the
"Ulster Guard" two field and one staff officer were
wounded, two captains and one lieutenant killed, five
captains and eight lieutenants wounded. [See List of
Killed and Wounded in Chronological Record, end of
Volume.]

As usual, in the Confederate Army, General Lee
says: "It is not in my power to give a correct statement of our casualties, which were severe, including
many brave men, and an unusual proportion of distinguished and valuable officers." Mr. Samuel Weaver,
who superintended the removal of the Union dead to
the National Cemetery, says: "In searching for the
remains of our fallen heroes, we examined more than
3,000 rebel graves. * * * I have been making a careful estimate, from time to time, as I went over the field,
of rebel bodies on the battle-field and at the hospitals,
and I place the number at not less than 7,000 bodies."

Mr. A. H. Guernsey, author of " Harper's Pictorial
History of the War," investigated the subject of the
Rebel loss at Gettysburg, and puts it at 36,000 men.
This includes the prisoners, whose numbers General
Meade reported at 13,621. Mr. Guernsey says: "The
entire loss to this army during the six weeks from the
middle of June, when it set forth from Culpepper to
invade the North, to the close of July, when it returned
to the starting point, was about 60,000." The Federals
captured three cannon, forty-one battle flags, and 25,000
small arms. Among the Confederates of high rank,
there were wounded Major-Generals Hood, Trimble,
Heth and Pender, the latter mortally ; Brigadier-Generals Barksdale and Garnett were killed ; Semmes mortally wounded, and Kemper, Armistead, Scales, Anderson, Hampton, Jones and Jenkins wounded ; Archer

was captured on the first day, and Pettigrew was mortally wounded during Lee's retreat.

The march of the two armies in parallel columns, on opposite sides of the Blue Ridge, after the battle of Antietam, was now repeated ; and, after an attempt, on Meade's part, to force Lee to battle near Front Royal, and its failure, he moved leisurely to the Rappahannock, while his adversary established himself on the Rapidan. A campaign of manœuvres followed without material results ; and, late in November, General Meade moved against the enemy at Mine Run. Finding him too strongly posted to justify an attack, he withdrew, without a battle ; and the two armies went into winter quarters, with the Rapidan between them.

The winter of 1863-4 was very unlike its predecessor, in regard to the spirit and strength of the Army of the Potomac. Now, instead of having Confederate cavalry raiding at their own sweet will in rear of the Federal Army, the latter's cavalry were performing this service between Lee and his capital, destroying his railroads and canals, and even riding into the outer line of fortifications around Richmond. Meantime recruits poured into the Union camps, and officers and men were busy in matters of picket, drills, inspection, reviews and the divers other occupations that fill the hours of the soldier's life when in winter quarters. Over all, and infusing an air of animation and cheerfulness into the bronzed faces of our men, was a feeling of confidence in the leader of the army and in its success in the coming campaign. How much of this feeling was owing to the fact that Lieutenant-General Grant had established his headquarters with the Army of the Potomac, I will not pretend to say, but the remark was frequent after this event, "Boys, the next campaign means business ; Uncle U. S. is going to travel with the Army of the Potomac."

Major-General Grant was nominated Lieutenant-

General and confirmed by the Senate on the second day
of March, 1864, and eight days afterwards, the President assigned him to the command of all the armies of
the United States. This gave him the direction of
affairs over the whole broad theatre of the war, and for
the first time during its existence we were likely to have
a general and co-operative movement of all our vast
armies, and thereby put an end to that facility with
which the rebels had heretofore re-enforced any one or
more of their armies, as occasion required, from other
of their armies. General Grant proposed to give all
their armies simultaneous and continuous employment
along the whole field of war. Regarding, however, the
contemplated campaign of the old Army of the Potomac as the chief one in the ensuing season, he came to
Culpepper early in the spring, and established his
head-quarters with that army, and sat down to arrange
the movements of each and all the Federal armies for
a final and crushing series of hard blows from the Rapidan in Virginia to the Red River in Louisiana. His
plans were soon matured and his clear, concise orders
issued to his subordinates commanding armies along
this vast extent of country His justice and modesty,
his reluctance to detract from the merit of another, are
manifested in a paragraph of his official report of the
operations of the armies under his command. He saw
that the fact that he had moved with the Army of the
Potomac would tend to confer upon himself the chief
share of credit for the successes won by that army, and
to protect General Meade, as far as he could, from any
obscuration of his just fame, he says this: "I may
here state that commanding all the armies as I did. I
tried, as far as possible, to leave General Meade in the
independent command of the Army of the Potomac.
My instructions for that army were all through him,
and were general in their nature, leaving all the details
and the execution to him. The campaigns that fol-

lowed proved him to be the right man in the right place. His commanding always in the presence of an officer superior to him in rank, has drawn from him much of that public attention that his zeal and ability entitle him to, and which he would otherwise have received."

On the fourth of May, General Meade issued the following Order to the army : "Soldiers! Again you are called upon to advance on the enemies of your country ; the time and the occasion are deemed opportune by your Commanding General to address you a few words of confidence and caution.

" You have been re-organized, strengthened and fully equipped in every respect ; you form a part of the several armies of your country, the whole under the direction of an able and distinguished General, who enjoys the confidence of the government, the people and the army Your movement being in co-operation with others, it is of the utmost importance that no effort should be left unspared to make it successful.

" Soldiers ! The eyes of the whole country are looking with anxious hope to the blow you are about to strike in the most sacred cause that ever called men to arms.

" Remember your homes, your wives and children, and bear in mind that the sooner your enemies are overcome, the sooner you will be returned to enjoy the benefits and blessings of peace. Bear with patience the hardships and sacrifices you will be called upon to endure. Have confidence in your officers, and in each other. Keep your ranks on the march and on the battle-field, and let each man earnestly implore God's blessing, and endeavor by his thoughts and actions to render himself worthy of the favor he seeks. With clear consciences and strong arms, actuated by a high sense of duty, fighting to preserve the Government and the institutions handed down to us by our forefathers—if true to ourselves, victory, under God's blessing, must and will attend our efforts."

Before this Order was distributed to the troops, they had set out on their last and finally triumphant campaign. As the sun rose on the morning of the fourth of May, its rays fell upon thousands of Union troops, marching towards the fords of the Rapidan, which they had crossed and re-crossed many times during the last three years, but over which they now passed for the last time. The army had cut loose from its base of supplies, and moved forward with the enormous train of four thousand wagons. On the 5th of May, General Warren, now commanding the Fifth corps, met and engaged the enemy outside his entrenchments, near Mine Run. As corps after corps of the Union army came up, they were put into the fight ; and all day long the battle raged with great fury. The scene of this engagement was the northerly side of the famous " Wilderness," through which Meade's line of march lay. Night put an end to the combat, but the morning of the 6th brought a renewal ; which was inaugurated by the Federals, and continued until nine o'clock at night, with unabated fury. That noble-hearted and gallant soldier, General Wadsworth, fell in this day's battle, while encouraging his division to hold their ground against a furious assault of the enemy, in the fore-front of the fight. On the next morning, it was found that the enemy had withdrawn to his entrenched lines, leaving a strong picket force where his line of battle had been. On the night of the seventh General Grant set his army again in motion, by the left flank, to thrust it between Lee's right and Richmond. On the ninth, the armies again encountered each other at Spottsylvania Court House; and, until the twenty-first, battle followed battle with fearful slaughter on both sides. On the night of the twenty-first, the Federal army again moved by the left, to the North Anna ; but the ever-watchful foe, having the shorter line, was found in position along the banks of the stream, ready to oppose a further advance. Here, another severe battle took place between General Warren's corps, which had crossed the river, and a portion of the Rebel army, in which the latter were repulsed with great loss.

While these events were transpiring, General Phil. Sheridan, whom General Grant had put in command of the cavalry, had swept around the flank of the Confederate army with a magnificent body of troopers, and totally destroyed the enemy's depots at Beaver Dam and Ashland—captured and destroyed four trains of cars loaded with supplies for Lee's army—destroyed many miles of railroad track—re-captured some four hundred of our men on their way to Richmond, as prisoners of war—met and defeated the enemy's cavalry at Yellow Tavern—carried the first line of works around Richmond, and threatened the second, but found it too strongly guarded ; and rejoined our army at North Anna, without a circumstance to detract from the brilliancy of this most successful raid.

While General Grant could direct what other armies should do, it was not possible for him to personally superintend the execution of his orders by more than one of them at a time. General Butler, commanding the Army of the James, should have marched into Richmond between the fourth and twenty-fourth of May, and if General Grant could have infused into this doughty commander one-millionth part of his own spirit, Butler would have done it, and shortened the war by six months. He was to move up the James River, from Fort Monroe and Suffolk, at the same time the Army of the Potomac began its march from the Rapidan ; Petersburg and Richmond, being his objective points. On the fifth of May he occupied City Point and Bermuda Hundred, without opposition, the enemy apparently giving all his attention to the other Federal Army approaching from the North—they had not yet begun to comprehend the new system upon which the war was to be waged, and they supposed Butler would remain idle until the Army of the Potomac was repulsed. On the sixth, General Butler had his army well in hand at the two points named, and, instead of advancing any farther, began to intrench. On the ninth, he telegraphed to Secretary Stanton, that he had reached the points designated, and that he had "got a position, which, with proper supplies, we can hold out against the whole of Lee's army." General Grant's view of this Falstaffian strategy is expressed in these words : "His army, therefore, though in a position of great security, was as completely shut off from further operations directly against Richmond, as if it had been in a bottle strongly corked. It required but a comparatively small force of the enemy to hold it there." Farther on he says : "The army sent to operate against Richmond having hermetically sealed itself up at Bermuda Hundred, the enemy was enabled to bring most, if not all the re-enforcements brought from the South by Beauregard, against the Army of the Potomac." And Butler and his army remained corked up until the Army of the Potomac crossed the James and uncorked the bottle, the fifteenth of June.

On the night of the twenty-sixth of May the order again passed along the Union lines, "By the left flank —March !" During the twenty-ninth and thirtieth, the army advanced under heavy skirmishing to Hanover Court House and Cold Harbor. At the latter place the fighting was almost continuous, and often desperate, until the night of the twelfth, when the army again moved by the left, and crossing the James River at Wilcox's Landing, moved up on the south side of the stream. The march from the Rapidan to the James had been attended by a series of battles and skirmishes that had strewn the route with the corpses of thousands of men, much the greater number of whom wore the Union blue.   Except in the battle of the Wilderness, the Federals were the assailants, and their losses on this long battle-field amounted to the frightful number of 54,551, killed, wounded and missing.

CHAPTER XXXVI

ON the 18th of June the army drew up in front of
Petersburg. Here manœuvres, attack and counter-
attack, consumed the summer, and thousands perished
in the fierce conflicts that raged around the "Cockade
City"

The enemy's lines were very strong, and were defended with unwavering courage and indomitable resolution. It was the last strategical point between the
Union army and the rebel capital. Even now the roar
of artillery rolled in ominous murmurs over the city of
Richmond.

But the lines could not be broken by direct attack.
Colonel Henry Pleasants, of the Forty-eighth Pennsylvania, of Burnside's corps, proposed to run a mine under
the rebel works in front of his (Pleasants') position, and
blow them up. General Burnside approved of the plan,
and the work began on the 25th of June. It had to be
carried on with great secresy, and was of herculean proportions. One of the difficulties was to dispose of the
immense quantities of earth excavated, that it might not
lead the enemy to suspect the plot. The main gallery
was 511 feet long, and was carried directly under a rebel
battery From this extended lateral galleries, right

484

and left, 38 feet each way, and parallel with the rebel fort above. Then, across these lateral galleries were four other short galleries, at equal distances apart, designed to receive the magazines. Each of these galleries was about four and one-half feet wide and of the same height.

Now, all the earth had to be carried out by hand in the night, and deposited in rear of our lines ; and then, to prevent the enemy seeing it from his observatories, branches of trees were cut and thrown over it.

The concussion of the enemy's guns over the lateral gallery produced a stunning sensation upon the men secretly burrowing beneath them, and sometimes excited a fear that they would cave through.

But on the 29th of July the work was finished, and 1,400 pounds of powder placed in each of the eight magazines—a total of 11,200 pounds.

Fuses and electric wires were connected with the magazines. The powder train of our army removed far to the rear, so that it might not be blown up by the concussion.

The morning of the 30th was fixed upon for the explosion of the mine, and it was to be followed by an assault all along the lines. An order was issued assigning to each corps its particular share in the momentous crisis. The columns for assault were to form before daylight, and every preparation made to take advantage of the breach and the enemy's expected surprise, the instant the report of the explosion was heard.

At half-past three Burnside was to spring the mine. His assaulting column was to move rapidly forward and seize the breach and the adjoining crest, and effect a lodgment. Ord was to follow on the right and Warren on the left. All the artillery in battery was to open on the enemy's lines at the instant of the explosion.

Thus was matured a plan which seemed to possess all the essential elements of success. The explosion was expected to tear an opening in the enemy's lines ; surprise and demoralize his forces, and thus give us a temporary advantage ; to be made permanent, if promptly and judiciously followed up.

At 3.20, ten minutes before the time fixed for the explosion, Gen. Meade telegraphed Gen. Burnside : "As it is still so dark, you can postpone firing the mine, if you think it proper." Burnside replied that he would explode it at 3.30. At 4.30 the explosion had not taken place, and Meade telegraphed to know the reason. At 4.35 Meade telegraphed : "The commanding general directs, if your mine has failed, that you make an assault at once, opening your batteries."

The fact was, the fuse had been fired at 3.30, and the flame ran into the gallery, but to the surprise of the operators, no explosion ensued. Whether the fire had gone out, utterly, in that long dark tunnel, or was smouldering, and might at any moment ignite the powder, no one could tell. Whoever should enter the gallery would be instantly killed in case of an explosion. But something must be done, and Lieutenant Jacob Douty and Sergeant Henry Rees, of the Forty-eighth Pennsylvania Regiment, volunteered to enter the gallery. They ascertained that the fuse had died out about 100 feet from the mouth. They re-arranged it, and nearly at the instant the telegram last quoted was passing over the wires from Meade's headquarters to Burnside's, heaven and earth seemed rent in twain, and the air was full of the debris of the rebel fort, and the bodies of its late occupants.

The mine had exploded, and now the assaulting columns rushed for the breach—Leslie's division in the advance—clearing the ground between our own lines and the rebel works before the enemy recovered from his surprise. The head of the division found itself confronted by a large crater produced by the explosion, 150 feet in length, 60 feet wide and 30 feet deep. The sides composed of loose, pulverized sand, piled up precipitately, from which projected huge blocks of clay. In the bottom of this pit were several rebel cannon and dead bodies of rebel soldiers.

The delay occasioned by this formidable excavation proved fatal to the enterprise. While the troops halted, the enemy recovered from his panic; comprehended the situation, and from right, left and in front opened a destructive fire of musketry and artillery upon the exposed column. To escape this fire, the leading brigade entered the crater, but only became more helpless and exposed. The enemy quickly covered several elevated points with cannon, and getting range of the crater, poured a storm of shell into it, while his mortars sent their fearful explosives into the dense throng of men, in this terrible slaughter-pen, with wonderful accuracy.

At midday the troops were ordered to be withdrawn, and now the rebel guns swept the ground over which they must move, by a tremendous perpendicular and cross fire. But to *remain* was to surrender or be slaughtered. So through this deluge of iron and lead the gallant fellows marched back again—"marched back what was left of them—while cannon to right and cannon to left of them vollied and thundered." Forty-four hundred of the assaulting column were killed or wounded and 246 captured.

So, while the red tide of battle daily ebbs and flows along the line, summer passes, and another winter wears away, and spring flowers again adorn the valley of the Appomattox. Petersburg, lying immediately in rear of a portion of the rebel lines, was unavoidably the target of a hundred cannon. In this long trial and amid the constant danger that surrounded them, it is said the women of Petersburg displayed wonderful courage and endurance. No murmurs—no shrieks—no flight, though shot and shell fell in their streets, and crashed through their houses—day and night.

During the winter of 1864-5, the Confederate army before Petersburg was in a condition of semi-starvation, and but half clad. The resources of the Confederacy were rapidly failing, and it became so patent that the natural results were experienced in General Lee's army Desertions were frequent, and the morale of the rebel army was greatly impaired, while the hope of a successful issue was fast fading away At the opening of the spring campaign, in 1865, the rolls of General Lee's army gave him less than 50,000 men, and upon this greatly diminished force really hung the last hope of the rebellion.

Lee is said to have resolved to abandon Petersburg and Richmond, and falling back towards Lynchburg or Danville, unite his forces with the army of General Joe Johnson, who was moving north before Sherman. But the Union forces had enveloped the right of Lee's army and covered roads by which he desired to move. To compel Grant to withdraw his left and uncover these roads, Lee resolved to assume the offensive and make a vigorous attack on Grant's opposite flank or centre.

At day-break on the twenty-fifth of March, two Confederate divisions under Gordon moved noiselessly out of their works, cleared the narrow interval that divided the lines, and crossing the Union intrenchments surprised and seized Fort Steadman, and captured most of the garrison, together with one brigade of the Ninth corps. The guns of the captured fort—which occupied a commanding position in our line—were immediately turned by the rebels on the adjoining Union batteries, 9, 10 and 11, which were thereupon abandoned by our troops and occupied by the enemy

The danger was imminent, but the rebel triumph was short lived. Training a hundred pieces of heavy artillery upon the doomed fort, it was rent to tatters by Union guns, when Hartrauft's division of the Ninth corps dashed upon the ruined work, and captured two thousand of its rebel occupants, while their comrades attempted to regain their own lines, through a deadly cross-fire of artillery, from all the adjacent works, which put 2,500 of them *hors de combat* between the lines. This effort was one of the expiring throes of a mighty giant, who began to feel that the thongs which were being drawn closer and closer around him must be broken soon or never. The failure of this bold attempt to compel Grant to relax his grasp on the roads to Lee's right was fatal to his plan of retreat.

On Saturday, the first day of April, Sheridan and Warren crushed the right of the enemy's line at Five Forks, capturing all his artillery and between 5,000 and 6,000 prisoners. That night the guns along the Union lines kept up a bombardment until four o'clock the next morning, when General Wright advanced his corps, and sweeping through the rebel lines in his front, captured several thousand prisoners and many cannon. Ord had meantime dispersed the enemy's forces on their extreme right, at Hatcher's Run, and then joining Wright, the two corps swung to the right and closed the southward outlet to the Confederate Army. Driven from his outer lines and with his numbers greatly reduced, the rebel leader yet clung tenaciously to his inner line of defences, and his men fought with the recklessness of despair. Gibbon now dashed upon two strong, enclosed works of the enemy south of Petersburg, and after a sharp fight carried them, and thereby materially shortened the line of investment. So success succeeded success throughout the day, and when the night arrived the Confederate Army was confined to its inner line of works and these so shortened as to promise but a brief resistance on the morrow. When the gray dawn of the morrow came the Union skirmishers advance upon the works so long and bravely held, but no shot is fired from them and they are found to contain but abandoned guns and

dead and wounded men. The remnant of the rebel
army had fled.

A Petersburger thus describes the events and emotions of that last day of battle around his city:

"With light came sounds of conflict, which grew
louder and more frightful. Did they not draw nearer?
It sounded so. And soon strange rumors filled the
streets. The church bells rang out their first call to
prayer, but no one heeded the summons. The clear,
sweet tones fell upon the agony of hearts that listened,
as bird notes sound to those who mourn the dead. Men
gathered in groups around the corners, and looked,
with straining eyes, towards the clouds of battle-smoke
that hung around the town—stood silently, and listened
to the dull reports of heavy ordnance, and the sharp
rattle of musketry, upon which their fate hung trembling.

"Men grew white in the agony of suspense, and
women wept.

"The old town-clock struck eight—the breakfast
hour—but the scanty meal stood on the board untasted.
The houses were deserted, and eager questioners crowded
around the men, who now came in with haggard faces
and wild eyes.

"What is it?

"And one answered, 'They have taken the River
Salient.'

"And another, 'Pickett and Johnson were overwhelmed yesterday, their line broken, and their commands beaten and crushed—cut off from the army, and
forced up the country'

"And another, 'Gibbon's Corps struck Wilcox's
front at daylight this morning, piercing his line; the
troops to the right were captured, those to the left forced
back. The enemy have reached the railroad and the
river, and our line is at the stone bridge.'

" And just then a cry of 'look !' was heard, and turning, we saw from the warehouses, where, by order of the military authorities, had been stored all the tobacco in the city, columns of black, thick smoke go up above a mass of lurid flames. ''Tis so,' was the speech of every white cheek and streaming eye. Few words told how like a whirlwind of wrath came to the thousand hearts the death of the hope of years. The groups dispersed and sought their homes. Agonizing suspense had become certainty, and they could weep now.

" Any attempt to tell of that day, with its hours of dull, dead hopelessness, its moments of wild hope, its feelings of utter wretchedness, of the end of all things to be desired. God spare us another such an experience !

" Now and then would fly from house to house some good report. 'We are pressing them back—Gen. Lee has re-established his lines,' and for awhile the feverish wish would be parent to belief. About 11 o'clock the Confederates did re-capture the lines at Rives', and a ray of real light came in upon the anxious souls. But the real danger was not there. On the right the work went resistlessly on. Fort Gregg fell, despite the most heroic defense of the war. The Union line advanced from Coghill's to Turnbull's, from Turnbull's to Woodworth's, and there, in a stone's throw of the corporation limits, marshalled their enthusiastic masses.

" At last Longstreet came. A strengthened line was formed, and at 4 o'clock the dispatch from Gen. Lee to his commanders across the Appomatox and James was, 'I can hold out until night, and shall then withdraw.'

" Its terms were noised abroad, and there was no more doubt or hope. The time passed in silent preparation. The Federal officers seeing the inevitable result of their successes, wisely and humanely forebore further assault, and the comparative stillness was oppressive.

" Dusk came, and with it began the evacuation

Noiselessly from the lines they had so gallantly defended, the Confederates withdrew ; and the long, dark
columns passed through the streets unattacked, un-
pursued. We were spared the horror of a fight through
the streets, which had been feared. Now began the
wild farewells and long embraces with which mothers
sent forth their sons to unknown fates, and perchance
endless partings.

"We draw the curtain over them. The darkness
fell, the silent march continued until the old bridge at
Pocahontas had re-echoed to the tread of the last Confederate soldier."

CHAPTER XXXVII

JEFFERSON DAVIS, sitting in St. Paul's Church, in
Richmond, on that beautiful sabbath morning, more
attentive to the thunder of distant cannon, that rolls
in sullen and ominous murmurs over the rebel capital,
than to the service he pretends to heed—his expectant
ear catches the sound of a hurried step and a clanking
sabre, approaching him, up the aisle. Every eye in
that congregation of anxious worshippers is turned upon
the chief of their expiring Confederacy He reads
General Lee's dispatch announcing the disaster to his
army, and his intention to retreat during the ensuing
night.

The dispatch is handed to the rector, who communi-
cates its contents to the congregation ; when groans and
lamentations take the place of songs and praise, while
the President of their short-lived government walks out

from among them to prepare for flight from his doomed capital.

General Lee held on to his contracted lines until night, and when darkness had enveloped the scene of Sunday's conflict with an impenetrable veil, he silently withdrew his army, now reduced to 25,000 men, and marching northward, to Chesterfield Court House, mid-way between Petersburg and Richmond, had placed sixteen miles between his and Grant's army at day-break on Monday morning, the 3d of April. Almost at the same moment a shock, as of an earthquake, rolled down the James, and for one instant the northwestern sky was lit up with a lurid glare. The rebels had blown up their iron-clad vessels and the bridges across the river, at Richmond. They had also fired the ware-houses, in that city, in which immense quantities of tobacco were stored, and the flames spread until the entire business portion of the city was a smouldering ruin. Thus did the enemy destroy and abandon the capital, in the four years defence of which he had sac-rificed so many lives and so many millions of dollars.

At Chesterfield, Lee turned the head of his column toward the west and resumed his flight, with Amelia Court House as his next objective point, 20 miles away, and where he had ordered supplies to be in waiting for his army, which had left Petersburg with but one day's ration.

General Lee's design seems to have been to unite the fragment of his army with the forces then under command of General Joe Johnson, near Raleigh, N C., and thus be enabled to present a front of opposi-tion, that would have given emphasis to a demand for favorable terms of capitulation, if not to negotiations for peace.

When Lee reached Amelia Court House on the fourth of April, he was met with the astounding intel-ligence that there was no food there for his army   A

train of cars, laden with stores, had been sent from
Danville to this point, in obedience to his orders, but a
command from the Richmond authorities met the officer
in charge of the train at Amelia, directing him to bring
the train on to Richmond. The purpose of the order
was to use the cars in the removal of the property of
the Confederate Government. But the officer understood it to require him to bring the train, not only, but
its contents also. So, he proceeded to Richmond, and
cars and contents were swallowed up in the Moscow-
like conflagration.

Few men could have rallied from the effects of so
dire a misfortune. A fleeing army in an impoverished
country, with an exultant and overwhelming enemy in
near and hot pursuit, and not a ration to issue to his
famishing men. Thus he was compelled to tarry at
Amelia Court House during the fourth and fifth of
April, while his foraging parties were scouring the
desolated country for food for his army. This untoward
delay enabled Sheridan, with the cavalry and the Fifth
corps, to swing across the Confederate line of retreat at
Jettersville, on the Danville railroad, seven miles beyond Amelia Court House. This was accomplished on
the afternoon of the fourth. On the fifth, Meade, with
the Second and Sixth corps, drew up at the same point.
Sheridan dispatched his cavalry right and left, to intercept the Confederate foragers, and on the morning of
the fifth General Davies struck a train of 180 wagons,
escorted by a body of Confederate cavalry, which he
defeated, destroying the wagons, and capturing five
pieces of artillery and a number of prisoners.

Finding the Union lines rapidly closing around him,
and his foraging parties cut off, Lee set his starving
army in motion, on the night of the fifth, for Farmville,
thirty-five miles west, where he purposed crossing the
Appomattox, destroying the bridges behind him, and
escaping into the {mountains ;beyond |Lynchburg.

Meantime the entire Army of the Potomac had concentrated at Jettersville, and on the morning of the sixth it advanced toward Amelia to give battle to the enemy, but the prey had fled. Grant now divided the pursuing forces, so that their lines of march threatened both flanks and rear of the retreating enemy At the same time, the Army of the James, under the grizzled veteran, General Ord, was thrown forward from Burkesville, diagonally across the front of pursued and pursuers, so that when the head of Lee's column reached Farmville on the sixth, they were saluted by the thunder of Ord's guns, while his infantry and cavalry were drawn up, ready for battle.

Meantime and on the same day, Sheridan had struck another Confederate wagon train under a heavy escort of infantry and cavalry Throwing upon it the divisions of Custer, Crook and Devens, the escort was defeated after a severe fight, and 400 wagons were destroyed, while 16 pieces of artillery and a large number of prisoners were captured. Ewell's corps, which was following behind the train, was thus cut off from its line of retreat, and after a desperate fight with the cavalry, re-enforced during the battle by the Sixth corps, Ewell was compelled to surrender, with four general officers and his entire command.

Lee had meantime entrenched himself in front of Ord, and remained behind his works until night set in, when he again resumed his flight, crossing the Appomattox near Farmville. Humphreys, with the Second corps, was so close on the heels of the retreating enemy that he did not give them time to destroy the bridges. Pressing the pursuit with unparallelled vigor, the heads of columns were now directed toward Appomattox Courthouse, twenty miles further west. At Farmville, 130 Confederate wagons were destroyed and the guard captured or dispersed. So, ruin and disintegration were constantly going on in the Confederate ranks, yet its indomitable commander would not yield to what he must now have known was inevitable.

Lee's attempts to gather food from the country, through which his march lay, were almost wholly frustrated by the activity of the Union cavalry, aided by the infantry, wherever it could come up in time. The blood of the triumphant pursuers was at boiling heat, and they were resolved to bring the hunted army to bay. Skirmishes were of almost hourly occurrence, and the way was strewn with the dead and wounded men and horses, and the debris of a fleeing army, while clouds of smoke by day and lurid flames by night, told of burning wagons and bridges. The poor remnant of Lee's army was reduced to the last extremity of weariness and hopelessness. Indeed, few troops had ever experienced so bitter a retreat as this. Hunger, sleeplessness, fatigue, despair ; *and yet, wonderful pluck.* An eye witness says : " Towards evening on the fifth, and all day long upon the sixth, hundreds of men dropped from exhaustion and thousands let fall their muskets from inability to carry them any farther. The scenes of the fifth, sixth, seventh and eighth, were of a nature which can be apprehended in their vivid reality, only by men who are thoroughly familiar with the har rowing details of war." Dropping down for a few moments of rest and sleep, the weary troops would suddenly be aroused by the boom of Union guns, and the thunder of charging squadrons of hostile cavalry, and again they must arouse themselves to fight or fly

Around the bivouac fire, on the night of the 6th of April, Lee's generals discussed the situation, and came to the conclusion that their chief ought to adopt one of the following courses : 1. Disband, allowing the troops to make their way as best they might to some fixed rallying point. 2. Abandon the trains and cut their way through the opposing lines ; or, 3. Surrender. General Pendleton was appointed to communicate these views

3 2

to General Lee. The latter did not assent to either proposition, and, in fact, the interview between the two generals was not concluded, when the outburst of musketry told that the Federals were again upon them.

On the night of the 7th, General Lee received this notice: "April 7, 1865. General:—The result of the last week must convince you of the hopelessness of further resistance on the part of the Army of Northern Virginia in this struggle. I feel that it is so, and regard it my duty to shift from myself the responsibility of any further effusion of blood, by asking of you the surrender of that portion of the Confederate States' Army known as the Army of Northern Virginia.

"U. S. GRANT,
" Lieut. Gen."

General Lee placed his reply to this note in the hands of an aide, to be delivered to General Grant in the morning, and pressed forward his weary columns, hoping against hope to find some way of egress from the cordon of bayonets that was closing around him. His reply was as follows: "General:—I have received your note of this date. Though not entertaining the opinion you express of the hopelessness of further resistance on the part of the Army of Northern Virginia, I reciprocate your desire to avoid useless effusion of blood, and, therefore, before considering your proposition, ask the terms you will offer on condition of its surrender." It is easy to imagine the struggle this note must have cost the commander of the Confederate Army. For nearly four years he had led it through all its vicissitudes, and it had come to be regarded as the chief bulwark of the Confederacy To surrender that army was to surrender the cause for which so many lives had been lost, so many millions of money expended, so much misery produced.

General Grant sent the following reply, bearing date

the eighth of April. "General: Your note of last evening in reply to mine of same date, asking the condition on which I will accept the surrender of the Army of Northern Virginia, is just received. In reply I would say that *peace* being my great desire, there is but one condition I would insist upon, namely : that the men and officers surrendered shall be disqualified for taking up arms again against the Government of the United States until properly exchanged. I will meet you, or will designate officers to meet any officers you will name for the same purpose, at any point agreeable to you, for the purpose of arranging definitely the terms upon which the surrender of the Army of Northern Virginia will be received." But Lee could not yet bring his proud spirit into subjection to the condition in which he found himself placed, and he temporized while he struggled to find some mode of escape. His reply was couched in the following diplomatic language : " General :—I received at a late hour your note of to-day. In mine of yesterday I did not intend to propose the surrender of the Army of Northern Virginia, but to ask the terms of your proposition. To be frank, I do not think the emergency has arisen to call for the surrender of this army ; but as the restoration of peace should be the sole object of all, I desired to know whether your proposals would lead to that end. I cannot, therefore, meet you with a view to surrender the Army of Northern Virginia, but as far as your proposal may effect the Confederate States' forces under my command, and tend to the restoration of peace, I should be pleased to meet you at ten A.M. to-morrow, on the old stage road to Richmond, between the picket lines of the two armies."

Grant received this note at midnight, and replied next morning, as follows : "April 9, 1865. General :—Your note of yesterday is received ; I have no authority to treat on the subject of peace. The meeting proposed for ten A.M. to-day could lead to no good. I will state, however,

General, that I am equally anxious for peace with yourself, and the whole North entertains the same feeling.
The terms upon which peace can be had are well understood.   By the South laying down their arms, they will
hasten that most desirable event, save thousands of
human lives, and hundreds of millions of property not
yet destroyed.   Seriously hoping that all our difficulties
may be ended, without the loss of another life, I sub-
scribe myself, &c."   Evidently General Grant did not
propose to enter into a diplomatic discussion with
General Lee, nor to meet him except to receive the surrender of his army   While this correspondence was
going on, military operations were not relaxed on either
side, and events were hastening to a climax.   On the
night of the eighth, the ubiquitous Sheridan reined up
with his eager troopers at Appomattox Station, on the
Lynchburg Railroad, five miles south of Appomattox
Court House.   The van-guard of Lee's army had just
arrived, and four trains of cars, loaded with supplies
for his starving men were approaching the station.
Sheridan threw a force in rear of these trains and captured them.   He then attacked the Confederate troops
and drove them back upon Appomattox Court House.
He had thus utterly annihilated Lee's last hope of adequate supplies for his hungry troops.   Then he planted
his bronzed veterans directly in front of Lee, and across
his only remaining line of retreat.   The Army of the
James was hurrying forward to join Sheridan in front,
and the Army of the Potomac was sweeping down upon
the Confederate rear.

Lee could only escape by cutting his way through
Sheridan's lines, and this he resolved to attempt.   At
dawn, on the ever-memorable ninth of April, he sent
orders to General Gordon, *to cut his way through at all
hazards.*   The rebel army was now reduced to about
8,000 armed men ; Gordon in front, and the wreck of
Longstreet's corps in rear.   Between them the *debris* of

the wagon-train and the gaunt figures of several thousand unarmed men, too weak to carry their muskets. The residue of that once grand army lay in the trenches around Petersburg, and in the roads and fields over which its frightful march had been made.

Gordon advanced to the attack with great spirit, and actually forced the cavalry to give ground. Sheridan directed his Lieutenants to fall back gradually, but to retard the enemy's advance, so as to give the infantry time to come up. By and by the bayonets of the Army of the James were seen advancing in serried ranks upon the field, when the Confederates gave up the assault and prepared to act on the defensive. Then Sheridan's bugles pealed forth the signal to mount, and soon 10,000 cavalry had swung around upon the enemy's flank, ready to charge on the baffled foe. But this further, and what would have been, terrible slaughter, was averted. At the last moment, and just as the bugles were raised to sound the charge, one bearing a white flag emerged from the Confederate lines with a letter from General Lee, asking for suspension of hostilities and an interview with General Grant. That interview took place that afternoon in a house at Appomattox Court House, where the two chieftains signed the compact which practically ended the war.

Walter H. Taylor, Adjutant-General of Lee's army, in his "Four Years with General Lee," thus portrays his chief in connection with the surrender of his army :

"On the evening of the 8th of April," General Taylor writes. "I became separated from General Lee in the execution of his orders in regard to the parking of our trains in places of safety and did not rejoin him until the morning of the 9th. After making my report, the General said to me, 'Well, Colonel, what are we to do?' In reply a fear was expressed that it would be necessary to abandon the trains, which had already occasioned us much embarrassment, and the hope was indulged, that relieved of this burden the army could make good its escape. 'Yes,' said the General, 'perhaps we could, but I have had a conference with these gentlemen around me and they agree that the time has come for a capitulation.' 'Well, sir.' I said, 'I can only speak for myself ; to me any other fate is preferable.' 'Such is my individual way of thinking,' interrupted the General.

" 'But,' I immediately added, 'of course, General, it is different with you. You have to think of these brave men and decide not only for yourself but for them.'

" 'Yes,' he replied, 'it would be useless, and therefore cruel, to provoke the further effusion of blood, and I have arranged to meet General Grant with a view to surrender and wish you to accompany me.'

" Shortly after this the General, accompanied by Colonel Marshall and myself, started back in the direction from which he had come, to meet General Grant as had been arranged.

" We continued some distance without meeting any one after passing our lines, but finally came upon a staff officer, sent by General Grant's order to say to General Lee that he had been prevented from meeting him at that point and to request that he would meet him upon the other road. General Lee then retraced his steps, and, proceeding toward our front in the direction of Appomattox Court House, dismounted at a convenient place to await General Grant's communication. Very soon a Federal officer, accompanied by one of General Gordon's staff, rode up to where General Lee was seated in a small orchard on the roadside. This proved to be General Forsythe, of General Sheridan's staff, who was sent by General Sheridan to say that, as he had doubt as to his authority to recognize the informal truce which had been agreed upon between General

Gordon and himself, he desired to communicate with General Meade on the subject, and wished permission to pass through our lines as the shortest route. I was assigned to the duty of escorting General Forsythe through our lines and back. This was scarcely accomplished, when General Babcock rode up and announced to General Lee that General Grant was prepared to meet him at the front.

" I shrank from this interview, and while I could not then, and cannot now, justify my conduct, I availed myself of the excuse of having taken the two rides through the extent of our lines and to those of the enemy, already mentioned, and did not accompany my chief in this trying ordeal.

" The scene witnessed upon the return of General Lee was one certain to impress itself indelibly upon the memory ; it can be vividly recalled now after the lapse of many years, but no description can do it justice. The men crowded around him, eager to shake him by the hand ; eyes that had been so often illumined with the fire of patriotism and true courage, that had so often glared with defiance in the heat and fury of battle, and so often kindled with enthusiasm and pride in the hour of success, moistened now ; cheeks bronzed by exposure in many campaigns and withal begrimed with powder and dust, now blanched from deep emotion and suffered the silent tear ; tongues that had so often carried dismay to the hearts of the enemy in that indescribable cheer which accompanied "the charge." or that had so often made the air to resound with the pæan of victory, refused utterance now ; brave hearts failed that had never quailed in the presence of an enemy ; but the firm and silent pressure of the hand told most eloquently of souls filled with admiration, love and tender sympathy for their beloved chief. He essayed to thank them, but too full a heart paralyzed his speech ; he soon sought a short respite from these

trying scenes and retired to his private quarters, that
he might, in solitude and quiet, commune with his own
brave heart and be still. Thus terminated the career
of the Army of Northern Virginia—an army that was
never vanquished, but that, in obedience to the orders
of its trusted commander, who was himself yielding
obedience to the dictates of a pure and lofty sense of
duty to his men and those dependent on them, laid
down its arms and furled the standards never lowered
in defeat.''

The men of the two armies at once mingled together,
and the starving Confederates found their late antagonists hospitable friends.

The Confederates were paroled and went to their
homes, many of them making their poor tables glad by
the abundance of Union rations, while the Union army
turned its face northward, and a few months later its
members had laid aside their arms and uniforms, and
were mingling with their neighbors in the ordinary occupations of life—valiant soldiers in war, good citizens
in peace.

Thus practically ended the great Rebellion—a rebellion that our incongruous system of government was
certain to entail upon the country, sooner or later. It
involved terrible trials and sacrifices, but we must
remember that,

> '' Not painlessly doth God recast
> And mould anew a nation.''

With the close of the war the dawn of a new and
better era burst upon our country We emerged from
the conflict triumphant not only, but we had shown
vitality and resources that amazed the world, while they
surprised ourselves. The blot upon our escutcheon had
been expunged, and we stood before the world in the
sublime majesty of a nation *free* in *fact*, as well as in
theory True, we yet bear the marks and scars of the

gigantic struggle through which we have passed, but with a people reunited and animated by that indomitable spirit which hitherto has enabled them to accomplish so much, they will march on, in the course of empire, until our continent shall be covered with towns and cities, and peace and good will shall dwell in all our borders.

NOTES.

NOTE I.

Letter from McD. Van Wagoner, Esq., in relation to statement on page 240.

KINGSTON, Sept. 3d, 1879.

GENERAL GATES :

Dear Sir :—As a member of one of the companies of the Harris Light Cavalry, and a participant in the fight of Brandy Station, and that of Rappahannock Station, in 1862, allow me to say I think you do injustice to General Kilpatrick in your criticism (on pages 240 and 241 of your history) of that gentleman's action.

An attempt was made to give the rebels a check, near Rappahannock Station, and Judson Kilpatrick, then Lieutenant-Colonel of the Harris Light Cavalry, was selected for that duty.

A portion of the regiment (Harris Light) was formed on a fine level piece of ground a few hundred yards from the brow of a hill, up which the enemy were expected to come in full force during their advance. There couldn't have been found a finer place for manœuvring cavalry, but as the rebels came up with a cloud of skirmishers, the dust which filled the air made their numbers look much larger than they really were, and the Harris Light being green, as it were, never having participated in a charge, or even seen one, when ordered by Kilpatrick to charge, didn't move forward immediately, and almost the next instant a column of rebel cavalry being seen coming on a gallop close to them, they broke and ran ;

Kilpatrick rallied probably fifty men, and with them made several charges ; and as for himself, being greatly excited, because of the lack of success of the charge, for a time he raved like a wild man, and fought like a tiger ; but he was finally run back in the crowd, and the dust became so thick, a man couldn't recognize his own officer. The regiment (or that portion of it) crossed the river in squads, when it was formed, having lost only a few men.

If General Kilpatrick made a mistake, it was in not starting the charging columns down towards the enemy at a trot, and then ordering a charge, when they would, no doubt, have swept the hill, for it was not a lack of courage that caused the men to fall back. At the battle of Bull Run, a few days after, when a charge was ordered by a staff officer, on the night of the first day, on the enemy, who were supposed to be retreating, though every one in the regiment knew it was almost certain death, when two companies, F and M, were ordered down the road, they did not flinch, but charged headlong, and as it was afterwards ascertained, actually charged a corps of the rebel army The result was, that out of the eighty men who made the charge, only four or five returned. The majority were shot down by a cross-fire of infantry, with grape from a battery in the road, directly in their front, and piled up with their horses on the road, killed and mortally wounded ; two went clear through the rebel lines and were captured, and as before stated, four or five managed to get back.

The record of the Harris Light Cavalry (afterwards the 2d New York), during the war, was of the best ; and whether mounted or dismounted, they could be depended upon to do good work, as General Patrick, and also General Custer (under whom the regiment fought several battles), were free in saying. Knowing that you would not intentionally do injustice to so creditable an officer as Judson Kilpatrick, or to so excellent a regiment as the Harris Light Cavalry, I have written these facts for your perusal.

                    Very truly, yours,
                         McD. VAN WAGONER,
                    Private Co. F, Harris Light Cavalry,
                         during the late War.

NOTE II.

ADDITIONAL LIST OF OFFICERS OF THE "TWENTIETH,"
PRIOR TO ITS DEPARTURE FOR THE WAR.

In addition to the list of officers given in Chapter III, as members of the regiment while it was commanded by Colonel Fiero, the records in the Adjutant-General's office, at Albany, show that the following named persons held commissions in the "Twentieth" between the time of Colonel Fiero's resignation and the departure of the regiment for the war, and whose names do not appear elsewhere in this narrative. It should be stated, however, that the regimental district had meantime been changed, and Greene County had been substituted for Sullivan. The additional list is as follows:

Surgeon.—James O. Van Hovenbergh, Kingston, November, 1857, in place of Cornelius G. Harlow, of Esopus. Sidney L. Ford, Lexington, and David B. Dewey, Catskill, Surgeon's Mates.

Chaplain.—Rev. Robert B. Fairbain, now Dean of St. Stephen's College at Anandale, N. Y.

Captains.—George Hartman, Rondout ; Daniel Gillett, John B. Davis, Olive ; Samuel Penniman, Samsonville ; James Diamond, Rondout ; Anthony Van Bergin, Rondout ; James Thompson, Esopus ; John Weber, Rondout ; Hezekiah Pettit, Lexington.

First Lieutenants.—Adam Smith, Cairo ; George W Mead, Jr., Cairo ; Lawrence H. Corbitt, Rondout ; Joseph Zemiski, Rondout ; Charles Shuman, Rondout William Golden, Rondout ; John Kline, Rondout

Platt J. Rowley; Hiram Davis, Windham Centre:
George Wheeler, Lexington, (promoted to Captain);
William Bertshe, Rondout : William Hammond, ; Cor-
nelius B. Bishop, Olive; John T. Dewitt, Samsonville;
John F. Ahrens, Rondout.

Second Lieutenants.—Philip V Moderse, Green-
ville ; George H. Masten, Greenville ; Joseph McElvy,
Samsonville : Hiram Boice, Shokan ; Nathan Leopold,
Ellenville ; John Henkel, Rondout ; Jacob Freelewich,
Kingston : George R. Scheck, Rondout ; George Bush-
nell, Claryville ; J Andrew Cross, Lexington ; Porter
J Schermerhorn, Westkill ; Albert Cohen, Saugerties ;
Henry Fox, Rondout ; Peter Claire, Rondout.

APPENDICES.

A.

CHRONOLOGICAL RECORD,

CONTAINING AN ACCURATE ACCOUNT OF THE MOVEMENTS OF THE REGI-
MENT DURING ITS ENTIRE SECOND TERM OF SERVICE—DISTANCES
MARCHED—PLACES OF ENCAMPMENT OR BIVOUAC—DUTY EMPLOYED
ON—DETAILS OF OFFICERS AND MEN—PROCEEDINGS OF DETACHMENT
ON VETERAN FURLOUGH—VISIT TO ALBANY—HON. JACOB LEFEVRE'S
RESOLUTION—IN THE ASSEMBLY CHAMBER—PRESENTATION OF COLORS
TO MASTER PRATT—ACCEPTANCE BY GOV. SEYMOUR—PRESENTATION
OF COLORS BY MRS. KUGLER—SPEECH OF HON. GEORGE T. PIERCE—AD-
DRESS OF REGIMENT TO COLONEL GATES—COLONEL HARDENBURGH IN
COMMAND—REGIMENT TO DEFENCE OF FORT SEDGWICK—GENERAL
COLLIS' ORDER—REGIMENT IN RICHMOND—HOW OFFICERS AND MEN
EMPLOYED—GENERAL TURNER'S ORDER—REGIMENT AT NORFOLK—
COLONEL HARDENBURGH IN COMMAND OF DISTRICT—MUSTERED OUT—
COLONEL HARDENBURGH'S ADDRESS—RECEPTION AND FLAG-PRESEN-
TATION AT KINGSTON—REORGANIZATION.

THE history of the original organization of the regiment
under Colonel Christopher Fiero, and its consolidation
with the Twenty-eight regiment ; the accession of
Colonel George W Pratt to the command, and its organization and departure from Kingston for its first
service under the United States Government, is given
in Chapters III, IV, and V of this work.

The following chronological record, after brief reference to the three months' service, carries on its
history from that time until its return in February,
1866.

About the middle of April, an order was received from the Adjutant-General of the State of New York, to prepare to march at an early day, and on the 26th of April, 1861, in pursuance of orders, the regiment left Kingston for Washington, about eight hundred strong.

The regiment was sent to Annapolis and thence to Annapolis Junction, where it did guard and picket duty along the Baltimore and Washington Railroad and the Annapolis Railroad until the latter part of June, when, on the occasion of the arrest of the Police Commissioners and Marshal Kane, it was ordered to Baltimore, and did guard duty there until its term of service expired ; but at the special request of General Dix, commanding at Baltimore, it remained a few days after its term was closed, when it returned to Kingston and was mustered out of the service early in August, 1861. It carried home a beautiful United States color, presented to it by the ladies of Baltimore.

The work of reorganization immediately began, and the regiment again marched from Kingston to Washington in the latter part of October, 1861, with the following field officers : George W Pratt, Colonel ; Theodore B. Gates, Lieutenant-Colonel ; Jacob B. Hardenburgh, Major ; and a total strength of a little less than one thousand, officers and men. It reached Washington on the 27th day of that month.

On the 7th of November, 1861, the regiment crossed the Potomac, and joined General Wadsworth's Brigade, General McDowell's Division of the Army of the Potomac, and did picket and foraging duty throughout the winter.

"*January* 1, 1862.—Regiment in camp at Upton's Hill, Va.

January 12.—Regiment on picket for forty-eight

hours in front of Falls Church, Va. From this date until March 10, engaged in drill, forage and picket duty.

March 10.—Regiment marched at 6 A.M., with General Wadsworth's Brigade, McDowell's Division, and bivouacked at 6 P. M., 16 miles from Upton Hill, and 2 miles east of Centreville.

March 14.—Two hundred and twenty-two men, under Captain Tappen, marched to and bivouacked on Bull Run battle-field.

March 15.—This detachment marched from that bivouac, joined the regiment, and the entire command marched to "Three Mile Run," near Alexandria, in a terrible storm of rain, 17 miles. The detachment marched 25 miles.

March 16.—Regiment marched to Upton Hill, 6 miles.

March 18.—Marched two miles below Bailey's Cross Roads, and bivouacked with brigade.

April 4.—Regiment marched with General Patrick's Brigade, from camp near Bailey's Cross Roads, at 3 P.M., and bivouacked at 7 P.M., 2 miles south of Anandale. Distance marched, 6 miles.

April 5.—Regiment resumed its march at 8 A. M., and marching through Fairfax Court House and Centreville, crossed Bull Run, and bivouacked 1 mile south of Blackburn Ford. Distance marched, 15 miles.

April 6.—Regiment continued its march at 8 A. M., and passing Manassas Junction, crossed Broad Run, and encamped near Bristow Station, at 2 P. M. Distance marched, 17 miles.

April 7.—A terrible storm of rain, snow and sleet, against which shelter tents afforded little protection, began to-day, and continued for sixty hours, occasioning much suffering.

April 16.—Marched to Catlett Station. Distance, 7 miles.

April 18.—Regiment marched at 6 A. M. ; obliged to leave forage, ammunition and sundries on the ground, for want of transportation, reaching a station 12 miles north of Falmouth, in a storm of rain.   Distance marched, 18½ miles.

April 19.—Marched at 7 A. M., reaching the hill-side directly opposite and in front of the city of Fredericksburg at 5 P. M., a distance of 14 miles.   The enemy have retreated, after a little skirmishing, across the Rappahannock, burning the three bridges and all their shipping, including the notorious Steamer St. Nicholas, captured by the " French Lady," Thomas.

April 28.—Moved camp half a mile further south.

May 5.—Three companies of this regiment, with two from the Twenty-third and one from the Thirty-fifth N Y Volunteers, all under command of Lieutenant-Colonel Theodore B. Gates, crossed the river at 5 P. M., and occupied the city of Fredericksburg, Virginia.

May 10.—Regiment crossed the river at 8 o'clock P.M., marching to a point 1½ miles beyond the city of Fredericksburg, on the Telegraph Road to Richmond, where it encamped.   Distance marched, 3½ miles.

May 11.—At 3 P.M. the regiment was ordered under arms, and moved some 2 miles down the Bowling Green Road, to repel a threatened attack of the enemy, under General Anderson, who was driving in a reconnoitering party, and advancing toward the city in considerable force. A few shots were fired, with a loss of one horse on our side, when the enemy withdrew.

May 14.—Companies B, C, H, and G, under Major Jacob B. Hardenburgh, on picket for twenty-four hours.

May 17.—Companies A, B, C, D, E, F, G, and K, relieved Thirty-fifth N. Y Volunteers, on picket for twenty-four hours.

May 20.—Companies A, B, C, D, E, I, and H, on picket for 24 hours.   At 10 o'clock, P. M., advanced our

picket line 1 mile, driving in the enemy and occupying
the Toll-Gate on the Plank-road, near Salem Church.

May 23.—Companies B, C, D, E, F, G, and K, on
picket for twenty-four hours. Enemy keeping up a
brisk fire on our men at the Toll-Gate. Regiment reviewed by President Lincoln.

May 26.—Regiment marched, with brigade, at 3
P.M., up the Telegraph Road to Massaponix Creek, and
encamped at 7 P M., on the ground occupied by the
enemy (the day before) under General Anderson. Distance marched, six miles. Companies C, and G, under
Major Hardenburgh, doing picket duty through the
night.

May 29.—Regiment marched at 12 M. to Hazel Run,
joined brigade, and continued its march through Fredericksburg, crossing the Rappahannock, through Falmouth, to a point six miles beyond. Bivouacked at 9
P.M. Distance marched, fourteen miles.

May 30.—Regiment marched, with brigade, at 8
A.M., and, after a very fatiguing march of twenty miles
crossed Elk Run, and bivouacked at 7 P M. Frequent
heavy rain storms.

May 31.—Regiment marched at 6 A. M., with brigade, crossed Cedar Run, and bivouacked at Catlett
Station, on Orange and Alexandria Railroad, awaiting
cars to transport it to Front Royal, Va. Wagon train
sent to Thoroughfare Gap by road *via* Haymarket, accompanied by company H, as escort. Heavy rain storms
during the night.

June 2.—Regiment marched with brigade at 12 M.,
from Catlett Station, Va., and bivouacked in a violent
storm at 6 P. M., on the bank of Kettle Run, on the road
to Haymarket. Distance marched, eight miles.

June 3.—Regiment marched, with brigade, at 7
A.M., and, crossing Broad Run, reached Haymarket, a
distance of five miles. Marched one mile south, and
encamped near Bull Run.

June 6.—Regiment marched, with brigade, at 8 A.M., and crossed Broad Run and Cedar Run, passed through the villages of Buckland and New Baltimore, and encamped one and one-half miles north of Warrenton, Va. Distance marched, twelve miles.

June 8.—Regiment marched, with brigade, at 4 P.M., passed through Warrenton, and bivouacked at 7 P.M., six miles beyond and two miles north of Warrenton Junction. Distance marched, six miles.

June 9.—Regiment marched, with brigade, at 6 A.M., passed through Warrenton Junction, and encamped on the bank of Elk Run, at 11 A. M. Distance marched, six miles.

June 13.—Marched with brigade at 3 P. M., crossed Elk Run, and encamped four miles south of Catlett Station at 5 P. M. Distance, three miles.

June 21.—Marched with brigade at 2 P M., crossed Power Run, and encamped at 6 P. M., twelve miles north of Fredericksburg, Va. Distance marched, eight miles.

June 24.—Regiment marched with brigade at 6 A. M., passed through Hartwood and Falmouth, reaching old camp, opposite Fredericksburg, at 2 P. M. Distance marched, thirteen miles.

June 27.—Moved camp two miles back from the river. Company C, Captain J. R. Tappen, ordered on special duty on the railroad between Fredericksburg and Richmond.

July 7.—Company C rejoined the regiment.

July 28.—Regiment marched from camp two miles back from the Rappahannock, to and across the river to Fredericksburg, where it divided, the four right companies, A, C, H, and K under Lieutenant-Colonel Theodore B. Gates, marched to Mrs. Stanbury's house, above Fredericksburg; the rest of the regiment to near Mrs. Fennihoe's house, below Fredericksburg. The regiment inclosed the city with a cordon of sentinels, preventing all communication with the interior. Distance marched by right companies, five miles; by rest of regiment, three miles.

August 4.—Right companies marched from Mrs. Stanbury's house, and rejoined the regiment at 2 P. M.

August 6.—Companies A, E, K, I, and C, two companies of Twenty-third New York Volunteers, one section of artillery, the whole under the command of Colonel George W Pratt, marched on a reconnoissance toward Bowling Green at 6 P M., in consequence of a report that the rebels had taken possession of Hicks' Hill, and returned at 3 A. M., August 7, having marched seventeen miles without seeing the enemy

August 7.—Regiment relieved from the duty of preventing communication between the city of Fredericksburg and the interior, by the One Hundredth Regiment Pennsylvania Volunteers.

August 8.—Companies B and D, six companies of Twenty-third New York Volunteers, four companies Third Indiana cavalry, and a section of the First New Hampshire battery, under command of Colonel Pratt, marched on a reconnoitering and foraging expedition at 7 P. M., to Round Oak Church, while Lieutenant Colonel Gates, with four companies of the Twentieth, marched up the Telegraph Road to Massaponix Creek, the bridge over which was found to be on fire, but the enemy had fallen back. The detachment then marched across the country, to the Bowling Green Road, and joined Colonel Pratt. The entire force returned at 3½ A. M., August 9, having marched twenty miles and captured two prisoners, twenty-five mules, thirty horses, and fifty head of cattle.

August 9.—Regiment marched, with brigade, at five P. M., to re-enforce General Pope, then engaged in battle near Culpepper Court House, and bivouacked at 10 P. M., on the Plank-road, eleven miles from Fredericksburg.

August 10.—Regiment marched, with brigade, at 5

A. M., crossed the Rapidan river at Ely's Ford at 11 A. M., and bivouacked at 4 P M., at a point four miles north-west of that river, near the road from Burnett's Ford of the Rappahannock. Distance marched, fourteen miles.

August 11.—Regiment marched, with division, at 5 A M., and bivouacked in line of battle three miles from Culpepper Court House, near battle-field of Cedar Mountain, at 12 o'clock midnight. Distance marched, twenty-two miles.

August 13.—The enemy having retreated, the regiment marched, with brigade, one mile nearer Culpepper Court House, where it encamped.

August 16.—Regiment marched with division at half-past eight, A. M., to Cedar Mountain battle-field, and encamped at 1 P. M. Distance marched, six miles.

August 18.—Orders to prepare three days' rations, and to be in readiness to march at a moment's notice, were received at 2 P. M. The baggage of the regiment was loaded immediately and sent off.

August 19.—Regiment marched, with division, at 9 A. M., and bivouacked at 11 P. M., three miles west of Rappahannock Station. Distance marched, seventeen miles.

August 20.—Regiment marched at 4 A. M., crossed the river at the Station at half-past five o'clock A. M.; encamped in the afternoon two miles north of the Station, one mile east of the river. Marched five miles.

August 21.—Were ordered forward to near the river at 9 A. M., to support Captain Reynolds' Battery L, First New York Artillery; and were there occupied during the day, the most of the time under a heavy fire from the enemy's battery, and a part of the time from his sharp-shooters also. At night, companies D and G, under command of Lieutenant-Colonel Gates, did picket duty along the river bank, and at the crossing at Norman's Ford—the residue of the regiment, under Colonel Pratt, forming the reserve.

August 22.—Were relieved at 5 A. M., by Twenty-second Regiment New York Volunteers, and returned to camp, which proved to be in range of some of the enemy's guns. Our loss was Sergeant Dopp, Company G, mortally wounded, and several others slightly.

August 23.—Marched with brigade at 10 A. M., and bivouacked at Warrenton, Va., at 8 P. M. Distance marched, 12 miles.

August 24.—Marched two miles beyond Warrenton, toward White Sulphur Springs, and encamped.

August 26.—Regiment marched at six o'clock for the Springs. As we approached them, the enemy opened fire upon us from two guns planted near a large yellow house on the opposite side of the river. Gaining the cover of the trees and buildings around the Springs, Company C was deployed as skirmishers. Subsequently the regiment marched across an open plain in full range of the enemy's battery, and took up a position on the hill east of the river, and about one mile from the Springs. The skirmishing continued all day, with a loss on our part of two men wounded. Distance march-ed, five miles. (See Chapter XVII.)

August 27.—Regiment marched from the Springs at 12 M., and bivouacked at midnight, eight miles beyond Warrenton, on the road to Gainesville. Distance march-ed, fifteen miles.

August 28.—Regiment marched at six A. M., and reached a point on the Centreville road, two miles be-yond Gainesville, where it halted, while the roads and woods in front were reconnoitered by General Hatch's Brigade, which, with General Gibbons, was in advance. The enemy were found in considerable force, and a brisk engagement ensued. The regiment was ordered up to support the troops engaged, but darkness put an end to the battle before it reached the field. Picketed road the rest of the night. Distance marched, seven miles. (See Chapter XVII.)

August 29.—Marched at 2 A. M., for Manasses Junction, which was reached about daylight. At 10 A. M. were ordered back to yesterday's battle-field, where the action had been renewed ; some three miles from Manassas, were ordered back, and returning to within one mile of the latter place, filed to the left, and, marching by the Sudley Ford, across a portion of the Bull Run battle-field, were posted in support of Reynolds' battery on the left of the road, and about one mile from Chinn's house. About dusk, were moved forward toward Groveton, to support Hatch's Brigade, which was engaged and likely to be turned on the right ; withdrawn about 10 P. M., and posting a portion of the regiment with Reynolds' and Campbell's batteries, the residue were detailed for picket on the front, under command of Lieutenant-Colonel Gates.

August 30.—Bull Run Second. (See Chapters XVIII–XIX.)

August 31.—Regiment marched at 4 A. M. to Centreville, and joined brigade.

September 1.—Chantilly (See Chapter XX.)

September 2.—Rejoined the brigade at 8 A. M., and, marching with it, at 2 P. M., passed through Fairfax Court House and Anandale, and reached Upton's Hill at 10 P. M. Distance marched, 13 miles.

September 4.—Regiment marched to Fall's Church, to repel a demonstration of the enemy, who had planted some guns on Bassett's Hill and driven in our cavalry Did picket duty that night. Distance marched, 2 miles.

September 5.—Regiment returned to camp, on Upton Hill, at 1 P. M. Distance marched, 2 miles.

September 6.—Marched at 2 A. M., crossing the Aqueduct Bridge at Georgetown, and marched through Washington, D. C., to Leesboro, Md., and bivouacked at 5 P M. Distance marched, 16 miles. (See Chapter XXI.)

September 8.—Marched, with brigade, 4 miles and bivouacked.

September 9.—Marched, with brigade, to Mechanics-ville. Distance, 9 miles.

September 10.—Marched from Mechanicsville, with brigade, to the farm of a Mr. Davis, 6 miles distant.

September 11.—Marched, with brigade, through Lisbon to Newmarket, a distance of 15 miles.

September 12.—Marched, with brigade, to Monocacy Bridge, and bivouacked. Distance marched, 12 miles.

September 14.—South Mountain. (Chapter XXI-XXII.)

September 15.—At daylight it was discovered that the enemy had retired, leaving his dead and wounded on the field. The regiment then rejoined the brigade, and, soon after, resumed its march toward Boonesboro, at which place it bivouacked two miles further south, on Antietam Creek, at 6 P. M. Distance, ten miles.

September 16–17.—Battle of Antietam. (See Chapter XXIV)

September 18.—In line of battle all day, but the action was not renewed. Endeavored to remove some of our dead where we were engaged yesterday, but the enemy's sharp-shooters have the range of the field.

September 19.—Regiment marched with brigade (the enemy have retreated) at 5.30 A. M. to the Williamsport Road, over the battle-field, and bivouacked in a wood half a mile northwest of the field. Distance marched, 2 miles.

September 29.—Marched with brigade at 2¼ P. M., to a point one mile northwest of Sharpsburg, near the Potomac river, where encamped. Distance marched, 1½ miles.

October 7.—General Patrick having been assigned to

duty at General McClellan's headquarters, as Provost-Marshal-General of the Army of the Potomac, took leave of the brigade. (See Order, Chapter XXV)

October 20.—Marched, with brigade, at 7 A.M., to Hagerstown Turnpike, up the pike about 2 miles, then taking a road to the left, passed through Bakersville, and encamped about one mile beyond. Distance marched, 5 miles.

October 26.—Regiment marched at 8 P.M., through a drenching rain; but the darkness compelled it to bivouac. Marched 1½ miles.

October 27.—Regiment marched, with brigade, at 6 A.M., and, passing through Keedysville, took the road leading to Crampton's Gap. Bivouacked at 4 P.M. Distance marched, 7 miles.

October 28.—Regiment marched, with brigade, at 5½ P.M., crossed South Mountain at Crampton's Gap, passed through Burkettsville, and bivouacked at 3 P.M., 2 miles north of Berlin. Distance marched, 13 miles.

October 30.—Regiment marched, with brigade, at 6 P.M., crossed Potomac river on a pontoon bridge at Berlin at 8 P.M., and bivouacked on the Baltimore and Leesburg Turnpike, 6 miles from Berlin, at 11 P.M. Marched 8 miles.

October 31.—Marched, with brigade, at 3½ P.M., towards Leesburg and bivouacked at 5 P.M. Distance marched, 2 miles.

November 1.—Regiment marched, with division, at 8½ A. M., passing through Wheatlands, taking the Winchester and Leesburg Turnpike, and bivouacking near Purcellville, at 3 P. M, Marched 8 miles.

November 3.—Regiment marched, with division, at 1 P. M. down the pike, about 2 miles, turned to the left, passed through Union, and bivouacked at 8 P.M. Distance marched, 12 miles.

November 4.—Regiment marched, with brigade, at

1¼ P.M., passed through Bloomfield, and bivouacked half a mile beyond at 4¼ o'clock. Distance marched, 4¼ miles.

November 5.—Marched, with brigade, at 8 A.M., and bivouacked 3 miles north of Salem, at 8 P.M. Distance marched, 18 miles.

November 6.—Regiment marched, with brigade, at 6 A.M., passed through Salem (General McClellan's headquarters,) at 8 A.M., through Warrenton at 5 P. M., and encamped at 7 P.M., one mile below that place, on the road leading to White Sulphur Springs.

November 11.—Marched, with brigade, at 1 P.M., and bivouacked near Fayetteville at 10¼ P.M. Distance marched, 5 miles.

November 12.—Marched down the road leading to Nolan's Ford, to do picket duty. Distance marched, 3 miles.

November 14.—Relieved from picket duty, and returned to camp at 4 P.M. Distance marched, 3 miles.

November 17.—Regiment marched, with brigade, at 11 A.M., and, passing through Liberty, Bealtown and Morrisville, bivouacked at 9 P.M., 2 miles south of the latter place. Distance marched, 18 miles.

November 18.—Marched, with division, at 8 A.M., reached Hartwood at 2 P.M., and, taking the road leading to Stafford Court House, bivouacked at 8 P.M. Distance marched, 10 miles.

November 19.—Marched, with brigade, at 8 A.M., (the roads in terrible condition), and bivouacked at 4 P.M. Distance marched, 4 miles.

November 20.—Marched at 8 A.M., half a mile, and encamped.

November 22.—Marched at 3 P.M., and encamped at 5 P.M., near the Richmond, Fredericksburg and Potomac Railroad, 1 mile southwest of Brooks' Station. Distance marched, 4 miles.

December 9.—Marched, at noon, towards Fredericksburg, and bivouacked at 5 P.M.   Distance marched, 4
miles.

December 10.—Marched, with division, at 9 A.M. :
bivouacked at 1 P.M.   Distance marched, 3 miles.

December 11.—Marched, with division, at 8 A.M., 1
mile, halted, stacked arms, and finally bivouacked at 5
P.M.

December 12.—Marched, with division, at 7½ A.M.,
to the Rappahannock river ; crossed the river at 2 P.M.,
near the Arthur Bernard House, 2 miles below the city
of Fredericksburg.   Soon after our crossing the river,
the enemy opened fire with his artillery.   Marched out
of range and bivouacked.   Distance marched, 3 miles.

BATTLE OF FREDERICKSBURG.

(For fuller details, see Chapter XXV

December 13.—At daylight the brigade was formed
in line of battle.   This regiment and the Twenty-first
New York Volunteers, forming the first line, advanced
to the left and toward a wooded ravine occupied by the
enemy   The enemy having been driven from this position, the brigade changed direction to the right, and
marched, under a heavy fire of the enemy's artillery, to
the Bowling Green Road, which was occupied by the
first line.   We remained in this position about an hour,
and until the advance had been checked on the right,
the enemy, meanwhile, pouring a constant shower of
shot and shell from their batteries, which were not more
than five or six hundred yards in front, when we were
ordered at a double-quick toward the right.   We had
proceeded about half a mile in this direction, when we
were counter-marched, and took up a position in a rav
ine to the rear, and a little to the right of the position
we had occupied in the Bowling Green Road, in sup-

port of several batteries, which drew on us a heavy fire
of artillery Soon after reaching this position, (the enemy having, during our march to the right, planted a
section of artillery on the road leading from the telegraph to the Bowling Green Road, and thrown forward
their skirmishers, who severely annoyed our cannoniers), Company F, Captain Corbin, Company K, Captain
Baldwin, and Company A, Captain McEntee, were deployed as skirmishers. They advanced rapidly, under
a heavy fire from the enemy's skirmishers, drove them
back, and took up a position in the Bowling Green Road,
where they soon silenced the section of artillery before
mentioned, killing several of the gunners and three
horses. These companies remained in this position until after dark, when they were relieved by the Twenty-
third Regiment New York Volunteers. At dark, the
regiment took up a position one hundred yards to the
right and rear, and remained there during the night,
being treated, in the early part of the evening, to a co-
pious discharge of grape and canister. At daylight the
line advanced about fifty yards, and Company B, Captain Leslie, and Company E, Captain Cornelius, were
thrown forward as skirmishers. They advanced, driving
the enemy back, and took a position by order of General
Doubleday, extending from a group of straw stacks to
the Bowling Green Road. The firing along this line was
brisk and uninterrupted during the whole day. The
ammunition of the companies having become exhausted,
they were relieved about 4 P. M., by Company H, Captain A. S. Smith, and Company C, Captain Snyder.
Captain Smith was severely wounded while in the discharge of his duty These companies remained on duty
during the night.

December 15.—Company G, Captain Cunningham
and Company I, Lieutenant Cook, relieved the above
named companies early in the morning, and, in turn

were relieved by Company K, Lieutenant Young. The picket duty along this line was very severe, as the line extended over an open plain, and the men were constantly exposed to the fire of the enemy's sharp-shooters, which was kept up during the entire day, and very frequently during the night.

December 16.—Regiment re-crossed the Rappahannock at 11½ P. M., and encamped on the heights beyond the pontoon bridge at 1 A. M., during a heavy storm of wind and rain. Distance marched, 5 miles.

December 17.—Regiment marched at 9 A.M., to a point opposite Fredericksburg, and a short distance south-east of the railroad station at Falmouth, where it encamped. Distance marched, 3 miles.

December 20.—Marched at 9 A. M. Passed White Oak Church at 11 A. M., and encamped at 5 P M., on the bank of Potomac River, three miles below Potomac Run. Distance marched, 13 miles.

December 23.—Regiment marched at 8 A. M., and encamped near Hall's Landing, Va., at 1 P. M. Distance marched, 4 miles.

December 27.—Marched half a mile, to a point north of Hall's Landing, and occupied log huts erected by the enemy last winter for troops stationed here to support a small redoubt, and a bastion fort, designed to command the mouth of Potomac Creek, and to obstruct navigation on the river. Furnished daily details for fatigue duty, at Hall's Landing, during the remainder of the year.

January 7, 1863.—Transferred from the First Corps, and placed in a provisional brigade, under command of Brigadier-General M. R. Patrick, Provost-Marshal-General, by Special Orders No. 6, Headquarters Army of the Potomac. [See General Patrick's letter, page 193.]

January 10.—Embarked on steamboat Rockland, at 8 A. M., and debarked at Aquia Creek, Va., at 10 A. M., and proceeded up the Potomac, Fredericksburg and Richmond Railroad, establishing guard-posts to Potomac River Station. Headquarters of the regiment at Brooks' Station.

January 21.—Marched·to Aquia Creek Landing to do guard duty. Encamped near the Landing. Distance marched, 6 miles.

January 22.—One company placed on picket duty along the Potomac River from Aquia to Potomac Creek. A sergeant and ten men on duty at Liverpool Point. Md., opposite Aquia Creek. The residue of the regiment doing guard duty at the Landing.

February 10.—Moved camp to a hill near the river.

April 29.—Marched from Aquia Creek to Brooks' Station, 6 miles ; establishing guard-posts along the river, and garrisoning the field-works at Accocac Creek, and *tete-de-pont* at Potomac Creek.

CHANCELLORSVILLE, OR FREDERICKSBURG SECOND, APRIL 30—MAY 6.

[See Chapter XXVI-XXVIII.]

May 9.—B Company proceeded from Brooks' Station to Washington, D. C., by rail and boat, to perform provost duty on Government wharf. Distance, 62 miles.

May 13.—B Company returned to Brooks' Station from Washington by rail and boat. Distance, 62 miles.

May 15.—Headquarters moved from Brooks' Station to Falmouth Station, 9 miles. Companies A, B, E and H moved to Falmouth Station. C Company stationed at Brooks' Station ; D Company at Potomac Creek Station ; E, I, F and K Companies at Aquia Creek ; G Company at Stoneman's Switch—all performing provost duty.

May 16.—D Company moved from Potomac Creek to Headquarters Army of the Potomac, 3 miles.

May 17.—K and I Companies moved from Aquia Creek to Headquarters Army of the Potomac. Fifteen miles.

May 18.—E Company moved from Falmouth Station to Headquarters Army of the Potomac. Two miles.

May 30.—C, D, E, I and K Companies, under command of Lieutenant-Colonel Hardenburgh, marched to Belle Plain, Virginia, to perform provost duty Seven miles.

June 14.—The different detachments of the regiment united at Aquia Creek—fifteen miles—at 12 M., and reported to Brigadier-General G K. Warren. At 3 P. M. moved by rail to Potomac Creek, to garrison field-works, perform picket duty, and remove Government property Nine miles.

June 15.—Marched at 7 A. M. to Brooks' Station, where remained doing picket duty and protecting the removal of Government property until 12 M., when, all being removed, proceeded by rail to near Aquia Creek, and garrisoned Forts Nos. 1 and 2. Eight miles. At about 3 P.M. a detachment under command of Major W A. Van Rensselaer, proceeded on a reconnoissance by rail to Potomac Creek Station, and returned at 5 P. M. Sixteen miles.

June 16.—Marched at 4 P M. to Aquia Creek, and embarked on steamer Hero, and debarked at Alexandria, Virginia, on the 17th, at 6 A. M. the next morning, 45 miles, and marched to Soldier's Rest, where breakfasted, when marched to the edge of the city, and bivouacked. Marched at 5 P. M. through Alexandria, across the Long Bridge, through Washington, to the Soldier's Home, where remained during the night. Eight miles.

June 18.—Marched at 5 A. M. through Washington and Georgetown, over the Washington Aqueduct, to near the Great Falls of the Potomac, where bivouacked at 7 P M. Sixteen miles.

June 19.—Marched at 6 A. M. to Great Falls of Poto-

mac, where embarked on canal boats on Chesapeake and
Ohio Canal, and debarked at Seneca ; and, marching
through Poolesville, bivouacked at 5 P M. a short distance beyond.   Twenty-four miles.

June 20.—Marched at 8 A. M. to the mouth of the
Monocacy, where encamped.   Six miles.   Regiment engaged in performing picket duty along the Potomac
river, and protecting Aqueduct of the Chesapeake and
Ohio Canal over the Monocacy River.

June 22.—Marched at 3 P. M. to Edwards' Ferry,
where encamped at 9 P. M.   Eleven miles.   While here
performed provost and guard duty

June 27.—Relieved by the One Hundred and Tenth
Regiment Pennsylvania Volunteers, and ordered to join
First Corps.   Marched at 10 A. M. to the Monocacy,
crossing that river over the Aqueduct, and bivouacked
at 6 P. M. four miles beyond.   Thirteen miles.

June 28.—Marched at 5 A. M., crossing the Katocton
Mountains at Katocton's Pass, passed through Adams-
town and Jefferson, and proceeded to near Middletown,
where, learning that the First Corps had gone to Frederick, the regiment took a by-road and recrossed the
Katocton Mountains at New Pass, and bivouacked at
8 P. M.   Sixteen miles.

June 29.—Marched at 6 A. M., and, passing through
Frederick and Lewistown, bivouacked at 5 P. M. on
Emmettsburg pike.   Sixteen miles.

June 30.—Marched at 4 A. M., and reached Emmettsburg at 12 M., where halted, and reported the arrival to
Major-General Reynolds, commanding First Corps,
where received orders to join Third Division under command of Major-General Doubleday.   On joining the
division, were assigned to the First Brigade, then on
picket.   Eighteen miles.

GETTYSBURG—JULY 1-3.

[See Chaps. XXXII-XXXIV.]

July 6.—Marched at 7 A. M., with the First Corps, and bivouacked near Emmettsburg, Md., at 7 P.M. Ten miles.

July 7.—Marched at 4½ A. M., and, passing over the Katocton Mountains, back of Lewistown, bivouacked beyond Hamburg, on the northerly side of the mountain, at about 7 P. M. Twenty-two miles.

July 8.—Marched at 5 A. M., through Belleville, Middletown, crossing South Mountain at Turner's Gap; formed in line of battle on north side, where barricades were thrown up. Fourteen miles.

July 10.—Marched at 5½ A. M., through Boonesboro, to right of our lines, and then threw up barricades. Five miles.

July 11.—Moved to the extreme right, under the mountain, and threw up intrenchments, putting our pickets in front.

July 12.—Marched at 11 A. M., passing through Funkstown and crossing Antietam Creek; took up a position on Funkstown Heights, one mile south of Hagerstown, and threw up intrenchments under fire of the enemy's pickets. Five miles.

July 13.—Lay in line of battle all day. Skirmishers pretty active in front. Our line of battle in range of enemy's sharp-shooters.

July 14.—Men aroused at 4½ A. M., and got under arms preparatory to an attack. Skirmishers of 20th advanced and found the enemy's works abandoned. Marched at 12 M., to near Williamsport, and bivouacked at 3 P. M. Five miles.

July 15.—Marched at 6 A. M., *via* Williamsport and Hagerstown Pike to Funkstown, and thence through Jones Corners, Keedysville and Bakersville to foot of South Mountain, and bivouacked at 7 P. M., near Crampton's Gap. Eighteen miles.

July 16.—Marched at 9 A. M., and crossing South

Mountain at Crampton's Gap, bivouacked at 4 P. M., near Berlin. Nine miles. At this place the regiment was detached from the First Corps and ordered to report to Brigadier-General M. R. Patrick, Provost-Marshal-General, for duty in his Department.

July 17.—Two lieutenants and thirty men being left at headquarters of Provost-Marshal-General, the regiment took cars for Washington as guard for seven hundred and twenty-five prisoners of war.

July 18.—Reached Washington at 6 A. M., next day.

July 20.—Returned to Berlin, and crossing the Potomac, marched ten miles to Wheatland, Va., where bivouacked.

July 21.—Marched at 6 A. M., and joined army headquarters near Union, Va., at 1 P. M. Ten miles.

July 22.—Marched to Delany's Farm and camped. Five miles.

July 23.—Marched at 8 A. M., with general headquarters, and bivouacked near Markham at 6 P. M. Twenty-two miles.

July 24.—Marched at 12 M., and bivouacked at 7 P.M., at Salem. Fourteen miles.

July 25.—Marched at 6 A. M., and camped at 6 P. M., in Warrenton. Twelve miles. Regiment doing provost duty in this town.

July 27.—Relieved by the One Hundred and Thirtieth New York Volunteers.

July 29.—Companies C and G proceeded by rail to Warrenton Junction, Va., to do provost duty. Ten miles.

July 31.—K Company ordered to guard Commissary Depot. Three miles.

August 11.—Broke camp at 6 A. M., and moved by rail to Warrenton Junction, to do provost duty. Ten miles.

September 17.—Moved by rail to Culpepper Court

House, to do provost duty in that town. Twenty-two miles.

October 10.—Marched at 4 A. M., and bivouacked at Rappahannock Station at 6 P. M.

October 11.—Marched at 6 A. M., to Bealton Station. Four miles.

October 12.—Marched to Catlett's Station, ten miles, where did picket duty at night.

October 13.—Marched at 6 A. M., for Fairfax Station. Twenty-one miles. General headquarters train being attacked by guerrillas, the regiment marched out to protect it, and then returned to station. Four miles.

October 14.—Proceeded by rail to Washington, as guard for three hundred and eighty-two prisoners of war. Twenty-four miles.

October 15.—Returned by rail to Fairfax Station. Twenty-four miles.

October 21.—Marched at 10 A. M., through Centreville, across Bull Run and Cub Run, and bivouacked at 6 P.M., at Gainsville. Twenty-one miles.

October 22.—Marched at 7 A. M., and camped at Warrenton, Va., at 1 P. M. Twelve miles.

October 26.—B company ordered to Manassas, to do provost duty   Twenty-four miles.

October 27.—Marched at 8 A. M., with general headquarters, to Auburn. Six miles.

October 30.—Marched at 10 A. M., to Three Mile Station. Six miles.

November 2.—Marched to Warrenton Junction. Three miles.

November 9.—Moved by rail as guard to one thousand eight hundred and eighty-six prisoners of war to Alexandria. Thirty-two miles.

November 19.—Moved by rail to Brandy Station. Sixteen miles.

November 26.—Marched at 12 M., and bivouacked at

8 P. M., near Germania Ford, on the Rapidan River. Ten miles.

November 27.—Marched at 7 A. M. Crossed the Rapidan River at Germania Ford, and bivouacked at the Lacy House, on Orange and Fredericksburg Pike, at 7 P. M. Ten miles.

November 28.—Marched at 7 A. M., to near Robertson's Tavern, where encamped. Four miles.

December 1.—Marched at three P. M., re-crossed the Rapidan River at Germania Ford, and bivouacked at 8 P. M. Ten miles.

December 2.—Marched at 7 A. M., and encamped at Brandy Station at 2 P. M. Eight miles.

December 24.—B Company moved by rail to Catlett's Station and Manassas, and A Company to Rappahannock Station and Warrenton Junction, to do provost duty.

December 26.—E Company moved by rail to Culpepper Court House Station, to do provost duty.

December 29.—Two commissioned officers and two non-commissioned officers and thirty men detailed as permanent guard on passenger trains running between Brandy Station and Washington, D. C.

December 31.—Headquarters of regiment at Brandy Station, Va., doing duty as above stated.

1864.

January 1.—Encamped at Brandy Station, Va., with officers and detachments at every station along the Orange and Alexandria railroad, from Alexandria to Culpepper Court House (both inclusive), acting as Provost Marshals and guards ; and one company at headquarters, Army of the Potomac, as guard for the Provost-Marshal-General. From this time to May 4th, the regiment was engaged in doing provost and guard duty on and along the Orange and Alexandria railroad, having charge of all mail, passenger and special trains run on that road : the granting of passes to all persons leaving the army ; and to all civilians to pass from one part of the army to another ; the registering of all civilians coming to the army ; the examination and general superintendence of all goods coming into the army ; and the conveying of all prisoners from the army to other places throughout the United States.

February 13.—Colonel Theodore B. Gates, Surgeon R. Loughran, Captains J. D. S. Cook, M. Snyder, Daniel McMahon, Lieutenants D. J France, M. J. C. Woodworth, J. Deils, and 161 enlisted men, left Brandy Station, Va., on thirty-five days' veteran furlough, and arrived at Kingston, N Y., on the 15th, where they were publicly received by an immense concourse of citizens, and after addresses of welcome, the battalion sat down to a bounteous dinner provided by the ladies whose presence graced the occasion.

February 17.—The officers visited the city of Albany, and were invited to seats on the floor of the Assembly Chamber, under the following resolution, offered by the Hon. Jacob Lefevre, Member from the Third District of Ulster County, and which resolution was unanimously adopted :

"*Resolved*, That the officers of the Twentieth Regiment, N Y S. M., now in this city, whose third enlistment in the service of their country during the present war has just taken place, and whose battle-flags in the Bureau of Military Statistics are their credentials, be admitted to the privileges of the floor of this House."

On taking seats they were addressed by Mr. Speaker Alvord, in patriotic and complimentary terms. He said the regiment was one of the old militia regiments of the State—from the good old county of Ulster. Thrice had they laid themselves upon the altar of their country Their lamented comrades slept upon many a well-fought battle-field. Their former Colonel,

Geo. W Pratt, fell in the second battle of Bull Run. As for the third time they go forth, God grant to preserve their lives in safety, and to return them once more to our State.

Colonel Gates replied as follows :

"MR. SPEAKER AND GENTLEMEN OF THE ASSEMBLY : I know not in what language to express to you the gratification we feel for the honor you have conferred upon the Twentieth Regiment, N. Y S. M., in inviting its officers to the privileges of the floor of this House. We came to Albany to-day, sir, on business of solemn import. We came here to pay, in the first place, our respects to the Governor of the State, the Commander-in-chief of the forces of the State of New York, and in the second place to tender to the widow of our deceased Colonel the compliment of a presentation of a stand of colors of our regiment to her infant son—the son of our ever-lamented Colonel. Knowing that we should be detained here till evening, we determined to come to the Assembly Chamber to witness the proceedings that might take place, but we had no expectation that we should be honored with the compliment of seats upon the floor.

" In behalf of the officers here, sir—in behalf of the regiment I have the honor to command, I thank you, sir ; and I thank the members of the Assembly for the honor they have conferred upon us. The Twentieth Regiment is a regiment of the Militia of the State of New York. On the breaking out of the rebellion they tendered their services to the Governor of the State of New York, and through him to the President of the United States, and were accepted. They marched from Kingston, in Ulster County, on the 20th April, 1861, for three months' service. At the expiration of that time they returned and were mustered out of service, but were mustered in again and marched in October, 1861. for the war.

" I feel it due that I should say to you, sir, and to the members of the Assembly, that the regiment has been faithful to the trust confided to it; that it has continued in the service up to the present time; that now we come back from the field of duty, for a brief recreation, only to return again to the defence of the Government, there to remain until the war shall close. The men I now have the honor to command in the place of the former Colonel, Geo. W Pratt, whose memory is sacred to us, and I believe to the people of the entire State—Geo. W Pratt, who was one of the principal men in perfecting the militia organization of the State of New York; whose heart was in the work which he took in hand: whose patriotism was above party and above everything, except the welfare of his country. On his death the regiment was assigned to me, and I have endeavored to be faithful to the trust confided to me. I endeavored to follow in the footsteps of my predecessor, and I only hope, sir, when this war is terminated, if I shall live to see its conclusion, that I may bear as good a reputation for the faithful discharge of my duty as an officer in the service of my country, as Colonel Pratt himself had.

" The regiment having passed through its three months; having re-enlisted for three years, and having served two and a half years of that term, has now availed itself of the offer extended to it to re-enlist for three years more. The regiment feels that the great duty now devolving upon every man able to bear arms is to fight this war out to the end. They feel, sir, that nothing is paramount to the duty that love of country, of government. of human liberty, devolves upon them.

" Now, sir, in conclusion, I beg again to thank you and the members of this House, for the compliment you have paid us, and I hope and trust that you may never have cause to blush that you invited the officers of the Twentieth N Y. S. M. to seats upon this floor "

February 22.—The battalion, accompanied by a large delegation of citizens of Ulster County, proceeded to Albany, to present to Master Geo. S. Pratt, son of the late Colonel Geo. W Pratt, the old regimental flag carried by the regiment when Colonel Pratt was mortally wounded at Bull Run. Arriving at Albany, the battalion was drawn up in front of Mrs. Pratt's resi-. dence, where His Excellency, Gov. Seymour, attended by his staff, in uniform, and a large number of citizens, were assembled.

Colonel Gates, speaking in behalf of his regiment, after alluding to the high-toned and unspotted character of the deceased, said :

" Seven years ago, the officers of the battalion induced him to accept the office of Colonel. At that time the militia of the State was in anything but a desirable condition, and the Twentieth was small in numbers ; but it was not long after Colonel Pratt took command before it reached proportions that none had anticipated, and occupied a position second to but few in the State. He was among the first to tender his services and his regiment to the country, when she needed soldiers, and his gallantry, his uniform kindness and heroic example on all occasions, inspired his men with a lasting admiration for him. Our love for his memory—our respect for his family—bring us here to-day. We come from the battle-field, where we have left many a comrade, to tender to his son one of the tattered banners under which his noble father fell. When the rebellion broke out, Colonel Pratt was one of the very first to tender his regiment. It seemed as though every missile hurled against Fort Sumter shook and thrilled his fragile frame, and, if possible, filled him with a deeper love for his country It seemed as though he felt that he could make no sacrifices too great in aid of his country against this unholy rebellion.   On the 26th of April, 1861, the regiment marched to the seat of war nearly one thousand strong.   It had then enlisted for three months, and after serving that term faithfully, returned home, reorganized, and again enlisted, this time for three years, and again under the lead of their favorite Colonel : and it was fated that our beloved and heroic commander should fall in the defense of his country.   He received his fatal wound in the second Bull Run battle.   Always kind, always generous, always good and noble, I cannot depict the grief of the regiment on learning of their loss.   He has gone to his long rest, and knowing him as well as I did, I cannot doubt but that his rest is both peaceful and happy We feel that his life was closed all too soon.   We know that it was not lived or lost in vain : and it should be, as it is, I believe, our study and hope to emulate his example, to the end that when peace is restored to our country, and the majesty of the law is again supreme, we may enjoy a portion of the general respect which was so largely his share, and which is now paid his memory.   In behalf of the regiment (addressing the boy), officers and men, and the men not less than the officers, I present you this battle-flag.   Its wounds were received when your father fell.   When it was presented to the regiment, he pledged himself that it should ever be religiously defended.   It has no marks of dishonor, all its scars are honorable, and we believe that it will be beloved and held sacred by you, as it has been and is by us, for the sake of the memory of your deceased father.''

Master Pratt said, in reply :

" I thank the Twentieth Regiment for these colors.

I thank them for remembering my father. I will try and be as good and brave a man as he was."

Governor Seymour, responding for Master Pratt, said :

"SOLDIERS OF THE TWENTIETH MILITIA : On behalf of a sorrowing and stricken father, on behalf of a mourning family—and speaking for the orphan children —I thank you for this manifestation of love for the memory of one who distinguished himself as your leader. They will treasure up this sad memento as among their most precious gifts. We have watched the history and course of every regiment that has left our State, with anxiety as well as with pride, and *none have challenged greater admiration than your regiment.* How many of your comrades have lost their lives, your diminished numbers tell in language more eloquent than words can utter ; and let me assure you that in the future there will be one household where you will ever be remembered with mournful interest ; one family that will always feel the deepest interest in your career and welfare : one house where it will be felt that, between it and your organization, a new relation exists. This banner will be dearly cherished by him into whose hands you have placed it to-day   It will speak to him of the spotless character of his father—of his virtues, and of the love borne him for those virtues by his comrades in arms : and God grant that he may emulate the example thus set him.

"Once more I thank you for this evidence of devotion to the memory of your late commander—for the generous, manly, soldierly affection that has led you to manifest, in this delicate way, your continued regard for his memory, and the respect that you entertain for his family ; and I again assure you that your invaluable gift will ever be most dearly prized—that there is one family where your happiness will be a source of solicitude—one family where everything that relates to your regiment will be of fireside interest."

Subsequently the officers were entertained at Mrs. Pratt's house, and the men, as the guests of Mrs. Pratt, sat down to a sumptuous dinner at the American Hotel. While there, Master Erastus Corning, son of E. Corning, Jr., and a nephew of the late Colonel Pratt, made his appearance among them, and presented each of the men with a tract, evidently to their great pleasure. Soon after 4 o'clock, the battalion took the cars for Kingston. Master Pratt, with numerous others, accompanied them across the river, and as the cars left, they gave him rounds of cheers.

During the time the battalion was at home, 140 recruits were added to the regiment.

March 18.—The battalion, with its recruits, was drawn up in line, preparatory to its departure for the army, when Mrs. Albert Kugler through Hon. Geo. T. Pierce, presented a beautiful silk color to the regiment.

Mr. Pierce spoke as follows:

"COLONEL GATES, OFFICERS AND MEN OF THE TWENTIETH: I am honored by being made the instrument of your fellow-citizen, Mr. Kugler, and his good wife, in presenting you this beautiful stand of colors— the work of their hands. Mr. Kugler was formerly a member of your regiment, who went out in the three months', and returning would have gone again, but was advised by his commandant that perhaps duty to an invalid wife and to his family demanded that he should remain at home. But chafing under his anxiety to serve his country, he determined to make due amends for his inability to go with you to the field. And his wife, desiring to make some slight compensation to the regiment for permitting her husband to remain at home, they have acted accordingly, and this magnificent flag, which I now present you, is the result. Would to God that every man and woman in the community would feel thus ill at ease with themselves, until they had done something half as noble for their country, in this trying crisis of its existence. But our German fellow-citizens have generally been loyal to the old flag, from the very commencement of our troubles—have kept the Star of the Republic steady in their eyes, and have not permitted party or personal considerations to divert their attention or detract from their devotion to one country—one Union—one destiny.

"You have just returned, Colonel, from visiting the shrine of your late commandant, Colonel Pratt, where you went to present to his widow and fatherless son, the remnant of the battle-flag which you carried with you for two years past. It was an offering well and worthily made. But it was this circumstance which suggested to Mr. Kugler that you would now stand in need of another flag. You have it; and in view of the record which you have brought back from the war already, and of the deeds which you have performed on the field, and which are known of all men, it would be presumptuous in me to charge you to keep that emblem sacred, and never permit it to be desecrated or disgraced. When borne aloft at the head of your columns, let each man remember it is no mere ornament there, but that it represents the sovereignty of the nation, and the majesty of thirty millions of people. And as it proved a scourge and a terror to tyrants in the hands of your fathers, so may it prove a scourge and a terror to traitors in the hands of you, their sons.

"Men of the Twentieth : It was over two years ago, and yet it seems but a few days, that you left us before, amid the mingled tears and acclamations of ten thousand of your neighbors and friends, your fathers and mothers,

brothers and sisters, wives and children. You returned
to be crowned with the blessings of 75,000 people, who
waited with open arms to receive you. You went out
as men—you returned as heroes. And if you shall return again, having accomplished the object for which
you go forth, and which every patriot has at heart, the
restoration of the authority of the Government over
every inch of its soil, and of consequent peace and prosperity to the country, you will be received by thirty
millions of people who will be ready to fall down and
worship you as little less than gods.

"Colonel, you return again to the field. Heaven grant
that it may be to see no more of the clash of arms or of
the conflict of battle—but to give the finishing stroke to
the rebellion and end the war. And the hideous shriek
of terror and dismay which emanates from Richmond
would seem to indicate that you had already struck the
monster a blow in his very vitals, and that he even now
totters to his fall. Your friends who fight from the
mountain tops of East Tennessee, above the clouds,
think they can discern the beginning of the end. God
grant that it may be so; and that it may be reserved to
you to become the bearers of food and freedom to those
of our brethren who are confined in Southern prison-
houses—to plant the standard of the Republic on the
turrets and temples of the Southern Confederacy, and
speedily to return to us again, bringing the joyful
tidings of the Union restored, the supremacy of the laws
maintained, and the rebellion crushed and overthrown.

"But whatever may be your fate in this respect—
wherever your lot may be cast—whatever may befall
you—it will be a consolation for you to know that the
people of this country are a grateful people. You have
had ample evidence of this at every step of your progress
since your return. They hold in constant remembrance

those of their kith and kin who have gone forth in defense of the country, and are in the field as the protectors
of their homes and their firesides.   The Twentieth,
One Hundred and Twentieth, and the One Hundred and
Fifty-sixth, are numbers indelibly impressed upon the
memory of the people of Ulster, and which will hereafter be engraven upon the granite of her mountains. To
those of you who survive the conflict and return to enjoy the fruits of your labors in a peaceful and undis-
severed country, we pledge a heartfelt welcome and
God's benison. To those who shall leave their bones
to bleach on a southern soil, we pledge a place upon the
monumental marble upon an equality with and alongside of your fathers of 1776, which every returning year
shall brighten with the halo of glory which the blessings
of increased millions shall shed upon it."

Colonel Gates responded in behalf of the regiment,
and after other addresses and an eloquent prayer, the
battalion moved off amid a vast throng of people to
Rondout, embarked on board the steamer Thomas
Cornell, and proceeded to New York.

March 29.—Battalion transported to the ocean
steamer America, and sailed for Washington, D. C.,
proceeding thence *via* Orange and Alexandria railroad,
to Brandy Station, Va., where it rejoined the balance
of the regiment.

May 4.—All detachments, except the one at army
headquarters, ordered to report at Brandy Station as
soon as the public property at their several stations was
removed.   At different times during the day the various
detachments reported at headquarters and were placed
on duty, guarding the public property at the depot and
picketing the country in the neighborhood.   At 11
o'clock P M., all public property having been removed
or burned, and the station destroyed, the pickets were
recalled and the regiment took its line of march to re-

join the army, then one day's march ahead. Marched to Stephensburg, a distance of five miles, and bivouacked.

May 5.—Resumed march, at 6 A. M., crossed the Rapidan at Gold Mine Ford, and reached Headquarters Army of the Potomac, at Wilderness Tavern, in "the Wilderness," at 7 P. M., having marched eighteen miles.

From this time until May 8, engaged in guarding prisoners of war.

May 8.—Marched at 1½ A. M. in charge of prisoners of war ; passed through Chancellorsville, and encamped at 7 P. M. near Pine Branch Church ; distance marched, twenty miles.

May 9.—Marched about six miles and encamped on north side of Fredericksburg and Orange Plank-road.

May 12.—Marched to near New Salem Church, on plank-road, six miles from last camp.

May 13.—Marched at six A. M., in charge of 7,000 prisoners of war (Johnson's Division, Ewell's Corps), through Fredericksburg, across the Rappahannock river to Belle Plain, on the Potomac river, being supported by the troops designated below, the whole under the command of Colonel Gates of this regiment. Distance marched, seventeen miles. Among these prisoners were Major-General Ed. Johnson and Brigadier-General Geo. H. Stewart.

May 14.—At daybreak, Colonel Gates orderd the cavalry to return, and at 2 P. M., having delivered the prisoners to the Veteran Reserve Corps, the infantry and battery took up their line of march, and at sunset, after reaching the Rappahannock river, opposite the city of Fredericksburg, bivouacked, having marched sixteen miles, part of the distance through a furious storm of wind and rain, which flooded the small streams, forcing the regiment to build bridges to allow the artillery to cross.

May 15.—Marched at 8 A. M., crossed the Rappahannock river, passed through and encamped in the rear of Fredericksburg. Distance marched, two miles.

May 21.—Colonel Gates ordered the battery of artillery to report to chief of artillery   G and I Companies marched to Belle Plain, in charge of prisoners of war. Remainder of regiment marched at seven P. M. to and through Fredericksburg, down the Bowling Green road, and bivouacked at 12 P. M. near the Massaponey river, having marched four miles.

May 22.—Marched at 5 A. M., following the Bowling Green road, and halted for the night near Welven. Distance marched, ten miles.

May 23.—Companies G and I joined the regiment, having marched forty-four miles. Marched at 7 A. M., and encamped at Milford, on the Mattaponey river, having marched nine miles.

May 24.—Marched at 3 P M., crossing the Mattaponey river at Milford, and encamped near Wright's Tavern. Distance marched four miles.

May 27.—Marched at 7 A. M., recrossing the Mattaponey at Milford, and encamped a mile west of the Mattacocy, having marched fifteen miles.

May 28.—Marched at 7 A. M., and passed through Newtown, encamped near the Mattaponey, opposite Dunkirk. Distance marched, twelve miles.

May 29.—Marched at 7 A. M. and encamped two miles north of the Pamunkey, opposite Newcastle. Distance marched, ten miles.

May 30. —Crossed the Pamunkey on a pontoon bridge, and encamped two miles from bridge, on the Hanover Court House road ; A and K companies guarding bridge.

May 31.—Moved back one mile nearer bridge. During this month the regiment was engaged in guarding prisoners of war and bridges, protecting wagon trains, doing picket duty, acting as rearguard to the army and

35

performing the general provost duty of the Army of the
Potomac. The total number of rebel prisoners received
by the regiment during the month was 10,315.

June 1.—Marched at 11 A.M. toward White House,
Va., and bivouacked near Old Church. Distance
marched, nine miles.

June 2.—Marching at 8 A. M., and passing Old
Church, encamped at Parsley's Corners, near Anderson's
Mills, three miles east of Coal Harbor, and five miles
from last camp.

June 11.—Marched at 3 P M., and bivouacked at 7½
P. M., at Tunstall's Station. Distance marched, eight
miles.

June 12.—Marched at 6 P. M., to near White House,
and bivouacked. Distance marched, four miles.

June 13.—Marched at 6 A. M., and taking the River
road, passed Cumberland Landing and Slatersville, and
bivouacked at 6 P. M., at Roper's Church, having
marched twenty miles.

June 14.—Marched at 5½ A. M., three miles and encamped.

June 15.—Marched at 3 P. M., crossing the Chicka-
hominy at 6 P. M., on a pontoon bridge, and bivouacked
at 3 A. M. Distance marched, fifteen miles.

June 16.—Marched at 5 A. M., to the James river, opposite Fort Powhattan, crossed the river at 3 P.M., on a
pontoon bridge, and bivouacked one mile beyond.

June 17.—Marched at 6 A. M., passed Merchants'
Hope church and bivouacked at Knox's Cross Roads at
4 P. M. Distance marched, eighteen miles.

June 18.—Marched at 3 P M. to City Point and encamped. Distance marched, three miles. Colonel
Gates appointed military commandant at City Point.

June 23.—Lieutenant-Colonel Hardenburgh, with a
detachment, consisting of Adjutant J. M. Schoonmaker,
Captain William H. Cunningham, Lieutenant Smith

and Assistant-Surgeon Wm. H. Taylor, and eighty men, embarked on steamer Guide, to proceed to Point Lookout and Fort Delaware, as guard for 700 prisoners of war.

June 25.—Regiment, pursuant to orders from Lieutenant-General Grant, embarked on transport and proceeded to Wilcox Landing, where it disembarked and marched toward Charles City Court House, to report to Major-General Sheridan. After marching five miles, was ordered to occupy earth-works two miles nearer the landing, under command of General Getty, where remained about three hours, when detachment returned to the landing and bivouacked.

June 26.—By order of General Sheridan, embarked on steamer and returned to City Point.

June 29.—Lieutenant-Colonel Hardenburgh and detachment joined the regiment.

During this month and July, the regiment was engaged in doing the general provost duty for the "Armies operating against Richmond," having charge of all trains running on the City Point and Petersburg railroad, all mail steamers running to and from Bermuda Hundred, City Point and points north, and the charge of the secret service boat, a detachment of the regiment being in that service and a large number of the officers on staff and special duty

August 9.—A vessel loaded with ordnance stores, lying in the harbor at City Point, blew up at 11 A. M., causing great destruction of property and killing and wounding a large number of men. The loss of the regiment by this accident was five killed and seventeen wounded. From this time till November the regiment continued doing the same kind of duty, nothing worthy of note occurring, except a march of the regiment a few miles and back in attempting to intercept Wade Hampton's cavalry, who had stolen a large herd of cattle. The regiment presented to Brigadier-General M. R. Patrick, Provost-Marshal-General "Armies operating against Richmond" (under whose command they had been for a long time), a magnificent sword, belt, sash and spurs.

On the 24th of November, Colonel T. B. Gates, who had commanded the regiment from the time that Colonel G. W Pratt was wounded, was mustered out on account of the expiration of his term of service, and Lieutenant-Colonel J. B. Hardenburgh assumed his place as Colonel of the regiment, and as military commandant of the post and defenses of City Point.

An address of the officers and men of the Twentieth Reg. N. Y S. M., was presented to Colonel Theodore B. Gates, on the occasion of his taking leaving of them at the expiration of his term of service, as follows :

"COLONEL GATES : The officers and men of your command approach you with feelings of deep regret on this occasion. We are well aware that it is no unusual occurrence for an officer who has faithfully done his duty to retire from his command, leaving behind him some of his old companions, and almost always bearing with him the regard and esteem, as also the affection of his men, but it has yet to be learned that *any* officer has ever left behind him in the field a body of men who more sincerely and deeply feel the loss they are sustaining than do the officers and men of the Twentieth Regiment, N. Y S. M.

"Having been so long together—having fought side by side—having endured hardships together—now, that you leave us, you carry with you the most profound esteem—the sincerest regard—and, above all, the deep affection of your fellow-soldiers.

"It is, beyond all question, a matter which concerns us deeply ; for we feel that, in losing *you* we lose one whose sympathies have ever been with us—whose voice has always cheered us—whose smile has ever encouraged us, and where *we* have failed in our duty, we know that *you* have never failed in yours.

" We make no allusion to your career as a gallant soldier—*that* is recorded in the *hearts* of your men, and will be read in the annals of this warfare. Trifling as may seem to you this small tribute of our esteem and affection, be assured that it is dictated by warm and loving hearts toward one, whose life and career, among us, has proved him to be a true patriot, a brave soldier, and an earnest-minded, Christian gentleman.

" It may not be inappropriate to say that this tumult of warm affection toward you, which your pro· posed departure has aroused among us, is not the spontaneous impulse of the moment, but it is the welling forth from the very depths of the fountains of our hearts of *that* feeling which can no longer be restrained within bounds.

" It may, perhaps, be some slight satisfaction to you, to know that it is to your example we are indebted for much that is good in us. We feel it and *know* it. It may be a greater satisfaction to you to be assured that that example shall always stand before us as a bright and guiding star, the luster of whose splendor shall not be dimmed by any fault of ours, in an earnest endeavor to sustain the enviable reputation which you have conferred on our regiment.

" Now that you are returning to your home and the duties of civil life, you bear with you our heartfelt and earnest wishes for the future prosperity and happiness of yourself, Mrs. Gates, and your family, and, since the storm of battle for *you* has passed, may the future, which lies before you, be as bright and glorious in its results, as the past has been distinguished by your nobleness and valor !

"That He, who has thus far preserved you, may keep you, with those who are dear to you, safe unto the end, is the earnest prayer of the officers and men of the Twentieth Regiment, New York State Militia."

During the months of November and December, the regiment continued in the performance of the same and similar duties as they had done since their arrival at City Point, nothing of particular interest occurring, except turning out twice during the night time, and marching to the defenses, to repulse threatened attacks of the enemy.

January 1, 1865.—Encamped at City Point, Va., doing guard duty and the provost duty for the "Armies operating against Richmond."

February 15.—Colonel Hardenburgh relieved from command of post of City Point by Brevet Brigadier-General C. H. T. Collis, and assumed command of the regiment—General Collis' regiment having been ordered to duty there. .

February 16.—Major J. R. Leslie was assigned to the temporary command of the Eighth Regiment Delaware Volunteers, lying at City Point.

During the balance of this month and the month of March, the regiment continued performing the same kind of duties as heretofore mentioned ; turning out once and marching to repulse the enemy, who had broken through our lines at Fort Stedman, but the enemy retiring, the regiment returned to camp.

April 2.—Received orders about 4 A. M., for the regiment to march, with brigade, to occupy the works which had recently been thrown up on the heights above City Point, to act as a reserve and support to an attack which had been ordered by General Grant, to be made at daylight, along the whole front of the lines, investing Petersburg and Richmond. The regiment marched as ordered and reached the position assigned it, just south of the City Point and Petersburg railroad at dawn. A portion of the enemy's works (including Fort Mahone, known more familiarly as "Fort Damnation"), having been carried by assault by the Ninth Corps, and the enemy having made several attempts to recover them, which had been repulsed, and it being feared that, as they were the key-point of that line, the enemy would again endeavor to take them at all hazards, the brigade, to which the regiment was attached, was ordered, at 7 A. M., to move to their support. With the utmost expedition they moved accordingly— most of the way at a double-quick—to Fort Sedgwick (generally known as "Fort Hell"). Upon their arrival they were immediately formed in line of battle, and ordered to move forward and occupy Fort Mahone ; the enemy still occupied the line to the left of Fort Mahone, and were thus enabled to keep up an enfilading fire over the ground the regiment was compelled to pass in moving from Fort Sedgwick to Fort Mahone. This fire was very severe, during the time the regiment was taking up its position, occasioning considerable loss to it. Just after the position was attained, the enemy having concentrated their forces, made a desperate charge, in hopes of re-capturing the fort, but were repulsed with heavy loss to them. They then retreated to their inner line of works, and opened a brisk musketry fire, which was kept up until about 10 P. M. During the night, the brigade moved forward and captured a lunette work in front of Fort Mahone, mounting two casemate howitzers, which enfiladed the works to the right of the fort. Shortly afterward, fires were seen at several points along the line, and in the direction of Petersburg and Richmond, and several heavy explosions were heard, showing conclusively that the enemy were evacuating those places.

April 3.—About 3 A. M. the brigade was ordered forward. They advanced rapidly on Petersburg, found the enemy's inner line of works abandoned, and reached the city just at daylight. The color-sergeant and color-guard proceeded to a conspicuous house near by and hoisted the Stars and Stripes over it. This was the first United States flag that waved in this city's limits after the passage of the Ordinance of Secession by the State of Virginia. The regiment remained in Petersburg until the afternoon, when it marched back to City Point and occupied its own quarters.

April 7.—The following order was promulgated:

HEADQUARTERS POST, CITY POINT, Va.
April 7, 1865.

General Orders No. 12.

In the recent operations which resulted in the capture of Petersburg and Richmond, the troops of this command have borne a conspicuous part, and their gallantry is the theme of universal praise. They were called upon to repulse a desperate enemy, flushed with a temporary success, which threatened to deprive us of ground which had already cost our troops dearly; and they moved forward to the work with such enthusiasm and determination that the enemy was driven from his stronghold in confusion. The skirmishers of this command were the first to enter the besieged city, and it is believed our colors were the first to float over it. We have lost many valuable officers and men who cannot be replaced, but it is a comfort to those who survive to feel that each of his fallen comrades was at his post, nobly doing his duty

By command of
Brevet-Brigadier-General C. H. T. COLLIS

April 14.—Pursuant to orders from Lieutenant-General Grant, the regiment was relieved from duty at the post of City Point, and ordered to report to Brigadier-

General M. R. Patrick, Provost-Marshal-General. On reporting to General Patrick they were ordered to proceed to Richmond. Embarked the same day, and proceeded to the city of Richmond, where disembarked, marched through the city to Howard's Grove, where occupied barracks formerly used by the rebels as a hospital.

April 22.—Pursuant to Special Orders No. 1, Headquarters Military Commander City of Richmond, this regiment and the Twenty-fourth Massachusetts Volunteers were constituted the provost guard of that city, "under the direction of the Provost-Marshal-General."

From this time until November, the regiment was engaged in the performance of provost duty in the city of Richmond, and the administering of the government of the same. While the regiment was in Richmond, in July of this year, Colonel Hardenburgh made a written application to have the regiment mustered out. The application was returned with the following endorsement of General Turner, who then commanded the District of Henrico to General Terry, who commanded the Department of Virginia :

HEADQUARTERS, DISTRICT OF HENRICO,
RICHMOND, Va.,
July 10, 1865.

Respectfully forwarded—disapproved. To dispense with the services of this regiment now would greatly disarrange the management of officers in the city of Richmond. *The regiment is very efficient,* and many of its officers are on special duty in the city The experience they have acquired makes them now very valuable, and their places could, with difficulty, be filled.

JOHN W TURNER,
Brevet-Major-General Commanding.

To show the extent of their duties and how multifarious they were, a list of the officers detached for special duty in the month of June is hereto annexed:

Colonel J. B. Hardenburgh, President of a General Court Marshal.

Lieutenant-Colonel J. McEntee, Provost Judge—duties same as Mayor of the city

Major J. R. Leslie, Provost Marshal Fourth District, City of Richmond.

Surgeon R. Loughran, Medical Director, District of Henrico.

Assistant Surgeon C. L. Humphrey, in charge of Alms House, County of Henrico.

Captain E. M. Misner, Company A, President of the Relief Committee.

Captain Isaac Buswell, Company B, member of General Court-Martial.

Brevet-Major, Captain Martin Snyder, Company C, Commanding Provost Guard, Fourth District.

Captain J. M. Schoonmaker, Company D, Aide-de-Camp to Brevet-Major-General Turner and Commanding Military Prisons, viz. : Libby Prison, Castle Thunder, City Jail, State Penitentiary, and Depot of Distribution.

Captain W. W. Beckwith, Company E, Aide-de-Camp to General Turner, and Assistant Provost-Marshal-General, District of Henrico.

Captain N. Hoysradt, Company F, Assistant Provost Judge, city of Richmond.

Captain M. J. C. Woodworth, Company G, officer Provost Guard, Fourth District.

Captain G. B. Mulks, Company H, officer Provost Guard, Second District.

Captain Charles S. Parker, Company I, officer Provost Guard, Fourth District.

Captain D. J. France, Company K, Commanding Provost Guard, Second District.

Lieutenant John I. Smith, Company A, in Command of Alms House.

Lieutenant Timothy Murray, Company B, officer of the Provost Guard, Fourth District.

Lieutenant Jacob H. Winfield, Company C, Aide-de-Camp to Brevet Major-General Turner, Commanding District of Henrico.

Lieutenant John H. Dunn, Company C, officer Provost Guard, Fourth District.

Lieutenant James Hatch, Company D, Street Commissioner, city of Richmond.

Lieutenant Lyman Hoysradt, Company F, Commanding Guard at State Penitentiary.

Lieutenant Isaac Thomas, Company G, officer Provost Guard, Fourth District.

Lieutenant E. B. Townsend, Company G, Aide-de-Camp to General Turner.

Lieutenant Eugene Subit, Company H, officer Provost Guard, Second District.

Lieutenant Remsen Varick, Company I, Commanding Provost Guard at Rockett's (steamboat landing).

Lieutenant S. F. B. Gillespie, Company I, Assistant to Provost-Marshal-General Department of Virginia.

Lieutenant Richard E. Houghtaling, Company K, officer Provost Guard, Second district.

November 27.—Regiment embarked at Rockett's on steamers, under orders to report at Norfolk, to Brevet Major-General A. F A. Torbert, Commanding District of Southeastern Virginia, leaving the following named officers at Richmond, performing the duties heretofore named, viz: Lieutenant-Colonel J McEntee, Captain N. Hoysradt, Surgeon R. Loughran, Captain J. M. Schoonmaker, Captain E. M. Misner, Captain W W Beckwith, Lieutenant J H. Winfield, Lieutenant L. Hoysradt, and Lieutenant S. F. B. Gillespie. During the balance of this month, the regiment was engaged in

performing Provost and Guard duty at Norfolk, Ports-
mouth Navy Yard, and the hard-labor prison.

December 18.—Pursuant to Special Orders No. 71,
Headquarters District of Southeastern Virginia, Brevet
Brigadier-General J. B. Hardenburgh assumed command
of that district, with headquarters at Norfolk. The
duties of the regiment, during this month, were similar
to those performed during November.

1866.

The regiment continued in the performance of the
same duties until January 29th, when it was mustered
out and returned home, after halting at New York City
to be paid off.

Previous to the dismissal of the regiment, Colonel
Hardenburgh, addressed the officers and men as follows:

"OFFICERS AND SOLDIERS OF THE TWENTIETH: The
time has at last arrived—which you have so long and so
anxiously looked forward to—when you are to be honorably discharged the service and permitted to return
to your homes. We are now about to separate—many
of us forever.

"What recollections come crowding upon our memory of common dangers and sufferings, joys and sorrows
—of the monotonous camp, the weary march and the
terrible conflict. What silent prayers go up from joyful hearts, that we are spared to return to our friends
and homes.

"I could not trust myself, if I could find words to
express to you all that I feel on this occasion. I have
been so long and so intimately connected with the 'Old
Twentieth,' that I feel as if I were about to part with a
dear old friend, whose familiar face I should see no
more forever. I cannot, however, permit the occasion
to pass without returning to you, briefly, my sincere
thanks for the uniform respect, cheerful obedience and

strict attention to duty you have ever evinced in your different relations to the regiment. Whatever my shortcomings may have been (and I know they have not been few), I have the satisfaction to know that ' I have endeavored to do my duty '

"The name and reputation of the Twentieth, have ever been most dear to me, and during my connection with it, I have endeavored to keep constantly in view its interest and honor.

"I exceedingly regret that the regiment could not have gone home as an organization and been finally discharged at its original rendezvous. There is nothing I more greatly desired, or that would have afforded me greater pleasure, and I am sure this is the feeling of a very large majority of the regiment.* But on account of the want of proper accommodation there for the men, at this season, during the time they would necessarily have to be detained, before receiving their final pay and discharges, the matter was deemed unadvisable and impracticable. It was supposed that at this place, which had been used so long as one of the regularly established depots for recruits and regiments to be mustered out, we would find everything which the season and climate rendered necessary, under the circumstances, for your health and comfort. But I regret to say that we have been most sadly disappointed. If I could have forseen the shameful and disgraceful state of things here, I certainly would have used every effort in my power to have had the regiment ordered to Kingston; for however we might have fared there, we certainly could not have fared worse than we have here.

"I regret the more that we could not have gone home as a regiment, because I know it would have afforded the friends of the regiment great pleasure to have extended to it a most cordial welcome. They have had in course of preparation for some time a new color, which it was intended to have presented to the regiment upon its arrival in New York. Colonel Gates came down for that purpose last Tuesday, but upon his arrival here he found that it was not finished, and so the presentation had to be deferred to some future time. It is now proposed by the citizens of Kingston, as a testimonial of the honor and esteem with which they have ever regarded the 'Old Twentieth,' to give an entertainment to the members of the regiment on the 22d of February next, and at that time to present the colors, and I am requested to give a cordial invitation to every member of the regiment on that occasion. I hope that all who can possibly do so will be present in their proper uniform.

"One word more and I am done. You are now about to quit the military service and return once more to the quiet walks of civil life. You belong to a regiment which has achieved a name and reputation which will go down through all coming time, and which you and those who may come after you will hereafter contemplate with pride and satisfaction. As you have been good and efficient soldiers, so I know you will be good and exemplary citizens, ever remembering that your duties as citizens are no less important.

> ' Peace hath her victories,
> No less renowned than war.'

"I hope you may long live to enjoy, through uninterrupted peace and prosperity, the rewards you have so richly earned, and that the choicest blessings of Heaven may ever abide with you and yours.

"And now, comrades, it only remains for me to pronounce the parting word—Farewell."

February 22.—Pursuant to previous notice, the regiment assembled to receive the flag which had been obtained for them by the citizens of Kingston. The fol-

lowing extract from one of the village newspapers narrates the circumstances incident thereto:

"On the 22d inst., the ceremonies attendant upon
the presentation of a regimental flag to the Twentieth
N Y.S.M., took place at the armory in this village.
A large number of citizens and soldiers were present.
Major Von Beck, of Rondout, was called to the chair.
That veteran vocalist, Mr. Bernard Covert, was then
introduced and sang an appropriate patriotic song. The
presentation speech was made by H. H. Reynolds,
Esq., of this village. [It may be found in Appendix C.]

"The color is of blue silk, with the State arms beau-
tifully embroidered in the centre. Over these, and
likewise embroidered, are the words 'Ulster Guard,'
Twentieth N. Y S. M., and worked upon the colors, in
different positions, is the following regimental record:
'Washington, April, 1861 ; Beverly Ford, August 21,
1862 ; Warrenton Springs, August 27, 1862 ; Gainesville, August 28, 1862 ; Groveton, August 29, 1862 ;
Second Bull Run, August 30, 1862; Chantilly, September 1, 1862 ; South Mountain, September 14, 1862 ; Antietam, September 17, 1862 ; Fredericksburg, December
12 to 15, 1862 ; Gettysburg, July 1 to 4, 1863 ; Petersburg, April 1 to 3, 1865 ; Richmond, April, 1865.'

"After the services were concluded, the soldiers were
invited to the upper room of the armory, where a most
bounteous collation was spread, and the tables were attended by fair women who gave our brave boys a cordial
welcome and a luxuriant repast. The entire affair was
a most gratifying success.

"On the evening of the same day the officers of the
regiment held a meeting at Brown's Hotel, in the village
of Kingston, at which it was unanimously resolved that
the regiment should be immediately reorganized under
the National Guard law of this State; and designating,
on motion of Colonel Hardenburgh, as their choice for

commandant. Colonel T. B. Gates. It was further resolved that Colonel J. B. Hardenburgh, Major W. A.
Van Rensselaer, Captain J. M. Schoonmaker, and Lieu
tenant Geo. North, Jr., be appointed a committee to
assist Colonel Gates in reorganizing the regiment.''

B.

COMPLETE ROSTER

OF

THE TWENTIETH REGIMENT, N.Y.S.M.

FROM SEPTEMBER, 1861, TO JANUARY, 1866.

Total number of Officers, ninety-six; of whom thirty-five were promoted from the ranks.

Seven Officers were killed in battle, and thirty-one wounded.

Four were promoted to higher grades in other regiments.

Eleven were discharged on account of disability resulting from wounds or sickness.

Thirty-three were mustered out by reason of resignation or expiration of terms, and six dismissed.

NOTE.—The muster-out of C. D. Westbrook, Captain of Engineers, and of the two officers whose names immediately succeed his, was on the ground that the regiment was not entitled to such officers.

COMPLETE ROSTER OF THE TWENTIETH REGIMENT, N.Y.S.M.

NAMES.	RANK.	JOINED FOR SERVICE. WHEN,	WHERE.	REMARKS.
Field and Staff.				
Jacob B. Hardenburgh...	Colonel	Sept. 5, '61	Kingston, N.Y.	Mustered as Major, Sept. 10, 1861. Promoted to Lieut.-Colonel, Sept. 11, 1862; Colonel, Dec. 19, 1864. Bvt. B. G. U.S.V.
John McEntee...	Lieut. Col.	Sept. 24, '61	Kingston, N.Y.	Promoted 1st Lieut. Sept. 11, '62; Captain, Dec. 19, '64; Lieut.-Colonel, Dec. 19, '64. Retained in service by order of Secretary of War on duty connected with Freedmen's Bureau. No discharge furnished.
John R. Leslie...	Major	Oct. 1, '61	Kingston, N.Y.	Mustered as 1st Lieut. Sept. 10, '61. Promoted to Captain Sept. 10, '62; Major, Jan. 11, '65.
George G. Masten...	Adjutant	Jan. 1, '64	Brandy Sta., Va.	Appointed Adjutant from 1st Lieut. C Co. March 6, '65.
Standish V. Cornish...	Q'rmaster	Mar. 10, '62	Po'keepsie, N.Y.	Promoted 1st Lieut. April 15, '65. Appointed Quartermaster, June 15, '65.
Robert Longhran...	Surgeon	Sept. 5, '61	Kingston, N.Y.	Mustered as Surgeon, Oct. 3, '61. Dept. Surg. at Richmond, Va. No discharge furnished.
William Taylor...	Ast.-Surg.	...	...	Mustered as Assist.-Surg. July 3, '63.
Former Com'ding Officers.				
Died.				
George W Pratt...	Colonel	Sept. 5, '61	Kingston, N.Y.	Died at Albany, N.Y. (of wounds received at Manassas), September 11, '62.
Discharged.				
Theodore B. Gates. ...	Colonel	Sept. 5, '61	Kingston, N.Y.	Mustered as Lieut.-Colonel, Sept. 5, '61. Promoted Colonel, Sept. 11, '62. Mustered out, Nov. 22, '64. Bvt. B. G. U.S.V.
John M. Schoonmaker...	Adjutant	Sept. 5, '61	Kingston, N.Y.	Mustered as Adjutant, Sept. 25, '61. Mustered out, Oct. 25, '64.
Cornelius D. Westbrook. ...	Engineer	Sept. 5, '61	Kingston, N.Y.	Mustered out by order Secretary of War, Nov. 17, '61.
Dumond Elmondorf. ...	Commis'ry	Sept. 5, '61	Kingston, N.Y.	Mustered out by order Secretary of War, Nov. 17, '61.
Selah O. Tuthill. ...	Paymaster	Oct. 23, '61	Kingston, N.Y.	Mustered out by order Secretary of War, Nov. 17, '61.

Name	Rank	Date	Place	Remarks
Walter A. Van Rensselaer	Major	Sept. 10, '61	Kingston, N.Y.	Mustered as Captain, Sept. 10, '61. Promoted Major, Sept. 22, '62. Promoted Major, Nov. 14, '64.
William S. Freligh	Q'rmaster	Nov. 18, '62	Upton Hill, Va.	Mustered out, Dec. 8, '64.
Resigned.				
John S. Griffiths	Q'rmaster	Sept. 5, '61	Kingston, N.Y.	Resigned Feb. 2, '63.
Cornelius Van Santvoord	Chaplain	Oct. 10, '61	Kingston, N.Y.	" Nov. 18, '62.
Thomas W. Street	Chaplain	May 28, '64	City Point, Va.	" May 17, '65.
Correl L. Humphrey	Ast. Surg.	Mar. 16, '65	City Point, Va.	" June 13, '65.
Transferred.				
George B. Mulks	Adjutant	Sept. 25, '61	Kingston, N.Y.	Appointed Adjutant Oct. 19, '64. Relieved from duty as Adjutant March 6, '65 (assigned to C Co.)
Amos B. Ferguson	Q'rmaster	Jan. 1, '64	Brandy Sta., Va.	Appointed Q'rmaster Dec. 9, '64. Relieved from duty as Q'rmaster June 15, '65 (assigned to K Co.)
Promoted in other Regiments.				
Robert K. Tuthill	Ast. Surg.	Oct. 3, '61	Kingston, N.Y.	Promoted and mustered Surgeon 145th N.Y.V., May 23, '63.
Howard E. Gates	Ast. Surg.	Aug. 19, '62	New York City	Promoted and mustered Surgeon 180th N.Y.V., Nov. 23, '64.
Officers of Company A.				
Elson M. Misner	Captain	Jan. 2, '65	City Point, Va.	Promoted from 1st Lieut. K Co. to Captain, and assigned to A Co. Joined for service Sept. 18, '61; re-enlisted as Vet. Vol. Dec. 31, '63.
Discharged.				
John J. Smith	1st Lieut.	Dec. 8, '65	Norfolk, Va.	Promoted Corporal, April 4, '64; Sergt. April 28, '64; 1st Sergt. Oct. 1, '64; 2d Lieut. May 8, '65; 1st Lieut. Dec. 8, '65. Has pay due for Comd of Co. (responsibility of arms) for the months of November and December, '65, and January, '66.
James Smith	Captain	Sept. 10, '61	Kingston, N.Y.	Discharged by reason of promotion to Lieut.-Colonel 128th N.Y. Vols. Sept. 5, '62.
Charles S. Wilkinson	1st Lieut.	Sept. 10, '61	Kingston, N.Y.	Discharged by reason of Surgeon's certificate of disability, Sept. 18, '63.
Joseph H. Harrison	2d Lieut.	Sept. 10, '61	Kingston, N.Y.	Dismissed from U. S. service, Sept. 5, '62.
Thomas W Rider	2d Lieut.	Sept. 10, '61	Kingston, N.Y.	Promoted from private to 2d Lieut. A Co. Nov. 1, '62. Discharged by reason of resignation, Feb. 2, '62.

NAMES.	RANK.	JOINED FOR SERVICE.		REMARKS.
		WHEN.	**WHERE.**	
Company A—_Continued._				
John Bevines	1st Lieut.	Sept. 5, '64	Utica, N.Y.	Transferred from Ind. Comp. to A Co. 20th N.Y.S.M. Nov. 6, '64.
Lewis Thomas.	2d Lieut.	Sept. 5, '64	Utica, N.Y.	Discharged by reason of resignation, June 18, '65.
Transferred.				
John W Carr.	2d Lieut.	June 6, '64	City Point, Va.	Transferred from Ind. Comp. to A Co. 20th N.Y.S.M. Nov. 6, '64. Dismissed U. S. service by order President, Dec. 28, '64.
J. H. Windfield.	2d Lieut.	Dec. 24, '64	City Point, Va.	Promoted from Sergt.-Major to 2d Lieut. and assigned to A Co. June 6, '64 ; 1st Lieut. (assigned to E Co.) Nov. 2, '64.
M. J. C. Woodworth.	1st Lieut.	Nov. 2, '61	Antietam	Promoted from private 120th N.Y. Vols. to 2d Lieut. Co. A 20th N.Y.S.M. Dec. 24, '64 ; 1st Lieut. (transfer'd to C Co.) May 8, '65.
John McEntee.	Captain	Oct. 13, '62	Lovets Ville, Md.	Promoted from 1st Sergt. I Co. to 1st Lieut. A Co. Nov. 1, '62 ; Capt. Dec. 23, '64, and assigned to G Co.
Officers of Company B.				Promoted from 2d Lieut. K Co. to Capt. (assigned to A Co.) Oct. 13, '62 ; Lieut.-Colonel, and assigned to Field and Staff.
Isaac C. Buswell.	Captain	Jan. 11, '65	City Point, Va.	Joined service as private Sept. 8, '61. Promoted Corporal Sept. 10, '61; Sergt. Nov. 14, '62; 1st Sergt. March 19, '63; 1st Lieut. July 2, '64; Capt. Jan. 11, '65. Has pay due for Comd. Co. (responsibility of arms, &c.) from Oct. 31, '64, to date of muster out.
Timothy Murray.	1st Lieut.	Feb. 18, '65	City Point, Va.	Joined service as 2d Lieut. from 4th U. S. Infantry, Dec. 25, '64. Promoted 1st Lieut. Feb. 18, '65.
Discharged.				
James Hatch.	1st Lieut.	Sept. 5, '61	Kingston, N.Y.	Joined service Sept. 5, '61. Promoted 1st Sergt. Sept. 6, '61; 2d Lieut. May 1, '62; 1st Lieut. Sept. 11, '62. Discharged for disability March 28, '63.
Charles R. Near.	2d Lieut.	Sept. 10, '61	Kingston, N.Y.	Joined service Sept. 10, '61, as 2d Lieut. Cashiered May 1, '62, by sentence of G. C. M, per G. Orders No.
Phillip Deits.	2d Lieut.	Sept. 5, '61	Kingston, N.Y.	Joined service Sept. 5, '61. Promoted Sergt. Sept. 6, '61; 1st Sergt. May 1, '62; 2d Lieut. Sept. 11, '63. Dismissed the service April 21, '64, per sentence of G. C. M. Gen. Orders No.

Transferred.				
Walter A. Van Rensselaer	Captain	Sept. 10, '61	Kingston, N.Y.	Joined service as Captain Sept. 10, '61. Promoted **Major** Sept. 11, '62.
John R. Leslie	Captain	Oct. 1, '61	Kingston, N.Y.	Joined service as 1st Lieut. Oct. 1, '62; Major, Jan. 11, '65. Promoted **Captain** Sept. 11, '62.
Amos B. Ferguson	2d Lieut.	Sept. 27, '64	City Point, Va.	Joined Co. as 2d Lieut. by promotion from Q'rmaster of the Regt. Dec. 10, '64. Appointed Q'rmaster-Sergt. Sept. 27, '64.
Officers of Company C.				
Martin Snyder	Captain & Bvt. Major	Sept. 22, '62	Sharpsburg, Md.	Joined service as 2d Lieut. Sept. 7, '61. Due for Comd'g Co. **$10** per month for the months of June, July, and August, '65. Promoted Captain from 2d Lieut. Sept. 22, '62; from Captain to Bvt.-Major, April 5, '65.
Jacob H. Winfield	1st Lieut.	May 8, '65	Richmond, Va.	On detached service at Richmond, Va. No discharge furnished. Vet. Vol. joined for service Sept. 25, '61, as private. Promoted Corporal March 23, '63; Sergt. July 11, '64; Sergt.-Major, Jan.
John H. Dunn	2d Lieut.	April 18, '65	Richmond, Va.	10, '65; 2d Lieut. April 18, '65.
Discharged.				
Andrew S. Schutt	1st Lieut.	Sept. 5, '61	Kingston, N.Y.	Discharged Sept. 5, '64, at City Point, by reason of expiration of term of service.
James Flemming	2d Lieut.	Sept. 10, '61	Kingston, N.Y.	Promoted Sergt. Sept. 10, '61; 2d Lieut. Sept. 22, '62. Dismissed by S. G. C. M. Sept. 22, '64.
Transferred.				
John Rudolph Tappen	Captain	Sept. 22, '61	Kingston, N.Y.	Transferred to 120th N.Y. Vols. by reason of promotion to Major, July 8, '62.
George B. Mulks	1st Lieut.	Sept. 27, '61	Kingston, N.Y.	Transferred from Field and Staff to Co. C, March 6, '65; promoted Captain, May 5, '65, and transferred to H Co.
George G. Masten	1st Lieut.	Jan. 2, '64	Brandy Sta., Va.	Transferred from C Co. to Field and Staff as Adjutant, Mar. 6, '65.
Officers of Company D.				
John M. Schoonmaker	Captain			On detached service at Richmond, Va. No discharge furnished. Promoted to 1st Lieut. Nov. 9, '64,
James Hatch	1st Lieut.	Nov. 9, '64	Near Petersburg, Va.	Vet. Vol. joined as private. Promoted to 1st Lieut. Nov. 9, '64, and assigned to D Co. Pay (from April 14, '65, to July, 31, '65—3 mos. 16 days) due for Comd'g Co. and responsibility for arms.

NAMES.	RANK.	JOINED FOR SERVICE.		REMARKS.
		WHEN.	WHERE.	
cers Co. D—Cont'd. bram D. Miller...	2d Lieut.	July 2, '65	Richmond, Va.	Vet. Vol. joined as private Sept. 15, '61. Appointed Sergt. Jan. 1, '63, and to 1st Sergt. Feb. 3, '63. Re-enlisted Dec. 30, '63; appointed 1st Sergt. at the same date. Promoted 2d Lieut. July 2, '65. Pay due for Com'd'g Co. and responsibility for arms, &c., from Oct. 31, '65, to date of muster out.
Discharged. aniel McMahon.	Captain	Sept. 15, '61	Kingston, N.Y.	June 28, '64, from wounds received. S. O. No. 227, War Depar't, A. G. O. June 28, '64.
enry Mick.... ..	1st Lieut.	Sept. 12, '61	Kingston, N.Y.	Promoted to 1st Lieut. Oct. 4, '61. Resigned Sept. 30, '62.
ames G. Wilson......	2d Lieut.	Sept. 5, '61	Kingston, N.Y	Joined as private Sept. 5, '61. Promoted Sergt. and to 2d Lieut. Oct. 4, '61. Resigned May 17, '62.
enry Clark....	2d Lieut.	.. ..	......	Promoted from Sergt.-Major to 2d Lieut. and assigned to D Co. August, '62. Discharged for disability from wounds received August, '63.
dward McMahon......	1st Lieut.	Sept. 5, '61	Kingston, N.Y.	Joined as private. Appointed 1st Sergt. Oct. 4, '61. Promoted 2d Lieut. May 17, '62, to 1st Lieut. Sept. 30, '62. Discharged for disability from wounds, Aug. 5, '63.
eorge B. Wollcott.	2d Lieut.	Sept. 5, '61	Kingston, N.Y.	Joined as private Sept. 5, '61. Promoted 1st Sergt. May 17, '62, to 2d Lieut. Feb. 3, '63. Mustered out by reason of expiration of term, Sept. 8, '64.
Transferred. andish V. Cornish. ...	2d Lieut.	....	.. ..	Assigned to D Co. Jan. 11, '65. Promoted to 2d Lieut. and assigned to G Co. April 15, '65.
cers of Company E. W. Beckwith......	Captain			Mustered as Captain May 15, '63. Absent D. S. on Staff. Pro.-Mar.-Gen. Richmond, Va. Promoted from 1st Lieut. 35th N.Y. Vols. to Captain Co. E 20th N.Y.S.M. No discharge furnished. Absent from Co. since May 15, '63.

Name	Rank	Date	Place	Remarks
Samuel Norfolk	2d Lieut.			Due Lieut. S. N. or responsibility for C. and G. equipage and ordnance stores. $10 per month. Sick in Post Hospital, Norfolk, Va. Severely wounded at Gettysburg, July 1, '63; Petersburg, Va. April 1, '65.
Resigned.				
Gilbert D. Cornelius	Captain	Sept. 8, '62		Resigned May 16, '63.
Albert S. Pease	1st Lieut.	Oct. 1, '61	Kingston, N.Y.	Dec. 24, 61.
J. C. Bouvier	1st Lieut.	Jan. 7, '63	" "	Oct. 5, '63, S. O. No. 267, Headqrs. A. of P.
John W. Carr	1st Lieut.	Oct. 9, '64	" "	May 26, '65, S. O. No. 142, Headqrs. Dept. Va.
Edgar T Dudley	2d Lieut.	Sept. 25, '61	Wawarsing,N.Y.	Jan. 30, '62.
Theodore Van Kleek	2d Lieut.	Feb. 10, '63	" "	Aug. 2, '63.
Mustered out.				
Abram Merritt	2d Lieut.	Apr. 17, '63		Mustered out at City Point, Va., by reason expired term service and disability from wounds, Sept. 23, '64.
Killed.				
Pelatiah Ward	Captain	Sept. 5, '61	Wawarsing,N.Y.	Died of wounds received at Manassas, Sept. 3, '62.
George Brankstone	1st Lieut.	Jan. 7, '63	" "	Killed in action at Gettysburg, July 1, '63.
Dismissed the Service.				
Oliver A. Campbell	2d Lieut.	Aug. 2, '62		Dropped from Rolls, Oct. 21, '63, G. O. 162, Headqrs. A. of P.
Discharged.				
Brankstone, George	1st Lieut.	Sept. 25, '61	Wawarsing,N.Y.	Promoted 1st Sergt., June 10, '62. Promotion to 1st Lieut., Jan. 7, '63. Discharged by reason of promotion to 1st Lieut. (Transferred from 231 N.Y.V.)
Norfolk, Samuel	2d Lieut.	Feb. 11, '63	Cape Vincent	Discharged G. O. No. 94, War Dept. A. G. O., June 15, '65.
Officers of Company F.				
N. Hoysradt	Captain	Aug. 9, '61	Kingston, N.Y.	Joined the service as 1st Lieut. Aug. 9, '61. Promoted to Captain March 1, '64. Due $10 per month for responsibility for clothing, arms, and equipments, &c., for the months of July, August, September, October, November, and December, '65. Retained in service by order of War Dept. No discharge furnished.

NAMES.	RANK.	JOINED FOR SERVICE. WHEN.	WHERE.	REMARKS.
Officers of Co. F—Cont'd.				
Thomas Leahey	1st Lieut.	Dec. 30, '63	Brandy Sta., Va.	Joined for service as Vet. Vol Dec. 30. Promoted to 1st Sergt. Sept. 25, '64. Promoted to 1st Lieut. Dec. 28, '64. Originally joined the service Sept. 13, '61.
Lyman Hoysradt.....	2d Lieut.	Jan. 27, '64	Kingston, N.Y.	Promoted to Sergt. Nov. 1, '64. Promoted to 2d Lieut. Dec. 30, '64. On duty in Freedmen's Bureau. No discharge furnished.
Discharged.				
George North, Jr. ...	2d Lieut.	Aug. 9, '61	Kingston, N.Y.	By reason of disability from wounds.
John Dellacroy	2d Lieut.	Aug. 11, '61	Kingston, N.Y.	By reason of disability from wounds.
Died.				
Joseph S. Corbin.....	Captain	Aug. 9, '61	Kingston, N.Y.	Killed at the Battle of Gettysburg, Pa., July 1, '63.
Officers of Company G.				
Isaac Thomas.. ..	1st Lieut.	Jan. 25, '65	City Point, Va.	Vet. Vol. Joined for service Feb. 21, '62. Promoted to 1st Sergt. Oct. 15, '62. Promoted to 2d Lieut. Dec. 28, '64. Promoted to 1st Lieut. Jan. 25, '65. $10 per month due for responsibility of ordnance and company property for months of November and December, '65, and January, '66.
Eddy. B. Townsend.....	2d Lieut.	Mar. 8, '65	City Point, Va.	Appointed from civil life to 2d Lieut. March 8, '65. Absent Freedmen's Bureau. No discharge furnished.
Discharged.				
William H. Cunningham.	Captain	Sept. 19, '61	Kingston, N.Y.	Joined Regiment as 1st Lieut. Sept. 19, '61. Promoted to Captain Sept. 17, '62. Discharged Oct. 6, '64—expiration of term of service.
M. J. C. Woodworth .	Captain	Oct. 10, '61	Kingston, N.Y.	Promoted from 1st Lieut. A Co. Dec. 23, '64. Discharged S. O. No. 79, Headqrs. R. S. Mil. Div. Atlantic, Nov. 8, '65.
James M. Van Valkenburg	1st Lieut.	Sept. 19, '61	Lexington	Joined as private Sept. 19, '61. Promoted to 2d Lieut. Sept. 24, '61. Pvt. 1st Lieut. Sept. 17, '62. Discharged Jan. 13, '63—disability.

Name	Rank	Date	Place	Remarks
James Smith	2d Lieut.	Sept. 16, '61	Lexington	Joined as private Sept. 16, '61. Promoted to 1st Sergt. Oct. 1, '61. Promoted to 2d Lieut. Sept. 17, '62. Dismissed by G. O. M. O. No. 26, July 26, '64.
Transferred. George B. Mulks. ..	1st Lieut.	Sept. 25, '61	Kingston, N.Y.	Promoted from Sergt.-Major to 1st Lieut. Jan. 13, '63. Appointed Adjutant Oct., '64.
Died. J. Talmadge Hendricks..	Captain	Sept. 7, '61	Kingston, N.Y.	Died Sept. 17, '62, at Washington, D.C.
Officers of Company H. George B. Mulks.	Captain	May 1, '65	Richmond, Va.	Promoted Sergt.-Major Nov. 1, '62; 1st Lieut. March 19, '63; Capt. May 1, '65. Has $10 per month due for responsibility of Company property for months of May, June, July, August, and November, '65. Joined service as private Sept. 25, '61.
Eugene Subit.	1st Lieut.	Dec. 30, '64	City Point, Va.	Promoted 1st Lieut. Dec 31, '64, from private 11th N. J. Vols. Joined service as private Sept. 27, '64.
S. F. B. Gillispie. ..	2d Lieut	Jan. 10, '65	City Point, Va.	Promoted 2d Lieut. from private of I Co. Jan. 10, '65. Joined service as private Sept. 6, '64. No discharge furnished. On S. D. at Richmond, Va.
Discharged. Abram S. Smith	Captain	Sept. 5, '61	Kingston, N.Y	Appointed Capt. of H Co. Oct. 9, '61. Discharged for disability from wounds, Feb. 19, '63.
Thomas Alexander.	Captain	Oct. 21, '61	Kingston, N.Y	Appointed Sergt. Oct. 26, '61; 1st Lieut. Oct. 26, '62; Capt. Feb. 23, '63. Discharged for disability, March 12, '65.
Ely R. Dobbs. ..	1st Lieut.	Oct. 9, '61	Kingston, N.Y	Appointed 1st Lieut. Oct. 9, '61. Discharged Oct. 21, '62, G. O. 162 A. of P
Alfred Tanner...... .	2d Lieut.	Oct. 15, '61	Kingston, N.Y	Appointed 1st Sergt. Oct. 30, '62; 2d Lieut. Feb. 23, '63. Discharged for disability, Dec. 8, '63.
Resigned. Edward A. Ross	1st Lieut.	Sept. 25, '61	Kingston, N.Y	Appointed Sergt. Oct. 26, '61; 2d Lieut. Oct. 21, '62; 1st Lieut. Oct. 23, '63. Resigned Nov. 1, '64.
Michael Farrell.........	2d Lieut.	Feb. 8, '64	Kingston, N.Y.	Promoted to 2d Lieut. H Co. Sept. 8, '64. Resigned May 17, '65.

NAMES.	RANK.	WHEN.	WHERE.	REMARKS.
Officers of Co. H.—*Cont'd.* *Died.*				
Martin Swarthout.. ...	2d Lieut.	Oct. 9, '61	Kingston, N.Y.	Promoted from 1st Sergt. A Co. Oct. 9, '61. Killed at Antietam, Sept. 17, '62.
Officers of Company I.				
Charles S. Parker	Captain	Apr. 15, '65	Richmond, Va.	Joined as 1st Lieut. Dec. 24, '64. Promoted Capt. April 15, '65. Due $10 per month for responsibility of Company property from June 1, '65.
Remsen Varick.. ..	1st Lieut.	Dec. 26, '64	City Point, Va.	Joined as 1st Lieut. Dec. 26, '64. Due $10 per month for responsibility of Company property for the months of January, February, March, and April, '65.
Discharged. James D. Balen.. ..	Captain	Oct. 10, '61	Saugerties.	Joined service as Captain. Dropped from rolls Oct. 21, '62, G. O. No. 162 A. of P. Restored and resigned, March 3, '63.
John D. S. Crook..	Captain	Oct. 10, '61	Kingston, N.Y.	Joined as 1st Lieut. Promoted Captain March 3, '63. Resigned Dec. 17, '64, S. O. No. 40 A. of P.
Frank Duval.	2d Lieut.	Sept. 23, '61	Woodstock.	Joined service as Sergt. Appointed 1st Sergt. Nov. 1, '62. Promoted 2d Lieut. March 4, '63. Mustered out; expiration term of service.
Transferred. D. J. France...... ...	1st Lieut.	Oct. 10, '61	Hurley.	Joined service as 2d Lieut. Promoted 1st Lieut. March 3, '63. Transferred to Co. K by promotion to Captain May 2, '64.
S. F. B. Gillispie. ...	2d Lieut.	Sept. 6, '64	Goshen.	Joined service as private B Co. Transferred by promotion to 2d Lieut. Jan. 10, '65, to H Co.
Officers of Company K. Demetrius J. France	Captain	May 2, '64	Petersburg.	Joined service in I Co. as 2d Lieut. Sept. 23, '61. Promoted to 1st Lieut. March 3, '63. Transferred to K Co. March 27, '64, S. O. No. 39, Headqrs. 20th N.Y.S.M. Promoted to Capt. May 2, '64. $10 per month due for responsibility of arms and accoutrements and C. C. and G. E. per months of May, June, July, August, September, and December, '65.

Name	Rank	Date	Place	Remarks
Richard E. Houghtaling.	1st Lieut.	Dec. 9, '65	Ft. Monroe.	Joined service as private Oct. 15, '64, in B Co. Transferred to K Co. March 2, '65, S. O. 49, Headqrs. 20th N.Y.S.M. Promoted 2d Lieut. March 2, '65; 1st Lieut. Dec. 9, '65.
Discharged.				
Alexander McFarland.	1st Lieut.	Sept. 28, '61	Kingston, N.Y.	Resigned Dec. 21, '61.
J. C. Bonvier	1st Lieut.	Jan. 7, '62	Acquia Creek.	" Oct. 5, '63.
Amos B. Ferguson	1st Lieut.	Dec. 31, '63	Brandy Sta., Va.	" Aug. 7, '65.
John M. Young	2d Lieut.	Sept. 2, '62	Brandy Sta., Va.	Dismissed April 7, '64, by sentence of G. C. M., S. O. No. 99, Headqrs. A. of P
Transferred.				
Elsen M. Meisner	1st Lieut.	May 1, '64	Kingston, N.Y.	Transferred to A Co. for promotion by S. O. No. 4, Headqrs. 20th N.Y.S.M., '65.
Chas. S. Parker.	1st Lieut.	Dec. 25, '64	City Point.	Transferred to I Co. for promotion by S. O. No. 86, Headqrs. 20th N.Y.S.M., '65.
Standish V Cornish.	1st Lieut.	Apr. 15, '65	City Point.	Transferred to D Co. for promotion by S. O. No. 87, Headqrs. 20th N.Y.S.M., '65. Appointed Regt. Q'rmaster, June 15, '65, S. O. No. 102, Headqrs. N.Y.S.M.
John McEntee	1st Lieut.	Sept. 11, '62	Aquia Creek.	Joined service as Q'rmast. Sergt. Sept. 24, '61. Promoted to 2d Lieut. Transferred to Co. A for promotion.
Died.				
Ambrose N. Baldwin.	Captain	Sept. 16, '61	Kingston, N.Y.	Joined service as 1st Lieut. Killed July 3, '63, at Gettysburg, Pa.
John R. Horner	2d Lieut.	Sept. 18, '61	Kingston, N.Y.	Killed at Manassas, Aug. 30, 62.

C.

List of Killed, Wounded and Missing in 1862.

KILLED.

NAME.	CO.	RANK.	DATE.	PLACE.
George W. Pratt.		Colonel	August 30,	Manassas.
Joseph Wells.	G,	Private	August 30,	Manassas.
J. P. Bloom...	G,	Private	August 30,	Manassas.
Michael Oats.	G,	Private	August 30,	Manassas.
Andrew J. Smith.	I,	Private	August 30,	Manassas.
James McAdams.	I,	Private	August 30,	Manassas.
Edwin Miles	F,	Sergeant	September 17,	Antietam.
Thomas Price.	K,	Private	September 17,	Antietam.
William H. Knowles.	C,	Private	August 30,	Manassas.
Wesley Shutlis.	D,	Private	August 30,	Manassas.
Jeremiah Townes.	D,	Private	August 30,	Manassas.
Stephen Van Velsen.	D,	Private	August 30,	Manassas.
Michael Coffee.	D,	Private	August 30,	Manassas.
John H. Davis.	D,	Private	August 30,	Manassas.
James P. Colligan.	F.	Corporal	August 30,	Manassas.
Hugh Wallace	F,	Private	August 80,	Manassas,
Bernard Garrety.	F,	Private	August 30,	Manassas.
Milton A. Smith.	B,	Sergeant	August 30,	Manassas.
Alfred Lasher (T).	B,	Sergeant	August 30,	Manassas.
Geo. H. Kelly (T)	B,	Private	August 30,	Manassas.
Lewis Redder (T).	B,	Private	August 30,	Manassas.
John Stewart (T).	B,	Private	August 30,	Manassas.
Rufus Warranger (T)	B,	Private	August 30,	Antietam.
Adam Bishop.	E,	Private	August 30,	Manassas.
Miles Anderson	E,	Corporal	August 30,	Manassas.
H. Goldsmith	E,	Corporal	August 30,	Manassas.
James M. Almy	H,	1st Sergeant	August 30,	Mannssas.
H. I. Pollock	H,	Private	September 17,	Antietam.
Patrick Sweeny	K,	Private	August 30,	Manassas.
H. M. Judd.	K,	Private	August 30,	Manassas.
William R. Dodd.	G,	Sergeant	August 21,	Norman's Ford.
Samuel J. White.	D,	Private	December 17,	Fredericksburg.
John P. Post.	F,	Private	September 17,	Antietam.
Peter P. Plass...	I,	Private	September 17,	Antietam.
M. H. Swarthout.	H,	2d Lieut.	September 17,	Antietam.
John R. Horner.	K,	1st Lieut.	August 30,	Manassas.

WOUNDED.

NAME.	RANK.	DATE.	PLACE.
Peletiah Ward.	Captain .	August 30..	Manassas.
J. Rudolph Tappen......	Captain .	August 30..	Manassas.
Abram S. Smith ..	Captain .	August 30..	Manassas.
A. N. Baldwin.	Captain .	September 17 .	Antietam.
Daniel McMahon........	Captain....	September 1..	Chantilly.
Abram S. Smith ..	Captain...	December 13..	Fredericksburg.
W. H. Cunningham. ..	Captain...	December 13..	Fredericksburg.
Philip Deits	2d Lieut .	August 30..	Manassas.
Edward McMahon ..	1st Lieut. .	August 30..	Manassas.
Henry Clarke..	2d Lieut ..	August 30..	Manassas.
O. A. Campbell	2d Lieut .	September 17 .	Antietam.
George North, Jr.	2d Lieut .	September 1..	Chantilly.
J. M.Van Valkenburg....	2d Lieut .	August 30..	Manassas.
J. D. France.	2d Lieut .	August 30..	Manassas.
Nicholas Hrynadt	1st Lieut. .	August 30..	Manassas.
James Smith..........	2d Lieut ..	August 30..	Manassas.
G. H. Brankstone	1st Lieut. .	December 13..	Fredericksburg.
Edward S. Bennett. .. .	Sergeant. .	August 21..	Norman's Ford.
Amos Travis.....	Corporal ..	September 17..	Antietam.
Henry Williamson	Corporal.	September 1..	Chantilly.
Jacob Cook.	Private ..	September 17..	Antietam.
John M. Crapser	Private .	August 30..	Manassas.
James Dykensan........	Private .	September 1..	Chantilly.
Abram C. Halstead......	Private ..	August 30..	Manassas.
Russel C. Harris........	Private	August 30..	Manassas.
Michael Kilroy.	Private .	December 13..	Fredericksburg.
John R. Morgan . ..	Private ..	December 13..	Fredericksburg.
Ona S. Payne.	Private .	September 1..	Chantilly.
Aaron Rhodes	Private ...	September 17 .	Antietam.
Charles H. Williams.....	Private .	August 30..	Manassas.
Henry Williamson .	Sergeant...	December 13..	Fredericksburg.
William A. Ingram. ..	Sergeant. ..	August 30..	Manassas.
John Stewart	Private	August 30..	Manassas.
Edward Babcock.	Private. .	August 30..	Manassas.
Philip Deits	Sergeant.	August 30..	Manassas.
Fred'ck Obermier (T)..	Sergeant. ..	August 30..	Manassas.
Michael Speedling.	Corporal. ..	August 30..	Manassas.
Andrew Yaple	Corporal. .	August 30..	Manassas.
Oswald Decker (T) .. .	Private .	August 30..	Manassas.
Thos. W Francisco......	Private .. .	August 30..	Manassas.
Theo. Garrison (T)......	Private	August 30..	Manassas.
Howard Joy	Private .	August 21..	Norman's Ford.
John Joy.	Private .	September 17 .	Antietam
Lewis Lamoyard. .. .	Private .. .	December 14..	Fredericksburg.
Isaac Lawrence	Private	September 17..	Antietam.
Chas. K. McNiff (T).. .	Private .	December 14..	Fredericksburg.
Adam Moore (T)	Private .	August 21..	Norman's Ford.
Michael O'Donnell .....;	Private ...	September 18..	Antietam.
Henry Plough	Private ...	August 30..	Manassas.
Wm. Rosenberger .. .	Private ...	August 30..	Manassas.

WOUNDED—Continued.

NAME.	RANK.	DATE.	PLACE.
Michael O'Donnell....	Private .	August 30.	Manassas.
Cyrastus H. Betts ...	1st Sergeant	August 30..	Manassas.
William Bates	Corporal. .	August 30..	Manassas.
John Knowls ...	Private .. .	August 30..	Manassas.
George Van Loan ..	Private . .	August 30..	Manassas.
George G. Martin ..	Corporal.	August 30..	Manassas.
William Knapp	Private .	August 30..	Manassas.
Philip Dillon	Private .	August 30..	Manassas.
Spencer Dederick	Private ...	August 30..	Manassas.
John Edleman	Private ...	August 30..	Manassas.
Henry Rose.	Private ...	September 17 .	Antietam.
George H. Banard. . ..	Private .	September 17 .	Antietam.
Ten Eyck O. France.....	Private .. .	December 13..	Fredericksburg.
Patrick Graney	Sergeant. .	September 17 .	Antietam.
Halsey Davis	Corporal. .	August 30..	Manassas.
Isaac E. Rosa	Private	August 30..	Manassas.
D. P Whittaker .. .	Corporal..	August 30..	Manassas.
Dubois Markle.	Corporal .	September 1..	Chantilly.
George Brown	Corporal. .	August 30..	Manassas.
John Connery	Corporal. .	September 17 .	Antietam.
Richard Burger	Private ...	August 30..	Manassas.
David S. Bell	Private ...	August 30..	Manassas.
Albert Collier..........	Private .	August 30..	Manassas.
Ebbin Higgins	Private .	August 30..	Manassas.
George Hinckley.	Private .	August 30..	Manassas.
Lorenzo Kibby.	Private .. .	August 30..	Manassas.
S. H. Lee.	Private .	September 1..	Chantilly.
Jacob P. Lattimore......	Private .	August 30..	Manassas.
George Moore.	Private .	August 26..	War't'n Springs.
J. M. Ostrander. .. .	Private .	December 13.	Fredericksburg.
Conrad Smith..... ...	Private .	August 30..	Manassas.
Watson A. Smith.. .. .	Private ...	August 30..	Manassas.
Peter Sparling	Private .	August 30..	Manassas.
Bealy Taylor...	Private .	August 30..	Manassas.
William Van Scoit... .	Private ...	August 30..	Manassas.
Stephen Van Velsan. ..	Private ...	August 30..	Manassas.
Michael Huger.	Private ...	August 30..	Manassas.
Hugh Donahugh ., .	Private ...	August 30..	Manassas.
Geo. H. Brankstone.....	1st Sergeant	December 14..	Fredericksburg.
H. H. Terwelliger. .	Sergeant. .	August 30..	Manassas.
Thomas Wallace	Sergeant. .	December 14..	Fredericksburg.
William Freeman	Sergeant. .	August 26..	War't'n Springs.
James W Whelpley.....	Corporal. .	August 30..	Manassas.
David H. Welch .. .	Corporal. .	August 30..	Manassas.
Miles Anderson .	Corporal. .	August 30..	Manassas.
George G. Barlow	Corporal...	August 30..	Manassas.
George P. Sanders. ...	Corporal. .	December 15..	Fredericksburg.
Ephraim Turner .. .	Corporal...	August 30..	Manassas.
Melvin Atkins	Private .. .	September 17 .	Antietam.
James Beers	Private .	September 17 .	Antietam.

WOUNDED—Continued.

NAME.	RANK.	DATE.	PLACE.
Andrew Carney	Private	September 17	Antietam.
Nicholas Cooper	Private	August 30	Manassas.
Martin J. Deponia	Private	August 26	War't'n Springs.
Alvin A. Hausehidt	Private	August 30	Manassas.
James Hansfeldt	Private	August 30	Manassas.
Henry H. Legg	Private	September 17	Antietam.
Samuel McCune	Private	December 13	Fredericksburg.
Lewis Payne	Private	September 17	Antietam.
Russel Powell	Private	August 30	Manassas.
John Swhab	Sergeant	August 3	Fredericksburg.
Calvin Sheeley	Private	September 17	Antietam.
Eugene F Thorpe	Private	August 30	Manassas.
Thomas J. Conlon	Sergeant	August 30	Manassas.
James F Colligan	Corporal	August 30	Manassas.
Peter Foley	Corporal	August 30	Manassas.
James R. Burke	Private	August 30	Manassas.
James Costello	Private	August 30	Manassas.
Thomas Doyle	Private	August 30	Manassas.
James Fitzgerald	Private	August 30	Manassas.
Bernard Gerrety	Private	August 30	Manassas.
Martin Jones	Private	August 30	Manassas.
John Kelly	Private	August 30	Manassas.
Valentine Lundly	Private	August 30	Manassas.
John Luft	Private	August 30	Manassas.
John Masterson	Private	August 30	Manassas.
William Mayer	Private	August 30	Manassas.
Philip Post	Private	August 30	Manassas.
George Patterson	Private	August 30	Manassas.
John Pratt	Private	August 30	Manassas.
Andrew Sweeney	Private	August 30	Manassas.
Cassander Warner	Private	August 30	Manassas.
Hugh Wallace	Private	August 30	Manassas.
William J. Miller	Private	August 30	Manassas.
Patrick Melia	Private	August 30	Manassas.
John Tieman	Corporal	September 17	Antietam.
J. M. Countryman	Private	September 17	Antietam.
James Green	Private	September 17	Antietam.
Thomas McAboy	Private	September 17	Antietam.
Patrick Nolan	Private	September 17	Antietam.
Edward Nolan	Private	September 17	Antietam.
John B. Barry	Private	September 17	Antietam.
James Smith	1st Sergeant	August 30	Manassas.
R. H. Barrett	Sergeant	August 30	Manassas.
H. K. Dopp	Sergeant	August 21	Norman's Ford.
George Butler	Corporal	August 30	Manassas.
William F. Smith	Corporal	August 30	Manassas.
James Higgins	Corporal	August 30	Manassas.
R. S. Hammond	Corporal	September 17	Antietam.
John W Tolland	Corporal	September 17	Antietam.
William C. Allen	Private	September 17	Antietam.

WOUNDED—Continued.

NAME.	RANK.	DATE.	PLACE.
P. S. Angle.......... .	Private .	August 30..	Manassas.
Albiner Fiero.	Private	August 30.	Manassas.
Chauncey Hogeboom....	Private .	August 30. .	Manassas.
John Haynes	Private ..	September 17..	Antietam.
Stephen Knapp	Private .	August 30..	Manassas.
James A. Lewis.	Private ...	August 30.	Manassas.
Joseph Bell..	Private ...	August 30.	Manassas.
William B. Rose	Private ...	August 30..	Manassas.
P. H. Wagner.	Private ...	September 17	Antietam.
Edward Rogers	Private .	August 30..	Manassas.
Isaac Cleaver	Private ...	September 17..	Antietam.
Wellington Butler.	Private .	August 30..	Manassas.
Albino West..	Private .	August 30.	Manassas.
George L. Hughson. ...	Private	September 17..	Antietam.
Lewis H. Wilkow	Sergeant. .	August 30..	Manassas.
George B. Coyle.	Private . . .	August 30..	Manassas.
Jacob J. Conway	Corporal . .	August 30..	Manassas.
Charles Bergher.	Corporal. .	August 30..	Manassas.
James H. Bunto.	Private ...	August 30..	Manassas.
Thomas C. France .. .	Private ...	August 30.,	Manassas.
John Haggerty..... ..	Private .	September 17..	Antietam.
James Rafferty.. .	Private ...	August 30..	Manassas.
Wm. H. Reynolds.... .	Private ...	August 30..	Manassas.
William Rosa	Private .	August 30..	Manassas.
John Sullivan...... .	Private ...	August 30..	Manassas.
Frederick Toothill.	Private ...	August 30..	Manassas.
James Van Elten..... .	Private .	August 30..	Manassas.
John Van Gasbeck ..	Private ...	August 30..	Manassas.
Aaron Woolsey	Private .. .	August 30..	Manassas.
Morris Hein	Private .	August 30..	Manassas.
Edwin Bruce	Private .	August 30..	Manassas.
Edward Higham..	Private .	August 30..	Manassas.
Apollos B. Fink	Private .	August 30..	Manassas.
James Mulvehill	Private .	August 30..	Manassas.
M. J. C. Woodworth.....	1st Sergeant	September 17	Antietam.
Michael Farrell	Sergeant...	December 14..	Fredericksburg.
Francis Clark..	Sergeant. .	August 30..	Manassas.
Henry M. Herring.	Corporal...	September 7..	Antietam.
Joseph Leonard	Corporal. .	August 30.	Manassas.
George Rossman .	Corporal. .	August 30.	Manassas.
Jordan A. Sickler	Corporal. .	August 30.	Manassas.
Michael Caughlan.... .	Corporal. .	August 30..	Manassas.
James Brady	Private .	August 30..	Manassas.
Romeyn Beach....... .	Private .	August 30..	Manassas.
John Camaton...	Private ...	August 26..	War't'n Springs.
Hezekiah Carle	Private .	August 30..	Manassas.
Myer Devall .. .	Private .	August 30..	Manassas.
Barney Fitch	Private .. .	August 30..	Manassas.
William L. Hanson......	Prvate i. .	December 13..	Fredericksburg.
Patrick Moran .. .	Private ..	August 30..	Manassas.

WOUNDED—Continued.

NAME.	RANK.	DATE.	PLACE.
John McKain	Private	August 30..	Manassas.
Edward McAdams	Private ..	August	Manassas.
John O'Brien	Private	August 30..	Manassas.
George W Peet.	Sergeant.	December 13..	Fredericksburg.
Peter S. Carle	Corporal...	August 30..	Mana s is.
Henry J. Newell	Corporal...	August 30..	Manas-as.
Joseph Hill.	Sergeant...	September 1..	Chantilly.
John B. Brush.	Private	September 17 .	Antietam.
John W Bradt	Private	August 30..	Manassas.
Amos J. Carle	Private	August 30.	Manassas.
Penj. W. Dutcher	Private .	August 30..	Manassas.
Maynard Decker	Corporal.	August 30.	Manassas.
Robert Drummond...	Private	August 30..	Manassas.
Daniel Greenwood.	Private	September 17..	Antietam.
Constant C. Hanks..	Private	August 30..	Manassas.
James Hooks ..	Private	December 13	Fredericksburg.
Charles Hansell.	Private	September 1..	Chantilly.
William Hapenward.	Private	September 1 .	Chantilly
Dennis Judd	Private	August 30..	Manassas.
Henry M. Judd	Private ..	August 30..	Manassas.
Horatio Lord	Private .	August 30..	Manassas.
John H. Pierce.	Private ..	September 1	Chantilly.
John Proper.	Private	August 30..	Manassas.
Edward L. Sealy.	Private	September 14..	South Mountain.
Henry Schutt. .	Private	August 30..	Manassas.
Hiram Travis..	Private	August 21 .	Norman's Ford.
William Winegard....	Private	August 30..	Manassas.

MISSING.

NAME.	CO.	RANK.	DATE.	PLACE.
Andrew Dile.	I,	Sergeant.	August 30..	Manassas.
John Tracy..	I,	Private ..	August 30..	Manassas.
Hugh Burns	H.	Private	September 17..	Antietam.
George Woolsey.....	C,	.. ..	August 10..	Manassas.

37

LIST OF KILLED AND WOUNDED IN 1863.

KILLED—*Commissioned Officers.*

NAME.	CO.	RANK.	PLACE.
Joseph F. Corbin.	F,	Captain.	Gettysburg.
Ambrose N. Baldwin.	K,	Captain.	Gettysburg.
George H. Brankstone. .. .	E,	1st Lieutenant...	Gettysburg.

KILLED—*Enlisted Men.*

NAME.	CO.	RANK.	PLACE.
Theodore Wheeler	A,	Corporal. .. .	Gettysburg.
Duane S. Bush. .. .. .,.....	A,	Private..	Gettysburg.
Henry Belcher.	A,	Private	Gettysburg.
Charles C. Babcock.	A,	Private	Gettysburg.
Francis I. Lee..	A,	Private	Gettysburg.
Dewitt C. Hamin ..	A,	Private	Gettysburg.
Ephraim Rosa	B,	Private	Gettysburg.
James Craig..	C,	Sergeant........ .	Gettysburg.
Constantine Van Steinburg.... .	C,	Private	Gettysburg.
Edward Coogan.	C,	Private . , ...	Gettysburg.
Walter S. Tyler.	C,	Corporal....	Gettysburg.
Luther W McClellan	D,	Sergeant..	Gettysburg.
Ebbin Higgins..	D,	Private	Gettysburg.
R. C. Van Leakin.	D,	Private	Gettysburg.
Amos C. Treat.....	D,	Private	Gettysburg.
Albert Collier.	D,	Private	Gettysburg'
Alexander Tice.	E,	Private	Gettysburg.
Leonard Van Jorder.	E,	Private	Gettysburg.
John Luft..	F,	Private	Gettysburg.
Lucius H. Decker.	G,	Sergeant........ .	Gettysburg.
James L. Hallock	H,	Private	Gettysburg.
James E. Angevine.	H,	Corporal	Gettysburg.
Eli A. Degrof.	H,	Corporal	Gettysburg.
Ansol B. Pierce.	H,	Private	Gettysburg.
Joseph Leonard.	I,	Corporal	Gettysburg.
John Tracy.	I,	Private	Gettysburg.
Thomas Hyatt.	I,	Private	Gettysburg.
Minard Decker.....	K,	Sergeant...	Gettysburg.
Nelson Southard...	K,	Private	Gettysburg.
George H. Babcock.	E,	Private	Gettysburg.
Squire Flanders.	I,	Private	Gettysburg.

WOUNDED—*Commissioned Officers.*

NAME.	CO.	RANK.	PLACE.
W. A. Van Rensselaer...		Major	Gettysburg.
J. M. Schoonmaker..... .. .	.	Adjutant .. .	Gettysburg.
John R. Leslie.	B,	Captain	Gettysburg.
Andrew S. Schutt.	C,	1st Lieutenant. ...	Gettysburg.
James Flenning.	C,	2d Lieutenant.. .	Gettysburg.
Daniel McMahon	D,	Captain ..	Gettysburg.

WOUNDED—*Commissioned Officers*—Continued.

NAME.	CO.	RANK.	PLACE.
George B. Wolcott	D,	2d Lieutenant. .	Gettysburg.
Abm. Merritt.	E,	2d Lieutenant. ..	Gettysburg.
John Delacroy	F,	2d Lieutenant.....	Gettysburg.
William H. Cunningham. ...	G,	Captain .	Gettysburg.
George B. Mulks.	G,	1st Lieutenant..	Gettysburg.
Thomas Alexander.... .	H,	Captain .. .	Gettysburg.
Alfred Tanner	H,	2d Lieutenant. .	Gettysburg.
J. D. S. Cook.	I,	Captain	Gettyshurg.
John M. Young...	K,	2d Lieutenant ..	Gettysburg.

WOUNDED—*Enlisted Men.*

NAME.	CO.	RANK.	PLACE.
John Boyle.	C,	Private.	Gettysburg.
James Gannon.	C,	Private	Gettysburg.
George A. Ackert.	C,	Private	Gettysburg.
John Edleman...	C,	Private	Gettysburg.
Thomas Wells....	C.	Private. .	Gettysburg.
George W Pardee	C,	Corporal	Gettysburg.
Joseph Shelightner	C,	Private . ..	Gettysburg.
John H. Dunn.	C,	Corporal	Gettysburg.
Jeremiah Kerrigan....... ...	C,	Private	Gettysburg.
Jonathan Dubois....... .. .	C,	Private	Gettysburg.
Abm. K. Van Buskirk. .. .	C,	Private	Gettysburg.
William Baker	A,	Private	Gettysburg.
James E. Doxie...	A,	Private	Gettysburg.
John Donnelly.	A,	Private.	Gettysburg.
John Ridings, Jr.	A,	Sergeant.....	Gettysburg.
William A. Stockings, (T).... .	A,	Private ...	Gettysburg.
Wansborough Bloxam, (T). ...	B,	Sergeant....... ...	Gettysburg.
Frank Bowman.	B,	Private	Gettysburg.
Isaac C. Buswell.....	B,	1st Sergeant ..	Gettysbur
Morgan Deneger, (T)	B,	Private	Gettysburg.
James Keegan....	B,	Private	Gettysburg.
Charles K. McKiff, (T)...	B,	Corporal ..	Gettysburg.
Adam More, (T)	B,	Private	Gettysburg.
William Risenberger, Jr...	B,	Corporal	Gettysburg.
John H. Swart.	B,	Corporal	Gettysburg.
Jacob F. Teal	B,	Private	Gettysburg.
H. C. Van Buren.......	B,	Private	Gettysburg.
James Yaple...	B,	Sergeant..	Gettysburg.
James A. Wescott...	B,	Private	Gettysburg.
Asa Bishop...	D,	Sergeant.	Gettysburg.
John Cudney	D,	Corporal.......	Gettysburg.
Charles Kniffin.	D,	Sergeant	Gettysburg.
Jacob P. Latimore.....	D.	Private	Gettysburg.
Martin Jerseneous.	D,	Private	Gettysburg.
Dewitt Rose.	D,	Private	Gettysburg.
Watson A. Smith	D,	Sergeant..	Gettysburg.
Lewis E. Champaigne. .. .	E,	Sergeant....... ..	Gettysburg.
Stephen L. Cudney	E,	Sergeant.......	Gettysburg.
William Fetterman.	E,	Private	Gettysbur
Lorenzo B. Healy.	E,	Private	Gettysburg.

WOUNDED—*Enlisted Men*—Continued.

NAME.	CO.	RANK.	PLACE.
James Housfall	E,	Private	Gettysburg.
Henry O. Irwin.	E,	Private .	Gettysburg.
John Johnson.	E,	Corporal.	Gettysburg.
Lewis Snyder	E,	Private	Gettysburg.
Enos B. Vail	E,	Private	Gettysburg.
John H. Winise.	G,	Sergeant..	Gettysburg.
James Higgins.	G,	Sergeant	Gettysburg.
John C. Parks.	G,	Private	Gettysburg.
Peter H. Van Wogoner.	G,	Private.	Gettysburg.
John Ovendorf..	H.	Corporal	Gettysburg.
William L. Snyder.	H,	Private	Gettysburg.
Joseph Sickler.	H,	Private	Gettysburg.
Morris Hein	H,	Private	Gettysburg.
William Fuller.	I,	Sergeant.	Gettysburg.
William Henson.	I,	Private	Gettysburg.
James Larrie..	I,	Private	Gettysburg.
John W. Plimly.	I,	Private	Gettysburg.
Henry Tompkins.	I,	Private	Gettysburg.
Edward Wright.	I,	Private .	Gettysburg.
Michael Farrel.	I,	Sergeant.	Gettysburg.
Moses Whittaker	I,	Sergeant.	Gettysburg.
Barney Fitch.	I,	Corporal.	Gettysburg.
George Rossman.	I,	Sergeant.	Gettysburg.
Jehiel I Judd.	K,	1st Sergeant	Gettysburg.
John Chandler.	K,	Corporal	Gettysburg.
Addison S. Hays.	K,	Private	Gettysburg.
George Hood	K,	Private	Gettysburg.
Joseph Hill.	K,	Sergeant	Gettysburg.
Henry Schutt.	K,	Private	Gettysburg.
Bernard Halstead	G,	Private	Gettysburg.
N Van Valkenburg	G,	Private	Gettysburg.
Charles C. Babcock..	A,	Private	Gettysburg.
James H. Beletier	A,	Private	Gettysburg.
Samuel Norfolk.	E,	Private	Gettysburg.
William H. Parkinson.	I,	Private	Gettysburg.
David E. Post.	I,	Private	Gettysburg.
Emerson Scott.	I,	Private	Gettysburg.
Ira B. Tait	D,	Private	Gettysburg.
Aaron Nichols.	H,	Private	Gettysburg.
A. Mullen	F,	1st Sergeant..	Getlysburg.
E. Becket.	F,	Sergeant	Gettysburg.
Ed. Ashley.	F,	Private	Gettysburg.
J E. Pells.	F,	Private	Gettysburg.
T Doyle.	F,	Private	Gettysburg.
I. Burns	F,	Private	Gettysburg.
John Knighton	B,	Private	Gettysburg.
Asa Jones	D,	Sergeant.	Gettysburg.
Charles Keegan.	A,	Private .	Gettysburg.
John Swart.	I,	Corporal.	Gettysburg.
N Rossman	I,	Private	Gettysburg.
James Boncsteel	G,	Sergeant.	Gettysburg.
T Croaks.	F,	Private	Gettysburg.
Stephen Strong.	I,	Private	Gettysburg.
William Shaffer.	G,	Private	Gettysburg.

D.

The regiment left the Strand by the steamer Manhattan, with a barge alongside, on Sunday, April 28th,
and after a stay of some days in New York City, dur-
ing which it was the first regiment to occupy the Park
Barracks, it proceeded to Annapolis, Md., where it was
mustered into the United States service by Lieutenant
Putnam, United States Engineers, and then went to
Annapolis Junction, relieving Schwatzewalder's Fifth
New York in guarding the line of railroad from An-
napolis to the Junction and a portion of the road from
Baltimore to Washington, with its headquarters at the
Junction.

The strength of the regiment when it left home
was 815.

Field Officers.—Colonel Gorge W Pratt, Lieutenant-
Colonel Hiram Schoonmaker, Major Theodore B. Gates.

Commissioned Staff.—Jacob B. Hardenburgh, Adjutant ; John S. Griffiths, Quartermaster ; Peter B.
Overbagh, Paymaster ; William Lounsbery, Commissary ; Major A. Crispell, Surgen ; Captain Leonard
Ingersoll and Lieutenant R. Loughran, Assistant Surgeons ; Daniel T. Van Buren, Captain of Engineers ;
William Darrah, Chaplain.

Non-Commissioned Staff.—P Freeman Hasbrouck,
Sergeant-Major ; Charles Schryver, Quartermaster's
Sergeant; Henry Mick, Sergeant Standard Bearer ;
Augustus Geoller, Drum-Major ; A. Webster Shaffer,
Sergeant of Sappers.

Line.—Company A, 73 men ; J. B. Webster, Captain ; A. G. Barker, First Lieutenant ; James Stevens,

581

Second Lieutenant. Company B, 113 men ; George H. Sharpe, Captain ; Jacob Sharpe, First Lieutenant ; Cornelius J. Houtaling, Second Lieutenant. Company C, 91 men ; J Rudolph Tappen, Captain ; W A. Van Rensselaer, First Lieutenant ; Peter S. Voorhees, Second Lieutenant. Company D, 74 men ; Davis Winne, Captain ; John Hussey, First Lieutenant ; John M. Schoonmaker, Jr., Second Lieutenant. Company E, 68 men ; William Lent, Captain ; Jacob A. Blackman, First Lieutenant ; Nicholas Sahn, Second Lieutenant. Company F, 63 men ; Patrick J Flynn, Captain ; Edward O'Reilly, First Lieutenant ; John Murray, Second Lieutenant. Company G, 80 men ; James T. Hendricks, Captain ; James D. Balen, First Lieutenant ; S. W Millar, Second Lieutenant. Company H, 87 men ; John Derrenbacher, Captain ; Jervis McEntee, First Lieutenant ; Lawrence Stoker, Second Lieutenant. Company R, 109 men ; Wade H. Steenbergh, Captain ; George Wheeler, First Lieutenant ; Cornelius C. Bush, Second Lieutenant ; Ambrose N Baldwin, Jr., Second Lieutenant. There was also a squad of sappers and miners consisting of nine men.

On the first of June Lieutenant-Colonel Schoonmaker resigned and Major Gates became the Lieutenant-Colonel, Adjutant Hardenburgh became the Major and M. W. McEntee was commissioned Adjutant.

On the 15th of December, 1862, the ladies of Saugerties, Ulster County, N. Y., presented to the regiment a
magnificent banner, made by Messrs. Tiffany & Co., of
New York City. The ceremonies took place in the
lecture-room of the Reformed Dutch Church, before a
large and intelligent audience. The exercises were
opened by the Rev S. Fitch, former chaplain of the
Twentieth, in a fervent and patriotic prayer.

The presentation address was made by the Rev J.
Gaston.

He commenced by saying, that before he entered
upon the discharge of the service which the patriotic
ladies of the town had devolved upon him, he desired
to call attention briefly to a few of the prominent features of the gigantic rebellion, which had necessitated
such ceremonies as those in which they were about to
engage.

He then proceeded to show the monstrous iniquity
of secession, and how utterly unjustifiable it was, and
how disastrous its consequences would be in any event.
He concluded as follows :

"Where is the man among us so unpatriotic, and
so lost to the political happiness of himself and posterity, that wishes to outlive this dire calamity? Our
country is worth preserving. Here our fathers lived,
labored and died. Here their graves are kept green
by the careful hands of filial affection. Here are all
our earthly hopes. And shall we let this noblest of all

republics perish, founded by the united wisdom, and cemented by the blood of our sires? Shall we consent to throw away the land of happy homes and Christian privileges? No! let the thought perish; this war, if needs be, must go on. It is a holy cause; a war of defence, not of aggression; not of invasion, but of resistance to intensified wrong.

"To draw back, in this the day of our nation's peril, would be ungrateful to our country, unjust to ourselves, and untrue to our children. We dare not suffer it to be rashly broken up without a patriotic struggle to defend and maintain it.

" In this fearful struggle for constitutional integrity, which has been waging for the past eighteen months, our noble Twentieth Regiment has borne a conspicuous part. On the outbreak of this wicked rebellion, when patriotic thousands rushed to the defence of the Government, Colonel George W Pratt felt that it was his duty to tender his services and the services of the Ulster Guard, the corps which it was his pride and honor to command, to his imperilled country Possessed of a large amount of military knowledge, which peculiarly fitted him for the field, and realizing that the cause of the Union was entitled to the earnest efforts of every true patriot, he felt it to be his duty to engage in the struggle. The offering that he laid upon the altar of his country was not that of impulse or necessity With him patriotism was not a blind instinct or passion, but of logic, of high and holy duty

"It was with this just appreciation of duty and obligation, that he went forth at the head of his command, on an errand involving principles most dear to his own heart and to the heart of every true American citizen. The most of us are familiar with the peculiarly efficient services rendered by our noble Twentieth Regiment, the pride not only of the county, but also of the State.

"Upon the expiration of the three months service, the Colonel immediately tendered the services of himself and his regiment to the Government—the tender was accepted and the regiment soon after started for the seat of war. The regiment formed a part of General Patrick's brigade, and was ever found prompt and efficient in obeying all orders, frequently being detailed for special and highly responsible duties. It was in the retreat under General Pope, from near Cedar Mountain to Bull Run, enduring much hardship and engaged in constant skirmishing. The regiment played a conspicuous part in the battle at Manassas, losing 280 men. It was in this engagement that Colonel Pratt and Captain Ward were mortally wounded, but not until they had nobly vindicated their manhood and their country's honor. We do not forget that the Regiment fought at South Mountain and at Antietam, under the gallant leadership of Colonel Gates, who, it was expected, would be with us this afternoon, to receive, at the hands of the patriotic ladies of the town of Saugerties, the most significant token of gratitude and confidence which it is possible for this community to bestow; but he was unexpectedly summoned to the command of his Regiment, in order that it might bear its part in that terrific battle now waging in the vicinity of Fredericksburg.

"It is enough to say, in closing this imperfect record of the services of the Regiment of our county, that at the battle of Antietam, being detailed for the special duty of guarding an important battery, so faithfully was the duty discharged, that out of 137 men on duty, 47 fell before the murderous fire of the enemy From such officers and men we may expect substantial benefits for the glorious cause so nobly espoused. Such men deserve to live in the hearts of a grateful posterity, and we cannot refuse to cherish and reward them.

"That the valiant corps, of whose exploits on the battle-field we have so much reason to be proud, de-

serves from us such words of high encomium, those
pierced and tattered colors most abundantly testify (the
old colors were suspended on either side of the altar),
as they speak in silent yet overpowering eloquence to
every sensibility of our nature. So nobly has that
solemn promise made by Colonel Pratt when those
colors were received, been kept, that if this land is ever
involved in war, they should wave with credit and
glory wherever danger is thickest and the fight is
warmest. I say, so faithfully has that promise been
kept that we feel that the Regiment is justly entitled to
receive at our hands this beautiful banner as an expression of our gratitude for the past and our continued
confidence in the future. It is, sir, with unfeigned
pleasure that we recognize you (T. R. Westbrook, Esq.,)
upon this occasion as the representative of those brave
and true men, who have reflected such glory upon the
county of Ulster. We regard the position you at present occupy among us as one full of honor. While the
gallant Colonel Gates and his brave compatriots are at
this hour so honorably representing this county upon
the field of battle, fighting like veterans for national integrity, indeed for national existence, it is right and
proper that you, sir, a distinguished citizen of Kingston,
should impersonate them in the significant ceremonies
in which we are now engaged.

"Receive then, sir, in behalf of the Twentieth
Regiment. N. Y. S. M., at the hands of the fairest and
truest among us, this regimental banner, which they
this day commit to your keeping; the only true emblem
of the country's hope. Though it has been disgraced
by those who should have died to save it from spot or
stain, yet, let it be your high ambition to transmit it,
pure and unspotted as when it was first received from
the hands of the Apostles of 1776. When this banner
shall float upon the breeze which echoes with your martial music, amid the din and carnage of the battle-field,

let it inspire you with hope, and let it nerve your heart
and hands to deeds of noble daring ; let the justice of
your cause ever give you courage, and let the favor of
kind Heaven ever grant you victory ; and let your days
of toil and your nights of watching be more than fully
requited by the glory of having given deliverance to
your country and security to your fellow-citizens !''

The banner was to have been received in behalf of
the regiment by Colonel T. B. Gates, in person, but the
recent conflict at Fredericksburg had compelled his absence. Mr. T. R. Westbrook, in the absence of the
Colonel, received, at his request, the colors, and after
the presentation address, spoke substantially as follows:

"Reverend Sir, Ladies and Gentlemen :

"No one can regret more than I do the absence of
the brave Colonel of the gallant Twentieth, who expected
to receive in person this beautiful banner—the gift of
the ladies of Saugerties. The sound, however, of booming cannon upon the banks of the Rappahannock, as it
reached his ears, spoke to him of duty ; and, with a
promptness and alacrity worthy of all praise, he at once
obeyed the summons, and is, even now, with his trusty
soldiers, perilling his life in defence of our cherished
Constitution and Government.

"I freely confess, nevertheless, that to be here in
his stead affords me personally no small degree of
pleasure. To have been deemed worthy, by an absent
friend, to receive in his behalf the colors of a regiment
whose fame is no longer hemmed in by county lines,
but has become national, is indeed an honor of which
any one might well be proud. And this feeling of mine
is greatly deepened and intensified by the reflection
that the fame which this gallant corps has attained for
bravery and good conduct, was won in a great struggle

for the right, for the perpetuation of the best Government ever given to man, and for the preservation of liberty and republican institutions.

"You, sir, in your very appropriate address upon this interesting occasion, have alluded to our old articles of confederation, and by arguments drawn from various provisions of our present constitution, have shown the folly and wickedness of those who are now seeking to overthrow that Union, under which our country grew and prospered as country never before had grown and prospered. In corroboration of your views, it will not be inappropriate for me to mention that our Union is older than the Constitution—older than the articles of confederation. When the first Continental Congress assembled in Carpenter's Hall, Philadelphia, in September, 1774, and when that same body, subsequently, on the fourth day of July, 1776, proclaimed the right of 'one people to dissolve the political bonds which connected them with another,' there was no written bond of union between the Colonies. It was not until the eleventh day of June, 1776, that a committee was appointed to prepare a form of confederation to be entered into between them. The plan submitted by this committee was not adopted by Congress until the fifteenth day of November, 1777, nor was it ratified by all the States until the first day of March, 1781. In the meantime a nationality had been declared, treaties formed, and a fierce and prolonged war most vigorously pursued and successfully conducted. How crushing and overwhelming to the modern argument in favor of the right of a State to secede from a union thus formed, are the remarks of America's great orator, Patrick Henry, uttered as long ago as 1774, and in that first memorable Congress to which allusion has already been made. 'All America,' said he, 'is thrown into one mass. Where are your landmarks—your boundaries of colonies? They are all thrown

down. The distinctions between Virginians, Pennsylvanians, New Yorkers and New Englanders are no
more. *I am not a Virginian, but an American.*'

"No, fellow-citizens, our Union was not originally
formed by a paper agreement carefully and coolly
penned by statesmen, each loving the section from which
he came more than the whole country, to which he was
proud to belong. It had a nobler origin than that. It
sprang into being from the common dangers and neces-
sities of the people of a widely extended country ; it
was cemented by common toils and sufferings, most
patiently and heroically endured, and made perpetual
and eternal by common blood most lavishly and pro-
fusely poured forth in its defence. Yes, *eternal!* I
use the word with a full knowledge of all its force and
meaning. Croakers, begone ! Timid men and traitors,
who would either consent to the dismemberment of our
glorious republic, or actively assist in this deed of
blackness, hide your heads in shame and confusion !
I point to these new-made graves, counting by thousands, and contained in every State where this foul rebellion has shown its hideous face—to that million of
volunteer bayonets, even now gleaming in this winter's
sun, girding our beloved Union round with rings of
steel, aye, with that which is stronger and better than
steel, their own loving, throbbing hearts. Those cold,
dead bodies, mouldering in stranger graves, and those
living forms, willing, if need be, to enter the same far-
off dwelling places, speak but one language and breathe
but one sentiment—*The Union: it must and shall be
preserved!*

"Before returning thanks in behalf of our noble
regiment to the fair donors of this beautiful banner, I
must crave their indulgence to utter one thought more,
which this occasion has suggested. During this interesting ceremony I have involuntarily asked myself the
question, Would you, if you could, blot out of our na-

tion's history, the record of the past two years? And
I confess, I paused as to the answer. I know full well
that there are, in every part of our land, vacant chairs
around the family table and fireside; that loving and
anxious relatives at home are, even now, waiting for
tidings from numerous battle-fields, which, when received, shall be to them tidings of grief and sorrow,
crushing and overwhelming. But I also know that our
country has a fame more enduring and sublime than
ever before. How has our patriotic love been rekindled
by this terrible baptism of fire and blood. We knew
not how closely the dear old flag of our fathers—the
glorious, ever-beaming Stripes and Stars—was wound
around our hearts and entwined with every fibre of our
affections, until traitor hands compelled its lowering at
Fort Sumter. What instances, too, of individual
courage and personal heroism has this war called forth,
worthy to be recorded side by side with any previous
exhibitions of which history informs us. Would you
witness a scene beyond the power of an artist's pencil,
then go with me to Hampton Roads. The iron-clad
monster, Merrimac, has already crushed in the wooden
sides of the brave frigate Cumberland; and now she
has drawn back for the final and fatal blow Not a
cheek blanches upon the decks of the noble ship,
though the rushing waters foretell the inevitable catas-
trophe. 'Boys!' says her captain to his men, 'shall
we give her one more broadside?' 'Aye, aye, sir!'
is the unanimous response; and the guns of the Cumberland belch out their iron hail as the gallant bark goes
down, but her flag is still floating proudly at her peak.
Look, too, at that spectacle near Roanoke Island. The
flames are leaping all over a vessel. One moment more
and they will reach a barrel of gunpowder, and then
vessel and men are lost. See now that heroic man, John
Davis, throwing his body over the terrible agent, and
protecting it thus from the raging fire. This is Ameri-

can bravery—this American courage kindled in the breast of one who felt that he was fighting for his flag, for his country. View one drama more. The scene is the Mississippi River—the curtain drops only as our national flag again floats over the Crescent City. What bravery, heroism, and deeds of noble daring. Stone fortresses, endless batteries, iron-clad rams, fire-ships! What are these when opposed to wooden walls manned by Union tars? An astounded world has answered the question, as it heard the thunder booming from the cannon of Farragut and Porter. No, no! We cannot, we must not blot the record of these glorious exploits from our nation's history, even though it be traced in tears and in blood. And that gallant act, too, which occurred but three days since upon the banks of the Rappahannock, of a hundred brave volunteers crossing that stream in the face of a murderous fire, and bringing back with them a hundred and one prisoners, must not be forgotten. This unflinching courage, this dauntless heroism, points only in one direction. Its unerring finger is ever turned to the old flag, floating as gayly in Charleston as in New York, and to one nation and one country, stretching from Maine to the Gulf, its unity unbroken and its Constitution still free.

"And now, ladies of Saugerties, in returning thanks for your beautiful and appropriate gift to our brave soldiers, what promises shall I make to you in their behalf? Need I say that the colors which you have this day presented to them, will be safely returned to the county, to be preserved among its most valued archives at the close of this unhappy struggle? I will not speak these words. Listen not to me, but hear what those (the speaker here pointed to the old colors of the regiment, which were present) mute but eloquent speakers have to say. Tattered and pierced by numerous shot, they tell you how Pratt, Ward and their gallant comrades fell. They recount the holding of the

wood at Chantilly and the support of the battery at
Antietam, and thus exhibiting to your view those
visions of the past, they ask you to commit, with full
confidence, to the care of the same men who have carried them so triumphantly, this new and beautiful
token of your love and respect. Yes, ladies, your flag
shall come again to our county, though riddled, as its
predecessors have been, by bullets. It shall come to
be preserved and pointed to in the future, if one solitary
member of the brave Twentieth survives to bear it
homeward. And that time will be, when peace shall
again smile in all the parts of that fair heritage which
our fathers bequeathed to us—when we shall shout,
with a feeling and tenderness we never knew before,
those immortal words of the great Webster, ' Liberty
and Union, now and forever, one and inseparable !' "

The old flags of the regiment were present on the
occasion, and their dilapidated appearance gave full
evidence that they had been through some very severe
struggles. The new banner cost $200, and is a very
beautiful gift.

As treasurer for the ladies, I would hereby acknowledge the receipt of the following sums for the purchase
of the new banner for the Twentieth Regiment:

SAUGERTIES.

Mrs. M. T. Trumpbour..	$5.00	Miss R. A. DeWitt. ..	$3.00
A. C. Hawley. ..	5.00	Mrs. P P Post	.50
E. J. Myer.	5.00	N. Brainard. ..	.50
B. M. Freligh ..	5.00	J. L. Butzel. ..	.50
P Cantine. ..	5.00	A. Preston. ..	1.00
Colonel C. Fiero.	5.00	Henry Turck.	.50
John Field.	10.00	Miss Sarah Whitaker...	2.00
Miss Laura Shaler......	5.00	Mrs. C. F Suderley. ..	.50
Hattie Shaler......	5.00	J. Kiersted, Jr.....	5.00
Mrs. A. J. Ketcham. ..	5.00	Wm. H. Trumpbour.	5.00
T. S. Dawes. ..	5.00	Miss Elizabeth DeWitt....	5.00
J. M. Boies.	5.00	Mrs. E. Simmons. ..	3.00
Luther Laflin.	5.00	C. F. Brill. ...	5.00

Mrs. A. Carnright.	$1.00	Mrs W. McCleur.........	$5.00
J. G. Mynderse.....	3.00	J. V. L. Overbagh....	5.00
Miss Catt Gay............	2.00	M. E. Williams....	1.00
Mrs. J. L. Montross......	2.50	J. Simmons.	2.00
F. L. Laflin.	5.00	W C. Hall..........	2.00
H. D. Laflin..	5.00	Misses Gosman..........	2.00
Miss J. Kearney..	2.00	Mrs. C. F. Field..... ...	5.00
J. E. Myer.	2.00	P. T. Overbagh	2.00
Mrs. S. Merclean.........	2.50	J. H. Myer.........	1.00
James Sickles.	2.00	W. Maginnis.........	1.00
U. Lockwood	1.00	J. B. Sheffield.......	10.00
J. H. Field.....	1.00	G, B. Matthews......	1.00
T. J. Barritt.	1.00	S. Bookstaver. ..	.50
Jeremiah Russell.....	1.00	H. P Heermans...	... 00
G. Wilbur..... ..	2.00	J. G. Smedberg..	1.00
Miss Annie Myer....	3.00	C. P Shultis.......	3.00

MALDEN.

Mrs. N. Kellogg. ..	$5.00	Mrs. F. K. Field..........	$1.00
Miss Kellogg.........	.50	Gelbert..............	.50
Mrs. Kays.	.25	O'Brien......	.25
John Maxwell.	1.25	Rightmyer..........	.25
Teal.	.25	Minnesley.....	.25
F Bell.	.25	Zulman...	.25
Wilson.	.25	Brink	.25
J. J. Buck.	1.00	J. E Kellogg... ...	5.00
D. Bigelow..	1.00	Miss A. Corcoran...	.10
C. Turpen.	1.00	E. Wolf.	.10
E. Bigelow.........	5.00	Mrs. H. Bogardus...	1.00
Miss E. Bogardus. ..	.25	Scott..............	.25
Mrs. J. Scutt...	.25	D. Snyder...........	.25
Knight...........	.25	E. Bell.	.25
Miss A. Coes.	.25	Miss R. Towner...... ..	.25
Mrs. Lewis......... ..	.22	Mrs. James Maxwell.......	.25
Miss C. Gillespy...	.50	Van Hosen...........	.25
Mrs. Elmendorf........	.15	Moore	.20
P. Bell.............	.20	Miller..	.25
O'Brien.	.25	Austen	.25
J..Terve.	.50	Paradeu........... ..	.25

Total............. .. ..$210.00

B. M. FRELIGH, *Treasurer.*

SAUGERTIES, December 22, 1862.

3 8

SAUGERTIES, Feb. 19th, 1863.

MESSRS. EDITORS: I have this day received from COLONEL T. B. GATES a letter of response *upon the receipt* of the New Regimental Banner, presented by the ladies of our town to the Twentieth Regiment, and I hand you the same for publication.

Yours, &c.,

B. M. FRELIGH.

HEADQUARTERS ULSTER GUARD,
Twentieth Regiment New York State Militia.
AQUIA CREEK, Feb. 12th, 1863.

BENJAMIN M. FRELIGH, Esq.:

"*My Dear Sir :*—Major Van Rensselaer, who has just returned from Ulster County, has delivered to me the beautiful banner presented to this regiment by the generous and patriotic ladies of Saugerties. I beg leave to express, through you, at whose hands I received a synopsis of the address of Rev. Mr. Gaston, and the reply of Hon. T. R. Westbrook, the sincerest thanks of the regiment for this most timely and apposite mark of remembrance and approbation.

"It would have given me much pleasure to have been present on the occasion of the presentation, and to have personally received this loyal offering from its fair donors, and to have listened to the eloquent remarks of their worthy representative. But this could not be ; and I regret it less, since the regiment was so fortunate as to have the Hon. T. R. Westbrook reply for it. With his usual eloquence, he most acceptably discharged the office he so kindly undertook. His self-sacrificing labors, which have contributed much to swell the enlistments from Ulster and neighboring counties, and his ardent devotion to the Constitution and the

Union, point him out as the representative of Ulster's absent soldiers.

" In delivering the Color to the custody of the regiment, I communicated to it the cordial and approving sentiments expressed in its favor on behalf of the ladies of Saugerties. I need not tell you that such words of commendation, and such tokens of confidence and esteem, sink deep into the soldier's heart. To know that at home—that around the hearth-stones where his friends gather, far removed from the scenes of strife and carnage which envelop *his* path—that in all the walks of civil life, where, in happier days, he mingled with his fellow man—to know that he is kindly remembered, and that his sacrifices and his trials, in aid of his imperilled country, draw forth the generous sympathy and warm eulogiums of its fair daughters—this is a knowledge that blunts the edge of many wants—that consoles, when hunger and fatigue add new burdens to his duty—that surrounds him with a genial warmth when storms are beating on him, and cold is pinching with its frosts.

" The bleak wind which now unfurls this much-prized symbol of woman's loyalty and regard, sweeps over the shivering forms of two opposing and embattled hosts, whose long lines of frowning guns seem eager for a renewal of the carnival of death, and the wild fierce scenes of war's ensanguined field. The hoarse thunder of their terrible anger now sleeps in their brazen throats, to be awakened again ere long, and summon to another struggle the Army of the Union with the hordes of rebellion.

" And this is but one of many similar pictures presented in the Rebel States. ' Grim-visaged war ' hath settled on their hills, and crouched within their valleys, and mustered its legions upon their plains, deforming the fair face of nature, and driving peace and its happy pursuits from the land.

" How difficult it is, even here, surrounded by frowning guns and bristling bayonets, to realize the fact of this demonic war—to comprehend the truth of the history we are now making. But two short years ago, peace reigned in every portion of our fair land—manufactories, trade, commerce, agriculture, arts and sciences flourished and adorned, while they enriched our people. The Nations of the Old World paid homage to the Giant of the New, and their people, by hundreds of thousands, annually sought homes and occupations under our liberal laws and venerated Constitution. The theory of self-government was thought to be fully vindicated and wrought into a living, enduring principle. The memory of the authors of our Federal Constitution was cherished and revered—our flag respected everywhere on land and sea. The murmurings of a few malcontents was as nothing in the universal happiness and prosperity which then did, and long had blessed our people, beyond any parallel in the world's history.

"That a nation thus circumstanced—thus seemingly secure in the enjoyment of domestic peace, could so suddenly, so causelessly, be torn away from its moorings, and dashed upon the rock of civil war, and reduced to the bitter ordeal through which we are now passing, challenges the wonder of mankind. That within the wide limits of our country was a man so treacherously vile, as to seek to render asunder the bond which held our Union of States together, was beyond my conception of human turpitude. No tongue has yet found language in which the wickedness of the authors of the rebellion can fitly be expressed—nor ever will. Aggregate the deaths and wounds—the widows' and orphans' tears—the wives' and children's watchings and anxiety—the soldiers' personal sacrifices and sufferings—the millions of treasure expended—and to these add what is yet to follow, and you have the sum of the guilt of the authors of this war. Is any human tribunal adequate to their punishment? None! God alone can measure their sin, and He, alone, in His own good time, will punish it as it deserves.

" Palliation or excuse? No! Satan's rebellion against the mild rule of Heaven was no more groundless or unwarranted. The Government had never infringed or attempted, or threatened to infringe any of their real or constitutional prerogatives. On the contrary, the rebellious States had been indulged and humored by governmental forbearance to a degree of unprecedented liberality Their sins of omission and commission (and the foremost of them had grievously offended) were generously overlooked or forgiven. They were allowed a basis of representation in the Federal Congress and in the Electoral College that was unequal, if not unjust, towards the non-slaveholding States, and they participated to their full proportion in the control of the Government and the direction of its affairs.

Among all the pretences by which it is sought to mask the iniquity of this rebellion, that which charges upon the Federal Government the beginning of the war, is the most impudent and brazen. Can any man, either South or North, with the truth of history before his eyes, help despising the knave or fool, who takes refuge behind this shallow sophism? The Government, still indulgent, looked calmly on, while armed traitors were congregating at Charleston, and while rebel hands were throwing up earthworks and planting batteries against the little band of United States soldiers, that, under the gallant Anderson, had fled from Fort Moultrie and now occupied Sumter. For days the work of preparation, under the guns of the Fort, went on, and yet the Government withheld the order that could have hurled the iron storm of Sumter upon the unprotected heads of these defiant and rebellious children. The Star of the West is fired into while bearing troops and supplies to the beleagured fortress—and finally, when all is

ready—when, by ill-judged forbearance, the odds are
all against the doomed fort, a hundred guns belch
treason against its walls, and its flag is lowered amid
fire and smoke, and shouts and rebel joy.

"Such were the first overt works of rebellion—such
the beginning of this desolating contest. The Federal
Government, still hoping against hope, hesitated to put
the hand of correction upon its erring children. But
all in vain ; forbearance was deemed pusillanimity, and
charity, imbecility   The hydra secession arose with the
fall of Sumter, and rivers of blood must flow to sa-
tiate its fury.   Oh, that the guns of Sumter had proclaimed the Federal authority, and vindicated its insulted dignity, when the first spade was thrust into the
earth to erect works against her !

"It was not in any pretended encroachment of the
Federal Government—it was not in the election of our
present Chief Magistrate—it was not from any fear that
the rights of the South would be invaded, that this unholy war was thrust upon the country   The seed of
this bitter fruit was sown as long ago as 1832, and has
been sedulously, but covertly nurtured by the slave-
holding aristocracy, until it burst full grown upon the
startled country in 1861.   An oligarchy, based upon
slavery, and controlled and governed by slaveholders,
was the dazzling vision which deluded them and the sole
incentive to their crime—a crime not only against their
Government and its Constitution and its laws, but a
crime against the liberty of the human race, against
Democratic Governments, against civilization throughout the world.   The question at issue, therefore, involves not only our Government, but also the principle
on which it is based ; it involves the establishment upon
this continent, and within the limits of the States, a
form of Government having slavery as its corner-stone,
and more despotic in its character than any European
power. *And should it succeed*, it involves ever-recur-

ring war, impoverishment and final absolute disintegration. Two such Governments cannot exist side by side
upon this continent.

"The South has thrust this issue upon the country, and
the Government must meet it. By every consideration
of duty—by every obligation imposed by the oath and
the Constitution and laws the Government must meet
and fight out this issue, though streams run crimson
with the nation's blood. There is no other alternative
if it were worthy to seek one. The rebels scout the
idea of a restoration by compromise, and laugh to scorn
the Brooks, the Van Burens and the Woods, who ask to
cement, by concession, the broken bonds of Union. No!
—let none be flattered by this delusive hope and cry
peace ; the instigators and managers of this rebellion
have cast their all upon the die ; with them it is success
or extinction.

"But, if it is the duty of the Government to marshal
its army and send it out to meet this domestic foe, how
much more is it the duty of *the people, who make the
Government,* to rally to its support, and, laying aside
all other considerations, give it their energetic, cordial,
determined aid in this its time of trial. If ever people
had a form of Government that was worthy of their
efforts to preserve and perpetuate—that justified the
sacrifice of lives and treasure to save—it is yours. Baptized in the blood of our fathers, built up and perfected
by the wisdom of giant minds, it has filled the land with
plenty and its people with honor and happiness. In
memory of the past ; with a full sense of the dangers of
the present ; with hope and faith in the future, let the
loyal people rally around the Government and fight
this question out. Then, and only then, can we be assured of permanent peace.

"If the principle of Secession is admitted, our Constitution was an idle phantasm of no real thing, and we
flourished eighty years and grew to a mighty nation in

blissful ignorance of the fact that we had no Government at all.   The idea is utterly repugnant to any conceiveable theory of Government, and only adapted to and productive of chaos, civil war. anarchy and the obliteration of all national obligations.   If South Carolina may ' secede,' then may any and every State ; and who would stand sponsor to the christening of such a child in the family of nations.

" This can never be conceded.   The battle we are now waging is for all time and for the principle of free Governments for all people.   The lives and money it may cost are as nothing weighed in the balance against the great issues involved.   If we fail, then farewell to the theory of self-government, and farewell to the rights of the *many* when poised against the aristocratic *few*.

" I banish all thought of eventual failure.   It cannot be that the history of our Union is completed, and the star of our destiny in its final decline.   We have not grown to our present magnitude as a nation only to be broken into fragments and partitioned off into petty States.   We shall come out of this contest with a vindicated Constitution, and with the bonds of union reunited and strengthened by the ordeal through which they have passed ; unless, indeed, loyalty and patriotism in the North and West give way before exactions of partisan considerations.   Nothing so much discourages the soldier in the field as rumors of discord and party strife which reach him from home ; while, on the other hand, he can receive no greater 'aid and comfort' than is afforded in a consciousness that the masses of the people are unanimous in sustaining the Government and the cause for which he fights.   Feeling, as he does, that there is no power under the Constitution to carry on the war but the Government, he cannot comprehend that loyalty which, while it professes to be in favor of a 'vigorous prosecution of the war,' indulges in constant attacks upon, and thereby weakens and embarasses the Administration, to whom alone, for the time being, is entrusted the prosecution of the war. Errors have doubtless been committed—wrongs, perhaps, have been done by the Administration, but this is not the time for the settlement of such questions. The present great business of the country is war, and if the people wish to see this business honorably finished, the Union restored, and peace again smile upon the land, they must not be lukewarm in their patriotism, or captious and fault-finding in their support of the Government. The army does not sympathise with the grumblers who vent their complaints upon the public and their lamentations upon every wind. But this semi-secessionism will pass away in the end, and the great heart of the North will beat true to the dictates of loyalty and freedom. It will realize. by-and-by, the imminence of the danger impending over the country and arouse itself to repel it. The people in the loyal States are too much absorbed by trade, commerce and pleasure—they hardly appreciate the existence of the war, or feel in any considerable degree its effects. If they would still have it a far-off evil, and a speedily-ended one, they must cease criticising and turn to supporting the Government, and then we may hope to see our standards advancing toward the heart of the rebellious districts, and the flag of treason humbled in the dust.

"LADIES OF SAUGERTIES!—In behalf of the Ulster Guard I thank you for the beautiful color you have bestowed upon it. It links us at once with fond memories of home and the history of our soldier lives. It reminds us of the hurried burials that have from time to time shut out from sight the forms of many who gallantly stood side by side with us when the traitor's

> " ball,
> The sabre's thirsting edge,
> The hot shell shattering in its fall,
> The bayonets rending wedge
> Scattered death."

'' The valleys of the Rappahannock and Hedgeman—the plains of Manassas and Antietam—the woods of Chantilly and South Mountain have drunk the blood of the 'Ulster Guard' and left it with ranks thinned and with many '' names we loved to hear'' underscored on our roster and muster rolls 'killed in action.' But their places will be filled, if not in our own corps, then in some other. Victory and defeat have alternated with our army, but in the end, and in God's own time, the right will prevail. For us this beautiful banner shall be an incentive to further and unrelaxing efforts in behalf of our imperilled country

'' The names inscribed upon it inspire, while they justify my confidence in the assurance I give you that, sooner or later, it shall be borne back to you floating over the remnant of the 'Ulster Guard:' torn and rent, perhaps, and its fresh beauties gone, but never, *never* dishonored!

'' If we ask you, then, to add some other names to those it already bears, let us hope that each may signify a victory, and the final one the extinction of rebellion and the restoration of union and peace.

I am, very truly,

Your obed't servt.,

THEO. B. GATES,

Colonel Commanding.''

FLAG PRESENTATION ON RETURN OF REGIMENT—ADDRESS OF MR. HENRY
H. REYNOLDS—REPLY OF COLONEL GATES—FOR DESCRIPTION OF FLAG
AND INCIDENTS OF PRESENTATION, SEE CHRONOLOGICAL RECORD OF
DATE OF FEBRUARY 22D, 1866.

*Colonel :—*Your fellow citizens of Ulster County desire to present this standard to the Ulster Guard—the
20th Regiment New York State Militia. They ask the
acceptance of it as a token of the interest with which they
continue to regard you all, and that it may *represent*
rather than replace your banners which have "borne
the brunt of battle" and are now deposited at our State
Capitol. With these few words my office (quite thank-
fully accepted) might be deemed to end—and perhaps
it was committed to such hands rather than to one of
younger years and feeling, that the precious gold of
silence might be more suggestive than most silvery
speech. And yet the day we celebrate, the occasion
and the presence—the crowding memories that have
made up so much of our lives in these five years in
which we have seemed to live for a generation, would
touch the lips of most trembling age with earnestness,
and stir within the oldest and coldest heart a fount of
feeling and of speech that would not be repressed. On
many such hearts the furrows this day are deeper than
the outward token, for the channels have been worn by
night and by day in anxiety, and fear, and sorrow, and
it now seems as if your return (the first to go, the last
to come back) were the final lifting of the dark cloud
that has so long enshrouded us. And so we come to
join the deep and solemn joy which here and elsewhere
to-day is touching elder lips than those of St. Simeon in
his day, with the lower refrain of the *nunc dimittis*—

"Now Thou dost let Thy servant depart in peace, for mine eyes have seen Thy salvation."

We go back irresistibly to the hour when first among the foremost you sprang responsive to the call for troops to defend our National Capital against an unnatural foe. The organization which, at the cost of so much labor and self-sacrifice, had been sustained for years, then showed its value ; and almost at a moment's warning you were ready for the field. Could we all have seen when first you went forth what was to be our loss and sacrifice in your onward path—could we have foreseen that one and another rank of 75,000 men then called for—more than seven times told were to be the sacrifice of our children to the southern Moloch—we should have needed more confidence in our cause and faith in Him who guides the destinies of nations to un- clasp the hands and nerve the hearts that would have held you back. Nay, how many of us would have turned hopelessly away from the effort to save our country. But could we have thought amid our despon- dency and despairing, when once and again you return- ed to recruit your wasted ranks, that we should this day, through the Divine blessing upon your and kin- dred efforts, stand in such a scene as this, amidst a rescued and unshattered country, would not many a vow have been recorded that nothing thenceforth should shake our trust in the cause of human freedom with its earthly and heavenly defences ? And now you have come back and we have looked upon your living faces, and with an inner vision have seen beside you the bless- ed form of every one who first or last went out to battle with you, and whom you have left behind to wait a lit- tle for us all, each now named softly as the household name

" Of one whom God hath taken."

In the watches of the night, in the rising storm, the

summer's heat, the winter's cold, rumors of defeat and victory, in the glare and through the darkness, we have seemed to hear your tramp and cry, your challenge and the sentry tread, the reveille and the tattoo. From the homes and hearts you left behind our eyes grew dim, and yet not weary, as with a passionate earnestness they followed your footsteps through the fields whose names are borne upon this standard. It was the wail of an English monarch, that on her pulseless heart would be found the name of a fortress lost by her armies. But on our living hearts, beyond the power of after memories are engraven Manassas and Gettysburg, South Mountain and Petersburg, Beverly Ford and Fredericksburg, Warrenton Springs and Chantilly, Gainesville and Groveton, Antietam and Bull Run. We did not ask whether the fields were lost or won, but you were there and there you did your duty ; there left precious seed for immortality beneath "the tree whose leaves are for the healing of the nations."

Nor were our eyes alone upon you. Our noble Regiments that successively followed you to the field listened, from however afar, to your clarion cry, shared in your reverses, gloried in your success, prouder of you than of themselves amidst all their hard-earned trophies ; nor this alone because they held you as " older, not better soldiers." Such is the presence to which you come to-day It needs no gift of second sight to see hands, not of flesh and blood, reaching out towards this standard, and dear pale faces translucent with the light of heaven. To such keeping it would seem as if your shot-riven banners had been given, to realize the fond conceit of an elder time that sought the consecration of its standards by priestly blessing.

Eight years ago on an occasion like the present, while yet no cloud was on our country's sky, your gifted Commander, who has won his rest before you, (" first falls the ripest fruit,") responded to a gift like this : " We appreciate the honor you have done us, and we promise that if this land is ever involved in war, that these colors shall wave with credit and glory wherever danger is thickest and the fight is warmest." Well did he keep—well have you kept the pledge. It is not now to be said whether we have been as faithful to you, though you have not lacked the oft-repeated assurance. One portion of us at least, the gentler and the fairer, they who are always going before or behind every great dispensation, smoothing the paths for rougher feet to tread, are here to-day to testify by their deeds on their own behalf and yours. Neither they nor we, nor yet yourselves, have counted up your heroes or your heroisms. Such have marked your marches and your watches, your hospitals and homes, as well as fields of battle, and not a few to-day are dwelling beneath the shadows of suffering or of sorrow. These are not ungladdened by the thought, that no sacrifice, or loss, or pain, that they or those most dear to them have known, but shall pass into benediction and blessing upon our own and other lands, a witness and an answer to the uplifted hand of the Ulster Guard and its legend—" This hand for our Country." We need no mythology, as of old, to give the place of honor to those who have done or suffered in the nation's cause ; and with the sad lessons of the few past years may not soon forget, that if our position among the nations is yet retained, it is, under the Divine hand, to you, and such as you, we owe it. You have bound the bars of our Nation's Flag together, and kept the stars shining in their orbit ; and while its crimson lines may indicate your path, its golden stars and azure field should be to all our eyes the over-arching heaven from which angels have come down to camp about our hearts and country in the times of peril. To all of us that flag will be the

dearer, because of the great danger through which it
has been borne.   Its rescue from those whom you

> " Forbade to wade through slaughter to a throne,
>   And shut the gates of mercy on mankind,"

gives to all its folds the significance of protection and of
safety.   Unlike the most of your brave brethren, you
have not returned to scatter to your peaceful homes,
and laying aside your armor forget the arts of war, but
under your old organization to stand as you stood before, ready for your country's call.

Take, then, this gift—nay rather, this part acknowledgment of the debt we owe you.   Its national escutcheon marks it as your own—yours by inheritance,
yours by conquest--and the names by which this is surrounded show how it has been defended.   But for
these we might have been a dismembered and scattered
nation, a shame and a hissing upon the earth.   Let this
be a memorial of our trust in you and your faithfulness
to us—a compact now baptized with the baptism for the
dead and the tears of the living.   We may not ask that
it may go with you to other fields of bloodshed, but in
the repose you have won so worthily, let it be a memorial of what you have done, and what we have striven
to do ; and above all, what has been done for us, in defense of a flag that to-day waves over an undivided land
in honor of him who first planted it among the nations.

> " Flag of the free heart's hope and home,
>   By angel hands to valor given,
>   Its stars have lit the welkin dome,
>   And all its hues were wrought in heaven."

Col. T. B. GATES received the color and replied as
follows :

Mr. REYNOLDS :—I am reminded, Sir, that eight
years ago a scene not unlike this was witnessed on our
Village Common.   The corporate bodies of Kingston

and Rondout united in presenting to the " Ulster
Guard " a stand of colors, in token of their official approbation of the soldierly appearance and good conduct
of the battalion then composing our local militia.

It was at a time when the people of the country were
beginning to shake off the apathy that had long distinguished the treatment of our citizen soldiery, and to
manifest some interest in and respect for these voluntary organizations which our forefathers intended should
constitute the bulk of our republican army.

But our destiny had latterly seemed to be only to
reap the sweet fruits of Peace, and gather the harvests
of ten thousand kinds of pleasant and useful industry.
We had been borne along on the flood-tide of individual
and national prosperity, and had become a learned and
wealthy people—an enlightened and powerful nation—
whose vast extent embraced all degrees of temperature
—every variety of soil—in whose bosom reposed the waters of an hundred inland seas, and whose extremities
were bathed by the waves of the two great oceans.

In our grandeur and self-sufficiency, we had come to
despise the simple means of national defense and internal peace contemplated by the founders of our Government, and our militia system had for years been the
laughing-stock of the country, and the butt of unthink-
ing ridicule.

The arms our forefathers wielded in establishing our
nationality, and which our fathers twice afterwards
siezed to vindicate our national honor, were rusting in
their undisturbed repose, and their uses were all but
forgotten. The rumor of foreign wars sometimes came
across the waters to us, but it could not induce us to
burnish up our own arms, nor divert us from our pursuits of pleasure or profit. Peace reigned throughout
our borders, and we were in amity with the whole world.
Why, then, we reasoned with ourselves, should we

mimic the "pomp and circumstance of glorious war,"
who nevermore shall see

"Battle's magnificently stern array ?"

Nor, Sir, was there any external sign of danger that
directed our attention to and begot some consideration
for our militia system, eight years ago ? There was no
single speck of war in all our tranquil sky But by one
of those changes which sometimes come over public sentiment, without an apparent cause, like the gradual rising of the billows of ocean, when the winds are locked
in their caves, our militia was lifted out of the slough of
despond, where it had lain so long in undeserved disgrace, and put upon a footing of respectability.

It was soon after this, Sir, that the scene you have
recalled to my mind, took place on our Village Common. Those of us who were present may have observed
the smile that lurked in many an eye, when our then
Colonel, in his earnest and heartfelt manner, declared
that the Colors he received should be protected and defended at the hazard of his life. To many, it seemed a
cheap pledge ; and to some, an absurd obligation.

And yet, within four years from that day, he had re-
deemed that pledge and paid that obligation with his
life-blood on the field of battle ; and within five years,
those Colors were deposited in the archives of your
State, torn and riven by hostile shot and shell.

But, Sir, may I add, that torn and rent as they were,
they had always gallantly floated over the Regiment to
which they had been entrusted, and although the enemy often saw, he never laid his traitorous hand upon
their sacred folds.

Serene as seemed our political horizon, when Colonel
Pratt pledged his life for the defense of those Colors,
we were even then, unwittingly, standing on the consuming crust of a national volcano, that was shortly to
crumble under our feet and carry a million of our peo-

ple to untimely graves. And in less than three years
thereafter, the quiet waters of Charleston harbor vibrat-
ed to the thunder of treasonous cannon, as they hurled
their iron power against the walls of Sumter, while
their echoes, sweeping over land and sea, called the
loyal men of the nation to arms.

Yes, Sir, we may justly feel some pride in the fact
that Ulster County was among the first to send her sons
forth to the defense of the country, and it was our
boast, later in the war, that she had three entire Regiments in the field, besides odd companies here and there,
and squads and single men in every New York Brigade.

And you will permit me to say, Sir, that no troops
excelled these hardy sons of Old Ulster in subordination
to discipline, in powers of endurance, or in bravery upon
the battle-field. They have fought, Sir, from Gettysburg in the north, to B Island, near the delta of the Mississippi, and everywhere with honor to themselves and
the county they represented.

This beautiful banner, which it is my proud office to
accept in behalf of the Regiment, is unlike its predecessor, to which I have referred, in that the former had no
foreign names upon its folds, while this is covered, by
authority of the Secretary of War, with what were
strange words to us four years ago. But now, alas!
they are all too familiar, and speak of battle scenes and
death struggles—of victories and defeats. And each
name is graven on the wrung hearts of fathers, mothers,
brothers, sisters, wives, for there, and there, and there,
some loved one fell, by battle or disease.

This beautiful Color, Sir, is an epitome of the war history of the Regiment that now receives it, and in a very
considerable degree, brings to our minds the leading
events of the Rebellion. It reminds us of the dark days
in April, 1861, when our National Capital, cut off from
communication with the loyal North, filled with and

surrounded by traitors, its safety seemed to depend upon the alacrity with which our militia should rally to the rescue. Then it recalls the memory of the brave, long, weary, desperate campaign of Gen. Pope, when for ten days a starving army marched by night and fought by day an opponent twice its strength, until its bleeding and shattered remnant found food and rest in the defenses of Washington.

Following that comes the more successful campaign of Gen. McClellan, with its fruitless termination in the escape of Lee's army across the Potomac.

Then the bold attack of Burnside, on the enemy's lines at Fredericksburg, and his frightful repulse.

Anon the loyal States are again invaded, and the three days struggle and glorious victory of Gettysburg ensue.

Finally, the dashing of the army of the Potomac upon, and the breaking of the enemy's lines around Petersburg ; the occupation of Richmond, and the termination of the war within a few days of four years from the date of the Regiment's first departure from this village, to which you have so eloquently alluded.

Through all these changing scenes the Regiment has been so fortunate as to retain the favorable regard of its friends at home. And if it should be needed to vindicate the more than ordinary esteem in which the people of this County always held the "Old Twentieth," I might be excused for saying, Sir, that its courage never was impugned—that it had on more than one occasion been selected from among its fellows for important and desperate service, and that it had been named in General Orders for gallantry on the battle-field.

The Regiment has had the fortune to serve under such General commanders as the Christian, noble-hearted gentleman and thorough soldier, Patrick ; the high-souled and chivalric Wadsworth ; the gallant and lamented Reynolds, and the impetuous, daring Hooker.

By the partiality of the first of these, the Regiment did not participate in the fighting between the Rapidan and the James, nor in much of that which took place around Petersburg. But during this time it had an important and the chief position, in the Department of the Provost-Marshal-General of the Army of the Potomac, and subsequently of the Armies operating against Richmond.

It was a great consolation, Sir, amid the fatigues and dangers of war, to be constantly assured, as we were, of the anxious and prayerful solicitude with which the career of the Guard was followed by the patriotic affections of the people of this County While such knowledge constituted a new tie, that bound our hearts more firmly to Old Ulster, it was also an incentive to the more earnest discharge of duty, for it ever whispered: "Friends at home are looking on you." And even in the last moments of the dying soldier, it gave the comforting assurance that here, where our thoughts so often wandered, the memory of the fallen should be forever green.

But these trials, Sir, are haply over, and what remains of the "Old Twentieth," has returned, among the last, to lay aside its bruised arms and the habiliments of the soldier, and to resume those of the civilian. Many, very many, alas! of those who went, came not back to meet the greeting of kindred and friends. The camp, the march, the bivouac, the battle-field, each claims its victims to the god of war. From the Blue Ridge of the Alleghanies to the fortressed lines around Petersburg—from Libby Prison at Richmond to the unparalleled horrors of the earthly hell at Andersonville, our dead are strewn like autumn leaves.

But, thank God! the cause for which they fell has gloriously triumphed ; and if our statesmen wisely employ that triumph, treason will never again raise its parricidal hand against the flag for which so many loyal men have died.

The remnant of the Regiment has returned to such reward as a loyal people will bestow upon its individual members. And its first duty is to thank you, Sir, (whom we are proud to recognize as once a member, and the revered religious guide of the Regiment), and through you the entire people of the County, for the kind sympathy, the encouraging words, the cordial greetings, and the substantial gifts which have so often gladdened the soldiers' hearts in their distant service.

And let me through you, Sir, bespeak for these returned soldiers an indulgent judgment, in the first flush of their new-found liberty from military restraint. If in the joyousness of present pleasure, enhanced ten thousand fold by the trials of the past, there sometimes springs up the spirit of mischievous excess, believe with me, it is as foreign to the nature of the man as this new freedom is novel and exhilarating to him.

And again, I ask that our citizens manifest the substantial respect I know they entertain for the private soldiers—the men who have carried the musket and borne the deprivations, the untold hardships, and the dangers of the field—the men who have done the actual fighting, and the reward of whose bravery and patriotism we now enjoy in peace restored and our Government preserved with all its former power and dominion. I ask that these men, Sir, shall find ready access to such honorable employments and fair remuneration as their several capacities may qualify them for. Most of them abandoned such occupations when their fellow citizens called upon them to go forth to the defense of the country It is but just that the means of comfortable livelihood be held out to them on their return.

The "Ulster Guard" resumes its position once more as a Regiment of New York Militia, and it will be the unremitting care of those upon whom its reorganization devolves, to make it worthy of its now historic fame. Its reputation is inseparably linked to that of the county whose name it bears, and whose partiality it has so often experienced.

The sneer that curled the fastidious lip at the name "Militia" in times gone by, has given place to a more generous and considerate sentiment, and hereafter the young and able-bodied men of the land will esteem it worth their while to swell the ranks of our citizen-soldiery, and thereby qualify themselves in some degree, for the discharge of the highest duty they owe their country—bearing arms in its defense.

I accept this historic banner, which you have entrusted to the keeping of the "Ulster Guard," and thank you in behalf of the Regiment for the flattering sentiments with which the gift is accompanied. The officers and men who may hereafter belong to the organization, cannot but be better soldiers, by the lessons this color will ever teach them. They cannot but prize more highly their religious and political privileges, when the banner that floats over them reminds them how much those privileges have cost.

I hope and trust, Sir, that this flag need never be unfurled to the storm of battle. But should the time come when our country calls for her citizen-soldiery to rally again to her defense, I have no reason to doubt the alacrity with which the "Old Twentieth" will respond to the call. And I pledge you, Sir, that her colors shall be as sacredly protected in the future as they have been in the past.

It is due to some gallant officers and brave men, who came from other counties and joined their fortunes to those of the 20th Regiment, early in the war, and who have shared its hardships and perils, to make this public acknowledgment of their services, and to thank them, as I do, in behalf of the "Ulster Guard," with which their connection now necessarily terminates, for

the faithfulness with which they always did their duty.
And I trust it will not be considered invidious if I express my particular obligations to Brevet-Lieut.-Col.
Leslie, who marched with us in 1861, as a Lieutenant,
and who has most richly merited his promotions, by a
devotion to duty that has known no deviation and
scarcely a respite.

To each and all of these officers and men who have
so long and faithfully served under a banner bearing
upon its folds a legend to which they would necessarily
be strangers on leaving the service, and yet who were
as jealous of the reputation of the "Ulster Guard," as
such, as though they were to the manner born—I pledge
to them, for all time to come, the same cordial affection
on the part of the Guard that they have borne towards
it through the wearisomeness of camp life, the fatigue
of the battle-field, the sadness of defeat, and the rapture
of victory.

May they ever feel when they put their feet upon
the soil of Ulster County, that they have a right to call
every loyal man they meet a brother, and may every
such be ready to give them a brother's welcome, for
the love they bore "the Old Twentieth."

And now, comrades, one single word of admonition
to each of you—do not be betrayed into any act, as civilians, that will sully your hard-earned renown as soldiers of the Ulster Guard. If it be true, as we were often reminded in the field, that the good citizen made the
best soldier, let us prove the converse of the rule, and
show that four years' wearing of the blue has not disqualified us for the decorous and orderly occupations of
civil life.

G.

The "Ulster Guard" still exists as the Twentieth Battalion N. G. S. N. Y., with the following

ROSTER.

FIELD AND STAFF TWENTIETH BATTALION.

Thomas H. Tremper. ....*Lieutenant-Colonel.*
Alfred Tanner ... .*Major.*
Stephen S. Hulbert.. *Adjutant.*
Vacant . . . . *Quartermaster.*
T. Beekman Westbrook. .*Com. of Sub.*
George C. Smith. .. .*Surgeon and Brevet Lt Col.*
C. William Camp. . . .*Chaplain.*
William S. Kenyon.. .....*Ins. Rifle Practice.*

NON-COMMISSIONED STAFF.

Samuel E. Jacobs. . .*Sergeant-Major.*
William S. Rodie .. .*Qr.-Mr Sergeant.*
Frederick B. Hibbard. *Com. Sergeant.*
James H. Tripp. .*Ordnance Sergeant.*
Charles A. Barnes .*Hos. Steward.*
Napoleon X. Avobambauet.*Drum Major*
Jerome Williams. .*Band Leader.*
Charles Dubois. *Sergeant Standard Bearer.*
Charles Rudnitske. .. " " "
William Gertach .*Right General Guide.*
Rodney Van Leuven. .*Left General Guide.*

616

LINE.

Company A.

Henry A. Hildebrandt   .*Captain.*
Vacant   .... .*First Lieutenant.*
Benjamin F Crump   .*Second Lieutenant.*

· Company B.

Benjamin J. Hornbeck   *Captain.*
John E. Dunwoody.   .*First Lieutenant.*
Charles B. Westbrook   ...*Second Lieutenant.*

Company D

Nathan A. Sims.......... *Captain*
Jacob C. Stephan.. ....*First Lieutenant.*
Richard Wiener ....*Second Lieutenant.*

Company F

Stephen Conwell .....   *Captain.*
Urban Hamburger ......   *First Lieutenant*
David Mulholland ....*Second Lieutenant.*

Company H.

John E. Kraft .. ..   *Captain.*
Wallace H. Smith ....   *First Lieutenant.*
N. Scott Haulenbeck......*Second Lieutenant.*

Present strength of battalion, 280.

H.

As an act of justice to General Fowler I insert the following extracts from his and General Wadsworth's official reports of the first day's operations at Gettysburg :

[*Extract from General Fowler's Report :*]

* * * * * "On entering the field the "Ninety-fifth N Y and Fourteenth N Y S. M. were "formed on the left of the Brigade, a house and garden "intervening between them and the right wing. We "were at once engaged by the enemies' skirmishers from "woods to our left and front, we drove them back and "I then found that the enemy were advancing on our "right, and were then to our rear and in possession of "one of our pieces of artillery I immediately ordered "my command, the Ninety-fifth N Y and Fourteenth "N Y S. M. to march in retreat, until on a line with "the enemy, and then changed front perpendicularly to "face them, the enemy also changing front to meet us. "At this time the Sixth Wisconsin Regiment gallantly "advanced to our assistance. The enemy then took "possession of a railroad cut, and I gave the order to "charge them, which order was carried out gallantly by "all the regiments, by which the piece of artillery was "recaptured. The advance was continued until near "the cut, when I directed the Sixth Wisconsin to flank "it by throwing forward their right, which being done "all the enemy within our reach surrendered, officers, "battle flags and men." * * * * * "The "loss of the regiment amounts to about fifty per cent. "of the force engaged." * * * *

(Signed) E. B. FOWLER,

Col. Cmdg. 14th Regt. N Y S. M.

[*Extract from General Wadsworth's Report :*]

*   *   *   *   *   "The Second Brigade Gen. "Cutler led the column followed by the Second Maine "Battery, Capt. Hall. The First Brigade Gen. Mere- "dith bringing up the rear. Here we met the advance "guard of the enemy

"Three regiments of the Second Brigade were order- "ed to deploy on the right of the road (Cashtown), the "battery was placed in position near the road, and the "balance of the division ordered up to the left of the "road, the right became sharply engaged before the "line was formed and at this time (about quarter past "ten A. M.) our gallant leader fell mortally wounded.

"The right encountered a heavy force, were out- "numbered and outflanked, and after a resolute con- "test bravely conducted by Brig. Gen. Cutler, fell back "in good order to the Seminary Ridge near the town, "and a portion of the command to a point still nearer "the town. As they fell back followed by the enemy "the Fourteenth N. Y. S. M. (Col. Fowler), Sixth Wis. "Vols. (Lieut.-Col. Dawes), and Ninety-fifth N Y. "Vols. (Col. Biddle) gallantly charged on the advance "of the enemy and captured a large number of prison- "ers, including two entire regiments with their flags, "the other regiments of the First Brigade advanced "further on the left, and captured several hundred "prisoners, including Brig. Gen. Archer.   *   *   * "   *   *   Maj. Gen. Doubleday commanding the "corps at that time (about quarter before twelve o'clock) "arrived with the Second and Third Divisions.   *   * "   *   *   The severity of the contest during the "day may be indicated by the painful fact, that at least "half of the officers and men that went into the en- "gagement were killed or wounded.   *   *   *   *

Very respt your ob't servant,

(Signed)   JAS. S. WADSWORTH,

Brig. Gen. Cmdg.